PRAISE FOR NANCY McKENZIE'S
QUEEN OF CAMELOT

"A rich and powerful tapestry of words layered in legend and myth . . .
Surely Merlin's magic reached out to touch Nancy McKenzie's pen."
—ELAINE COFFMAN

"Guinevere comes alive—a strong, resourceful, and compassionate woman,
accessible to modern folk . . . McKenzie makes a quantum leap in defining
the character of Guinevere as a real, flesh-and-blood woman. The Arthur-
Guinevere-Lancelot triangle comes alive as well—believable, poignant,
and bearing the seeds of tragedy."
—KATHERINE KURTZ

"A lovely story, a wonderfully human retelling of the Arthur and Guinevere legend, one touched with passion and enchantment."
—JENNIFER BLAKE

"McKenzie brings immediate freshness to her entertaining reworking of an
often-told story by focusing on the girl destined to be queen."
—*Publishers Weekly*

Also by Nancy McKenzie
Published by Ballantine Books

QUEEN OF CAMELOT

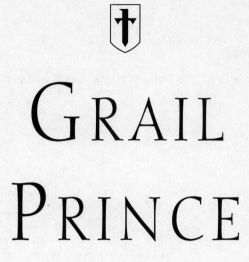

GRAIL PRINCE

NANCY AFFLECK McKENZIE

BALLANTINE BOOKS

NEW YORK

To Meg Affleck, Deborah Hogan, and Mary Stewart

A Del Rey® Book
Published by The Ballantine Publishing Group

www.delreydigital.com

Library of Congress Catalog Card Number: 2002094133

ISBN 0-345-45648-3

Cover photo by Elizabeth Barrett
Cover design by David Stevenson

Manufactured in the United States of America

First Edition: January 2003

1   3   5   7   9   10   8   6   4   2

ACKNOWLEDGMENTS

No writer I know writes without the help of other people. *Grail Prince* would never have been written without the pivotal influence of three women: Meg Affleck, Deborah Hogan, and Mary Stewart.

After I had sent my first Arthurian novel (*The Child Queen*, republished in 2002 as *Queen of Camelot*) off to an agent, I languished in postpartum doldrums, wondering what to write next. My sister Meg suggested I write a book about Galahad. At first I was appalled—what was there to say about a perfectly virtuous, perfectly boring man? But of course no one is perfect, and in the end it was the challenge of creating an imperfect character—more, one capable of downright despicable deeds, who nevertheless was the kind of man to inspire legends of stainless virtue—that won me over. Thanks to Meg, I decided to give it a try.

This wasn't an easy task. I both loved and hated Galahad. More than once I sought the advice of Deborah Hogan, professional editor and friend, without whose expert assistance I would still be wrestling with Galahad. Her perspective, her appreciation of dark characters, her ability to perceive the best structure for a manuscript, were instrumental in bringing the work to publishable form.

I owe my greatest debt to Mary Stewart, author of my favorite Arthurian novels: *The Crystal Cave, The Hollow Hills, The Last Enchantment, The Wicked Day*. Her imagination and skill brought fifth-century Britain alive for me and helped shape my own vision of Arthur's time. I took to heart her wish, expressed at the end of *The Last Enchantment*, that her books might be a beginning for some new enthusiast. I can think of no greater homage to Lady Stewart than to openly acknowledge that I strive to follow in her footsteps.

Heartfelt thanks are also due to Shelly Shapiro and Kathleen O'Shea David, editors at Del Rey Books, and to Jean Naggar, my agent, for their advice and assistance in shaping and publishing *Grail Prince*.

Finally, thanks to all my friends on Arthurnet for their words of encouragement, their erudition, and their unflagging interest in all things Arthurian.

—Nancy Affleck McKenzie
September 2002

CONTENTS

PROLOGUE 1

BOOK ONE

BOOK TWO

Part I: Fields of Battle
In the twenty-sixth year of the reign of Arthur Pendragon

Part II: The Return of the King
In the twenty-sixth year of the reign of Arthur Pendragon

BOOK THREE

Part I: Three Women
In the seventh through tenth years of the reign of Constantine

Part II: The Once and Future King
In the eleventh year of the reign of Constantine

ABOU BEN ADHEM

Abou Ben Adhem (may his tribe increase!)
Awoke one night from a deep dream of peace,
And saw, within the moonlight in his room,
Making it rich, and like a lily in bloom,
An angel writing in a book of gold:—
Exceeding peace had made Ben Adhem bold,
And to the presence in the room he said,
   "What writest thou?"—The vision raised its head,
And with a look made of all sweet accord,
Answered, "The names of those who love the Lord."
"And is mine one?" said Abou. "Nay, not so,"
Replied the angel. Abou spoke more low,
But cheerly still; and said, "I pray thee, then,
Write me as one that loves his fellow men."

   The angel wrote, and vanished. The next night
It came again with a great wakening light,
And showed the names whom love of God had blest,
And lo! Ben Adhem's name led all the rest.

—JAMES LEIGH HUNT
(1784–1859)

✝ PROLOGUE

In the twelfth year of the reign of Arthur Pendragon, High King of Britain, the full moon rose on the night of the autumn equinox. On that night Niniane, the Lady of the Lake, walked out the curved gates of Avalon unattended and ascended the Tor by secret paths to hear the Oracle of the Great Goddess.

She walked alone in her white robe to the clearing near the summit of the Tor. Below her stretched the glittering lakes, orchards, marshes, fields, meadows, flowing rivers, rich woodlands, and rolling hills of a land at peace: Arthur's Britain. It had not always been so. She remembered well the years of war, the long fight against Saxon domination, the burned fields, the desecrated shrines, the rape of women, the savage butchering of children, the mortal terror of coastal villages at the sight of a Saxon sail.

Niniane stood by the Black Stone, waiting for the moment when the moon would rise above the pines and send her first shaft of light onto the concave surface of the rock. She recalled the morning, over a decade past, when her predecessor, old Nimue, Chief Priestess of Avalon, had descended at dawn from her night on the sacred Tor. She had babbled at first. Perhaps that was why the Ancients called the oracle the Sacred Speaking. It had taken days to get sense from her. But what she had told them—that their young war leader would grow into the greatest king Britain had ever known; that he would unite the warbands and the kingdoms, from Lothian to Cornwall, into a single kingdom and win for Britain a breathing space of peace from barbarian invasions; that Merlin the Enchanter would die entombed inside a rock; that for all his power the great king would fail to breed an heir of the woman he wed—all had come to pass.

Niniane shivered. Her dark hair was washed and dressed, pulled back from the pale oval of her face, her body bathed and scented, her robe as white and flawless as a thousand bleachings could make it. She was prepared. But in her heart she knew she did not want to receive this oracle. The land was at peace. She served Arthur, a man she liked and trusted against all her expectations, even though he was a Christian. She did not want anything to change. But she knew well that time turned, nothing stayed the same.

Overhead the heavens wheeled. The pines trembled as the great virgin disc rose brilliant and majestic above their branches. The first bright shaft of light stabbed down at the rock. Niniane took her curved knife from her belt and cut her wrist, letting the blood spill into the stone's concave bowl. When it was full to overflowing she bound up the cut, lifted her hands to the moon, and murmured the ritual greeting. Light-headed, she staggered against the rock. The bowl of her blood looked black in the moonlight, glittering silver on the surface like a shining skin. Niniane blinked. There in the blood was the face of the Goddess, blank, white, inhuman. Niniane winced at the sudden sound of a strident, metallic voice.

The wheel is turning and the world will change. Those who are weak shall grow in power and the mighty shall be cut down. A dark prince from the Otherworld shall arise and slay the Dragon. A great serpent shall wade forth from the sea and swallow the Dragon's remains. The Dragon himself will be borne across water and buried in glass. Forever. And a son of Lancelot, with a bloody sword and a righteous heart, shall renew the light in Britain before the descent of savage dark.

The voice stopped. Hands pressed hard against her ringing ears, Niniane slid to the ground. Overhead the night breeze sang sweetly in the pines. Somewhere below her on the hill a nightingale took up its song. Crouching in the shadow of the great rock, huddling from the moonlight, Niniane covered her face with her hands and wept.

BOOK ONE

PART I
In the Shadow
of Camlann

In the first year of the reign of Constantine

1 ⛨ WOLF

Galahad woke instantly. It was cold and dark. Silence breathed on his neck, and his heart raced. Where was he? He lay still, holding his breath, listening hard. He could see nothing, but something was there. The very air was thick with menace. He knew, without knowing how, that death was near.

Suddenly he heard again the sound that had jerked him awake: the shrill bleat of a horse in terror. *His* horse! Memory flashed back: Farouk tied at the back of the vaulting cave, Percival tucked in his bedroll against the rock face, a fire lit in a circle of stones at the mouth to keep away wolves—

He raised himself cautiously on one elbow. Two feral golden eyes stared at him out of the night, ten feet away, throat high. His breath stopped. By the dark light of dying embers he made out the thin gray-black body of a mountain wolf, head down, ears forward, ruff bristling, nose alive to living scent. Without moving his body he let his fingertips slide toward his belt and his dagger hilt. But even as the weapon slipped into his hand, he knew it was no use. He would never have enough time. At the first threat of movement the animal would attack. Already the lips stretched in an ugly snarl, revealing the great fangs. He stared back at the golden eyes as hard as he could. The wolf did not blink. A low, rumbling growl sprang from deep within its belly. Behind him the frightened horse swung around on his tether, nervous footfalls vibrating through the earth.

"Jesu God!" Percival's terrified whisper split the silence. The wolf's head shot up, turned. Galahad's arm drew back and whipped forward as the animal, sensing its mistake, whirled and flung itself at him. The wolf fell dead as it hit his chest, the dagger's hilt stuck in its throat.

"Galahad!"

"Shhh!" Galahad rose to a crouch, shaking, and scanned the darkness beyond the cave, but he could see no other eyes.

"My God!" Percival stifled a sob and wriggled out of his bedroll. "It's my fault! The fire died—I fell asleep—he might have killed you! Oh, Galahad, after all we've been through—to think we might have ended as a meal for a mountain wolf! A *wolf*, of all creatures, when we're on the road home to Gwynedd!"

"Be quiet, will you, for pity's sake?" Galahad glanced at Percival's shoulder badge, where the Gray Wolf of Gwynedd stood proudly guarding the

Irish Sea. Did the boy think the creatures knew who he was? "Get busy with that fire. There may be others about."

Forcing his breath to normal, Galahad looked down at the wolf's emaciated body. It had been a hard year for wolves as well as men: a late, cold spring, a dry summer, a hot, desolate autumn, and now winter looked to be early. It must be bitterly cold in the heights to drive them down into the valleys so soon.

It's a new world now. The thought came back to him unbidden, rising in his throat like vomit. *Everything is changed.*

He dragged the wolf's body back to the cave mouth, pulled the dagger out, and slit its throat. Blood spilled out onto the rock ledge outside the cave, and dribbled down into the blackthorn thicket hedging the brook below. Percival lay on his stomach, cupping the precious embers as he blew gently on their only hope of fire. Galahad watched him a moment, saw the glow brighten and strips of whittled kindling curl and dissolve into little flames.

He nodded. "Keep your eyes open and your dagger nearby. The stench of wolf's blood may deter any others, but fire's better. I'm going to settle the horse."

The black stallion snorted and flung his head at the end of his rope, but calmed when he felt the reassuring touch of his master's hand. Galahad took his time with the horse, running his hands over the sweating coat and speaking calmly. "Rouk, Rouk, steady on, my boy. It's only a wolf. You've faced worse: Romans in Gaul and Saxons in Britain. It's all over now." But underneath the steady flow of assurances, the fear he had lived with for six long weeks clutched him again. *It is a new world now. Arthur is dead. Oh, dear God, Arthur is dead. . . .*

He bowed his head against the horse's flank as hot tears escaped his hard control. It was only last spring—a lifetime ago—he had left Britain with Arthur's army to join the kingdoms of Less Britain in their stand against the Romans at Autun. That battle had ended the threat of Roman domination, but it had come at such a cost! So many men had died! His own father— He shrugged the thought away. He did not want to think about Lancelot.

And after Autun, disaster had followed hard upon disaster. Was it only six weeks ago, the Battle of Camlann? Six weeks ago half of Britain had died near the banks of the Camel within sight of the towers of Camelot.

Angrily he pushed away that memory. There was no point in remembering. Even the last six weeks were growing more difficult to recall. He had spent most of them at Percival's side in Avalon's House of Healing. That was a time shrouded in grief. Or had the Lady of the Lake drawn a living mist across his mind to guard the secrets of Avalon? He wouldn't be at all surprised. Niniane, chief priestess when Arthur was King, was a powerful enchantress, a witch of the first order. And young Morgaine, who took her place after Camlann, was a gifted healer. Although it was widely claimed they used their power only for good, he did not trust them. He would have preferred a pile of bracken on the floor in one of the mean cells at the Christian monastery atop the Tor, rather than sleep in a real bed with a down pillow as a guest of pagan priestesses in the orchards of Avalon. But they had saved Percival's life. For that, he owed them courtesy.

What would happen now? He glanced toward the cave mouth, where Percival crouched over the growing flames. Percival of Gwynedd, his cousin, was eleven years old—too young to be a warrior king. He was one of twelve, the Lady said, to survive Camlann. But he had barely survived it. It had taken six weeks in Avalon and all the healing power the Lady could summon to close the sword cut in his shoulder and put color back into his face.

Galahad ran his hand over the stallion's flank. The horse had cocked a hind leg now and slouched in boredom. How lucky animals were to forget fear so quickly! His own fear pressed down upon him like a bird of prey crouching on his shoulder, with every faltering step digging talons in. Once, he had had a future. King Arthur had given him a mission, a quest—the witch Niniane had sent him a dream about it—but now Arthur was gone and Niniane had disappeared. Nothing was the same as it had been. What on God's sweet earth would happen now? Slowly, like a man in sleep, Galahad walked forward toward the fire.

"I'm sorry I shouted," Percival mumbled. "I thought he was going to kill you." He crouched over the pile of brush and branches they had gathered before dusk, searching for the right size tinder for the nascent flames.

"He might have, if you hadn't drawn his attention. Your shout probably saved my life." Percival colored shyly and reached for a branch. Galahad watched him struggle to break it across his knee. The boy had no strength yet in his injured arm. "Do you want some help?"

"Certainly not! Any village child of six can do this. And I'm nearly twelve."

"No man of twenty could do it if he'd had his shoulder cut clean through six weeks ago."

Percival flashed him a grateful look. Beads of sweat had formed along his brow, as cold as it was. "Nevertheless, let me try. I'll get it."

"You'll open the wound again. And this time you won't go to Avalon. You'll have to settle for whatever care your kin can give you in Gwynedd."

If we get there. Again the unbidden voice of fear whispered in his ear. Two boys traveling through Welsh hills left lawless by the decimation of Camlann—they could so easily be killed by a couple of bandits with decent knives, or by a starved wolf, or even by a night out in the cold without a fire. . . .

Impatiently Galahad shrugged off the weight of his fear and went out to the rock ledge beyond the cave. He lifted the wolf carcass by its heels until it was drained of blood. Then he dragged it back inside the cave, slit it open, and began to skin it.

"Sharpen a stick or two. Let's roast the pluck."

In the end they roasted all the flesh they could get off the bones, and stuffed it into their saddlebags for future meals. They ate the liver and the heart, and finding there was not enough dirt on the cave floor to bury the bones and entrails, threw them off the rock ledge, a feast for night's creatures. They stretched the wolfskin to dry by the fire and then sat down, looking at each other. Neither of them made a move toward his bedroll. Instead, Percival brought out the skin of wine the Lady had given him at parting, and offered it to Galahad.

"We're still in Guent now, aren't we?" he asked. "A day out of Caerleon? How many days until we reach Gwynedd?"

"I was going to ask *you* that. I've never been to Wales. You live here."

Percival looked uncomfortable. "Yes, but until I sneaked away to join Arthur's army I had never been out of my own valley. I don't even know where the border lies. I won't know where we are until we get to land I recognize."

Galahad tried a smile. "Then we'll have to hope the commander at Caerleon was telling us the truth. Northwest, he said. Gwynedd lies northwest of everything."

"You didn't like the Caerleon commander, did you? What was his name, Sir Bruenor? I thought he was courteous enough."

"He's a Cornishman. Sir Caradoc and the men from Caerleon I knew all died at Camlann. Bruenor is Constantine's man. Caerleon is Constantine's. Camelot is Constantine's. So is Britain, if there is a Britain still."

"You didn't like him because he was Cornish? Cornishmen are Britons, too."

"Under Arthur they were tame enough. But the dukes of Cornwall have always been ambitious. Constantine has wanted the High Kingship all his life. Now he has it. But I wonder how many will follow him."

"We have to begin again somewhere. It might as well be with Constantine."

Galahad smiled at his young cousin. "Will you follow Constantine, then, King of Gwynedd?"

Percival colored. "I am king only because my father was killed at Autun. My uncle Peredur is appointed regent until I'm fifteen. Those were Arthur's orders."

"Arthur is dead. There is no one to enforce those orders now. You can be king from the day of your arrival home, or your uncle can snatch it from you. There's no one to stop him."

"He wouldn't!"

"I'm glad to hear it."

"I *know* he wouldn't!"

"We'll find out as soon as we get to Gwynedd."

"My mother wouldn't let him. Or my sister."

Galahad shook his head. "Peredur has a sword. They don't."

"He wouldn't harm them!" Percival cried. "He wouldn't dare!"

Galahad moved closer to him and slung an arm around his shoulders. "Calm down, and keep your voice low. I didn't mean that. I only meant to point out your position. Who's been ruling in Gwynedd since your father left for Brittany with Arthur? Your mother or Peredur?"

"My father appointed Peredur regent in his stead."

"You see? For six months he's been in command of every soldier there. He's got their loyalty by now; he's appointed his own captains. If he's any sort of leader he's in full control of the house guard, too. He already has the power in his hands. It's a small step from regent to outright king. There's only you in the middle."

Percival gulped. "What are you saying? That I'll have to fight him for my birthright?"

Galahad shrugged. "You wouldn't be the first. He's Maelgon's brother. He has a claim to it. You're the only one in his way." He paused. "What kind of man is he? Direct or devious? Selfish? Cruel?"

"N-no. Not cruel. Direct, yes. We breed men so in Gwynedd."

"Well." Galahad handed him back the wineskin. "You're a long way from fighting him for your birthright. You can hardly move that arm of yours, much less hold a sword. And even if you could, you know little enough of swordplay. You had better let me be your sword. I'll stay with you in Gwynedd, at least until we see which way the land lies."

"Will you?" Percival's eyes were shining. "Thank you, cousin. *Your* sword is protection against any man in Britain! But there won't be any need. Wait and see. Uncle Peredur will welcome you with open arms. After all, you're his nephew, too. My whole life he's always bragged to others how his sister Elaine married Lancelot of Lanascol, the High King's second-in-command. He's prouder of his kinship bonds with Lancelot, which are only through marriage, than he is of his blood cousin, the High Queen Guinevere. He'd never raise a sword against Lancelot's son."

"That was in the old days," Galahad said levelly. "Now everything has changed. Lancelot's name will not be as bright as it was."

"Why not?"

"He's gone home to Lanascol. For good. He's given up on Britain. On the future. He said his time is past. He'd never back Constantine. And I wouldn't be surprised if he's not alone."

Percival sat silent, staring moodily at the flames.

"Britain lies on the brink of disaster," Galahad muttered. "Everything

Arthur fought for, the peace and unity of the past twenty years, is already undone. As soon as the Saxons realize what has happened, the Kingdom of the Britons could go up in smoke."

Percival looked up and met his eyes. "But it won't. We'll unite. We'll rebuild."

Galahad managed a smile. "Who's *we*? A fourteen-year-old Breton nobody likes and an eleven-year-old boy from the northwest corner of Wales? Who would follow *us*? I'm not so certain Britain can be put back together. Too many men are dead. Too few left living who dreamed Arthur's dream."

A wolf howled mournfully in the distance, and the hairs rose on the backs of both their necks. Percival threw a log on the fire and shuddered.

"Go ahead and sleep," Galahad said gently. "I'll stand watch. You need your rest. We'll get an early start in the morning."

Galahad gazed into the deep heart of the fire as Percival's breathing slowed toward sleep. This creeping journey, this covert slinking through the Welsh hills toward the protection of Percival's home, might prove to be the end of his and Percival's fortunes—for they were powerless against any man with a force at his back—or it might be a beginning. It all depended upon what they found when they reached Gwynedd.

2 ✝ GWYNEDD

In the steep mountains of North Wales the first snows were falling. Bare hardwoods raked leaden skies with naked fingers while dark pines spread green skirts to catch the swirling flakes, and the earth settled grudgingly to sleep under her cold blanket. Streams froze slowly at their edges. Hard ground crunched underfoot. Every breath was captured, timeless, by the still, unmoving air.

At the top of a narrow ridge Galahad led his horse carefully along the slippery track, past rocky outcrops and ledges that overhung sheer drops to the valley far below. Percival, sitting on the horse's back, stared glumly down through the veil of snow at the misty outlines of his father's castle.

"Home at last," he muttered. "Now that we're upon it, I'd rather be anywhere else."

Galahad looked down at the silent valley. The castle was well placed, nestled between the high hills with a wide view of the sea. The sea itself lay shrouded in fog, but he knew it was there, cold, gray, and forbidding. He could smell it. "Putting it off won't make it any easier. Besides, we're out of food. We've been a week too long as it is, thanks to the weather."

Percival glanced down at his bandaged shoulder and the stiff sling cradling his arm. "Do you think I'll ever use this arm again? It doesn't feel like it will ever heal."

"Don't you remember how it felt the day I found you at Avalon? Why, you were half out of your mind with pain. And look at you now—able to ride."

Percival snorted. "I don't call this riding, sitting upon your horse while you lead us both. I can't get a decent grip on the reins, and I'm on the verge of falling off every other step. Why can't you use a saddle, like other men?"

"Oh, well," Galahad said lightly, "if you'd rather walk . . ."

"Oh, no! Thank God for your horse, my dear cousin. Good old Farouk! I'd never have made it walking, and horses are scarcer than hen's teeth since Camlann." He shuddered. "I still have nightmares. It seems like only yesterday—I thought for certain I had lost my arm."

"In six months you'll be wielding your sword again with the best men in the kingdom."

Percival grimaced. "To tell truth, I have lost my taste for battle. And you were right, I think, to have doubts about the future. Between Autun and Camlann, what kings are left in Britain?"

"The King of Gwynedd, for one."

"Exactly. Boys and babies who cannot rule their own lands. Who will protect us, with Arthur gone?" He scowled. "And when we ride up to the gates of Gwynedd, what shall I say to them all? Here I am, but no one comes with me—I have lost our army. Every last man of it is dead!"

"They died in Arthur's service, defending Britain. There is no higher honor for a soldier."

"But I live!" Percival cried. "What kind of king am I, to return alone without my men? They probably have lookouts posted along the shore, expecting my father to come sailing in, triumphant, with all his men gathered on the deck. Whatever will they say when they see it is only me?"

"You're working yourself up. Your fever will return. Surely your family will forgive you your recovery. They will all be glad to see you safely home, even without Maelgon, even without the army. I will tell them of your courage at Autun, and how you drew your father's troops together after he fell, and how you led them against the Saxons at Cerdic's Field, and how Arthur trusted you. You will be a hero to them all, Percival, young as you are."

"Oh, of a certainty," came the bitter reply. "A boy who left home without permission, defied his father, and sneaked across the sea, who lived to see the death of every man who served his homeland—the death of his father and his king—yes, indeed, how welcome I will be!" He coughed violently, and wiped his sleeve across his eyes.

Gradually, as they descended the steep hills, Percival's chatter turned from memories of war to healing dreams he had dreamed at Avalon. His favorite was of a lovely maiden who had appeared to him three times and whose kisses had eased his pain.

"The most beautiful girl on earth, cousin! Skin as white as snow, hair as black as a raven's wing, and lips as red as new blood. When she kissed me my pain vanished and I felt like an emperor!"

"Healing dreams, indeed! This is strange talk for a beardless boy."

Percival's face was flushed and his eyes gleamed overbright through the curtain of falling snow. Remembering Percival's fevers in the House of Healing at Avalon, Galahad hurried the horse down the steep and slippery path. Behind him Percival continued his banter and, because it was preferable to hearing him worry about his reception at home, Galahad let him talk. It was not until they reached the lower slopes that Galahad realized Percival's jabber no longer made sense. He turned. The boy's face was dark and hot, his eyes half-closed and unseeing. His whole body shivered as it burned. Galahad leaped onto the stallion's back, hugged Percival tightly against him, and grabbed the reins.

"Come on, Rouk; you'll have to carry us both the rest of the way."

It took another hour to reach the valley floor, and twenty minutes at a swift canter to reach the castle gates. By then Percival had gone cold and silent, a deadweight against Galahad's body.

The guards at the gate sounded the alarm. Men came running as Galahad slid from the steaming horse with Percival senseless in his arms. The guards among them drew their swords. Before Galahad could speak to defend himself, a chestnut mare pounded up at a hard gallop, and the rider, a slender youth royally appointed, sprang from the mare's back in the middle of a sliding stop, gravel and dirt flying everywhere. Even as he opened his mouth to protest on Percival's behalf, Galahad admired the skill the stunt required. The youth raced to Percival's side and stared down into his ashen face.

"It's Percival! Call the queen—it's Percival!" Cold green eyes narrowed at Galahad. "You villain! What have you done to my brother? How dare you treat him so! He is a king!" The boy spun on his heel and pointed. "You, and you, and you, send for the queen and the physicians! And *you*, sir, you will answer for his pitiable state! Give me your name and family!"

Galahad stared into the young, furious face and found he could not speak. The youth was a prince, for certain, dressed in a fur cap, soft boots, and a good, thick riding cloak. Wide, gray-green eyes shot at him a hatred as intense as any he had seen on a battlefield.

"I asked your name. Men, arrest this rogue and throw him in the dungeon! If my brother dies, he dies. If he recovers, this blackguard will speak to me or I'll have his tongue out!"

No one stepped forward to restrain him, and Galahad pushed past the youth toward the castle and warmth. Clearly, the boy was a mere child, not a prince of standing, not to be taken seriously. He stopped when he felt a dagger point touch his back.

"Don't trifle with me, princeling. Or I will have your life. I can do it."

"Sir," Galahad croaked, wondering desperately what had happened to his throat, "I do not doubt it. Kill me if you must, but first let me get Percival to a fire."

"Oh!" The youth gasped, withdrawing the dagger. "A fire! Bryll, take him to the meeting chamber; there's a log fire going, and—and light the brazier in Val's room. Tell the queen Val is home—" He whirled toward the motionless guards. "Cowards, all of you! Afraid this intruder might *be* somebody, with his fine clothes and his bearing? What about my brother? Percival is your king!"

Galahad strode away after the servant. So they knew already of Maelgon's death. Was that the reason no one disciplined this unruly child? Would he find the widowed queen prostrate with grief? But prince or no prince, the lad deserved a whipping.

In a large room with a snapping log fire, Galahad laid Percival on the hearth and knelt beside him. An old hound, displaced from his rest, licked Percival's face, with a gently wagging tail. Percival lay absolutely still, his flesh as livid as a serpent's belly. Galahad bent his ear to the boy's chest and to his relief heard the sounds of life. He turned quickly as footsteps sounded behind him, but it was the young firebrand again, finished scolding the guards.

"Is *that* the best you can do? No blankets? No bedding? Did you find him thus in the forest? Or did you do this to him yourself?"

Galahad bristled. "I am Percival's friend!"

"A friend! May the blessed saints preserve me from such a friend! He's perfectly blue! Where are the blankets? The hot bricks? The broth? He's chilled to the bone—*and* senseless! Hadn't you even a bedroll to wrap him in? Bryll! Goran! Lucan! Broth! Bricks! Blankets!"

The boy knelt down and put a slender hand to Percival's face. "Oh, Val, Val. You're so cold! And you've been away so long! I've given you up for dead a thousand times and it was all my fault."

Galahad stared at him. "*Your* fault? How is it your fault?"

"Never mind. When it's your business to know, I'll tell you."

"Take care you don't knock his shoulder," he said in exasperation. "He's been wounded."

"Wounded! Sick *and* wounded? When did that happen? King Arthur would never have let him fight; he's far too young. Wounded! What in God's name were you doing in the mountains in winter with a wounded boy, sick with fever? Trying to kill him?"

"Dandrane!" A sharp voice rang out between them. "You should get lashes for swearing and rudeness to a stranger." Galahad looked up to see Queen Anet—it had to be Percival's mother; she looked exactly like him—come through the door with a crowd behind her. Small in stature, dark in coloring, she was not a pretty woman, but her face reflected her well-known kindness and gentleness of soul.

"Percival!" She fell to her knees and clasped her son's cold hand to her breast. "Does he live?"

A physician, bending over Percival's face, muttered pessimistically, but Galahad found his voice at last.

"Yes, madam, do not fear. He is weak from traveling—we have been too long upon the road—but he has had the best care in Britain. And he's as strong as anything."

Her dark eyes flew to his face. "You are his friend," she said suddenly, almost smiling. "And you brought him home. God bless you."

"Serious, most serious," the physician muttered.

"Some friend," Dandrane whispered behind the queen. "With such a friend, he needs no enemies!"

"Still, I may be able to save him." The physician laid his ear against Percival's chest.

"Hush, Dandrane." The queen spoke patiently, her eyes on Percival's face. "You know nothing of where they have been or what has happened to them. No doubt they have both been through hard times. Winter's come early; they might easily have been stranded in the mountains or attacked by wolves. Behave yourself, child, and take off your cap in the house. Do try to remember who you are."

It was not much of a rebuke, to Galahad's mind. He thought the lad deserved at least a beating. But the pale face flushed with color and the gray-green eyes stared hard at the flooring as the prince reached up and obediently snatched the cap from his head. Down tumbled a wild tangle of chestnut curls. Galahad's jaw dropped.

"I'm sorry, Mother." The voice from behind the curtain of beautiful hair was small and contrite. "But I'm scared for Val." The pale face lifted and Galahad blinked twice. He found himself staring at a pretty girl.

She grinned at his discomfort. "You're not as smart as you think you are, are you, princeling?"

"Hush, child! Tame your tongue. Apologize for your behavior, Dane, and beg this young man's pardon."

The physician straightened. "I can save him, my lady, but only with a leeching."

Anet shuddered. "Very well. His chamber is being prepared. But I pray you, sir, let him rest here until he is warm." She turned to her daughter.

"I know you are frightened, my dear, but that is no excuse for rudeness. You are awfully quick to judge. Apologize to Percival's friend for your behavior."

"What has he done to deserve such deference? We don't even know who he is!"

Scandalized at her defiance, Galahad's face flamed, and he was spared further embarrassment only by the sudden arrival of blankets, hot bricks, and bedding. The physician soon had Percival wrapped warmly, and gradually his shivering diminished and his color improved. They carried him to his own room and laid him on his bed. Galahad noted the bare walls, the meager furnishings—one clothes chest, one table by the uncarved bed, no lamp. By Camelot's standards it was hardly fit for a prince, never mind a king. But the floor was swept clean, the mattress was plump with stuffing, two thick blankets of finely combed Welsh wool covered a bleached linen sheet, and the single table, intricately carved in the old style of the northern Celts, held a candlestand of silver.

Glowing coals in the brazier struggled against the brisk whistle of wind through cracked window shutters. It was a losing battle. The room was cold and growing colder. Two blankets would hardly be enough. The place smelled musty from disuse, more like a tomb, Galahad thought suddenly, than a sleeping chamber. He shuddered and glanced quickly at Percival's ashen face. In the small cell at Avalon, hung with fragrant herbs and warmed by an applewood blaze, Morgaine had prophesied a glorious future for Percival of Gwynedd. But one would be a fool to trust a witch. Galahad crossed himself quickly. Queen Anet took his arm and gently led him away, leaving the physician to his awful art.

3 ✠ A HEARTHSIDE TALE

"I cannot bear to watch a leeching," Anet confided with a shudder. "Come with me back to the fire, and tell us about yourself. You must be nearly as cold as Percival. We will give you hot soup and honey mead, and if you will oblige me, I am afire to hear all about your travels with my son."

As they passed through the hall the main door opened and a burly man strode in, covered with snow. He stamped his feet and shook himself as the servants hurried to relieve him of his cloak.

"Damned storm covered the tracks," he growled. "But it was a big boar—we'll get her before the winter's out."

"My lord Peredur!" The queen dipped him a quick curtsy. "Percival is home! He is ill, and wounded, but at last he has come back!"

Peredur embraced her warmly. "Thank God! Anet, our prayers are answered. Where is he now?"

"In his bed, asleep. Timonius is leeching him."

"He lies near death!" Dane cried, pushing forward. "Oh, Uncle, he's been horribly wounded and nearly frozen to death in the snow!"

Galahad scowled furiously at her but she paid him no attention.

"What's this? He's wounded? How so? How did he get here?"

Anet turned toward Galahad. "This brave young man brought him home. Timonius assures me Percival will live, but we may have this young lord's help to thank for that."

Peredur's blue eyes regarded Galahad. He was a thick-bodied man of middle years with a bushy brown beard going gray at the temples. Although not as tall as Galahad, he was twice his weight, with a bearing of authority.

"Who are you, sir, and how do you come here with my nephew Percival?"

Galahad bent his knee to the floor. "My lord, my name is Galahad. My homeland is in Less Britain, a place called—"

"Galahad!" Peredur stepped forward and raised him. "Of Lanascol? Aye, lad, I know it well. Why, you are my sister Elaine's son, and my nephew!"

Galahad took an instant liking to this rough Welshman. It was the first time in his life he had been welcomed as Elaine's son instead of Lancelot's.

"You see now what you have done," Anet said quietly to Dane. "It is your own cousin you have insulted by judging so hastily. Are you not ashamed?"

The girl's face was already crimson. She turned to Galahad and made a pretty reverence, contriving somehow to look feminine in her boots and leggings. "I beg your pardon, cousin. Please forgive me."

To his fury, Galahad found his tongue tied. A nod was all he could manage, and he saw her eyes flash green with amusement before he looked away.

"Let's sit before the fire and hear your tale," Peredur cut in. "Tell us where you've been and how you came to meet Percival. Of my brother Maelgon and of Arthur we have already heard, may they rest in peace. We had a courier from Gaul telling us of Maelgon's death, and as for Arthur— news as bad as that travels on the wind. But come, Galahad, and give us the details. Tell us how young Percival came to be wounded."

They sat before the great log fire in the room where Percival had so recently lain. Servants arranged chairs and benches around the hearth, brought a bowl of rich, steaming broth for Galahad and cool mead in a silver pitcher. Peredur took the central chair and stretched his legs out to the fire while his servant stripped off his soaking boots. Anet settled herself beside Galahad with a few of her women behind her. The unruly girl curled at her mother's feet, hugging her knees, placed, he noticed, so that she could watch him and yet be unobserved by her guardians.

"Tell us, my lord," Anet began, "how you met my son."

"I met him the night after Arthur's ships landed in Brittany."

"Did Maelgon present him to King Arthur?" Anet smiled. "Perhaps Percival has told you how he begged to go with his father to the wars, and how Maelgon refused even to consider it. We thought him too young. He had no sword training; he did not even have a sword. But I suppose the truth is, we did not want to risk him. Of course he was wild to go and serve King Arthur. At the last moment, as they boarded the ships at Segontium, Maelgon relented, for we had a courier with the news he had taken Percival after all."

A slow blush spread across Galahad's face. He knew the truth of that tale: Percival had sneaked aboard the ship without his father's knowledge, and Dane had lied to Anet that Maelgon had changed his mind and decided to take Percival with him. Dane had presented Anet with Maelgon's ring as a token of it, pretending it had come from Maelgon's courier, although she had stolen it from her father's chest weeks before when the plan was hatched. Galahad looked down at the girl's upturned face. She glared defiantly back, daring him to tell the truth. He was tempted to do it and see if she got the beating she deserved, but the thought of Percival stopped him. Percival, lying ill and senseless, bled by the physician's leeches, needed every bit of a hero's welcome.

He faced Anet. "He met Arthur the next morning. Then we moved off to Kerrec with the army and met King Hoel of Brittany. And Childebert, King of the West Franks."

"And Lancelot, of course," Peredur prompted.

Galahad nodded woodenly. "Everyone was there. Everyone united under Arthur—Britons, Bretons, and Franks. From Kerrec we marched south and east into Gaul and met the Romans at Autun."

No one spoke. All their eyes were on him. He described the great battle as best he could, seeing still in his mind's eye rank upon rank of foot soldiers and cavalry clear to the horizon, hundreds of banners—boars, bears, hawks, wolves, dragons, and, of course, eagles—the bright blaze of armor amid whirlwinds of dust, the blinding flash of sword blades in the sun. As he spoke he heard again the tremendous roar of clashing armies, the incessant din of the battlefield, screaming horses, screaming men, bellowed paeans, and sobbing wails of pain. The very earth trembled beneath his feet. Again his blood ran hot with excitement and his flesh pricked cold as the black shadows of circling ravens passed overhead. That brilliant June day had been a day of glory: Arthur of Britain and his allies had defeated the legions of Rome and sent them packing. But so many, many Britons had died. . . . Anet wept silently to hear again of Maelgon's falling. It had been quick, at least, and honorable, a warrior's death. Afterward, Arthur had handed Percival his father's sword and given him the kingship of Gwynedd.

Here Galahad stopped and glanced swiftly at Peredur. The ice-blue eyes were already fixed on him, narrowed slightly at the corners, perhaps in amusement, perhaps in assessment. Peredur nodded. "Arthur did Gwynedd the honor of sending us a courier directly from Gaul with the news of Maelgon's death and his acknowledgment of Percival as his heir." He smiled lightly. "And my appointment as regent until he is of age." He leaned forward. "You suspect me, don't you, young hawk? Don't. I also acknowledge Percival's claim. I will keep his kingdom strong and whole for him. It is not in Gwynedd's best interest to divide the royal house, especially at a time of such uncertainty in Britain."

Galahad inclined his head. "Percival will be a strong king, my lord, I am sure of it, when he has a little more training. Why, he has already fought more Saxons than most knights twice his age!"

"Saxons!" Dane's head lifted, like a hound's who scents the fox. "What Saxons? You said it was Romans you fought at Autun."

Color washed across Galahad's face. He glanced hurriedly at Anet and Peredur, who watched him with polite, expectant faces. "Percival and I . . . we didn't actually fight at Autun. We were too young for Arthur's army."

"*You* were too young?" Dane cut in before anyone else could speak.

"A year too young. I'm fourteen."

"But, surely"—Peredur frowned—"he could have fought with Maelgon's troops. That decision was Maelgon's, not Arthur's. As you surely could have fought with Lancelot."

Galahad looked away. He did not want to explain his refusal to fight with Lancelot. Let the past lie quiet in the shadow of Arthur's passing. It was a new world now.

"I served King Arthur. So did Percival. Arthur did not want to risk both sons and fathers in the front line of the battle."

"Bless him," Anet whispered.

"Then what did you do?" Dane asked sharply. "Or were you both just watching?"

"The High King put me in charge of the field guard," Galahad retorted. "Percival was my lieutenant. We organized the grooms and pages and servants, and went among the fallen to see who could be saved, and killed anyone who tried to rob the bodies."

"Scavenger hunters!" Dane snorted in disgust, using the soldier's term for the unpleasant but necessary duty usually assigned to the injured, the inept, or the cowards. "God in heaven! Percival a scavenger hunter!"

"Hush, Dane!"

"If he didn't fight, how did he come to be wounded?" Peredur's voice had lost some of its warmth.

"That was later. After we got back to Britain. We fought and beat a Saxon army a day's ride from the Giants' Dance. At a place called Cerdic's Field."

"Is that where Percival was wounded?"

"No. He was wounded after that . . . at Camlann."

"Camlann!" Even Peredur paled, and Dane went perfectly white.

"Only twelve survived Camlann, they say," she whispered, her wide eyes as gray as spring storm clouds, dark and alive.

"Percival was one."

"And you another."

"No." Galahad's lips thinned. Leave it to the wicked girl-child to ferret out his shame. "I did not fight at Camlann."

"You did not fight? My brother nearly died and you did not fight! Then you are a coward."

"Dandrane! Please!" But even Anet's protest was not as strong as it had been before.

Heat rose to Galahad's face and he stared hard at the floor. He would tell them the truth, but not the whole truth. The whole truth was impossible. "I couldn't fight . . . because I wasn't there. Arthur sent me on a secret mission to Camelot. He gave me a message for the Queen. I had to get past Mordred's lines, and sneak in and out of the castle without being seen."

"You saw Guinevere?" Anet asked quickly. "How does she fare?"

"The King sent her to Amesbury, to the monastery there. To await him while he dealt with Mordred. That was the message."

"Thank God," Anet said under her breath, crossing herself. "So that's where she is! I have wanted so much to know. Peredur, this explains Constantine's anger. When he took Camelot, he found her gone."

Peredur nodded. "The ambitious swine. Marriage to her might have brought him the allegiance of all Britain."

"Ah, God, poor woman. I have thought of her so often these weeks past. Still as lovely as a girl. And now, for all her beauty, she's alone in the world, a widow as I am, but with no home, no place to call her own. Arthur and Mordred were her only family."

"I'm surprised she didn't go home with Lancelot," Peredur said. "There are a thousand men in Britain who would be willing to give her a home, if she'd deign to have them. I thought Lancelot might be the one she would accept."

"Poppycock!" Anet cried. "You've been listening to kitchen gossip! There never was a woman more faithful to her lord than Guinevere was to

Arthur. The faith between them was absolute—a thing rarely seen—stronger and more lasting than the ties of life. She'd never go with Lancelot, even as a widow. And I don't believe Sir Lancelot would ever ask her."

Galahad shut his eyes and hung on desperately to his manners. They did not know Lancelot as well as he did. . . .

"Well," Peredur grumbled, "it's a damned shame if she didn't. The thought of that beautiful woman in a nunnery!" He shuddered. "And it's a damned shame about Camlann. With Arthur gone to Gaul, Mordred had to take the kingship or the Saxons would've been at our throats. But we all thought he'd yield up his crown again if his father returned. Yet it seems they had to fight it out."

Galahad gulped. If only they knew the truth, they would weep for weeks at the injustice of it. He felt Dane's eyes upon him and forced himself to ignore her.

"Father and son," Anet said slowly. "It seems that fate was against them."

In the long silence that followed, the only sound was the strident snapping of the fire.

Predictably, it was Dane who spoke first. "So where were you during Camlann, that you did not fight?"

She should have been a hound, Galahad thought. She never lost a scent. "After my visit to the Queen, I went to Avalon with a message for the Lady Niniane. I delivered the message, but she would not let me go to the Christian monastery atop the Tor, where I wished to spend the night. Instead, she gave me a bed in their House of Healing. And sent me a dream."

He looked at their faces, Anet's polite and waiting, Peredur's lightly frowning and slightly bored, Dane's still and intent. He wondered if they would believe him. "The next thing I remember, I woke up in a cell at the monastery. And the Battle of Camlann was over."

No one spoke. He looked down at his hands. The knuckles were white.

"How did you wake up in the monastery if you fell asleep in Avalon?" Dane asked quietly.

He expected the question. It surprised him she exercised restraint in asking it. "I don't know. That's the truth. I don't know. The witch of Avalon cast a spell upon me, I suppose. She's famous for them."

Dane bit her lip and her eyes flashed. He could not tell if she was angry or laughing at him. "You were *asleep* while Percival and Arthur risked their lives for Britain?"

No protest this time from Queen Anet. He flushed darkly. "You could call it that, I suppose. It was not a sleep of my own choosing."

"No, no, certainly not," Peredur said easily. "No one doubts your courage, I am sure. Where did you find Percival, then? On the battlefield?"

"No. Next morning at Avalon. It was where all the wounded were taken. Lancelot . . . went back to Lanascol, but when I found out Percival was alive, I stayed with him in the Lady's House of Healing until he was well enough to travel. Then I brought him north. It was a bad wound, and he was senseless or wandering for a fortnight, but Lady Morgaine promised him it would heal cleanly, and he would be able to use a sword."

"I thought you said Niniane was Lady of the Lake," Dane said sharply.

"She was. But after Camlann she left. The Lady Morgaine has her power now."

"Where did Niniane go?" Anet asked.

"I don't know. They don't answer questions outright, even if you ask. Some said she had gone back to her husband's home. Pelleas, King of the River Isles, was one of the twelve survivors. He was wounded and she might have gone home to tend him." He shrugged. "It does not matter."

"But it does," Peredur said warmly. "It matters to me. Pelleas's kingdom is in Guent, which is part of Wales. I'm going to try to unify Wales, if I can, and I don't want that pagan witch messing things up."

Galahad straightened. "I'm sorry, my lord. I didn't think of that. I wish I knew for certain where she went, but I don't."

"Perhaps you can tell us something else the whole kingdom wants to know: Where does the High King lie? Have you any idea?"

Galahad swallowed. "Yes, my lord." Dane's head whipped up. "But I have sworn an oath of secrecy. Lancelot bound me, so that the Saxons will never find him. It was what Arthur wanted."

"So Arthur anticipated the Saxons coming that far west into Britain?" Peredur fingered his beard. "I don't think Constantine expects it. Well, well. And your father went back to Lanascol? And you didn't go with him."

Galahad felt Dane's eyes upon him and lifted his chin so he could not meet them. "My lord, I . . . I couldn't. We, er . . . I had to find Percival. Dead or alive, I had to bring him home."

"For which we thank you, Galahad," Anet said, warmth returning to her voice.

"Didn't Lancelot even *try* to see the Queen?" It was Dane again. Inevitably she threw the sharpest barbs.

"Yes." The admission came bitterly. "When we parted he was headed for Amesbury. He did not want her to learn of Arthur's death from a stranger's lips. Even though she is in a monastery with comfort all around her."

"Quite right." Anet nodded.

"Cold comfort for such a queen," Dane said sadly.

Galahad scowled. "I advised him not to go."

She met his eyes. "I believe it."

Unaccountably, Galahad felt heat in his face. "He'd be better off if he never saw her again."

"Only a man would think so," Dane shot back.

Anet rose, silencing them. "The leeching must be finished. Let us see how Percival is doing."

Peredur rose with her, and took her arm. "An excellent idea. Thank you, Galahad, for sharing your tale with us. It was good of you to let us know how my brother died."

Galahad and Dane rose together. She put her hand on his arm. "Cousin. A moment." Her tangle of hair hid half her face, giving her a fragile, childlike look. He was not fooled.

"What do you want?"

"I owe you thanks for not betraying our secret. Val's and mine. About how he stowed away."

"I kept silent for Percival's sake."

"I know." The changeable eyes met his directly. "It was my plan. He was the one who wanted to go, but I made it happen. If he'd been killed—" She swallowed suddenly.

"He wasn't."

"But he so nearly was. I . . . I couldn't have lived with myself if he'd died."

"You should have thought of that before you sent him off."

"I did. I did. But he wanted to prove himself so desperately. And our parents were so afraid to risk him. They never let him near a weapon. He's their only son."

"He's not out of the woods yet."

She smiled fleetingly. "Oh, he'll live. I know he will. Now that he's home." She paused. "I'm sorry if I trod on your private ground. I didn't mean to. But I can't abide not knowing things."

He stiffened instantly. "Never mind."

She nodded, dropping the subject at once. "How long are you going to stay here?"

"I don't know. Until I'm certain of Percival's future."

"Do you mean, until he is recovered?"

"That's part of what I mean."

Her eyes widened and she smiled. "Your thoughts run with mine. You do well to have doubts. Let's call a truce, shall we? For Percival's sake? We are twins, you know. I can't be angry at you if you're his friend."

He looked down at her. For a girl she was remarkably perceptive. He lifted his shoulders. "All right. But private ground is private ground."

She grinned, suddenly looking a lot like Percival. "Agreed. I'll keep off yours if you'll keep off mine."

"What is that, I wonder?"

She laughed. "You'll never know."

4 ✝ EAVESDROPPING

Dane huddled in a corner of the turret, drawing a thick wool blanket closer around her shoulders. This was her favorite hiding place, this niche in the tower wall. It had a narrow window that looked down over the courtyard where her father's soldiers trained, and a ledge just wide enough for her to sit. A sharp wind gusted in from time to time, more reminiscent of winter than of spring, and she wriggled deeper into her warm cocoon. She prayed her mother would not miss her and come looking. She was not worried about Peredur's wife finding her. Lady Ennyde was too wrapped up in her own concerns to know, even after all these years, where Dane hid when she wanted to escape her duties.

Dane shuddered. The winter had been long and cold, penning the women indoors in the workrooms, and she was sick of spinning. She loathed it. It amazed her that grown women could stand the tedium. She liked weaving better; at least that required thought. But she was too young and small to work the looms herself. Once in a while Anet would let her help. She enjoyed that. Her mother was a master weaver whose tapestries were the pride of all Wales. Several of them hung in Camelot itself, for Queen Guinevere had prized them above the work of her own women.

But spinning! There was nothing so mind-numbing as spinning. Her thread was forever uneven and her fingers blistered after an hour of it. It was all right for her mother's women; they were old hands; they sat and gossiped and made wishful matches for their daughters and nieces while the lumpy wool raced through their fingers and onto the spindle as neat thread. She would *so* much rather watch sword practice than spin!

She looked down again at the sun-washed courtyard. Sir Maldryn, Maelgon's master-at-arms, was sparring with Percival. She had never liked Sir Maldryn and she wished Peredur would appoint someone new. But good swordsmen were impossible to find these days. Between Autun and Camlann, everyone with an ounce of skill or courage was dead. Maldryn had a mean streak in him which surfaced from time to time. It made him untrustworthy in her eyes. She watched as he instructed Percival on a new defense, demonstrated it, let him practice.

Percival's arm was daily growing stronger and more mobile, but it had been a long recovery. His fever had lasted a fortnight, despite leechings, and it had been a month before he could swallow more than broth. From Christmas to midwinter he had been abed. By the time of their twelfth birthday, a week beyond the spring equinox, he had been able to last an entire day up and about, and had been able to attend the feast held in their honor. That had been wonderful, staying up until they were weary and not being sent to bed as soon as the wine went round.

Dane frowned suddenly. Her twelfth birthday had also been the day Ennyde spoke to her mother about marrying her off to the king of Powys. How dare the old witch act as if she were queen! Thank God Anet had refused to consider making a match for her yet! Most girls weren't married until fifteen or so, but twelve was not too young for betrothal. Anet, whether from wisdom or from kindness, thought her unready and refused to discuss the subject. Dane grimaced. Even such a fool as Ennyde ought to be able to see she was unready. Her body was as straight and slender as a boy's with no hint yet of any change. And Dane was determined to keep it that way. She did not care if she had to bind herself like a barley sheaf; she was not going to let Ennyde's sharp eyes detect change when it came.

Boys were so lucky, she thought glumly, watching Percival swing his sword in the glinting sun. They could ride and hunt, and play with swords and cudgels, and go exploring alone in the summer hills. They were encouraged to be strong and independent. Yet *she* was scolded for all these things when she was caught at them. *She* was made to spin and weave and sew until she was half-dead with boredom. Sighing, she shrugged off her annoyance. This was an old complaint, and years of protest hadn't changed a thing. Fighting it only made her bitter and unhappy. She did not want to grow up ill-humored like Ennyde.

In the courtyard several of Peredur's men were throwing spears at targets of stuffed animal hides hung from poles. They kept a respectful distance from the center of the square where Sir Maldryn pushed Percival to greater effort. To one side, leaning casually against the shield rack, watching, stood her cousin Galahad. She studied him a moment. Although he had been five months in Gwynedd he was still an enigma to her. That he was devoted to Percival was clear, and as far as she was concerned it was his saving grace. He rarely addressed her willingly, and when he did she found him taciturn and haughty. Val, however, worshiped him. Whenever she found fault with Galahad, Val defended him vehemently, and it wasn't just his natural loyalty to someone who had saved his life. Val genuinely admired him. She supposed they shared that mysterious brotherhood born between men who had been to war, but she sensed that the source of Val's worship went deeper than that. She wished she could understand it, but they never shared their counsels with her. In fact, if she came upon them talking together, Galahad always went silent until she passed out of earshot.

She supposed she ought to hate him for it, but she couldn't. There was something about her tall, black-haired Breton cousin that intrigued her. He was not everything he seemed to be. Percival thought him the soul of honor, valiant, honest, and devout, but for all his inward calm and enviable self-possession there were times when he seemed to Dane, oddly, somehow lost.

From the corner of her eye she saw two servant girls blush and curtsy in Galahad's direction as they passed by. Dane smiled when she saw their efforts were in vain. He didn't even see them. He never noticed women. Percival said he had made a vow never to marry. It was what she liked best about him. But he was fifteen, tall for his age, with eyes as deep blue as a cloudless day in summer and features of astounding beauty. *And* he was Lancelot's son and heir to Lanascol. No wonder every maiden in Gwynedd was vying for his attention! With such gifts, it would be a miracle if he kept his vow.

Suddenly she saw Galahad straighten and his hand fall to his sword hilt. Her eyes flew to Percival. He was tiring. His legs had stopped moving and his sword strokes had lost all their finesse. He was doing little more than heaving the weapon about with all his strength, but Sir Maldryn would not let him stop. Instead, the master taunted him, rebuking him for his weakness, and ran his own sword in once, twice, and sliced his tunic. Percival staggered, exhausted. Dane had opened her lips to cry out when Galahad appeared at Percival's side and Sir Maldryn found his blade crossed by the Breton's sword.

For a long moment no one moved. Then Sir Maldryn sneered and made Galahad a mock bow. Galahad said something she could not hear while Percival limped to the courtyard wall, clutching his shoulder. Slowly the two men began to circle. She had seen enough instruction to follow some of the tactics. Sir Maldryn feinted but Galahad was not fooled. Maldryn lunged and dodged, moving quickly, but Galahad's blade was always there to meet his, and Galahad did not seem to move at all. Several of the spear throwers turned to watch, and began laying bets on the contest. It was a game to them, but Dane's knuckles whitened against the stone sill and her heart thudded in her ears. She could see Percival's face as he leaned sweating against the wall. He was not smiling.

Game or not, it was over quickly. Sir Maldryn, never a patient man, charged in a fury, his blade flashing faster than the eye could follow. The next instant he found himself standing unarmed, gripping his wrist, his blade winking in the dust at his feet, Galahad's sword point at his breast. In the stunned silence that followed, no one moved. Galahad stepped close to Maldryn until they were nearly face-to-face. He spoke slowly and distinctly. Dane could not hear what he said, but she saw a grin tug at the corners of Percival's mouth. Then, still inches from Maldryn's face, Galahad sheathed his sword, turned on his heel, and left by the nearest door.

Sir Maldryn flushed a dark red and stared back at all the watching faces. The soldiers quickly went back to their spears. Maldryn turned to the door where Galahad had disappeared and spat loudly in the dust. Then he bent for his sword and left the courtyard without so much as a glance in Percival's direction.

Dane hugged her knees and shivered. She would see to it Peredur learned of his master-at-arms' arrogant behavior. Peredur had better send him packing. Her father, Maelgon, would have killed the man for such insolence, but she knew Peredur was less violently tempered. Dismissal was probably the most she could hope for, dismissal and a blackening of his name.

She had swung her legs from the ledge when she heard women's voices approaching. Quickly, she retreated back under the blanket, pulling it tightly around her and hiding her face in its folds. She knew the voices instantly: Lady Ennyde and one of her fawning women.

"Three years is a long time, my lady. There's no need to get your feathers ruffled now."

"I do not have feathers, Cressa," Ennyde returned coldly. "And they are not ruffled." Under her blanket Dane giggled and pressed her hand tight against her mouth. "He's not only a boy; he's a weak boy. He'll never be a man of Peredur's stature. The other kings of Wales are a vicious, power-hungry wolfpack. Without a strong hand in Gwynedd to guide them, I don't like to think what might happen. Our lives might even be at stake."

Unsmiling now, Dane strained to listen. They were close enough to see her. She hardly dared to breathe.

"Sweet heaven! But surely, my lady, that's unlikely. You told me Prince Peredur is binding the Welsh lords into a federation—surely it won't take three years to do that. You told me he had already put out feelers."

"And what would happen, do you suppose, to such a federation should he hand over his power to an untried boy?" *Untried!* Dane thought furiously. *What did she think Camlann was? A hunting party?* "A federation of lords is only as strong as the leader who binds them. Look at Arthur and Britain. For twenty-six years Britain was a single kingdom because a strong king held the kingdoms together and bound the lords to his side. Now that he is gone, what has happened? No one follows that Cornish maggot, Constantine. He holds Camelot and Cornwall, but little else. No, Cressa, my dear, had Maelgon lived it would be different, but as it is"—she lowered her voice—"only Peredur can save Gwynedd, and as king, not regent. For all our sakes."

"Can it be done? Queen Anet will never allow it."

Ennyde laughed softly. "Dear Anet. What can she do, besides spread slander? She is the least of the obstacles in our way."

Our way! Dane's blood ran cold as she fought against her rising temper.

They were walking away. She slid off the ledge and tiptoed forward, keeping her back to the wall.

"It's Peredur himself I must convince, Cressa. He likes the boy, God knows why. I must convince him it is necessary for Gwynedd's sake."

"And he might think of his own children and his wife, from time to time, when he has the chance."

"Indeed." Ennyde's voice warmed. "Meanwhile, I must get rid of that Breton creature who protects Percival."

"What a taciturn, brooding soul he is."

"He's dangerous. Without him Percival is nothing. I need him gone."

"And then what will you do about Percival?"

Ennyde laughed again, without amusement. "Are you afraid I'll poison his soup? No, my dear. I'd hardly dare anything so obvious. Less direct means are far more effective, and less traceable to their source. Let me get rid of his handsome cousin and marry off his little bitch of a sister, and we'll have nothing to fear from Percival. He's a weakling like his mother. It's that wretched girl who inherited Maelgon's will."

Cressa made some reply but they were starting down the stairs and Dane could no longer hear their words. She leaned against the wall, sweating, trembling so violently she could hardly stand. She must run to tell her father— Ah, no, alas, he was gone forever, that stalwart, thickheaded oak of a man. She must tell her mother— She bit her lip in despair. She could not go running to her mother with such a tale. Anet, bless her sweet soul, would never believe it. She never credited other people with motives by which she herself was never moved.

Slowly, carefully, Dane gathered the blanket in her arms and folded it, forcing herself to calmness and her whirling thoughts to order. It was up to her to think of some solution. There must be a way to foil Ennyde's plans.

Long after dark Dane crept past her sleeping nurse and out into the dimly lit corridor. Slipping from shadow to shadow between the torches, she reached the men's quarters, melted up the winding stairs like a wraith in mist, and scratched lightly on Percival's door. After a long moment it opened. She looked up into Galahad's frowning face.

"What are *you* doing here?"

"Let me in! Quickly! I must speak with Percival!"

Grudgingly he let her pass, closing the door behind her.

"Why, Dane!" Percival lay propped up in his bed, his right arm bent across his waist as if he still carried it in a sling. She knew without asking that his shoulder pained him. For an instant anger at Sir Maldryn bit at her, sharp as a knife blade, but she quelled it.

"Forgive me, Val." She sat beside him and slipped an arm about his neck, pressing her cheek to his. "Princes' council. It's urgent or I wouldn't have come."

Percival regarded her with open affection. "Princes' council. Ah, Dane, how I miss those days!"

"What," Galahad addressed Percival, "is a prince's council?"

"Oh, it was just a name between us—our private signal for secret conferences in our childhood days. We met at prearranged places to plan our outings and adventures."

Galahad grunted. "Your sister is hardly a prince."

"I'm as much a prince as you are," Dane retorted with a shake of her head. Her wild hair half tumbled from its bonds. In irritation she reached up and loosed the rest, letting it fall about her shoulders in an unruly jumble.

"Yes, and you're a better one than I am," Percival cut in, pushing her hair from her face with a tender touch. "If *you'd* been at Camlann we'd have won the battle."

Dane flushed with pleasure. "Now you're being silly. I've come about something serious, Val, and it's just as well that Galahad's here. Both of you are going to have to leave Gwynedd."

They stared at her. "Why?"

"Because to stay is dangerous."

Galahad stiffened and turned his back on her.

"This isn't about Maldryn, is it?" Percival wondered. "He's been demoted. He's being punished."

"He ought to be whipped and driven out of Wales!" Dane cried, trembling. "Father would have killed him publicly! What you call punishment is barely a slap on his wrist! It's insulting!"

Percival smiled. "Well, you and Galahad are agreed on that."

"And so should you be, Val. Maldryn's in Ennyde's pocket. It's thanks to her he got off so lightly. Don't you know that? He married Ennyde's niece two years ago—she's got Peredur convinced he risks war with her family if he exiles Maldryn!"

Galahad turned and glanced sharply at Percival. "Is this true?"

Percival shrugged. "It is if Dane says it is. I don't remember."

"It's only a small sample of her influence. That's why I've come, to warn you of Ennyde's plans. I overheard her on the stairs." She repeated the conversation and saw both their faces darken. "So you see"—she turned to Galahad—"you must get Val out of here. Even if his arm is not yet healed. He is better off anywhere else at all between now and his fifteenth birthday."

"But Dane," Percival protested, "I just got home. Now you want to send me off again for three whole years? I can't just vanish—what possible excuse could I make for going? You must be exaggerating. Ennyde isn't queen."

"Not in name. But she's wife of the regent, which is much the same thing in her eyes. As it will be in Peredur's, if she has her way."

"Nonsense. Mother can put a stop to it."

Dane rolled her eyes. "Mother has *never* seen through *any* of Ennyde's devices. And of course Ennyde is careful always to present a smiling face to Mother, so Mother thinks her a pleasant enough companion. A little vain, perhaps, but certainly not a blackguard. And besides"—her voice saddened—"don't forget Mother's not Queen of Gwynedd any longer. Ennyde will run roughshod over her if she gets in the way."

"And Peredur?" Galahad asked. "If you told him what you heard, would he believe you?"

"It's my word against Ennyde's," Dane replied. "Would you believe your twelve-year-old niece against your own wife?"

Galahad shrugged gracelessly. "I don't know. All women lie."

Dane jumped to her feet. "No more than men!"

Percival waved them silent. "Do you really believe I'm in danger from Peredur?"

Dane still glared at Galahad. "Not now. Perhaps not for quite a while. But yes. I believe Ennyde has the power to persuade him to almost anything. And she's ambitious."

"He has publicly acknowledged my right to kingship."

"That was then. Next year he may publicly acknowledge his own."

"But even if you're right, I can't just run away. That's cowardice."

"No, it's not; it's wisdom. There'll be plenty of chances for bravery when you come back to claim the kingship. But in order to get that chance, you'll have to leave."

"But why? I don't understand why."

"Listen, then. Ennyde wants to drive Galahad away so she can weaken you in Peredur's eyes and in the eyes of his men. That fight with Maldryn was only an example. Imagine how you'd have felt if Galahad hadn't been there."

Percival flushed lightly. She returned to his side, kissed him quickly, and held on to his hand. "It's important that you have the men's allegiance," she said softly. "You must, to be their king. You can't afford to let Ennyde shame you, even a little. Three years is not a long time. The men will remember. Birthright or no, they will want to follow a strong king, not one who's been pushed aside and left sitting in the shadows. And what's to keep you from being pushed aside? Only your sword arm, and that's not ready yet." She squeezed him gently. "I'm sorry, Val, but it's truth. You know it is. Galahad might be able to protect you, but it wouldn't help you much— the men would not respect you for hiding behind him. And it's the men of Gwynedd who will make you king."

Percival stared miserably at his lap. At last he nodded. "What shall I do for three years? Where shall I go?"

"It doesn't matter. Anywhere. Get away from here and learn the things you will need to know to come back and claim your inheritance. Improve your swordsmanship, for one thing. Galahad can teach you. Go to Lanascol and train with Sir Lancelot. Travel. Meet the kings of other lands. Do them service; earn their favor. Come back with allies at your back. I shall hate to lose you again so soon, Val. I shall cry myself to sleep for a solid year. But it's the best thing, really it is, to bring about the future we've always planned for Wales. You are the strong king Gwynedd needs, all Wales needs—and you know it's in you. Camlann proved that. But you cannot become that king if you stay here."

"But what excuse can I give for leaving?" Percival cried. "I've not been home six months! How can I turn around and say that I am going off again?"

Dane hesitated, and then looked quickly at Galahad, chewing her lip. "Well, I thought perhaps you could go with Galahad when he leaves. Wherever he goes. Er, that's what I came to ask you, cousin. Will you take him away with you, for Gwynedd's sake?"

Galahad looked at her coldly. "You've a strange way of asking a favor."

She glared up at him. "You said yourself you would stay until Val was strong enough to fend for himself. Ennyde will *never* let him get strong enough if he stays here. Do you want to see him shamed in his own country? And denied his birthright? You didn't bring him all the way from Avalon for that. You can't be planning to live in Gwynedd forever—take Val home with you when you go. That's all I ask. Is it so very much?"

"I'm not going home."

He stood half-turned away, a brooding shadow against a dark wall. Dane forced herself to speak quietly. "Where then?"

He ignored her. "What's to stop your uncle from making himself king before Percival and I are across the border?"

"He won't, because he's not ready to. For now, being regent is enough. Ennyde has yet to convince him he's made for better things."

"Peredur's wife will still be here in three years' time."

"I know. Leave Peredur's wife to me."

"To you!"

Dane looked up at him defiantly, her untidy curls framing her face in a wayward halo. "I'm not ineffective just because I'm small."

"Believe her, cousin!" Percival cried. "She got me off to war behind the backs of both the king and queen. And they never knew it!"

Dane flashed Percival a look of affection. "And you came back a hero."

"What will you do to Peredur's wife?" Galahad asked quietly.

She grinned suddenly. "Are you afraid I'll poison her soup? No, half-wit. Less direct means are more effective. I'll play by women's rules. Don't trouble about your conscience. In three years' time she'll be alive, but with luck, out of favor. Wait and see."

"My conscience is none of your concern. Neither is our destination. That's between Percival and me."

She rose. The top of her head barely reached his chin. "We are twins, Val and I. Two sides of one coin. We share everything."

Galahad turned, walked across the room to the single window, and stood staring out, a shadow belonging more to that vast, deepening dark beyond than to the solid warmth of the lighted room. When at last he spoke, Dane and Percival both jumped. "I am going away on a quest Arthur gave me. Even though he's dead I think the mission is important. I don't know if I can find the things he wanted found. I only know I have to try."

"Would you let me come with you?" Percival asked softly, his face alight.

"I might as well."

"Oh, Galahad, a thousand thanks!"

"What quest?" Dane cried. "What are you looking for? Val, what is he talking about?"

Galahad turned to face them. His eyes burned blue even in shadow. "I go at a time of my own choosing. I don't know when it will be."

"I'll be ready," Percival vowed.

"What quest is this?" Dane turned toward her brother. "What do you know about it?"

Galahad lifted an eyebrow. "One person, are you?"

"Tell me what you're talking about."

He shook his head. "This is something you can't share. It's private ground." To forestall her protest, which he could see already rising to her lips, he walked past her, opened the door, and strode down the corridor to his own chamber.

But sleep came hard. He lay for a long time staring at the ceiling, his hands folded beneath his head. He was half-afraid that if he slept, he would dream again the dream Niniane had sent him that night in Avalon, the dream that had cheated him of Camlann. And he was half-afraid that he would not. An hour before dawn his eyelids finally closed and he sank into sleep with the swift inevitability of a stone down a well.

He rode out of a dark forest by the banks of a flowing river. In the middle of the river stood a castle on an island. The river swept by, deep, swift, silent, while the castle beckoned to him. But he saw no bridge, nor any fording place, only a man asleep by his boat at the water's edge.

"Good sir!" he cried. "Can you tell me how to get to yonder castle?"

The man leaped up, a stout pole in his hand. "Aye, my lord. You have come to the right place. A bronze coin will get you across."

He tossed the man a coin, then slid from his horse and got into the narrow boat. The craft looked small for such swift water, but the ferryman was skilled; soon he stood on the green verge of the island.

"What place is this?" he called out. "What lord lives here?" But the ferryman was already too distant to hear him, and just nodded politely as he poled back across the river.

Now that he stood at the door, he saw the castle was really a rambling house built on several small islands and connected by arching bridges. A quaint place, he thought, but probably deathly cold in winter.

He drew his sword and pounded on the door with the hilt butt.

"Who goes there?" cried a voice within.

"A traveler!" he called back. Slowly the door swung inward, revealing an old man who leaned upon a staff.

"Ah, Sir Galahad." He bowed low. "Welcome, my lord, to Corbenic. We await you at dinner."

He followed the old man through corridors, up steps, over bridges, past doors which opened onto beautiful rooms, lavishly appointed.

"Old man, stop a moment! Where are we going? And how do you know my name?"

"Ahhh"—the old man grinned—"those are questions easily answered. Not like some." He cackled. "I know you by your badge, of course." Galahad plucked the badge from his shoulder and was shocked to see not the Hawk of Lanascol, but a red cross on a white field. "We are going to meet your host. The Fisher King."

"The Fisher King? Who is he? Does he fight for King Arthur?"

But they had reached the great doors to the dining hall; the servant bowed and disappeared.

The doors swung open upon a huge chamber, big enough to seat a thousand men, its rafters lost in darkness. Before him on a dais stood a long table draped in white cloth and lit by forty candles. At one end of the table sat a handsome man of middle years with a short, graying beard and a pleasant smile. All the other chairs were empty.

The man rose and beckoned to him. "Ah, Sir Galahad, you've come at last. Welcome, my lord, welcome. Sit here by me, so I can have speech with you." He wore a crown upon his head and carried his left arm in a sling.

"How fares your arm, sir?" Galahad inquired politely as they took their seats. The king waved the question away with a light laugh.

"Oh, it's nothing. An old war wound that still festers from time to time."

No sooner were they seated than serving maidens appeared with rich dishes of every sort, fatted meats, roasted fowls, vegetables simmered in broth, nuts and breads, honey cakes with raisins, fruit fresh from tree and vine, sweet water and neat wine. Galahad had never seen such a feast. He ate until he was full to bursting and still they came, with sweetmeats, cakes, and iced fruit drinks, each serving maiden prettier than the next.

"Please!" he finally gasped. "No more!"

In an instant they were gone, and he was alone with the Fisher King.

"Now watch," said the king, "and I will show you a marvel. Pay attention, for I will ask you a question later about what you see."

A question, Galahad thought, not so easily answered.

The candles dimmed of their own accord until the hall glowed with a soft light. Someone unseen struck a harp, and sweet, vibrant music moved the air, singing to his soul. From a doorway at one end of the hall a maiden came forth, dressed in white, with pale, glowing skin, hair as black as a raven's wing, and lips as red as new blood. In her hands she held a krater of ancient make, shallow and wide-lipped, shining with the sheen of beaten silver, studded with tiny amethysts and delicate golden chasing. In the hollow dimness of the hall it shone with its own light and seemed to float of its own will between her hands. Galahad gulped, dry-mouthed. He had never seen anything so beautiful or so compelling. The maiden approached him with the krater, stepping gracefully to the music, and passed him by. There were words etched upon the krater's lip, but he could not quite read them. He tried to reach out and touch it, just once, but his arms would not obey him.

A second maiden followed, as lovely as the first, bearing a spear. Galahad caught his breath. It was over six feet long but so beautifully balanced she carried it with ease. The shaft of dark, dense wood was polished to brilliance; the honed spear tip shone deadly bright. Again he saw writing etched along the shaft, dancing in the light. What a magnificent weapon! His palms began to sweat as the maiden approached and passed by. What ancient hero king had made that spear, had feasted from the krater? The music faded; the candles flamed; the maidens were gone.

Galahad turned to his host. "Sir, I beg you! What are these treasures? Where do you keep them? Bring them back and let me see them once again! I have searched everywhere to find them!"

The Fisher King turned. His eyes shone blue and green and blue, changing like the water outside his door, deep and unreadable.

"Galahad," he said slowly, "what do you seek?"

"Sir, that is a question easily answered. I seek the Grail and Spear."

The Fisher King smiled. "Why?"

"Why, to bring to Arthur! That Britain might be whole and he might be King forever!"

At once the candles blew out and left Galahad in darkness. From far away he heard the laugh of the Fisher King.

Arthur has no need of the Grail and Spear! His time is past; his time is yet to come. Go, Galahad, seek far and wide for the Blessed Gifts whose power can heal Britain. In the soul of darkness will you find them. In the heart of light they lie. Find them for the hand that will hold them. Thou art the Grail Seeker. Find the Grail and Spear.

The words eddied around him, spinning ever faster about his head like stars gone wild. Flashing light beat against his vision. He staggered once and fell. Even as he lay rigid and sweating in Percival's castle, hands clutching the bed frame, knuckles white and eyes open, he fell down, down, hurtling through endless darkness in a sickening plummet into nothingness.

5 ✝ PRIVATE GROUND

S ea fog blanketed the low hills and snaked up the mountain valleys, hugging the crevasses and deadening the forest noises. Galahad rode slowly along the track, letting his stallion pick his own way through the clogging damp. He did not much care where they went—he only wanted a day's escape from that wretched castle. The winter had been hard and the long spring wet. Seven months penned in by rains, snows, and tempests, with no soldiering and little hunting, daily fighting a thousand small battles to preserve his wits in a household made up of a grieving widow grown over-protective of her son, an ambitious regent who had begun to thirst for kingship, a friend reduced to petulance at the slow speed of his recovery, and an ill-bred girl who was good for nothing at all except disobedience and rebellion—seven months of such companionship was enough to ruin anyone's humor. That and this foul Welsh weather. Everywhere else in Britain the sun shone on the first of June.

He shrugged and wiped the cold damp from his face. One good thing had come from such forced inactivity: Percival was at last nearly healed of his wound. The arm was stiff but serviceable, and would loosen up with time and use. He was beginning to chafe under Maldryn's patronizing, Ennyde's hauteur, and Peredur's astounding tolerance of their behavior. Only last night he had solemnly told Galahad, "I'm ready to go when you are."

Why, then, did he still delay his leaving? Galahad did not understand his own reluctance. Had not his mother always told him he was meant for something special? That he would one day do something so glorious, so magnificent, he would eclipse his father's fame? Had not King Arthur himself sent him to find the Grail and Spear? Surely his dreams lent force to that request. Why, then, did he continue to put off the moment of departure?

The longer he stayed, the more teasing he would have to bear from Dane. He scowled as he thought of Percival's sister. Her bold tongue and ready wit tried his patience. She could argue her way out of anything and always ran circles around him when he opposed her. She spent little time with the women of the house, where she belonged. She went where she willed, usually to the stables, or to the yard to watch sword practice, or wrestling, or contests of strength among the soldiers. It did no good to resent her presence, or to point out to her the unfitness of her behavior. She only laughed at him.

The stallion picked his way along the narrow, rocky path and quickened his pace as the trail broadened into a pine wood. Dane rode better than many of Peredur's soldiers and could handle a bow and arrow, cut down for her size, as well as anyone. Her aim was true—more than once her day's catch had fed the entire company at dinner. It was exasperating to come home empty-handed from a boar hunt to find Dane waiting with a pouch full of fat hares.

He had heard many of Arthur's soldiers make the same complaints of Guinevere. Bold, beautiful, and certainly capable, but unwomanly. He smiled to himself. No one in his right mind would call Dane beautiful. Pretty she might be, with all that wild hair, but she did not have a single feminine grace to recommend her. On the other hand, she was truly devoted to Percival. She cared more for his health and his honor than about anything else, including her own freedom. She had certainly risked her family's wrath by helping him to stow away to Less Britain. His future as King of Gwynedd meant much to her, as much as it meant to Percival himself.

Galahad knew that, alone of all the men in Gwynedd save Percival, he had her admiration. She admired him for his horsemanship and his skill with a sword. Something so hard to win had a value of its own, and half against his will, he felt honored by her esteem. He only wished that now and then she would drop her banter and show it in her speech.

The stallion's ears pricked forward. Galahad did not know where they were, but it hardly mattered. No matter how far he had ridden up into the hills, the horse could always find his way back to his own kind. He let the reins fall slack across the stallion's withers; through the fog the horse strode surefooted, climbing higher, quickening his pace. Suddenly he stopped, threw up his head, and whinnied. Galahad awoke with a start from his brown study and reined in sharply.

Directly ahead of him a fire burned at the mouth of a large cave. With a gasp of dismay he slid to the ground and covered the stallion's nostrils with his cloak, holding him fast, and looked quickly about. But no one came forth; nothing stirred; the thickening mist bathed everything in silence. He loosed the horse and drew his sword. The stallion's head lifted, nostrils quivering, searching the air. The horse stamped once, blew, and lowered his head to graze. Exhaling slowly, Galahad tethered the reins to a tree and advanced cautiously toward the cave.

It was of comfortable size and only recently deserted. A bed of bracken lay against the wall, covered by a blanket of fine, combed wool. Near the fire a place was laid for a meal with Samian ware as fine as any in the king's house. He held his sword at the ready and trod cautiously forward. Bold thieves, indeed, to steal from Maelgon's very castle and live in his hills! How strange that Percival had not mentioned ruffians so close to home. A woven basket sat against the far wall. He lifted the lid, half expecting to find more stolen goods, and was surprised to find it full of clothes—tunic, mantle, a pair of leggings, and a good, thick cloak. He paused. This was not the hiding place of thieves, after all. Perhaps a hermit lived here; perhaps he had fled when he heard the stallion scream.

Near the bed of bracken an oil lamp, just like the ones in the castle, perched on a shelf of rock. He trimmed the wick and lit it with a stick of kindling. After a moment's hesitation it caught, and shed a bright, steady light over the rest of the cave: jars of oil and provisions stacked in a corner near neatly folded blankets, bits of candle scraps lined up carefully on a ledge; a small bow with a quiver of carved arrows, and half in shadow, a sword.

He lifted the weapon carefully. It was thick and unbalanced, old, practically useless, the blade dull and chipped. But the hilt was ivory inlaid with enamel in an ancient Celtic pattern. Such a weapon predated the Romans' coming. Who had the need for it now? He replaced it and turned. Beyond the bed was an old oak chest, handsomely carved and silver with age. He sheathed his sword and knelt down beside it. It was not locked and opened easily at his touch. He stared in astonishment at a stack of scrolls. Twenty at least—a veritable library! He picked up the thickest of them and was astounded to find it written in Greek. Another was a child's prayer, written in Latin by an amateur hand. There were drawings, too, of swords and horses, a harness, a wheel, some kind of loom. At the bottom of the chest lay an assortment of quills, knives for sharpening them, and small pots of ink. He sat back on his heels, frowning. Surely this was the abode of a wise man, a learned recluse. Why had Percival not told him?

He closed the chest and rose. Something lay in the shadow behind the chest and he bent down to pick it up. It was furred, soft to his touch: a wolf's pelt, well cured and neatly rolled. As he stared at it he realized it looked familiar. He unrolled it quickly; yes, there were the jagged edges where his dagger had cut unevenly across the neck and paws—he'd been in a hurry that night in the cave; the light had been dim; it was not a job he was used to—this was *his* wolf pelt that he had given to Percival! What on God's sweet earth was it doing here?

His stallion nickered; he whirled, sword drawn, toward the entrance. From the blank mist a dark form slowly took shape, coming closer, growing solid and real as it neared the fire.

"Halt and declare yourself!" he cried.

"Put down your sword, cousin. I won't hurt you. Even though you've found my private ground. You're just in time for dinner."

He blinked twice at the slender shadow. As she set down the sack of firewood she carried, the firelight danced over the fall of auburn hair escaping in reckless abundance from her hood. "Don't stare so. It's only me. You've found my secret place, but I forgive you. Are you hungry? I've made some honey cakes."

"Dane!"

She stopped, startled. "What?"

"What . . . what are you doing here? This is a hermit's lodge!"

She laughed. "Yes, well, I'm the hermit. I live here, when I'm not at home. It's where I come when I want to be alone."

He gaped at her. "*You?* But why?"

"Why are *you* out in the hills today? Why is Val out fishing off the point? To get out, of course. Another day of it and I'm sure I'd have gone perfectly mad. Put your sword away; there's no one here but us."

"But"—he gestured toward the chest—"but these things cannot be yours."

She smiled. "Why not?"

"Because . . . because they are books!"

"Books and sketches. I don't usually take them out in such wet weather. But now that you have let in the damp, we might as well have a look at them." She slid off her cloak and laid it neatly to dry by the fire, then approached him.

Hastily, he sheathed his sword. The wolf pelt was still in his hand.

"And *this*." He held it out to her. "This is *my* wolf pelt. What's it doing here?"

"Percival gave it to me. He said it was a gift from you, along with his life."

"But—"

"Do you mind that he gave it to me? I asked him for it. As a caution against hubris." She looked up at him solemnly. "As a reminder of how close he came to death when he was almost home. It's another danger I sent him to when I helped him sneak away to war." She glanced around the cave. "I keep all my dearest treasures here. But you can have it back if you want it."

"No, no," Galahad said quickly. "I didn't mean that. You're welcome to it."

Dane reached into the chest and retrieved the thickest scroll. "I see you found my Xenophon. It's my own copy." She held it lovingly against her breast. "It was my birthgift from Queen Guinevere herself."

"But surely you can't read it," Galahad spluttered. "It's not in any tongue you know!"

"I can so read it. It's only Greek." She unrolled it carefully and held it toward the lamp.

"Ἐπειδὴ διὰ τὸ συμβῆναι ἡμῖν πολὺν χρόνον ἱππεύειν οἰόμεθα ἔμπειροι ἱππικῆς γεγενῆσθαι, Βουλόμεθα καὶ τοῖς νεωτέροις τῶν φίλων δηλῶσαι, ᾗ ἂν νομίζομεν αὐτοὺς ὀρθότατα ἵπποις προσφέρεσθαι.* There."

Galahad gaped at her. "Wherever did you learn it?"

"I had an old Greek tutor when I was young. Iakos. He taught Guinevere as well when she was a girl here. And your mother."

"My mother couldn't read Greek."

"Perhaps she wasn't as apt a student as her cousin."

Galahad's face flamed. "What nonsense! What do you need Greek for, anyway?"

"Why, to read Xenophon, of course." She laughed at him and dug deeper in the chest. "Here, look at this. This is a poem I wrote when I was six. It's a prayer, really. Go on; you can read it; it's in Latin."

"I've read it already." He reached into the chest and pulled out a drawing of a horse in strange trappings. "What's this?"

"A harness I invented to enable my mare to pull things without getting sores. It's simple to put on and releases quickly if she gets stuck. I can ride her at the same time, you see, and control her better."

Galahad bit back a smile. "What you need more is something to control your hair."

Dane flushed and grabbed her hair, braiding it swiftly behind her. "There. Now think of me again as Percival's brother. We shall get on much better that way."

"And have you invented new arrows and sword hilts as well?"

"You *have* been reading my scrolls. I didn't think I'd been out that long."

"What makes you think of these things?"

"Oh, I think about lots of things," Dane replied, diving back into the

---

* "Inasmuch as we have had a long experience of cavalry, and consequently claim familiarity with the art of horsemanship, we wish to explain to our younger friends what we believe to be the correct method of dealing with horses." Xenophon, *On the Art of Horsemanship, Scripta Minora,* trans. E.C. Marchant. Cambridge: Harvard University Press, 1968.

chest. "Winters are so deadly dull, I have to do *something*. So I think about better ways to do things. And then I come up here and try them to see if they will work. Just the other day when Mother set me spinning I thought of a better way to do it, so my fingers won't get so sore and blistered. I do hate spinning. And I don't do it very well. But if I had a wheel I could control the tension and the speed would be much faster. I thought of a way to connect the wheel to the spindle—"

"Never mind!" Galahad laughed. "I've heard enough!"

"And if she will let me make one, I will give Mother a present for her loom. I've found a way to move the shuttle faster. She will spend half as much time weaving and get twice as much done. But I shan't tell her about it if she doesn't let me make my spindle wheel."

"Well, I'm sure if anyone can talk her into it, you are the one." He turned and lifted the sword from its corner. "And where on earth did you get this?"

Dane smiled. "Isn't it a beauty?"

Galahad held the blade across his palms and examined it by lamplight. "It's primitive work, except for the hilt. It must be very old."

"It's ancient. I found it in one of the inner caves, not far from here. It lay half-buried with a jumble of bones. It's probably a grave gift from the ancient days."

"You disturbed a grave?"

Dane shifted her shoulders and said quickly, "I didn't disturb anything. There were plenty of old badges and buckles about. All I took was the sword. They're my own ancestors, anyway. Just look at the inlay—isn't it beautiful?"

"It's very fine, indeed. Is that why you took it?"

"Well . . ." She dropped her eyes. "Not exactly. I took it because it was a sword and I was jealous of Percival. He gets to receive sword training, and I get to spin!" Galahad grinned as her voice rose. "I spy upon his lessons, and then come up here and practice. I'm better than he is at some moves, he'll tell you so himself." She looked up, her face alight. "And I've invented a tactic that cannot be defended. Do you want to see it?"

"By all means, princeling. Show me your skill."

Deftly she took the sword as he drew his own. After a few halfhearted feints she began to attack on his left side; graciously, he allowed her to back him toward the wall. She was quick, he saw, and graceful, and had acquired a surprising degree of skill, especially as she had learned it all from observation. But she certainly was not dangerous.

"Now here is my invention," she announced, breathing fast. "As you're right-handed, I'll strike down like this, pinning your arm like that—"

Smiling, Galahad twisted his wrist, turned his hip, whirled out of her trap, and before she had moved a step, held his sword point at her breast.

"Oh!" She gasped, and her shoulders sank. "I . . . I hadn't thought of that evasion. I didn't know your wrist could be so strong. Percival's isn't. I suppose you've seen that move before?"

To comfort her, he spoke gently. "Well, once or twice. To make it work, you can't allow me this much room."

She sighed. "Well, the other problem is, I'm not very strong. I suppose I never will be." She set the sword down lovingly. "And as handsome as this old sword is, it's nothing beside yours. I've often admired it from a distance. May I take a closer look?"

After a moment's hesitation, Galahad yielded his weapon. She took it gingerly, and looked at it in awe. "Why, it's so thin and supple!"

"And sharp. Take care."

"And this silver work upon the hilt—that was done by a master. Rubies set deep to form a cross, how dark they are! This is a magnificent weapon, Galahad. Worth a king's ransom. Where did you get it? Was it a gift?"

He took it back in silence, and slid it home to its scabbard. "It was my father's sword."

"The one that Arthur gave Lancelot? I remember the tale. But it's yours now."

He nodded slowly. "He gave it to me the night after Camlann. Before he headed home. He knighted me with it after we buried Arthur. It was made by the High King's swordsmith to use in Britain's defense, and my father is done defending Britain."

Dane's features softened. "He has passed that duty on to you, now that you are a man." She smiled quickly. "You see, I haven't forgotten. You turned fifteen when we turned twelve."

"How did you know? I've told no one."

"Percival told me you were born on the equinox. A week before us. It's a propitious time, isn't it, when the world nears rebirth? Why didn't you tell us your father knighted you? It's not a thing to hide. We've not celebrated that and we ought to. Come, are you hungry? We'll have a little feast in your honor."

Galahad suddenly realized he had not eaten since dawn, and it must be by now near the middle of the afternoon. He helped her put the scrolls away and built up the fire while she brought forth a plate of sweet cakes and a small skin of wine which she set near the fire to warm.

"Welcome to my table, Sir Galahad. May God bless you and keep you and make His face to shine upon you." She closed her eyes as she spoke the blessing and poured a small libation on the ground.

"And be gracious unto you and give you peace," Galahad finished. "Amen." They ate in silence for a moment. The cakes were surprisingly good and the wine sweet and warming. He looked around the cave in wonder. Clearly, it was more a home to Dane than her father's castle. Why had Percival never told him about it?

"Did you ride up here? Where is your mare? Is that what Rouk smelled?"

"I've built a shelter for her around back. There's a fissure at the back of this cave just big enough to squeeze through. It leads into another cave, a small one, which opens out on the side of the hill. I've made a stable out of it, and stored up some hay. We can last out here for days without discomfort. There's a spring up the track a little farther."

"Then you come here often?"

"Whenever I can."

"How did you get all this stuff up here? The hay, the chest, and jars of oil?"

"Most of them I carried. Mother was throwing the chest out—it's old-fashioned Celtic work and she's had a new one made. I fashioned a sled and strapped it on. Gilla pulled it up for me. I used my new harness on her. She didn't mind at all."

"You mean you got all this stuff up here by yourself?"

"And without anyone knowing. Not even Val knows about it. It's my own, you see."

Galahad gaped at her. "You didn't tell Percival?"

"No, and I wouldn't have told you, either, but you stumbled upon it. Or your stallion did. This is my private ground. You must swear, Galahad, on your honor, to keep my secret. You've broken bread with me. You must."

The gray-green eyes were intent. He nodded slowly. "All right. I swear upon my honor not to tell Percival or anyone else about it so long as I live."

Dane grinned. "After you're dead you can tell anyone you want."

He shrugged at her jest and stretched his legs out toward the fire. It was very pleasant to lie warm and dry and comfortable on such a cold, damp day, watching the fog drift by the cave mouth, listening to the steady sounds of the stallion's grazing. The honey cakes were the best he'd ever tasted. He began to think that Percival's sister had her uses, after all.

Dane added another stick to the fire. "Galahad, where will you go with Percival? Why won't you go home to Lanascol? What exactly is this grail you're seeking and why didn't you tell me about it?"

6 ✟ MACSEN'S TREASURE

Galahad stared at her.

"Fair is fair," she retorted. "Your private ground for mine. I vow to keep it secret." She leaned forward, curious and intent. "What is the grail? Why is it so special?"

His heart began to pound. It served him right, he thought suddenly. He should have left Gwynedd already. If he had, he wouldn't have to endure this. "It's none of your concern."

"But it *is*," she responded softly. "Val is afire with this quest of yours, and he's my brother. My twin. We're one person."

"You are not. You're completely different."

"We are as close as one. Nothing can come between us, not even you. He tells me everything, you know." Her voice was gentle. "Everything you tell him, he tells me."

"Then you don't need to ask me questions. Ask Percival."

"He doesn't know the answers. He thinks this grail you're after is some old feasting krater of Macsen Wledig. He thinks the recovery of it will unite Britain."

"I told him that. It's true."

Dane laughed. "Then you don't know much about Macsen, do you?"

"And you do?"

"There are thousands of tales about him here in Wales. Gwynedd is where he lived, you know. He was a greedy old devil of an emperor—oh, yes, he was a fearless commander, and his men adored him. But he could never have enough of the things he liked. Half the women in Northgallis bore him children. He led his men into wars they didn't need to fight because he grew too fond of praise. That's why he died on a battlefield fighting the King of Rome and not at home in bed. I'm sure his feasting krater is beautiful—no one loved a lavish display more than Macsen—but, Galahad, it isn't magic! It isn't sacred. It doesn't carry any power. It's been in the ground a hundred years or more; it's probably in pieces by now. Why on earth are you looking for it?"

Galahad's gaze sharpened. "How do you know it's in the ground?"

"I don't. But the hillmen have a song about it:

> *Ravens sing*
> *Blackthorn ring*
> *Under stone*
> *Myrddin's home.*
>
> *Water weathers*
> *Stones alight*
> *Macsen's treasures*
> *Burning white.*
>
> *Llud's gate*
> *Open waits,*
> *Blessing stays*
> *A thousand days.*

She smiled nervously at him. "Strange, isn't it? The middle rhyme is different, as though it was added later to some older song. I don't know what it means. But I think it implies that Macsen's treasure is buried."

Galahad sat up quickly. "Where did you hear this? You don't know any hillmen."

"Oh, don't I? There are hillmen all over Wales. Haven't you ever seen them? They're small and dark; they slip in and out of shadows. They call themselves the Ancient People, the Forgotten Ones. They were here before the Romans, even before us Celts. They've come into this cave from time to time, for food if they are starving, for help if they are hurt. The cave was theirs before it was mine. Goll, one of their leaders, gave it to me with his blessing. I've spoken with them, you see, pretty often. Their tongue is not unlike ours, only simpler. "

"Who is Llud?"

Dane grinned. "Don't you know anything? Are there no Ancient Ones in Less Britain anymore? Llud's the god of the Otherworld." She spread an arm out to encompass the cave and the hill behind it. "This could be one of Llud's gates for all I know."

Galahad shuddered. "Old wives' tales, nothing more."

"Oh, very well, then, if you know everything." Dane tossed her head in annoyance and her hair flew free from its braiding. Galahad couldn't help smiling. Angrily she pushed it back from her face. "So what do you want to dig up the emperor's treasure for, anyway?"

He hesitated. "Macsen's treasure has the power to heal Britain."

"And my mother can cure warts. Who told you this nonsense?"

"Arthur." He was pleased to see her completely taken aback.

"King Arthur? Himself?"

"He called them things of power and asked me to find them for him. He told me that when he held all three together—the Sword, the Spear, the Grail—Britain would be safe forever. Unconquered and unconquerable. And even though he is dead, they still hold power. They are Britain's best hope for preservation."

She frowned. "But you can't get Arthur's Sword. It's buried with him."

"No, it's not. It's at the bottom of the Lake of Avalon. Where my father threw it."

She stared openly at him. "Lancelot threw the High King's Sword *away*?"

"At Arthur's command. He was dying and commanded it be done."

Dane nodded. Everyone knew the dying wishes of kings were sacred. She gazed back at the vivid blue eyes watching her. "Let me understand this. You are seeking the Grail and Spear, and when you find them you'll retrieve the Sword, and then Britain will be whole forever, no matter who is sitting in Camelot?"

Galahad nodded slowly. "I think so."

"Does Constantine know this?"

"No. No one does but you and Percival. And he doesn't know quite so much. He doesn't ask so many questions."

Dane grinned. "I like to learn. How will you know these things when you see them?"

"I have seen them in a dream. Twice."

"So *that's* the dream. Percival told me you had an enchanted dream in Avalon." She eyed him askance. "I suppose that's the one that kept you sleeping throughout the Battle of Camlann. I can understand that you'd want to make amends. Do you know where to find these treasures?"

"No. But I know who holds the key. A man who is called the Fisher King. Have you ever heard of such a person?"

"No, but it could be a local name. It might not be known outside the village where he lives."

"He lives on an island."

"Then search along a river. There are islands in the Eden River, they say. And that's where Excalibur was found, which was Macsen's sword."

Galahad considered this. "That might be a good idea."

"Of course it's a good idea. It's also a good idea to take Percival to Lanascol so he can train with Lancelot."

Galahad glared at her and crossed his arms over his chest. "I'm not going home. I told you that."

"Not even to visit? Why not?"

"That's none of your business."

"Percival worships Lancelot. He'd love nothing better."

"Percival's been in Lanascol. We spent two weeks in Benoic on the way home from Autun."

"That's different. Lancelot was wounded then and confined to bed. Take Val there now and let your father teach him to be a king."

Galahad shook his head. "There's no point. My father has given up."

"On Britain, perhaps, but surely not on Lanascol. Perhaps he's just war weary. Perhaps you could convince him to return."

"No. Not even if I could."

Dane's eyes narrowed until they were slits of green. "In heaven's name, why not? What is there between you?"

"It's . . . it's . . ." Galahad stammered, coloring furiously. "Leave it alone, can't you? As long as he's there I'm not *ever* going home."

For the first time since he had met her Dane was at a loss for words.

"We've never done well together, he and I," he continued swiftly, propelled by the need to fill the silence, "and more than once I've sworn to kill him. I won't—probably—but he does better when I'm not around and so do I—" He stopped, appalled at all he had revealed.

Dane reached for his hand and squeezed it. "I'm sorry, Galahad. I shouldn't have asked. You are right: it doesn't concern me. I just assumed— But it must be hard to be Sir Lancelot's son. I never realized—I beg your pardon."

"What do you mean?"

She smiled shyly. "He's such a great man, so renowned for his daring and his skill; it must be difficult to have people expect as much of you."

Galahad stiffened and withdrew his hand. "I'm not *jealous* of him, if that's what you mean. Good God, you've got it backward! I'm ashamed of him."

Dane's jaw dropped. "What on earth for?"

"How can you not know? The whole world knows!"

"*You* believe the rumors about Lancelot and the Queen? His own son?"

He couldn't answer. The words stuck in his throat.

Dane was shaking her head. "You shouldn't. The rumors are lies. My mother was a great friend of Queen Guinevere's. It's all malicious slander. A man can love a woman without betrayal. I believe that's possible, don't you?"

"Not if the woman is another man's wife!"

"Nonsense! Of course he can. He can love her at a distance without dishonor to anyone."

Galahad laughed bitterly, his face burning as he recalled all the times he had inadvertently caught Lancelot and Guinevere together: sometimes hand in hand, sometimes in a long, ravenous kiss, once in a torrid embrace which he had been certain would lead to his father's death. They had always had the same look of helpless, hopeless longing on their faces. "There was never any distance."

"Well," Dane returned, "there was enough. He didn't betray Arthur's bed. He didn't even steal Guinevere's affection from the King."

"What romantic hogwash!" Galahad snorted. "You don't know the first thing about it. He coveted another man's wife. That's a sin. And he's never been sorry about it. That's another. He's better off in Lanascol, where he can't easily get at her. Let him make peace with my mother's memory. He treated her abominably. He left her there to wither and die in Lanascol, all because he couldn't stay away from Guinevere."

Stung, Dane retaliated. "You expect him to make peace with her memory when she's the one who betrayed Guinevere? It was *Elaine's* plan for King Melwas to abduct the Queen and ravish her—her own cousin, for pity's sake! And it was *Elaine* who tried to take her place in the King's bed while she was gone. Why else did Arthur banish her from Britain?"

Galahad stared speechless at her.

"You didn't know? It's known in Wales. My aunt Elaine was jealous of her cousin all her life—if you lived with her, you ought to know that."

Galahad's lips moved stiffly. "You ignorant girl—she never betrayed anyone. She was herself betrayed."

Dane shook her head vigorously. "You've got it wrong, Galahad. She betrayed Guinevere to Melwas and tried to take her place in Camelot. But Arthur threw her out—you didn't know that either? He banished her forever from his presence. That's why when Lancelot married her he took her to Lanascol. He had orders never to let her come back."

Galahad leaped to his feet. "You lie! You ignorant, interfering gossip! What can you know about it? It's a barefaced lie!"

Dane jumped up to face him. Her unruly hair tumbled free about her shoulders, lending her face a wild ferocity. "Who are you to call *me* ignorant and interfering? You apparently know *nothing*! My whole family knows King Arthur banished Elaine—that's why they had to go to Lanascol to see her!"

Pale, sweating, Galahad backed along the wall of the cave.

"Leave my mother alone!" he gasped. "She was a better woman than *you'll* ever be! And Lancelot betrayed her with Guinevere."

Dane hooted. "You poor blockhead! Marrying Lancelot was the only honorable thing she ever did. And he deserved a better wife than Elaine of Gwynedd!"

Galahad's throat went dry. He stared at her vivid face, half-hidden by her hair. "You're nothing but a stupid, meddling girl. I don't have to listen to your half-wit lies." He backed away, feeling blindly along the wall.

Dane followed. "You call *me* stupid and meddling? What would *you* call a woman who devised a plan to have her cousin raped? What would *you* call a woman who tried to trick the High King into her bed? She was false, Galahad. It was Lancelot who saved Guinevere from Melwas—you can't blame her for loving him. . . ."

Galahad bolted from the cave mouth and fled to his horse. "Witch! I won't listen!"

"Witch, am I? Then I'll curse you!" She pointed a finger at him. "May your arrogance consume you; may your road meander! May you follow in your father's footsteps and love a woman you cannot in honor have!"

He stumbled, grabbed the reins, and threw himself upon his stallion's back. They galloped down the track, the horse slipping and sliding in the mud and fog. Galahad clung blindly to the whipping mane, wondering if it was possible to get across the border into Northgallis before dark.

Dane stood before the fire in the cave mouth and watched him go. She was already ashamed of calling him names, but she could scarcely bring herself to believe that he knew so little about his parents. Who had closed his eyes? What kind of a childhood could he possibly have had to know so little and be wrong about so much? How could he hate a man as upright and revered as his own father, a man all Britain held in such high esteem?

She shook her head and shivered, drenched in fog. There could not be a boy more ignorant, more backward, more stubbornly contrary than her cousin Galahad. What on God's sweet earth could have made him so?

PART II
The Hawk of Lanascol

*In the seventeenth year of the reign
of Arthur Pendragon*

7 ✟ AIDAN

Galahad shivered in his big bed. He hated the dark. It wasn't the loneliness of it; he had never minded being alone. It was the unseen menace in the corners that terrified him. Warmth and comfort were nearby, next door in the nursery where Maida slept with his little brothers. Sometimes he ached to sneak in and cuddle with her as he used to do, sucking dreamily at her milky breasts until sleep gently closed his eyes. But those days were past—he was nearly five years old and he was Prince of Lanascol. He was entitled to his own chamber. Dark corners and all, it must be endured. Wet nurses were for babies.

He sat up suddenly when he heard footsteps in the corridor. It wasn't the watch changing, the tread was too light. He slipped out of bed and pattered to the door. Cold struck upward from the stone floor, numbing his bare feet, setting him shaking. Pulling with all his might at the heavy handle, he slipped the latch and opened the door a crack.

Cressets burned smokily in the hall sconces, but even in the dim light he recognized his mother, her blue gown, her golden hair, the proud lift of her head. He dared not move. At her side, stern and silent, soft-footed in fine, doeskin boots, walked the king himself. Biting his lip, Galahad watched them go by. He had only a glimpse of her face, cold and shuttered, but it filled him with rage. Why couldn't he leave her alone?

He opened the door a little further and stuck his head out. They stopped outside the queen's chamber and his hopes rose. Perhaps the king would not go in. He heard their voices: his low-pitched and commanding, hers shrill and heavy with contempt. He waited a moment, hopeful that the argument would end in the king's leaving. It had been so often enough before. But the king took her arm, opened the door, spoke briefly to the sentry, and followed the queen in. The door shut behind them with a loud thud.

He hesitated, but it was freezing and his feet were already numb. He hurried back to bed and pulled the soft wool blankets tight around him. He closed his eyes and tried to shut out the picture of the king's strong hand on his mother's arm. He tried to think of things that pleased him, as Maida had taught him to do when he was angry. He thought of his mother's hair with the sun on it, dark gold and glowing. And his uncle Galyn's sword, which had silver chasing on the scabbard and a golden cross upon the hilt. And the new chestnut stallion with the white blaze which Galyn had promised he could sit this coming spring.

He thought of his mother's small white hands as she sat stitching by candlelight, her dancing hands moving with swift, sure grace over some bright fabric. Sometimes she would take him on her lap and caress him with those pretty hands. How sweet she always smelled! She was so different from anyone else in Lanascol, with her fair complexion and accented speech. He knew she had been born in a far-off land at the very edge of Britain, and that the king had taken her away from her people when he wed her and brought her to Lanascol. Whenever she spoke of her homeland her eyes would mist with tears.

She was always sad in winters when the king was home. But in spring, summer, and autumn, when the king was gone across the sea to Britain, she would smile and sing; she would dance with Galahad in the garden; she would hold court in her own name and everyone did her bidding. From equinox to equinox she ruled Lanascol. Everyone scurried to obey her, and when she was not pleased grown men trembled before her anger.

The scrape of metal on stone interrupted his reverie. He slid out of bed and ran to the door. The sentry was gone from the queen's chamber; he could hear his footfalls on the stair and those of his replacement. Galahad slipped quickly out into the hallway. Everything was cold, still, and silent. Surely the king had gone. They had little enough to say to each other at the best of times. He ran down the corridor, his bare feet making no sound at all on the icy stone.

The door was heavy but unlocked, and he got it open. The queen's serving women lay on pallets in the antechamber, fast asleep. Old Grannic, grown almost deaf, snored in her bedroll near the door to the bedchamber. It was easy to slip past them. Without a backward glance he put a hand to the latch and opened the inner door.

The first thing he saw was the sword. It lay balanced on a stool against the wall close by his hand. Light from a candle on the little table gleamed on the oiled leather scabbard and picked out the dull glow of rubies set in a cross upon the hilt. He knew—everyone knew—the sword was the gift of the High King Arthur and a weapon of sacred power. He had never seen it so near. He reached out a furtive hand to touch it, then froze as it dawned on him what the sword's presence meant. In the same instant he heard sounds in the darkness beyond the candle: the bed's rhythmic creak, low-pitched grunts, and a woman's hiss.

"Animal! Swine!"

Galahad stood motionless, fist in mouth, and began to shake. The king himself was here!

"Vermin! Viper! I spit on you! There!"

He recognized his mother's voice and, stepping closer, shaded his eyes against the candle and peered into the darkness.

She lay naked with her hair flung untidily across the pillows, pale and helpless, pinned beneath the man's brown body. He held her wrists to the bed and moved against her, pushing her, crushing her flesh, his dark head bent near her face. She gasped each time he moved, struggling against his weight and cursing him in furious whispers. One heavy breast flopped sideways, ghostly in the dimness, jiggling, its dark nipple staring at him like some baleful eye. Even as he watched, the man gasped, groaned, fell still, and bowed his head, releasing her arms. Weeping, she clawed his back with her nails.

"Oh, God, what have I done to deserve this?" she cried. "Get off me, you heavy oaf! You are a beast, no better! Get off!"

"Mama!" Galahad wailed, but his lips were too stiff to move and no sound came out.

The king raised his dark head from the woman's breast. "For God's sake, Elaine," he said wearily, "you are my wife. Be still."

"I will not! You will not take your pleasure without cost! You are an animal! Let me go!" She pummeled his shoulders with her fists, trying futilely to push him away. "You rutting beast! I loathe you! Go back to Britain—take your filthy lusts to Britain's great whore—"

His hand took her throat; his long fingers encircled her neck. She lay instantly still, whimpering.

"If her name passes your lips," he said slowly and very clearly, "I will have your life." They stared at each other in silence. The boy did not dare to breathe.

"I hope you roast in Hell."

His fingers tightened and she began to scream. Too quick for thought, Galahad grabbed the great sword with both hands, pulled it free of the scabbard, heaved it over his head, sobbing with the effort it cost him, and lurched toward the bed.

"Leave her alone! Leave her alone!" The words burst forth at last, unstoppable and shrill. "Leave her alone!" Straining with all his might, he swung the heavy weapon and brought it down. The king's startled face turned toward him; his strong hand whipped out, caught the boy's wrist, and the sword pulled free.

The woman gasped and grabbed for the blankets. "In front of your own son! Are you not ashamed?"

But the king lay still, watching him calmly, holding the sword without effort.

"Galahad. Son. Could you not sleep?"

The boy gulped. "Leave her alone! You are hurting her! Why can't you leave her alone? Go away! We don't want you here!"

The king moved off her, then, and carefully set the sword down. Slowly and with deliberation, he swung out of bed and faced the boy, a naked giant of a man, tall and lean, war-hardened and battle-scarred, a king's man, a king. The boy stepped back. His mother's hand pulled him close against the bed and held him. She whimpered something to him but he did not listen. He could not take his eyes from the man before him.

"I am not ashamed," the king said. "She is my wife. It is my right. But even so"—and the voice softened slightly—"I would not hurt her. Go ahead and look. There is not a mark on her. She is not in pain."

"You hurt her!" Galahad blurted, fighting tears. "I saw you!"

The man said nothing, but reached for his leggings and pulled them on, then his boots, his tunic and mantle and royal brooch. Finally he reached for his sword.

"Galahad. Be easy, son. Your mother is well and whole. If I have hurt her, it is in her vanity only, and does not touch her honor—"

"Honor!" she howled, pointing a finger at him. "Oh, yes, let's talk about honor! How you lust after one woman and lie with another! What precious honor!"

"Hush, Elaine," he replied in irritation. "This does not help him to understand it."

The boy listened as the familiar bitterness of their arguments eddied past him, making him feel alone and small. All he understood was that the king had admitted to causing her pain. He stepped forward from her embrace.

"I will kill you for it," he said firmly, standing straight as a soldier and looking his father in the face. "When I am grown. I will kill you."

His mother squeezed his arm but the king did not move. The gray eyes pinned him with the swiftness of a dagger blow. Although his heart was pounding, Galahad could not look away from his father's face, from the black hair and straight black brows, the clean lines of cheekbone, jaw, and chin, and the crooked nose, broken in childhood, that women said robbed him of beauty. Slowly the king raised the sword and touched the blade to his forehead in salute.

"When you are grown, we shall see," he said with a grim smile, and turned away. At the door he stopped and looked back. "Soon, Elaine, I will take him with me. Next summer, perhaps. He is ready. He has been too long with you."

"Take him, if you dare!" she spat. "I will kill you myself first! He is all I have! Go back to Britain, where everyone values you so, and leave us alone. The great Lancelot! No one wants you here." She clutched the boy to her breast as the door closed.

He turned and kissed her face. "I'm sorry, Mama. The sword was heavy."

A tear slipped down her cheek as she ruffled his hair. "My fierce little protector, you couldn't have stopped him. Not tonight. His blood was up. It's not your fault, my brave boy. It's the fault of that wicked Queen, that sorceress, Guinevere. The whore of Britain."

The day Lancelot left for Britain, Galahad and his brothers gathered in the forecourt with their nurses, waiting with Lancelot's brother Prince Galyn and his new wife, Adele, to bid the king farewell. The escort waited with them, a hundred horses in five neat rows stamping their feet, flicking their tails, tossing their heads and playing with their bits until the shuffle and jingle of their impatience filled the courtyard, raucous in the peace of early morning. Overhead, cool spring clouds hung low, promising rain.

In the center of the courtyard a groom held a riderless black stallion who danced and snorted, refusing to be still. A saddlecloth was strapped to the horse's back, embroidered with the Hawk of Lanascol. Galahad watched the stallion prance. Alone of all the men in Lanascol, Lancelot rode bareback, even in battle. He was, Galyn had once said in envy, music in motion on a horse. Suddenly the stallion quieted, pricked his ears toward the king's house, and nickered.

Elaine and Lancelot came out the door together and down the shallow steps of the king's house. Even from where he stood Galahad could hear the hushed murmur of their voices and knew at once they were arguing. His mother's face was cool and proud, his father's strained.

"I'll be back for him before the summer is out," he heard Lancelot say as they came toward him. "He's old enough. There are lads in Camelot as young as he."

"Over my dead body."

"Try to see reason, Elaine. He is my son, too."

She looked away, her face hard. "Attempt it at your peril. You will regret it."

"I regret so many things." Lancelot spoke grimly. "One thing more. This year I'm leaving Galyn in command of Lanascol, since he's not coming with me. His orders, *all* his orders, are to be obeyed."

Galahad glanced swiftly at his mother. Her face froze, but a slow blush crept upward from her throat.

"Do not try to thwart him, Elaine. You will answer to me for it. And I might as well tell you now that I've sent to the bishop for a new priest—an honest one. His name is Patrik and he'll be here soon. Galyn will see him installed in the chapel. As for Aidan—keep that filthy charlatan out of Benoic and away from my sons. I'll not tell you twice. If he shows his face inside the gates, Galyn has orders to kill him."

Elaine's blue eyes widened, and then narrowed. Her lips moved stiffly. "How like you, Lancelot, to kill a man who does not suit you. Even a man of God."

Lancelot grunted. "He's as much a man of God as I'm a Saxon. I'm not the fool you think me, my dear. Be warned."

Her chin lifted in defiance but she said nothing. Lancelot gazed down at Galahad. "Galahad, my son."

"My lord."

"I have agreed to let your mother keep you here in Benoic a while longer. But before the next equinox I'll return to take you back to Britain. It's time you came to Camelot and joined the fellowship of soldiers who serve Arthur. It's where your place will be when you are grown."

"His place is here with me!" Elaine snapped. "At least until Arthur has freed himself of that profligate witch of a wife! She'll not have charge of my son! Not while I live!"

Lancelot's face whitened and his nostrils flared. "Mind your promise to me," he said in a flat voice, "or I'll take him with me now."

"I have not said her name. That is all I promised."

Lancelot drew a deep breath and looked down at Galahad. "Judge by actions, Galahad, not by words, and strive to make truth your companion. I must be going—stay by your mother and keep her from harm. I'll be back by summer's end."

They watched as Lancelot leaped lightly onto his stallion's back. He raised an arm as the nervous horse swung round, and the soldiers drew their swords and touched them to their foreheads in salute. Lancelot sketched a salute in return and, whirling the stallion on his haunches, started down the road toward the gates of Benoic.

The onlookers watched silently until the galloping horses were no more than a low vibration on the heavy air. Then, as if a signal had been given, everyone began to move at once.

Elaine reached for Galahad's hand. "Galahad, come with me."

She led him to her garden, where Grannic huddled on a carved bench, wrapped in a cloak. Elaine began to pace back and forth along the stone-paved walk, wringing her hands and moving in short, sharp strides.

"Who does he imagine he is, to order me about so? I, Elaine of Gwynedd, to take orders from his *brother*? Have I not ruled Lanascol in his absence these four years past? And now I am unworthy to be obeyed by his kin? He uses me as a doormat; he wipes his boots on me!" She spun around, snapping her fingers. "*That* for his commands! I shall do as I please. What can he do to me that he has not done already? He has abandoned me here in this cruel country, so far from home! Let him have me horsewhipped, if he dares!"

At this Grannic stirred. "Calm yourself, my lady. Sir Lancelot has never horsewhipped anyone, and you know it well. You will throw yourself into one of your weeping fits, if you're not careful."

"I don't care!" Elaine cried, flinging her arms out. "Why shouldn't I weep? He has left me with little else to do!"

"Prince Galyn is a kind man. You will have the running of the household, not Adele. You will not be powerless."

"A queen of chamberlains, cooks, and gardeners?" She held out her arms to Galahad and he ran into her embrace. "I am not even queen of my own bed! Ask Galahad. He knows."

"Shame!" Grannic cried, rising. "He's but a child!"

"Perhaps, but he knows more than most boys twice his age. Don't you, my handsome prince?"

She sat next to Grannic on the bench and let Galahad climb into her lap. "My little warrior," she said fiercely, hugging him close. "You will be strong one day, stronger than all of them. It has been foretold. Strong enough to protect me from him, won't you, little prince?"

"Yes, Mama."

She stroked his hair and spoke solemnly. "One day you will outshine your father. Remember the prophecy of the Lady of the Lake. He is corrupt, but you will be pure. One day you will raise the sword of righteousness in Britain, and the light of your glory will eclipse all other lights."

Galahad had heard this many times before. It was her favorite refrain in her injured moods. The words meant little to him, but he loved to see the way her eyes lit when she spoke.

"It means you will destroy your father," she said firmly, "and that is a sight I should dearly love to see."

Old Grannic shook her head. "Shame on you, Elaine. It's wrong to turn a lad against his father. Just because your nose is out of joint."

"Out of joint!" Elaine's great blue eyes filled with tears. "Grannic, you were born and raised in Wales, as I was. Don't you miss it? Don't you ever miss those solemn mountains, those narrow valleys, and the cold, gray sea? Don't you dream of it every night? Doesn't the longing for it fill every waking hour of every interminable day? I tell you, I shall die if he does not take me home. A year, a single year, was all I asked."

Grannic sighed. "Elaine, my dear, from a child you've always wanted what you couldn't have. You are queen of a kingdom larger than your father's. You have three healthy sons. What more do you want?"

"What more?" Elaine cried. "Are you jesting? You are no help to me anymore, Grannic. You're so old your wits are gone. Go inside and leave me alone with my son."

Elaine hugged Galahad tightly and pulled his head to her breast. "You know the wrongs he has done me, don't you, Galahad? You remember the things I've told you? He has taken me from my home and all my kin, and for what? To sit alone in this dark fortress, surrounded by an impenetrable forest, while he waits hand and foot upon my wicked cousin, King Arthur's wife! Oh, God! What has she ever done to deserve such homage? Why cannot Arthur *see* with the eyes God gave him? Your father, Galahad, worships her—he worships her before even God." Her voice broke; she wiped her tears fiercely away. "He will do *anything* to please her; he will grovel; he will beg to be allowed to kiss the ground she treads. But *I* am not worthy to receive his brother's bow! How unfair it is! She, who was born in a tiny kingdom without hope of power, she has them both! And I, Princess of Gwynedd—who am owed such adulation by right of birth—I have no one!"

Caught in the whirlwind of her emotion, Galahad gripped her hand and held it hard between his own. "I'm here, Mama."

"Ah, Galahad!" She clutched him and wept into his hair. "I will be revenged. By God I will!" She smiled weakly down at him. "You'll be a thousand times the man he is! What a gall you will be to him!"

"What is a gall?"

"He is cruel to me, Galahad; you don't know how cruel. And this latest insult! Your father thinks he can rule my life even when he is not here. But I have never, *ever* submitted to his will, except when he has forced me. You know that, don't you?"

"Yes, Mama." Galahad looked away.

"Did you hear what he said about Father Aidan?"

Galahad nodded and Elaine smiled bitterly. "Pay no attention. Aidan will come to me when and where I will. Lancelot is powerless to prevent it." She cast a quick glance beyond the garden wall. "I will tell you a secret, Galahad. Aidan has been here for weeks now, but in hiding. Let the new priest come. Your uncle Galyn will officially install him and Lancelot will be content. But Aidan will still be here in secret. You see, Galahad"—and suddenly she turned to him, her bright blue eyes holding his own—"no worldly power can keep him out. Father Patrik, or whatever his name is, may have the bishop's blessing, but Father Aidan has God's own. He is a wandering holy man and beholden to no one, not to a bishop, not to a pope. He lives as the lilies in the field, from season to season with only God's protection. And this summer, Galahad, he will be your teacher. Learn well from him. But make this our secret. Don't tell even Maida or Renna. And certainly don't tell Galyn. The young fool thinks he must kill him because Lancelot wants his death."

A bird called somewhere in the silence, sweet and shrill. Elaine went suddenly still. The call came again and she rose, pushing Galahad from her lap. "Now go. Renna must be wondering where you are."

Although she did not move, Galahad sensed excitement in her. He followed her gaze, but could see nothing unusual in the corner of the garden which held her gaze. "Mayn't I stay with you? Please, Mama?"

She bent down quickly and kissed his cheek. There was a gaiety about her that he had not seen all winter. "No, my sweet prince. Not right now. Later I shall send for you and we'll sup together. Will that do? Now run along and find Renna. There's a good boy."

He obeyed, walking slowly back the way he had come. But on the threshold of the house he turned. His mother stood where he had left her, running a hand over her gown to smooth the wrinkles, her eyes on the low door in the garden wall. And slowly, very slowly, the latch lifted and the door began to open.

"*There* you are!" Strong hands spun him around and Renna lifted him bodily from the ground. "Where have you been, you young scamp! I've been searching the place from the rafters down!" She laughed just a shade too loudly, shut the door behind him, and took him away.

Galahad awakened suddenly from a dreamless sleep. Heart racing, he slipped out of bed, pulled on his tunic, and belted it tightly around his narrow waist. Then he slithered onto the stone sill and paused, looking out at the night. It was moonless and chill, with clouds hanging low over the surrounding forest. He did not stop to wonder where he was going or what it was that called to him from the silent dark. Without any thought beyond anticipation, he dropped silently to the ground, slipped into the shadows, neatly avoided the sentries, and made his way beyond the grounds of the king's house, through the twisted alleys of the town to the postern gate. Here he stopped, suddenly uncertain. A single sentry stood watch under the dim light of a burning torch. Galahad hid in the shadow of an old oak and waited. Before long he heard footsteps. The sentry heard them, too.

"Who goes there, in the king's name?"

"It is I, Gilles. As arranged."

"My lady." The sentry bowed low and, without lifting his eyes, backed away into the dark.

Two figures appeared, walking side by side along the wall. The man wore a monk's robe tied at the waist with a braided leather thong. His face was hidden by his cowl. The woman wore a light cloak over her gown and a hood that only half-hid her golden hair.

"You've heard the prophecy," she was saying. "He needs to be directed and prepared. He's easy to instruct; you'll find him quick and obedient. Use care, though. If he's riled beyond endurance he can fly into a passion. It's more than temper, I promise you. In that, he's like his father. I will leave him in your hands, but don't delay. We have only months. Lancelot will be back at summer's end to take him." She paused. "I intend to go with them, but if I am refused, you must keep him from taking Galahad. I don't want him going to Britain until he's old enough to wield a sword. I want revenge."

A low voice answered, deep, rich, and authoritative. "You will get your revenge in time, beauty. Lancelot's glory will be as a candle to Galahad's sun. This every seer worth his salt has already seen in the stars."

Elaine stopped in front of the gate and put a hand on his arm. "I want to see that day! I want to see Lancelot's face!"

"That I cannot promise."

"But you must. And you will, for me. Can't you come earlier tomorrow? There is so much to discuss. And"—she pressed closer—"my need of you is great."

The robed figure bowed over her hand. "Not until moonset."

"An hour ago you scoffed at the regent's power—now you are afraid of being caught by his soldiers?"

The man stiffened at her bantering tone. "I fear no man. Nor any woman."

The queen laughed. "The bravest of all men, no doubt. I have heard that boast before. "

"No man can harm me when God is my shield."

"Indeed? Even so, you might do well to fear a woman. . . . Come at moonset, then. Send the usual signal. Tomorrow I will bring the boy."

"No need. He will come at my call."

"Without my leave? You overstep yourself."

"I have already summoned him. He is here. Now."

Her head whipped round, scanning the shadows. "Where?"

"Hiding. You might do well, beauty, to remember this one thing: What is between your son and me is nothing you can share."

"There is nothing at all between you until I give you leave!" she retorted angrily. "Understand this, if you wish to live until morning!'

The tall man laughed gently and bowed low. "You will get your due, beauty. Never fear it."

"You will be ruled by me."

"By God first."

"Agreed. And you will not harm my son."

"Indeed, I will not. He is more precious to me than you can guess."

"Good. I bid you good night, then. Come tomorrow and be on time." She turned away with the characteristic lift of her chin, and then she paused. "Is he really here?"

The robed figure turned toward the oak tree and went still. Galahad felt silent fingers reach out to him, close about his will, and move him forward three steps into the outer reaches of the light.

Elaine gasped. "Galahad!"

Galahad did not turn to look at her; he could not. He was drawn to the deep black space inside the cowl. As he stared, the outlines of a face gradually appeared, lit by a pair of light, feral eyes. He tried to call out. His lips moved but made no sound. *Aidan! Inside the gates!* The wild eyes smiled. Galahad fainted.

8 ✟ GALYN

"You know, don't you, that he's here, that she meets with him every day." Adele paced back and forth across the chamber, plucking at her gown.

Galyn stood as still as the carved chair he leaned on. "Are you sure? Have you seen him?"

"No." Adele turned. Her dark eyes narrowed with worry; damp tendrils of hair escaped her net and danced in agitation as she moved. "She's very clever, Galyn. I don't think Lancelot knows half how clever she is. She sneaks away and no one knows where she's gone, not Pella, not Desse, not even Grannic."

"What makes you think she's meeting *him*?"

"The triumph on her face. The sly smiles. The condescension. The veiled references to Galahad's instruction. To his 'higher' calling. It's as if she's daring us to ask her outright if the man is here."

"Have you?"

Adele flashed him a quick look. "Indeed, no! That's man's work, if there ever was! She's Lancelot's queen; *I'm* not crossing her path if I can help it. *You* ask her. You're regent."

Galyn lifted his shoulders a fraction. "I don't want a contest of wills this soon after Lancelot's departure. I'd rather find out another way. When she disappears, does Galahad go with her?"

"Sometimes." Adele wrung her hands together and then made herself stop. "Galyn, what if— I know Lancelot is worried about the boy's corruption, but what if . . . what if it's Elaine who's really in danger?"

"What do you mean, 'in danger'?"

"I think—I'm not at all sure, because she conceals it—but I think there's something more between them than the boy's education."

Galyn straightened slowly. "Speak plainly."

She stepped closer to him and lowered her voice. "Why did Lancelot marry her, Galyn? We both know it wasn't for love, and surely he could have had his pick of women. Why her?"

"He got her with child."

"Yes, but why?"

Galyn frowned. "He's never told me, Adele. And I've never asked. I only know the stories you know."

"That he was drunk and took her by mistake, thinking she was Guinevere?"

"It must have been more than drink."

"What, then?"

Galyn hesitated. "Lancelot's a man of hard control. But when the control breaks, it's like a dam smashing. All his passions break their bond at once and sweep his sense away. He does things that in his right mind he would never do. It serves him well in battle; it makes him well-nigh invincible. But it happens at other times as well, when he's been pushed too far. It's his only flaw. He himself calls it his curse. I've always imagined his bedding of Elaine must have come at such a time."

Adele sighed sadly. "A moment's derangement he's paid for with his life. And I don't believe that's the whole story, either. Do you know what I think? I think Elaine planned it. Elaine plans everything." She looked up at him and spoke in a whisper. "But this I know. He doesn't lie with her now, except when he's driven to it."

Galyn gasped. "Are you suggesting . . . are you suggesting they aren't his sons?"

Adele smiled. "No, no. You have only to look at them to know they're his. No, I meant, what would a woman do in such a circumstance? What would Elaine do? She has a nature that demands admiration. She cannot deny herself the satisfaction of her smallest whim. As little as she loves Lancelot, she resents the insult of his inattention."

"I don't know." Galyn frowned. "What would she do?"

Adele glanced quickly behind her. "She would find herself a man she could command. She would find herself a lover."

"She would not dare!" Galyn said softly. "He could kill her for it!"

"Yes, but he wouldn't. Not Lancelot. He might kill the man. And hasn't he given you those very orders?"

Galyn let out a low whistle. "I wondered what was behind the banishment. It's not like him to treat a priest so. When he told me it was on account of the man's corruption, I thought he was worried about the boys. My God. This sheds a clearer light on everything."

"But he was right to be worried about the boys. Galahad's secretive

NANCY AFFLECK McKENZIE • 63

enough as it is, but lately he's been more so. He spends all day bent over the Sacred Scrolls, working out the words and learning them by heart."

"Well, what's wrong with that?"

"It isn't natural!" Adele cried. "He should be out with the other boys, fishing in the river, riding his pony, rolling about in the dust with his companions, playing with wooden swords and daggers, out in the bright sun of summer, in God's blessed light. Instead, he hides away in a corner with a candle and his scrolls, and memorizes verses until his little head ought to burst with the knowledge! Who inspires him to this, Galyn? Not Elaine—she says she can read, but I've never seen her glance twice at a scroll. He has no friends. Who sets him these tasks?"

Galyn frowned. "Have you asked him?"

"He doesn't answer. He just politely apologizes for disturbing me and vanishes to another corner. Something is very wrong, my dear. I'm sure that priest is here. Somewhere."

Galyn came forward and took her in his arms. "I'm indebted to you, Adele. I'll keep an eye on Galahad from now on. I have an idea or two how his interest might be diverted from his studies. Underneath that serious demeanor of his, he *is* a boy."

Adele looked at him worriedly. "I suppose so. But sometimes I wonder."

Galyn pushed open the stable door, and the warm, musky odor of horses, hay, and rubbed leather engulfed Galahad in a wave, drawing him inside. He had always found it a heady scent, enticing and impossible to resist. From his corner tether a gray pony whinnied hopefully.

Galyn laughed. "Little pig." He slapped the pony hard on the rump as they walked by; the ears went flat. "You've had enough already."

"Watch out, Uncle Galyn. He'll kick you."

"No, he won't. Look at his eyes. He's still watching your pouch, looking for carrot tops. How's your riding coming? Have you had a chance to try the new course Lancelot set the cavalry?"

Galahad nodded. "I can do it. But Cherub is awfully slow."

Galyn grinned. "You'll get a faster mount in time. Then we'll find out if you've got your father's skill. Come see the surprise I told you about. Ho, Nedric, bring the new stallion out."

The groom led out a gleaming liver chestnut with large, dark eyes and a white blaze down his forehead. Neat-footed as a pony, the stallion sidled against the groom, tucking his head until his bent neck was a long, bulging curve of smooth-coated muscle. The groom made him stand quietly, and the horse looked at them eye-to-eye, unafraid.

"What's his name?" Galahad asked softly.

"Oh, I don't know. I haven't gotten around to that. What do you think I should call him? Anything but Blaze."

"Caesar!" Galahad cried suddenly. The stallion snorted and his ears shot forward. The groom pulled on the halter rope and laid a hand against the horse's neck.

"Why Caesar? What made you think of it? It's a Roman name, and he's hardly a Roman horse."

"It's the highest rank. Higher than generals."

"Ahhh. I see. But you're forgetting the High King of Britain. That's a higher rank than caesar."

"It is?" Galahad stared wide-eyed at his uncle, who went forward to stroke the horse.

"It is indeed," Galyn replied, and then under his breath finished, "but God save Arthur if he ever has to prove it."

"Call him Arthur, then."

"No, no." Galyn laughed. "I'd not do such a thing to Arthur. Caesar is good enough. Ho, Caesar, stand while I handle you. Now, Galahad, are you ready? Come on. I'll give you a leg up." Galyn swung him aloft and settled him onto the stallion's back. "There you go. Grip his mane; it'll keep you steady."

But Galahad did not need to grip the mane. He sat up straight and looked past the horse's ears to the far wall, all his concentration on the animal beneath him. He could feel every muscle, every sinew as it moved, stretched, shifted, every breath taken and released, every lift of the tail behind him—all this he could *feel* from the warm back beneath his seat. This was nothing like sitting his pony, which was not much different from sitting in Grannic's chair with the curved braces that rocked back and forth. This was like sitting on living magic, powerful beyond imagination, capable at any moment of breaking free of the groom's control and speeding him away. He thought about what that would feel like, racing over meadow grasses, leaping streams, flying down forest tracks— His legs tensed, the horse stepped forward, was brought up short by the rope, and snorted in frustration, pawing the ground.

"Not yet, my handsome devil. Not yet." Galyn's voice had an odd quality about it, and Galahad turned to look at him. His uncle was smiling. "I knew it. You're born to it—it's in your blood already. You just think it and the horse obeys."

"He wants to run. He's tired of the stable and he wants to run free."

Galyn smiled. "Exactly. It's what he does best. He's young yet, and hasn't got all his manners. Come on, princeling. That's enough for now. Pretty soon he'll talk you into setting him free in the Wild Forest and we'll never see him again."

But Galahad ached to stay on the horse. "Uncle Galyn," he said quickly, ignoring the uplifted arms, "why is my father wicked?"

Galyn stared. "What! Lancelot wicked? Who has been telling you such tales? Why, he's the best man alive and the best knight on either side of the Narrow Sea, second only to Arthur himself! There's not a man in all of Less Britain, never mind Lanascol, who can touch him for skill with a sword. The only man in Britain who can best him is Pendragon himself. Of course, it's not his prowess as a soldier that makes him a good man. Lancelot's word of honor is as good as gold. That's why kings, dukes, knights, common folk, children, and wise graybeards all hold him in such high esteem. Everyone trusts him. He's foremost among Arthur's companions. No one challenges Lancelot. He's the best there is."

"Mama hates him."

Galyn waved the groom away and took the halter rope himself. "Surely 'hate' is too strong a word. Married people have . . . differences. . . ." He paused, but the boy's puzzled expression did not change. "They say things to one another they don't mean, in a moment's passion. It is because they love one another that they are so sensitive to slights."

"But he went away. To see the wicked Queen."

"Wicked Queen? You must be— Now listen." Galyn gripped him firmly and lifted him down from the horse. "Listen to me, Galahad, I will tell you truth." He knelt down to the boy. "Your father is the best man I know. He is beloved by all who know him, who truly know him. He cherishes virtue; he fights for Arthur and Britain; he worships God. He loves honor above all. And *that* is goodness."

Galyn beckoned to the groom and handed back the horse. He took Galahad by the hand. "Now come with me. I've something to show you."

Galahad followed obediently. "He makes Mama cry."

His uncle stopped at the stable door. "Galahad," he said slowly, "when you are older you will understand this better, but women cry for many reasons. It's not always a man's fault. And as for love, love between men and women is a tricky matter. It's not always as it seems. But I can tell you this: Lancelot treats Elaine honorably. He defends her name. He gives her rule of his household. He gives her children. These things encompass a woman's domain. He honors her, he protects her, and he keeps her from harm. He does his duty by her."

Galahad looked at him steadily. "Is that love?"

Galyn shook his head with a rueful smile. "Perhaps not. But it's respect. And in marriage, respect is often more important. We can't choose whom we love, but we can always pay respect where it is due. I'm lucky that the woman I love, loves me, and was free to wed me. It doesn't happen that way to many."

Galyn swung open the stable door and led Galahad out into the misty sunshine of a soft, spring day. They had gone fifty paces toward the kennels and Galyn had begun to feel relief that the subject had lost the boy's interest, when Galahad spoke again.

"He hurts her."

"Never," his uncle scoffed. "Not Lancelot. He doesn't beat women. Feelings, of course, are another matter. He may, perhaps, from want of tact, hurt the queen's feelings. Women are oversensitive that way."

"That's not what I mean." Galahad trotted to keep up with his uncle's strides.

"What do you mean, then? Galahad, what have you seen?"

"I saw him hurt her. I was there."

"He hit her? With his hand?"

"No."

"With what then? Not with a weapon, surely!"

"No. His sword was on the stool. But he hurt her. I saw him."

Galyn frowned. "I'm sure it was not intentional. Striking women is beneath him." He paused. "Even good people, Galahad, make mistakes from time to time. It doesn't make him a bad man. All men sin. And sins may be forgiven."

Galahad did not immediately reply, and Galyn quickly whistled for the houndsman. "Ban! Ho, Ban!" He smiled at Galahad. "He's named for your grandfather, did you know that? My father, Galaban. Ban of Benoic he was called. Rescued Lanascol from the Franks, and helped King Uther hold Britain after Ambrosius died."

A short, squatly built man emerged from the kennel sheds and bowed low when he saw them. "Prince Galyn! Prince Galahad! Good morning, my lords. A fine day, eh? By God, I'll be glad when the rains are over! Mud's a danger to colts and puppies."

"We've come to see Dia's litter," Galyn said. "The pups should look like something by now. What's it been? Three weeks?"

The smile faded from Ban's weathered face. "Aye, my lord, but they look like bastards, they do, except for the two."

Galahad followed his uncle into the dimly lit shed. In a corner a thin black bitch lay stretched on a blanket with a row of fuzzy puppies at her teats. Her tail beat eagerly as Ban approached. He spoke softly to her and she lay quiet. "Y'see, my lord, only two black. The others tan and white, or spotted. It's my belief a village stray got to her before we bred her to Apollo." He hawked, turned, and spat. "The king won't be pleased. But by the time he returns, with any luck she'll be heavy with another litter. All by Apollo."

Galahad knelt down and touched the tiny, wriggling bodies. "What will happen to the tan ones?"

"God knows what they're good for," Ban muttered, pulling one from the bitch's teat and holding it frozen in midair by the loose skin on its neck. "Food for foxes. I'll need to know soon what you want to do, my lord. No need to make Dia nurse nine of them when we're keeping only two."

Seeing Galahad's face, Galyn lifted a hand to silence Ban. In a gentle voice he explained to Galahad, Lancelot's theory of breeding and why they could not keep the puppies of a village stray. "If you have a bitch and a dog with good noses, their puppies will have good noses, too. Perhaps even better. If you want to improve the skill of your hunting dogs, you take care which dog you breed to. We don't know anything about the father of these bastard pups. He might be slow; he might be cowardly; he might be vicious. But because we don't know, we can't take the chance that when they're grown, they'll breed to one of the king's bitches, just as their father did. The whole work of the past ten years will be for naught if we don't destroy them."

Galahad looked down at the puppies. Three of them had left the bitch and lay fast asleep on the blanket, their pale stomachs swollen with milk. Galahad picked up one of them, a spotted pup, and felt in his hands the racing beat of a tiny heart. "Can't I keep this one, Uncle Galyn? Can't he be mine? I'll keep him away from the king's bitches. I promise I will."

Galyn hesitated, then smiled. "All right. It might even be a good idea. This summer you can learn how to handle dogs. I'll teach you how to train him. Of course, we'll have to geld him once he's grown. And you'll have to get Lancelot's permission to keep him."

"Thank you, Uncle Galyn!" Galahad reached an arm around his uncle's neck and hugged him. Startled, Galyn drew him into an embrace. He could not remember ever having seen Galahad weep, but the child's brilliant blue eyes glistened with tears.

"You can't take him now, son," he said softly into the silky black hair pressed against his cheek. "He needs his mother's milk for a few more weeks. But you can come and visit him as often as you like. What will you call him?"

Galahad drew away, wiped his eyes quickly, and looked down at the sleeping puppy. "Valiant. Because that's what he will be."

Galyn smiled. "A good name. Now you'd better put him back with his brothers. See how the bitch is watching you. Come visit him every day, and she'll get used to you and trust you better. Ban," he said, rising, "this one belongs to Galahad. When you've time, you can get rid of the others."

9 ✝ BLACK LAKE

Galahad sat on a three-legged stool in the center of the hut. Through the open doorway blew the sweet-scented breezes of early summer: honeysuckle, larkspur, and wild roses. Above his head sunbeams picked their way through dilapidated thatching and lit the hard dirt floor in tiny pools of brilliant light.

Outside the day grew hot. The steady drone of bees among the wild-flowers drowned out the nearer human voice reading interminably from the Sacred Scroll. The voice droned on, the bees droned on, the light-dappled air shimmered with heat. Not far away, lake waters lapped gently against the shore of the little island. His eyes slowly closed, his head fell quietly, in gradual stages, against his shoulder. He never heard the distant, soft splash of oars.

"Galahad, you are not attending." He jumped. Eerie golden eyes fixed upon him from the shadows.

"I'm sorry, Father Aidan."

"You were sleeping. Sloth is a deadly sin."

"Oh, no, Father, I was, um, I was thinking. About my father."

"Don't lie. Never lie. You were sleeping."

Galahad flushed. "Yes, Father."

The golden eyes sharpened to bronze points. "Why did you say you were thinking about Lancelot? Does he concern you?"

"Uncle Galyn says he is a good king. My mother says he's wicked."

The eyes watched him unblinking. "He is good with a sword. Swift killing impresses such men as your uncle Galyn."

"Uncle Galyn says he is good because he loves honor and fights for Arthur."

"Ahhh. Arthur Pendragon. The soldier's god. But you have doubts, Galahad, or you wouldn't be asking. What are they?"

The boy shrugged, suddenly uncomfortable, but the golden eyes held his gaze and he couldn't look away. "I don't know. He hurts Mama sometimes. She yells at him."

The robed figure came out of the shadows and into a shaft of light. A tall man stood before him, lean-featured, with a full beard and long, cascading curls of light brown hair. He looked down at the child. His rich, vibrant voice filled the small spaces of the hut. "I will tell you a tale about Lancelot. It's a true tale. It happened in the village where I grew up." The priest's long fingers deftly rolled up the scroll and tucked it into his robe. "There was a miller in our hamlet who had the great good fortune to marry the girl he loved. She had no dowry, but the miller did not set great store by earthly goods. He loved her dearly. He loved her more than life itself. Perhaps that was a sin."

Aidan walked slowly to the single window. Sunlight struck his face and lit his flowing hair. "Every day he thanked God for this great blessing. On the day their son was born, he felt his cup of earthly joy run over and wept aloud in thanksgiving. For three years his life was a wonder of happiness, a daily heaven. He had everything he had ever wanted." He paused. Galahad waited. Aidan stood so still for so long the boy thought he had forgotten the rest of the tale. But when he finally spoke, the powerful voice struck like a hammer blow.

"Then your father came to our town. On that day, the miller lost it all."

Galahad gulped. "How?"

"King Ban was dead. Lancelot was just eighteen and back from Britain to take up his crown. He was a great hunter in those days, always galloping headlong about the country in pursuit of one beast or another. That day he and his companions raised a she-boar, wounded her but could not kill her. She went mad with pain." Aidan paused again, as if gathering strength to go on. "Have you ever seen a boar stuck with spears like a giant hedgehog, bleeding her life away and blind with rage? That day our village saw her. The miller's wife saw her. She had gone a short way into the Wild Forest of Broceliande to gather acorns along the forest track. Her son was with her. As children will, he wandered from her side—only for a moment—but it was the last moment of his life. The boar broke through the brush, ran him down and gored him, flung him into the air, then fled in her terror toward the town. The woman grabbed the child, screaming, as the king's horses thundered down the track. They passed by her, every one, without even a second glance. She ran with the child toward the river—who knows why? To clean the blood from his little body? To take him to her husband, though he was not a healer and the boy was past human help? It is too late to ask her. She reached the river, and then she stumbled. She could not swim. The miller watched as his wife and son were swept downstream beyond his reach. Two days later they surfaced in the Green Pool. Bloated. Unrecognizable." Aidan's voice went flat. Galahad shivered. "And the young king killed the boar at sundown on the day this family died, and held a great feast in Benoic in honor of his deed."

After a long moment Aidan turned back to face the boy. His eyes were veiled. "The miller went mad, they say, and never returned to the village. Three lives wasted on a summer's day and all for nothing." Aidan moved toward him. "From that day to this, Lancelot has not passed a happy day in Lanascol. The miller's curse pursues him, though he knows it not." A long finger pointed right at Galahad's face. "Goodness in a man is a simple thing. It is obedience to God's commands. That is why you study here, to learn what the Lord requires of you. For you, Galahad, will do God's bidding. So it was prophesied while you were still within your mother's womb." His voice thrummed in the warm air like a plucked harp string. "You will hear the Lord's voice one day, and you will obey it."

Galahad's throat was dry. He swallowed quickly.

"Christ commanded us to care for our neighbors. Lancelot cared for nothing but the glory of his hunt. The village, the people, his own people he was sworn to protect, meant no more to him than a bar across his way. They meant less than the boar herself." The golden eyes suddenly blazed and Galahad shrank back. "He will pay for that. Yes, he will pay. For that, and for other sins. For causing your mother pain. For putting Arthur's service before Christ's. For sins of the flesh he commits as freely as breathing— a root bearing poison and wormwood, the wicked woman is—she has his soul!" Aidan paused, his fist raised before his face, and let his arm fall slowly to his side.

"What woman?" Galahad whispered.

Aidan shrugged off the question. "Abhor wickedness, Galahad, all the days of your life. Of all these sins and more, Lancelot is guilty. Damnation awaits him if he does not repent. And he will not repent because he loves his sins too well. Remember this, Galahad: Repentance must come from the heart, and not the lips only. God sees into our hearts with the ease and clarity of sunlight through a window. Remember the tenth commandment."

The boy responded eagerly: " 'Thou shalt not covet thy neighbor's house, thou shalt not covet thy neighbor's wife, nor his manservant, nor his maidservant, nor his ox, nor his ass, nor anything that is thy neighbor's.' "

"That sounds easy to obey, does it not?"

"Yes, Father."

A long arm reached out of the dimness; a thin-fingered hand gripped his shoulder. "It is impossible for most mortal men. Because it commands not only your actions, but your will." The hand withdrew. The hard voice softened. "Attend me carefully. Not only is it sin to lie with another's wife—that is adultery, clear and simple. It is sin even to *desire* another's wife. A man may keep himself as chaste as he will, and yet sin against God if he lusts after what is not his own. Do you understand, Galahad? Your very daydreams may betray you. You may be damned for what you long for. Your thoughts, your aspirations must be trained and guarded and kept pure. It is not just the actions of your flesh that condemn you; it is your thoughts as well, your wishes, your desires. These you can never hide from God. It is the same with repentance. To repent of a sin you must give up what you gain by its commission. You must hate in your heart what you loved before."

Aidan cocked his head. They both heard the distant scrape of a boat upon the shingle. He leaned down to Galahad, fixing his golden stare on the boy's uplifted face. "Remember the prophecy: You will raise the sword of righteousness in Britain. To be a righteous man you must abhor evil in your heart. Turn against it wherever it lies. Consort not with abomination. Sin is anathema, and those who commit it. Put them all away. Don't make ex-cuses for a man because he is your father. If thine own eye offend thee, pluck it out! Cruelty may be kindness in disguise. A good man is like a white robe, clean of dirt. Remember that."

The resonant voice rang in Galahad's ears. Aidan turned, releasing Galahad from his gaze. Quick, firm steps approached up the pathway. The boy slid quietly off the stool and waited. He, too, recognized the steps.

A woman's silhouette appeared in the bright rectangle of the open door. "Aidan? Are you within?" Aidan moved so that a shaft of light fell on him. "Have you finished with Galahad for today? Let him go. I must speak privately with you. Now."

Aidan bowed with the slow grace of one who is never in a hurry. "As you will, my lady."

"Mama." Galahad came forward to embrace her, but she kissed him hurriedly and pushed him toward the door. "Not now, not now. Go see what that oafish son of Dessa's is doing with the rowboat. He nearly upset me in the middle of the lake. That's a good boy." She swept into the hut, throwing off the light shawl that hid her hair. Aidan closed the door behind her.

With a shrug Galahad walked down the footpath toward the shingle, where Renna dozed under a pine tree. The lad who had poled Renna and Galahad across was fishing off the end of his barge, head bent in concentra-tion over the dark lake waters. Nearby Dessa's son stood beside a rowboat, glancing nervously around the island, making the sign against enchantment with a furtive hand.

"What's the matter?" Galahad asked him, wondering why Elaine had gotten Dessa's son to do her rowing and not one of the soldiers. Everyone knew Brith was terrified of water.

The youth rolled his eyes. "Don't you know about this island? Black Lake's been a sacred place time out of mind. And here in the center is worst of all—it's haunted! There are spirits everywhere!"

"I don't see any spirits."

"They're here, though. Folk say there are a thousand of them living here. Spirits of the pagan dead. And I've seen one myself."

"You have?"

"Aye. And I know who it is, too. My father told me."

"Who, then?"

"It's Vivienne, who used to be the Lady of the Lake and live in that very hut, although it was nicer then. Full of silks and cushions. Fit for a king's son." Brith grinned nervously at him and winked.

"What king's son?"

"Why, come on, you *must* have heard that tale. Sir Lancelot—when he was young—used to come here all the time to visit the Lady, even though his father whipped him for it. They say he bore the whippings gladly to be with the Lady Vivienne. She was a magnificent beauty, they say, and a powerful priestess. She's the spirit I've seen, I'm sure of it. Tall and raven-haired and golden-skinned. Come out here on the night of the new moon, and I'll show her to you."

"No!"

"Ha ha! You're frightened now yourself! Serves you right for trying to make me feel a fool."

"I'm not frightened! You're making this up! My father didn't come here. There aren't any spirits. There's only Father Aidan."

"And the queen . . ." Brith winked again, more boldly. "Wonder what they're doing in there, all this time. Kissing, do you think, like last time?"

"You lie! You lie!" Galahad cried.

"I do not. It's all over Benoic. You might as well know."

"It's not true! Take it back!"

"I won't!"

With a strangled cry, Galahad threw himself at the older boy.

Elaine stood in the shadows and watched the sunbeams play over the rich riot of Aidan's curls. "Well, Aidan. Where have you been? I was beginning to think you had tired of Lanascol."

"You shouldn't have come."

"I have a reason."

"Send your messages through the boy."

Elaine shrugged and walked slowly around the hut, assessing the mean furnishings, the ramshackle construction, the poverty of possessions.

"It is about the boy I have come." She stopped and faced him. "Exactly what are you doing to him, Aidan? I want to know."

The cool golden eyes met hers. "I am teaching him, beauty. As you instructed. I am preparing him for his future."

"Hmm." She looked slowly about. "I see no tablets, no stylus, no scrolls. What exactly are you teaching him?"

From the fastness of his robe he drew forth a thick scroll bound with a ribbon. "I teach him the Word of God. It is all he needs to know. The rest is chaff."

An eyebrow lifted. "Indeed? Then why are we ruled by kings instead of priests? Government, warfare, lettering, history, star-reading—these are useless pursuits, I suppose. Even for a priest, yours is a limited idea of education."

Aidan laughed lightly and set down the scroll. "All those things he will learn elsewhere. In Camelot, no doubt. You did not bring him to me for that. You asked me to make him single-minded. To make him pure because his father is corrupt. To teach him righteousness that he might fulfill the Lady's prophecy. I am doing that." His voice softened. "What did you really come for, Elaine?"

She clasped her hands in agitation. "I came for help. Lancelot is taking my son to Britain at summer's end and he still refuses to take me!"

"You've had an answer to your latest plea?"

"Yes! The courier rode in this morning. Don't look so smug, damn you!"

"Surely it was no surprise."

"You've got to help me, Aidan! You once told me everything was within your power but wielding weapons. Were you boasting or can you make Lancelot change his mind?"

"I can get you to Britain, certainly." He gazed thoughtfully into the distance. "Are you certain that's what you want? To go to Britain with Galahad? Or would it serve you just as well to keep him here?"

"I want to go to Britain! I want to see my homeland again." She looked up at him, her round blue eyes enormous with tears. "I want to go home, Aidan. It's been six long years since I've seen the mountains of Gwynedd. I want to see my homeland. I want to see Camelot. And the King."

The golden eyes flickered. "Ah, yes. Arthur, King of the Britons. Beloved of every man and ruler of every woman's heart, if half the tales are true."

"You know nothing about him," Elaine retorted hotly. "He's not an ordinary man. You and I are not fit to breathe the air he breathes."

Aidan turned away and stood by the window. "You are as transparent as shallow water. It is easy to see where your heart lies."

Elaine colored lightly. "Do not be angry with me, Aidan. Half the world worships Arthur. You would, too, if you but knew him."

For a long moment Aidan did not reply. Then he turned toward her. "How much do you want to go?"

"It's life and death to me!" Elaine cried. "Galahad *must not* go without me! I will lose him, Aidan—she will taint him, my wicked cousin, she will blind him with her charm and spin him lies by the hour—she will malign me; she will cast her spell across him and everything I've done with him, everything I am to him, all will be lost!"

The golden eyes held hers in a long, steady stare. "Keep the boy here, then, if you are afraid of the High Queen."

"Afraid!" Elaine's chin jutted forward. "Afraid of that skinny, spiteful bitch? Don't make me laugh! But Galahad must not go near her. I've known her from childhood, Aidan. She will do *anything* to thwart me!"

"Is girlish spite reason enough to steal your child?"

"It is Lancelot's child she wants. It is Lancelot's son she wants to make her own—it is Galahad. I *know* this, Aidan"—she thumped her fist against her breast—"as I live and breathe, I *know* this. She is barren and cannot bear to Arthur. It is a pain she lives with, day in, day out, and would do anything to ease—she will take my son from me if I am not there to protect him. And Lancelot will let her."

Aidan regarded her in a long, assessing stare. "It is possible to give you what you wish. But there is a price to pay. Will you do what is required?"

"I will do *anything*, Aidan! Anything!"

Aidan turned back to the window. "You speak with passion, but I fear your desire is stronger than your will. You are a woman, after all, and weak."

"I could have you whipped for that!" Elaine snarled. "How dare you insult me so? Do not forget, sir, who is queen and who is servant!"

Aidan regarded her, unsmiling. "You speak from your husband's power. But how much strength have *you?*" He paused. "I will tell you what I find surprising. That in six years Lancelot has not allowed you back even for a visit. I wonder. It's almost as if he were obeying orders."

"Orders!" Elaine bristled. "What do you mean? Who would give him such an order?"

"Who indeed?"

"Don't be a fool, Aidan. When did I *ever* obey an order of Guinevere's? High Queen or not, she's only my cousin. I'm *not* afraid of her."

The golden eyes narrowed. "Perhaps it was not the Queen."

Elaine went still, and paled. "Arthur? Do you mean Arthur himself? But . . . but he wouldn't. . . ."

"You don't sound very certain." Aidan watched her face. "What did you do to him, my dear, that he would banish you for?"

Elaine began to tremble. "Nothing. Nothing. Nothing at all . . . Nothing that a man might not forgive." His golden stare forced the words from her against her will. "Once, when Guinevere was away, I went to his bed without his knowing—I wanted to show him how much better a wife I could be to him—all the women in my family are great breeders of sons . . . but when he discovered me, he . . . he would not approach, but had me taken out." Bright color rose in patches to stain her face. "I forgave him, as I am sure he has forgiven me."

"I see. He preferred to lie alone than to lie with you. And yet you and I are not fit to breathe the air he breathes." Aidan leaned forward suddenly. His voice went through her like an arrow of ice. "You can go to Britain, beauty, as soon as your husband dies."

Elaine gasped. "Death?" She stepped back a pace. "He's never ill. He's in the prime of life. The country's at peace. It won't happen."

"Do not pretend to misunderstand me."

She drew a long, unsteady breath. "No. I can't be part of that. There must be another way."

"Must there?" He watched her coldly. "A moment ago you were ready to chance *anything*. But I knew you had a coward's will."

"Coward! How do you dare?" She was shaking, her eyes wide with fear, but she spoke defiantly. "I am queen of this land and you speak treason to my face! I have only to say a word to see you die on a stake."

His hands reached out to her, took hold of her, and drew her roughly into an embrace. He covered her mouth with his until he felt her body weaken. "That is how I dare," he whispered, his lips moving against her own. "Stop me if you will."

She collapsed against him. "Aidan, my sweet Aidan, lend me your strength! Why have you stayed away from me so long? Nights are interminable without you! Do what you will with Lancelot, then. Only come back to me."

His hand slid down her gown and pressed against her little belly. "And what is this? Three months gone, at least. It is Lancelot's, then, and not mine."

Elaine gasped. "It was not my fault! Oh, Aidan, I have been so careful! All winter I denied him every time he asked! But one night he took me by surprise—I had no time for preparation and he brooked no excuse. Who would think . . . from a single bedding—"

Aidan smiled. "You're an excellent breeder of princes, my dear, that is true enough. Well, well. Some things we cannot prevent. He is your husband, after all. You owe him service."

"Oh, do stop, Aidan! It was an accident."

Aidan laughed softly and ran a thin finger along the line of her jaw. "You weakened, Elaine. Confess it. You weakened at midwinter. You wanted that brooding fire and that warrior's body. You and your lust could not wait for me."

"He forced me, by all that's holy! I wanted nothing to do with him! I never have!"

"Except when you seduced him." His hands gripped her hips and pulled her forward hard against his unyielding body. "Do not forget you chose him for a husband."

"I chose him," she spat, "to spite Guinevere! Oh, yes, and how I enjoyed watching her turn green with envy as his child grew within my belly! To cause her pain I'd have done a deal worse than bed Sir Lancelot!" She paused, breathing heavily. "Do not imagine, Aidan, that I wanted him twice."

White teeth gleamed as his lips spread in a slow smile. "What a carnal creature woman is."

She slipped her arms around him, pressed close, and moved eagerly against him, breathing heat into his face, wildfire raging against his still calm. "I despise him, Aidan! I curse the day he was ever born! He's never loved me. He abandons me without a backward glance; he doesn't care what hurts me; he cares only for the woman he cannot have! But you, my fine lover, my hot-blooded priest, you keep my bed warm, you understand what it is like, to be alone. . . ."

He allowed her lips to caress him, he let her roving hands seek beneath his robe, he let her whisper promises, let her rising passion beat helplessly against his unmoving will.

"Curb your desire," he said finally, taking her wrists and holding them in his hands. "This unbridled lust of yours—it blinds you and endangers us. Control it. Bend it to your will. Be patient. The future can be ours if you have the stomach for it."

"What future is there for me here but slow decay? He will take my sons from me, one by one, and give them to *her*!"

"Choose, then, my loving queen, between your husband and your sons. If he lives, you lose them. If he dies, they are yours."

She looked up at him, all her defiance drained away. "What choice is there in that? My sons are my future. My husband I never wanted."

"Do you assent, then?"

She swallowed in a dry throat, but said nothing.

He let go of her hands. "I can help you. But the price must be paid. And you must give the order for it."

"This is not something Arthur could forgive," she whispered, closing her eyes, pressing her face against the rough cloth of his robe. "He will blame me. He will exile me again."

"Not if the deed is laid at someone else's door."

"Whose?"

"It is better you do not know."

"Not you! No, no, ahhh, God, Aidan, his men will tear you limb from limb. You are the first person they will suspect."

"No. Not me. I am not ready to exchange my life for his."

"Who, then?"

Aidan stroked her belly. "Patience, Elaine. All things come to him who waits."

Elaine smiled bitterly. "It's easy for a man to be patient. Change shoes with me, Aidan! *You* bear this child and put up with the dizziness and the vomit, the swelling and the pain, and see if *you* can be patient."

He pushed her gently away. "Sit down on the stool. I will bring you a cup of water."

He lifted a clay pitcher and poured clear liquid into a glazed cup while Elaine composed herself. "Galahad tells me his cousin is coming to Benoic to visit. Who is this cousin?"

Elaine's hand trembled as she took the cup. "It's only Bors of Ganys. Galyn's invited him. He has a son around Galahad's age." She shrugged. "They are nobodies. Hillmen. Uncivilized."

Aidan raised an eyebrow. "What is he like, this Bors of Ganys? It's possible he might be useful."

"How?"

"Aren't we looking for a scapegoat?"

"Bors?" Elaine began to smile. "His own cousin Bors? It's all he can do to put two thoughts together!"

"Is he at all ambitious? Has he ever shown signs of envy or of spite?"

Elaine shrugged. "God knows the poor sod *ought* to be ambitious. He's been buried in the mountains all his life. His side of the family has had nothing but rocks to rule for generations; he ought to be ready to sell his soul for a scrap of power! But you can't tell with Lancelot's kin. What they call family honor means more to them than land or cattle. I told you before, they're a simple-headed lot."

Aidan stroked his beard. "Observe him well. Tempt him a little and see how he responds. If you judge him weak, bring him to me. I can bend any willing mind. It's a risk, but it might be worth it."

She gazed up at him, blinking in the dappled light. "Is that how you will do it, then? You will weave a spell about him and convince him he is Lancelot's doom? If it doesn't work, he's likely to kill you."

The golden eyes drilled her. "It always works."

"Are you able to command *any* will weaker than your own?"

"Yes."

She rose and handed him the empty cup, smiling coyly. "Is that what you've done to *me*? Stolen my will?"

He laughed softly. "The test of that will come when you wish to send me away."

"When I wish to be rid of you, believe me, you will go. Willingly or not."

He bowed politely. "My lady queen. I am your servant."

"As long as you know it."

Aidan regarded her. She stood in a shaft of sunlight with motes dancing like fireflies around her yellow hair. In many ways she was the embodiment of everything he hated. Her firm lips, her fine nose, her small but definite uplifted chin, her smooth hands which had never done a moment's labor, her upright carriage, the graceful assurance of her movements, all signs of the easy certainty of power—here, in one person, was the essence of his life's resentment: the unthinking arrogance of the highborn. Yet how could he hate what gave him such wonderful satisfaction to control? In a way it was better than kingship, for she did not even know that she obeyed.

He smiled gently and held out his hand. Immediately she turned to him, her eyes widening, every feature softening as her trembling will felt the touch of his.

"Are we agreed, then?" he said softly.

"About . . . about Lancelot?"

He took her hand and slowly lifted it to his lips, holding her eyes.

"About Lancelot's murder. Do you assent?"

He pressed his lips into her palm, watching her. She was breathing quickly, her flesh warm, her body calling out to him, beseeching him in the only way she knew. "For God's sake, Aidan—"

"Choose, Elaine. Yes or no." He slowly lowered her hand, let it go, and straightened.

Tears shone in her eyes. "Please."

He said nothing, but gazed at her in silence. Although he did not move, he seemed to grow colder, grayer, more remote, his vibrant presence slowly fading. She reached out and grabbed his hand, pulling it to her breast.

"All right! I submit! Kill him, then, if it pleases you! I order you to do it. Kill him any way you will, only rid me of Lancelot."

1O ✝ PROMISES

"There is one other thing."

"What?" she cried. "What else? For Christ's sake, Aidan, what else could there be?"

"I must conduct a ceremony for Galahad. You must be there."

She frowned. "What kind of ceremony?"

Aidan went again to the window, glancing quickly about. "You asked me to give his life a center. I have done that. I have given him God. The ceremony will seal that gift. It will be a sort of dedication."

"Dedication to what?"

"Think of it as a ritual marking transition to another life. Like a wedding, or funeral rites, or the making of a knight. Something to pass through and achieve. When it is over, he will belong to God and not to Lancelot."

Elaine considered this. "Surely it's unnecessary if you are going to deal with Lancelot anyway."

"It is necessary, whatever happens to Lancelot."

"All right. All right. When is this ceremony?"

"The closer to the time of Lancelot's return, the better."

"Will it do Galahad any harm?"

"On the contrary, my dear. It will do him good. It is the final culmination of all his learning. It is the first step on the path to his destiny. He will remember it all his life. When it is over he will no longer be Lancelot's son."

"I don't see how you can change his parentage. Are you filling his head with gibberish, Aidan? I won't have that. Whose son will he be, then?"

"God's."

Elaine grimaced. "That's what I meant by gibberish. Don't fill him with notions of holiness, and turn him into a priest—what use will he be to me then?"

Aidan smiled lightly. "I suppose I should take offense at that."

Elaine walked up to him. "If you *are* a priest, you are one I understand. You deal in sin. I've known for a long time you want my husband dead. But up to now, as you so delicately put it, I have not been willing to pay that price." She smiled and ran a slow hand down his robe. "What is this ceremony worth to you, Aidan? How important is it?"

The golden eyes flashed. "Don't trifle with me. You will regret it."

"I am paying a price for my son, a heavy one. You can pay a price for him as well."

Aidan looked down at her, his face expressionless. "What do you want?"

Elaine pressed against him, pulled his head down to hers, and kissed his mouth. "*You* are the price, priest. I want *you*. Come to my chamber, yes, into my very chamber, where Lancelot begot this child. Come to me tonight. And every night that I send for you. Do it, and you can have your precious ceremony."

"Your husband's brother will kill me if I am found."

She smiled up at him. "Risk makes it more exciting, don't you find? Well? What is your answer? Choose now."

His thin lips spread into a slow smile. "I will pay your price with pleasure." He spun her around, lifted her in his arms, and strode to his pallet.

"Not here!" She laughed, wrapping an arm about his neck. "Not now! Submit to me! I command you!"

He set her down, his eyes aflame. "You said you liked risk."

She wriggled out of his arms and straightened her gown. "I like risking *your* future, Aidan, not my own. I won't risk Galahad finding us. It's not the kind of thing he would forgive."

"No," Aidan said coolly. "He knows all the commandments."

"My son will be a great knight and a strong king. Fill him with your rage, if you will; just don't fill him with aspirations to holiness. You will take the life out of him."

Aidan spoke slowly. "Your son is made of finer stuff than you imagine. He's bright, sharp metal that will, with time, be forged into a cutting blade. But we must both take care. It's a weapon that can turn in the hand."

"Not if you manage it right," she replied impatiently. "Come, Aidan, you know perfectly well what I require of you. The Lady said he will live forever in glory. If that is so, I will live in glory with him. Make it happen. And a hundred years from now no one will remember Lancelot's name." She bent to retrieve her shawl. "And you'd better hurry. Galyn's beginning to sniff something in the air. He has me watched and guarded, you know, now that I carry Lancelot's precious seed." She paused. "That reminds me. You've often told me how skilled you are with herbs. . . ." Her hands touched the soft curve of her belly. "I need your help."

"If it's death you want, go to a Druid. I don't kill children."

"Neither do I!" Elaine retorted. "Who spoke of death? Cure me of my illness, priest, not my child. Children are a woman's tools to power in this warrior's world. I may not bear this one willingly, God knows, but I'll bear him." She drew a deep breath. "I only wanted something for my sickness."

Aidan bowed politely. "It has already been done."

Elaine stopped, startled. "What do you mean?"

"How do you feel?"

A look of amazement crossed her face. "I do feel better."

Aidan gestured toward the clay pitcher. "I had heard the rumor, you see. I brewed the medicine this morning." He withdrew from his robe a small, clay vial stoppered with cork. "Take some with you now, for tomorrow. I will send it with Galahad in future."

Elaine stared at him. Spots of color flamed her cheeks and her nostrils flared. "Don't ever do that again! Do not *dare*. Don't *ever* give me anything without telling me first. Or Galahad. Promise it. Swear it."

Aidan's lips twisted in a smile. "Trust me, Elaine."

"I do *not*! Promise!"

He bowed obediently. "Very well. I promise."

Elaine grabbed the vial and strode out of the hut. Aidan stood at the window and watched her go.

"My proud, highborn beauty," he said softly. "How your fury becomes you! Have I underestimated you? I think not. If only your son were made of your clay. Then would I have a vessel I could shape to my will as easily as drawing breath! But he is already iron, young as he is." He turned and walked to a shelf where several small clay jars stood in a neat row. With a long, bony finger he touched them, one by one. "How shall I deal with Galahad? How shall I shape that blade to my hand? Which of these will weaken him, make him pliant, prepare him to accept the deed he must do?" Then, recalling the day when Galahad had thrown himself into the cold lake waters in an attempt to swim ashore because Aidan had refused to let him bring his puppy to the island, Aidan mused, "Which of these will touch the spring of revolt inside him? Which will turn that streak of mindless passion into blood lust?"

He turned and looked around the empty hut in open contempt. "After all I have endured, I will *not* be thwarted. Bors may serve as a smoke screen, but it will be Galahad who frees my soul from Hell." He closed his eyes and drew a deep breath. "I will have my revenge upon Lancelot, and it will lie sweet upon my soul. A wife for a wife, and a son for a son." He sank to his knees, clasping his hands before his face. "Let the son destroy the father, as the father destroyed my son. Let justice be done, and the blood of my enemy sprinkled upon the ground beneath my feet. All the days of my vengeance shall be accomplished, and I shall go back to my village with a quiet heart. I shall be a miller again."

When the queen came down the path Galahad was lying on the barge, trailing a finger through the green-black water while dragonflies hovered around his head.

"Renna! Asleep again! Why do I retain you, I wonder, when you cannot keep your eyes open more than half the day? Get up and take Galahad back before he's missed." Galahad looked up. His face was swollen and a dark ring was forming around his eye. "What's this?" Elaine cried. "What's been going on? Galahad, who attacked you?"

She looked at once toward Brith, who stood sullenly by the rowboat. His tunic was torn and a puddle of crusted blood darkened one nostril. "You, Brith! Did you dare to strike my son?"

"No," Galahad cut in. "I fell down. But look!" He pointed to the distant shore where three horsemen waited. One sat a liver chestnut with a brilliant blaze. "Uncle Galyn."

Her lips thinned. "So he's found us at last. It took him long enough."

Brith rowed them back across the lake and Elaine made a pretty curtsy to Galyn on the beach. "My lord Galahantyn."

"So. This is where you have been bringing the boy."

She smiled sweetly. "How clever of you to have discovered it, my lord. After all these weeks."

Galyn ignored the provocation. "I suppose that's where the charlatan is hiding out?" He jerked his head toward the island.

"Black Lake is a sacred precinct," Elaine said calmly, "as you know well. It has never been in the king's domain, even when Ban of Benoic ruled

Lanascol and your sweet brother came here to spend his time in ways better not mentioned in front of children."

"That is not what I asked you."

"If Father Aidan chooses to reside there because he is banned from the town, it is his right to do so. There is not a thing you can do about it."

Galyn's features hardened. "No. He can stay there if he wills. But I can prevent the boy from visiting. Lancelot gave orders he was not to traffic with him. You knew that."

"I am his mother." The queen's voice sharpened. "Surely I have a right to educate my son as I see fit, at least until his war training begins." Elaine dropped her eyes suddenly and softened her tone. "Lancelot never took the time to know the man. And you, Galyn, admit that you don't know him, either. What is there against him, after all?"

Galyn's eyes flicked briefly to Galahad and then back to the queen. "You know what the accusations are."

Elaine smiled her gentlest smile. "Is it such a sin to admire me? Am I so old and ugly no man may look at me twice without having suspicion laid at his door?"

Galyn flushed. "Of course not, my lady; that is not what I meant. You are beautiful, indeed. No one denies it. But it is not a priest's place to—"

"Lancelot misunderstood it, Galyn." She spoke very softly, her hand on Galahad's head. "He jumped to conclusions. Why don't you make the effort to know the man yourself? Go on, question Galahad about him, if you like."

Galyn's gray eyes widened. "That is what I came to do," he admitted. "You will allow it?"

"Certainly. I have nothing to hide. Galahad." The tone of her voice changed. "Ride back with your uncle Galyn and tell him about Father Aidan." The lake seemed to ring with the words she had not spoken: *You know what to say.* . . .

Perched on the saddle in Galyn's lap, Galahad watched the world speed by at a thrilling pace. The stallion's canter was easy to sit, even without his uncle's strong arm about his waist, but Galahad resented the saddle. He could no longer feel the horse beneath him. It was like riding a swiftly bobbing log, not a living beast. When they were clear of the forest and reached the open meadows ringing the walls of Benoic, Galyn slowed the horses to a walk.

"Well, Galahad, you've been in a scuffle, I see."

"Yes, sir."

"And your opponent?"

"Brith, sir."

Galyn chuckled. "No wonder you won, though he's twice your age. He's full of a thousand fears. I've not seen much of you lately, boy. I've missed you in the stables and the kennels. Valiant's missed you. Caesar's missed you. Now I know where you have been."

"Mama wants me to study."

"Hmm. Your mother's got a narrow view of education. A prince must learn to hunt and fight as well as read. What do you say we get you something new to ride? The horse trader's due next week."

"Can I have a horse?" Galahad asked eagerly.

"Well, something bigger than your pony, surely. A small horse, perhaps. To suit your size." He paused. "Tell me what you do with Father Aidan."

"I learn the Word of God."

"Prayers and psalms? Invocations? What, exactly?"

"Commandments. Verses. Stories. Father Aidan has scrolls and scrolls, all packed in an old chest."

"What's in the chest beside books?"

"Nothing."

"No weapons? Not even a dagger for food?"

"No."

"Not a sword for protection?"

"He has spells for protection."

"Is he an enchanter, then? Have you seen him use magic?"

"No," Galahad said slowly. "But he has funny eyes."

"Indeed! How are they funny?"

"He looks at me and I can't look away. I have to do what he wants."

"Ah." Galyn's voice was grim. "I know that kind of spell. It's called a Watching. To defend against it, think of something you love very much, your dearest friend, your happiest memory. Love is the only barrier that Watch-spells cannot brook."

Galahad nodded obediently, but privately he doubted Father Aidan's spells could be so easily conquered.

"Do you go to him willingly, Galahad?"

"Oh, yes."

"Do you like him, then?"

Galahad paused so long that Galyn leaned down to see his face. "What's the matter? Is that a hard question to answer?"

"Yes."

"Why? Is he not friendly?"

"Not very."

"Do you not feel safe when you are with him?"

"He frightens me sometimes."

"How? With threats?"

"No. It's just his eyes. He's a holy man."

"Is he? You believe that?"

"Yes."

"Holier than Father Patrik?"

Galahad considered the plump, jovial priest newly come to Benoic, a good man and well-meaning, but overfond of the king's food and wine. "He's much, much holier than Father Patrik."

"Galahad," Galyn said carefully, his arm tightening around the boy, "what does Father Aidan want of you? What are you studying so hard for?"

The boy shrugged. "To be a great knight and serve King Arthur. And to keep my robe clean."

"Well, well. Those are admirable goals. No harm in that."

" 'Consort not with abomination. Sin is anathema, and those who commit it. Put them all away.' What is anathema?"

Galyn smiled. "Death to the spirit. Well, Galahad, I can't fault his teaching. It's good advice. And I'm pleased he wants you to be one of Arthur's knights. Those are your father's plans for you, as well. If you can follow in *his* footsteps, my lad, you will be a great man, indeed. There is no one more worshiped in Britain than Lancelot. Excepting only Arthur."

"Father Aidan calls King Arthur the soldiers' god."

Galyn laughed. "And so he is, in some ways."

"He says a wicked woman has my father's soul."

Galyn hesitated. When he finally spoke his voice was sad. "That's not true. The woman isn't wicked. She has his heart, perhaps, but not his soul. Your father worships virtue, like every good knight, in a woman as well as in a man. But there are those who, for reasons of jealousy, fear, or hate, will twist the truth and find evil and betrayal where none exist. Rumors start and men will believe them, even men who have the truth before them, plain to see. If you hear rumors about your father, don't believe them. Watch with your own eyes and judge truth yourself. Promise me that."

Galahad nodded obediently. "I promise."

Galyn smiled. "Now it's time to get back to Benoic. You tell Caesar it's time to move on. Go on and try." At once the stallion paced forward and Galyn laughed. "Yes, we must find you a mount to test your skill. And we must find you a lad your age to play with. You are too much alone with women and priests. Bors's son Cordovic is about your age. A little older, perhaps, but you'll get along well enough. They'll be here within the month. At last you'll have someone to wrestle with, to race against, to test yourself against in swordplay. That's a healthier life for a boy than memorizing commandments and living beneath a priest's skirts. Why, in two months' time you'll be ready to test yourself against any boy in Camelot. And that's *my* promise to *you*."

11 ✠ CORDOVIC

B ors arrived on the hottest day of the whole summer. When his escort
trotted through the gates and up the hill to the king's house, the ground
shook and the shimmering air filled with dust.

"Bors!" Galyn cried, coming forward with arms outstretched.

"Galyn, you young dog!" A black-bearded giant of a man slid from his
charger's back and embraced him. "You're looking well and I don't wonder
at it, knowing how you spend your nights! Is this your bride? What a beauty
you are, my dear. Let me welcome you to the family. We're a rough lot, I'm
afraid, here in Lanascol, uncivilized by some standards, but we stand by one
another." He swung an arm around Galyn and kissed Adele.

Galahad's eyes ran swiftly over the ranks of cavalry behind Bors. In the
first row a sturdy boy of middle height with thick brown hair and a dusty
face sat astride a small, fine-boned horse. Galahad stared at the animal. She
was a blood bay, quick and fine, with a small head and big, dark, soulful
eyes. She lifted her tail delicately as she danced in place, sidling this way
and that in a nervous struggle to relieve the pain in her mouth. Galahad's
fists clenched at his sides. The mare's nose bobbed in the air, her mouth
open, froth dripping from her lips. The thick muscle on the underside of her
neck told a tale of long abuse, of a head held high to escape bits too cruel
and hands too heavy. Galahad winced as the boy absently hauled at her
mouth in yet another vain attempt to make her stand still.

"Beautiful Lady Elaine!" Galahad's head jerked around. In the shaded
doorway of the king's house Elaine leaned against the doorpost, fanning
herself slowly. Her long white arms gleamed with silver bracelets. Her hair
was drawn back from her face and coiled in golden braids upon her head.
Around her brow she wore the queen's crown of Lanascol, silver, garnet,
and iridescent mother-of-pearl. Her light shift was belted high above her
waist to hide the growing roundness of her belly.

Bors knelt in the dust before her. "How is it you grow lovelier every
year? Why, if I didn't know better, I'd say you were eighteen and not a day
over!"

Elaine smiled and stepped out into the sun to greet him. Light flashed
on her bracelets, her crown, her hair. "You must get a good deal subtler than
that, my dear Bors, before I'll believe a word you say." She extended her
hand to him and he drew it to his lips. "How fares your lady wife? You left
her in good health?"

He rose and grinned. "I left her well enough, but not, I'm sorry to say, in your bloom. He's done it again, hasn't he, my randy cousin—planted his living seed in your fertile soil. Bless you, my dear girl, I wish I knew how you do it—breed them one after the other, you do, all of them healthy, handsome sons. All branches off the tree of Lanascol."

Bors looked pleased with his turn of phrase, but the light had left the queen's face. "You talk like a common gardener. Where are your manners, my lord? Pray, speak of something else before I'm ill."

"Manners and I have never seen eye-to-eye!" Bors laughed. "As you know well! And if you're ill, it's your husband's doing and none of mine! But I mean no offense," he added hastily, seeing her expression. "It does you honor to bear princes to Lancelot."

Elaine forced a smile but her voice was cold. "Did you say you had brought your son, my lord? Pray, let me see him."

Bors turned and beckoned eagerly to the boy on the bay mare. "Aye, my lady, I've brought him along as company for your Galahad. It's about time Lancelot's sons met their kin."

Elaine watched the sturdy boy come toward her, dusty from the road, with thick, badly cut brown hair and small, sullen eyes. Her nose wrinkled in distaste. "I doubt your son and mine have much in common."

Galyn drew a sharp breath, but Bors had already turned away to sling an arm around Cordovic's shoulder. "Here he is, my lady. This is my son Cordovic. My firstborn. Cordovic, this is your kinswoman Elaine of Gwynedd, Lancelot's wife and Queen of Lanascol."

The boy touched his knee to the ground and mumbled stiffly, "My lady."

"As to what they have in common," Galyn put in firmly, "they have Lanascol. And that is all they need."

"Indeed?" Elaine looked down at the boy's filthy hair. "One to lead and one to follow. It is bond enough, I suppose."

Galyn's face flamed. "My God, Elaine—" he began, but Bors only shrugged and laid a hand on his arm to stop him.

"No matter, Galyn. It's true enough. Galahad's bound to be Cordovic's king someday. Better they meet now, in kinship, than later, when there may be more between them." He turned and scanned the onlookers. "Where is the boy, anyway? There? Not still with the nursemaids? A strapping lad like that? Galyn, whatever are you thinking?"

"He is my son, Bors," Elaine snapped. "Not Galyn's. Don't forget it."

Bors opened his mouth to protest and then thought better of it. Elaine beckoned Galahad to her side.

"Galahad, this is your cousin Cordovic. This is my son Galahad. Prince of Lanascol."

The two boys looked at each other. Although Cordovic was older, he was short and stockily built like his father, and the boys stood almost eye-to-eye. Neither of them blinked.

"Cordovic," Elaine said loftily, "kneel to your prince."

There was a stunned silence. Bors's heavy hand fell on his son's shoulder, pushing the boy to the ground as Galyn found his voice.

"Rise, Cordovic! Christ, Elaine, I did not invite them here to be insulted. They are kin. We owe them the best we have."

"They are no kin of *mine*," she retorted. "I'm Welsh, not Breton. Remember that." She turned on her heel and without another word strode back into the house.

"Whew!" Bors exclaimed. "There's a tongue that's a weapon!"

Galyn's face was flaming. "I beg your pardon, cousin. She is with child again and it plays havoc with her temper, I'm afraid."

Bors raised an eyebrow. "Is it that, or is it you, Galyn? He left *you* regent this time, didn't he?"

Galyn smiled. "As always, your aim is true. But come, more of this later. Let's get your men settled and the horses out of the sun."

The boys headed for the river path.

"I'm sorry she made you kneel," Galahad offered. "It was wrong."

"Bring it up again and I'll make you eat dust."

Galahad glanced at the sulking boy and let the challenge pass. He led the way through the winding streets of the town and down to the water meadow. He assumed his cousin must want to wash the dust of travel off. They were nearing the towpath when Cordovic finally spoke.

"So you're Galahad. What kind of a sissy name is that?"

"It's not a sissy name."

"It's the stupidest name I ever heard. What do they call you? Gal?" He sniggered.

"I don't have a nickname."

"Christ! They actually call you Galahad?"

"You shouldn't swear."

"I'll swear if I damn well want to. Don't *you* tell me what I can do! I'm twice your size!"

This was a patent falsehood, but Galahad let it pass. "Aren't you called Cordovic?"

Cordovic grinned suddenly. It was nearer a sneer than a smile. "*Prince* Cordovic, to you. No nicknames or I'll bust your head in."

"You can try."

Cordovic launched a sidearm punch. Galahad ducked.

"Son of a bitch!"

Smiling, Galahad turned away, when suddenly Cordovic landed him a blow across the shoulders that spun him to the ground. He spat dust out of his mouth. Cordovic stood above him, chuckling.

"Just you try to rule over me, you little mother's whelp! I'll tan your hide!"

Galahad rose, wiping his hands on his tunic. Cordovic swung at his head; Galahad ducked and butted him in the stomach, knocking him off balance.

"Race you to the river!" he cried, and fled down the path. Cordovic was after him at once, pounding heavily behind him, gaining with every stride. Galahad reached the river with Cordovic's fingers grasping for his tunic, and dove into the water. When he surfaced in midstream he saw Cordovic standing among the reeds, gasping for breath and cursing.

Galahad grinned. "Come on and get me."

"Come back here, you little coward!"

"You can't swim. But I can."

"Damn you, you little weasel! You pampered brat!" Cordovic sneered. "Think you're pretty smart, don't you?"

"I got away from you."

Cordovic splashed the cool water on his face and shrugged. "I'll learn to swim when it pleases me."

Galahad swam closer. "It's not that hard. I could teach you. Starting tomorrow. Starting today."

Cordovic eyed him warily. "What would it cost me?"

"Let me ride your mare."

Cordovic laughed. "When Saxons fly! My father bought her off a trader from southern Gaul last winter when I turned eight. Ten pieces of gold he paid! And now you think I'm going to let you ride her?" Cordovic threw back his head and howled with laughter. His foot slipped suddenly and he went down with a splash, his head ducking underwater. He came up screaming, "Help! Help!" His arms flailed as water filled his mouth.

Galahad picked up a thick branch of driftwood that lay lodged in the reeds and held it out to Cordovic just beyond his reach. "Change your mind!"

"Help!" Cordovic choked, going under a second time. "Help! I'm your cousin, damn you!"

Galahad bent toward him. "Change your mind."

"All right!" Cordovic screamed, and Galahad tossed him the branch. The boy clutched at it, gasping and sputtering, sobbing out curses and recriminations. "You were going to let me drown! I take back everything! It's not fair—you can't force me at the point of drowning!"

"Stand up."

"What?"

"Go ahead. Stand up."

Struggling for composure, Cordovic got his feet under him and stood. The river came only to his thighs. He flushed darkly. "I hate you."

Galahad shrugged. "Father Aidan says many men will hate me."

"Who's Father Aidan? I like him already."

"A holy man. He lives on an island in the middle of Black Lake. He's my teacher."

"Serves you right to have a priest for a teacher. What do priests know about anything? They've never ruled anywhere or killed anyone."

"Father Aidan knows everything. We built a coracle together. You can come see him with me if you want."

Cordovic grunted. "I'm not fond of priests. Too much kneeling."

"When you can swim you won't be afraid to go."

"I'm not afraid! Get that through your thick head, all right?" Cordovic climbed out of the river and sat heavily on the bank. "This is the first time I've been cool in days. . . . It might be fun to swim. I'd be the only one in Ganys. . . . Maybe I'll think about it."

"And the mare?"

"You teach me to swim, first."

Galahad smiled. "It's a bargain, then."

Cordovic and Galahad stood naked on the riverbank an hour past sunrise. Galahad pointed to a spit of land upstream of the reed bed.

"Stand there. Go on, it's shallow." Galahad pulled from its hiding place among the reeds a small raft he had made of driftwood bound tightly together with long reed stalks. "Hold on to this."

"What for? It's not very sturdy."

"It floats. Hold the raft out in front of you and kick your legs out behind. You'll go forward, across the river. I'll swim next to you."

Cordovic eyed the makeshift raft with contempt. "You're crazy. This stupid thing won't hold me up."

"Yes, it will. It's how I learned."

Cordovic made a face. "All right. I'll try it."

At the end of an hour of crossing and crossing again, Cordovic threw himself on the bank, exhausted. "I don't see how pushing a raft around will teach me how to swim," he complained. "All it does is make my legs tired."

"It's simple," Galahad replied, stretching on the grass and letting the strengthening sun warm his skin. "Every day I take away a piece of driftwood. When there's none left you'll be swimming."

"Or at the bottom of the river."

Galahad smiled.

They donned their tunics and headed uphill toward the king's house. As they passed the kennels Galahad said, "After breakfast I'll show you my puppy. His name is Valiant. He's out of one of the king's own bitches. You can play with him, if you like. And then I want to see your mare."

Cordovic scowled. "I don't care about your flea-bitten puppy. I've got a hound of my own at home. And as for my mare, I don't think I'll tell you where she is."

"I'll find her. What's her name?"

"Swifty."

Galahad wrinkled his nose. "Swifty? I'm going to call her . . . Glory."

Cordovic sniggered. "Glory? That's a sissy name for a horse. What's the matter with you, anyway? Been spending too much time with that strange priest?"

"Father Aidan isn't strange."

Cordovic's face lit. "I've heard he is. I've heard plenty about him. It's all over Benoic how he slips through double-locked gates like a practiced thief and lurks around the queen's garden when everyone knows Lancelot banned him from the town. Nothing keeps him out. They say he's a ram in priest's clothing who's only after kisses from your mother!"

Galahad's fist smashed into Cordovic's jaw. Cordovic found himself lying on his back with Galahad straddling him, pounding his fists into his chest. "Take it back! Take it back! You dirty coward! Take it back!" Cordovic could not stop him. The child's eyes blazed with inhuman fury; he neither felt nor responded to Cordovic's blows, but only increased the maniacal drubbing of his fists.

"Help!" Cordovic screamed. "Get him off me!"

Adults appeared from nowhere. Someone lifted Galahad off. Someone helped Cordovic up. Stunned, Cordovic stood rubbing his jaw while Galahad was led away, still shouting insults.

Bors looked down at his son. "Be careful of that boy, Vic. He's got a lot of Lancelot in him. Better pick on youths your own age."

"But isn't he?"

"He may be tall for his age, like his father, but he just turned five at the equinox, Galyn tells me."

"*Five?*" Cordovic stared in disbelief at the doorway where Galahad had been taken in. His chest still hurt from the pounding of those fists. "Son of a bitch," he whispered.

12 † THE BARGAIN

"Ready!" Galahad shouted. He waited on the riverbank with Galyn and Bors while on the opposite bank Cordovic stood on a spit of mud among the reeds, staring down at the passing river with concentration. Galahad wondered why it still held terror for him. Now, at midsummer, the river was so low he could almost walk across. Suddenly Cordovic shut his eyes and flung himself into the water, surfacing with wildly splashing arms and kicking feet.

"He's off!" Bors cried. Valiant turned excited circles in the dust and barked furiously. Very slowly for all the effort he expended, Cordovic drew closer. Galahad thought in growing excitement about the mare. Every morning at dawn for the past month he had gone to the horse lines with Valiant at his heels, just to stand beside Cordovic's mare. She had soon become accustomed to his presence, to his voice and touch, and to Valiant's curious sniffs and growls. She had even begun to nicker at him as he approached, just the way Lancelot's stallion always greeted his father. He was always gone before the grooms came by with hay and water. No one knew of his visits, not even Father Aidan. He did not know why he kept it such a secret. It just seemed of paramount importance that no one else should know.

Not once in the long, hot weeks since the bargain had his attention wavered from his goal. While he sat on Aidan's stool and recited verses, while he stood in the river with his cousin and patiently bore his curses and his insults, while he ate and slept, he thought only of Cordovic's mare. He twisted his hands together. He was so close now! Cordovic, the selfish brat, would never drown himself to weasel out of the bargain, and that was what it would take.

Bors shifted anxiously from foot to foot as Cordovic reached the middle of the river where the water was well over his head. Galahad wondered briefly why his mother spent so much time with Bors. He knew she despised him, yet they were constantly together. Bors hung on her every word, laughed at her jests, openly admired her skin, her gown, her golden hair, even though she laughed at him for his compliments and made fun of him behind his back. That made Galyn angry, but Bors seemed not to mind. Galahad shrugged. Adults were impossible to understand. Even Aidan had told him to mind his own business.

Bors let out a great whoop as Cordovic struck shore, gasping, and pulled himself up the grassy bank.

"Well done!" Galyn said warmly.

Bors slung an arm proudly around his son. "That's a damn sight better than I ever did in a river!" he cried, handing the dripping boy a tunic. "Well done, boy! I told you coming to Benoic would be good for you—look, now, you've befriended your young cousin and learned to swim! A good month's work, if you ask me."

Galyn's hand fell on Galahad's shoulder. "Well done, Galahad." He nodded toward Cordovic. "You boys have had some merry times together. I'm sorry it has to end."

Galahad looked up swiftly. "End?"

"We're leaving, lad," Bors told him. "Been here long enough—settled some matters that, er, needed settling. I must be getting home. We set off tomorrow at first light."

Stunned, Galahad turned to Cordovic, who grinned. "Sorry, cousin. I guess I forgot to tell you."

"But—"

"There'll be a feast tonight," Galyn interjected, seeing his face. "I'm sure your mother will let you stay up extra late this time."

"But—"

"What, then?"

Bors and Cordovic had turned and were already walking away. "Nothing."

Galyn considered him a moment. "Come. I've promised the queen to have you back by midday. She wants to see you. But first, let's stop by the stables. I've a new pony for you to look at. Bigger and faster than old Cherub."

Galahad swallowed hard and clenched his fists against his sides. Valiant whimpered and jumped against his leg, licking the nearest hand. "No, thank you, Uncle Galyn. I don't want a pony."

He turned and ran in desperate, pounding strides up the long hill to the king's house with Valiant bounding beside him.

Elaine stood at the window and looked out at the brilliant summer sun. The heat was a living creature, immense and suffocating, breathing its hot, fetid breath into the oven of the room. She pushed a damp tendril of hair from her sweating brow and placed her hand against her belly.

"The pain again?" Adele asked, looking up from her stitching.

Elaine shrugged. "Again and again. It's ever-present now. Oh, this awful heat! I won't be at all surprised if I lose this child."

"Touch wood!" Adele cried. "You tempt fate to say such a thing. Sit down and put your feet up on a cushion. I'll send for a cool drink."

"No." Elaine turned from the window and lifted a hand. "I want no servants near." She slumped into a nearby chair. "I don't care if I tempt fate. You must know by now I bear this child against my will. . . . You needn't gawk at me; I'm not the first woman to resent the unborn."

"No," Adele agreed uncertainly, "but you are young to feel so."

"I am five-and-twenty," Elaine continued wearily, "and what has life brought me? I sit here exiled in this backwater, away from all that's happening in Britain. I have no power; my husband has seen to that." Tears sprang to her eyes. "Is it honorable to treat a woman as a broodmare? What do they do but pen me in my quarters and keep me from the companionship I choose? I may not ride out, I may not chance myself to a boat, I may walk only as far as the garden—and all because I am carrying Lancelot's precious child!"

Adele said nothing, but dipped her kerchief in her water cup and pressed the cool cloth to Elaine's brow.

Elaine gazed up at her. "Surely you must know by now that Lancelot does not love me. Has not cared for me one single moment we have been together. My sons are only tokens of his lapses in control."

"Oh, Elaine!" Adele said softly, laying a hand on her arm. "That's a wicked thing to say!"

"Would it surprise you to know that I do not love him, either? No, I see it would not. But I will tell you something few others know: I lost my heart long ago to a greater man than he. I had a destiny once. From childhood my mother planned it. She raised me to be King Arthur's bride. As I should have been."

"But Lancelot is second only to the High King," Adele said quickly. "Bearing his sons is no less honorable than bearing Arthur's."

Elaine rested a hand on her belly. "I'm not talking of honor. I'm talking of love." She looked into the younger woman's eyes. "I love Arthur Pendragon as a man, not as a king. I love everything about him: his voice, his eyes, his hands, the sound of his laughter, the cold fury of his rage. I love him with every fiber of my being, and I've loved him every waking moment of every waking day since I first set eyes upon him."

Adele paled. "Why then did you marry Lancelot?"

Elaine's eyes narrowed in amusement. "Why do you think? What future does a woman have without a husband?" She shrugged. "I married him to make my cousin weep. And weep she did. The memory of her anguish is still a balm to my soul."

Adele retreated a little, staring at her, but Elaine did not notice.

"Do you have any idea what I would give to go back to Britain? To spend a summer in Gwynedd by the western sea? Or a month in Camelot? I have a pain"—she struck her breast lightly with her fist—"here, waking and sleeping. It is dread that I shall never see my homeland again."

Adele sank to her knees at Elaine's side and took her hot, moist hand between her own. "Never is a long time. Perhaps, in a few years . . . Wait until your sons are of fighting age, and you can find them wives in Britain—"

"My sons!" Elaine cried. "He is taking away my sons! He will take them away and I will never see them again!"

"What nonsense is this? Of course you will—"

"Do you imagine I have power over my sons? Just look at Galahad! I can count on the fingers of one hand the times I've seen him alone this past month! Galyn and Bors have thrust him into the world *they* chose for him, because they do not trust Aidan and they do not trust me. And what is he become but another dirty urchin wrestling with his fellows in the dust? A common boy who smells of dog breath and horse sweat, that's what he is become."

"Dirty? Nonsense, Elaine. Galahad is always—"

"That boy is a fine, virgin cloth woven of godly thread, and they have used it to wipe the mud from the soles of their boots! Have you forgotten the prophecy? 'He shall wield the sword of righteousness in Britain. . . .' How can he do that if he is not trained? But now that Bors is finally going I shall remedy what I can, I shall—" She stopped suddenly at the sound of footsteps racing down the corridor.

"What will you do, Elaine?"

A frantic pounding sounded at the door. "Mama! Mama!"

Elaine rose unsteadily. "I shall set his feet upon a new path." She turned to face the door. "Enter!" Galahad came in, white-faced, and fell on his knees at his mother's feet. "Galahad! What has happened?"

"He's a cheat! Cordovic is a cheat! Let me kill him! Please?"

"Don't be ridiculous." Elaine glanced quickly at Adele. "Leave us." Adele made her reverence and, after a long hesitation, went out and closed the door behind her.

Elaine waited until she had gone. "If he's a cheat, he's no worse than the rest of his family. What has he done to you?"

"He made a bargain with me! He made a promise and he broke it!"

Elaine stroked his hair and kissed him. "Tell me about it."

In fits and starts, Galahad told her the whole story, describing the mare, revealing his daybreak visits, confessing the drudgery of the tedious hours spent in the river with Cordovic. "Today he swam across the river. And now he's leaving and he still won't let me ride his mare!"

Elaine snorted. "Cordovic's not fit to wipe your boots. Forget him. If you want his horse so badly, take it. He owes it to you. But I can't see why you make such a fuss about an animal. One horse is much like another. Now attend me, Galahad. I have an errand for you. It's important."

Galahad looked up into her pale face. Her blue eyes, so like his own, looked enormous. "What is it, Mama? Are you ill?"

"I am today. It is this child of Lancelot's that sickens me. You must take a message to Father Aidan."

"Shall I bring you more medicine?"

"Yes, yes, I would be grateful for it, but that is not the message. Attend me now. Tell him . . . tell him Bors has proved to be a worse fool than I thought him. Tell Aidan that well is dry. He will know what I mean." Her clammy hands gripped his. "Tell him that. Have you got it?"

"Yes, Mama."

"And tell him this also. Bors spoke to Galyn about me. Galyn sent a courier to Britain—to Lancelot. Tell Aidan it is time for the ceremony. You and I will beg off from this farewell feast. I am too ill to attend it, and you . . . we will find some excuse for you. Tell Aidan to be in the chapel an hour past moonrise. We will meet him there."

"Am I going with you?" Galahad stared up at her. "To the chapel with Aidan? What for?"

She smiled and bent down to kiss his forehead. "Tell Aidan an hour past moonrise. Don't forget."

He ran lightly down the road, his heart soaring. He darted into the stable-yard with Valiant leaping at his side, past grooms busy fetching water, and slipped around back to the horse lines. Everything was quiet. All the horses had their noses deep in hay. One pretty bay face turned toward him and nickered softly.

"Glory!" Valiant danced jubilantly in the grass as Galahad untied the mare from the ground lines and stood with the lead rope in his hands. There was no time to run for her bridle. The bit only caused her pain, anyway. The halter would have to do. He led the mare to a corner of one of the outbuildings where a wooden tub stood half-full of dirty clothing. He turned the tub over and climbed up on it. Grabbing Valiant and stuffing him into his open tunic, he threw a leg over the mare and slid onto her back. She shied sideways, and then stood patiently.

"Glory! My beauty!" he whispered, stroking her neck. The puppy squirmed against his chest and yipped with glee. "Shhh!" Galahad laughed. "Ready, Valiant? Let's go!"

His legs moved against her side and she threw up her head in alarm, out of long habit, and danced sideways. Galahad grabbed for the mane, startled at the bounce in her step. Thrice he nearly lost his seat and only just managed to save the pup as the mare tossed her head and spun, fearing the yank on her mouth that always followed the weight on her back. Finally, Galahad dug his heels into her side. She bolted.

The town flew by in a blur as they thundered down the winding road.

Galahad prayed aloud the great gates might be open—he knew he could not stop her. But the unsettling bounce was gone. She was as easy to ride as the coracle on a breezy day, with her head stretched out before her and her legs reaching for the ground in a steady rhythm. He could feel her life, her pride, her joy as she fled from imprisonment and followed her eager will. Against his heart the dog lay still, a curl of fur, cowed by the whip of speed. Miraculously, the gates opened to admit a wagon full of timber. Galahad crouched low on the mare's neck and swept past the guards in a blur. He held firmly to the halter rope. The mare leaned comfortably against his hand and increased her speed. Her excitement filled his entire being until he laughed aloud and clung to her whipping mane, willing her onward, past the open fields and into the forest.

Finally, in the sweet, pine-scented cool of the forest shade, she slowed. He sat up as she shortened her stride into a canter, holding her head relaxed now, arching her neck in a long, lovely curve. Her coat was dark with sweat, but he could feel the undaunted eagerness in her stride. She had plenty of run in her still. They cantered down the forest track at an easy pace, the thick carpet of pine needles muffling the beat of her hooves. He knew, without knowing how, that he was meant for this, that horsemanship was part of his destiny, that things that came so easily to him, things he seemed to know already how to do, were part of his future, part of God's plan. He'd been right to take the mare. She was meant to be his.

Eventually Galahad drew her to a trot, and then a walk, as they neared the edge of the lake. Valiant poked his head out of the tunic and sniffed excitedly. Galahad slid off her back, set the dog on the ground, and ran his hand down the mare's chest. Her sweated coat was drying; she was cool enough to drink. He led her to the water, where Valiant was already playing in the shallows, and then tied her lead rope to a sturdy branch.

"You stay here, Glory. We'll be back soon and we'll do the ride again. Come on, Valiant. Find the coracle!"

He dragged the coracle and paddle from their hiding place. Valiant leaped in eagerly and sat between Galahad's knees all the way to the island. A robed figure awaited him on the shingle.

"Father Aidan! I have a message from my mother."

The priest nodded slowly, his face hooded even in the heat. "I thought as much. Tie the dog."

He turned and walked slowly up the path to the hut. Galahad loosed the thong from his waist and bound Valiant to a sapling. "Be a good boy and stay here. You can't come this time. He must have his medicines out. Wait for me."

He followed Aidan into the hut and stood solemnly by the door. "My mother needs her medicine. She said Sir Bors is a fool and the well is dry.

Uncle Galyn sent a courier to Britain. Tonight we're going to the chapel an hour past moonrise. She said to tell you it is time."

Aidan said nothing. He went to the shelf by his pallet and lifted down a small glazed vial stoppered with cork and marked with a label impressed in wax. He held it in his hand and looked down at it a long time. Then he straightened.

"This is what she asks for. Give her this. Tell her not to take it until dark."

For a moment Galahad was afraid. It was not the same vial he usually carried. "It's for sickness, isn't it?"

"Oh, yes," Aidan said softly. "It's a cure for earthly ills." His keen eyes flashed at Galahad and the boy froze. "Take it to her in this linen bag. Keep it well inside your tunic and let no one see it. If you are asked about it, do not answer. It is no one's business but the queen's. Do you understand?"

Galahad nodded. Aidan lifted his chin and searched his face. "Has she told you what will happen in the chapel?"

"No."

"You will face your destiny. Tonight you will be dedicated to it. Do you know what that entails?"

Galahad gulped. "No."

"You will be offered to Almighty Living God. If you are worthy, if He accepts you, you will be His. When you are given to the Almighty, you belong to Him absolutely. No longer to your father, to your mother, to your king. God becomes your Father and your King. It is His commands you follow. This requires courage, Galahad, and discipline. You will be set apart. You will never be the same as other men."

Galahad stared up at him, hardly daring to breathe. Aidan's firm hand clasped his shoulder. "But you will not be alone. I will guide you. I will not leave you."

"How . . . how do you know what will happen?"

Aidan smiled. "The Lord has given me eyes that see. During the ceremony He will give them to you, as well. When you look into the Cross of Visions you will see your destiny and the man you will become."

"The Cross of Visions?" Galahad asked. "What is that?"

"You will see soon enough," Aidan said, leading him to the door. "Now go home and prepare yourself. Pray for strength and courage. Remember the prophecy. Your future beckons and it is time to begin. You will not be the same afterward, ever again."

Galahad stared at the golden eyes and trembled.

"Wear white. Tell your mother to do the same. Wear white and come barefoot into the sanctuary." Aidan turned away without smiling. "One more thing. Give that horse back to the boy it belongs to. Rid yourself of the desire for earthly possessions. After tonight, you will have no need of them. Go now. I need time to prepare."

Galahad clutched the vial to his breast and fled.

Halfway back he saw a small group of soldiers riding fast toward him. He slowed the mare and waited. Valiant, asleep in his tunic, did not stir. Galyn and Bors led a troop of men. They surrounded him in a semicircle. Cordovic was there, too, riding a large pony he'd never seen before and looking ready to spit flames.

Galyn's face was grim. "What the devil do you mean by this, Galahad? Stealing Cordovic's horse and sneaking hell-bent-for-leather out the gates? Are you mad, son? What possessed you?"

"I didn't steal Cordovic's horse."

"The hell you didn't!" Cordovic screamed. "We've caught you red-handed! Who gave you permission to take her?"

Galahad glanced at him coldly. "You did."

"Liar!"

"You're an oath breaker!"

"Liar! Thief! Swine!"

"That's enough, son," growled Bors. "Let's hear his explanation."

Galyn raised an eyebrow at Galahad. "Well?"

"He promised I could ride her when he swam the river."

"Liar! I said we'd talk about it! I never gave you leave!"

Galahad lifted his chin defiantly.

Galyn frowned. "You should have asked him. It's his horse."

"He broke his oath."

"You royal bitch's whelp!" Cordovic wailed. "I'll—"

"That's enough!" Galyn cut in, lifting his hand for silence. "Galahad, what's that in your tunic?"

Galahad froze. "Um . . . there's nothing—" He bit off the lie as Galyn's face darkened. Suddenly warm fur wiggled against his chest and the puppy's nose pushed out.

Galyn smiled. "Valiant! Well, why didn't you say so? I'm amazed he stood for it."

"It's that damned ugly dog!" Cordovic muttered. "He takes it *riding!*"

Galyn sobered. "Well, Galahad, in the matter of Cordovic's horse you acted rashly and without permission. For that I must punish you. You will spend the evening in your room and miss the feast tonight."

"Yes, my lord." Galahad fought to hide his relief. God was here; God was working; God was following Aidan's plan.

"What about my horse?" demanded Cordovic, yanking the pony's head around and battering its ribs with his boots. "Make him get off her and ride his own!"

"As to that," Galyn said dryly, "that's not his pony yet. I haven't paid for it. And seeing how you treat your mounts, I think I'll spare your mare."

"What!" Cordovic was aghast. "Father! Do something!"

"Shut up!" Bors snapped. "Galyn's right. I wish you could ride half so well as Galahad. That mare goes like a dream for him. Haven't you been watching? You should have had him teach you to ride, too, while you were about it."

Cordovic's face flushed an ugly red.

"Enough," Galyn said quietly, swinging his stallion around. "That can't be taught. It's in his blood. Now let's go home."

13 ✝ AN HOUR PAST MOONRISE

Galahad lay on his bed in his best tunic of white combed wool. Outside his narrow window a nightingale sang, alone and confident. The night was warm with haze, the stars hidden. Dimly he heard the sounds of talk and laughter. The feast had begun. He smiled secretly. A guard stood outside his door, but Galyn had forgotten how easy it was for boys to slip through windows.

He heard his mother's step before he heard her call, and he was through the window before she had finished speaking his name. He went down on one knee when he saw her. Waves of glimmering, golden hair cascaded over her shoulders. Her white robe shone in the mist like a beacon on a dark sea. She was a maiden again, highborn and lovely. She smiled at his awe and took his hand. They walked slowly through the garden and down the narrow trail behind the king's house. Galahad held the candle and guided her steps, for she was unused to going barefoot and her feet were tender and easily bruised. He did this solemnly, holding in his excitement and his pride.

"Did you take the medicine?" he asked. "Are you feeling better?"

"Yes, I took it, much good it did me. I feel worse." She shrugged. "I will feel better presently, when Bors is gone."

"What did he do to you, Mama?"

"Do?" She laughed bitterly. "Nothing. Absolutely nothing. He has less ambition in his whole body than I have in my fingertip. He's a fool." She stopped suddenly and clapped a hand to her belly. "Dear Christ!" She bent over, gasping, eyes screwed shut, clutching his hand with clawlike fingers.

"Mama!" he cried in panic. "Mama, stop!"

The spasm passed; she drew breath and straightened. But her face was the color of her robe. "Let us go on, Galahad. In the chapel I will sit down and rest."

He led her down stone steps and past the old well built by ancient men in times unknown. Nearby stood a small, square chapel built of pale, polished marble as smooth as silk to touch. It shone in the moon-bright haze as if its stones carried light.

A hundred candles burned around the altar, haloed in mist. Stone walls, stone bench, stone floor grew warm and welcoming in their soft, resplendent glow. Elaine and Galahad moved forward slowly. In the center of the altar hung a golden cross, heavy and crudely fashioned, polished to a dull sheen. In the center of the cross a garnet glinted, set deep and oddly cut, as big as a gull's egg and a dark blood red.

"I've never seen that cross before," Elaine whispered. "Have you?"

Galahad shook his head. They sat together on the bench. Outside, night sounds filled the air: the nearby chirrup of crickets, the far-off wail of a wolf, the scurry and rustle of small forest creatures followed by the slow, heavy beat of wings as death passed by.

Galahad shivered. "Mama, can't we go home? I promise to be the best knight that I can."

"I know you will, my sweet boy. But you must promise it to God. Aidan says it needs a priest to summon the presence of the Almighty. You must be offered, found worthy, and accepted. I don't know what it all involves. But don't fret, Galahad. You will find the courage when it is necessary."

He swallowed but his throat was dry. The arching cavern of the chapel rang with emptiness.

Elaine gasped. A spasm of pain crossed her face. "Galahad!" He took her hand. Her fingers bent stiff like claws. Sweat glistened pale on her cold brow; the skin around her mouth looked drawn and tight. Her hand upon his arm was ice. "Something . . . something is not right. Listen to me. I brought you here at Aidan's bidding. He has a plan for you. But if . . . if Aidan's plan does not work, or if I . . . I . . . things somehow go awry, if I fall ill of this cursed child within me, I want you to promise me—"

"Only ask it! I will do it!" cried the shaking child. "What is wrong? Who is hurting you?"

She looked down at him, her face as pale and lifeless as a death's head. "Avenge me. Avenge me upon Lancelot. He is the root cause of all my suffering. From the beginning, the source of all my pain. He has killed my spirit." Her eyes closed slowly as she drew breath; the lids were blue. "I will not rest easy, in Heaven or in Hell, until he is dead."

Suddenly from behind them came the sound of Aidan's voice. "Be still, Elaine." Galahad whipped around. Aidan walked calmly toward them, robed in white, his rich curls falling in profusion about his shoulders. He carried a horn cup full of steaming liquid. As he neared them, Galahad caught the heavy scent of poppies. Aidan put the cup into Elaine's hand. "Drink this. It will ease your pain and enable you to endure."

She looked up quickly at him and clung to his hand. "Aidan, what was in that potion?"

"You disobeyed me, didn't you?" The golden eyes were metal. "You took it before dark. Impatient woman. I will mix another poppy draft for you later. But take this now." His voice commanded her, and she drank.

Then Aidan stood before Galahad. "Rise, Galahad. Are you ready?"

Galahad tried to still his shaking, but could not. "No, Father."

Aidan smiled. "At least you are honest about it. He who comes before God without fear in his heart is arrogant and doomed to perdition." Aidan placed a golden cushion at the foot of the altar. "Kneel here, Galahad, and pray. Ask God to grant you courage." Galahad obeyed. The cross hung before his face, the great, dull jewel at eye level.

Aidan placed three cups upon the altar, one of horn, one of silver, and one of gold. Galahad's eyes slid sideways. He could not keep from staring. Where had all this treasure come from? He had never seen any sign of wealth in the hut or on the island. Aidan lifted a wineskin and filled each cup half-full. He looked suddenly at Galahad. The boy ducked his head and closed his eyes.

"Pray, Galahad. The Lord is watching. Your curiosity will be satisfied soon enough."

From his pouch Aidan withdrew three linen bags tied with silken cord. From the first bag he took a pinch of gray powder and dropped it into the horn cup, mixing it with the wine until it dissolved. From the second bag he took white powder and dropped it into the silver cup, and from the third bag, black powder into the gold cup. Then he tucked the bags away, folded his hands within his robe, and lifted his eyes to the vault above his head.

"Almighty God, I bring you Galahad, whom You have chosen. Inspect him; look into his heart. If he is found wanting, dry up his courage and send him away from this place. But if he proves worthy, anoint him with Light." Aidan's deep voice echoed around the glowing walls.

"Rise, Galahad. Stand before the altar." Galahad rose. "Rise, Elaine. Stand by me."

She looked better, Galahad saw with relief. The poppies had restored color to her cheeks and life to her eyes.

Aidan made the sign of the cross over the horn cup, touched it to his lips, and handed it to Galahad. "This is the Cup of the Servant. Drink, Galahad, that you may serve God."

Galahad's hand shook as he took the cup from Aidan. The golden eyes bored into him, steadied him, and he drank. The wine tasted oddly bitter. He swallowed once and put it down.

"You shall serve the Lord, your Father, with your body, with your spirit, with your life. No one else commands you. You are become the servant of God. Swear it."

Galahad repeated the oath. His head felt light and a little dizzy. Aidan made the sign of the cross over the silver cup, touched it to his lips, and handed it to Galahad.

"This is the Cup of the Soldier. Drink, Galahad, that you may become a soldier of the Lord and one day carry his mark upon your shield."

The wine slid sweet on his tongue, but stung his throat as he swallowed. His head began to spin and he gripped the altar to steady himself. He seemed oddly disconnected from his body, as if he were watching himself from a distance.

"You shall serve Arthur and you shall serve Britain as the king's soldier. But when you are grown you shall go forth on a mission of your own, for the greater glory of Almighty God. You, Galahad, are become the soldier of God. Swear it."

Again, Galahad repeated the oath. With glittering eyes, Aidan raised the golden cup. He did not touch it to his lips but held it out to Galahad. His voice fell to a whisper.

"This," he said, "is the Cup of the Sword. Just as a sword slashes its way through all opposition, he who drinks of this cup will see only the straight path, the Path of Light, and will be blind to the twists and turns of the dark roads that surround him. Drink, Galahad, that you may follow the path of righteousness. Drink, that you may strike down evil in the name of God."

Galahad took the cup. It was heavy. The wine it held had turned a dark, muddy blue and smelled sharply of rotten eggs. He glanced quickly at Aidan, at the voracious eagerness on his face. It flashed across Galahad's mind that the wine might not be safe to drink—but a will beyond his own commanded his flesh. He lifted the cup with both hands and drained it.

Aidan smiled triumphantly.

Elaine looked up at him, frowning. "Aidan, what—" But he waved her silent, not taking his eyes from Galahad's face.

The fearsome liquid lay on Galahad's tongue like ambrosia. When he swallowed it down, it sank sweetly into his body, filling his limbs with an airy lightness and a welcome warmth. Aidan and Elaine seemed to waver and melt before his eyes, dispersing into nothingness.

"Galahad, look at me." Aidan's voice brought him back out of the void. "It is your destiny to lead men to the light. Be strong. Be stainless. Be unforgiving. Judge men without mercy. Falsehood and wrongdoing are your only enemies. You are become the true blade, God's own weapon, forged in the refiner's fire. Pure. Swift. Clean and deadly. Where the Lord points His finger, you will strike men down. You are Galahad, the sword of God. Swear it."

The golden eyes trapped him. He struggled briefly, suddenly afraid, but he was as helpless as a butterfly newborn from the chrysalis, caught in the hunter's net, pinned by Aidan's will.

"I swear it."

"Swear also to keep the secret of this dedication. What we do tonight, what you have seen and are yet to see, must never be revealed. To anyone. On pain of death. Swear it."

"I swear it."

"Kneel, Galahad," Aidan whispered. "Look into the Cross of Visions. See what lies before you."

The dull surface of the gem dissolved even as he watched. It began to gleam, light from the candles reflected in a thousand facets behind the garnet's face. In one of them he saw himself, pictured small. He leaned closer. There he was again, a youth now, with silk-black hair, bright blue eyes, and features of surpassing beauty. The handsome youth raised a sword—Lancelot's sword—with a cross of rubies on the hilt. On his arm was a white shield with a crimson cross. The light began to shiver and beat around the youth, around Galahad himself; the whole world began to pulse with light and shadow.

Bloodred facets flashed before his eyes with the images they carried: a battlefield of gore and horror where corpses stared with open eyes into the beaks of ravens; a young woman's body, naked in dim torchlight, her eyes closed and her hair tangled with dirt; a weary commander, tight-lipped, sitting his stallion on a hilltop, looking down on the open field where his betrayer approached; an island in a river where a wounded king awaited his coming; a tower where girls were imprisoned who reached out to him with eager arms and dulcet voices; a wild ride in cold, whipping rain to an empty garden; a black horse carrying him wearily into a dusty town where a small boy played with a wooden sword; a royal bier winding slowly uphill with a dreadful burden; a lantern on the floor by an altar, at the edge of a deep pit; a king's hall lit with a thousand candles and filled with the song of angels; a shield on the wall above a dying man's body; an old, blind blacksmith holding Lancelot's sword across his lap; a secret room where a dozen ancient chalices lay hidden in the dark; himself kneeling in a dusty storeroom in the bitter cold, a rotting scabbard in his hands; a young woman crouching before a fire, smiling at him, a smile that turned his bones to water; a dark wasteland spread out before him in the driving rain, a place of fearful desolation and disgrace. The images flashed faster as the pulsing light quickened—Lancelot's body, drowned in a pool of blood; the white walls of a holy house; the white veil hiding a woman's face; and then, in the flash of glittering, reflected light, a dazzling spear, a gleaming krater encrusted with gems, held aloft between a woman's hands; himself again, a grown man, bathed in light, glory shining about him and in his hands, the blessed Grail—his breaths came in short gasps; pain pierced his head; he sought to look away but failed.

Suddenly he saw Aidan in the facets, robed and cowled, standing in a bower, waiting for a woman. The woman approached, blue-gowned and golden-haired, and Aidan took her in his arms and kissed her. His hands reached inside her gown, her body opened to him—Galahad cried out as he saw her face. Aidan whipped around, the golden eyes fixing on him, and drew a red curtain firmly across his vision—a red curtain of blood! Blood thick and oozing and dark, splashing everywhere, staining the marble floor, flowing up the walls, clogging his nostrils with its sweet stench!

Sobbing, Galahad fell to the cold floor. "Aidan! Aidan!" Screaming filled his ears. It was not his voice! *"Aidan!"*

Above his head candle flames bobbed and danced, drawing together in a circle, a halo of light, coalescing slowly into a globe, a brilliant sphere of solid flame. A voice, hollow and unreal, pierced the light. *Attend me!* The sphere of flame swelled and pulsed, resolving by infinitesimal degrees into the outline of a face. His breath caught in his throat. Cool, golden eyes burned down into his soul. A low hiss sounded in his ears. *You are mine now. Mine forever. There is no going back. Galahad, I am your God. Submit to me.* He pressed into the marble floor, shrinking from the horror, mouth open in a silent scream. His whole being shuddered, revolted, his spirit heaved in refusal. The flaming face came closer. *Kill your father. Soldier of God, I command you. It is time to act. Submit to me. You are my sword. Lancelot is coming to take you away. He is corrupt and will take you into the heart of corruption. Fear him not. You are the sword of God. Strike him with your dagger! You will get no peace until he's dead. I promise you this.*

Galahad fought for breath, clutching at his memory. Someone, somewhere, sometime, had taught him the key to Watch-spells. *Attend me. I am your God.* He whimpered as the flames bore down and terror seized his soul.

Suddenly, through the numbing fear, he remembered. And just as suddenly another presence came to his aid. A companion. *Hold on to me.* A warm voice spoke, calm and powerful, more felt than heard. *Out, demon! Leave my son alone.* Slowly, the flaming apparition began to change. The eyes faded from gold to silver to gray, the pulsing face withdrew and reformed into the outlines of a human face, a face he knew, a brooding face with straight black brows and a crooked nose.

Father! His lips would not move but his spirit screamed the name. *Father! Help me!*

Slowly the lights above his head began to spin, reduced now to whirling candles. Someone nearby whimpered in pain, "Aidan!" Galahad sobbed aloud, "Lancelot!" and the world went dark.

Something touched his cheek. He struggled to breathe. A great stifling weight seemed to sit upon his chest, but even as he fought to awaken, he recognized it. It was fear. His eyes flew open. All he saw was white. He gasped once, twice, heart pounding, and screamed.

He heard, away in the distance, a feeble cry that died to nothingness. "Galahad?" It was a human voice! Warm fingers clutched his arm. "Galahad, can you hear me?"

He turned his head and saw Renna's face bending down to him.

"Praise be to God, the child's awake at last!" She smiled, and pulled back the white cloth they had fixed above his bed to protect him from the morning sun. He gazed at his own chamber wall. He lay in his own bed.

"Renna!" It came out a whisper. "Where's my father?"

Renna put a hand to his forehead. "Well, well, little Galahad, and it's about time, too!" She stepped lightly to the door and spoke to someone outside.

He struggled to sit up, and failed. "Where's my father?"

Renna returned. "In Britain, of course. Where else? Here, drink this."

Gradually his head cleared and he was able to sit up. He pushed the proffered cup away. "What happened, Renna? How did I come here?"

She laughed sharply, shaking out his doeskin tunic. "You're asking *me*? That's the question all Benoic is asking. *I* don't know. Come, put this on."

Galahad looked down in surprise at his naked body. "Where's my tunic? My white one?"

Renna shuddered and tried to conceal it. "They burned it, most like," she muttered. "Stank like a slaughter pit."

"Blood!" Galahad gasped as memory flooded back. "There was blood! It was real! I know it was! I smelled it!"

"Hush now. Don't excite yourself. You'll fall down in a faint again."

"Whose blood was it, Renna? Who bled on my tunic? It's not me—see, I'm whole. I'm not hurt. Renna, whose was it?"

Something like fear touched Renna's face, and was instantly hidden. Soft steps sounded in the corridor. Renna spoke quickly. "Your aunt Adele is coming to see you. She will answer all your questions. Ahhh"—with a sigh of relief—"here she is."

Adele sat gracefully beside Galahad on the bed. She took both his hands and he clung to her. Her lips were the color of the queen's rosebuds, dark pink and unblemished. Her eyes, liquid brown and deeply set, were not the eyes of the royal family of Lanascol—"Benoic eyes" people called them—long-lashed and gray. But then, she was a stranger here. As he was now.

"Galahad." Even her voice was beautiful, gentle, and very kind. "Your mother is taken ill."

He nodded. He had known it from the moment she entered the room.

"Strange things went on last night," Adele said slowly. "It would help us, it would help the physicians and your mother, if we could learn what they were."

"Was the blood hers?" he blurted. "Was it?"

Adele frowned lightly. "What are you talking about?"

"There was blood—in the chapel. All over everywhere."

"Galahad, can you tell us what went on in that chapel? Why were you there?"

"First tell me! Was it her blood?"

"I don't know."

"What's the matter with her? Does she bleed now?"

Adele paused. "She is . . . she is very ill, and in pain. The physician fears she may lose the child she carries."

Galahad's eyes widened. "Send for Father Aidan! He can cure her!"

Adele's hand trembled as it smoothed the hair back from his face. "Galyn has been out since dawn looking for him. At the lake, through the forest, all over Benoic. Aidan has disappeared." Galahad stared at her but Adele continued calmly. "Galyn came to check on you when the feast was over, and found you gone. The alarm was raised. Then it was discovered the queen was not in her chambers. Grannic finally confessed how she had dressed her in her white ceremonial robe but she did not know where the queen was going, or why. When Galyn came to the chapel in the dead of night, he found a hundred guttered candles, you in a faint upon the floor, and the queen lying . . . on a bench. Aidan was not there."

"What about the silver cup? And the golden Cross of Visions?"

Adele's eyes widened. "He certainly found no such treasures as you describe. Who in Lanascol has such a cross? Did you see really such a thing, Galahad?"

"Oh, yes. I . . . I . . . and a golden cup, too. It was heavy. I drank from it."

"What?" Adele said quickly. "What did you drink?"

"Only wine. Blue wine."

"Did your mother drink anything?"

"Not the wine. It was for me. For the ceremony."

Adele frowned. "What kind of ceremony?"

Galahad shuddered. "I can't tell you."

"But you *must* tell. It could be important."

"But I swore not to."

Adele sighed and kissed his forehead. "All right, then. If you swore an oath."

"There *was* a cup that Mama drank. But it was only poppies. Father Aidan gave it to her. She had a stomachache."

"Are you sure she was in pain *before* she drank it?"

"Yes."

"Perhaps she took something earlier in the day," Adele said thoughtfully, and rose. "Well, we will talk about this again later, when things have calmed down a bit. I must get back to your mother now. Renna will bring you something to eat. But take it slowly, Galahad. You've been drugged, and we don't know what it may have done to you." At the door she paused and turned back. "Try to remember what you can of the ceremony. The physician thinks your mother drank something, a potion of some sort, with poison in it. Think if you can remember anything she might have taken."

The door closed silently behind her. Galahad stared wildly at the space where she had been.

As soon as Renna left to get him food, he slipped out of his window and raced barefoot down the winding path to the chapel. A guard called out, but Galahad ignored him. He stopped when he came to the ancient well. The midday sun blazed on the hot stones. Nothing moved in the bright stillness. The chapel glittered, making his eyes ache.

Inside it was cool and quiet. He moved slowly toward the altar. There were no guttered candles. Taking a deep breath, he stole a glance at the floor beside the altar. The pale marble was perfectly white and unstained. His knees began to shake and he sat heavily on the bench. The place had been cleaned, and cleaned well. Even the long, congealed fingers of cold wax had been scraped from the altar sides. But they could never have scoured so much blood away in so short a time. It must have been a dream, a nightmare vision in the gemstone, like all the rest.

With a sigh of relief he bowed his head to pray, and froze. There under the bench, where two slabs of marble met, was a thin, dark line. He scanned the floor—only here, only beneath the bench were the blocks of marble outlined by whatever dark substance filled the cracks between them. Shaking, Galahad knelt on the floor and ran his fingernail along the tiny space between the marble stones. The stuff flaked off as he touched it. It was dark red.

Clutching his stomach, Galahad ran to the side door and fell to his knees near the bushes. His hands pressed into the cool, damp earth. Damp! He looked around wildly. The dirt path bore the marks of soldiers' boots, still clear along the muddied edges. Mud! With a trembling hand he reached for a fistful of the moist dirt: it was reddish brown, slightly sticky, and smelled of death.

Galahad threw himself headlong to the ground and wept.

14 ✝ THE KING OF LANASCOL

For five days Galahad huddled in the nursery with his brothers, where Maida and Renna went about with lowered eyes and voices, Galahodyn wept openly and Gallinore played, uncomprehending, with his blocks. Galahad sat stone-faced in the corner, refusing food, saying nothing. He was never left unguarded. A pallet had been made for him in the nursery, but he slept little. The same dream pursued him night after night: He paddled madly across Black Lake in his coracle, the stoppered vial tucked against his breast, knowing death was close on his heels. When he ran aground on the shingle, he reached for the mare's reins, and instantly plunged into a black pit, screaming as he fell, a long, high-pitched, never-ending wail—for there was no bottom and he fell forever. He awoke in a sweat and sat for the rest of the dark hours hugging his knees and listening to the sonorous rhythm of the women's snores.

The days were not much better. He tried to pray, but when he closed his eyes he saw only the candlelit altar and his mother's waxen pallor, so he kept his eyes open. About the ceremony he did not think at all. Renna, Maida, his brothers were always around him, but their movement and their noise swirled formlessly by him, making no impression against the rock-hard stillness of his grief.

No one told him anything. Everyone tiptoed about and spoke in whispers, sent for physicians and then for the priest, but no one thought to warn him death was near. First Hodyn, and then even little Gallinore looked to him for solace, but he was powerless to help them, he who could not even help himself.

Finally, on a gray day warm with summer rain, Galyn walked into the nursery with Adele. The lines in his face, the deep sorrow in his eyes told Galahad before he spoke what they had come to say. Adele drew the younger boys onto her lap, and told them with great tenderness that God had taken their mother into Heaven, with the daughter she had borne too soon. They must be strong princes, all, and say prayers for their mother and their sister. They must wear their best tunics and do what Renna told them, and say nothing at all until they were bidden.

The house rang with the women's keening until Galahad covered his ears against the noise. He saw her body once, swathed in rich cloths and spices, but it was the face of a stranger, gray and old. Gone forever was the golden presence of his boyhood, the bright-armored beauty he had always known.

The sun shone the day they buried her in the birch grove. He was afraid to look into the yawning pit, and they did not make him. Renna took him back as soon as Father Patrik had pronounced the blessing, so he did not have to watch them shovel earth into her grave.

Galyn came to him later, and drew him aside from his brothers. "I have sent for your father," he said gruffly. "In a week or so, when Arthur is back in Camelot, he should be here."

Galahad nodded. Of course it was what they would do.

"Eat something," Galyn said suddenly. "Even if it's only broth. You are nothing but skin and bones."

On a dark night touched with the first hint of coming cold, Galahad heard the thud and jingle of cavalry galloping up the hill. He slid out of bed, drew on his tunic, and slithered out the window. The grass under his bare feet was cold and wet, and he began to shiver. He slipped wraithlike through the dark, neatly avoiding the sentries, and hid in the shadows of the courtyard. Galyn stood on the steps under the torches, the king's seneschal and a handful of servants behind him. Six horses came up the hill at a neat hand-gallop ahead of the rest of the escort. The black stallion in the lead slid to a stop at the foot of the steps. In one fluid motion Lancelot leaped down, threw the reins to a groom, and embraced his brother.

"Galyn!"

"Oh, God forgive me, Lancelot! I am so sorry."

"Please God, it was not your doing. I blame myself I was not here. Tell me, was it swift?"

"Alas, no. She suffered dreadfully."

"Where does she lie?"

"In the birch grove. Near Father."

"And the child?"

"In her arms. Stillborn an hour before she died."

Lancelot bowed his head. "May God forgive me, to reap such a harvest for my sin."

"My dearest brother . . ."

Lancelot turned suddenly, sensing eyes on his back, saw the thin child standing in the shadows, took four long strides, and scooped him up in his arms. "God give me peace! My son!"

Strong arms pulled Galahad hard against a dusty shoulder, rough lips kissed his cheek. The warrior's body, trained to endure every kind of hardship, began to tremble. It lasted only a moment. The king straightened and drew away. Looking up, Galahad saw his eyes were wet.

"Galahad!" Galyn cried. "What are you doing here?"

Lancelot waved him silent as they started up the steps. "It's all right. Let him stay with me." The king's arm tightened around his body as he carried the boy through the corridors into a lamplit room.

"Light the fire," Lancelot ordered. The chamberlain unclipped his brooch and pulled off his cloak. "Get me a blanket, Jules." He wrapped Galahad in the great black cloak and sat by the hearth in his carved chair, holding the boy on his lap. "Galyn, see the men are fed. We've stopped for nothing since the ship landed."

"At once, my lord. And what about you, yourself?"

"Broth and bread will do. And wine."

"Right away, my lord."

Servants scurried to light the tinder, to draw off the king's boots and bring his doeskin slippers, to fetch food and set wine to warm over the flame. Throughout the bustle, Lancelot sat as still as stone with Galahad on his lap. Nestled in the thick cloak, Galahad felt for the brooch, loosed it, and held it in his hand. It was heavy and round, made of black enamel with a silver emblem on the face, the emblem of Lanascol, the screaming hawk with outstretched wings. Galyn had one just like it, and he would, too, he knew, when he was old enough. But Lancelot's hawk alone had a ruby eye. As he held it in the lamplight it winked at him, glowing red, taunting him with memories of another stone. He thrust it into his father's hand.

"Not for you tonight, is it?" Lancelot took the brooch, glanced at it once, and tucked it away. "A fierce badge. Not for me, either. Not in the face of such tragedy. Two such needless deaths."

Galahad shivered and drew the cloak closer. Beneath him Lancelot's legs were as hard as iron. And the gray eyes, glowering at the hissing flames, were hard eyes, cold and deadly as a drawn blade.

Galyn returned to his chair across the hearth, followed by servants with bowls of steaming broth. Lancelot lifted his eyes to Galahad and offered him a bowl. The boy shook his head; the king let him be.

"Tell me," he said to Galyn. As he ate, Lancelot listened to the story of Elaine's illness, agony, and death. Galahad, too, heard for the first time what had been happening during those long, empty days in the nursery. Each word from Galyn's lips struck his heart like a hammer blow, yet he felt the tremors from those blows shake the king's body with his own.

He stole a curious glance at his father's face. The gray eyes, the black hair, the crooked patrician nose, the long, lean jaw, now dark with stubble, the lips pressed hard together and stiff with pain—this was a mask, this face, like the ancient thespian's mask in the nursery chest, carved of elmwood, blank and unyielding, with dark eyeholes whose fathomless depth had always frightened him.

Galyn came to the end of his tale as Lancelot finished his meal and reached for the winecup. Waiting servants whisked the bowl away and replenished the wineskin. Jules appeared at his side with a fine wool blanket.

"My lord is cold from the long ride?"

"No, not for me. For Galahad. That cloak is stiff with mud and sea spray. The blanket's warmer." Jules tucked the blanket around Galahad and draped the cloak over his arm.

"I will have it cleaned. Is there anything else you require, my lord?"

"See that there's bread and wine, and a jug of hot broth in my chamber. Light the brazier and bring an extra blanket for Galahad. I want him with me tonight."

Galahad looked up at him swiftly, but could read nothing in the king's face. He drew the blanket tighter around him and shivered. The servants withdrew, leaving the two men and the boy alone.

A heavy silence descended. Flames licked the logs, hissed and spat. Light and shadow played across the faces of the brothers, so alike in feature, so differently lined by experience. Finally Lancelot drew his eyes from the flames.

"And the priest?"

"You mean Aidan?"

"Of course."

"Gone. Vanished. No one's seen him since the night in the chapel. Black Lake's deserted. The hut's been burned. He must have done it himself, before he left. He's probably in Brittany by now."

"Hoel won't shelter him."

"Gaul, then. I'm sorry, Lancelot—I did my best to keep him out of Benoic. But I couldn't keep her from going to him. And she insisted."

"Mmm."

It was a grunt of assent, and Galyn lightened a little. He drew a long breath. "He has some sort of treasure with him, apparently. He'll be killed by outlaws for what he carries before he gets far; I'll wager gold on it."

Galahad's eyes flew to Lancelot's face. Lancelot waved Galyn silent. "Or he'll find another protectress. Let him go for the moment. He can do no more harm here."

Galyn fidgeted, looked swiftly at Galahad, then leaned forward in his chair. "But there was more to it than you suspected, brother. They had a plan, the two of them. You won't believe it. Bors told me. She broached it to him and then, when he objected, tried to buy his silence. With gold, and . . . and with her charms."

Lancelot sighed wearily and shook his head. "It's an old song, Elaine's ambition. It doesn't matter. Whatever she brought upon herself, it wasn't death. *I* brought that upon her. No one else."

Galahad stared at his father, his mouth open, his throat dry.

"Don't, Lancelot," Galyn whispered. "Don't blame yourself. She took something, the physician said, some medicine or potion, she took it deliberately, she even told Adele she didn't want to bear the—"

"No." The word fell flat and final into the stream of Galyn's pleading, and stopped his tongue. "These are excuses. She died of the child. It was my child, begot on her against her will." Lancelot paused. His eyes darkened. "Her death is mine to bear." He rose slowly, lifting Galahad in his arms. "I owed her more than I ever gave her, and now the debt can never be repaid." He turned and without another word strode out of the room.

The king's sleeping chamber was simply furnished. A big bed stood against one wall, a carved oak chest against another. Two double-flamed lamps shed a warm light on the bare plank floor. Near one of them a low table bore a basket of bread, a bowl of fruit, and a jug of broth. Between the narrow windows a brazier glowed, shedding gentle heat into the calm cool of the spacious room.

Lancelot deposited Galahad on the bed, then turned to unbelt his sword as his chamberlain reached into the chest for a nightrobe. Galahad looked around the room with interest. He had never been in here before. The chest, carved with the Hawk of Lanascol, was very old—the oak had the silver sheen of great age and the carving was crudely done—perhaps it had belonged to his grandfather Galaban, or even to Gorlan before him. On the wall above the chest hung an embroidered hanger for the king's sword. That was a recent gift, he knew. He remembered the day his mother had first seen it, and scoffed at it, belittling both its use and its necessity. It was certainly beautifully embroidered in neat, tiny stitches and vibrantly colored thread. A great silver hawk floated majestically against a dark blue sky, every feather somehow iridescent, as if lit by moonlight. His eye was red, his beak cruelly curved, and in his talons he clutched the king's sword of Lanascol with the cross of rubies on the hilt. To either side of the great bird was an intricately worked "L" in tiny crimson stitches, ornate and convoluted in the style of the ancient Celts. No one in all Less Britain had the artistry or skill to make such a hanger. It must have come from Britain, from the heart of the High Kingdom, from fabled Camelot. The sword itself in its old leather scabbard rested comfortably in the hanger. The hawk seemed to be carrying them both, the real sword and the stitched one.

Lancelot followed his son's glance and smiled. "Amazing work, isn't it?"

Galahad nodded. "Where did it come from?"

The chamberlain stood at Lancelot's elbow with a ewer of hot water and a towel. Galahad waited while the king washed his face and hair and toweled them dry. "Thank you, Jules. I'll need your skill with a razor in the morning. But that's all for tonight."

"My lord."

The door shut behind the servant. Lancelot looked down at his son.

"It was a gift from a dear friend of mine. Queen Guinevere of Britain made it herself."

Galahad stared up at him. How could such an evil woman make something so beautiful? He gulped. "But she's wicked."

"Wicked! No better woman has ever drawn breath. Who has been telling you tales?" A bitter smile touched the king's lips. "Never mind. I can guess. Well, my son, you will be able to decide for yourself one day which tale is true, mine or your mother's." He closed his eyes suddenly. "God rest her soul, I will not speak ill of the dead."

Lancelot sat heavily on the woolen coverlet and frowned. "Galahad, I have not asked you if you wished to stay the night with me or in your own chamber. There is a reason for that. I . . . you might well be able to do without me, but I . . . tonight, son, I cannot do without you."

Galahad looked into the lined face and hard gray eyes. "It's all right with me."

"Thank you." Lancelot hesitated. "Will you tell me what went on in the chapel?" Galahad shook his head solemnly. "Very well. But tell me this—you owe this truth to your mother, if to no one else—did Aidan do anything to harm her? While you were there, did you see anything that would give me, as king, a reason to seek him out for vengeance?"

Galahad licked dry lips and swallowed. "Not while I was there."

Lancelot exhaled deeply. "I thought as much. It was in his interest to keep her alive and well. If she took a remedy for her condition, well, that may be laid to my account as much as to hers." He rose. "Tomorrow, will you take me to her grave? We will say a prayer over her together."

Galahad nodded.

"Now," Lancelot said, "I will pray for her departed soul. Eat if you will, or blow the lamps out and sleep. Pay me no mind."

He knelt by the edge of the bed, crossed himself solemnly, bowed his head, and began to pray. Galahad sat still and watched the bent black head and the clasped, long-fingered hands, listened to the beautiful, flowing Latin of his prayers, delivered not in the nasal staccato of Father Patrik, but in the strong, resonant baritone of a warrior king. On and on they went, while the wind rose and cleared the clouds from the stars, while the pale moon lifted above the trees and swung past the window, while the lamps burned low, guttered, and went out. On they rolled, bearing Galahad with them as on a tide, lifting his terrible guilt from his small shoulders and sweeping it away, such a minuscule addition to such a powerful torrent of sin. Here was a penitent who understood sin, whose voice reached God, who took his son's fearful secret and confessed it as his own, unlocked the gates of Hell and set his young soul free.

Galahad slid softly out of bed and went to the table. Quite suddenly, he was hungrier than he had ever been in all his life. He devoured half a loaf, drank hot broth from the jug, and ate a pear from the bowl. Satisfied at last, he crawled into the great bed, pulled the blanket around him, and yawned. The king had not stirred, although the chamber had darkened and grown chill. Still his black head was bent, his hands clasped, his clear voice steady and beseeching. Galahad laid his head down upon the pillow and slept a dreamless sleep.

In the bright cool of early morning Galahad awoke. The chamber was empty, but a jug of fresh water had been left on the table and a new tunic laid across the foot of the bed. He dressed quickly and swilled water over his face and hair. A scratch came at the door and the king's chamberlain entered with a tray of bread and honey, hot willow tea and porridge, and a bowl of fruit.

"Well, my young lord, I see you slept well. You look twice the lad who went to bed last night."

Galahad grinned. "I feel better, too. I'm starving!" He helped himself to bread and honey as Jules set down the tray. "Did the king get any rest?"

"Very little, I'm afraid. He slept for about an hour. I wouldn't call it rest."

"Where did he go?"

"To the birch grove."

Galahad reached for another thick slice of bread and tucked it in his tunic. "I'm going to the kennels. I've got to show Valiant to my father. He'll let me keep him, won't he, Jules? When he sees all the things I've taught him?"

"Aye, young master." Jules smiled and tossed him a pear as he headed for the door. "I wager he'll let you do about anything you want."

Valiant was not in the kennels. Ban greeted him warmly, but he shook his head in answer to Galahad's query. "He's not here, my lord. Didn't he sleep in your room last night?"

"I . . . I wasn't there. And Renna doesn't let him in. She doesn't like his fleas."

Ban laughed. "Isn't that just like a woman? Like as not he spent the night outside your chamber window, then."

Galahad walked back up the hill to the king's house, whistling to himself, wondering what Lancelot would say when he saw the brown, spotted coat of Dia's bastard. Would he laugh, as Galyn had? Or curse, like Ban?

He turned the corner at the back of the house and stopped in his tracks. Four large ravens plucked at something hidden in the dying grass. Two of them screamed at him in their raucous voices. He forced himself forward, unable to take his eyes off the dark huddle they scavenged. The birds flapped their wings excitedly as he approached, screeching in their foul tongue, their beaks bright with blood. He picked up a stone and hurled it at them.

"Be gone! Be gone! Get off him!" His own shriek resounded in his ears, wild and uncontrolled, a stranger's voice.

He looked down at the stiff carcass of his dog. Flies and ants were already at work. The eyes were gone. The head lolled sharply sideways, one ear flopped over, the pink, tender skin on the inner surface all that still reminded him of his dearest companion.

"Valiant," he whispered. He knelt down. He touched one of the big, lifeless paws, the pads still puppy-soft. A slow fire began to burn in his breast. Hot tears welled. With shaking fingers he pulled off his tunic and wrapped the pup's body in it. He knelt for a moment, shutting his eyes tight, squeezing back the tears. "I'll kill whoever did this! I'll kill him!" A glint of color in the trampled grasses caught his eye. He bent down. His fingers closed upon something cold and rounded, a clip, a badge. He stood alone in the slowly warming sun and stared unseeing at the object in his hand: on a field of black enamel, the screaming silver hawk with a ruby eye.

Lancelot stood in the birch grove gazing down at Elaine's grave. Galahad walked up and faced him across the dark scar of earth. He waited, fists clenched at his sides, but Lancelot did not look up.

"She was fourteen when I met her," Lancelot murmured. "What is it now—eleven years ago? My God, it seems like yesterday. There in her father's house, in Pellinore's wild corner of Wales, I met them both. Elaine and Guinevere. When Arthur sent me to Gwynedd to fetch back his bride." He paused. "She was a pretty girl. And a lovely woman. It was not her fault her cousin outshone her as the sun outshines a candle. But that, alas, she couldn't bear. . . . Eight or nine of the Companions sought her hand. She'd have been better off with any one of them than with me. . . . What a future she might have had. . . . What a tragedy life can be." He looked up and met the accusing glare of bright blue eyes. "She gave me many blessings, Galahad. You are the foremost. Here, I have something for you."

He reached inside his tunic and brought out a dagger with a horn handle, carved with the head of the hawk, and a slender blade tapered to a narrow point. The newly sharpened edge glinted silver in the sun. "I was about your age, I think, perhaps a trifle older, when my father gave it to me. But you're ready for it. You're a brave lad. It will serve you well."

Lancelot extended the dagger across the grave to Galahad. The boy stared at it, wide-eyed. *Strike him with your dagger! You will get no peace until he's dead!* He shook his head vigorously. Lancelot blinked, and for the first time took note of the boy's disheveled condition, the dirt on his hands and leggings, the naked torso, the rage on his face.

"Galahad, what have you been doing? Where's your tunic?"

The boy gulped. "I buried my dog in it."

Lancelot frowned. "What dog?"

"The dog you killed! Because he was a bastard!" Furiously Galahad blinked back tears. "He wasn't like the others. I trained him—he was only a puppy—and he loved me."

"*I?*" Lancelot said blankly. "I would never harm your dog. I didn't even know you had one."

Galahad thrust his hand out, palm upward, displaying the badge. "I found this next to his . . . him."

"Galahad. Son. I would never do such a thing. It's mean-spirited and contemptible."

"It's your badge!"

"Yes," Lancelot said unhappily, taking it from him. "It's mine. You held it in your hand last night. And here are shreds of my cloak still attached. Someone has taken pains to lay a scent for you. Someone who knows his way around my house." He tucked the badge away and looked down at the boy's taut face. Great, wretched tears glistened on his cheeks. His jaw was clenched so tightly he could not speak. "Galahad," Lancelot said gently, "tell me about this dog. He must have been a loyal beast to win your heart. Where did you get him?"

"Uncle . . . Galyn . . . gave him to me. He was one of Dia's bastards."

"Dia had bastards, did she? How many?"

Galahad wiped away his tears with the back of his hand. "Seven. They drowned the others. Uncle Galyn said I could have this one." A sob caught in his throat and he forced it down. "Until you came home. I was going to show him to you . . . to see if . . . you would . . . let me keep him."

Lancelot looked gravely at the ground. "I see. What was his name?"

"Valiant."

"An excellent name. Had he a good nose?"

"Yes! Especially for fowl." Galahad's voice steadied. "He loved ducks. He loved to swim."

Lancelot smiled briefly. "He must have gotten that from his father. Dia's not fond of water. We will bury him with the other dogs of Lanascol. I will move the grave myself. You can lead the ceremony, if you like." Galahad looked up at him. He knew Lancelot was paying Valiant a great honor to allow him burial near the king's best hunting dogs, none of them bastards, but in his grief the honor brought him little joy.

"In order to find out who did this, Galahad, I must ask you some questions about what you saw. How do you know the dog was killed?"

"His neck was broken. Last night. Outside my chamber window."

Lancelot frowned. "What was the ground like? Are there boot marks?"

"It's grass. It's all trampled."

"By one man or two?"

"I . . . I don't know. I don't know how to tell."

"I'll come and look at it later, as soon as we're finished here." Galahad started. Until that moment he had forgotten that they stood beside his mother's grave. "It takes a strong man to do it alone," his father was saying, "even to a puppy. Did he leave no other sign behind him?"

"I . . . I didn't see. I only saw the badge."

Lancelot nodded. "Our best hope is that the dog marked him. A man with a dog bite shouldn't be hard to find. They always fester."

Galahad looked down at the mounded earth. Golden birch leaves had already fallen in a light blanket over the new grass. The shape of the long, curved mound terrified him. It looked so solid, so cold, so permanent. And already it looked forgotten. He wished suddenly that he were anywhere else on earth.

" 'The Lord giveth,' " Lancelot said quietly, " 'and the Lord taketh away.' "

"I'm sorry I thought it was you," Galahad whispered, staring hard at a golden leaf. A voice brushed against his ear like a cold wind: *Avenge me! I will not rest easy, in Heaven or in Hell, until he is dead.* He squeezed his eyes shut. "I know it wasn't you."

"You had cause." His father's gentle voice, light as a caress, stilled his trembling. Galahad looked up into warm gray eyes. "You had the badge. You don't know I'm not the kind of man who would do such a thing. You don't know me, son, and that is my fault. I've been away too long." He paused. "I'm going back to Britain, Galahad. I'd like you to come with me. We will put all this behind us and start over."

Lancelot offered him the dagger, but still Galahad did not take it.

"But Lanascol is home. Can't we stay here?"

"The time will come when I come home to rule. But just now, we are building such a kingdom in Britain as the world has never seen. Arthur and I and all the Companions. Britain's a big place, and no one man can hold it by himself. We work together. You will see how it is. Come with me to Arthur's court, and I will show you how the young men of Britain are growing up in the High King's city, how the future of Britain—your future, Galahad—is taking shape under the High King's hand. You are not too young to serve Arthur, and it's time you took your place there. It's time you learned the principles we live by." He paused, watching the child's face. "I know it's hard to leave the only home you know. But Camelot will soon be another home. You'll like it better than staying here with Renna and your baby brothers, watching your aunt Adele take your mother's place. Your brothers are too young to go, but you've lived long enough beneath women's skirts."

Galahad gulped. "Cordovic's older than me, and he's never been to Britain."

A smiled touched Lancelot's lips. "Cordovic! No, indeed. It's not for everyone. Bors is a good man, as solid as the earth, but Cordovic has yet to prove what kind of soldier he will make. You, Galahad . . . you are my son. Because Arthur is who he is, you won't have to wait until you're old enough for warrior's training to prove yourself. You may come to Camelot now. Permission has already been granted." The boy's eyes widened. "There are other boys in Camelot. You won't be lonely or afraid for long."

"I'm not afraid!"

Lancelot smiled. He held out the dagger again. "Then will you come with me?"

Galahad looked down at the leaves on the grave and took the dagger from his father's hand.

15 ✝ THE GOLDEN CITY

Two days after crossing the Narrow Sea, Lancelot and Galahad reached the rolling hills of the Summer Country and headed north along the Roman road toward Caer Camel. From his perch atop his father's stallion Galahad had a fine view of the magnificent country all around them. If he had to share a horse, he was glad it was Nestor. Nestor was the finest horse in the kingdom. His strength and speed made Glory seem like a half-grown yearling.

"Almost there." Lancelot's voice sounded in his ear, taut and eager.

Galahad noted the change in him. In all those long winters at Benoic, Lancelot had scarcely spoken above a dozen words in Galahad's hearing. But on the swift journey to Camelot he could not keep still. Hesitantly at first, and then in an unbroken flow, words poured out in a constant stream. Some Galahad took in, but most swirled by uncomprehended: talk about the rolling downs, the local kings, tales of Saxon battles as they passed nearby the border, vivid descriptions of Arthur's brilliance as commander, a history of the ancient wars, gossip about this lord and that—on it flowed in an eager torrent until, in spite of his misgivings, Galahad began to feel light-headed. The man's pleasure was impossible to resist. Lancelot was so happy that he could not hold it in. Now, as the horses' hooves clattered on the worn stone blocks of the Roman road running straight as an arrow up the wide Camel valley, he exuded a joy that engulfed the men around him and sent everyone's spirits soaring.

Every night of the journey Lancelot talked to Galahad of Camelot and the things that he would see there, but even so, the boy's first sight of the great fortress amazed him. High on a green hill sat a castle built of golden stone, banners flying gaily from her towers, protected by a triple ring of fortifications. In the southwest corner a wide road paved with stones curved upward to the huge double gates, King's Gate, the soldiers called them. Never in his life had he seen anything that took such skill to build. Through these gates and down this broad causeway King Arthur and his companions had ridden forth a hundred times to the Saxon wars.

The soldiers at the guardhouse saluted Lancelot and called out welcomes. As they passed down the streets of the thriving town, folk came out to greet them. Men saluted, women curtsied, smiling, children hid behind their mothers' skirts and stared, faces alight with admiration. Galahad felt the strong arm tighten about his waist. The wave of affection engulfed him, too. He realized with a distinct jolt that here in Camelot, Lancelot was openly beloved. Everyone acted as though he were a long-lost son, coming home.

In the castle courtyard grooms appeared from nowhere to take their horses. Lancelot greeted them all by name. Galahad stared at the arching stonework and curved windows of the castle, at the magnificent stableyard glimpsed through a line of trees, at the very grooms whose boots were better than his own. It was all too magnificent to be real.

Up wide marble steps they went, side by side, and through a pair of stout oak doors carved with dragons. In the cool, dark vestibule servants brought them bowls of clean water and they washed the dust of travel from their faces, hands, and hair. Lancelot thanked the servants and greeted them by name. They turned down a long corridor. Galahad had to trot to keep up with Lancelot's long strides. There was hardly time to admire everything: glazed floor tiles in the Roman pattern, like the ones they had in the great hall at Benoic, only newer; the shiny armbands the sentries wore, and the dragon buckles on their swordbelts; the hall sconces, intricately worked in old Celtic patterns, every one the same and yet different; and above all, the air of order, peace, and power that pervaded everything. Excitement filled him as he trotted along beside his father. To be a part of this! To be the son of Lancelot in this wonderful place!

They came to a door with double guards. Both sentries saluted Lancelot and he greeted them like old friends. Within was a large room which gave onto a garden. All the benches had cushions worked skillfully in many colors, very much in the style of his father's Hawk hanger. The windows were glazed and thick tapestries hung upon the walls. Near the open garden door stood a heavy table with curved feet where a man in a plain robe sat, chin on fist, dictating to the scribe at his elbow. The table was piled with scrolls and clay tablets. A bowl of cut glass filled with roses scented the air with rare perfume. Beneath the table a handsome white hound scratched lazily for fleas. There was no one else in the room but man and scribe. In vain Galahad looked around for the King.

The man at the desk looked up as they entered and his smile lit his face.

"Lancelot!"

"Arthur!" Lancelot knelt. The man rose and came swiftly around the table to raise Lancelot and embrace him. Galahad stared in disbelief. Although tall and broad-shouldered, with the carriage of a warrior, this man wore a brown robe of simple woven stuff without a single stitch of adornment. His sandals were old, soft and worn. He had no sword, no badge, no armband, no shiny buckles. Yet this was Arthur, High King of Britain.

"You are earlier than I expected."

"There was no need to stay. Galyn is there. I have brought my son Galahad to meet you."

The High King turned to him. As he had been instructed, Galahad took the King's hand and, bending his knee, kissed the royal ring. This was of heavy gold and held a great ruby with fire in its depths and the Dragon of Britain carved small upon its surface. He swallowed in a dry throat and stared up at the man he had mistaken for a servant.

"My lord Arthur."

The High King looked amused. "Welcome, Galahad, Prince of Lanascol. Welcome to Camelot. I expect you will like it here, even if I am not what you expected."

Galahad flushed and bit his lip. Arthur squatted down so his face was at Galahad's level. Like Lancelot and the rest of his Companions, he shaved his beard and it gave him an air of youth. His warm brown eyes seemed to look straight into Galahad's heart. He smiled again. "You will be a fine soldier one day, Galahad, a knight of stainless honor like your father. I hope that, like your father, you will serve me and not one who stands against me. I want your sword on my side."

Galahad hardly dared to breathe. The High King of Britain spoke of swords and service, man to man, to a boy who had just received his first dagger! Galahad straightened to make himself taller. "I will serve you, my lord. You have my word."

The High King nodded gravely. "Thank you, prince. I will remember your promise."

He rose and with a wave of his hand dismissed the scribe. Picking up a scroll from the table, the King turned to Lancelot and then paused. "Galahad, would you do me a kindness and leave me alone with your father for a moment? Perhaps you would await us in the garden. The fountain might interest you—there's not another like it in the world."

Obediently, Galahad slipped out the open doorway into the sunlit garden. The fountain was an alabaster dragon, smooth and white, standing on hind legs with water streaming from its mouth instead of fire. Its claws were tipped with gold and its nostrils painted red. Though fierce of face, it looked happy enough to be there, surrounded by sunlight, bright flowers, and joyful music. Indeed, who would not be happy in such a place? He wondered if even the Garden of Eden could have equaled this.

It took him a moment to realize that the music was not coming from the fountain. He heard a woman's voice, high and sweet, from somewhere farther off. After a swift glance at the doorway to see if his father was still in conference, he went in search of the singer. His mother used to sing to him now and again, nursery songs in a language he had never understood—Old Welsh she had called it, the tongue of bards—but she had never sung like this. This was a pure voice, sweet and glorious, that drew him onward without his knowing he was drawn.

He turned a corner of the walk and stopped in his tracks. There she was, singing while she cut armfuls of fragrant roses, a woman lovelier than any woman he had ever seen. She might have been an angel of God, for she was fair beyond any human fairness, with white-gold hair so light, so radiant, it could have been a halo about her head. Tall, slender, dressed in a gray-blue gown, she sang to herself as she stretched forth a long, pale arm toward the glowing blooms. Her graceful movements, the pretty way she held her head, the flush of health that sprang beneath the creamy skin—he recognized that this was beauty, undeniable, unsurpassable, supreme, as real and as encompassing as the daylight itself.

On the thought, she saw him from the corner of her eye and turned toward him, the song dying upon her lips. Her eyes were a deep, dark, amazing blue, alive with an intensity that transfixed him. She smiled shyly, and the world about him seemed to grow soft, sweet, and vibrant. He was seized by a desperate longing to do anything to please her.

"Hello," she said. He swallowed hard. She put down the sheaf of flowers she carried and laid the cutting knife carefully beside them. Then, to his complete astonishment, she bowed her lovely head and made him a low reverence. "Good day to you, my lord." She sat gracefully on a stone bench near him, and he walked up to her without knowing that he moved. He could not take his eyes from her face. When he looked at her he felt like singing.

"I do not know you, sir," she said, reaching out a hand to him. "Are you a visitor in Camelot? Will you stay long with us?"

Her flesh was warm and firm and fragrant. He longed to climb up on the bench and sit in her lap. "Beautiful lady," he said softly. On impulse, he kissed her fingers.

She smiled, the color rising slowly to grace her cheeks, and he smiled back, entranced. "You are a gentleman, I see. With princely manners. Where is your home, my lord? Who is your—"

Suddenly she broke off, hearing something, and rose, gazing past the hedge at someone he could not see, joy suffusing her features, her whole being alight. Someone was coming down the walk, someone she was awaiting. Politely, knowing he was forgotten, Galahad withdrew, and only at the last looked back.

Lancelot turned the corner. With a cry of joy she ran into his arms, held him tightly as he kissed her lips and whispered in her ear, his eyes closed, his heart manifest upon his face.

"Guinevere! My dear love, it feels like years I've been away."

Galahad stood motionless. Around him the day grew dark, shot with light and shadow. It beat against his chest, pounded at his temples. Lancelot's lips caressed the woman's face as his hands slid over her gown. She leaned into him and they clung together, one soul, one longing, in the radiant sunlight of the High King's garden.

He turned and ran. He ran until he could run no more and collapsed, blind with tears, against the cold stone of a deserted outbuilding. He wept with a force that frightened him, pounding the earth with his fists, sobbing for Aidan, for his mother, for Almighty God. At last, his young fury spent, he dozed off, still whimpering in exhausted sleep.

He awoke to the touch of gentle hands. Strong arms lifted him with care and held him close and warm. "Galahad," said a man's voice in his ear, "to please God you must live well, and that takes courage." He stared through swollen eyes at Arthur's face, so near his own. "You are a brave lad," the High King said softly, "but you have a lot to learn. Some things will not be easy. Always keep a little mercy in your heart."

"I saw them . . . together . . . I saw . . . my father and—"

"Shhhhh." The High King kissed his wet cheek and held him closer. "I know. But remember this: Always keep a little mercy in your heart."

"My lord." Galahad sobbed into the High King's shoulder, exhaustion leaving him defenseless against compassion, the dark truth of his secret shame spilling into this stranger's calm, accepting heart. "He never loved my mother so!"

PART III
Three Tokens

In the second through fifth years of the reign of Constantine

16 ✝ THE SMITH'S TALE

It was almost dark when Galahad and Percival stopped to rest. Behind
them lay the valley of the Deva River and ahead, shadow upon shadow,
the rising mountains of Rheged. The long summer twilight lingered as they
staked their horses, laid out their bedrolls, and gathered firewood. As night
drew near they sat down to their meal.

"I'll take first watch, if you like," Percival offered, licking his fingers.
"I'm not at all tired." Galahad nodded, stoppered the wineskin, and un-
buckled his swordbelt. Without speaking he lay down on his bedroll and
turned his face away.

Percival watched him, wondering for the thousandth time what was
the matter with him. It hadn't been difficult, after all, to leave Gwynedd.
That foggy afternoon when Galahad had come galloping in and ordered
him in clipped tones to pack his belongings and a bedroll, he had doubted it
would really be possible to leave. What could he say to Peredur that would
not sound like an affront? *Uncle, I want to go with my cousin to look for something, we don't know exactly what, that's hidden someplace, we don't know exactly where, until I'm old enough to come back and reclaim my birthright from
you. . . .* He smiled to himself. He should have known he could leave it
safely in Galahad's hands. Galahad addressed Peredur as one knight to another and begged his leave to take Percival as his companion on a mission
he had sworn to Arthur he would perform. Sadly, he had needed to say little
more than that. Peredur was so relieved he almost smiled. Regret had
shown upon his features—Percival had always liked his uncle and the liking was returned—but his relief at having his rival gone was too great to
conceal.

Percival's brow furrowed when he thought about Dane. She had reappeared just as they were leaving, kissed him and slipped him her lucky rabbit's foot, whispered her good wishes and farewells, and then, without a
word to Galahad, vanished within doors. Such behavior was so unlike her it
astonished him still. What could have happened to upset her so? Whatever
it was, she was no doubt past it by now—unlike Galahad, who had scarcely
spoken a word to him the entire week they had been on the road.

A wolf called, low-voiced and mournful. Percival drew his sword and
inched closer to the flames. For the first time in his life he was free to do as
he pleased. No more yielding to the demands and desires of older people.

All his life he had been under someone's yoke of obedience: his father, his mother, Arthur's commanders, even the priestesses at Avalon. Now he was alone with his silent cousin. There was no one about to tell him what to do and see that he did it. He felt both free and uncomfortably uprooted.

"Drop the sword, bitch's whelp, or die!" A sword point pressed into his back. He froze. The sword point prodded him sharply, and he let his hilt slide from his hand.

"Galahad!"

A fist smashed against his head. "Silence!"

The world swam dangerously and Percival lay still, unable to breathe. Hands searched his body, took his dagger from his belt—his grandfather's dagger! He pushed up to one elbow and shook his head to clear his vision. In the firelight he could see three big-boned men in rags. Two of them held Galahad; the third held Percival's sword.

"Who are you?" Galahad demanded. "What do you want with us? If you are thieves, we have little of value."

"Ha!" snorted his captor, pulling Galahad's sword from its scabbard. "Lies won't help. Just look at this sword, Ralf! What a beauty! The hilt's inlaid with gems!"

Ralf grinned, showing blackened teeth. He brandished Percival's sword. "Aye, and this one be worth something, too! Garf, we be rich men now!"

"Nothing of value," Garf mocked. He hawked and spat. "Where did you two mewling brats steal these weapons?"

"That's my father's sword."

Garf laughed aloud. "It's mine now, princeling. Dinias, check the saddle packs." Dinias loosed his hold on Galahad and lumbered toward the horses.

Galahad spoke calmly. "I don't have a saddle pack. I don't use a saddle."

"Don't you, indeed?" Garf, still gripping Galahad, looked him up and down. "Who do you think you are, you pretty little catamite? Lancelot du Lac? Ha ha ha!"

Galahad went white. They all laughed heartily. Dinias had reached the horses and put a hand out to Farouk. Galahad whistled sharply. The stallion rose, screaming, on his hind legs, pulling the stake from the ground and striking out with his forelegs for Dinias's face.

"Look out!"

"Christ Jesus!"

"Son of a bitch!"

Galahad drove his knee into Garf's groin, twisted free of his grip, dove to the ground, rolled, came up with his dagger in his hand, and threw it. Garf howled and grabbed his wrist, dropping the sword. Galahad sprang, got his hand around the hilt just as Ralf leaped for him, sword raised. Percival stuck a leg out; Ralf sprawled headlong. Percival reached for his sword, got a kick in the head and an earful of curses. But it was enough to give Galahad a chance to back away, sword in hand, and face his attackers.

All three of them came at him at once. Percival sat up, hunched in pain, and watched. The ruffians fought from pain and fury; Galahad was cool. They flung themselves at him, striking wildly, shouting. He dodged, moving swift and sure as a cat, every stroke of his finding flesh while the other blades whirled uselessly around his ears. Although it looked one-sided, Percival knew it was no contest at all.

Garf was the first to kneel, his wrist bleeding from the dagger blow. Ralf had Percival's sword knocked from his hand, and one good blow from Lancelot's sword shattered Dinias's weapon.

Galahad looked down upon them in disdain. "Percival, take back your sword."

"I have it, cousin."

"Are you all right? You're swaying on your feet."

"I'll be fine in a minute. You saved my life, Galahad."

"Nonsense," Galahad said grimly. "These are poor excuses for fighters. You could have taken them yourself in daylight. You'd better pack up the horses, though." He gestured toward the leader. "We'll have to find the nearest village. This one needs tending to."

"You are merciful, my lord," Garf whimpered, clutching his wrist. "We don't deserve sparing."

"It's beneath me to kill you," Galahad returned flatly.

Percival gathered up the weapons and the bedrolls. He paused before the kneeling men. "Think twice before you set upon innocent men. You don't know who you'll come across. Tonight you made a grave mistake. No one in all Britain can take *this* man." Three pairs of eyes looked dumbly at him. "This was child's play to him. I've seen him take six of my father's men in the training yard, all seasoned soldiers, all at the same time. This is Sir Galahad of Lanascol. Lancelot's son."

Garf threw himself to the ground. "Sir Galahad, I beg your pardon! I'd never have harmed you if I'd known—I fought with your father, sir, against the Saxons—there never was a better man!"

"Give me your name, soldier."

"Garfalon. Garfalon of Roundhill."

"How does a soldier in the High King's army sink to banditry?"

Garfalon began to weep. "Oh, my lord, that were my shame! But my wife's been dead these three years and my children are starving. The garden failed this summer and the stream's run dry. And the game's gone up into the hills. Ralf's my cousin, and Dinias, he's a half-wit. Strong as an ox, but not a featherweight of sense. Don't blame them, Sir Galahad. It's all my fault."

Galahad sheathed his sword. "Is there a village hereabouts, Garfalon?"

"Aye, my lord. I'll show you the way. My sister keeps a roadhouse there."

"Your sister can bind your wounds. And perhaps give us a place to sleep."

Dinias made a torch from a stout branch and an oily rag. Galahad and Percival rode behind the three bandits down the ridge to where a hamlet lay nestled at a crossroads. The crescent moon hung silver among the pines and nightingales sang sweetly in the wood. Somewhere a dog barked at the sound of horses. The night air breathed chill on the back of Percival's neck and he was glad when they reached the open door of a tavern. A stout woman stood silhouetted against the background glow of a cooking fire.

"Garf?" she called out. "Is that you?"

"Aye, Grainne. And I've brought you company."

"What have you been up to, you lazy lout? I thought you went to chase those poachers from our woods!"

"Now, now," Garfalon said hastily, "no poachers, Grainne. Princes."

"Princes, my left foot. Is that blood? You've been wounded!"

"No more than I had coming to me." He turned as the boys slid off their horses. "This is Galahad, Sir Lancelot's own son, and young Percival, King Maelgon's boy. Give 'em the best you have, Grainne. I done wrong by 'em."

"Come in and let me dress that. Dinias can stable the horses."

The silhouette backed toward the light as the woman made way for them. She was thickset and ruddy-complexioned, with meaty arms and a fierce, distrustful eye. "Why, they're only boys! Where's the man who cut you?"

"Boys they be, but I've never seen a faster blade than Sir Galahad's. Make them welcome, Grainne."

The woman curtsied clumsily. "Welcome, young lords. The fire's only peat but there's a skin of wine by it. Help yourselves while I dress this hand."

"They'll be wanting beds," Garfalon added, "seeing as we kept them from their sleep."

The woman grunted. "There's straw in the shed. I can make up pallets as soon as I've tended my brother. Will that do?"

"If it's clean straw," Galahad replied, "thank you, yes."

The woman stared at him a moment. "Sir Lancelot's son, are you? We'll see about that. My father went to Caer Camel in his younger days to make swords for Arthur's troops. He knew Lancelot. Didn't you, Da?"

The boys turned and saw an old man in the corner, sitting upright on a stool with a stout staff in his hand. His eyes were the cloudy eyes of a blind man and his beard had gone gray, but his face lit at the mention of Arthur's name. "Aye, daughter, I did indeed."

"Were you a smith, then, sir?" Percival ventured.

"I was."

The boys moved their stools closer to the old man and Grainne, nodding to herself, led Garfalon into the back room to bind his wound.

"Tell us about Camelot," Percival begged, "and the weapons you made. They say the finest swords in all the world were forged in Camelot."

The old smith smiled. "Aye, that's true enough. Smiths from all over Britain left their forges and traveled to the High King's fortress to try their hands at making weapons worthy of Arthur. We all had skill, but only a few of us had the Blessing."

Percival looked blank. "What blessing? The High King's blessing?"

"Ah, no, lad. This be a Blessing older than any king." The old smith's face took on an expression of reverence and his sightless eyes looked far away. "Without the Blessing a smith is only a man who wields hammer and tongs at a forge. Horseshoes, such a man can make, and plowshares, hooks, and hoops. But weapons?" He smiled knowingly. "Such men as yourselves don't want weapons forged by such a man. A sword forged without the Blessing will fail at the moment of its testing and betray the man who wields it." He shook his head slowly, as if aware of the wide eyes that watched him. "No, no, young lords. You want a strong and supple weapon that will defend you in your hour of need. You want a sword with life in the blade. Mark my words: Best find a smith who has the Blessing."

"But what Blessing?" Percival wondered. "Christ's blessing? Or do you speak of other gods? We are Christians."

The old smith chuckled. "And so be we, lad, good Christians all these thirty years and more. Yet the truth of the land is age old, older than the nailed God from the east, older than the three-faced Goddess from the west, older than Mithra, older than Yahweh, as old as the earth herself. This is a truth other gods cannot destroy." He paused. "Have you ever walked into an oak wood and felt eyes on your back? Or looked up at a high place with reverence? Or witnessed a dawning with awe? Some things bear a holiness from time's beginning. The ways of going, the places where roads and waters meet have been sacred time out of mind. And that's where you'll find us smiths, son, near a ford, a crossroads, or a watersmeet." He laid a bony finger next to his long nose and stared at them with cloudy eyes. "A good smith, a born one, knows where to build his forge. The land tells him. He hears her voice and obeys her and she blesses the work he does."

Percival coughed uncertainly.

"Take me lightly if you dare," the smith growled, "but I speak no more than truth. I'll prove it to you. I'll tell you boys the secret of the Blessing, which is not a secret many know outside the forge." He grunted appreciatively as their attention sharpened. "When a smith has the Blessing, the iron takes shape in his hands almost without his willing. He hears a voice no one else can hear—the shape of the thing-to-come calls to him from the fire." He nodded solemnly. "A smith knows if he has the Blessing. He hears the voice. And you will know it by the weapon he makes."

"In Camelot," Percival whispered, "did you make swords for the King himself?"

The old man shook his head sadly. "Not I. I made them for his soldiers and for two of his Companions. There was only one among us who made swords for the High King. The greatest smith I ever knew. Elludyn of Lothian. Named for a god. He was a master."

"I've heard of him," Galahad said. "I've heard it took him a month to fashion a sword."

The smith grinned, showing gaps between his teeth. "Oh, aye, a month sometimes, for a blade without blemish. I remember a sword he made, it seems a lifetime ago, now. I was younger then, with the strength still in my back and my arms. I took a turn at the bellows for him just to watch him work. He fashioned the blade from the finest steel and chilled it with water melted from ice brought all the way from Snowdon and packed in straw in the cellars." His voice sank to a whisper and the boys leaned closer. "Every single time before he put the iron into the fire, he shut his eyes and listened. Some took it for praying, or casting spells, but it never was. Elludyn appreciated silence. He listened. For the voice of the sword-to-be. He always heard it. He was the best."

"And what became of the sword you helped him make?" Percival asked. "Did King Arthur use it in battle?"

"No," the smith replied, "he gave it as a gift. Elludyn fashioned a cross of rubies in the hilt, and Arthur gave it to his dearest friend, the Breton Lancelot."

Galahad gasped aloud. "But that sword is mine now! I have it here!"

The old smith turned his head toward Galahad. He went very still. "Where?"

Galahad rose, drew the sword from its scabbard, and placed it in the smith's hands. The gnarled fingers moved over the sword with consummate skill, testing its edge, its springiness, its heft and balance, caressing the jeweled hilt and the grip worn smooth with use. Tears sprang to his unseeing eyes and slid down his weathered cheeks.

"Aye," he whispered, "this is the one. The very one. Feel how it sings of glory, how it breathes with the joy of battle. A weapon made for a king! I honor you, my lord. A base man could not wield it."

"It was my father's," Galahad acknowledged. "He made me knight with it."

"Knighted by a sword of Elludyn's! What a future awaits you, young prince! You've honored me just by letting me hold it. It is a great gift. I am ashamed I have nothing to offer you in return."

Galahad took back the sword and sheathed it. "There might be a way you could help us. We are looking for the Grail and Spear that once belonged to Magnus Maximus, Emperor of Britain. Have you ever heard tales of such things here in Rheged? Songs, perhaps? Or of a man called the Fisher King?"

The old smith went very still. His lips worked silently for a moment before the words came out. "Who are you?"

"My name is Galahad."

"Galahad," the old man repeated in a whisper.

Percival and Galahad exchanged quick glances. The smith put out a trembling hand and touched Galahad's hair. "You are—you might be—the one who is awaited. The Grail Seeker."

Galahad drew a sharp breath. "I seek the Grail, certainly."

Now the old man's head bobbed up and down. "Your coming has been foretold." His thin lips split into a toothless grin and his weathered face shone with excitement. "I knew you would come to a smith someday, but I never dreamed it would be to me."

"Old man," Galahad said sharply, "what have you heard? Or are you wandering?"

The smith cackled. "You are the wanderer, lord, not I. I stay where the land calls me." He leaned forward, as if willing his dulled eyes to see. "The legend of the Blessed Gifts has come down, smith to smith, since the Treasures went into the ground. A hag foretold that the man who would find them would come to a smith, asking directions, and that he would be known by the sword he carried." The smith's fingers twitched in his lap, where the sword had so recently lain.

"What hag?" Percival wondered.

"Honored smith," Galahad whispered, "will you tell us what you know of these Treasures?" He filled a clay cup with warm wine from the skin and placed it in the smith's trembling hand. The old man sipped it gratefully.

"Aye. For my bones tell me that you are the one. The Spear was made by a blacksmith along with the Sword, and they were fashioned here in Rheged. A silversmith made the Grail. They say Maximus—we call him Macsen Wledig in these parts—searched the isle of Britain for the best smiths in the land, and that he put them to death afterward, for he wanted no one to have treasures as beautiful as his." He paused, and the cloudy eyes blinked before a vision only he could see. "That might be truth, that might be a tale, but this much I know for certain: Once he got the Treasures, an ancient hag came down out of the hills to warn him of his doom. She warned him that if he took them out of Britain he would lose them."

"And so he did," Percival supplied. "Macsen died fighting the King of Rome, but the Grail, Spear, and Sword came home to Britain. Elen of Gwynedd, his wife, hid them for safekeeping."

The old smith shook his head. "Not for safekeeping. She could have given them to her sons, but she wished to propitiate the power which protected them at the price of her husband's life, so she buried them in the ground to return them to their source."

"Do you know where they are?" Galahad could not help the question.

The blind eyes turned toward him. "No, lord. I know the signs, they've been handed down, but not where they lead."

Signs! Galahad hardly dared breathe.

The smith held up one hand, displaying three bony fingers. "You must find three tokens—all hidden—and pass three tests." With his other hand he touched his fingers one by one as he spoke in a singsong voice:

> *One is empty, one is crossed,*
> *One's full of laughter and desire.*
> *One for feasting, one for fighting*
> *One forged in a smithy's fire.*
>
> *Three tokens there be,*
> *And find them must he*
> *Who seeks the treasure of kings.*
> *In shadow, in light,*
> *In darkness bright,*
> *Three tokens to hidden things.*

The smith fell silent and Galahad looked at him blankly. "What does it mean?"

The smith shook his head.

"What are the three tests?" Percival asked eagerly. "Is there a rhyme for those, too? Are they difficult?"

The smith grunted. "No rhyme. But difficult enough for any man. You must set free what ignorance has imprisoned. You must polish what fire has tarnished. You must kneel before the virtue of a woman."

Galahad drew back, startled. "Kneel before a woman? Are you jesting?"

The smith laughed heartily. Grainne's voice from the other room warned him to pipe down. "So you don't like women much, do you?" the old man cried. "I can't blame you there. But you'll have your fill of them before you're through, like it or not. You must kneel of your own will before the virtue of a woman—not because you wish to pass the test, but because you honor her goodness. And what's been imprisoned by ignorance is female, as well. And so is what's been tarnished by fire. Three women will set you tests that you must pass. And you must pass them all unknowing."

"How do we find them?" Percival asked quickly, seeing Galahad's face.

The smith chuckled. "Not by looking, lad. You must put yourself into the way of going and follow the signs you see. I don't know how long it will take or where you will go. You may travel together to find the tokens, but he must pass the tests alone, the Grail Seeker."

"How will he know if he's found the right tokens and passed the right tests?" Percival pressed. "They could be almost anything."

"After he finds the tokens, he'll see a sign. Don't worry; it will be impossible to miss. The three tests follow shortly after. When the tests are passed, he'll be led to the Grail and Spear. By an innocent." He held up the back of his hand before Percival could draw breath for another question. "That's all I know. Won't do no good to ask more."

"I have only one more question," Galahad said slowly. "You said the Sword and Spear were made in Rheged. Do you know where?"

The smith nodded. "They were forged in a tributary of the Eden River, where the water runs fast and cold from the mountains. My grandfather told me it was Weland Smith himself who made the sword, but I don't know if that's fact or bragging. Plenty of kingdoms beyond Rheged lay claim to Weland's forge. But it's well known that Arthur drew Excalibur from the great stone under Lludyn's Hill on an island of the Eden. That might be where the forge once was."

"Thank you," Galahad said gravely. "I believe we must see this island."

A door slammed behind them, shattering the silence. "Your beds is made," Grainne announced belligerently. "That hand of Garf's is cut deep, but I wager it might heal." Galahad met her level stare and she dropped her eyes. "Has Da talked your ears off yet? He's a great one for runnin' on and it's perishin' rare he gets strangers to badger."

"On the contrary," Percival responded. "He's told us something of great value."

Galahad prodded him sharply in the ribs. Grainne regarded them both darkly. "He don't know anything of value. He just likes to remember the days when he was a man who counted in the world. It makes him feel young again."

The smith struck his staff sharply upon the floor. "Enough of your twaddle, Ygraine. Go to bed and leave us be."

Color spread in a vivid blush across the woman's blunt features and her expression hardened. "You'll have your little joke, won't you, Da, at my expense? But your glory days is over. You'll never serve Arthur again, more's the pity, and that's that." She turned as she went out the door. "Yer beds is out back, upstairs of the kitchen. Garf told me he wronged you, so tonight I won't charge you nothing. But tomorrow's another matter." She slammed the door behind her as she went out.

The smith cackled wickedly, rocking back and forth in his chair.

Percival looked bewildered. "What's so funny?"

"He named her Ygraine," Galahad murmured.

The smith wiped a tear from his eye as he struggled against his laughter. "I did it a' purpose, to get at her ma. She's looked like that from a baby, she has, big as a house and ugly as sin. And I named her after Ygraine of Cornwall, Arthur's mother. The loveliest woman in Britain. Ha ha ha!"

They left the smith still laughing. Outside, darkness engulfed them like a cloth across the face, and they stopped to wait for their night sight. The moon had long since set and the thick crowd of stars shed only enough light to discern the general shapes of the outbuildings, shadows darker than the night itself.

A whisper drifted out of the blackness. "My lords?"

"Garfalon?" Galahad turned as a hand touched his arm.

"Follow me, my lords, and I'll show you the way. Don't mind Grainne. It's just her nature. Here, up these steps. She's left a candle burning. Look, there are your beds, under the eaves. Clean straw and plenty of it, and blankets from her own bed." He stood in the doorway, his wrist bound in a cloth and held tight against his body. "I've seen to your horses. The meadow was cut last week and we've plenty of sweet hay." He lingered as Galahad and Percival stripped off their tunics and washed their faces in the basin of water by the door. "My lords, I know I've no right to ask, but would you let me . . . would you let me serve you? I can't go back to soldiering. The army's gone. Near everyone I know died at Camlann. And the King of Rheged's got more men than he can feed. To tell truth, I can't abide life with Grainne and Da much longer. All they do is pick at each other all day long. If he weren't old and blind, I'd fear she'd kill him, angry as she gets. Yet it's on account of him we're first in the village here, and Grainne's the mistress of the tavern. He was a smith, once." He ran a tongue over dry lips. "I'm handy with most things, my lords. I can hunt and cook; I can sharpen swords and mend tack; I'm good with horses. Though," he added quickly, "not so skilled as yourselves."

"I thought you were worried about your children," Percival countered, glancing uncertainly at Galahad. "I thought that was why you tried to rob us."

Garfalon shuffled from foot to foot. "Yes, well, and to clear you from our woods. Grainne's particular about poachers. But she'll keep my girls for me if I leave. She'll be glad to have them—they can do work around the tavern. And although I owe you the service for what I done"—color washed his face—"if you could spare me a coin now and again, it would help us mightily."

He cleared his throat and stood awkwardly, his injured hand clamped against his side. Galahad reached in his pouch and tossed Garfalon a silver coin. "I accept your offer. Have the horses ready an hour past dawn. If your hand doesn't serve you, get Dinias to help."

Garfalon stared openly at the coin and bent his knee to the ground. "God bless you, my lord! It will be done. Don't give a thought to my hand—it will heal. I'll bring along a mule to carry our gear. Where are we bound?"

Galahad stared beyond him into the distance. "A place called Lludyn's Hill. Near Caer Eden."

17 ✝ CAER EDEN

The fortress of Caer Eden stood on the site of an ancient hillfort overlooking a broad turn of the Eden River. The Romans had enlarged the fort, paved the roadways in and out, built villas and barracks, and replaced the wooden palisade with a high, encircling wall of quarried stone. They had also changed its name to Luguvallium. For ten generations bands of northern Picts had sent their warbands south to harass the Romans. Even the Great Wall, running east and west across the breadth of Britain just north of Caer Eden, had not entirely kept them out. Roman commanders had been forced to keep a thousand troops at Luguvallium—foot soldiers, cavalry, and archers—to fortify the wall defenses.

Now the place was crumbling, half the barracks lay in ruin, many of the stables had been torn down for firewood, the roads had gone weedy, even the battlements were roughly patched. The town itself had shrunk to three hundred souls, including the small contingent of troops left to guard the valley. Thanks to the unity of Arthur's Britain, the kingdoms of Strathclyde and Lothian now lay as buffers between Rheged and the Picts. As the fortress shed its Roman size and Roman ways, it shed its Roman name as well and became known again as the hill fort of Caer Eden.

On a hot evening in late summer Galahad, Percival, and Garfalon rode up the hill to the fortress just as the gates were about to close. They found the place full of Rheged's troops, for Rydor, King of Rheged, had ridden in just the day before on his way north to Dunpeldyr to a meeting of the northern lords. There was neither bed nor pallet to be had in all of Caer Eden and the boys had to be content with such comfort as they could find in the tavern hayloft. Leaving them to see to the bedrolls, Garfalon elbowed his way into the crowded tavern to see what he could find in the way of dinner.

"He's a good man," Percival said as soon as he was out of earshot. "I'm glad we brought him."

"He's honorable at heart. And he *has* made the journey easier."

"Yes," agreed Percival, thinking of the fat hares and waterfowl Garfalon had snared and cooked, the sweet fish he'd netted, split, and stuffed with pine nuts, acorns, blackberries, and roasted over a hickory fire. "He certainly has."

They sat on their bedrolls and shared a skin of water. The thick, heady odor of horse sweat and manure drifted up from the stable and eddied around them, mingling in the warm night with the dry, sweet scent of hay. Distant voices sounded from the tavern, raised in laughter or drink, and all around them, as pervasive as the air itself, the incessant cacophony of locusts filled the night.

Percival regarded his pensive cousin. "Galahad, there's been something eating you ever since we left Gwynedd. You can tell me. I'm your kin. I won't say a word to anybody."

"It's nothing."

"Garf says you're broody."

The vivid blue eyes turned toward Percival. "Perhaps I am."

"Is it Dane? I knew something wasn't right that foggy afternoon when you both rode down out of the hills, one after the other, too furious for words. What did she do to upset you?"

Galahad scowled. "Forget it, can't you?"

"You may think it's none of my business, but Dane's more than my sister. She's my twin. We share *everything*."

"Not everything," Galahad muttered, thinking of Dane's hideout in the hills.

Silence fell between them. Above the din of locusts and the shifting beasts below they heard raucous laughter from the direction of the tavern. The stable door flew open and a man stumbled in, half-supported by a woman. He did not even wait until they reached a bed of straw before he fell with her to the ground and began fumbling under her skirts. The horses shifted and blew and returned to their hay.

Galahad turned away quickly, his eyes fierce. "Your sister told me lies about my mother. She told me King Arthur banished her from Britain."

Percival dropped his eyes. "Oh, that."

"You mean . . . you *knew*?"

Percival said in a small voice, "I thought everyone knew."

Below them the couple began to writhe and grunt. Galahad's lips set in a thin line. "Your sister called my mother false. If she'd been a man I'd have drawn my sword!"

Percival looked alarmed. "She was foolish to say so. I'm sure she'll apologize."

"She told me . . . terrible things my mother had done. Things that turned Arthur against her. Have you heard those stories?"

Percival nodded nervously.

"She accused her of arranging the Queen's abduction!"

Percival nodded again. "You have to remember, Galahad, your mother and the Queen grew up together. In Gwynedd. They were cousins, like you and me. They were friends. But they were rivals, too, for the King's notice."

Below them the woman's cries and the man's grunts rose in a quick crescendo. Both boys covered their ears until the lovers finished and all they could hear was their heavy, exhausted breathing.

"Women have no honor," Galahad said bitterly. "You and I would never stoop to such measures, rivals or no."

"Of course we wouldn't. But it's not fair to judge all women by the acts of one—"

The stable door opened again to admit two drunken soldiers and Garfalon with a basket over his arm. The lovers, half-undressed, looked up sleepily.

"A copper coin!" the woman cried out to the soldiers. "I'll make it worth your while, I will. Ask Stannic here. Look how tired he is!"

One of the soldiers fell to his knees beside her and fumbled in his pouch.

Percival grinned. "Look! Here comes Garf. Saints be praised, he's got food! Come on, Galahad, make room for him. We're going to have a feast!"

Garfalon was full of tavern gossip. As the boys delved into the basket and brought forth half a roast fowl, sausages nestled in bread fresh from the ovens, a handful of peaches, and half a comb of honey, Garfalon settled himself between them and took a long pull at his wineskin.

"You haven't heard the half of it, my lords," he began. "Rydor may be headed north to a meeting that determines Rheged's future, but he most desperately wants not to go—and wait until I tell you why!" He leaned forward and in a low voice related what he had heard. Within a day of Rydor's leaving his castle in Glannaventa, his young sister had been abducted on her way to a nunnery, and although he had three-quarters of his troops scouring the countryside to find her, ten days had passed and he had heard nothing of her. He was waiting in Caer Eden, just south of the Strathclyde border, for two more days in the hopes he would hear of her recovery. After that, he would have to press northward with all speed in order to get to Lothian before the meeting began. He had that very day offered a reward of three talents of gold to the man who found her and brought her back.

Garfalon sat back, eyes shining, and regarded the boys with obvious excitement. "Well, my lords, what do you think? Worth pursuing, no?"

"Three talents of gold!" Percival exclaimed. "That's a fortune!"

"Aye, my lord, 'tis indeed. A man could buy whatever his heart desired with three talents of gold. And I can track anything that leaves a trail."

"Does he love the girl so much?" Galahad asked. "Or is it his pride he holds so dear?"

"Well, my lord, they say he loves the girl, has been fond of her all his life and wanted her to marry well. But that's not to say his pride is not involved. She's turned down every suitor he's proposed, including his neighbor, Kastor of Strathclyde, for all she's barely past fifteen. Now *that* would be an alliance of importance. Rydor had words with the Lady Elinor after *that* rejection—a row, more like—and he swore she'd marry Kastor or he'd send her to a holy house. She refused to yield—as stubborn as a mule, just like her brother—so Rydor promised her to the abbess at the Christian house in Brocavum. The escort got as far as the foothills when she just disappeared."

"Disappeared?" Percival asked. "You mean, there was no fighting?"

"Not according to those of the escort who had the courage to return. At sundown she was in her tent; at dawn she wasn't." Garfalon's eyes narrowed wickedly. "A pretty little thing she was, too, they say, as fair as Rydor, with hair like spun gold and eyes the color of honey."

"And a dose of his pride as well," Galahad added. "Depend upon it, she's escaped to her lover and feigned abduction to fool her brother. It's an old trick among women."

Percival shot Galahad a swift look.

Garfalon hesitated. "Then it's our duty to restore the naughty child to the king. Believe me, my lords, let us get into those foothills and I'll wager half my share of the treasure I can track her."

Galahad's cold blue gaze lifted to his. "It's a waste of time to look for her. Married or not, she belongs to another man now."

"But, my lord, there are bandits in those hills! Anything could have happened."

"It's pointless. By now she's either dead or well protected. Somewhere."

But Garfalon turned to Percival. "Three talents of gold, my lord! This grail and spear you're after—they're no more than a pile of rusted metal after all this time, and they'll still be wherever they are afterward. Whereas this princess—"

"No." Galahad's voice was hard. "If you wish to go alone, I won't prevent you. Go, then. Seek your fortune. But we—Percival and I—are on a larger quest."

Garfalon swallowed audibly. "But, my lord, I have no sword. I only thought . . . you could do this on your way."

Galahad rose and dusted off his tunic. "That's not what you thought. It's the gold that lures you. We knew already that you're a greedy man. You attacked us for what we carried." Garfalon flinched. "But I thought, when I let you come with us, that you might grow to value higher things. I thought it was the beginning of something better in you." Galahad's shoulders sank. "But I'm often wrong." He turned and descended the ladder down to the stable floor, and went out into the night.

Garfalon looked sourly at Percival. "Who is he to be disappointed in me? He's not my father. He's only a boy."

"He's not just any boy. And he's easy to disappoint. I'm sure I do it every day."

"Every soldier in that tavern was bewailing the fact he had to ride north with Rydor and couldn't go looking for this girl. I was the only one among them who was free. At least, I *thought* I was free."

"You are. You heard him. You're free to go."

Garfalon looked up hopefully. "Will you come with me?"

Percival shook his head. "Oh, no. I'm with him."

"But why? What's so wonderful about this old grail you keep talking about? It's nothing but a feasting krater. Every king has a dozen of them."

"Not like *this*. There's nothing on earth like *this*. King Arthur himself sent Galahad to bring it to him, that Britain might be unconquered for all time." Percival paused. "The Grail is the heart of Britain. What are three talents of gold beside that?"

Garfalon's eyes narrowed. "Will it keep the Saxons off?"

"Yes, in the hands of the High King."

"But Constantine the Cornish dog is High King!"

"Even so." Percival tilted his head and looked at Garfalon. "At what price would *you* keep the Saxons off?"

"At any price!" Garfalon replied fervently.

"Well, then."

Garfalon scratched his head and pulled at his beard. "All right," he said at last. "It sounds like one of my Da's tall tales, but if you believe it's true . . ."

"I do believe it's true."

"That Galahad, now—he's an odd sort, and no mistake."

"He's different," Percival insisted, "because he's the one destined to find the Grail. The Lady of the Lake made a prophecy about him: 'A son of Lancelot will wield the sword of righteousness in Britain, and save her from the dark!' "

"All right. All right. I'm in with you both. Britain's future's worth more than three talents of gold"—he grinned—"even to a rogue like me."

Percival smiled. "I knew you were a good man."

Mist swirled upon the surface of the Eden River, drifting knee-high along the banks and blanketing the forest noises. Galahad sat alone on his black stallion as the sun set behind him in a red haze and the river mist glowed pink. He stared unmoving at the island in the center of the river, the famous hill now nothing more than a low hump, a ruin of landslide rubble and dirt, empty of wonders. Whatever it had once held—a great cavern, a gate to the Otherworld, a Faerie sword embedded in a stone, an emperor's treasure—was long gone. The tales lingered; that was all.

Percival and Garfalon had climbed the low ridge behind him to make camp and start a fire. He could smell the acrid sting of woodsmoke and hear the faint laughter of their voices. But although he knew that Lludyn's Hill held nothing for him, had been a waste of time to seek, he made no move to join his companions. He sat and let the still summer evening fall around him, content for the moment to empty himself of hope and disappointment, to sit in the quiet peace and listen to the river glide over its shallow bed. Here was the fork, the watersmeet. Here was the island. Here was the ford. If the old smith was right, this had been a sacred place since time began. If any shreds of awe still clung to it, as the mist clung to the nettles at the water's edge, he wanted to feel them. He emptied himself of thought and waited.

Nothing moved in the long dusk but the river mist, which thickened perceptibly and now and then trailed a cold finger across his cheek. The woods darkened; the trees began to blend indistinctly into a single, solid mass, shadowing the river black. The mist, imprisoning the last of the light, glowed white.

Impatiently, his stallion pawed the ground. Galahad corrected him absently. The horse sighed, stretched his neck, dipped his nose into the blanket of mist, and began to graze. Suddenly the animal's head whipped up, ears flicking forward. In the same instant Galahad saw a flash in the mist, the wriggle of a silver fish rising from the river. He peered between the stallion's ears and saw a shadow on the bank below him, shoulder-high in the mist, a small man snagging the fish from a line and thrusting it into a pouch. Galahad slid off the horse's back. The mist swirled waist-high, so bright against the forest dark it was impossible to see anything that was not itself enveloped in the mist.

He approached the figure cautiously. Words rang in his memory: *Hillmen, they're small and dark; they slip in and out of shadows. They call themselves the Ancient People, the Forgotten Ones.* Hillmen. The elusive descendants of the first Britons who had lived here long before the Romans, even before the Celts. Hillmen, who were rumored to remember a time when Britain was a land of ice and mountains, inhabited by giants. Hillmen, whose forefathers were gods.

The fisherman eyed Galahad warily. He was small in stature, dressed in ill-cured skins which still stank of goat, and carried no weapon that Galahad could see. He leaned on a stout ash staff as he tossed his line out again, and Galahad was surprised, when the man turned to pull in another fish, to see gray at his temples and in his beard. Such marks of age seemed incongruous in one so small.

"Fisherman," Galahad ventured. "Good evening."

The little man grunted and tossed out his line again. He muttered something in a guttural language Galahad could make nothing of.

"My name is Galahad. Do you live here?"

The fisherman ignored him until a third fish was safely in his pouch. Then he wound his line around his finger and turned to Galahad with a long, considering glance.

"You," he said suddenly. "Son of Lancelot."

The words were thickly accented and barely distinguishable. Galahad bowed politely. "I am. And you?"

All he could see now in the dark were the whites of the man's eyes and the silhouette of his head against the mist. The deep voice spoke gravely.

"Bran. Son of Bran. Son of Bran. Son of god."

Galahad bowed again. "I am honored. Do you . . . live nearby?"

The hillman grunted and jerked his head eastward toward the rising Pennines.

"I came to see Lludyn's Hill," Galahad ventured. "I heard it was a place of wonders."

Bran's dark eyes glinted. "Empty. Forgotten. Llud gone." He pointed to the island floating above the mist. "Long time gone."

"Yes. I was afraid of that."

"Otherworld. Many gates."

"Indeed?" Galahad paused. "I wonder if— Have you ever heard of the Grail of Maximus? Macsen Wledig?"

The fisherman shook his head and said something in his own tongue. "Fisher King," he announced abruptly.

"*What?*" Galahad gasped. "What did you say?"

Teeth gleamed white in the dark face. "Take care. Take care. Beware. Beware. Fisher King. Blackthorn ring." The little man was dancing in circles, pointing east, reciting the words in a guttural singsong. When he had turned thrice around, he ducked into the mist and disappeared.

"Bran? Bran! Come back! Please!" Galahad called his name and searched the riverbank, but the man was gone. The mist, thick as cloth, clogged his throat and nostrils and forced him back from the water. In the distance he heard Percival calling his name. He whistled softly for the stallion and leaped up on his back.

From that height he could see past the island to the narrow finger of mist that moved up from the Eden east into the foothills. A tributary! Excitement ran up his spine. Hadn't the old smith claimed that Weland

Smith's forge was on a tributary of the Eden River? And hadn't the ancient Briton as good as told him that the abode of the Fisher King lay east? He swung the stallion around and sent him up the ridge toward camp at a fast canter.

18 ✝ MARRAH'S PRAYER

Marrah swept the chapel steps and yawned. Around her the forest awoke to life in the dawning light. *A new day,* she thought, stopping for a moment to gaze around the clearing, *and what will it bring me? I'll be another day older and still unwed.* Turning, she glanced behind her at the chapel door, always open to welcome visitors. A single candle gleamed upon the altar. The dirt floor was packed hard and strewn with clean straw. On the cracked, curved wall behind the altar her father had hung his sword. It was the only cross in the place, for it had been a pagan shrine, time out of mind, until her father had quit the King's service and retired from a soldier's life. It still looked like a pagan shrine to her mind, low and rounded with curved, ill-fitting doors and narrow windows.

And the shields made it look positively secular—more like a weapons room than a chapel. Her father had hung thirty shields upon the walls, most of them gathered from the battlefield at Camlann, some left by occasional travelers, some found in the aftermath of skirmishes around Castle Noir. One of them, according to her father, was a special shield indeed: a blood-red cross upon a field of spotless white. She shrugged. Her father had grown witless since her mother died. He honestly believed the tale the hillmen told, that one day the best knight in all the world would come to this forlorn, forgotten place, and claim this simple shield, out of all the others, for his own. Such patent hogwash! As if an honest Christian could believe that bandit race of dwarves! As if any knight in his right mind would pick such a plain shield when most of the others bore the fierce faces of wolves, eagles, wildcats, and boars. As if any knight with pride would choose a shield that lay hidden in the shadow behind the door, when all the others hung in the light! She shook her head. And yet her father polished that silly shield every month, more religiously than he said his prayers, believing that someday the knight would come who would bring honor and glory to the chapel and its caretaker.

Marrah wiped away a bitter tear. If her mother hadn't died, if her father hadn't been wounded in King Mordred's army, she might have grown up at a prince's court and been married by now to some likely lord. As it was, in these deserted hills she would be lucky not to die a virgin.

She set aside the broom and flattened her rough gown against her body, running her hands over the curves of her flesh, imagining what she looked like to other eyes. Her breasts felt firm and full, her waist narrow, her hips gently rounded—she closed her eyes and let her breath out slowly. She knew she must be desirable; she was eighteen; it was past time and she was ready—her body swelled, aching, under her touch, but it was no use. She was a flower bursting into bloom alone in darkness.

She stood in the middle of the chapel and uttered a quiet prayer, whether to Mary or to Modron or to the ancient earth Goddess, source of fecundity, she neither knew nor cared. *Mother, hear your daughter! I am an empty vessel, a fallow field, a sweet wine untasted. I languish in a wasteland! O Mother, before my youth is gone, bring me a man!*

The yellow dog came charging from her father's hut, barking wildly. Startled, Marrah opened her eyes and turned. There, down the forest track where the dog was pointing, rode a horseman. She rubbed her eyes and looked again. *Two* horsemen, *young men*, knights, by the look of them, well mounted, well clothed, and, she crossed herself quickly as her heart lifted, fair of face! She reached for her broom and clung to it.

"Silence, Red!" Her father strode around the corner and grabbed the dog by the scruff of his neck. "Silence!" The dog, hackles raised, contented himself with a low growl.

The horsemen pulled up in the clearing. The younger of the knights was little more than a beardless boy, slightly built, but with a man's sword nearly as long as his legs. His mount was a thick-boned gray that had already seen its prime. The second animal was a tall and beautiful warhorse, smooth-coated and large-eyed, with a long, graceful neck and a coat that gleamed blue-black in the early sun. Marrah's heart began to pound. The knight who sat astride this horse was the handsomest man she had ever seen. His hair was as black as his horse's coat, and his eyes a devilish, brilliant blue. His tunic was finely made; he wore deerskin boots and a cloak of good, combed wool. He could not be less than a king's son. But he wore no wristbands, no torque, no buckle, no ornaments of any kind, only a badge at his shoulder with a hawk device.

"Be welcome, my lords," her father said, tugging at the growling dog.

"Thank you, sir." The beautiful young man slid from the stallion's back and gathered the reins in his hands. Marrah stared. He had only a cloth strapped to his horse's back, no saddle at all, no spear, no shield! Her eyes flew to his hip. But he was not weaponless, after all. He wore a sword. The jeweled hilt glinted red as he turned. "What place is this we have come to?"

"It is known as the Chapel in the Green, my lord. It is an old name. I am only the most recent caretaker. My name is Ulfin, my lord, at your service."

"Sir Ulfin, if I am not mistaken. You carry yourself like a knight."

Ulfin bowed. "I was once in the High King's service." Ulfin's eyes slid to the young man's hip. "You're a knight yourself, I'll wager. What lord do you serve?"

The blue eyes flashed. "I serve no lord." The beautiful knight gestured to his companion, who slid from the gray's back and bowed low to Ulfin. "My name is Galahad, and this is my cousin, Percival of Gwynedd."

Marrah saw a third man coming up the trail into the clearing. He rode one of the rough-coated mountain ponies that bred freely in the hills all over Britain and he led, with difficulty, a mule.

"And this," the beautiful knight continued, "is Garfalon, once in the High King's service like yourself. And, like yourself, reduced by war to harder times."

Garfalon grinned and ducked his head. "No complaints, my lord. Could be a sight harder, I wager, than questing about for a—" He saw Galahad's face and stopped. "Than riding all over Britain in your service," he finished.

"What we seek," Galahad said firmly, "is a place to rest. We followed a tributary of the Eden up into these hills, but I'm afraid we lost it. We found this track instead."

Ulfin grinned. "There's no wonder in that, my lord. Llud claims the river halfway up the mountain, but the spring's out back behind the chapel." He jerked a thumb toward Marrah, who blushed.

The beautiful knight seemed to freeze in place. "Llud?"

Ulfin laughed and let go of the dog, who had ceased his growling and was wagging his tail in greeting. "Oh, that's how the hillmen talk. All it means is that the stream runs underground up here. It has its source in the spring. That's probably why the chapel was built, to honor the god of the spring. We keep the chapel, my daughter and I, but in the Christian way." He nodded to the princes. "You're welcome to stay for as long as you like. We have fodder for your horses and food enough for all. This is a rich country, and game's been plentiful all summer. My daughter Marrah"—he gestured toward her and she colored again as she curtsied—"is an excellent cook. You haven't tasted a mealcake until you've had one of Marrah's."

All three men bowed in her direction. The gaze of the black-haired knight seemed to scorch her flesh. Ulfin coughed warningly. "Take the horses to the shed, Marrah, and be quick about it. Stake the mule under the trees. It'll do until nightfall. I've lit the oven fire. Be sure we've bread enough, and bring out the mead from the cellar hole. I'll hie down to the stream and try my luck with the trout."

"And I with you," Garfalon offered. "I've a way with fish. They just leap into my net."

Ulfin laughed. "If you can catch mountain trout with a net, you're a better man than I! Wait a bit and I'll fetch my pole."

"I'll take care of the horses," Percival declared as the men moved off. He winked at Marrah. "Why don't you show my cousin Galahad around the chapel?"

Marrah's face flooded with color and she dropped her eyes, but not before she had seen a blush darken Galahad's cheek. She hid a smile.

"He's not very subtle, is he, my lord?" she murmured when Percival had led the horses away.

"He's supposed to be learning," Galahad replied sourly. "What's in the chapel?"

"Not much." Marrah turned, conscious of his eyes on her. She thrust her thin shoulders back so her breasts pushed tight against her gown, and stepped forward with careful grace. "See for yourself, my lord. It's a small place, and dark without the candles. But there's the altar and the cross. That's my father's sword. He doesn't use it anymore. He says his fighting days are behind him."

Galahad stood in the center of the chapel and looked around slowly, his gaze sliding over the shields, past the dim shadow of the door, without a flicker of hesitation. "Then these must be quiet hills. What are the shields for?"

"Camouflage. There's an old legend that— Have you never heard of the Knight of the Shield?"

The blue eyes turned to her, intent. Marrah trembled, hardly able to breathe but unable to look away. "No. Who is he?"

"The best knight in the world. My father believes he'll come someday and lift down the shield that's meant for him, all unknowing. And with that shield he'll save Britain." She smiled shyly. "It's nonsense, my lord. It's just an old tale the hillmen tell. I don't believe half their stories. They claim they see gods everywhere and talk with Faerie folk. It scares me. Father listens to them, but that's because they please him. He loves to hear them call him the Fisher King. It goes right to his head—"

"What?" Breathless, Galahad gripped her shoulders and stared down into her face. *"What did you say?"*

But Marrah hardly heard his words, her heart was pounding so. She gazed up into his burning eyes and her body blazed, her blood roared in her ears and her head tilted back, lips parted. He froze. She saw in his eyes the moment when he felt her heat and understood it, when the question that had been on his lips died, forgotten, and there were only the two of them together in the dimness, so close, so eager, so long desiring, with nothing between them but the silence of the chapel and the thin fabric of her gown.

With a cry like a gasp he thrust her away.

"My lord," she whispered, swaying on her feet.

"No!" he cried in a strangled voice.

"But, my lord—"

He whipped around, turning his back on her. "Leave me! Get out!"

She hurried to the door, but then looked back. He knelt at the altar, bent over his clasped hands.

"Gracious Mother," she whispered, breathing swiftly and leaning against the jamb. "He's the one. He must be. It couldn't be anyone else. Dear God, let him be the one!"

As the sun lifted above the encircling pines, they gathered for breakfast in the clearing. Ulfin cleaned and spitted five fat trout while Percival got a fire going. Garfalon dragged a cool flagon of mead from the cellar pit and Marrah produced a batch of mealcakes hot from the clay oven and a basket of blackberries fresh from the woodland thickets.

"A feast!" Ulfin cried in satisfaction. "Surely the king at his table eats no better! Come, my lords, sit where you will, but join me and partake of these blessings. I feel in my bones it will be a glorious day, this day of your coming. May the Lord of Heaven bless you and all your endeavors. Amen. Marrah, my dear, mead for the young lords."

The mead slid smoothly over Galahad's tongue, tasting faintly of peat smoke and mountain heather. Around them the forest grew golden with light, the sky deepened from azure to sapphire, and the morning blossomed with pine scent, birdsong, and woodsmoke. The yellow dog dozed in the warm dust at the back of Ulfin's hut, his paws twitching in some dreamy escapade, as the awakening locusts took up their scratchy song and the very air thickened with their noise.

"A coin for your thoughts, my lord."

Galahad started at the touch on his elbow. Ulfin, Garfalon, and Percival were deep in talk about fighting tactics, but Marrah sat at his side, gazing shyly up at him.

"Nothing," Galahad said stiffly. "I was daydreaming, that's all."

"You looked so serene, I thought you must be thinking of something wonderful. Your wife, perhaps? Or your lover?"

Galahad flushed brightly. "Don't be ridiculous."

"What, then?"

"If you must know, I was taken by the peace of this place. It's very beautiful."

Marrah sighed. "I suppose it is. Father loves it here. He'll never leave."

"And you wish to? Are you unhappy?"

Marrah grimaced. "Wouldn't you be, my lord? It's so far from the main road we hardly ever see another human face. Nothing ever happens. The whole world and all that's in it passes us by."

Galahad shrugged. "The world outside is a violent place. You are safe here, at least."

"Safe! So safe I'm nearly dead of boredom! If we'd stayed in York I'd be wed to a lord by now. I was born there, you know. York's a real city. My father served Sir Lucius, the garrison commander. My mother was a lady. We had a villa and a farm. And servants." She gestured lightly toward the hut and the sleeping dog. "It all seems like a dream, now."

"What happened?"

Marrah dropped her eyes and trailed a finger through the grass at her feet. "My mother died. My father suffered a war wound. A sword in the hip. He was a long time recovering. We could not keep up the farm between us, and in truth, he had no wish to. He was determined to spend the rest of his days in the mountains of his youth. So here we are."

"He was born here, then?"

Marrah flicked him a curious glance, noting the sudden interest in his voice. "Near enough. Why?"

The blue eyes turned to her with a sudden intensity that transfixed her. "Why is your father called the Fisher King?"

Marrah's jaw dropped. "It's just an epithet. It doesn't mean anything."

"How do you know?"

"No one calls him that but hillmen."

"And why do they?"

"Because he beat their leader in a fishing contest." A smile tugged at the corners of Marrah's mouth. "Why should you be disappointed? What did you think it meant?"

"It doesn't matter." Galahad paused. "Have you ever heard of Macsen Wledig?"

"Who?" Marrah frowned.

"His Roman name was Magnus Maximus."

"Oh, of course, the Emperor Maximus! Why didn't you say so? He's well known in these parts. Sir Brastias keeps the Cup of Maximus at Castle Noir."

Galahad gasped aloud. "The *what*? *Where*?"

The men paused in their conversation and turned.

"Castle Noir," Marrah repeated in a bewildered voice. "Just over the ridge."

"Ah, we were talking of Castle Noir ourselves," Ulfin interrupted. "Imagine that!"

Galahad struggled for command of his voice. "Tell me about it, would you, sir?"

"Why, certainly. It stands at the head of Dark Valley on the other side of the mountain, and commands the hill country east of here. Sir Brastias holds it. I've just been telling your companions about Sir Brastias. He's an odd duck to have for a neighbor, but he's done us no harm. He's really a prince of Strathclyde but he dislikes being addressed so. He's the youngest brother of King Hapgar, that was king in Arthur's day. Hapgar died at Autun, and his brother Pertolys at Camlann. Brastias, I've heard men say, should have been next in line for kingship. But he had long since disappeared into his mountain fastness here in Rheged, having, he says, seen the handwriting on the wall. So young Kastor, Hapgar's son, now sits in the king's chair at Caer Farne, although he's barely twenty. And his uncle Brastias hides himself away in Castle Noir, amusing himself with his music and his scrolls and," he added with a lift of his eyebrows, "his magics and enchantments, if rumors are to be believed."

"An enchanter?" Galahad said under his breath.

Marrah nodded but Ulfin shrugged. "It's a matter of opinion. He's feared by many, and I've heard him cursed as a devil, although I know him to be a Christian. If he has power, he keeps it to himself. He's a peaceful man and wants no part of any fighting. A man like that, so odd, so full of mystery, is bound to stir up interest. He has his hands full keeping thieves and bandits out of Castle Noir. He needs a house guard of trained men but dislikes the company of soldiers, so he must defend himself with what skills he has. Thus far, no one has gotten in who did not come in peace."

"What is this . . . this Cup of Maximus that Marrah says he keeps? Is that what the thieves are after?"

Percival and Garfalon turned excited faces to Ulfin, but the old soldier laughed. "Hardly. It's a drinking cup like any other of its time, I imagine. But because the place itself is so mysterious, and Brastias so private, rumors have swept like wildfire across Rheged that he is guarding some great treasure from Roman times. Thus the constant attacks by bandits, groups of errant soldiers, any greedy soul with a blade on his hip and time on his hands."

"You imagine?" Galahad repeated. "You haven't seen the cup yourself?"

Ulfin shot him a swift look under lowering brows. "No. And you won't, either, even if you manage to get inside the gates, which I doubt you can. He doesn't let strangers in." Ulfin rose suddenly and gazed fiercely at his guests. "I hope you didn't come all this way just to lay your hands on a treasure that's none of your concern. As soon as I saw you, I thought more of you than that."

Galahad stiffened, but Percival went on one knee and raised supplicating hands to the angry soldier. "Oh, no, Sir Ulfin, you mistake us, indeed you do! We bear no ill feeling toward Sir Brastias—quite the contrary, I promise you! We are on a quest, that much is true, but it is not for ourselves.

King Arthur himself set Sir Galahad the task of finding the Treasure of Maximus, that Britain might be saved from barbarians forever."

Ulfin frowned, watching their faces. "But King Arthur is dead."

"What these noble lords seek," Garfalon said quickly, "they do not seek for their own enrichment. Why, I bade them leave their quest and take up the hunt for the missing Rheged princess—King Rydor is offering a fortune to the man who finds her—but they refused. They wish to restore the emperor's treasure to its rightful place, that Britain may be preserved forever, no matter who sits in Camelot."

Ulfin turned to Galahad. "Did Arthur tell you this himself?"

"Yes." Galahad got slowly to his feet. "I know what I am looking for. I have seen these things in a dream. That is why I wish to see the cup at Castle Noir."

Ulfin's eyes widened. "A dream?" Awe crept into his voice. "You could be the one, my lord. The one I have waited for."

Marrah shook her head quickly. "He has been inside the chapel, Father. The shields meant nothing to him."

"That does not matter," Ulfin whispered. "He who is to come will choose it, all unknowing."

Galahad looked at them both in growing consternation. "Listen, Sir Ulfin, I beg you to believe me. I am not the Knight of the Shield. I don't know what ancient legend the hillmen told you, but it does not refer to me. My companions and I will travel to Castle Noir tomorrow, but today we would spend in your service, to repay you for your generous hospitality, and to prove to you that we are men of goodwill and not bandits greedy for gain."

Ulfin hesitated and then shrugged. He smiled at them. "Ah, well, I suppose my hope ran away with my sense. Old dreams die hard. If you will forgive me, I will accept your help, my lords. I was going into the forest today to cut wood for winter."

"We will do it for you," Percival cried. "Spend the day with your daughter and let us fell trees and chop them for you. It's the least we can do." He grinned at Marrah. "And maybe pretty Marrah can send us on our way with more of those wonderful mealcakes!"

The woods grew quickly cool when the sun went down. Marrah checked the new bread in the oven, then walked around the outbuildings into the clearing to add wood to the cooking fire. An old iron stewpot hung on its stand above the flames. She stirred it absently, staring down into swirling chunks of rabbit, wild onions, garlic, pine nuts, carrots, and sage, but seeing instead a pair of brilliant blue eyes and straight black brows. Behind her a raven rasped loudly, settling on its branch with much commotion and fixing her with a beady stare.

She scowled. "Bad luck, ravens." She let the cover fall on the stewpot. Something moved in the woods beyond. "Father?" she called, straining to see through the deepening dusk. "Is that you? How many did you catch tonight?"

The yellow dog trotted to her side, nose twitching, head lowered. A low growl issued from his throat and his hair stood up along his spine from ruff to tail. Marrah's heart began to pound.

"What is it, Red?" she asked softly. "Bear? Boar?"

The dog stepped forward, stiff-legged, his eyes fixed on something she could not see, his lips curling back around long, curved fangs. Marrah backed closer to the fire. Shapes appeared out of the dusk, six men, raggedly dressed, holding weapons and glaring at her with wild eyes.

"Father!" she cried. One of the men carried a drawn sword. He took no notice of the dog, but looked around the clearing in swift assessment, and then smiled at her, showing a line of broken teeth.

"Where's the man of this place?"

"Man?" Marrah repeated dumbly. Red's growl escalated to an open snarl. His whole body vibrated with promised violence.

The man stood still. "Your father. Your husband. You called out for someone just now. Who was it? Who protects you?"

Marrah drew a deep breath and clutched the stick she had used to stir the stew. Behind her back she lowered it into the coals. "My . . . my brothers. Giants. Great warriors. They protect me. They . . . they're just coming up from the stream."

"Of course they are," the leader sneered. "I can hear the army thundering at their backs. Come on, men, it's ours for the taking."

"Who are you?" Marrah cried. "And why do you come with weapons against a woman? What do you want?"

The leader laughed, and so did his companions. The dog went stiff with fury.

"These weapons are not for you, lass!" He clapped a hand over his groin and thrust his hips forward. "*This* is the only weapon we need against you. And I promise you, you shall get the feel of it later, when we've time. You'll get to burnish all our spears, again and again, until morning. Ha ha!"

"No!" Marrah hiccuped, blinking at them, unable to comprehend the enormity of the threat, thinking only of her father, due any minute to return from his evening fishing.

The leader came toward her and reached out for her arm. She whipped the burning stick from behind her back and lunged for his throat. At the same moment the dog launched himself at the man's arm. The flying body of fur knocked Marrah sideways; she fell to the ground, narrowly missing the fire. Gasping, she rolled quickly into the shadows, picked herself up and half ran, half crawled toward the chapel. From the corner of her eye she saw Red hanging from her attacker's arm, still snarling. The bandit swore viciously and struggled for a moment with his sword; then the blade swung in a glittering arc through the firesmoke and the dog fell dead in a heap of fur and innards.

"Get her!" the leader cried, hugging his bleeding arm against his side. "Don't let her get away! Hold her for me!"

His five companions howled excitedly and ran toward Marrah. They caught her halfway to the chapel door, grabbed her arms and legs, and pinned her to the turf.

"Father!" Marrah screamed. "Help me!"

"Father, eh?" the leader snarled, walking over to her. "What happened to your brothers? Gorn, Lemas, keep an eye out for the old man. That'll be the keeper of the chapel we heard about. And this will be his virgin daughter." He laughed aloud as Marrah struggled, sobbing, in the cruel grasp of his men. "We've heard that you keep a treasure hidden in this chapel. Tell us where it is."

"What treasure?" Marrah cried. "There are only shields! My father's shields! There's no treasure!"

The leader leaned down until the stench of his breath made her retch. "There is a treasure. Where is it?"

"Sir!" Marrah quavered. "I beg you! Go into the chapel and look! There is one shield more valuable than all the others, but I . . . I . . . I don't know its worth!"

"Liar!" He grabbed her shoulders and wrenched her bodice open. "Sweet little liar. I'll enjoy taking you almost as much as I'll enjoy killing you. Tell me which one it is, maiden, or you'll feel the prick of my spear right now!"

"Take your hands off my daughter!"

The leader straightened. His men whipped around. There on the chapel steps stood Sir Ulfin, the old sword in his hand wavering in the trembling light.

"Father!" Marrah sobbed, pulling herself to her knees and holding her gown closed. "Oh, Father! Let them have the shield! They will kill you else!"

Ulfin's sword steadied. "These men did not come here for a shield. Not vermin like these. They'll want everything we have."

The leader grinned his broken smile. "You're right about that, old man. I'll start with your daughter."

"Never!" Ulfin said, the sword lifting. "Let her go, you heathen swine!"

"Ah, that's good! Heathen swine! Did you hear that, men? Listen, you old, dried-up fool, put down that sword or I'll slit her throat!" He swung around and laid the edge of his blade against Marrah's neck.

"Damn you!" Ulfin shouted. In the next instant he staggered, a dagger deep in his chest, as two of the ruffians swarmed up the steps, grabbed the sword, and knocked him down.

One of Marrah's captors cried, "Look out behind you!"

Horses thundered into the clearing. Marrah looked up in time to see a great shadow swoop over them, a blade like a flash of starlight arc down across the leader's neck, and the headless body sway, buckle, and topple to the grass, spraying blood everywhere. She screamed as the head rolled toward her, its dead eyes frozen in surprise. She jumped up. Her captors had gone, running into the woods, howling like mad dogs.

"Father!" She staggered toward the chapel, aware of commotion behind her, unable to see clearly through her tears. She found her father's body just inside the chapel door. He lived, but barely, his breaths coming quick and shallow, bubbles frothing pink on his lips. "Father! Dear Father!" She gathered his head in her arms and kissed his brow.

"Does he live?"

She looked up. Galahad stood above her, his eyes blazing. The sword at his side dripped blood. "Only . . . only just. The . . . the dagger—"

"Don't touch it!" He bent down closer.

Ulfin's eyes glistened gray. His lips moved. "The Shield."

"Tell him we're off to get the others. They've not gone far. Garfalon will stay and guard you until we get back."

"Wait!" Marrah looked up beseechingly. "Take a shield with you. He wants you to take a shield."

"What for? I've no need, and there's no time—"

Ulfin struggled for breath, his blind eyes searching the dark. "No time. Dying now. Take the Shield from the wall."

"Please," Marrah begged, tears sliding down her cheeks. "Please. Just do it. It doesn't matter which one. Just take a shield. It is his dying wish."

"Very well." In the dimness the round shields all looked the same. Galahad reached up for the nearest one, behind the door above Ulfin's body, and ran his arm through the straps. "I've taken one, Sir Ulfin. May God bless your eternal soul." He made a sign of the cross in the air, turned, and was gone.

Marrah sat on the rushes of the chapel floor and held her father's head in her lap. Outside the window a nightingale began to sing. Behind the music she heard the rustle of mice somewhere in the straw and then the steady *thud, thud* of Garfalon stacking the wood the knights had brought into the clearing. He had built up the fire and a soft, golden glow shone through the chapel door and washed Ulfin's pale, cold face with a last touch of color.

"Marrah . . . did he—"

"Hush, dear Father. Yes, he did. He took the Shield. Just as you said he would."

An expression of peace, of satisfaction, of serene joy settled over Ulfin's features. He almost smiled. "I knew he was the one."

"Yes, Father," Marrah whispered. "You knew as soon as he rode in this morning. Just as you knew it would be a glorious day." She bent her head over his body and wept.

19 ✝ THE MASTER OF CASTLE NOIR

The road through the mountain pass to Castle Noir, once paved with neatly fitted, broad-cut stones, was now slashed by gullies and buried in debris, all the work of rushing torrents in the spring snowmelt. What track there was dipped steeply down from the ridge crest to a narrow valley ringed by towering pines. The stronghold of Castle Noir nestled at the head of the valley, and before it, covering the valley floor, stretched a long, glittering lake.

At the top of the pass Galahad paused and narrowed his eyes to see the fortress better. From this distance outbuildings were just visible at the back of a sprawling wooden structure punctuated at uneven intervals by three stone towers. He wondered why anyone called such a place a castle. It looked more like a rebuilt Roman villa fortified for defense. Greenery showed—trees or meadow or both, he could not be sure—between the buildings and the encircling wall. Strange as the castle was, the wall looked even stranger. From this distance it glittered silver, protruding here and there in its meander about the grounds—never Roman built, that was sure—a bent but shining crown around an odd, misshapen brow. For all its oddity, Castle Noir was excellently placed. There was only one road in and only one road out. At its back ranged the steep hills and before it lay the water. Even for a small company it would be easy to defend.

Behind him Percival and Marrah rode together on the old gray, followed by Garfalon on his sturdy mountain pony and the mule. Thank heaven the girl had not balked at leaving the Chapel in the Green. They had buried Ulfin as soon as it was light enough to see. She had wept, of course, but said very little. She had done as he asked and gathered her meager belongings and slung them on the mule. Even more surprising, she had kept her eyes lowered and her thoughts to herself. He had not expected such meekness from her. The only time life showed in her features was when they passed a cloud of ravens, circling and screaming above the trees a short way off the path, and he had told her that that was where he and Percival had caught the ruffians and killed them by the light of the waning moon. Marrah blessed him then, but otherwise stayed silent. He glanced down at the shield. Perhaps it was a lucky token after all.

As the pine woods thinned toward the lake verge, Galahad raised a hand and halted. "We'll stop here and water the horses if the shore road is not patrolled. What do you know about Brastias's defenses, Marrah?"

She shrugged apologetically. "Not a thing, my lord."

"What did you see the last time you were here?"

"I've never been to Castle Noir, my lord. Father came here for supplies twice yearly, but he never brought me. Sir Brastias lives there with his son. My . . . my father met Kynor on his last trip there at winter's end. He had been away at the wars but came home to heal his wounds."

"A warrior, then. Does he command the troops?"

Marrah looked at him blankly. "I never heard Father say anything about troops. Except for Kynor and a couple of servants, Sir Brastias lives alone."

"Alone! That's impossible!" Percival cried. "How does he eat? Or keep himself warm in winter? Or keep out the thieves?"

Marrah's eyes widened. "With magic, of course."

Silence fell. Garfalon cast a worried glance at Galahad, who scowled. "We will see about that. But if there are no troops to patrol the shore road, we can safely take the horses down to drink. Follow me."

Running straight along the edge of the valley floor toward the castle, the shore road looked as though it had once felt the touch of Roman hands. But time, decay, and overgrowth had narrowed and bent it until in some places it was little more than a winding track, squeezed between the encroaching forest and the lake. Six mountain streams slashed their way across the road. Once culverts had contained them but now they ate freely away at the road's foundations, creating steep-banked gullies too broad to jump. In late summer the streambeds were nearly dry and easy to ford, but Galahad imagined that for six months out of the year such hazards would slow an enemy's approach. He wondered if the road's neglect was intentional.

The sun was fast disappearing behind the western ridge when at last they neared the castle. The treetops, catching the last rays, burned gold, but the lake glimmered cold and green in shadow. They stopped in the weedy, level yard before the gate-place and stared. There was no gate. The sinuous wall glittered unbroken before them, an impossible thing, but true.

"Perhaps it's around back," Garfalon ventured at length. "I'll go see." Galahad nodded and Garfalon kicked his pony into a trot. Galahad himself went up to inspect the wall. Its smooth surface puzzled him. It was white as lime-washed plaster but had the feel of rock. Thousands and thousands of glittering, hard flecks were embedded in the whiteness, so that it caught and reflected light from the sky and the lake. It was both beautiful and mysterious, wonderful and very cleverly functional. His opinion of Sir Brastias began to rise.

"Look!" Marrah cried suddenly, pointing with a shaking finger at the lake. Even as they watched, a warm mist rose off the cooling water and thickened, gathering strength. Her voice rose to a nervous shriek. "It's coming for us!"

"Don't be ridiculous," Galahad said sharply. "It's only mist."

Percival cleared his throat as the mist rolled off the water and up the reed-lined shore to where they stood. "Well," he ventured, "there's mist, and then there's mist."

They turned, startled by the frantic hammer of hoofbeats. Garfalon rounded the far wall, bent low on his pony's neck. "My lord! My lord!" He pulled up, breathless. "My lord, let's be gone, and quickly! There's a great mist rising! Oh!" He gasped sharply as he looked toward the lake. "And another one falling!"

"*Another one?*" Percival croaked.

"Aye. Look yonder." He pointed behind them to the castle, where a feathery whiteness descended from the dimming sky. Already the tops of the stone towers were lost to view. The horses shifted edgily, tossing their heads. Marrah whimpered.

Galahad turned to Garfalon. "What did you see along the wall?"

"No gate, my lord. There's a ditch dug most of the way around, and water in it, too. At the back it runs right up to a cliff. The only place to scale the wall is here." He gulped audibly. "And I pray you won't try it, my lord. I'll wager there's something nasty waiting on the other side."

The first cold fingers of mist drifted between them. The mule snorted, rolling the whites of its eyes.

"Sir Brastias may like his privacy," Galahad muttered, "but we come in peace. He has no reason to keep us out." He raised a shout and heard his voice echo off the hills. Silence followed. The mist thickened visibly, rolling by in solid clumps, clogging their nostrils and throats, blinding their eyes.

"Please, my lord," Marrah begged. "Let us camp farther down the valley. We can try again in the morning."

"What makes you think it will be any different then?" Galahad turned back to the wall, which he could barely see, though it was less than a horse's length away. "Ho! Sir Brastias! We come in peace! We are four only, and one a woman, Sir Ulfin's daughter from the Chapel in the Green. We have news, and need of help. We will pay for a night's shelter and a hot meal."

Nothing stirred. Then suddenly they heard movement behind them in the water, in the reeds, a soft rustle and a low chorus of frogs. The mule brayed, backing wide-eyed, and Marrah cried out as frogs swarmed up from the lake and surrounded them, thick upon the ground, a shifting, hopping carpet of green, silver-eyed creatures all croaking and calling at once.

"Mother of God!" Garfalon cried, struggling to keep the pony and mule from bolting.

"They're only frogs," Galahad said sternly. "Hold hard to your horse, Percival, and force him to be still. He thinks the ground has come alive. Get his attention off the frogs and onto you."

Percival managed to control the gray, and Garfalon held tight to both sets of reins. Eventually the frogs returned to the lake as mysteriously as they had come. "It's that damned enchanter!" Garfalon quavered. "He called them forth!"

"Frogs!" Galahad snorted. "He must be jesting."

Marrah whimpered. "If we don't leave, what will be next?"

Galahad shouted again and asked for entrance, and again nothing stirred in the shrouded night. The white wall glittered in the shifting fog and Galahad's stallion skittered nervously.

"Easy, Rouk. What is it?"

Percival's voice trembled. "I've never seen a moment's fear in that horse before. He didn't move a muscle at the frogs."

"He's not afraid of frogs. Snakes worry him, but that's all."

A shriek issued from the fog. "Look!" Marrah cried. "Snakes!"

Galahad stared, blinked, and stared again. Sinuous dark shadows slithered over the wall and down to the ground, hundreds of them! The stallion danced and the other horses fidgeted uneasily. Galahad drew his sword, a flash of light in the mist, and lifted one of the snakes onto the blade. The stallion shuddered, backing, as the ground around his hooves silently writhed and glittered.

"For pity's sake!" Galahad cried. "Garden snakes!" He pushed the stallion forward to a standstill. "A silly, common trick, that's all it is. And it means that someone's on the other side of that wall. Hallo! We come in peace!"

For a long while no one answered. Then finally a voice came dimly out of the mist. "Put up your sword."

Galahad shook the snake off the blade and sheathed his sword. How could anyone see them, when they could see nothing themselves? "In the name of God, in the name of Arthur, who will come again, have the courage to meet me face-to-face. I will do you no harm."

They stood silently in the rolling mist, waiting for something to happen. The snakes disappeared quickly into the long grass and the horses stood still. Gradually the mist began to thin and draw back along the wall, and as it withdrew a man appeared, suddenly and completely, where the mist had been. They all cried out together and Galahad's sword whipped from its scabbard of its own accord.

The man, wrapped from head to toe in a brown monk's robe, pointed to the blade. "Is this how you come in peace? Then you may go back again." And he began to turn away.

"Stay!" Galahad cried. "My hand moved faster than my thought, that's all! You startled us. See, it is sheathed again now."

The robed figure turned back to them. "Is this all of you? Where are your men? Your supplies?"

"We've no men. The mule carries our supplies. We are travelers, except for Marrah, Sir Ulfin's daughter. He was killed last night by bandits. We buried him this morning and brought her with us. She cannot stay there alone."

"I didn't know Sir Ulfin had a daughter." The man lifted a hand and pushed back the hood of his robe. He was young and fair-haired, with broad shoulders and a warrior's carriage beneath the robe. "I see no wounds upon you."

"We were not there when they attacked him. But we killed them afterward. Every one."

"Was the leader a big, dark-bearded brute with a piece out of his ear?"

"Indeed," Galahad said sharply. "Do you know him?"

The young man grimaced. "Hardly. They attacked us first, and then must have headed over the ridge. A bloodthirsty group, they looked. I am sorry to hear about Sir Ulfin. My father will be distraught." He drew off the robe and stood before them in full fighting gear, heavy leather leggings studded with brass and a shirt of mail, finely linked and flexible, over his tunic. At his hip the hilt of his sword gleamed silver in the dusk. He bowed politely. "My name is Kynor. Sir Brastias is my father. On his behalf I welcome you all to Castle Noir."

Galahad slid off his horse and introduced his companions. Kynor bowed to each, but took Marrah's hand in his own and raised it to his lips. "I am so sorry to hear of your father's death. I deeply regret sending those ruffians away instead of fighting them myself, as I wished to do. We never thought they would find the Chapel in the Green. So few ever have."

Marrah blushed and then paled. "Thank you, my lord."

"What made them leave?" Percival asked. "The frogs or the snakes?"

Kynor grinned. "Neither. He only uses frogs and snakes with women. It was the moving wall that sent them howling into the night."

"The moving wall?" they all repeated together.

Kynor smiled. "Aye, the wall moves. That's why it's built so. If men try to scale it, it moves with a thunderous roar. I'd love to show you how it works, but I'm forbidden. You touched it"—he turned to Galahad—"but you also called out for entrance in Arthur's name. Had you not done so, I would not be standing here." He turned away. "Come. Follow me."

Kynor headed into the woods beyond the lake until he reached a hillock covered with holly and blackthorn. He pulled some tangled growth aside, revealing a great, rounded door in the side of the hill. It led to a tunnel dug beneath the wall, floored in stone and supported by columns of wood, tall enough to lead a riderless horse through.

"Unfortunately," Kynor said, "you can't ride through it. A great shortcoming, to my mind, but I was only a child when my father built it and he did not ask for my advice."

"Sir Brastias built this?" Galahad stared at it in wonder.

"Yes. When he designed and built the wall." Kynor winked. "This is the gate you were looking for."

They came out of the tunnel into a broad, paved courtyard flanked by the wooden house and a square stone tower, and lit by slatted lanterns slung on posts. A servant appeared to take charge of their horses and Garfalon went with him. Kynor led the way up broad, shallow steps to a pair of carved oak doors. He paused before them and pressed his hand against the lintel. With a groan, the doors swung inward of their own accord.

They walked into a large hall brilliant with light. Tapestries woven in the golden days of Arthur adorned the walls; rich, imported carpets covered the tiled floor; the carved chests were inlaid with glazed enamels and banded in silver; cushions of bright needlework decked benches and chairs; and thirty candlestands, in bronze, silver, and even gold, held aloft a hundred blazing candles. In the center of the hall stood a wide bronze kettle filled with logs but unlit.

Galahad, Percival, and Marrah stood blinking at the wealth such magnificent furnishings and profligate use of candles implied.

Kynor sighed. "It isn't necessary, Father. It's just wasteful."

"Oh, but I think it is," a voice replied. In a corner of the room, in the only shadows, a narrow stair twisted upward. Halfway down this stair a tall man in a monk's robe stood perfectly still. "We must honor these guests, Kynor. One of them is our kinsman, and the other—did you see the shield he carried slung across his stallion's back? No, I thought not. Then you don't know who he is."

"This is Galahad," Kynor replied, with an edge to his voice. "And this is—"

"Yes," the voice interrupted, a peremptory voice, used to command. "That was the name."

Sir Brastias came down the stairs and into the light. The resemblance to Kynor was clear in the straight features, broad shoulders, and carriage. But the older man wore his coarse, brown robe with the ease and familiarity of daily living, not as a cover for something else. He had a mane of rich, brown hair going gray at the temples, and a beard already more gray than brown. The ring he wore on his right hand, a black stone set in gold, was his only ornament. His eyes were unsettling. To suit his coloring they should have been brown like Kynor's, but they were silver-gray and utterly unreadable, more mirrors than eyes. Galahad shifted uncomfortably as they gazed at him.

Suddenly Brastias smiled, and the room warmed. "Welcome, Prince Galahad. You are Lancelot's son. I remember your father well. I fought with him when the kingdom was green and we were young, before I gave up the arts of war. He saved my hide at the battle of Agned. And he made me knight. A more honorable man I have never had the pleasure to know. You honor me by coming to my house." He bowed.

"Lancelot's son!" Kynor stared. Marrah gaped in awe and crossed herself quickly.

Galahad returned the bow. "Thank you, my lord," he said stiffly. "You honor us by sharing your house with us tonight."

A glint of amusement flashed in the silver eyes, and was gone. "I wouldn't have missed it. Besides, you called on me in Arthur's name and I could not deny you." He turned to Percival and held out open arms. "Percival of Gwynedd—my nephew, by all that's holy!"

Before he knew what was happening, Percival found himself wrapped in a bear hug. "Uncle?"

Sir Brastias laughed. "You've never heard of me, I have no doubt. But your mother, Anet, is my sister, and nearest to me in age of all our father's children. She was last born of the twelve and sent to a nunnery as soon as she could talk. She'll not remember me, but I remember the day our brother Hapgar gave her to Maelgon of Gwynedd." He slapped Percival gently on the back. "Tell me, have I any other kin in Gwynedd I should know about?"

"My sister Dandrane." Percival gulped. "My twin."

"Twins, eh? They run in the blood of Strathclyde. I was sorry to hear of Maelgon's death. But what are you doing so far from home if you are now king in his stead?"

Percival flashed Galahad a quick look and flushed lightly.

"Ah, it's like that, is it?" Sir Brastias nodded slowly. "And who has usurped your place, young prince? One of my wild kinsmen, or one of your own?"

"My father's brother, Peredur." Percival licked his dry lips. "He's not really king—he's only regent. Until I'm fifteen."

A sad smile flickered over Brastias's features. "Gone are the days when boys could afford such innocence. Gone with the greatest king the world has ever known." He sighed. "No, lad, he is king, not regent, for you cannot go back without his leave. Accept your fate or fight it, but at least know it for what it is."

Percival nodded dumbly and Sir Brastias turned to Marrah. "And who might you be, child?"

Kynor stepped forward. "This is Sir Ulfin's daughter, Father. Those bandits we sent away yesterday found their way to the chapel and killed Sir Ulfin. These young lords have brought Marrah to us for safekeeping."

Brastias's face went utterly still and the light left his eyes. He took Marrah's hand and held it between his own. "May God forgive me. Not for all the world would I have sent death to Ulfin. He was a good man, with a generous heart and a tongue that abhorred a lie. God rest his soul and bring him peace."

"Thank you, my lord," Marrah said in a small voice. But the gray eyes looked beyond her into a distance none of them could see.

"I should have foreseen it," Brastias said softly. "He died because his time had come. The Shield had no more need of him." He turned, his gaze narrowing to focus on Galahad. "It was your coming, Galahad, that made it so. For you are the Knight of the Shield."

Galahad straightened. "*I* did not kill him! I was in the forest with Percival. We killed his murderers. Ask Marrah."

"Be easy, son." Brastias's voice was low and kind, the master's caress on the raised ruff of his hound. "No blame attaches to you. It is a thing beyond your will, and certainly beyond your power. Think no more of it than of the tide turning. Inevitable change. Even predictable, to those with the means to know." A furrow appeared in his brow. "If you wish to blame someone, blame me. I should have seen it coming. The signs were there. But I was too . . . distracted . . . to read them." He let his breath out slowly and smiled lightly at their confused faces. "Forgive me if I seem to ramble. Do none of you know the legend of the Shield?"

They all shook their heads. Sir Brastias clapped his hands and summoned a house servant. "Arath, we will have some wine."

When the wine came Sir Brastias himself poured it and served it. Galahad thought he had never tasted anything so good, not even in Gaul. Dark red, smooth, and dry, it slid down his throat and beguiled his senses until his fatigue and hunger vanished, and he was dreamily content to sit on a cushioned chair and listen to Sir Brastias's tales.

"The Shield last belonged to one Vausanius, a Roman who made his home here. Castle Noir is built on the remains of his villa, which the Saxons burned nigh on fifty years ago. Vausanius was a cavalry commander who served with the Sarmatians posted at the Wall. The Shield was a gift of their commander, whose life he saved during a Pict attack. It had an ancient history, even with the Sarmatians, and a legend already attached to it. In the ensuing years, more than once the Shield meant the difference between life and death, and Vausanius counted it his most prized possession. When he retired to this villa at the end of his service, he kept it always by him. His children were daughters and understood little of weapons. They thought him besotted to prize it so. When he felt death approaching, he thought where he could hide it for safekeeping, for so powerful a death defier cannot be handed down like a painted pot or a beaded necklace, and certainly not to a woman. So he gave it to Nog, chief of the Ancient People hereabouts, and told him the Sarmatian legend. It was a shield of heroes, god-blessed and sacred to their god of war. They believed the man who raised it had to fight the spirits of its former owners before he could claim it for his own. Thus it became a symbol of the best warrior in all the world. It was made to keep the flame of civilization alight against the darkness of a barbarian foe." Brastias paused. The silence of deep attention lay like a blanket over his listeners. They did not dare breathe. "Nog, of course, got the instructions by heart and obeyed them to the letter. He hid the Shield in the sacred place of the Ancients, a beehive hut surrounded by standing stones in the heart of the mountains. Generation after generation followed his example and kept it safe. Sir Ulfin was its last keeper, and a Christian at that. He tumbled down the standing stones and made a clearing to let in the light. He turned the hut into a chapel, and even disguised the Shield's hiding place by hanging up every shield he could lay his hands on. Until you came, Prince Galahad, in the hour of his death, to take it down."

Galahad felt the weight of their eyes on him. "I took it because it was handy," he protested. "I did not know what it meant."

"Nevertheless," Brastias said gently, "it is the only shield ever to leave the chapel. It is no accident you chose that one, lad. No accident at all."

Percival leaned toward Galahad, his face lighting. "Cousin! The token!" he whispered excitedly. "You found it in shadow, remember? And it's crossed! It must be the first of the tokens!"

"Yes," Galahad responded quietly. "I had thought of that."

"What tokens?" Brastias interjected. "Tokens of what?"

"A private jest," Galahad said quickly. "Beyond the reach of your magic."

Brastias smiled. "Then you admit an admiration for my powers?"

Galahad laughed outright. "Frogs? Snakes? Mist? You're no enchanter. You have a book of charms, that's all."

"And a wall that moves," Kynor muttered defensively.

But Brastias chuckled. "If by 'enchanter' you mean someone like Merlin,

who could move megaliths with a song, travel as the wind, and see the future in the fire, no. Of course not. What I have is sight, not vision. Cleverness, not power. And don't let Kynor fool you. I use an engine, powered by
water and levers, to move the wall. I use music to charm the frogs and
snakes. And every student of the Old Arts can call a mist out of the air on a
cool summer night. I have a crystal, it is true, where, with luck and concentration, I can see things that have not yet come to pass. But merely seeing
them means nothing—interpretation is the key, and that takes a great deal
of wisdom. I have learned to turn away from most of what I see, and rely on
good sense and caution. Now and then a message comes clear as a ringing
bell from the future, urgent and compelling, but this is rare. I will show you
my study in the morning, if you like. And my scrolls, and the mathematical
shapes I have cast in bronze. It would delight me to give you a tour about
my home. But not tonight. I will send for a meal and have you shown to
your bedplaces."

He rose. The wine held them all motionless and he seemed to look
down on them from a great height. "Please forgive me for not staying to
keep you company, but I am promised elsewhere. Until morning, then."
Brastias bowed, turned in a swirl of robe, and vanished back up the twisted
stair.

"Promised elsewhere?" Galahad repeated stupidly, through the pounding of a headache. "What does that mean?"

Kynor shrugged and then winked. "Don't tell him I told you, but he's
newly married. And God help him, for the girl is young."

In the middle of the night Galahad rose from his pallet and searched in the
dark for the wastepot. The candle had long gone out. His head felt heavy
and stuffed with wool. He relieved himself and was feeling along the wall
with one hand to guide himself back to bed when he pushed against the
door accidentally and it swung open into the corridor. The torches were still
lit. As he looked out he saw a girl come up the stair, carrying a pitcher. She
was small-boned and slender, wrapped in a robe of white wool, with fine
tresses of spun gold cascading over her slim shoulders and down her back.
She looked up suddenly and met his gaze directly before she flashed him a
quick smile and ducked into the doorway on the opposite side of the hall.

Honey-colored eyes. Hair of spun gold. Galahad stood rooted, his mind
spinning dazedly. Where the certainty came from he did not know, but
he would have wagered his horse and his sword that he had just seen Lady
Elinor, Princess of Rheged, taking a pitcher of mead to the master of Castle Noir.

20 ✠ THE CUP OF MAXIMUS

When Galahad awoke the next morning he found himself in a large bed hung with crimson hangings and covered with a blanket of stitched ermine pelts. He ran his hand over the furs in disbelief. He did not remember seeing these luxurious trappings when the servant had led him upstairs last night. He did not remember anything beyond the grateful dark and the delicious plummet into senselessness. He looked around him now like a stranger awakening in a foreign land.

Rich tapestries hung from the walls, and mats of intricately woven reeds dyed green, gold, and blue adorned the tiled floor. Four large clothes chests, all beautifully carved and polished, stood against the walls. Four chests! He slid cautiously out of bed and counted them again. He had never heard of anyone owning four clothes chests. Not even Queen Guinevere in Camelot had had so many. Two double-flamed lamps flanked the bed, and a tall mirror of polished bronze rested on its tilted stand near three narrow windows.

Galahad moved tentatively toward the windows and jumped as his reflection flashed back at him from the bronze. Then he stared, lured by the fascination of the image he had never seen.

He saw a tall, naked youth, well made and lean, with long arms and shoulders beginning to broaden into a man's strength. The face was slender, with fine-boned, regular features set off by a fall of shining, coal-black hair. But the beauty of the face was marred by the fierce gaze of startlingly intense blue eyes. He frowned, and immediately stepped back. The youth in the bronze glared at him, the brilliant eyes ferociously afire. In spite of himself, Galahad's heart pounded in his chest. He turned away quickly and forced himself to take slow, deep breaths. With such a face as that, how had he ever befriended Percival? How had he ever befriended anyone at all?

Bread still warm from the ovens, fruit, water, and wine waited on a tray at the foot of his bed. His tunic had been shaken out, his boots cleaned and oiled, and his sword and dagger, burnished to gleaming point, lay in easy reach of the bed. Galahad ran a slow hand through his hair. He did not remember undressing. He did not remember any servants but the one who had led him to his door. Except . . . had he not seen a girl come up the stairs? Or had he dreamed it?

He dressed quickly, strapped on his swordbelt, took up his dagger, and went out into the corridor. He stopped before the only other door, ornately carved with winged lions and unicorns, and knocked firmly.

"Enter!"

He pushed open the door. Sir Brastias sat at an immense table littered with scrolls and odd-shaped objects, his head bent over a clay tablet. At his feet a spotted hound regarded Galahad with the calm assurance of one who knows he is master of the meeting. Opposite the door a pair of windows gave a fine view of the valley. Even as he watched, clouds piled high over the western mountains and swung slowly eastward toward the young sun, throwing the shining lake in shadow.

"Sir Brastias."

Sir Brastias raised his head from his work and watched him gravely. "Come in, my lord; come all the way in. I have been expecting you."

Among the odd objects on the desk was a milk-white sphere half-covered by an ornately embroidered doeskin bag.

Sir Brastias followed his gaze and smiled. "Not by divination, Galahad. By logic. You have come to question me about the girl you saw in the corridor last night."

Galahad nodded. "Indeed, my lord, I have. If she was real and not a dream."

Sir Brastias smiled lightly. "Oh, she was certainly real. But let that wait for a moment. I neglect my duties as a host. How did you sleep last night?"

"My lord, like a felled tree. I confess when I awoke this morning I hardly knew where I was—such a richly appointed room! Do you treat all your guests to such splendor?"

Brastias laughed. "Would that I could afford to! No, that is my room you slept in. I fear you will find that your companions fared less well in the old soldiers' barracks."

"Your room!"

Sir Brastias bowed. "You are my honored guest. I take no responsibility for the furnishings, however. Blame my wife for that. Women adore such trappings."

"Your wife?" Galahad said in evident relief. "Oh, I see. Then that girl could not be—"

"I meant Kynor's mother." The silver eyes flickered. "My late wife. The lady Aileth." Silence hung in the air between them. "A disappointed woman," Brastias continued evenly. "She was thoroughly aghast when I laid down my arms and retreated to these hills. She wanted a public life, an opportunity to display her status as the wife of a prince of Strathclyde." He paused. "We were not well suited. I gave her a free hand with the furnishing of Castle Noir, except for this room, which is mine. You can see well enough what she has done with it."

"It is very fine." Galahad paused.

"Far finer than it needs to be." Brastias beckoned him closer to the desk. "Come, Galahad, let me show you what I've been working on. You will find it interesting, I think."

Galahad gazed down at tablets and parchments covered with numbers and lines, indecipherable pictures and symbols, all drawn in a firm, knowing hand. Brastias was telling him how he had diverted the stream that fed the lake to run through the castle grounds in order to make fetching water easier, but now he wished to devise a means of getting the water uphill from the streambed into the house without the physical labor of carrying buckets.

Galahad's head spun. For a heartbeat he was back in Dane's cave, confronted by an intelligence that dwarfed his own.

"Because there are so few of us here," Sir Brastias was saying, "and there is so much to do. I am always trying to think up new devices to save us time."

Galahad stared down at the maze of scrawl. "What does it mean?"

"Nothing at all," Sir Brastias reassured him, "unless you have studied mathematics. I am a student of Pythagoras the Greek." He gestured at the collection of bronze weights that held the open scrolls in place. "I had these made—the sphere on its stand, the cube, the pyramid—because he is said to have had these in his own study. A little vain of me, no doubt. But they are pure shapes, defined by formulae and pleasing to the eye."

Galahad gazed about the room. It was a plain room and simply furnished, with only the desk and chair and one old, much-mended Roman couch. A harp, a lyre, and a lute leaned together in one corner near an old blue curtain. The wall facing the windows held shelves spilling over with scrolls.

"So many books, Sir Brastias!" Galahad cried, wondering what Dane would think of her own prized collection if she could see this. "Surely you are wealthier than even the King in Camelot!"

Sir Brastias smiled. "Better read, perhaps. It would amaze you how little a book costs, precious as it is, when compared to the cost of keeping a barracks full of knights for one's defense."

"And this is enough to keep you busy?"

Sir Brastias's smile widened. "A young warrior might find it hard to credit, but there is more, much more, to living than killing men in battle. Life is more precious if you have time to study it."

Galahad's brow furrowed. "That's all you do, then? Study and think?"

"Not quite all." The silver eyes narrowed in amusement.

Color washed Galahad's face. "Of course. Last night Kynor told me you were newly married."

Sir Brastias's lips thinned and his face shuttered closed. "He ought not to have told you that." He turned away and walked to the window. "It was the wine's doing, and I must blame myself for that. I served it."

"The girl I saw last night, who came in here. She is your new wife?"

Sir Brastias turned back. His eyes were as dark as the storm clouds behind him. "She is," he said firmly, with a lift of the chin.

"She is the King of Rheged's sister, is she not?"

The storm-flecked eyes went flat and still. "And what, Prince of Lanascol, gives you the right to ask me that?"

"You must know her brother is looking for her. You must take her back to him."

"Nonsense," Brastias snapped. "Who are you to tell me what I must do?"

"You yourself called me the Knight of the Shield. It is not an appellation I asked for."

After a long pause, Brastias nodded. "You *are* the Knight of the Shield. How can you doubt it when your sword carries the same emblem? Very well, truth dealer. If you want truth, you shall have it. But I must have her permission first."

He strode across the room to the blue curtain and pulled it aside, revealing an alcove with a plump pallet strewn with furs and blankets. In the middle of the furs sat the golden-haired girl, wrapped in a bleached robe, her bright hair falling arrow-straight over her shoulders. Sir Brastias reached down a hand to her; she took it and nimbly rose. Standing beside him, the top of her golden head no higher than his breast, her youth a vibrant aura that made his craggy warrior's face look suddenly tired and old, she could have been his daughter, or even his granddaughter, but certainly not his wife.

"Elinor, this is Galahad of Lanascol, Sir Lancelot's son. Galahad, my wife, Elinor."

"Of Rheged," she added defiantly, making a small reverence.

Galahad bowed. "Lady Elinor. I am glad to find you safe."

The honey-colored eyes fastened on him. She tossed back her hair with an arrogant shake of her head. "I would never have been safe if I had not made it here."

"I think," Brastias said gently, "we had better tell him the whole story, don't you, my dear?"

She shrugged, the delicate gesture enhancing her look of fragility. "As you will."

"You must know your life is forfeit, my lord," Galahad blurted. "All Rheged is in turmoil. King Rydor has sworn openly to kill the man who took his sister from him."

The mirror eyes glittered. "Rydor is a fool. He himself drove her away."

"He would have married me to a pox-ridden goat!" the girl cried. "Or thrown away my future to a house of holy hags—death, either way! That is the choice my loving brother gave me."

"Be it so—he has men looking for her everywhere. Rydor gives out she was abducted, but some believe she ran off to join a lover." He swallowed in a dry throat. "And if that is true, Sir Brastias, you are a dead man. He has publicly offered three talents of gold to the man who brings her back."

"My God!" The girl gasped.

Sir Brastias's features hardened. "And you wish to be that man."

"If you think I want the gold," Galahad said stiffly, "you do not know me. Take her to him yourself."

Sir Brastias returned to his desk and began rolling up his scrolls. A fitful breeze sprang up, ruffling the gray lake waters and whispering among the harp strings.

"I did not marry her for the reasons old men marry children, to recapture my youth, to bask in a young girl's admiration, to indulge an unseemly appetite for youthful love. We were not lovers before I took her to wife. I married her because she fled to me, alone and afraid, and begged my protection. How could I keep such a royal lady under my roof, all alone in this valley, without ruining her name? There was only one way. I gave her mine."

"Do you think it was easy crossing the mountains alone?" the girl demanded. "Do you think I enjoyed it? I nearly died of starvation, having no way to hunt, and too afraid to show myself to ask for food. The Ancients helped me, may the Mother of men bless their spirits forever! They fed me and showed me the path to take. As it was, I was skin and bones when I got here."

"But why here? Surely there were closer places to seek shelter—"

"All in Rheged! All under my brother's thumb!"

"Castle Noir is in Rheged."

"But not a part of Rheged Rydor rules. Sir Brastias is my brother's subject in name only. When Sir Brastias came to Glannaventa last year with his pox-ridden nephew, Kastor, I saw he was a man well respected by all, a man even Rydor bowed to. I thought even then he was a safe harbor I might run to, come the storm."

The steel went out of the old soldier as he gazed at her elfin face. His voice gentled. "You see, Galahad? More a father than a husband. Even so, I am not able to give her up."

"I should say not!" She ran to his side to nestle in the strong crook of his arm. "I am better here than with the holy women who deny themselves innocent comforts for the sake of their male God. Rydor wanted alliance with Strathclyde—and I am wed to a Strathclyde prince. I have not done anything worse to him than he was doing to me!"

Galahad regarded them solemnly. "Then give him this news face-to-face."

Sir Brastias stiffened. "He is a young fool. He will destroy us. He will destroy this place."

Galahad lifted a shoulder. "Perhaps. Perhaps not. I will vouch for you, if you like. But you cannot keep her hidden. You must tell him, because you owe him that. You married her without his leave. It was his right to bestow her where he would."

"Oh!" cried Elinor. "You are so cruel! I pray no woman ever loves you!"

"And if we do not tell him?" Sir Brastias demanded.

"Then I must."

"Serpent! Swine!" the girl said in a hiss.

Galahad flushed, but stood adamant. Sir Brastias twirled his stylus thoughtfully in his fingers. Then he turned to the window and lifted a hand. The dark thunderheads rolled down the valley like cotton boulders. "Do you see that storm, Galahad? I can bring it down upon us in a lightning flash, or I can send it away to spend its fury on the foothills. I can call up the rain, or the mist, and pen you within my doors for as long as I like. Do not take me lightly."

Galahad met his eyes. He knew from his experience before the mirror what his face looked like. "Then call up the water from the streambed into the house, and be done with all your mathematics."

Sir Brastias glowered, and then suddenly laughed. "You have courage, lad, I'll give you that. You are Lancelot all over again. He would stick at nothing to defend a principle. And like him, you are prickly to live with." He sat down on the edge of his desk and narrowed his eyes. "I will set you a puzzle. If you solve it, I promise to take Elinor back to Rydor and ask formally for his blessing. If you fail, you promise to leave this valley and never tell anyone where you have been or what you know. What do you say? Are you a man for a wager?"

"That depends. What is the puzzle?"

Sir Brastias drew a long breath. "In the days of the Emperor Maximus, when Vausanius lived in this valley and the roads were far more passable than they are now, Maximus and his train stopped here on their way across the mountains. Vausanius entertained them for a week. It's true—we found his steward's records in an old clay jar in the wine cellars. They must have had a rollicking good time, for when Maximus departed, he left behind his drinking cup. It might have been a gift, it might have been by accident, but Vausanius kept it. It happened to survive the destruction of his villa, and I have it now."

"The Cup of Maximus!" Galahad said softly.

"Did Sir Ulfin mention it to you? I keep it with the other drinking cups that survived from that Roman household. The puzzle is this: Pick out Maximus's cup from the others. I give you one try. Are you game?"

Galahad glanced from the soldier to the girl and back again. "And if I refuse the challenge?"

"Then," Sir Brastias replied evenly, "I must face you, sword to sword, in the courtyard. One of us must die."

"And in either case," Galahad said slowly, "I will never see the cup." He bowed low. "I accept the challenge, Sir Brastias."

Relief flooded the girl's face. "Thank you, Sir Galahad!"

Brastias led the way to the stone wall beside the blue curtain. For the first time Galahad noticed a tiny crack in the mortar, the telltale outline of a door. Sir Brastias pulled back a block of stone and set his hand to a lever hidden behind it. The stone door pulled outward.

The dark space behind smelled musty with long disuse. Elinor brought a candle and Sir Brastias stepped in front of Galahad. "Follow me."

They stood in a small, cold vault with a wide stone ledge along one wall where fifteen ancient drinking cups were clustered in various stages of deterioration.

"Some of these I found in the rubble of the villa," Sir Brastias said in a hushed voice. "Some belonged to my father, Caw of Strathclyde. One or two I found in mountain caves while sheltering from storms on some hunt or other. For all I know they may be grave gifts. Two I took from a burned-out Saxon camp after battle. Take the candle. I will give you an hour to make your choice."

He took Elinor's hand and walked out into the lighted room behind him.

Galahad gazed in dismay at the assortment of drinking cups. He had hoped beyond hope that he might find the Grail, but none of these cups resembled what he had seen in his dreams. Some were copper, some were pewter, some were horn, some were glazed, baked clay; some were carved of wood, three were silver, one was glass, one was gold. Most bore etchings of some sort, a few were banded in metal, two were pitted with rusted settings where gems had once lain. All of them were speckled with age and fragile. He had no idea how to tell their ages or their styles. A man like Brastias would know what culture had made them, whether they came from the north or the south, from rich kingdoms or hill tribes or invaders. But Galahad had never seen a drinking cup that did not belong to the royal house or to one of Arthur's subjects, and none of these cups looked like any he had ever seen.

He whispered a quick prayer and started by lifting them up to the candle, one by one, to study the etchings on them. The gold cup and one of the silver vessels bore Latin inscriptions in praise of the Emperor Theodosius. Certainly they were old enough to have belonged to Maximus. But they had a formal, ceremonial look and were hardly dented. He doubted they had traveled in any baggage wagon all the way from Wales. He set them aside.

The glass cup had a curved lip, ill formed, and a much-mended handle shaped like a snake. Surely the emperor's workmen could do better work than that. He set it aside with a shiver. The snake made him think of Druids.

The second silver chalice was etched with strange-looking symbols. It was black with age or tarnish or fire, and had held gems once around its base. Galahad shrugged. He did not recognize any of the symbols and there was no way of knowing if they were Welsh, Druid, or Saxon. He discarded the third silver cup and a copper one because they were too small. Made for children, he guessed, or for hillmen.

But the other copper cup, the horn ones, the wooden ones, the clay and pewter—he did not know what to make of them. His palms began to sweat and he placed the candle on the ledge. With great concentration he studied the pictures carved, painted, or etched upon them. Some were done with great skill, some with little; some showed pictures of hunting scenes, of battles, of processions, of crownings, of joyous celebrations. None of them had a maker's mark that meant anything to him.

"It is nearly time," Sir Brastias called.

Galahad jumped. Surely not! He had just begun his examination!

"One moment more!"

Sir Brastias laughed. "Very well. I'm a merciful man."

Galahad's hand shook. He put down the clay vessel so he would not drop it and lifted for the third time a stout, wooden cup, primitively carved. Its wide, deep bowl was banded in rotten silver. It could not possibly be the one he sought—it had a procession of women carved upon the bowl!—but he liked the heft of it in his hand. It gave him something solid to hold on to while he studied the rest.

"Come, my lord Galahad," came Brastias's voice again. "It is time to make your choice."

Galahad swallowed hard. There was nothing for it but to admit defeat or choose blindly. But in the act of putting down the wooden cup to reach for the painted clay, he froze. The shifting candlelight lit the wood from a different angle and suddenly he saw what the women in the procession carried in their hands. The first carried a great sword with a gem in the hilt, the second a spear held balanced in her hand, and the third—he blinked in disbelief—the third woman carried a shallow feasting krater!

His heart pounded like thunder in his ears. Rooted to where he stood and deaf to Sir Brastias's repeated calls, he stared at the cup until he heard the man come up behind him.

"Come, lad. I confess I set you an impossible task, but you agreed to the wager."

Galahad turned, clutching the wooden cup to his breast. "This is the Cup of Maximus," he whispered.

Sir Brastias paled. Awe swept his features and he made the sign against enchantment. "It is indeed. But how did you ever know?"

"Brastias!" the girl cried, hurrying to his side and clutching at his sleeve. "He can't have found it?"

"But he did, my dear. That is the cup."

Her wide, golden eyes turned full upon Galahad. "But how? You told me it was impossible."

"That's something I'd like to know myself. How did you choose it, Galahad? Was it luck?"

Galahad shook his head. The world swam before his eyes and he struggled to bring the pale blurs of their faces into focus. "No. Not luck. I've seen these . . . these treasures the women carry. I've seen them in a dream."

There was a moment of absolute silence. "In a dream?" Sir Brastias murmured. Slowly he slid to one knee and pulled the girl down beside him. "Who are you?"

Galahad shrugged, clutching the cup. "If I knew that," he said softly, "if I only knew that . . ."

Golden-haired Elinor glanced from one to the other. "Does this mean I have to go back to Rydor?"

"Yes, my dear, I'm afraid it does."

"He will never let me leave Glannaventa again!"

Galahad shook himself awake. "He is not in Glannaventa. He's gone north to Dunpeldyr to a meeting of all the northern lords. We'll go north and meet him there."

"We?" Brastias asked quickly. "You will go with us?"

Galahad nodded. "I told you I would. It seems to me that somehow things are falling into place. This is not the Grail I seek, but it might be a token—a sign that the road is straightening itself before me." He extended the cup to Sir Brastias, who rose slowly, and the girl with him. "Tell me, Sir Brastias, do you know if Magnus Maximus was ever in Dunpeldyr?"

"I've no idea. But"—he gestured toward the cup—"you keep that. It isn't mine any longer. You seem to know more about it than I ever could discern with all my arts. How you come by such knowledge I do not know. If it is truly from dreams, then it is from God, and I will not stand in your way."

21 ✝ DUNPELDYR

On a bitter day in late November a small party of horsemen straggled down from the windswept moors to a narrow river and a cold ridge of dark rock bordering the sea. In the east the sky leaned leaden on gray hills, and a cruel, fitful wind hurled biting snow hard against their cheeks. They plodded on, numbed with weariness and cold, until they splashed across a paved ford and topped a rise that gave them, at last, a view of their goal.

Galahad raised his hand and signaled the halt. They huddled close together, the horses haunch against haunch for warmth, in a thin, bare wood of alder and beech. Ahead of them great, forbidding crags rose straight from the valley floor, their summits crowned with blowing mist. On the far horizon the steely waters of the firth frothed white under the wind. Nearer, at the feet of the closest crag, mean wattle huts crouched in abject submission against sheer walls of naked rock. As they watched, strands of mist tore free from the summit and there, a blemish on a blighted landscape, rose the dark fortress of Dunpeldyr.

"A devil's land," Garfalon muttered. "And the devil's own house, so help me God." A squall whipped across the water and up the valley, tearing past the fortress and flinging sleet into their faces. They drew their cloaks tighter.

"Do you think the meeting is still going on?" Percival asked anxiously. "Or did we miss them all when we got lost in the Caledonian forest?"

Galahad shrugged. "It depends on whether they were able to settle their disputes in six weeks' time. Rydor can't have been here much longer than that. In any case, we must go on. We're out of food and water."

"You don't know the northern lords if you think they could settle anything between them in less than half a year," Brastias replied dryly. "They'll all be there."

Galahad nodded and turned in the saddle to look behind him. Lady Elinor still clung to her mare's saddle, although her face was ghostly with fatigue and her lips blue with cold. "Another hour should do it, if Lady Elinor can last."

Elinor lifted her chin proudly. Galahad touched his heels to his stallion's flank and they began the long climb toward the spine of black rock ahead. In the month they had been traveling she had not addressed him once, had not even turned her glance his way except when his back was turned. But her obedience, her silence, her determination to carry the journey through as best she could, impressed him. He knew no woman like her. Once or twice he even imagined he understood what Sir Brastias saw in her.

On the other hand, he was glad to be rid of Marrah. She had opted to stay at Castle Noir with Kynor and keep the place until Sir Brastias should return. He had no doubt she would manage to seduce the young warrior— she had already begun, it seemed to him, before they left—and Sir Brastias might well return to a new family, if not a wedding.

That Sir Brastias would return, he did not doubt, either. Over the past month his respect for the man had grown into admiration. Brastias, in turn, had honored his every wish, had paid him deference he was not due, and had taken pains to give him information about the lords he would meet inside Dunpeldyr, for Brastias had known these men, or their fathers, all his life.

As they rode shivering inside their cloaks in the lee of the crags, Galahad considered the northern lords. First, of course, was Rydor, a young hothead, according to Brastias, who angered easily but cooled and forgave just as swiftly—if the insult did not touch his honor. He was capable of great affection and great bravery, but of great foolhardiness as well.

Kastor of Strathclyde, Brastias's nephew, was a weak man by his uncle's own account, a man of appetites and vices with little stomach for the discipline of war. He had the makings of a cruel man, although he was only twenty. He delighted in women, horses, and dogs and was perfectly willing to send his men to die against the Saxons, so long as he did not need to go himself.

Owaine of Gorre was a forty-year-old veteran of war against the Picts. A tough man, he used men hard and had few friends except among his battle captains. He could be counted on to fight, but only when he could see that fighting lay in Gorre's best interest. He thought of no one outside himself. How Arthur had managed to keep him an ally for twenty years, no one knew.

Talorc of Elmet, who had lost his elder brothers at Autun and his noble father, Drustan, at Camlann, was a clever, agreeable man who saw the sense in uniting against a common foe. Indeed, the Anglii had been at Elmet's throat for nigh on three generations. Talorc was young, but had married well and given Elmet the promise of stability in the wake of his father's death.

Valvan of Lothian, their host at Dunpeldyr, was, in Brastias's opinion, the only truly wicked man among them. Sir Brastias referred to him as "the crab" because he came sideways at everything. He even came sideways at the crown of Lothian, for he had been Lot's distant cousin and inherited the kingship only after all four of Lot's sons had died in Arthur's service. He could be counted on to do and say whatever gained him immediate advantage. His word was so much chaff in the wind, his promises writing in water.

"Why do you think the northern alliance is meeting in Dunpeldyr?"

Brastias had grumbled. "Because Valvan won't go to anyone else's strong-hold. He can't be bothered. If they want his men, they must come to him. He says he's too busy keeping the Picts from his door."

"Might that not be true?" Galahad had asked. "His kingdom lies the farthest north."

Brastias had laughed loud and long at that, and said he would learn soon enough to take the scales from his eyes.

Galahad frowned to himself as he set his stallion up the twisting road to the fortress. They did not sound like the type of men to welcome the intrusion of such an uninvited party as his own. For the thousandth time he wondered if he had been right to force Sir Brastias and the girl to make this journey. Back there in the quiet safety of Castle Noir he had been so certain, but now he began to realize what his certainty might cost. The girl might die of the hardship and Sir Brastias would be his enemy forever, and Rheged's as well, if she did. Britain, Arthur had always said, could not afford enemies among her own kings, or they might wake one day to find Saxon fangs in their throats. Death, the death of many, hung on his decision, and now, in the cold sea wind and fading light under the walls of the dismal fortress, the deadweight of uncertainty and self-doubt dragged at his heart.

"Ho! You there! Declare yourself!"

Galahad jerked upright to face a ruddy-complexioned, ill-tempered outpost guard. "We come in peace."

Cold light eyes met his. "State your name and business or I'll cut you down where you stand."

Sir Brastias rode forward to Galahad's side. "I pray you, my lord," he murmured, "say nothing to him about our true business here. If you do, Valvan will cut us down, as this man threatens, and claim the gold himself."

"What shall I tell him, then?"

"Tell him . . . tell him you are the Knight of the Shield."

Something glittered behind Brastias's eyes, but in the dimming light Galahad could not guess what. He turned back to the guard. "Go to your master Valvan of Lothian and tell him the Knight of the Shield begs entrance."

The guard gasped. "*What!* What sort of nonsense is that? You . . . you are no Faerie knight—"

Galahad shifted the white shield into the guard's view. His eyes blazed. "Go. Tell him. Or it shall fare the worse for all of you."

The guard's jaw dropped. He made the sign against enchantment before his face, turned, and ran uphill to the gate as if pursued by demons.

Percival whistled softly. "I don't know if I'd have said *that*. That's as good as a challenge."

"Yes," Sir Brastias agreed in satisfaction. "Now the fur will fly."

* * *

Valvan of Lothian sat in the middle of the long table at the end of his drinking hall. His quick, dark eyes darted among the gathered lords, drunk, all of them, except for Talorc. His own men crouched around the log fire in the center of the smoky hall, muttering among themselves, while the foreign troops slept snoring with the hunting dogs in the rushes on the floor. He had seen to it his own men got heather beer, well watered, while the wine he served his visitors was neat.

With a lift of his hand he signaled to have the food platters taken out and more charcoal added to the braziers around the table.

He rose. "Gentlemen. The time has come to give me your answer to my proposal."

Rydor slammed his goblet on the table. "Wine!" he shouted. "More wine! My throat is dry! Where the devil is the steward?"

Valvan signaled the wine bearer, who rushed to refill his cup.

Kastor sighed. "Talk, talk, talk. What good are words? What have you got tonight, Valvan, for our entertainment? Any more dancing girls?"

Valvan smiled, showing small, even teeth. "After what you did to them last night, my lord, they can hardly walk, never mind dance. I'm afraid you will have to give them a day or two to recover."

Kastor laughed as he gulped down his wine. Some of it dribbled from the corner of his mouth in a thin, red stream and stained his beard. Valvan shuddered lightly and straightened the already straight folds of his robe with a delicate hand.

Owaine looked up blearily, but when he spoke his voice was perfectly clear. "A pox on your proposal. It strengthens you at our expense. We'd be fools to agree to it."

"You would cut all ties with the southern kings," Talorc pointed out, "which splits Britain in twain, a fate Arthur spent his life trying to avoid. We are stronger with those alliances than without them."

"What have the kings of Logris, or Cornwall, or Dumnonia, or Wales ever done for us?" Valvan countered softly. "They want *our* assistance. We don't need theirs. We've kept the Picts, the Anglii, and the Saxons at bay for over a hundred years. Why should we send our troops south to fight against longboats in Cornwall? It only weakens us here. What need have we of such alliance? Let them build up their own defenses, as we have, if they wish to remain unconquered."

"Oh, aye," Rydor added wearily, "and form a new alliance, with you as High King of the North. I'm better off now with no High King but Constantine, who's either too busy or too far away to call on me too often. I've a mind that you'd be sending for my men two months out of three, just to have the commanding of them."

Valvan stiffened. "Don't be a fool."

Rydor leaped to his feet, his dagger in his hand. "Who's calling me a fool?"

Valvan's lips parted in a mirthless smile. "Sit down, my lord King of Rheged. Do you have a death wish?" He gestured to the drinking hall, where Valvan's men had sprung to their feet at the threat, each with a weapon to hand. Rydor's men, however, were asleep on the floor. Rydor sheathed his dagger and sat down, grumbling. Valvan rested his hands on the table and leaned forward, gathering all of them with his gaze.

"Listen now and listen well. We have bandied this about for long enough. You have a choice before you. You can be slave dogs of Constantine the Cornishman, who will bleed your kingdoms dry just as Arthur did, with no honor to yourselves but plenty to him. Or you can live independently and alone, without alliance, and be devoured by the Picts, the Anglii, the Gaels, or whoever it is that tests your borders every spring. Or we can band together and form a kingdom of the north. We will be a council, with a king and war leader picked from among ourselves. Let the tribes of the north reclaim our former glory; let us reclaim the power we had before Pendragon! The south of Britain can go to the Saxon dogs, for all I care. I've had a bellyful of southern domination. Constantine has given me his last order. I am my own man from now on." He paused. "Where has your spirit gone? Has Pendragon turned you into bleating sheep? Where is the old conquering spirit of the independent north?"

Talorc rose. "The independent north is dead, and with good reason. Let our own experience be our guide. Together we have withstood the barbarian onslaught—Picts, Anglii, Gael, and Saxon combined. But divided— remember the days before Arthur—under Uther, under Ambrosius, under Vortigern. Remember how we bled and suffered then! We need to unite, yes. Who doubts it? But let our union be larger than five kingdoms of the north. Let us keep our treaties with the south, as our fathers promised. Without southern troops to swell my ranks the Anglii on my borders would have devoured Elmet long ago."

Owaine pushed himself to his feet. "And who would be high king of this new kingdom? I will submit to no man's domination, Valvan, not even yours."

"Well," Kastor drawled, leaning back in his chair and staring insolently at Valvan, "I'm willing to be bought. But it will cost you. Yearly."

Valvan's eyes flickered, but he turned to Rydor.

Rydor sighed deeply. He rose, swaying slightly on his feet. "I'm all for the union of the north. But breaking our ties with the south will make us enemies. I don't see that we gain by making enemies where now we have friends. Lukewarm they may be, but they're allies nonetheless. I'm not sure it's a wise move, Valvan. Not sure at all."

Valvan straightened. "So. That's how it is," he said softly. "A month of talk and all we have to show for it is words."

"The wine's been good," Kastor murmured.

Valvan's quick eyes narrowed. "You leave me with few choices, my friends. What you will not give me, I must take perforce."

"What do you mean?" Talorc asked quickly.

Valvan lifted his shoulders and smiled. "Only this—that what you will not help me do, I will do alone. I should advise you"—his voice softened—"to consider your position." His gaze slid to the wine-drugged troops, to his own guards, armed and ready in the doorways, a gaze that seemed to encompass not only the drinking hall, but the corridors and stairways, the very fortress, the hill it stood on, the land it commanded.

Owaine's chair shot back with a screech as he leaped to his feet. "You are bound by guest law, Valvan! You will protect us, and those who ride with us, while we are in your halls! Or else—"

"Or else?" Valvan's teeth gleamed between his lips. "Are you threatening me, Owaine? Who said you are not safe here? Not I. I merely ask you to consider your position." He lifted a heavily ringed hand and gestured casually to his troops. "Use your eyes."

Owaine's face darkened. "You filthy, serpent-tongued rogue, I'll—"

A guard rushed in at the door and threw himself on his knees before Valvan. "My lord! My lord! Come quickly! There is a stranger at the gate! He has threatened you—me, us, the kingdom—with dire harm if I do not let him in!"

Valvan turned. "A fool with a death wish—who is he?"

"He will not give his name, my lord. He has the eyes of a wildcat! He said to tell you he is the Knight of the Shield!"

For an instant Valvan paled. The other lords stared at him.

"What the hell is that supposed to mean?" Rydor demanded.

"Oh, it's an old legend they tell in the ice-capped hills," Valvan said lightly. "A hero killed before his time walks through the gate of the Otherworld and returns bearing an invincible shield. A white shield—"

"With a red cross," the guard finished wildly. "My lord! My lord! It is the very one! The Spirit King has come for us!"

"Take him away, for God's sake," Valvan said sharply to his captain. "If you can't shut him up, lock him in. I won't have such rumors spreading among the men."

But already they could hear the buzz of low-voiced murmurs from the corridor. The soldiers glanced nervously at one another and made the sign against enchantment behind their backs. Valvan cursed swiftly under his breath. "I'm going down to get a look at this madman. While I'm gone, think about what I've said."

"The hell you are!" Owaine shot back. "You're not leaving without me!

I wouldn't trust you not to slip a knife between my ribs while my back is turned. I'm coming with you."

"And I," replied Rydor and Talorc together.

"Oh, very well," Kastor grumbled. "If *no one's* going to stay."

Snow whipped and whirled in circles in the courtyard, a steady, light snow which curled across the cobbles and licked the walls. From the parapet above the gate Valvan looked out across the broad, encircling ditch to the crest of the road, where a small group of horsemen huddled together. Their faces were indistinguishable but their leader was recognizable nonetheless. On his arm, unmistakable through the blowing snow, was a white shield with a red cross.

"Beckon him to come within shouting distance and ask him what he wants here," Valvan commanded the sentry at his side. He turned to the other kings who had come up behind him. "What do you say, my lords, to a little sport? He looks a likely warrior, whoever he is. Shall we test his strength against ours as the price of entrance?"

"Price of entrance?" Talorc repeated. "And if he loses, you will let those people freeze?"

"They are at my mercy within the walls or without," Valvan snapped. "Their fate is mine."

"If that knight meets whatever test you set him, you will shelter those people within your walls and grant whatever request they have come to ask of you." It was a statement. Valvan saw Talorc's hand drop to his sword hilt and rest there. Behind him Rydor nodded and Owaine grunted in assent. Even Kastor's eye had lit.

Valvan's lips thinned. "I will grant them shelter. I promise nothing beyond that. Here is the test: Let him fight and disarm all five of us with no help from his companions."

"No man can win at five to one!" Rydor cried.

"Except Lancelot," Talorc said softly. "May God preserve him. He did it more than once."

"Let us go out one after the other," Owaine demanded, "and see which of us can disarm him in single combat. Let the strength of our sword arms decide who among us is to be High King of the North." He grinned at Valvan. "I'll go first."

"A decision of such import is better made in the council chamber," Valvan returned icily. "But as for this upstart knight, by all means take him on. One after the other or all together, it matters not to me."

"Upstart!" Talorc exclaimed. "What has he done but ask for shelter?"

"He has threatened me, and I am Lothian." Valvan snarled as he turned to the sentry. "Go on. Ask him to ride to the gate. Alone. Then put our challenge to him. I will tell you what to say."

The black-cloaked knight rode forward, alone, and listened to the sentry. Slowly he lifted his face and looked at the row of kings watching from atop the battlement.

"He's but a youth!" Talorc whispered.

"He rides without a saddle!" Rydor gasped. "Whoever heard of such a thing among warriors? Only farm boys—"

"And Lancelot." Kastor peered through the falling snow at the knight's face. "Lancelot never bothered with a saddle. And never came off his horse."

"Who *is* he?" Owaine demanded. "He can't be Lancelot."

"Ask the fool for his name," Valvan called down to the sentry.

But as he spoke the knight unsheathed his sword, touched the blade to his forehead in salute, whirled his stallion neatly, and cantered back to his companions.

"Now we're for it," Talorc grumbled. "He's accepted."

"What name did he give?" Valvan demanded of the sentry.

The man shook his head. "None, my lord. He said you had not earned the right to know his name."

Color rose to Valvan's face. "No? Let him wait out in the cold until he freezes, the insolent puppy!"

Owaine thumped Valvan hard on the back with his bear-paw of a hand. "Too late for that, fox! You're bound by your own challenge now! I'll go down to my horse. Open the gates when he's ready."

Talorc pointed to the far side of the ditch, where all the knight's companions were gathered around him, gesticulating wildly. "Look. They argue with him. They are friends, then, not troops. He does not command them."

"So much the better for us," Valvan muttered. "When he falls, no one will dare to take his place. Let's see what that oaf from Gorre can make of him."

Owaine charged out the open gate. The knight whirled to face him and shouted to his friends, who cantered a safe distance away and then turned to watch. Owaine's first blow fell on the white shield, and his horse, a heavy, big-footed beast, carried him past the unknown knight for three full strides before he could be slowed and turned. But in that space of time the knight spurred his own horse to Owaine's side and with a well-placed blow, knocked Owaine's shield from his arm. Owaine bellowed and hauled his horse around, slashing wildly with his sword. But the knight had already galloped away and stood waiting at the edge of the ditch ringing the fortress. Owaine gathered his mount under him and charged again. The knight waited, sword held ready, shield up. Owaine raised his sword high over his head and shouted his battle cry. At the last moment the black stallion whirled neatly away. Too late, Owaine saw the gaping ditch and yanked hard on the reins. But the lumbering horse could not pull up on the frozen ground and plunged headlong into the ditch with a screaming whinny. Owaine pitched face-first into the icy dirt. He lay stunned for a moment, struggling for breath, then pushed himself up to look for his sword. He saw, instead, a bright blade inches from his face. He raised his head slowly. The black-cloaked knight stood over him, holding Owaine's sword in his other hand.

"Who are you?"

Owaine spat dirt from his mouth. "Owaine of Gorre, lord. Who are you?"

"A stranger seeking shelter. Why did you attack me?"

Owaine shrugged. "It was Valvan's idea. He thinks you're a spirit from the Otherworld. It's some old legend about a shield. Didn't the guard tell you? You must fight us all to gain entrance."

"I didn't believe him." The knight spoke quietly. "How many more?"

"Four." Owaine looked up into his face for the first time. "Why, you're a beardless boy! I have two sons older than you! How did you defeat me?"

"I have a better horse. Can you stand?"

"Aye." Owaine pushed himself to his knees. Nearby his horse stood, head lowered, on trembling legs.

The knight pointed. "Go take your horse and stand in the lee of the wall. I will leave your weapons in the ditch. When this tyrant's game is over you can return and fetch them yourself."

Owaine nodded. "Better look quick behind you, my lord. That's Rydor of Rheged coming out the gate."

Rydor halted at the edge of the ditch where the riderless black stallion waited, reins dangling. He leaned over, grabbed the reins, and smiled down.

"Yield, stranger! I have your horse."

The knight looked up. "But can you keep him?" He whistled sharply and the stallion jumped. Finding his head restrained, the horse reared and lashed out with his forelegs. Rydor's stallion snorted, screamed, and reared, ears pricked forward, answering the challenge. Rydor clung to his neck and turned him away, but the black's reins slipped out of his hands and the horse slithered down the steep-sided ditch to his master.

Rydor was a brave, forthright fighter but he could not get his sword past the white shield, and he had trouble controlling his stallion, who was more interested in the other stallion than in the battle. As many blows as he withstood himself, he could land none on the other knight. Feeling his horse tire beneath him, Rydor made one last, desperate thrust, only to find his sword wrenched from his hand altogether.

"I yield!" he cried. "Whoever you are, you are a better man than I! Where on earth did you learn to fight like that?"

"In Camelot," replied the knight.

Rydor stared at him, going pale. "They are all dead, who lived in Camelot."

Brilliant blue eyes stared levelly back. "Not all."

Rydor's weapons joined Owaine's in the ditch, and Rydor joined Owaine against the wall. Together they watched Talorc ride out.

Talorc saluted the knight, and instead of charging, engaged him directly. He had seen enough of the horse's ability and the knight's moves to know he was facing a real test of his skill. But he had led the men of Elmet against the Anglii warriors for four years and knew his own strengths well. Patience, endurance, a bold move at an unexpected moment, these were his weapons. He was a thinking fighter; no man who could not overpower him could beat him quickly. All this proved so, and yet as the fight progressed, Talorc discovered that the young knight fought from instinct as much as from brains, had such fluid communication with his horse that he no sooner thought of a maneuver than the horse performed it, and had the ability to create new moves, new strategies, new defenses when the standard ones proved unavailing. Gradually Talorc found that he was losing. He was stronger, and perhaps more patient, but his thoughts moved more slowly than the other's intuition, and he was struck more times than he struck back. At length, when rivulets of sweat dripped from his nose and chin, and his stallion was frothed with sweat and blowing, he raised his hand into the air.

"My lord, I yield. I have given you my best, but you have gotten the better of me today."

He was rewarded with a quick smile. "Had you held on a little longer," the youth said in a gasp, "I must have yielded or died. As it is, I am easy meat for the next man. What a worthy fighter you are, my lord! May I have your name?"

Talorc bowed. "Talorc, son of Drustan. King of Elmet. And yours?"

The knight paused. "I have sworn not to give it to the cowards who make us pay for shelter with blood. How can such a man as you be one of them?"

Talorc's face darkened. "I would sooner cut my throat than be one of them. Yet I have Elmet to think of. Without allies in the north, it may come to throat cutting soon enough."

"I see. And who is this riding out to meet me now?"

"Kastor of Strathclyde. A lazy fellow, but not a stupid one. Be on your guard." Talorc smiled. "I will fling my weapons into the ditch on my way to the wall."

Kastor rode forward and stopped his horse ten paces away. He stared at the weary knight, sheathed his sword, and slid off his horse. He walked to within three paces of the black stallion and stared up into luminous blue eyes.

"Who the hell are you? Are you flesh or spirit?"

"Flesh."

"If you are flesh, then you can die."

"As easily as you."

Kastor's teeth flashed in a brief smile. "We shall see." He made to turn away, then drew his dagger and flung himself toward the horse's belly. The stallion reared, screaming, as the dagger, missing the belly, plunged into the inside of his flank.

"Coward!" the knight yelled. He slid off the horse, whipped out his dagger, and threw it. Kastor caught it with his shield, rolled quickly away, and reached to draw his sword. He froze when he felt the sharp edge of cold steel against his neck. "You filthy coward! I ought to kill you for it!"

Kastor turned slowly and saw fierce blue eyes blinking back tears. He shrugged. "Fair is fair. That horse is a weapon. Like the dagger."

"He's worth a thousand daggers!" the knight whispered. He prodded Kastor's chest with the sword. "Get up. Drop your shield and swordbelt."

Kastor smiled. "Shall I not drop them in the ditch, as Talorc did?"

"You are not the man Talorc is. Leave them at my feet. Who is left inside that blighted fortress? Just Valvan?"

"Just Valvan. King of Lothian. Give some thought to what may happen to you if you harm him. The place is thick with his men."

"I have given a lot of thought to Valvan of Lothian."

Kastor moved off toward the wall, but the gates did not open. The knight went to his stallion, ran a calming hand over the shaking horse, then pulled the dagger from his flesh. The wound bled lightly, but the animal was lame, unable to bear weight on the injured leg. He talked to the horse a moment, cradling the stallion's head in his cloak. Then he drew off his cloak and flung it over the horse's back.

He strode to the gate clad only in his heavy tunic and leggings.

"Valvan!" he shouted. "Come out and meet me, if you dare! I have defeated your champions! You cannot freeze me out without freezing your allies, too. Come spring, the whole north will rise up against Lothian!"

A horn sounded somewhere, and the gates swung open.

Valvan rode out on a proud white horse, regally robed in a crimson cloak with the crown of Lothian around his brow. But he wore no battle dress and carried no weapons. A phalanx of foot soldiers followed him.

"And who are you, to beg entrance uninvited?" he demanded when he had come within a dagger's throw of the young knight. "What do you mean by such effrontery? Why, you're only a boy! Tell me why I should bother to truck with you. I've more than half a mind to throw you in the dungeon."

"Is there no guest law in this country?"

As Galahad spoke, a sudden gust of wind tore across the headland, catching Valvan's cloak and whipping it around his body. His horse squealed and backed, throwing his head up and showing the whites of his eyes. The foot soldiers stared at Galahad as Valvan struggled to control his mount.

"You shall have your night's shelter and your bowl of gruel," Valvan snapped, "when you tell me what I wish to know. We are too near Pictish lands to trust strangers. Who are you, and why are you here?"

Snow whirled between them, shedding silence. Sir Brastias slid off his horse, pulled his hood close around his face, and walked quietly forward to gather up the black stallion's reins. His face shielded by the horse, he approached Galahad.

"Say nothing to him, my lord. Lift up your shield arm, that his soldiers may see the device."

Galahad obeyed. The men in the front line of the phalanx gaped openly. A low murmur went through the ranks like wind through a wheat field. One by one, and then by twos and threes, the soldiers laid their weapons down and sank to their knees.

Valvan cursed and threatened, gesticulating wildly, but his men paid no attention. They stared at Galahad in dumb and fascinated awe.

Owaine strode forward. "Honored knight, Spirit King or man of flesh and blood, we welcome you to Dunpeldyr on behalf of our host, who would invite you in himself if he could catch his breath." He glared at Valvan as the King of Lothian began to protest. "Consider your position, my lord. Use your eyes."

"Yes, come in with us," seconded Talorc, "and the rest of your party, too. That horse needs tending and you all must be frozen from the cold."

Galahad nodded silently and gestured to his companions. With Owaine and Talorc at the head of the procession, they walked right past Valvan and his troops into the fortress.

22 ✠ THE SCABBARD

Whispers ran like wildfire through Dunpeldyr. Soldiers and courtiers peered around corners to get a glimpse of Galahad. Servants shrank and trembled as he passed by. He and Percival were given rooms in the part of the fortress built from stone—not quarried, square-cut Roman stone, but piled boulders cemented with wattle and supported by beams in the round, uneven style of northern builders more ancient than the Romans. When they were shown into a large, round chamber with a newly lit brazier, their chamberlain quaked so badly he leaned against the doorjamb for support and was glad to be told they needed nothing beyond hot water and fire.

"Thank God!" Percival exclaimed, extending his hands to warm over the log blaze. "I thought they'd never let us in! I can't feel my fingers or my toes. However did you fight them all in this bitter cold?"

"Fighting's warm work."

"Thank you, cousin, for taking it upon yourself to pay the price of entrance. Who does this selfish tyrant think he is?"

"You owe me nothing. Rouk paid, not I."

Percival laid a hand on Galahad's shoulder. "He'll recover. Didn't you hear the stablemaster? It's not so deep. All it needs is a month or so."

Galahad nodded glumly, dropping his bedroll on a plump pallet near the fire. "I will see to it myself. But first, there is business even more important to attend to."

"Ah, yes!" Percival rubbed his hands together. "The feast in your honor! I'm as hungry as a bear in springtime. I'd have settled for dinner, or the promised bowl of gruel, but now there's to be a feast!"

Galahad scowled. "I don't mean the feast." He changed his tunic and leggings for a cleaner pair and buckled on his swordbelt. "Hurry, Percival. We must take Sir Brastias and Lady Elinor to Rydor before the feast begins."

With Brastias, Elinor, and Percival behind him, Galahad followed the servant to Rydor's door. They were shown into an anteroom where a sulky coal fire smoked in the brazier and a pair of spotted hounds lay curled in its circle of warmth. The dogs leaped up as they entered, stiff-legged, showing fangs. Then one of them began to wag its tail; in an instant they were writhing about Elinor in a riot of delight, whining for pardon and pawing eagerly at her cloak. Rydor's attendant opened the inner door.

"The Knight of the Shield, my lord. With his companions."

Rydor came out at once. He was richly dressed with plenty of gold showing at his shoulder, wrists, and waist, and a magnificent silver torque about his neck.

"My lord king." Galahad bowed low.

"Sir." Rydor returned the reverence. He snapped his fingers sharply. "Hawk! Fang! Here!" Obediently, the dogs skulked to his side.

Galahad drew a deep breath and introduced himself and Percival. "We have come about your sister," he finished.

"What?" Rydor cried, paling. "Have you news of her? Does she live? Tell her all is forgiven, if only she lives!"

"Your sister lives," Galahad said quietly. "She has been in the protection of a wise man, and a brave one." He stepped aside and gestured to those behind him. "He will tell you himself."

Rydor looked eagerly at the two hooded figures who had not been introduced. Sir Brastias flung back his hood and bowed.

"Brastias!"

The smaller figure hesitated, then broke into a run and threw herself into Rydor's arms, much to the dogs' delight. They danced and whined around the embracing pair as the King of Rheged wept openly, kissing the girl and hugging her close. "Thank God! Thank God! I was a fool, Elinor! Say you'll forgive me! You needn't marry—but don't leave me anymore!"

"No, brother, no—it was wrong of me to run off, but I couldn't help it! I saw only two paths to take, but had I stopped to consider, I would have seen there was a better way. I would never have hurt you, Ry, but you treated me so cruelly!"

"I did," he owned. "I know it. But, Elinor, I have suffered dreadfully on account of it. I have thought you dead these many months, and as good as by my hand. Say you will come back to Glannaventa with me when we are finished here, and live peaceably at home again."

Elinor pulled away from him and lifted a hand to his face, the hand with Brastias's golden ring shining on her finger. "Alas, brother, I cannot. For when I left you I took a husband."

Rydor grabbed her hand and stiffened. "What? Without my leave?" His face darkened. "Where is he? Brastias, what do you know of this? Who is the lad? Can he be bought off?"

Elinor clung to her brother's cloak. "Rydor, Rydor, have you learned nothing? It was a wedding of my choosing! We can never go back to what we were, you and I. But you must accept my husband, or it *will* be the death of me!"

"Accept your husband?" Rydor cried. "When you have never asked my leave?"

"I ask it now!"

Sir Brastias stepped forward and bent his knee to the ground. "My lord Rydor," he said firmly. "I am the one she begs you to accept. She ran to me for shelter and for comfort, and I married her."

Rydor gaped. *"You?"*

With a lift of her chin, Elinor moved to Sir Brastias's side and took his hand. "Sir Brastias is my husband. We have come to ask your blessing."

"Brastias?" Rydor roared. "It's Brastias you ran to? Why, in God's name?"

"Because I love him," Elinor shot back, coloring brightly. "He's been a better friend to me than anyone in Glannaventa, including you!"

Rydor stared from one to the other. The two hounds planted themselves between the couple, panting joyfully. At last the king lifted his shoulders. "Well, well. What's done is done. You are alive and well, and it could have been much worse. Brastias is an honorable man. I have no quarrel with him. It's just that . . . my own sister . . . why didn't you ask my leave?"

"Would you have granted it?"

Rydor grunted. For answer, he reached out and grasped Brastias's arm in the soldier's embrace. "Welcome, Brastias. It seems we are brothers now."

Brastias cleared his throat gruffly. "Indeed, my lord. But there is a small matter still unsettled. A small matter of three talents of gold."

Rydor froze and color washed his face. "So that's it! You wanted my gold!"

"No, no, you have it wrong. You owe it to Galahad, not me. I would have stayed in Castle Noir, warm, safe, and silent, but for him. He is the real reason we are here."

Rydor turned slowly to Galahad. "Is this true?"

"It is true I persuaded them to come and ask your blessing."

"To get my gold? And you a son of Lancelot?"

Galahad's hand slid unthinking to his sword hilt. Rydor blanched at the look in the blue eyes. "Then why did you do it? Why bring her all the way here, in winter? A message would have been good enough."

"A message," Galahad replied evenly, "would have dishonored you. And it would not have been enough. You know full well you'd have sent half your army to Castle Noir to get her back."

Rydor shrugged, but Elinor came forward and took his hand. "The truth, Ry. You know you would have."

"All right," Rydor growled. "A promise is a promise. But you must follow me back to Rheged, my lord. I don't travel with three talents of gold."

Galahad bowed. "I don't want your gold, Rydor of Rheged. I want your pledge, instead."

"What pledge is that?"

"A pledge against the future. You owe me a battle. Swear now that you will come when I call, to wherever I need you, without hesitation and without fail."

Rydor laughed. "You may call me to battle anytime you wish! I shall not balk at that. And I will certainly exchange such a promise for three talents of gold. You have my word upon it."

They grasped hands to seal the bargain. "And will you," Galahad continued, "help me extract such a promise from the other kings at this evening's feast? For I defeated them all, except Valvan, and for the moment I am master of his men. They owe me a battle, all of them."

Rydor considered the proposition carefully. "It might be done, at that," he said at last, slinging an arm around Elinor and Brastias. "Come, we shall all go in together. I will show him I support you, and I wager Talorc will, as well. Kastor is Brastias's kinsmen and my neighbor; we will persuade him without much trouble. As for Owaine, he is so delighted a threat to Valvan has suddenly appeared on his own doorstep, I wager he will do whatever you bid him, and with pleasure."

Galahad smiled. "Good. For I've no doubt there will come a time when Britain will need the support of all the men of the north."

* * *

The winter proved a hard one. For week upon week bitter winds blew cold from the north and wet from the east. Blizzard upon blizzard battered the barren land, freezing rivers and blanketing the woodlands in snow the height of a horse. Damp blew off the cold sea into every corner of Dunpeldyr. Within doors tempers flared as personalities, penned within the stronghold in forced inaction, chafed against one another in constant meeting. Although Galahad had procured the promises he sought, most of the northern lords avoided his company. Owaine did little but drink, wrestle, and dice. Kastor spent his time in drink and fornication, tolerating Valvan but openly contemptuous of Rheged. Rydor put this down to wounded pride. Upon learning of Elinor's marriage to Sir Brastias, Kastor had openly sneered, "Well, well, how like her to choose the goat over the ram. An ill-brought-up girl, if I ever met one. It's your doing, Rydor. You always indulged her. Now you've reaped what you've sown. I wish her joy of her bed, much fruit may it bring her."

Rydor colored but held on to his temper. "It is not an ignoble choice. He is a prince of Strathclyde and could have worn your crown had it suited him. He's a good man and a wise one, a veteran of many battles."

"Who has given up war," Kastor added. "For books."

In public conference with the other lords, at dinner, at sword practice, at hunting when the weather allowed, at gaming when it did not, the tension between all the men was kept alive and sharp by Valvan's bitter contempt for them all and his relentless insistence that they accept him as High King of the North. Valvan sought to prove his fitness for this honor by pointing out their own unfitness in great detail. Such insults, however subtly or pointedly made, could not be avenged by open attack, for the undeniable fact remained that all of them were prisoners in Dunpeldyr while winter storms raged across the north, and Valvan's men outnumbered their own by ten to one.

Galahad might have stilled Lothian's tongue, for the aura around him still shone bright in the eyes of Valvan's men, but he spent as little time as possible in the company of the northern kings. For the first month he practically lived in the stables, tending Farouk. The dagger wound was shallow, but it festered, and Galahad nursed the stallion back to health with hot compresses, soaks, and constant walking. Even when the horse was healed, he clung to the stables as to a refuge, and often fell to talking to the grooms and stableboys about the Emperor Maximus. None of them had heard the legends. Their general ignorance led Galahad to conclude that Maximus might well have never traveled this far north, and that neither his treasure nor the third token was likely to be found in Lothian.

Percival spent long days in sword practice, often staggering back to his chamber, exhausted, bruised, and bloodied from repeated blows with blunted weapons, to bathe in a tub of snowmelt and fall into delicious sleep. He grew slowly tougher, hardier, more skilled. He found in Garfalon the perfect companion to help him sharpen his fighting skills, and Garfalon found the king's son eager to learn all he could about everything from fighting to hunting to woodlore to dressing wounds. Through Percival, Galahad learned of Garfalon's longing to rejoin Rheged's forces. Galahad spoke to the king on his behalf, and Rydor willingly granted his request. Garfalon was so ecstatic at the news he threw himself to the floor and kissed Galahad's boots, much to the boy's dismay and Percival's amusement.

At night, in their bedrolls around the peat fire, they talked of the day's events, where they might go, come spring, and what the third token might be. This was Percival's favorite subject.

"You've found two of them, for certain," he would begin. "The shield was forged in a smithy's fire, and it's crossed, and you found it in shadow. And the cup, although it doesn't look like much now, it must have been used for feasting, and the wine it held made the emperor merry. And you found it in darkness."

"Darkness bright," Galahad corrected. "I had a candle."

"Yes. So that's two of them. I wonder what the third could be? I can't imagine what could be both empty and used for fighting, can you? And if you're going to find it in daylight we might have to wait for spring. I've never seen such a gloomy place as Dunpeldyr in all my life!"

"Which"—Galahad smiled—"covers so many years."

They spoke of where they should go when spring made the roads passable.

"We'll put ourselves in the flow of events," Galahad decided. "As the smith advised. That's what we've done so far, and every place we've been has led us somewhere else."

"And at each place we've found a token. At this rate we'll find the third token and receive the sign of success before the summer solstice!"

Galahad shuddered. "I almost hope not."

"Why not, for heaven's sake? You'd be halfway to your goal."

"You forget what follows the finding of the tokens."

Percival propped himself up on one elbow and grinned. "Ah, yes. Kneeling before women." In the low light of the fire he could just make out Galahad's dark head, the liquid glimmer of open eyes gazing at the ceiling. "I wish I could do it for you. I think women are wonderful. All of them. They're not without courage or sense. Look at Marrah; look at Lady Elinor. Brave, courageous in loneliness, loving and kind. They're the equal of men, most of them, although we don't give them credit for it."

The glimmering eyes turned toward him. Even in the dark Percival could see their blue blaze. "What utter nonsense, Percival. You're deluded by their charm, which is just what they intend. Marrah brave? It was her scream that drew her father from the river when the bandits attacked. Had she been brave, she'd have sacrificed herself in silence and so saved his life."

"But then those ruffians would still be a living menace and you wouldn't have found the shield."

Galahad shrugged. "As for Lady Elinor—she has borne much discomfort, that is true. But she ought to have obeyed her brother's wishes. Instead, she's put him and his soldiers through months of distress and she's completely disrupted Sir Brastias's life."

"I don't hear him complaining about it. Would you really have married that girl to Kastor? Ugh! She's better off with Sir Brastias, and he with her."

"My point is, women have the power to manipulate men. They glory in that power. The more highborn and beautiful they are, the more deftly they control us. Even the strongest men are no more than puppets to them. Look what Guinevere did to Arthur. He was never able to put her away, a courageous man like that! They're all capable of the grossest deception. Lying's as easy as breathing to them. You will never get anything straight out of a woman. I promise you this, Percival: I will never succumb to the power of women. They may lie and weave their intrigues all about me, but it will avail them nothing."

"Never is a long time, cousin. Someday you, too, will be moved by love."

"No. When we desire them, we give them power over us. I will not allow that to happen."

Percival laughed merrily. "Easy to say when you've not yet met the woman who'll drive you mad, but you will. And I can hardly wait to see the day!"

Galahad shivered. He remembered the day in Brittany when he had felt the first stirrings of desire, had tasted madness. "Then you will wait forever."

Winter blustered into spring with no diminution of cold or violent wind. But the day of the equinox broke clear and still without a tremor of moving air. To ears so long accustomed to the roaring of the wind, the sudden silence was deafening. By midmorning a mild breeze from the southwest started icicles dripping from the eaves and cheering echoed across the snow-swept ridge of rock.

On his way back from the stables Galahad met Sir Brastias in the corridor. That noble knight, who had spent the winter snugged down with his bride or bent over his scrolls, looked suddenly ten years younger. His step was springy, his color fresh, his smile benevolent.

"Well, well, Knight of the Shield! Good day to you. Your handsome horse must be quite recovered now."

"Yes, thank you, Sir Brastias. He is. I don't need to ask how you do. Yours is the only even temperament in all of Dunpeldyr."

Brastias laughed and slung an arm around his shoulders. "I'm a young man today, Galahad! You're a man of discretion—I'll tell you why. My lovely wife has just told me she's with child! My child, Galahad! Can you imagine it? I feel like an emperor this morning!"

Galahad congratulated him because he obviously expected congratulations, but he did not understand the older man's joy. He wondered what Kynor would think of it.

"Come with me," Brastias said suddenly. "I'll show you a room of wonders, right here in Dunpeldyr." He began walking toward a spiral stair at the end of the passage, pulling Galahad along with him. "Valvan gave me the keys to this room during the first snowstorm. Why he keeps it locked is beyond me, but without books I promise you I should have gone mad cooped up here this long winter."

"Valvan has books?"

Brastias laughed. "I was surprised, too. He has no use for them, of course. He believes everything he needs to know he can learn by doing himself. When he took over Dunpeldyr he piled all the books and old belongings of his predecessors into this one storeroom, locked it shut, and forgot about it."

They came to a small, curved door halfway up the tower and Brastias struggled with a great iron key. "There's a lot of junk," he said, pushing the door open and beckoning Galahad to precede him, "but some of the scrolls are priceless. He told me to help myself to whatever was here. Perhaps you'd like to do the same." He smiled again, that wide smile of joy. "It's a day for sharing."

The room was small, with curved walls and a round window facing east. The morning sun, still low in the sky, lit the small space like a beacon. Every dust mote, every cobweb stood out in bright detail. Trunks, boxes, sacks, and piles of junk lay everywhere. Dust lay thinnest on two old trunks closest to the door, and it was to these that Brastias led him.

"See?" He lifted the lid of the nearest one. "All the classics are here! Virgil, Ovid, Tacitus, Cicero, Herodotus, Homer, Plato, to name just a few. Histories, metaphysics, poetry, politics, books on healing, on magic, on mathematics! With these added to my library at Castle Noir I shall be the wealthiest man in all Britain!"

Galahad surveyed the piles of discarded boots, coils of rotting rope, rusted weapons, and broken crockery that littered the floor. He moved closer to the window, peered into a loosely bound sack, saw only a bundle of old, stained clothes, and knelt down to a small chest which lay full in a shaft of sunlight. Besides being smaller than the others, this chest was bound with an iron strap etched with strange runes along the top, and locked. "What's in here?"

"That? I don't know. I haven't gotten that far. It's taken all winter just to read my way through these. Go on and open it up. Perhaps there'll be some clue to its owner. For the life of me I can't imagine who collected this treasure. None of the kings of Lothian in my lifetime has even been able to read. Nor did they employ scholars. Use your dagger. I tell you, Valvan has no interest in any of these things."

The lock was brittle with age and rust, and yielded to the persistent pressure of Galahad's dagger. Sir Brastias came over as he swung the lid up and peered inside. There appeared to be only one object within, wrapped in oilcloth: a thick collection of parchments, cut square and pressed flat between two heavy squares of leather, all of it sewn together along one side so that everything lifted out as one.

Brastias took it gently from Galahad's hand. He lifted one edge of the leather cover and fingered the separate pages with great care.

"What is it?" Galahad wondered.

"I don't know. But look! There's writing on every parchment. It's a woman's hand, I believe. These are recipes, yes, and chants. Directions for . . ." Brastias looked up, and his voice rose in pitch. "These are spells! My God, Galahad, this is the property of an enchantress! Do you know what that means? There was ever only one witch in Lothian worth the name, and she'd have had access to the king's house—Morgause, King Lot's wife. King Arthur's sister!" He began thumbing through the pages, reading quickly. "Most of it's in Latin, but some of it's in a tongue I do not know. Aye, here's the spell against seasickness. That's fairly harmless."

"Will you add it to your library?"

Sir Brastias shuddered. "Heavens, no. Morgause was a mistress of the black arts. I'm not interested in her kind of power."

Galahad turned back to the chest. It was not empty, after all. Something long and dark lay at the bottom. He lifted it out carefully. It was an ancient leather scabbard, cracked and dry, the stitching that held it together half rotted away. But as he held it across his hands in the brilliant light, a queer feeling of awe stole over him and he sat back on his heels, staring at it.

"Look at this," Brastias said softly, absorbed in his reading. He pointed to a scrawled verse beneath a set of symbols. "This is her curse for barrenness. Look at the name at the bottom. It's for Queen Guinevere." His voice began to tremble. "Is it possible the Witch of Lothian was responsible for that poor woman's fate? It makes sense, doesn't it? Since Queen Guinevere bore the King no children, he made Mordred his heir. Mordred, his only son, who was his doom. Mordred the bastard, begot on Morgause herself. She stood to gain so much if Guinevere did not bear! My God, Galahad! Do you see what this means? We have uncovered the root cause of the whole disaster."

But Galahad did not hear him. His head was spinning with rhymes and his eyes could see nothing but blazing light. *One is empty . . . One for fighting . . . In shadow, in light . . .* The thing in his hands was empty, but he could almost feel the weight of the living blade it had sheathed and protected for so many years.

"Sir Brastias." Galahad looked up, dazed. "What do you know about the King's sword, Excalibur?"

He did not speak loudly but something in his voice stopped Sir Brastias cold at the height of his excitement.

"That it was Maximus's sword which Merlin found for Arthur and fixed in the stone of Lludyn's Hill by magic arts so that none but he who was rightwise born King of all the Britons could pull it out. Also, that it disappeared at Arthur's death."

Galahad nodded slowly. "And what do you know of the scabbard which held it?"

"Why, that it was made for the sword by the Ancients themselves, who were on friendly terms with Maximus then. They wove their power into it, and so long as the king wore it, no blade could touch him in battle. Had Maximus taken it with him to Rome, he might have triumphed, who knows? But he was drunk on his own successes by that time and had a jeweled scabbard made to take on that campaign."

"What happened to the old one?"

"It was buried with the sword, I believe. And raised with the sword from the stone. Arthur wore it during the Saxon wars. But afterward, in the years of peace . . ." Brastias stared at him blankly. "I've no idea. I'm not sure anyone knows. It just disappeared."

Galahad lifted up his hands so he could see the cracked leather sheath. "This is it."

Brastias opened his mouth to protest, then came closer and peered at the leather. Symbols had been burned into the scabbard along its length. Even in the strong light they were barely discernible.

"Runes!" he whispered. "Wait . . . let me see . . . this one is for strength . . . here is eternity . . . faith . . . kingship . . . protection . . . and here, my God, here it is: 'To the One Unconquered'." He stared at Galahad. "That was Arthur's epithet. He was the only unconquered king."

Galahad nodded.

"Of course!" Sir Brastias cried. "His witch-sister stole it from him. Should he fall in battle, her son would become High King. And she so nearly succeeded, for Arthur didn't have it to take to Autun against the Romans!"

Sir Brastias trembled violently, but Galahad was filled with a serene calm. He rose, holding the scabbard carefully.

"I have found what I came to Dunpeldyr to find."

23 ✝ DINAS BRENIN

Lady Niniane, Queen of the River Isles and former high priestess of Avalon, once the most powerful woman in Britain during her years as King Arthur's chief advisor and Lady of the Lake, paced back and forth across her chamber in ill-controlled impatience. Her pale face still retained the lineaments of beauty. Her dark hair showed not a single strand of gray. Her bearing had lost none of its arrogance, her personality none of its force. She paused once in her pacing to pick up the bright green crystal on her worktable, polish one of its facets, and set it impatiently down.

"Where is that good-for-nothing dwarf? What *can* be taking him so long? Hurry, Naceyn! They are coming and we must be ready for them!"

She strode to the window and gazed out at the river, swollen and churning brown with the spring flood. They were coming, those two wandering boys; they were nearly within the reach of her power. She resisted the temptation to go down to the still pool and call up their images once more. They couldn't be more than ten leagues closer than they had been at dawn, when she had seen them last. In another five days, if they kept heading west, they'd be in Guent and within her grasp at last. Three years! What in the Goddess's name could they have been doing for three interminable years so far from Wales? What could have driven that tormented son of Lancelot out of Gwynedd without her knowing? She smiled bitterly. Time was, her power could have reached across the length of Britain to find him and draw him back.

Angrily she turned and strode back across the chamber, nearly colliding with a small, squat figure who came in at the door. "Naceyn!"

The dwarf bowed low. "Lady Niniane. Your servant."

"It's about time. What kept you?"

"Beg pardon, lady. I came as swiftly as I could." The little man had silver hair and a silver beard, and blue eyes made for laughter. But he did not laugh now. He kept his large head demurely bowed and watched her from the corners of his eyes. She was always chancy to cross, but in these moods even her smiles were dangerous.

"I sent for you because the time is upon us—nearly past, unless your donkey has wings. Galahad and Percival are in Logris and heading west. In five days they'll be here."

Naceyn's silver eyebrows shot up. "*Here*, my lady?"

"Don't be ridiculous! Galahad would never come *here* of his own will. That's why I need you: to bring him here. In five days they'll be in Guent. I believe they're headed for Gwynedd, but I will direct them to Dinas Brenin. Do you know the place?"

"Aye, lady. I was born there."

"Were you, indeed? Born in the Wolf's lair?"

"Near enough. But no one remembers old Vortigern now."

A glimmer of a smile touched Niniane's lips and her voice softened a trifle. "Vortigern's ruined stronghold is a perfect place for your meeting. It was no coincidence I chose it."

She turned to her worktable and picked up a small linen bag bound with a black cord. "You will leave at once for Dinas Brenin. You must get there before them. Build yourself shelter. Pretend it's your home." She placed the bag in his hand. "Put this in their food. It will prepare them for the dreams I will send them, and in the morning they will part. Let Percival go home to Gwynedd. Bring Galahad to me."

"On what pretense?"

"He is looking for some sort of sign. That is all I have been able to discover." She laughed. "What imbeciles they are! They have been three years looking for a sign, but have they once gone to a wise woman or a seer? No. They have been to Elmet, and York, and Logris, fighting Saxons, Anglii, and bandits. There's no apparent pattern to their wanderings. They befriend kings and fight for them. When the slaughter is over, they move on." She paused and her eyes grew brittle. "Time was, I could have closed my eyes and seen into their minds. Or looked into a candle flame and told their future . . . Bring Galahad to me, Naceyn, and I will show him such a sign he'll be back on his quest like a dog after a sausage."

She laughed suddenly, a buoyant laugh Naceyn had not heard in years. "We are almost there, Naceyn! We are so close, at long last! How wise I was to have Arthur nurture the boy's thirst for glory! A word whispered here and there, a hint, a suggestion, and then, when Arthur sent him to me at Avalon and I had him under my roof, a powerful dream to send him mad with ambition! I will drive him to his destiny, Naceyn. I will do all but lead him to the Grail. And when he finds it"—her eyes widened, although she stared at nothing—"then all Britain will be in my debt. Forever."

"You foretold his destiny, as I remember," Naceyn murmured. "At the Sacred Speaking. Or was that not the Goddess, but your own invention?"

A shadow passed across Niniane's face. "Of course that was not my own invention. What She prophesied for Galahad will no doubt come to pass. But She said nothing about the Grail of Maximus. I am the one who discovered how his destiny was to be fulfilled." She frowned at the dwarf. "Do you doubt me? Believe me, Naceyn, I have seen farther into the future than even Merlin. There is more at stake here than defeating the Saxon kings. Britain's very future hangs in the balance. If we succeed, we preserve our homeland for eternity. If we fail, she goes down into the savage dark and all our names will be forgotten, even Arthur's. For time without end."

Naceyn bowed low. He tucked the linen bag into his tunic and put his hand to the door. "Then the sooner I am off, the better our chance for success."

Niniane watched him go. She picked up the emerald crystal from her worktable, held it up to the window, and saw the river outside roaring by, yellow-green, the color of oak buds. *Show me*, she commanded, bringing her concentration to bear, *how soon Arthur will return!*

A fitful March wind blew cold from the east, throwing dark clouds against the high Welsh hills in uncertain fury. In a narrow valley a rain-bloated stream slashed through its bed in a fierce torrent, filling the valley with the roar of its passing. At the head of the valley stood a tower of rock, treeless and steep, glistening with wet. Atop this tower the ruin of an old stone wall meandered around a jumble of quarried building stones amid deep pools of mud, and skirted a small stone hut, domed like a hive, sitting beside a cairn. Behind the hut a wooden lean-to sheltered a pair of horses from the pelting rain. At the low, curved mouth of the hut a sullen fire hissed and spat, smoked wickedly, and went out.

"Well, so much for warmth and a decent meal," Percival grumbled, poking viciously at the embers. "What shall we do? Eat the fish raw or go back to the jerky? Damn, but I'm tired of jerky."

Galahad huddled in his bedroll, for although the hut was well wattled and perfectly dry, it was wretchedly cold. "I don't care. I'm not hungry."

Percival cursed under his breath. It was suddenly too much—his cousin's black temper, the five days of storm that had slowed their progress through Wales, the incessant cold that had crept into their bones and refused to leave. "I'll be damned if I eat another piece of jerky. I'll eat this fish raw. At least it will be a change."

Percival pulled out his dagger and split open the two fat trout the swollen stream had thrown up on the bank that afternoon. They had no money, they were nearly out of food, it was horribly cold and damp, and for weeks now they had had little to say to each other. He scowled. Two long years ago they had left Dunpeldyr in such high hopes! They had accompanied Talorc to Elmet, sure that somewhere in that noble king's domain lay the sign they were awaiting. But all that had awaited them were swarms of Anglii, battle-ready and desperate for land. It had taken six months of nearly constant fighting to subdue them. True, his arm had strengthened and his skill improved under such constant use. But nothing had happened that Galahad recognized as the sign he sought.

Nothing had happened in York, either, where they fought the following year, nor in the rich lands of Logris after that. This past winter Galahad had begun to grow sullen and aloof. He had snapped at Percival's suggestion that perhaps the tokens they'd found were not the right ones after all, and once had stormed off in cold fury at Percival's suggestion that he would never accept anything as the sign because he did not want to be tested and found wanting by three women. Since then, Percival had not ventured any more of his opinions, had not crossed his cousin in any way. Galahad had said little enough in return. Neither of them mentioned the Grail anymore, or asked after anyone called the Fisher King. It made for dull companionship, but at least they could tolerate traveling together.

But it could not go on like this much longer. Percival's fifteenth birthday was days away and he was ready to go home. This time he did not want Galahad to go with him. Winning back his kingdom was something he must do alone if it was to have any value, but although he knew in his heart he had the courage to face Peredur, he doubted he had the courage to tell Galahad of his decision. Savagely he sliced the head off a fish.

"I think you'd better go home." Galahad's voice startled him, coming firmly out of the gloom behind him.

"What?"

"Go back to Gwynedd. It's time. I've taught you everything I know about swordplay. You're good enough to defeat Peredur. Go back home and claim your birthright."

"Of course," Percival said bitterly, furious that his cousin should have the courage he himself lacked. "After accompanying you for three years, I'll just up and leave you to fend for yourself in a land you don't know."

"I *can* fend for myself," Galahad retorted. "Wherever I am."

"You're a lousy cook." Percival turned around to look at him. All he could see in the dark was the liquid blaze of eyes. "Are you going to continue the . . . quest?"

"Of course. But the rest I have to do alone."

Around them the rain hissed so furiously it drowned out the river's thunder, but within the hut silence was complete. Percival's hand dropped to his dagger. Did Galahad mean to imply that the sign had not come because Percival was with him? That it was *his* fault? This was the last straw.

"Well, are you going to cook that fish or aren't you?" A gruff voice spoke from the doorway and Percival whirled. Just beyond the remains of the fire a short, thick figure, no higher than the hut door, blinked at him from under the hood of a cloak. Beneath the cloak he wore a coarse robe tied at the waist with braided twine. His small feet were wrapped in oiled cloth. The heavy sack over his shoulder was held by a broad, fat, but unbelievably small hand.

"Who are you?" Percival's dagger slipped into his hand. "What do you want?"

"A little hospitality in my own home," the figure growled.

"*Your* home?" Percival gulped. "You live here? Our pardon, sir! We thought the place was deserted. We thought it had been empty for generations. Where have you been?"

"Away. You've made yourselves free with my shed, too. Two great lumbering horses and barely enough room to squeeze my donkey in."

"I beg your pardon, sir," Percival said hastily. "But . . . may we beg your hospitality a little longer, until the rain lets up? Your house is big enough for three—and well built, too, dry as a bone. Come in, come in."

The short man grunted. "You may stay, Percival of Gwynedd, and your cousin, too, if in return you'll let me have those fish."

"How do you . . . you can't possibly know who we are!"

The stranger barked a short laugh. "Can't I?"

Percival pushed the fish at him. "Take them, take them. But I don't know how you'll cook them. All the kindling's wet."

"Stand aside."

Percival backed away from the door and the little man entered. He reached out a chubby hand and pointed a finger at the dead fire. His voice rose and fell in a quick incantation, and suddenly a blue flame sprang to life amid the sodden ashes. It hissed as it devoured the rain, licked upward, grew, and blossomed into a yellow-red, beating blaze. In the stunned silence he threw off his robe, revealing a miniature, squat body, an overlarge, misshapen head, and a square, ugly face.

"Who *are* you?" Percival whispered.

"My name is Naceyn." He nodded politely at Percival and Galahad. "You are princes. I am a Druid. We are equals of a sort." He smiled briefly at the expression on Percival's face. "No need to fear me. I come in peace. You have shared your dinner with me, and in return I will give each of you a gift."

As he spoke, he withdrew two stout, sharpened sticks from the pack he carried, skewered the fish, and held them over the fire. He cocked a bright eye at Percival. "Reach into that sack. I've a rabbit, cabbages and apples, a jar of olives, and a bag of raisins. All yours."

Percival dove eagerly into the sack and withdrew several packages wrapped in oiled cloth, a small jar of olives, and a small iron pot. Naceyn handed his roasting sticks to Percival. "Roast my dinner for me, prince, and I'll make you a rabbit stew you won't soon forget."

With amazing speed he pulled a small dagger from his belt, skinned and cut up the rabbit, added it to the pot with a cabbage, water, three wild onions from one of the cloth packages, a handful of raisins from another, and a sprinkling of herbs from a small linen bag. Then he placed the pot at the edge of the blazing fire, neatly rewrapped his packages, replaced them in the sack, and took back his sticks from Percival. He winked at Galahad, who sat cross-legged at the rear of the hut defiantly chewing a strip of jerky, nearly as tall sitting as Naceyn was standing.

"You will see, my fierce Christian friend, there is nothing to fear from a Druid's stew. It will do you no harm and tastes a deal better than six-month-old jerky."

Galahad put down the jerky and frowned. "Where did you come from and how did you get here? You didn't cross that stream in full flood."

Naceyn's smile revealed a row of white, even teeth. "You forget you're not a native of these parts, Sir Galahad. You don't know the secret paths and twisting byways that lead in and out of this valley. I do. I've lived on Dinas Brenin for forty years."

"Dinas Brenin?" Percival said softly. "Is that where we are? Isn't this where wicked King Vortigern tried to build his tower? That fell down three times in the building when the walls reached man-height? It's a cursed place!"

Naceyn grinned. "On the contrary. It's a sacred place to those who serve the Mother. This is where the Druid Merlin flushed Vortigern from his lair out into the open, where Ambrosius killed him. The High Priestess Vivien sanctified this place and built the cairn. A small community of Druids has lived here ever since. I am the last living. I was born here."

"Merlin the Enchanter was no Druid," Galahad broke in stiffly. "He served King Arthur all his life."

Naceyn's eyes flickered. "Only ignorance speaks without fear of contradiction. Merlin was the most powerful Druid ever born. He brought Arthur into being. Although," he added lightly, "I own that Uther Pendragon and Ygraine of Cornwall played their parts."

"Whom do you serve?" Galahad asked, the jerky forgotten. "You with your tricks of magic. Some pagan enchanter? A local witch?"

Naceyn regarded him thoughtfully. "I serve the Mother. And you?"

Galahad's nostrils flared. "Who is your mortal master? And don't lie to me if you value your skin."

The dwarf did not flinch. "Who is yours, son of Lancelot? And don't forget you are a guest in my house."

"You do not live here. There are no signs of habitation anywhere. The wattle between these stones is fresh. Why did you come here so full of lies?"

For a moment silence hung between them, sharp and dangerous as a bared blade. Then, with a little smile, Naceyn bowed. "I came to find *you*, my lord."

"Why?"

"The queen I serve bade me bring you to her."

"Do you pretend you can take me against my will?"

Naceyn laughed quietly. "Of course not. It is my hope that I can persuade you to follow me."

"And if you can't?"

"Then you will go your way and I will go mine." He smiled. "Be easy, son of Lancelot. I did not come to cross blades with you. I came because you are searching for something and I believe I can help you find it."

Galahad started and Percival looked at him eagerly. "Cousin! This could be—"

Galahad waved him silent. "If you know what I seek, tell me what it is and where it lies. Then I can find it myself."

"Ah," Naceyn said softly, "but it is not that kind of thing. You must come with me to Guent and the key to finding it will be shown to you. That is all I know about it."

Galahad stared at him a moment and then shrugged. "Perhaps I will come. Perhaps I won't."

Naceyn bowed politely, then reached into his sack and brought forth a polished pewter plate and a wooden bowl. He set them both near the fire and laid the skewered fish carefully on the plate. After giving the stew a stir, he ate his fish, neatly and quickly, pulling out the bones with a practiced hand. He washed the plate in rainwater and dried it with the hood of his coarse robe, then replaced it in the sack. "An excellent dinner. I thank you for it. I'm overfond of trout. I've never been able to catch them myself. It's a disappointment to me."

"Why don't you charm them out of the water, if you're a Druid?"

Naceyn turned slowly to face Galahad. "That is a misuse of power, to manage trivial things, to smooth the way for personal comfort. He who misuses a gift, loses it."

He poured the stew into the bowl and gestured the cousins to sit closer together. "I've only one bowl. You'll have to share. But I've plenty of wine and it's excellent stuff, imported from Gaul. Drink as much as you like." He handed them his wineskin and watched them eat. Then he settled himself opposite them and folded his hands in his lap.

"Tonight I will give each of you a great gift. In your sleep you will see part of the glorious futures that await you. In each dream is a key to understanding. If you grasp the key you shall achieve your destinies."

Galahad looked up sharply. "Send me no dream, Druid. No one but God can know the future."

"Believe what you will, my lord. But I will be here in the morning, and if you are displeased with your dream, you may kill me if you choose. I have no weapon but my little dagger. I am at your mercy."

"Perhaps I should kill you now and save myself your dream."

Naceyn's eyes flickered. "Then you are no son of Lancelot, but a coward. And my curse would follow you all the rest of your days."

Galahad shuddered. A Druid's curse was no laughing matter. The bravest soldiers in Arthur's army had feared them worse than death in battle. It was said a Druid's curse could follow a man for years and strike him at the least expected hour. All he ever heard was the warning whistle of a dagger in flight seconds before it struck. "I've had enough of killing. You are safe from me."

Naceyn nodded. "A wise decision."

Sleep came quickly to Percival, but Galahad lingered on the edge of sleep for a long time, listening to the gentle hiss of rain. Finally, with Naceyn curled in a corner of the hut, snoring steadily, Galahad gave up the battle and closed his eyes.

He rode out of a dark forest by the banks of a flowing river. In the middle of the river stood a castle on an island. He looked about, and saw a man asleep by his boat at the water's edge.

"Good sir!" he cried. "Can you tell me how to get to yonder castle?"

The ferryman took him across and the porter led him by familiar paths to the hall of the Fisher King, who rose and beckoned to him.

"Ah, Sir Galahad, you've come at last. Welcome, my lord, welcome. Sit here by me, so I can have speech with you." He wore a crown upon his head and carried his left arm in a sling. A feast followed, more food than thirty men could eat, and, when he was finished, a trio of pretty serving maidens cleared it all away.

"Now watch," said the king, "and I will show you a marvel. It is my guest-gift. Look sharp, and you will see your heart's desire."

The candles dimmed of their own accord until the hall glowed with a soft light. Someone unseen struck a harp and sweet music sang to his soul. From a doorway at one end of the hall came a maiden dressed in white, with skin as pale as winter's snow, hair as black as a raven's wing, and lips as red as blood. In her hands she held a krater of ancient make, shallow and wide-lipped, shining with the sheen of beaten silver, studded with tiny amethysts and delicate golden chasing. In the hollow dimness of the hall it shone with its own light and seemed to float of its own will between her hands. Galahad gulped, dry-mouthed. He had never seen anything so beautiful or so compelling. The maiden approached him with the krater, stepping gracefully to the music, and passed him by. There were words etched in Latin upon the krater's lip, shimmering in the light: *Whoso thirsts, drink ye and be restored.* How he longed to reach out and touch it—he was so thirsty! A second maiden followed, lovelier even than the first, her features half-hidden by the luxuriant fall of chestnut hair. Galahad caught his breath. The spear in her hand was over six feet long but so beautifully balanced, she carried it with ease. The shaft of dark, dense wood was polished to brilliance; the honed spear tip shone deadly bright. Again he saw Latin writing etched along the shaft, dancing in the light: *Whoso trembles, take this and fear not.* What a magnificent weapon! His palms began to sweat as the maiden approached, and passed by. What ancient hero king had made this spear, had feasted from the krater? The music faded; the candles returned to light; the maidens were gone.

Galahad turned to his host. "Sir, I beg you! Where have they gone, the Grail and Spear? I have searched everywhere to find them!"

The Fisher King turned. His eyes shone blue and green and blue, changing like the water outside his door, deep and unreadable.

"Galahad," he said slowly, "what is it you seek?"

"Sir, that is a question easily answered. I seek the Grail and Spear."

The Fisher King smiled. "Why?"

"To . . . to . . . to heal Britain. To restore her, to make her whole, to return her King!"

"A noble quest," his host replied. "But only a worthy man can find the way. Do you know what makes a man worthy, Galahad?"

"To love God, to fear evil, to avoid sin, to uphold truth."

At once the candles blew out and left Galahad in darkness. From far away he heard the laugh of the Fisher King.

He who knows when he is thirsty can be restored; who knows when he trembles can be preserved. You have eyes, but they see not. Go, Galahad, seek far and wide for the Blessed Gifts whose power can heal Britain. In the soul of darkness will you find them. In the heart of light they lie. Find them for the hand that will hold them.

The words eddied around him in the darkness, spinning ever faster.

"What shall I do?" Galahad cried in panic.

"Go south. Go south. Go south," repeated the fading voice of the Fisher King.

* * *

Galahad sat bolt upright. Outside the stone hut a weak sun glittered in pools of standing water. He shrugged off his bedroll as Percival stirred and opened his eyes.

"Galahad! Oh, cousin! I've had the most amazing dream!"

"And so have I."

"The most beautiful girl in all the world appeared to me—I've seen her before, in the dreams I had at Avalon. She told me . . . she told me to go home."

"And I must go south."

"It is time for us to part, then, cousin. I . . . I'm sorry about it. I shall miss you."

"And I you." They stared at each other. In a single night the animosity between them had vanished and they spoke to each other as they had when they first set out. Together they turned toward the corner where Naceyn had slept, but found it empty.

"Where's the dwarf?" Galahad wondered.

"He really did send us dreams, didn't he? He is a Druid, then."

Galahad stretched. "It was probably a drug that did it. When Niniane put me in an enchanted sleep she gave me an apple first. We two ate the stew Naceyn prepared. He didn't. He ate our fish. Did you see what he put in the stewpot?"

"N-no," Percival replied uncertainly. "Not everything."

"Well, then. Perhaps the secret lies in herbal lore. Old Merlin was famous for his knowledge of plants and what could be distilled from them." He smiled suddenly. "Perhaps that's all Druids are—herbalists who guard the secret of their preparations and frighten people with rumors of their power."

Naceyn coughed behind them. "I shall disregard that remark."

Galahad flushed but Percival grinned. "Thank you for the dream, Naceyn! You have given me my own quest—for the maiden I saw there!"

Naceyn's face creased into a smile. "I warn you, you must earn the right to her hand. And you, Galahad, how was your dream?"

"It's one I've had before," Galahad said slowly. "But with a new ending. Percival is going home to Gwynedd, but I . . . am going south."

Naceyn nodded. "Then I shall be able to accompany you. Guent lies south. Come, let's break our fast and I will show you the separate paths you are to take. It looks to be a beautiful day."

In the strengthening sun Percival and Galahad readied their horses and parted at last with expressions of affection and promises to meet again as soon as circumstance allowed. Percival followed the westward trail Naceyn pointed out. As Galahad leaped onto Farouk's back, Naceyn pulled his donkey from the shed.

Galahad hesitated. "If the dream was your gift, I can hardly refuse your request. You have given me back hope and I am in your debt. You may accompany me south." Naceyn bowed politely. "But tell me this: Is it no coincidence your way lies south as well?"

Naceyn did not answer at once. All his effort and attention seemed to be engrossed in mounting the recalcitrant donkey. At last, safely aboard, he straightened his robe and met Galahad's eyes directly.

"Do you suspect me? Do you imagine I could force you anywhere against your will?"

"Why is your dream the same one I dreamed at Avalon?"

"Ah." Naceyn smiled knowingly. "That's a good question, as it happens. Perhaps because they spring from the same source." Galahad frowned but the dwarf pulled his donkey's head around and started down the steep trail to the valley floor, effectively ending conversation. Galahad watched him for a moment and then put a leg to his horse. It did not matter. Naceyn was right. One thing he had learned in the years since Arthur's death was that very few men could force him to do anything he did not wish to do.

By midafternoon they wound their way out of the valley and found a well-worn track leading to the Caerleon road. The warm sun sent rainwater steaming off trees and grasses, so that most of the way they rode in a knee-high mist. Galahad said little, all his thoughts focused on what lay ahead. After months of dragging disappointment, to have hope renewed! He could not take the dream as the sign he awaited, for he had seen it twice before, but after three long years of struggle he had seen the Grail again, and he sensed with growing excitement that he was back on its trail.

So deep was he in thought he was nearly taken by surprise. The air began to vibrate with the approaching thunder of hooves, and a troop of armed men rode out of the mist at them.

"Halt, in the King's name!" the captain cried, raising his arm and bringing his company to a standstill. Galahad pulled up. The captain's eyes widened when he saw Galahad's shoulder badge. "You, sir! Are you of the House of Lanascol?"

"I am. My name is Galahad. And this is—" He turned to introduce Naceyn but the dwarf and his donkey had disappeared. Only a narrow flattening of young growth on the verge indicated where they had faded into the forest.

Galahad turned back to face the soldiers alone, his heart racing. First the dream, now this! Events were moving again, and fast. The captain and his men wore the Boar of Cornwall on their badges. "Greetings, Sir Galahad. This is luck, indeed. You are the very one we seek. We come from the High King Constantine, who wants you in Camelot without delay. He needs your help."

Galahad raised an eyebrow as the men surrounded him. "Do I have a choice?"

The captain had the grace to blush. "I doubt we could force you against your will, my lord, but we'd have to try."

"No matter. I'll come with you. I was heading south anyway."

24 ✠ THE SEAT PERILOUS

G alahad rode southeast with the escort, past the marshes bordering the Lake of Avalon, waiting with ill-concealed impatience for the turn in the road that would bring him the first sight of Caer Camel and the magnificent fortress that for nine years of his boyhood had been his home. Set high on a green hill, commanding a view of many leagues in every direction, the towers of Camelot glittered like burnished gold in the late sun. From a distance it looked unchanged. But as he drew nearer he saw with a sense of foreboding that the fortress, like the rest of Britain, showed everywhere the marks of slow decay. Grass grew unchecked between the paving stones. Bushes and scree had sprung up in the greensward at the top of the hill between the trees and the castle walls. Arthur had always kept this growth cut back for a hundred paces all around the outer fortifications, so that no enemy could approach unseen.

Inside the gates it was much worse. Gone was the air of orderliness and discipline that had characterized the place in Arthur's day. The sentries at the gate diced in a corner, hardly casting them a glance as they rode in. No one guarded the approach to the castle, and two guards lay drunk and snoring under a tree near the forecourt—in broad daylight!

The town of Camelot was half-deserted, the training grounds a pool of mud, the horse meadows empty of the glorious animals once bred in the Camelot stables. The poor steeds who stood at the paddock fences gazing at him as he rode by looked like mountain ponies straight from the hills, rough-coated and thin.

When they slid from their horses in the courtyard no grooms came running to lead their mounts away. One of the escort gathered up all the reins and led the horses away himself.

The captain bowed. "This way, my lord. The High King awaits you."

Galahad followed silently. At least the golden stone of the castle itself still stood firm; the marble steps were not yet worn into unevenness; the great oak doors were still carved with fighting dragons, Arthur's emblem, and had not been replaced with the Boar of Cornwall. But his relief was short-lived. Inside, dust had been allowed to gather in the corners, spiders had been at work on the ceilings, even the guards looked grimy and discontented. No one came with bowls of water to let them wash the dirt of travel from their faces, hands, and hair. The captain did not even pause to wipe the mud from his boots, but set off down the corridor at a swift pace. He stopped at the door of Arthur's workroom, signaled Galahad to wait, entered, and bowed low. "My lord King. I have brought Sir Galahad, as you commanded."

A chair shrieked as it was pushed suddenly back against marble flooring. "He is here? Now? That was fast work, Darric. I commend you. Bring him in."

Galahad entered. In his mind's eye he pictured the room as he had first seen it that morning in high summer when he was a boy: a graceful room with tall, glazed windows looking out on a lovely garden, polished benches adorned with beautiful cushions stitched by the Queen's ladies and by the Queen herself, handsome tapestries depicting glorious battles lining the stone walls, Arthur's heavy marble-topped desk with dragon-claw feet at the far end of the room near the opened doors to the garden, his white hound scratching lazily for fleas in its shade. And behind the desk, a tall man in a plain robe and sandals, dictating to a scribe, an ordinary man he had taken for a servant until he saw Lancelot bend his knee to the ground.

Galahad shook his head to clear the memory. It was the end of March, not high summer, and the windows were shuttered, the doors closed. Old, stained rushes covered the floor. The tapestries showed threadbare in places. The cushions had gone brown from lack of cleaning, their bright colors barely discernible in the gloom. Two oil lamps threw off a sullen, smoky light. Only the brazier by the desk at the far end of the room burned bright enough to see by.

The man behind the desk was magnificently robed, his garments trimmed in fur. Gold gleamed on his fingers and wrists, at his shoulder, waist, and neck. Around his brow, unbelievably, he wore the crown of Britain. Galahad nearly gasped aloud. Arthur had rarely worn it, reserving its use for only the most important occasions, thus preserving its solemnity and power to impress. But then, Arthur had considered himself a soldier first and a king second.

Constantine's dark eyes glared at him from either side of his eagle's beak of a nose. Galahad dipped his knee and bowed. "My lord Constantine."

Constantine's features lightened and he almost smiled. "I thank you for coming, Sir Galahad. I am aware that the escort I sent could not have forced you. I've, uh, heard, of course, about how you defeated the men of the north single-handedly. I congratulate you. I have wanted to speak with you for a long time. But you must be hungry and thirsty after your long ride." He clapped his hands to summon a page. "Meat, cheese, and a flagon of mead for Sir Galahad. At once." The page darted away. "Come, Galahad, have a seat by the brazier and warm yourself. Tell me all that you've been doing since Camlann. I've been hearing strange stories of your travels in the north."

Galahad had never met Constantine before but was not surprised at his instant dislike of the man. "What stories, my lord?"

"I hear you've stirred up those northern kings. Rubbed their noses in their own high and mighty arrogance. That true?"

"No, my lord. Not exactly."

"Are they still a federation? Determined to hold their own and the rest of us be damned?"

"I wouldn't call them a federation. They're loosely organized."

Constantine grunted and looked at Galahad through narrowed eyes. "They say you carry a magic shield that protects you. Is that true?"

"No, my lord. An ordinary shield I found in a hermit's hut."

"But you've not been touched by a sword since you took it up, I hear. Is that not true?"

"Yes. But not on account of the shield." Unseen by Constantine, Galahad's hand slid to his scabbard, Excalibur's scabbard that he had oiled and sewn and strapped on to sheath Lancelot's sword. He believed now in its power. When he oiled it the cracks in the leather had virtually disappeared, and after two years of use, not only had it conformed to the shape of Lancelot's sword as though it had been made for that weapon, it had protected him from so much as a scratch in battle.

Constantine chuckled. "No one doubts your skill, prince. What are you now, eighteen? Even at eighteen you've more of a reputation than any of my battle captains. It's all I've heard for three years past from every traveler coming south, Galahad this and Galahad that. They say you personally defeated all the northern lords at Dunpeldyr." He cocked an eyebrow at Galahad.

"In a manner of speaking, that is true. We engaged in a sort of contest. I won. But no kingdoms were at stake."

"Hrmmm." Constantine cleared his throat and spoke carefully. "How would you describe your relations with those arrogant bastards—Rheged, Strathclyde, Lothian, Gorre, and Elmet? Friendly? Cordial? Hostile?"

Galahad regarded the hard eyes that never left his face. "Friendly with Elmet. Talorc's a good man. As to the others"—he shrugged—"civil at best. I spared their lives and they owe me a service. But they will not do it willingly. I will have to force them to it when the time comes."

"I see." Constantine turned and stared moodily into the fire. His next question, when it came, was casual. "Why did you go north in the first place? Why not go home? With Lancelot."

Galahad dropped his eyes. "My lord, there comes a time when a boy must leave his father. To learn to make his own way."

Constantine nodded. "Indeed. It can't have been easy having Lancelot for a father. There was nothing he couldn't do. Cador, my father, was the same."

Galahad hid his surprise as best he could. He wondered if Lancelot would be amused or annoyed to hear himself classed with the ambitious, hard-nosed Cador of Cornwall.

A light scratch sounded at the door. Constantine sat back in his carved chair as the page appeared with Galahad's food and drink. The boy set the tray down and retired at the king's quick wave of dismissal.

Constantine gestured at the food. "Eat up, eat up. You're thinner than you ought to be to serve me. I want your sword arm strong."

Galahad ate with a sense of relief. Constantine was interested only in his fighting skills. But he did not see what connection such service might have with the dream which had sent him south.

"You're an odd man, Galahad. They say that no king yet has won your loyalty, not even Lancelot. That gold does not tempt you, that neither your service nor your heart can be bought. This interests me. I want the chance to win your loyalty. For Britain."

The dark eyes flicked briefly to Galahad in a quick, assessing glance. Then Constantine leaned back and stared at the ceiling. After a long moment he began speaking quietly. "I've heard it said that in his last days Arthur expressed an interest in unearthing the treasures the Emperor Maximus brought back from Rome." Galahad froze. Constantine sighed a tiny sigh and kept his voice light. "I don't know what those treasures are, but I called upon a bard in Cornwall, old blind Trefayne, to tell me what he knew of them." As he spoke his voice grew lighter and more offhand. "He knew a fair bit, it seems. And he told me something I didn't know. If these objects—there are three of them, the Sword, the Spear, the Grail—are ever again united in the hands of Britain's king, then Britain herself shall remain invincible. Forever." He smiled quietly. "Imagine it, Galahad! Safe from Saxons! From Gaels, from Picts and Anglii! To enter a battle with the outcome never in doubt! Now it is a dream I nightly dream. But it was Arthur's vision before it was mine."

Galahad did not speak. He did not even breathe.

Constantine sighed deeply. "I know where Excalibur is. Your brave but misguided father threw it into the Lake of Avalon. I've no doubt I can dredge it up, in spite of Morgaine's objections. But what's the use, unless I can discover the whereabouts of the other two?" He looked sharply at

Galahad but met only two blank blue eyes across the table. "I've no doubt it would take a lot of searching. I've never heard of anyone who knows where these things are. It would take a certain kind of man, a man indifferent to power and gold and the pleasures they buy, to find such treasures and return them to me. A man like you. I've heard the prophecy about you: Your future is a marvelous one. It occurred to me this might be the way to fulfill it."

He paused and watched Galahad carefully. During the speech Galahad had not touched his meal or moved an eyelash. Now he carefully lifted the mead cup to his lips, drank, and set the cup down with a steady hand.

"Is this what you want of me, King of Britain? To find you another man's treasure? I would rather kill Saxons for you."

Constantine's lips thinned until his teeth showed. "You shall have your chance, prince, never fear. There are plenty of Saxons about. But does this other matter not interest you? You would be the most honored man in all Britain if you could find these things. And I did hear you had gone north to seek a marvel. Is that not true?"

"It is true."

Constantine watched his face for any sign of change, and then sat forward, slapping his hands on the desk. "Well, well, enough of this for now. We will speak of it again another time. As for marvels, this is the place for them. There are plenty of marvels in Camelot. Let me show you around a bit before you go to your rest."

He rose and Galahad rose with him.

"My lord has forgotten that I grew up in Camelot." By the startled look on Constantine's face, Galahad saw he had not known, and that the knowledge was a blow to him for some reason. "I lived here from the age of five until fourteen. "

Constantine's frown made him look instantly angry, but a moment later he wiped the frown away. "Come see the Round Hall at least," the King said quickly. "It's changed a bit since Arthur's day."

Arthur's day, Galahad thought bitterly as he followed Constantine down the corridor, was only four years ago. It seemed a lifetime. He did not want to see the same slovenly deterioration in the Round Hall that he had seen in the workroom, and he held his breath as Constantine pushed open the door.

To his unutterable relief the Round Hall looked unchanged. The large, round, white oak table nearly filled the room. Thirty chairs sat around it, the King's chair taller than the rest, with a dragon carved in the crest. Above the King's chair Excalibur's hanger still hung from the wall, beautifully stitched by Queen Guinevere herself. It was empty. At least Constantine had not yet had the effrontery to hang his own sword there and pretend that a blade forged in Cornwall could be the symbol of victory for all Britain.

Constantine was walking slowly about the room, touching the chair backs as he passed, and talking. Galahad followed and tried to attend.

"—had each knight's name carved in his chair," the king was saying. "It pleases them, and gives them the sense that their place in council is a permanent one, although it takes but three days to carve in another man's name." He paused at the chair directly opposite the king's seat. "But this one, as you see, is uncarved. It is the Seat Perilous."

"Yes, I know—" Galahad began, remembering that it was first known as the Chair of Complaint, where people brought unsettled grievances before the High King himself, and had been given the name "Perilous" on account of some harsh judgments rendered.

But Constantine was telling a different story. "—reserved for one person, an unknown knight of perfect valor who will one day take his seat here. The greatest knight in Britain. It has been foretold. Anyone else who tries to sit here suffers dreadful torment. Three have tried it. All of them took violently ill with cramps and bleeding the same night. The third one died, and no one's tried to sit here since."

Galahad masked his disbelief and nodded obediently. The chair was clearly newer than the rest, unworn and well polished. Constantine stood before it a long time, talking about council meetings and the knights who served him. Galahad waited patiently, remembering only too well the last time he had seen this room. Nine years ago he had witnessed the knighting of Gareth of Orkney, his boyhood companion. A week later Galahad had gone off to Brittany in Arthur's train. He had never seen Gareth again.

"Gryff will show you to your quarters now, my lord." It seemed Constantine had finished. "If you know the castle, you'll recognize them. Tomorrow after breakfast we'll drill the troops and you can judge for yourself the quality of men I keep."

Galahad followed the page through corridors and up a winding stair. The rush mats that had once served as a carpet were long gone, and his boots resounded sharply on the cold stone flooring. The page stopped by a solid oak door and bowed. "My lord."

Galahad pushed open the door with a sense of homecoming. They had given him Lancelot's chamber. A youth in a ragged tunic and rough-knit leggings bowed low as he entered. "My lord. I am Brynn, your chamberlain."

"Good evening, Brynn." He noticed his bedroll in a corner. His meager belongings had already been unpacked. "Where are you from?"

"Cornwall, my lord. My father's family has always served the Dukes of Cornwall."

"I hope you don't mind serving a Breton. Our kingdoms have not always been on friendly terms."

"It is an honor, my lord," Brynn responded eagerly, "to serve *you*. My father knew Lancelot. They fought together at Autun."

Galahad raised an eyebrow. "Constantine's son Prince Meliodas led the Cornish troops at Autun." He turned to let Brynn unbelt his sword and unlace his tunic.

"Yes, my lord. But so many were killed—toward battle's end Sir Meliodas and Sir Lancelot fought together."

"Did they, indeed? I did not know that." He had seen that battlefield. Too well he remembered the spent, gray faces of the dead, the green field trampled to mud and soaked with gore, the butchered bodies of his kinsmen sprawled facedown in filth. He shut his eyes to blot the memory out. "And how does Meliodas? I know him; he's an excellent commander. Is he here in Camelot?"

"No, my lord. He's in Cornwall."

Galahad paused as Brynn drew off his boots. "Surely, as heir to the High King, he ought to be here."

Brynn averted his eyes. "Aye, my lord, so many say behind the High King's back. But a year or two ago King Constantine quarreled with Sir Meliodas, not liking his son's choice of wife. Since then he's had Sir Markion, his second son, serving him here instead."

"What? Are they not yet reconciled? What kind of woman did he wed?"

Brynn sighed as he bundled Galahad's clothes and set them by the door for later cleaning. "I never saw her, my lord, but they say she was very beautiful. She was the daughter of a bard. She grew up in Amesbury, cared for by the nuns at the monastery while her father traveled. She brought Cornwall neither money nor land nor honor. That's what infuriated the High King, that Sir Meliodas should marry her only for love."

"You speak of her as if she lived in the past. Did Meliodas put her away?"

Brynn filled a basin with water from a pewter pitcher, and began to sponge the dirt of travel from Galahad's body. "No, my lord. She died in childbirth, leaving him a strapping son. I don't think he's gotten over it yet. He does not speak to his father. Or to his brother, Markion."

"A shame," Galahad said thoughtfully. "Meliodas is a good leader and an honest man."

"Oh, my lord, he is beloved by every man in Cornwall! To a man, we would die for him." He lowered his voice to a whisper. "He is a better king to us than my lord Constantine ever was. If we have our way, Sir Meliodas will succeed his father. No one can abide Markion."

Brynn bent over a trunk, brought out a nightrobe, and pulled it over Galahad's head. Galahad fingered the garment in wonder. It was finely woven of lightweight gray wool, but lined with some fabric of magical softness. When he moved, the garment caressed his skin like a warm breath.

"Where did you get this, Brynn?"

Brynn gestured to the old carved trunk at the foot of the bed. "It belonged to your father, my lord. He left many clothes here."

"This . . . this is an unbelievable garment. I've never worn anything like it."

Over the breast the Hawk of Lanascol was intricately stitched in tiny, delicate blue threads. He remembered the hanger for his father's sword that hung on the wall in Benoic and a cold misgiving assailed him.

"That's because it was made by the High Queen herself. She made two of them, the first as a wedding gift to Arthur, the second for Lancelot when his son—when you were born."

Galahad clutched at the garment and tore it off over his head. "Take it away! I will wear something plain to bed or nothing at all."

Gaping at him, Brynn retrieved the nightrobe from the corner where Galahad had flung it, and hurried to pull another—plain and brown—from the trunk.

Galahad was shaking from head to foot. "Go through the trunk, Brynn, and throw out anything that witch has touched. I will not have her handiwork against my skin. I will not have it in my chamber. Give it away or burn it, but get it out of my sight."

"Yes, my lord. Of course, my lord. I did not understand, my lord, but now I see—I quite see."

Galahad turned on him, blue eyes blazing. "You're a font of information because you're a gossip. If I hear a single word of this from anyone else's lips, I shall cut out your tongue. Do you understand me?"

Brynn whimpered as he clutched the robe to his chest. "Yes, my lord! I will say nothing, I swear it!"

Galahad pointed to the door. "Then go."

Brynn bent to gather up the clothes, bowed hastily, and disappeared. Galahad sighed and sat heavily on the bed. The vehemence of his outburst had surprised even him. He plucked at the brown robe in agitation. Would he never be free of the past? Ever since he had set foot back in Camelot, memories he thought he had locked away in darkness had begun breaking loose into the light. Perhaps it had been a mistake to come here, after all. Perhaps he should have followed that Druid dwarf to Guent. But it was too late now. Constantine clearly meant to keep him in Camelot. He had put himself in the way of events and they had led him here, so here he would stay. Perhaps somewhere in this place of fables he would see the sign he awaited.

In the morning Constantine introduced Galahad to the lords and battle captains who made up his courtiers. There were twenty of them, not even enough to fill all the seats at the Round Table, and all of them Cornishmen. They regarded Galahad with wary respect, not entirely unmixed with awe, and Galahad wondered what tales Constantine had been telling them.

He was taken to the training field to inspect the Camelot troops. Constantine clearly expected him to be impressed, but these men were nothing, either in equipment, skill, or bearing, to the least of Arthur's troops, and Galahad kept his expression carefully neutral. Suddenly a page came running from the castle and threw himself at Constantine's feet.

"My lord! My lord! A marvel! You must come and see! In the Round Hall!"

Galahad glanced sharply at Constantine. Neither the High King nor his men questioned the page, but turned as a body and hurried toward the castle. In the Round Hall Constantine's seneschal stood across the table, staring down.

"My lord!" he cried. "Here's a marvel! Look!"

The king and his men gathered around the Seat Perilous in subdued excitement. "There's a name carved on it!"

Galahad exhaled slowly and kept his face straight. So this was why Constantine had shown him the Round Hall last night.

"Galahad!" the king cried. "Come look at this!"

There on the back of the Seat Perilous he saw his name carved deep into the shining wood: *Sir Galahad*. He bowed politely to Constantine. "My lord does me great honor."

"Not I, my lad, I assure you," the king said quickly. "It is a day of miracles! You have been sent to us—here is the sign! I have prayed long for such a warrior to join our ranks!"

Galahad noticed some of the knights glancing at one another but he kept his own face solemn before the king. Constantine need not have bothered. He had already decided that he might as well stay and serve him. All the man strove to do was keep the Saxons from Briton lands, which was no more than Arthur had fought for all his life. It was known ground. He would fight for Constantine as he had fought for lesser kings, as he had fought for Arthur. He would quell the demons of his memory until he could walk past the Round Hall without thinking of Gareth. Besides, for all he knew this rather obvious trick might, in spite of Constantine, be the sign he sought. He was obviously expected to take it as a marvel.

He went down on one knee. "I accept your offer, my lord. I will swear service to you, faithful service, until the time comes that God calls me away."

Relief flooded Constantine's face and he smiled. Around the two of them the Round Hall erupted with cheering.

25 ✝ AN ILL WIND

Late that night, stuffed with rich foods at Constantine's table and half-drunk on his miserable wine, Galahad fell at last into a restless sleep. The crowding memories that had assailed him at every turn since his arrival in Camelot, memories so fiercely resisted by his waking mind, now found that resistance melted away and in sleep swamped him. He did not dream, but remembered.

He was nine years old when Arthur took him along as page on a visit to King Hoel of Brittany. A host of Briton kings accompanied him—but not Lancelot—to discuss the growing unrest among the Franks in Gaul. All went smoothly until they were on their way home. Galahad was eager to get back to Camelot and share his adventures with Gareth, his only friend. He had no way of knowing, as Arthur's cavalry galloped flat out on the Roman road, that it was already too late.

Overhead the wild wind tore across the night, flinging cloud against cloud in thunderous fury, hurling stinging pebbles of rain at the huddling earth, screaming in a wanton crescendo that deafened even the pounding of the horses' hooves. It was a dream, Galahad thought, or a nightmare: the animal beneath him ran and ran, sides heaving, slippery with sweat, yet he could hear nothing of its movement above the raucous, raging violence of the storm.

If he lifted his head into the onslaught, he could just see the backs of the foremost riders and dimly, through sheets of rain, the streaming tail of Arthur's gray. He could barely make out the road. In all his life he had never ridden so fast. Thank God they were already across the Camel—they might get home in one piece yet.

Until today they had taken it easy coming home from Brittany. King Hoel's council of kings in Kerrec had been a great success. Treaties of alliance had been signed and feasted over, and Arthur had journeyed home at a leisurely pace. Even the sea had complied with the High King's wishes and given them an easy crossing. It wasn't until today, more than halfway home from the coast, as they cantered along the dry November roads and began to think about a meal and rest, that this madness had begun. Arthur had stopped to question a horseman riding south. Constantine of Cornwall, the traveler had reported, was rumored to be moving north with troops. At that, Arthur had sent a courier flying off to Camelot, had handpicked the twelve best riders in his train and headed north at full speed in the courier's wake.

Galahad hunched against the horse as cold rivulets ran down his neck. A wicked gust tore at his cloak and threw sharp needles of rain against his face. He shuddered involuntarily. There was something sinister and ominous about this storm.

At last Caer Camel loomed before them, a solid shadow darker than the night. They turned up the broad, paved ride toward King's Gate, the tired horses straining hard against the hill. Not until they were at the gates and had hailed the sentries could they see a light.

"It's the High King!" someone shouted from the guardhouse. "Quick, men, to the gates!"

Galahad rode forward, shivering, as the great gates swung open. He was close enough to see the captain of the guard come out to Arthur, a smoking torch held high over his head.

"My lord King! Stay a moment! An urgent message from the Queen!"

"Guinevere!" Arthur reined in sharply. "How does she fare? Is she well?"

"Aye, my lord, as far as I know. The message concerns your nephew, Sir Gawaine."

Gawaine, who had ridden up to Arthur's side, sidled closer. "What's this?"

Arthur frowned. "Give me the message, man! Don't keep my horses standing!"

"Yes, my lord! The High Queen begs the King to place Sir Gawaine under guard and seal him away from any intercourse with others, even servants, until the King has spoken to the Queen. She begs, my lord, that you will trust her judgment and see the order carried out, or death may follow that might be otherwise prevented."

"What nonsense is this?" Gawaine cried. "It's house arrest! Don't be absurd! I'm not going to kill anyone. Let us get in out of the wet—"

Arthur raised a hand for silence and Gawaine stopped. "Augus, do you know aught of this?" the King asked the captain.

"No, my lord. But Sir Kay gave me the message himself."

"Very well. I will have the Queen's order obeyed. Gawaine—"

"Uncle, this is utterly ridiculous—"

"Do it anyway," Arthur snapped. "Augus, take five of your men and escort Sir Gawaine to the Round Hall."

"For pity's sake, Uncle!"

Arthur looked at him coldly. "Have you ever considered it might be for your own good? That *you* are the one she is afraid for? Quit blubbering like a spoiled child and wait in the Round Hall for me. I'll come to you as soon as I know what this is all about." He looked around uneasily. "It's an evil night. And something is amiss."

Reluctantly, Gawaine slid off his steaming horse and allowed himself to be surrounded by the guards. Arthur raised his arm and the rest of the cavalry cantered through the gates and up the hill to the castle. Arthur dismounted at the door, but Galahad and most of the others rode on to the stableyard, cold, wet, and grumbling, and after seeing their horses rubbed down and fed, hurried off to the barracks for hot porridge, warm wine, and a change of clothes.

Galahad hesitated at the barracks door. He was afire to know what the trouble was. What could have happened to put Gawaine's life in danger? Pulling his soaking cloak close around him, he slipped through the shadows to the castle's scullery door, ran quietly through the deserted kitchens and up the back stairs to Gareth's chamber. Gareth was Gawaine's youngest brother. He would know what the trouble was.

But Gareth's room was empty. The bed had been slept in, Gareth's cloak lay on the chest, but his boots and his sword were gone. The candle at his bedside had burned to the hour mark, but if he wasn't coming back, then he'd have snuffed it. Galahad stood uncertainly a moment and then sat down on the chest to wait. He doffed his wet cloak and wrapped Gareth's around himself. The shuttered window faced south, in the storm's lee, but the wind's chill fingers still reached in, seeking everywhere, to steal his warmth.

To keep his teeth from chattering, Galahad forced himself to think about Gareth. The youngest of the four sons of King Lot of Lothian and his queen Morgause, Gareth was the only one without a killing temper. Gawaine, Agravaine, and Gaheris were as hotheaded as their royal father. Gawaine was, at the moment, imprisoned in the Round Hall, but Agravaine and Gaheris might be anywhere, up to anything. Gareth was too sensible to be caught up in their schemes. Besides, where could he have gone without his cloak on a night like this?

He could have gone to visit his betrothed, Linet of York, the Queen's waiting woman. But if he'd meant to visit Linet, he'd not have gone to bed.

He rose and began to pace fitfully. Someone shouted in the corridor. He ran to the door in time to see sentries running by.

"What's the matter? What news?"

One of them turned and shrugged. "Don't know. Sir Kay's in a passion. Sir Bedwyr's sent for a physician. Rumor is, there's been murder done. Drunken Orkneymen in the High Queen's chamber!"

Orkneymen in Guinevere's chamber! Not Gareth—Gareth seldom drank, and Mordred was never drunk. But the twins, Agravaine and Gaheris, were seldom sober. They were notorious troublemakers, besides, and leaders of a small band of rabble-rousers who thirsted for glory in a land at peace. Still, none of them had any business in the High Queen's chamber.

No one had any business there but the Queen herself and her women. And, of course, the King. But King Arthur had been away for six long weeks. . . .

Galahad's palms began to sweat. He would not let himself think the thought. He got up again and searched the corridor, but no one was about. Who was dead? Who had been in that room? An ache clutched at Galahad's throat until he could hardly breathe. He saw again the dark head bent in prayer, urgent prayer, hour upon hour, praying for something he had needed so much more desperately than sleep. *Forgive me, forgive me, forgive me, O Lord, forgive my sin.*

Galahad found his knees were shaking. He sat down again. Curling himself in a corner beyond the bed, he forced all speculation from his mind and settled down to wait. Weary as he was, he could not close his eyes, but dully watched the candle burn. From time to time he heard voices, shouts, barked orders, the quick tramp of booted feet. No one came to Gareth's door. Once he thought he caught the sound of weeping, but on such a night the wind played tricks with sound. Finally, a chamberlain came in to replace the candle.

"What news, Fayn?"

The man jumped. "Who's there? Sir Gareth?"

"No. It's Galahad. Over here."

Color seeped back into the man's ashen face. "Oh, my lord! What are you doing in the corner? You gave me a fright, you did!"

"I'm waiting for Gareth. Do you know where he is?"

"No, my lord. He's been gone a long while. Sir Lancelot came to fetch him hours ago."

Something twisted hard in Galahad's gut. "Lancelot came himself?"

"Aye, my lord. They went away together."

"Was . . . was Lancelot armed?"

The chamberlain tugged at his beard and paused. "No. Now I think on it, he had neither boots nor sword. Sir Gareth, he pulled his boots on and took his sword. I recollect Sir Lancelot grumbled about it and said they had not time."

"Were they sent for?"

Fayn said nervously, "Aye, my lord. By the High Queen."

Galahad's throat tightened until he could not speak. He simply stared at Fayn.

The chamberlain rolled his eyes and edged toward the door. "Oh, my lord, there's evil doings aplenty, I hear tell. Dead men everywhere. Thank all the gods the High King's back and in command." With that, he went out and closed the door. Galahad sat still, staring at nothing, suddenly afraid that the future trembling on the edge of knowledge was a nightmare, like the storm outside. He no longer wanted to know what had happened. He wanted to be back on the Roman road, riding recklessly in driving rain, back where he could hear nothing but screaming wind.

Slow, heavy footsteps came down the corridor. He held his breath as the door swung open. There stood Lancelot, pale as a nether spirit, armed, booted, and dressed for the road in his thickest cloak.

"Galahad?" he whispered. "What—"

"I'm waiting for Gareth."

Lancelot stared at him, standing stiffly, drawing breath as if it were a labor. His black hair was wet from recent washing. His red-rimmed eyes glistened in the candlelight. His face, mirthless and exhausted, looked suddenly old. He entered the room, moving as if every step gave him pain. Above Gareth's bed a small cross of beaten silver hung on an old thong. Slowly and with deliberation, Lancelot took it down from the wall and slipped it over his head. He mumbled a prayer, lifted the cross to his lips and kissed it. Then he turned to go.

"Father!" Galahad heard the note of panic in his own voice and tried to still it. "Father, where are you going? Why are you taking Gareth's cross? What has happened?"

Lancelot looked back. A tear slid down his lined cheek but his eyes were hard as metal. "Gareth is dead and I am exiled. If you hate me for the rest of your long life, it is no more than I deserve." Before Galahad had time to draw a second breath, he was gone.

He was jerked back to consciousness by a stab of pain in his ribs. Gawaine kicked him again.

"Get out! Get out, you filthy Breton swine! Get out before I kill you! Aye, that's what I ought to do! A life for a life! Murderer's whelp!"

Galahad scrambled to his feet, dodging the next blow.

"Murderer's brat! By God, don't gape at me! Pretend you don't know, is that it? That won't get you far!" He struck Galahad in the side of the head with a heavy fist, knocking the boy across the room.

"That's enough, Gawaine." Arthur stood in the doorway, his face lined with weariness, the dust of travel still upon his clothes. "Beating the boy won't bring your brother back."

A woman slipped by Arthur soft-footed into the room. She knelt by Galahad. "Arthur, he's bleeding. Give me your kerchief, Gawaine. You owe him that."

The cloth against his head smarted dreadfully, but the smooth, cool hands were gentle and caressing. Galahad looked up into wide, dark blue eyes and alabaster cheeks that bore the tracks of tears. He struggled to sit up.

Gawaine slammed his fist into the wall. "I'll kill him if he sets foot in

Britain!" His voice, half scream, half sob, broke upon the words. "I'll kill him! I've taken an oath upon it!"

"Yes," Arthur agreed quietly. "I've heard your oath."

"You exiled him so I couldn't take my vengeance!"

"I've made you King of Lothian and Orkney. Go take charge of your inheritance. Tonight."

"I know what you're doing, Arthur! I see right through you! You're trying to keep me from getting at him."

Arthur smiled bitterly. "You might say I'm trying to spare your life."

Gawaine waved a fist before the High King's face. "Oh, I'll kill him. This is one battle *I* will win. One day I'll kill him, even if no one is looking but me."

Arthur shrugged. "That's as may be. But you won't kill him tonight. Now go."

"Let me have my brother's sword."

"No." Arthur's voice was sharp. "It's not your gift. Lancelot gave it to him. I'll dispose of it as I judge best."

"But—"

"Enough. I've had enough of killing for one night. You are dismissed."

Gawaine paused, scowling, and then nodded curtly. "My lord King." He strode out.

"Galahad," the woman whispered. "Can you see straight? Can you speak?"

He looked up, his temples throbbing. Her white-gold hair was spattered with blood, but she seemed unharmed. The blood must belong to someone else. Even her pallor looked lovely in candlelight. Her beautiful eyes searched his as her trembling warmth enclosed his fear, soothed him, held him safe in the sanctuary of her affection. He fought a strong desire to lie back in her arms.

"Go away!" he whispered fiercely. "Leave me alone."

The King reached down, raised her, and took her in his arms. "He will be all right, Gwen," he said in a low voice. "Let me speak with him awhile. Go and see to Mordred. He's been asking after you."

"He's been weeping, Arthur. He must have cried himself to sleep before Gawaine came in. And he's wet to the skin. He needs a fire."

The King touched his lips to her cheek. "He's a strong boy. He'll live."

She nodded, managing a smile, kissed him quickly, and left them alone together.

Arthur lifted Galahad, wrapped him in Gareth's cloak, and sat him on the bed. He reached for his traveling flask and poured a dark liquor into the horn cup on Gareth's table. "Drink this." It was a command. Galahad drank. Somehow the fiery liquid got down his throat. He coughed, and found that he could speak.

"My lord, Gareth's not dead?" His voice shook. "It's not true, is it? It can't be!"

Arthur walked to the window and stood with his back turned. When he spoke, his voice was low and heavy. "It is an old, old story, Galahad. Envy, greed, ambition, distrust, and betrayal. Everyone has lost. No one has won. My fellowship of knights is torn asunder. If the kingdom itself survives this night's work, I shall count myself lucky."

"It can't be true!"

Arthur turned. "Tonight your father, my dearest friend and my companion of twenty years, was attacked by my own nephews. My own nephews and six others. All of them drunken fools who put more faith in gossip and rumor than in men." The King's eyes blazed. "He was alone and unarmed when they attacked him. And he killed them all."

Galahad trembled. "He was alone?"

"I meant he was the only warrior. He was in the Queen's chamber. But he had no sword, and neither had she."

Galahad stared unbelieving at the King.

Arthur's face hardened until it looked like stone. "You too, Galahad? I thought you knew your father better." His voice was cold. "The Queen sent for him in haste. She had received a message from a courier at a late hour. It was my message. I sent the courier. You saw me do it." He paused. "I commanded her to send privately for Lancelot and Mordred, to tell them Constantine was reported moving toward Camelot with troops. Secrecy was important because Constantine has spies in my household. I did not want anyone but these three—whom I would trust with my life—to know I'd be home tonight." He passed a weary hand across his face. "She was well attended. Three of her women were in the room. And Lancelot brought Gareth." Their eyes met. Arthur was the first to look away. "What happened only happened because fools believed the talk about them."

"But . . . Gareth . . . Gawaine said . . ." He could not finish. Arthur sighed heavily and came and sat beside him on the bed.

"Imagine yourself, Galahad, unarmed, set upon by eight drunken ruffians. You are sworn to protect the Queen, you have sworn that oath to *me*, and these men have burst into her chamber, waving swords, which is treason. How do you suppose he killed them all?"

"I don't know."

"I do. He went into a rage. He went mad. I have seen him so in battle. I have seen Saxons flee who only looked into his face. Soldiers call it blood lust. He doesn't know who or where he is. He simply kills everything that moves." Arthur's voice grew quiet. "That's just how the Queen described it, and she was there. She saw it all. . . . When the last sword fell, he stopped, but he did not know what he had done. Imagine his horror when he found that, in addition to his attackers, he had killed Gareth and knocked

Mordred senseless, although they had each come to his aid. But in his fever he knew them not."

"My *father* killed Gareth?" The King put an arm around him. "My *father*? How could he? I'll . . . I'll . . . I'll kill him for it!"

"You don't mean that. And it is not in your power to inflict a worse punishment upon him than he will, every day, every night, for as long he lives, inflict upon himself. Gareth's death will lie upon his soul forever. He has loved Gareth as a son since the day the boy came to Camelot—he would sooner have killed himself than kill Gareth. But he did not know what he was doing."

Galahad sobbed wildly against the King's chest. Arthur kept talking in a quiet, steady voice. "And poor Linet saw it happen. She was one of the Queen's attendants. Ah, God, but this is a black day for Britain! We are divided now and I fear we shall never be whole. Gawaine has sworn to kill Lancelot—not for Agravaine or Gaheris; they were doomed by treason as soon as they entered the Queen's chamber—but for Gareth. Gareth's death is just cause for vengeance and I cannot deny him his right. I can only hope to keep them apart as long as I can." He stroked Galahad's hair. "And Mordred, who took a sword in the shoulder, has cause for vengeance, too. He followed his Orkney brothers to the castle, and when he saw what they intended, went to fetch the house guard. He feared for the Queen's life. He did not think Lancelot could defend against them all." He paused. "But he will not seek vengeance. He told me what the Queen has told me. Lancelot saw only the sword before his face, not the man behind it. For my sake, for her sake, and for Britain's, he will not hold Lancelot to account."

Arthur looked down at Galahad. The boy's face was puffed with weeping and his eyes swollen half-shut. "Come, Galahad, put away your tears. It is time now to be a man. Gareth is with God; he does not share your grief. Your father escaped death tonight, and he saved the Queen's life. For that alone I forgive him all his other sins." He paused. "But you do see, don't you, that I had to exile him? For his own good, I have sent him back to Lanascol. We who are left, you and I and Guinevere and Mordred, we must see that his name is not blackened here in Britain. For Gawaine's tongue will not be idle long."

He rose and in the shadow of the door picked up a swordbelt and scabbard. "And we must bury Gareth with honor." Galahad's sobs subsided to hiccups but his breaths still came in gasps. The King came toward him, drew the sword, and held it flat across his palms. It was the same sword Galahad had seen on Gareth's hip a thousand times. The hilt was inlaid with blue enamel in the shape of twined sea serpents, as on the badge of Orkney, and down the blade ran Latin letters: *For the glory of God, the glory of Britain, the glory of Arthur.*

"This is Gareth's sword. I remember the day Lancelot gave it to him." Arthur smiled sadly. "He was only ten, but worth any two of his brothers in loyalty, piety, sense, and kindness. His brothers went out of their way to make him feel small and useless. It was Lancelot who saw his heart and knew him to be noble." He held out the sword to Galahad. "I give it to you. You were more a brother to Gareth than any who shared his blood. It is fitting you should have it. You are nearly eleven, aren't you?"

"No, my lord," Galahad said in a small voice. "I'm nine."

"Nine!" The King smiled. "Imagine my forgetting! I beg your pardon. Nevertheless, you are ready for it. You are nobly born and nobly raised; in your heart you serve the light."

Galahad accepted the sword gingerly. "I will do my best," he whispered, staring at the weapon.

Arthur raised an eyebrow. "You have promised me service, do you remember? It would give me great pleasure to see you wield that sword for me." He turned and looked out at the dark, howling night. "What we need," he said slowly, "is a good clean fight out in the open air, a bloody battle to cleanse our souls. It is the cure for jealousy and rank ambition, for boredom and the restlessness bred of peace. Let us face a foe of merit, an enemy so deadly we quake to meet him, and we will all stand together. Then we Britons will regard ourselves as brothers once again, and put away petty quarrels to save our skins." He rested a hand on Galahad's shoulder. "What we need," said the King, "is a war."

✝ BOOK TWO

PART I
Fields of Battle

In the twenty-sixth year of the reign
of Arthur Pendragon

26 ✠ THE LANDING

A n hour before sunset the first of Arthur's ships rowed into the Breton harbor on a sea as smooth as glass. A great crowd of men thronged at the wharfside, jostling for position, horses sidling, banners held aloft, shouting welcomes.

"Arthur! Arthur! Arthur of Britain!"

Galahad stood at the rail well aft of the group clustered around the King. He had not seen Breton soil since that awful journey, five years ago, which had ended in Gareth's death and Lancelot's banishment. He scanned the crowds for the banners of the men he knew. In the failing light he picked out the Black Boar of Brittany over King Hoel's men. He doubted that ancient warrior was there himself—they were probably led by Riderch, Hoel's eldest son, a man older than Arthur and still only a prince. And there . . . there was the one he looked for, the Hawk of Lanascol lifting proudly in the evening breeze. He leaned forward, searching intently for the face he dreaded seeing. But it was his uncle Galahantyn who led the Lanascol contingent. He waved, but Galyn's attention was on the High King and he did not notice.

The ship sidled up to the wharf; the great hawsers were swung down and secured. Men and horses shuffled into position as the procession ashore began. Arthur led, with Mordred and Gawaine at his heels, and then the companions and the kings and princes of Britain with all their trains. After a short ceremony of formal greeting, which Galahad was too far away to hear, the High King was given a horse and rode slowly away with Prince Riderch, the massed troops following in an orderly march out of town.

The full unloading of the ship would take half the night. Men and horses on the following ships would not come ashore till morning. The army, once encamped, could not move off toward Kerrec for three days at least. There was plenty of time. But Galahad hurried ashore, jostled this way and that by soldiers, pages, and servants, badgered by merchants with trays of goods to sell: sweetmeats, trinkets, copper armbands, cheap daggers for the unwary, charms and talismans of victory for the superstitious, tankards of ale for the thirsty, and every sort of worked leather from sandal straps and bootlaces to scabbards and thick gloves. He fought through the crowd to where the men of Lanascol had been.

They were no longer there. He was alone in the bustling throng where

Galyn had stood only twenty minutes past. They hadn't waited for him. Slowly he retraced his steps along the wharfside, following hundreds of others in a dusty procession out of town. Probably they thought Arthur had left him home. What use, after all, could he be? He was just fourteen, a full year too young for the army. In the coming glorious battle he could take no part.

"Galahad! There you are, at last!" He spun around as a long arm caught his shoulders and drew him into a warm embrace.

"Uncle Galyn!"

"Where have you been, lad? I looked for you everywhere. I was beginning to think you had not come. And if I hadn't seen your badge I'd not have known you. You'll be my height in another year, by God! Come and sup with us, won't you? We are camped up on the hill behind the town. The High King's tent will be near enough. And we want to hear your news."

"And I yours. King Arthur tells me I have another cousin. Congratulations."

Galyn laughed. "Three girls now, each one as pretty as their mother. They want to see you, Galahad, and so do your brothers. I hope you'll stop at Benoic if you get the chance."

Galahad avoided his eyes. "That depends. Who is with you, Uncle?"

"Bors and Cordovic, Menaduke with all his sons, young Hebes—though he's not half the swordsman you are—Lavayne, Nirovar, Sadok, Palomides and his brother Saffir, even old Selysus—"

"You've named every lord in Lanascol! Who is left to hold Benoic?"

Galyn grinned. "Your aunt Adele. Why do you frown so? She is as able as I am, except in warfare. Lancelot chose her himself and does me great honor by it. Don't worry, Clarres leads the house guard. He is loyal."

"You know Aunt Adele is dear to me," Galahad murmured. "It's not that. But . . . it's utter foolishness to let a woman rule a kingdom!"

Galyn looked amused. "Your own mother did not think so. Don't be so stiff-necked, boy. Arthur left Guinevere regent in Britain—what say you to that?"

"I'm not the only one who thinks it a mistake."

In the long May dusk they passed the wharfside warehouses and the inns with their doors flung open. Welcome scents of roasting meat hung in clouds above the dusty street; snatches of soldiers' songs drifted out to them as they trudged by, in step but silent. Galahad's stomach growled audibly. Beyond the wooden palisade that marked the village boundary they found themselves walking alone together, with no one near enough to overhear.

"You haven't yet asked after your father."

"I saw he wasn't here."

"He's in Kerrec with King Hoel. He wanted to leave me there and come himself to greet you and Arthur, but . . ."

"He knows Gawaine travels with the King," Galahad finished, "and he didn't want to chance that meeting in a wharfside village."

"Don't be absurd!" Galyn snapped. "You can't think he fears Gawaine!"

Galahad shrugged. "All of Britain is waiting to see *that* meeting. I know plenty of soldiers who've had bets laid on for years."

Galyn flushed. "That's *not* the reason he stayed away. You can't think so little of him. You, his own son."

"Can't I?" Galahad's face darkened. He kept his eyes on the ground.

"You still cannot forgive him? Five years is a long time."

"Gareth still lies in a bed of dirt."

"You honor him with your mourning, Galahad. But it is time for that to pass."

"Let's talk about something else. Please."

After a long moment Galyn nodded. "Tell me about the crossing, then. Had you good weather? How many men has Arthur been able to raise? The courier said ten thousand, but that number is beyond belief."

"Twelve thousand," Galahad said proudly. "Every able-bodied man in Britain answered his call."

"Twelve thousand! This is wonderful news! What with the men of Lanascol, Hoel's army, and King Childebert's men, we will be nearly twenty thousand strong! No one dared hope for so many."

"King Childebert! Must we fight with Franks? They have been our enemies so long."

"Not since old Clovis died. Childebert's a man who values peace. He soon saw sense in making an alliance with Hoel and Lancelot. And now that trouble has arisen"—Galyn hawked, turned, and spat—"he is doubly glad. Who would have thought that Rome would ever be our enemy again!"

"I thought the emperor asked only for tribute."

Galyn clapped a hand on his shoulder. "An old ploy, weakly veiled. The demand for tribute sent to Hoel and Childebert and Lancelot is more than any of them could ever pay. Rome knows it. And whom does she send to collect it? General Hiberius himself! It's clear enough: We must fight, or we must surrender. There is no middle ground."

"Then this war is with Rome? I thought we came to fight the Burgundians."

"We're fighting both. Burgundians are nothing but Rome's lackeys. Dogsbodies. Boot-licking catamites. At Rome's instigation, they attack us. If we pay the tribute, Rome will call them off."

"Are the Romans afraid to challenge us directly?"

"Aye, that's what your father thinks. It might be a war unpopular at home. Lancelot also thinks they might be shy of attacking Arthur outright. They know well he has never been beaten."

Galahad nodded gravely. "The Unconquered King."

Galyn grinned. "So is he known even among the consuls of Rome."

"The Franks have always been stiff-necked and proud. Will they acknowledge his command?"

"Aye, that is already settled. When we get to Kerrec he will be formally proclaimed chief commander. Then it is up to Arthur to win the respect of Frankish troops."

"Give him a week; they will follow him to the ends of the earth."

Galyn laughed with pleasure, and ruffled the boy's hair. "Well done! Spoken like a son of Lancelot! Thank God for the time you live in, that you have known such a man. When he is gone, we will not see his like again."

"Not propitious words, Uncle Galyn, when in a month we go to war."

"Well, well, with any luck, this war will come to nothing or be over by the solstice, and you can pass the summer with us in Benoic before returning."

"Not," Galahad said slowly, "if my father is there."

Galyn's hand slipped from his shoulder. They walked a while in silence. When Galyn spoke at last, his voice was low and sad.

"Lancelot wanted nothing more than to lead our contingent to greet King Arthur, his oldest and dearest friend. But he did not—he stayed in Kerrec with King Hoel and sent me instead—because he knew you would be near the King, and he wanted to spare you the pain of a public greeting, should you still hold Gareth against him."

Galahad kept his eyes on the rutted road and said nothing.

"Galahad, can you not find it in your heart to greet him as a son should? He loves you dearly and you repay him with grief."

Galahad did not respond and Galyn shook his head. "Well, well, perhaps it must wait until you are old enough to know him as a man. Come sup with us and bring us up-to-date on events in Britain. It's going on two years since I was there, and Cordovic, poor fellow, has never seen it. He is green with envy. Tell us about Camelot and the gathering of all the kings for war with Rome."

The Lanascol encampment was in a place of honor near that of Riderch, not far from the crest of the hill where the High King's tent stood, the Dragon of Britain already flying, red on a field of gold. Everyone came to greet Galahad, sons and fathers, lords and soldiers. This was but one more mark, Galahad knew, of the love they bore his father. He himself had never seen any of them since he was five years old.

They placed him in a seat of honor at the campfire and served him first. The food was rich and steaming, the wine mellow. In answer to their questions he told them all of Britain's preparations, named the kings and princes who had come, and with how many, and all the knights who traveled with them, and who was left to hold the kingdoms in their absence. But of Guine-vere, the Queen regent, he said nothing. It seemed everyone already knew.

To a man, they were delighted that so many had united behind King Arthur when Britain herself was not directly threatened. It was more than just repayment for the aid the kings of Less Britain had given to Arthur in the Saxon wars. But it was like Arthur, they said, to repay tenfold what had been given as a gift.

"There is one lord you have not mentioned," Bors growled. "What of Constantine of Cornwall? I saw the Cornish banner, but it was young Meliodas who led them. Where is Constantine?"

"He stays as guardian of the west. I heard the High King say Constan-tine had lately quarreled with Childebert, so he did not like to bring him. And clearly some trustworthy warrior must be left to safeguard Britain."

Bors snorted. "Arthur did not say *that*, I warrant. Those are your words, Galahad. I'd trust old Constantine about as far as I could catch him with my spear."

Galahad flushed. "Well, sir, the High King left him to guard the west. I heard him say so. If that is not trust, I don't know what is."

Bors laughed heartily, and downed his ale. "It's prudence, lad. What to do with a man who's a poisonous spider and can't be trusted? If you can't take him with you, give him a sop to his pride and a set of clear orders to obey. If he disobeys them, why then, you have the excuse you've been look-ing for to rid yourself of the pest. And mark my words, that's what the King will do." He glanced at Galahad, whose face was burning. "Well, well, this is only speculation. Forgive me, boy. Didn't mean to ruffle your feathers. We'll know in time. Come on, drink up, there's a lad. No hard feelings."

Galyn leaned forward. "It's true, Galahad, that Arthur has not trusted Constantine since he publicly named Mordred his heir. Remember, Con-stantine grew up knowing his own father had been named the High King's heir. But then, with Cador dead and Constantine himself next in line, to have an outland Orkney youth, and a bastard at that, take his place—"

"I grant you that he has reason to hold a grudge."

"Indeed he does, but if he does not see that the future of Cornwall lies in the unity Arthur has brought to Britain, he's a half-wit. If he risks offend-ing Arthur by trying something while the King's away, he will only do him-self irreparable harm. Young Meliodas knows this—that's why he's here with us—so Constantine must. Yes, Britain will be safe in Arthur's absence. The Queen is well protected, and believe me, she is no fool."

The talk soon turned to the coming meeting between Gawaine and Lancelot. Everyone in all Less Britain knew of Gawaine's oath to kill Lancelot, and within the week the two men would meet in Kerrec face-to-face. No one knew what might happen. No one could match Lancelot's skill with a sword, but Gawaine was fifteen years his junior and known for his great strength. It might be a close fight. To a man, the men of Lanascol declared themselves ready to defend Lancelot against Gawaine.

Galahad rose suddenly. "With your permission, my lords, I must report to the King. He will be wondering where I am."

"There is room for your bedroll in my tent," Galyn offered. "We would be happy to have your company. Why don't you stay? Surely Arthur can spare you."

Galahad shook his head. "Thank you, Uncle Galyn, but I must be there when he looks for me."

"What for?" Cordovic sneered. "You're not a soldier yet, and surely you are a little old to be a page!"

"I serve him as his personal guard," Galahad replied coldly.

"Ha!" Cordovic laughed. "A likely story! He has bodyguards aplenty! With an army of proven soldiers all about him, what need has he of a child of fourteen? He only tolerates you because he loves Lancelot so. Everyone knows it but you, fool."

As Galahad spun on his heel his sword leaped to his hand. Before any man there could draw breath to speak, the weapon flashed in the firelight and whipped down, slashing the leather lacings on the breast of Cordovic's tunic. The fabric fell open, revealing his flesh, unmarked, untouched by the blade. The sword slid softly home to its scabbard as Cordovic gasped and belatedly stepped back.

"If I'm a fool, what does that make you?" Galahad turned and walked coolly out of camp. No one stopped him.

27 ✝ THE PROMISE

It was dark when Galahad arrived at the High King's tent. Two sentries stood at the entrance, Gabral and Bryddon, the night watch. He moved to his accustomed place between them at the edge of the skins that closed the entrance and, drawing his sword, took up his stance. Gabral raised a hand in greeting; Bryddon turned his head to one side and spat.

"Where've you been, young lord?" Gabral whispered with a grin. "The King's missed you, he has. We been laying bets whether you was took sick from the crossing or whether"—with a sharp nudge of his elbow and a lurid wink—"whether you was bedded down with a lass in the bushes outside of town."

Galahad colored and Gabral chuckled. "I was hopin' you'd'a caught one o' they lasses down at wharfside. I seen a redhead"—he leaned closer and Galahad stiffened to keep from reeling at the stench of his breath—"I seen a redhead could lift a man's spear with a glance." He cackled and clapped a hand to his groin. "She lifted mine, right enough!"

Galahad smiled. "By your own account, that's not hard to do."

"Shut your trap, Gabral," Bryddon snapped. "Have you been at the wineskin? Think of war instead of women, just this once. If the King hears you, it's as much as your post is worth."

Gabral sobered and straightened. "Beg pardon, Bryddon. Just tryin' to lighten him up a bit. When he came up that hill he had such a face on him—I thought he was bit by a poisonous snake."

"Save your breath," Bryddon returned. "It's his natural expression."

Galahad glanced at Bryddon. The man had never liked him and he did not know why. "Is Arthur in council within?"

"Aye."

"With how many?"

"Ten." Bryddon grunted, avoiding the boy's brilliant eyes and staring instead over his shoulder.

"Who?"

The sentry's tone grew clipped. "Mordred, Prince of Britain. King Gawaine of Lothian and Orkney. King Bedwyr of Brydwell. King Urien of Rheged. King Maelgon of Gwynedd. King Melwas of the Summer Country. King Hapgar of Strathclyde. My lord Sir Gereint and my lord Sir Meliodas of Cornwall. And Prince Riderch of Brittany."

"Have they eaten?"

"Oh, aye, a while back," Gabral supplied eagerly, his glance flicking from boy to man and back. "And the wine's gone in. They be at council now. For hours p'rhaps. There be no trouble— Who goes there?" he cried suddenly, drawing his sword and taking a step forward. But no one answered, no one moved, no sound met their ears but the night whispers of the forest. All the same, Galahad sensed that someone was out there in the dark, beyond the flare of torches. He felt the presence. And he would trust Gabral's hearing beyond any doubt of his own. The man had the ears of a fox; he could hear a leaf fall. Thus he earned royal guard duty even though he was a half-wit. They waited a long moment, weapons poised, but heard nothing. Galahad felt the presence slip away. Gabral had already sheathed his sword.

"Scared him," he whispered, grinning. "Gone away to find food."

"Good man, Gabral," Bryddon grumbled and Gabral straightened proudly, throwing him a look of frank affection.

Galahad stood between them in silence. He did not understand the deep friendship between these men, the sour soldier and the half-wit, but it was a real thing, tangible and enduring, and he envied them for it.

The night deepened. The moon swung toward her setting and far away in the hills a wolf howled mournfully. Suddenly a great cheer went up within the tent. "To Arthur of Britain! Long may he live!" Galahad stepped back from the curtain just in time to escape a collision with Riderch, who came out laughing and staggered drunkenly, his arms slung around the shoulders of his companions. The sentries stood at attention, eyes forward, faces carefully neutral of expression. But Galahad watched the lords as they went by. Maelgon followed, with Urien, Hapgar, and the rest of Britain's honored princes, all in exuberant spirits, all rosy-cheeked and buoyant with the effects of wine. Last came Gawaine with Mordred, who was never drunk. They paused at the entrance.

"I promised him, Dred, in front of everyone. Why isn't that enough for you?" Gawaine's speech was thick, but he was steady enough on his feet. There was no need for Mordred's hand upon his arm.

"I know your temper, cousin—"

"Brother!" Gawaine snapped. "And don't forget it."

"Cousin *and* brother," Mordred agreed calmly. "And how could I forget it when I am so often reminded?"

Gawaine grinned maliciously. "Less Britain is swarming with Christians. There are plenty hereabouts who will hate you on account of your birth."

Mordred refused to be drawn. "No doubt. But I fear them not. We are come together in a great cause that overrides all others. My only fear, brother, is that you may forget this when you stand before Lancelot face-to-face."

Gawaine straightened and shrugged off Mordred's arm. "I tell you, Mordred, I will do as Arthur bids me. I will stand before my brother's murderer and forswear my vengeance while we both fight in Arthur's service."

"If you do this, Gawaine, I will honor you for it."

"I have sworn to do it. But I make no promises beyond the battle. When the fighting is behind us, then let him look to his defense. Before I leave Less Britain I will kill him."

"That day is your death day," Mordred said sadly.

"There you are wrong, fisher-boy. Our witch-mother saw my future in her glass. I will die by the hand of an enemy of Britain. So you see, if I live beyond this battle, I need have no fear of Lancelot."

Mordred's face went cold and his voice sank to a growl. "Call me 'fisher-boy' again at your peril."

Gawaine laughed loudly. "My pardon, Prince of Britain! You wish to leave your past behind you? No fault of yours when your future looks so bright!" He lowered his voice and leaned closer. "A word of advice, brother-cousin. Don't count your catch until the net is in." He hiccupped, turned to leave, swayed on his feet, and staggered into Galahad, who pushed him upright with a grimace of distaste.

"Get off me, you filthy— Who's that? *Galahad?*"

Gawaine glared at him but it was the look in Mordred's eyes that made Galahad blanch.

"My lords." He bowed to the space between them.

"So," Gawaine sneered, "the High King's spaniel has returned. Did you know that's what we call you behind your back? Ha ha!"

"Gawaine!" Mordred said sharply.

Gawaine thrust out his chin. "How long have you been there? How much have you heard?"

Galahad did not reply.

"Everything, no doubt," Mordred said coolly. "He always knows more than he lets on."

"I'll teach him a lesson!" Gawaine raised a fist, only to find it caught fast by Mordred. "Let me go, Dred! He's naught but a murderer's brat who dogs my poor uncle more closely than his shadow."

Mordred smiled. "You ought to befriend him, Gawaine. I believe he's the only man alive who despises Lancelot as much as you do."

Gawaine shrugged free of Mordred's grip and spat on the ground. "Man, indeed! He's a child. I bid you good-night, Mordred." And he strode away into the darkness.

Mordred looked steadily at Galahad, who trembled under his gaze. "I will tell my father you have returned." He disappeared into the tent and when he emerged some moments later he said nothing, did not even turn his head, but walked silently away and melted into the night.

Galahad exhaled and Gabral smiled. "He's a dark one, ain't he?" he whispered. "Got a devil spirit in him, ain't he?"

"Hush, Gabral," Bryddon growled. "Remember where you are."

"Mordred," Galahad asserted, "is abomination."

At that moment the skins parted and Varric, the High King's chamberlain, looked out.

"My lord Galahad, the High King would like a word with you."

Galahad swallowed and followed him inside. Arthur was seated amid a pile of skins and carpets, looking tired and sober. In the center of the dirt floor a small fire burned, encircled by stones, and all around it were the marks where the other kings had sat. Over the fire hung a flaccid wineskin, nearly empty. He rose as Galahad entered and the boy fell to his knees, kissing the great ruby on Arthur's hand.

"My lord Arthur."

"Come, Galahad, sit here by me and tell me what has passed with you. I lost you in the bustle of landing. I assumed you met up with Galahantyn and were taken to camp to greet your kinsmen?"

Arthur listened patiently as Galahad related the details of his day, nodding gravely and watching the boy's face with worried eyes. Galahad had met his kinsmen for the first time in nine years, had been offered the chance to join them, but had passed it by.

"Well, Galahad," he said slowly when the boy had finished. "Think twice about the choice you have made. Do you wish to stay and serve me, or would you rather join your countrymen and your kinsmen? I will not prevent your going, if you wish to."

"My lord, I will stay with you."

"Even though it means sleeping outside with Gabral and Bryddon? I wouldn't have thought they were much company for a lad like you."

Galahad smiled. "If I can't sleep, I can always listen to Gabral's tales about the women he wants."

"Gabral thinks of nothing but women because he has never had one," Arthur said, laughing. "He fears them."

Galahad's smile faded. He looked away. "So do I, my lord."

Arthur's hand came down on his shoulder. "That is common enough at your age. That kind of courage will come without thought when you are ready." He searched Galahad's face. "Consider the choice you've made, son. You can fight with the men of Lanascol. They will give you a place of honor among them and you can wield your sword in our joint defense. But I cannot offer you that chance, much as I would like to. Skilled as you are, you are too young for my army. I am bound by the rules I myself have set, and I cannot break them, even for you."

Galahad looked up at him and swallowed hard. "My lord, do you need my sword?"

"One sword, more or less, will not win or lose this battle. What I want is to see you and your father reconciled."

"Sir, I would rather serve you than my father. But I do not want others to think I fear the fighting."

Arthur smiled. "There is not a man in Britain who believes there is a drop of cowardice in you. And those who will say it, say it to rile you. Pay them no mind." He sobered, then, and regarded Galahad with the grave, assessing look he was known for. "Before you go, I want you to make me a promise."

"Anything, my lord."

"I have this night extracted Gawaine's oath to forswear his vengeance and deal civilly with Lancelot while they both fight in my service. If you wish to serve me, you must promise me the same. Behave toward Lancelot as a son should toward his father. Whatever is between you, let it die."

"I can't!" Galahad cried, fighting unexpected tears. "How can I?"

"Gareth was Gawaine's brother. Yet Gawaine will put his grief aside for a space of time, for my sake. I know he was your friend. But you have had five years to mourn him. Put that grief behind you now or it will do you harm."

Galahad struggled against the words he wished to speak. How could he tell the High King to his face that it was on Guinevere's account—not Gareth's—he could not love Lancelot? A *root bearing poison and wormwood, the wicked woman is*.

"I do not ask you to love Gareth any less," the King was saying. "Only to let go of the bitter grief that wears upon your spirit. Do this for your own sake, if not for mine."

"My lord," Galahad whispered, "I don't know how."

"Are you man enough to forgive your father? However much you have suffered from Gareth's loss, he has suffered a thousandfold."

"Sir, Gawaine has *not* forgiven him. I heard him say himself he will kill Lancelot before he leaves Less Britain."

"Well," Arthur said wearily after a long pause, "Gawaine has taken a first step toward forgiveness. They will fight side by side against the Romans. Gawaine has done the best he can. What, Galahad, is the best that you can do?"

With an effort the boy stilled himself and faced the King.

"For your sake, my lord, I will greet him as your battle captain. As your Companion. As king of my homeland. And . . . and as your friend."

Arthur placed both hands on the boy's shoulders and gazed into his face. Galahad trembled beneath that searching look.

"Not," Arthur said very softly, "as your father?"

"No. Sir, I cannot."

Arthur sighed deeply, and dropped his hands. "I cannot ask for what you cannot give. I will take what you offer me. You are bound by this oath, Galahad."

"Yes, my lord. I am bound."

"I wonder," Arthur murmured as the boy made his reverence and turned to leave, "if Gareth is the real source of all your pain. Had he died in battle, you would not feel so. There is something else hounding you, isn't there, son?"

Galahad fled from the tent.

28 ✟ THE STOWAWAY

Galahad knelt on the forest floor. All around him the great pines kept silent watch beneath the sliding stars. Small creatures rustled in the underbrush, now and then an owl called to its mate, and dark wings fluttered on the edge of sound far above his head. This was night's music, the song of the hallowed dark, and he welcomed it.

He bent his head in prayer. It was so hard to be a good soldier, to be like Arthur, to think of nothing but the coming fight and Britain's need. Why could he not forgive his father? Everyone else could. Why should it gall him that his father was so beloved, even after five years' banishment? Why did Aidan's tortured voice still ring in his ears? *Sin is anathema and those who commit it. Put them all away.*

From the bushes behind him came a stifled sob. He whirled and drew his sword. "Who's there? Show yourself." The sound ceased abruptly. Nothing moved. Even the owls were still. "Declare yourself, or it shall fare the worse for you. Come out, or I'll call the High King's men!"

The bushes trembled, then parted. Slowly a boy crawled out. All Galahad could see of him were large, glistening eyes in a filthy face.

"Come forward into the moonlight. I will not harm you unless you try to flee." He sheathed his sword and beckoned the youngster out. The boy was slightly built, thin to the point of weakness, and his ragged clothing hung limply from his body. But he did not carry himself like a beggar or a thief.

"Who are you?"

The boy looked up and twisted his hands together. "Please, my lord, do not ask me. Let me go, I beg you. Let me hide."

"Give me your name."

"Oh, no, I dare not!"

Galahad's hand went to the hilt of his sword. "Give me your name." The boy bit his lip, backing away. "In the name of Arthur, to whom you shall go if you evade me, give me your name and family!"

The boy fell to his knees and clasped his hands before him. "Oh, sir knight, I pray you, don't take me to the High King. He would give me into my father's hands, and I have disobeyed him!"

Galahad looked at him with new interest. "Indeed? What have you done? Have you killed anyone?"

"Oh, no! I'm not old enough—or strong enough—and besides"—he gulped suddenly—"I'm not sure I could."

"What a strange accent you speak. Are you an Irish dog?"

"Oh, no, my lord! I am a Briton. And a loyal one."

Galahad hesitated. The youngster's collarbones stood out so far from his flesh they cast shadows even in moonlight.

"How long has it been since you have eaten?"

The boy licked his lips and swallowed. "Days and days," he whispered. "Not since I left home."

"How did you get here? Who protects you? You cannot be a soldier, nor a page either, by the look of you."

Miserably, the boy shook his head. "My lord, I am a stowaway."

"Are you indeed? Is that what you have done? Disobeyed your father and stowed away to war? Sit here in the shadow of this tree. No one will see you. I have some jerky and a heel of bread, and a small skin of wine. For such courage you shall live until morning."

"Oh, sir knight, I thank you!" The boy grabbed his hand and kissed his fingers.

Galahad recoiled in surprise. "I am not a knight. Here. Eat. Perhaps it will give you the spine to tell me who you are."

When he saw how the boy attacked the food, Galahad believed his story. After he had finished and taken a long pull at the wineskin, the boy sat back, licking his fingers, and looked up at Galahad.

"Thank you, sir. May God and his angels bless your kindness. I think you saved my life."

Galahad grunted and sat beside him on the soft carpet of pine needles. "At least you are a Christian. Your clothes aren't much, but your manners speak of good breeding. You must have been raised in a civilized house."

The boy faced him, chewing his lip, and suddenly nodded. "My name is Percival, my lord. My father is Maelgon, King of Gwynedd."

Galahad whistled softly. "Prince of Gwynedd! How old are you?"

"Eleven, my lord, near the time of the last equinox."

"That's my birthday, too. I am fourteen."

Percival looked at him shyly. "You look older. I suppose it's because you're so tall. I took you for a king. You must be a king's son, at least."

"My name is Galahad."

Percival gasped. "Galahad! You are Lancelot's son! Why, we are cousins— your mother was my father's sister." He threw his thin arms around Galahad and hugged him tightly. Awkwardly, Galahad returned the boy's embrace.

"Be welcome, cousin. All my mother's kin are dear to me, for her sake. But why is it I don't know you? Your father has been to Camelot many times, yet not with you."

"He never takes me anywhere," Percival grumbled, straightening his filthy tunic. "I've never been out of our own valley, if you can believe it, until now. I don't know how he expects me to learn about the world if I don't see it. But he's well known to be shortsighted. I suppose he expects to live forever."

Galahad smiled. "So you saw your chance and took it. I like your spirit. And what did you expect to happen here in Less Britain, if you must keep hidden from your father?"

Percival grinned. "I suppose, like my father, I didn't give it enough thought. Truly, Galahad, God sent you in answer to my prayers. I thought for certain I should die here of starvation before the battle even began!"

"You might have. We are a long way yet from battle. Do you expect to fight in it?"

"I expect to try," Percival said firmly, lifting his chin. "Will you stop me?"

Galahad smiled. "I will do all I can to help you. But I thought you said you couldn't kill anyone."

"Well . . . there's a first time for everyone. When I don't think about it too much, it seems an easy thing to do."

"And where is your sword?"

Percival gulped. "I, well, I don't have one yet. But I have an excellent dagger." He drew this from his belt, raising the blade so it shone milk-white in the moonlight. Gravely, Galahad admired it. It was a fine, heavy weapon with a keen edge; it would take strength to throw.

"It's beautiful. Have you practiced with it?"

"Yes. I'm . . . I'm pretty good, too, until my arm gets tired." His eyes slid to Galahad's hip. "But you have a sword."

Galahad drew it and let him hold it, get a feel of the balance. "When you fight with it—when it crosses another sword—you can feel the life in the blade. It moves by itself, almost."

Percival's eyes shone with admiration. "I wish I had one! My father won't allow it. I have to wait until I'm fifteen to start sword training."

"Fifteen!" Galahad cried. "Why, that's unheard of, surely, even in Wales! I started when I was nine."

"But you were in Camelot. There is no backwater in all of Britain like Gwynedd." Percival lifted the sword, which shone deadly pale in the dark. "And I bet you have a fine horse as well. I have a runt, little better than a pony. Not fit for a prince of any age."

Galahad smiled at the boy's disgust, remembering his own envy of Cordovic's mare. "Yes, I have a fine horse. A young stallion from the High King's stables. His name is Farouk. He's still on shipboard. All the horses should be ashore by morning. Then we can go down and get him."

"We?" Percival spoke bitterly. "You, you mean. I'm not going anywhere in daylight."

"Then how are you going to fight in this battle? Are you going to sneak along behind the army all the way to Kerrec? It's a walled town, you know. And there are outlaws in the forest. How will you eat? Your clothes are almost gone. Who will you fight under? Who can protect you, if you stay in hiding?"

Percival handed him back the sword. "I left that part to God. And He sent me to you. Why can't I fight with you?"

Galahad shifted uncomfortably. "Go to your father and beg him to accept you, now that you've come across. What you did took courage. Perhaps he'll let you stay and serve Gwynedd."

"You don't know my father. First he'll whip me; then he'll hold me up to public scorn; then he'll put me on the next ship back. He'll take it as a slight that I came against his orders. No. I'm not going to my father."

"I suppose you *did* ask him straight out to let you come?"

"Of course! I pleaded. I begged. I fasted. He would not listen. He said I was too young. And he well knows the King takes youths my age as pages. But he would not allow it. He gave all the usual excuses. The truth is, I'm his only son and my mother is afraid. She fears everyone will die in this campaign. She made my father promise not to take me and he agreed because he, too, is afraid." He said this sadly, plucking pine needles from his leggings and averting his eyes. Galahad felt a sudden rush of great liking for this boy whose father was such a disappointment to him.

"Will not your mother get word to him when she discovers your absence? The courier may already be upon the sea."

Percival brightened. "Oh, no. My sister has seen to that."

"Your sister?"

"My sister, Dane. We are twins. She is a wonder, Galahad; she is afraid of nothing. She helped me get aboard the ship without being seen. By now she will have told my mother that at the last, my father relented and brought me with him. She will have given Mother one of Father's rings as a token of it." He giggled in delight. "We stole the ring a month ago, when he first refused me. It was Dane's plan. She can always tell what Father will do long before he does it, or even knows himself."

"Does she not risk your mother's anger when the ruse is discovered?"

Percival sobered. "She risks a great deal. But by the time the news gets home, we shall have won the battle and be returning victorious. At least, that is the plan."

"Then you had better fight in the battle."

"Let me fight with you, Galahad."

Galahad frowned. "You can fight with Lanascol. My uncle Galyn is your kinsman by marriage. He has room for one more bedroll in his tent."

Percival's restless fingers stripped a pine twig of its needles, and he stabbed the ground with it in irritation. "My father would demand my return. Would your uncle dare to deny him his rights? No, he could not do it. King Arthur would not allow dissension within his ranks, and I don't want to be the cause of argument. Why can't I fight with you? You are Lancelot's son—my father would not cross Lancelot for all the world."

"You can't fight with me. We must think of another way."

"But why not? We were meant to be together, don't you see? God sent me straight to you as soon as we landed. Tonight, as I was hunting about for scraps, I came across the tent you guarded and saw you there. Later, you came out to my hiding place and found me. You were led. It's a sign. Please, cousin, let me serve you."

"But you can't fight with me," Galahad said desperately, "because . . . I'm not going to fight."

"What?" Percival stared blankly at him. "What do you mean, not fight!"

Galahad drew a deep breath. "I serve Arthur, not Lancelot. And I'm not old enough for the army."

"So what? You're not a common soldier; you're Lancelot's son."

"Arthur can't break his own rules just for me."

"But that's nonsense!" Percival sputtered. "Fight with Lanascol, then! You said yourself there's room for you there. Lancelot would let you fight, however old you are. He'd never be afraid, like my father."

Galahad looked grim. "I don't serve Lancelot. I'm in Arthur's service."

"But they're best friends. Surely the King will let you go."

"He said he would. But I refused his offer." Percival stared at him incredulously. Galahad added stiffly, "I'm not afraid. But I won't fight under my father."

"When the future of Britain is at stake? In God's holy name, why not?"

Galahad's eyes, dark in the moonlight, glittered hard like precious stones. "Because. I just can't."

"Of course you can! It would be a great honor to fight in Lancelot's company."

"Not if . . . not if you couldn't obey his command. And I couldn't." Percival looked quickly away and Galahad flushed. "I'm not afraid! I . . . I don't shy at killing. It's just that . . . I can't forgive him. I've tried to, but I can't. He is my enemy. That's why I can't serve him."

"Forgive?" Percival said softly. "What has he done?" Galahad said nothing. Percival peered into his face. "Come on, cousin. What can he possibly have done, a man like Lancelot? Why, I would trade him for *my* father in a heartbeat!"

Galahad lifted his sword into the moonlight. "He killed the man who owned this sword."

"I thought it was your sword."

"It is now. King Arthur gave it to me the night its owner died. And the man who owned it . . . was my friend." He laid the sword across his knees. "Look at the hilt. Can you see the sea serpents? That is Orkney's badge. This sword belonged to the High King's nephew, Gareth of Orkney." Quickly he sketched in the events of that awful November night.

"So *that's* why everyone wants to see what happens when Sir Gawaine comes face-to-face with Lancelot!" Percival cried. "But why would Lancelot kill Sir Gareth, if he had come to Lancelot's aid?"

"According to Arthur, he didn't mean to do it." Galahad's face grew hot. "It wouldn't have happened—none of it would have happened—if he hadn't been in the High Queen's chamber!"

"Oh!" Percival gazed at his cousin. "What was he doing there?"

The innocence of the question took the heat from Galahad's fire. He scowled. "The King had sent a courier to the Queen with a message to share with Lancelot. The hour was late and she was already abed. So she sent for the regent in her chamber. She was well attended, the King says, and so was Lancelot."

"Well, of course they were. Where's the harm in that?"

"I've just told you what harm came of it."

"But that wasn't Lancelot's fault."

"It was," Galahad said slowly. "He didn't go to her chamber just as regent. He has loved her, he has worshiped her, since the day he met her. He has loved her all these years, and he has never loved any other woman."

Percival gazed at him steadily. "If he went to her at the Queen's command, you can't blame him for it."

"He was regent. He could have commanded her to come out."

"Oh, come on, Galahad. When Father's away in Camelot it's my mother who rules Gwynedd, no matter whom my father has appointed. You're blaming him for the wrong thing."

"He murdered Gareth."

"An accidental killing. Which he must regret as much as you."

"If he hadn't been there, it never would have happened. Gareth's brothers were trying to catch the pair together—and they did."

"Catch them at what? Were they abed?"

Galahad shrugged. "No."

"Then what you really blame him for is loving the High Queen."

Galahad sprang to his feet. "Yes! That is his sin! He loved her, he has always loved her past bearing—and he cared nothing for my mother!" Percival shrank back against the tree. "He never cared a straw for her. He took her from her home in Britain and never let her go back, even to visit. He was cruel to her; he made her weep. And all because he loved another woman. The High King's wife. A woman he couldn't have." He stopped, shaking, and looked down at the wide-eyed boy. "I ought not to have said all that. I beg your pardon. But it is a stain so black, so deep, so permanent, I can hardly breathe, sometimes, for the shame of it."

Percival rose to his knees and clasped his hands before his face. "Oh, cousin, do not be ashamed on my account; I will pardon you anything. Let me serve you, Galahad. Let me serve you and, through you, the King."

Galahad sheathed his sword. "You are Prince of Gywnedd, Percival. You cannot serve me."

"Oh, please, Galahad—I must take service somewhere if I am not to be sent home, and I would rather serve you than anyone. Please."

After a moment's hesitation, Galahad raised him and slid an arm around his shoulders.

"Let me take you straight to Arthur. He is the only one who could overrule your father in this matter. Since you have been so kind to me, I will do you a kindness in return. I will plead with him on your behalf."

The boy's mouth dropped open. "Do you know him so well? He will listen to you?"

"He listens to everyone. In the morning I will take you to him."

"Galahad." Percival gulped. "Does he know that Lancelot . . . loves Guinevere?"

"Oh, yes," Galahad replied sadly. "He knows. He has known that for a very long time."

29 ✝ PRINCE OF GWYNEDD

Arthur stood half-naked at the washbasin, splashing icy water over his face and chest and arms, when his chamberlain, Varric, ushered the boys inside the tent at dawn. Percival huddled behind Galahad, trembling uncontrollably.

"Tell him the truth, the whole truth," Galahad muttered under his breath for the twentieth time, "and all will go well."

Varric took a clean cloth from the traveling chest and toweled the High King dry.

"Well, Galahad, what is it? Don't bring me bad news, I pray you, for this has all the earmarks of a fine spring day and I intend to enjoy it. How did you pass the night? Did you sleep well?"

"Yes, my lord. Thank you. Passing well."

All traces of last night's fatigue had left the King; he looked strong and fit and eager, the warrior King of Britain. He had not looked so for years. He drew on his tunic as Varric toweled his hair. The beard he had grown on shipboard was newly shaved away. He looked nearer thirty than forty, which was his age. He looked, Galahad thought suddenly, like Mordred.

"Sir, I have brought someone to meet you."

Arthur pushed the towel aside, saw Percival, and waved Varric away.

"So you have. Come forward, young man."

"King Arthur!" Percival whispered, falling to his knees and kissing the great Pendragon ruby. Arthur raised him and looked him over well.

"That is my name, sir, but you have the better of me there."

"Oh!" Percival blushed to the roots of his hair. "I'm so sorry! I mean . . . I . . . my name is Percival, my lord. Son of Maelgon of Gwynedd."

"Maelgon!" Arthur looked at him again sharply, and then began to laugh. "I'll wager a talent of silver your father does not know you are here."

"No, he does not! I stowed away secretly and last night Galahad found me. I would have stayed hidden, but he said I must come to you."

Arthur grinned. "Stowed away to war? Brave lad. I'd have done the same myself in your place. You're old enough to join us, by the look of you. You must be twelve."

Percival looked pleased. "Nearly, my lord." Galahad prodded him gently in the ribs. "Er, I mean, eleven at the equinox just past. But even so, my lord, I am old enough to serve. Many of your pages are even younger."

"Why did your father leave you home?"

The King stood before him, hands clasped behind his back, looking calmly down upon him and awaiting his reply. It dawned on Percival that he was being questioned—alone and man-to-man—by the High King of all Britain, the man of a thousand legends, the Saxon-Slayer, the Dragon himself, who bathed in ice water before breakfast and who glowed with vigor, strength, and health. He shifted from foot to foot and stared nervously at his toes. Galahad poked him fiercely in the back.

Then the King reached out a hand and gently raised his chin until he looked into the boy's face. Percival met his eyes, warm and brown and kind, and his fear slid away. He took a deep breath. He could tell this man anything.

"I know you asked him," Arthur said gently. "Tell me, what was his reply?"

"Sir, he said I should stay home and protect my mother."

"Ah. Do you think that an unreasonable request?"

"No, my lord. Only, she is well protected. My uncle Peredur was left in charge. He is a good fighter and a skilled hunter. He can keep my mother and sister safer than I could."

Arthur nodded gravely. "No doubt. But is that what your father meant?"

Percival stared. "What else could he mean?"

Arthur shrugged lightly. "Only that your uncle has a wife and children of his own. It is only natural that their interests will be foremost in his thoughts. However loyal he is to Maelgon—don't misunderstand me, Percival. I know Peredur. He has not the makings of a traitor in him. Your lady mother will be safe enough. But safety is not all, especially to women. Will she be first in any man's thoughts while you and your father are both away?"

Percival swallowed hard. "I did not think of that, my lord."

The King placed a hand on the boy's shoulder. "What's done is done. It is hard, after all, for a youth your age to understand what a soldier feels when he must leave the ones he loves so completely in the hands of others." His voice trailed off and for a moment he stood lost in thought. Percival and Galahad exchanged quick glances. "But you have made the effort," he said briskly, coming back to himself, "and will be the wiser for it. There is no going back now."

"Oh, my lord! Then you will not send me home? You will allow me to stay and take service with Galahad?"

Arthur looked amused. "So that was the plan. No, I don't think I can allow that. Varric!"

"My lord?"

"We will be three at breakfast. That is, if my young lords will do me the honor?"

Percival and Galahad gaped, then spluttered eager acceptance. Varric spread a carpet on the ground and the King bade them sit down beside him. Within minutes Varric brought them wooden bowls of steaming porridge studded with raisins, a plate of new bread, sliced thick, a comb dripping with honey, strips of jerky, and a flagon of milk still warm from the goat. The boys ate like young wolves; Percival had a second helping of everything and licked the honey from his fingers. The King ate sparingly and drank only water.

"My lord." Varric poked his head through the curtain. "Prince Mordred is here."

"Bid him go ask Maelgon to attend me here as soon as he has broken his fast. Then tell Mordred I will meet him by the horse lines. Keep everyone away, Varric, until Maelgon leaves."

"My lord King," Galahad ventured when Varric had withdrawn, "must you send for King Maelgon? I persuaded Percival to come out of hiding and place himself in your hands. Must you . . . must you give him to his father? Percival will think I have betrayed him and regret the day he met me. And . . . and he is my kin, besides."

"Oh, no!" Percival cried. "I would never think so, Galahad—you saved my life!"

Arthur looked gravely at them both. "What would you have me do?"

"Let him serve *you*, my lord, if he cannot serve me. He could be a page, perhaps, if . . . unless . . . maybe you need another guard?"

Arthur smiled. "So short a time you have known one another, and already friendship has taken root and grows." He pushed his plate aside and leaned forward, chin on fist, watching their faces. "King Maelgon is a staunch ally. He commands a strong force of fighting men. I need them. I cannot afford to dishonor him before this gathering of kings. And I would not do it if he commanded no one. He is the Queen's cousin, and thus kin to me. If I dishonor him, I insult her. And I would not do it even if we had no ties of kinship. For he is a man, and deserving of honor, until he betrays my trust." He paused. "What say you to this?"

The boys glanced swiftly at each other. It was Galahad who spoke.

"Certainly you are right, my lord. King Maelgon must not be dishonored."

"Young Percival has disobeyed his father's command. He admits himself that it was not an unreasonable command to obey. If I take him into my service without Maelgon's permission, what is that but a slap in the face to his authority?"

Percival flushed and lowered his eyes. "You are right, my lord."

"So," Arthur continued calmly, "we will ask his permission."

"But he will never grant it," Percival whispered. "You do not know him."

At this the King laughed outright. "Not know him? I daresay I know him well enough. I would make you a wager, my dagger against yours, that he will give you permission to stay. But I will not make it, because I know that I will win and that looks to be a weapon much beloved."

"Indeed, my lord, it is," Percival replied, brightening as he drew it forth. "It belonged to my grandfather King Pellinore. My grandmother Alyse gave it to me on my birthday. I think she foresaw I would have need of it."

"It would not surprise me. She is a shrewd woman." Arthur turned the sheath in his hands and drew the blade. "So this was Pellinore's, was it? It's a fine example of Celtic craft; the art of its making is known to few."

They heard raised voices in the distance. Arthur handed Percival back his dagger and said swiftly, "Be penitent, boy. Bend yourself to the strong wind, and you will still be standing when the storm is past."

"My lord King Maelgon!" Varric announced. No sooner were the words out of his mouth when Maelgon strode into the tent. He bowed low.

"My lord Arthur . . . *Percival!* By God, how came you here?" His face darkened and the very bristles of his beard seemed to stand out straighter from his face. Arthur motioned him to sit.

"Come join us, Maelgon. Sit here at my right hand, and you will learn how it came about."

"I told you to stay and protect your mother!" Maelgon shouted. In the corner, Varric coughed warningly. Maelgon saw suddenly that he was standing while the High King sat. Angrily, he seated himself across from his son.

"Varric, a pitcher of ale for the king," Arthur called. What followed was a lesson in diplomacy Galahad never forgot. Arthur toasted Maelgon's health and the success of their joint venture against the Romans, forcing Maelgon to drink of the ale for courtesy's sake. When, scenting delay, Maelgon demanded to know how his son came to be there, Arthur calmly related how Galahad had found him and brought him to the King. "We are all family here," he said, thereby reminding Maelgon he was Galahad's uncle, and that anything said in that small circle was between kin. Maelgon grunted, but acknowledged it. He was clearly furious, but since the High King was so pleasant and courteous, his righteous indignation was out of place. At Arthur's signal, Percival went on his knees before his father and confessed every detail of his disobedience, justifying nothing, bowing his head in submission and letting his father's rage wash over him in waves. He offered no resistance, accepting scorn and insults without batting an eye, agreeing to whatever punishment Maelgon threatened to give him. Gradually, Maelgon's anger abated. No one offered him argument or challenged his right. At last he sat back and drained his tankard, which Varric hurried to refill.

"Can you give me one good reason why I should not send you back on the next ship to Britain?"

Percival hung his head. "No, my lord."

"Hand over my father's dagger." Percival went white, but obeyed. Maelgon tucked the dagger in his belt. "You are not worthy of your birthright as Prince of Gwynedd."

Percival's eyes filled with tears. Galahad shot a desperate glance at Arthur, who was watching Percival with great compassion.

Maelgon, satisfied at last, sighed deeply. "It grieves me to do it," he said to the King, "but I cannot keep him here. He is too young to fight and all the men know I commanded him to stay."

"And your lady wife?" Arthur murmured, half to himself. "Surely she will suffer great distress when he returns in shame."

Maelgon colored. "Aye, my lord. But there is no help for that."

"Well," Arthur said easily, "perhaps there is another solution." Maelgon looked up sharply, but the King's face was blank and guileless, his eyes focused on some distant thought.

"What have you in mind, my lord?"

"I am thinking of your honor, Maelgon, and of your lonely queen, Anet. If you sent her, instead of Percival, a message saying you had changed your mind and decided to take him, it would make her proud, would it not?"

Maelgon's face darkened. "Perhaps, my lord. But I have not changed my mind. He cannot serve me."

"Perhaps not. But he can serve *me*."

Arthur smiled, and Maelgon was forced to swallow his anger. "I am organizing the pages and the grooms, and all the other boys now in my service, into a small corps to serve as hospital guards and scavenger hunters during battle. I will need every able-bodied man upon the field. They all have a weapon of some kind, a sword or a dagger, and while we fight they can at least protect our wounded behind the lines. Galahad will have the training of them." Galahad's eyes widened, but he kept his surprise from showing on his face. "With your permission, and if the lad is willing, I would welcome your son in this group. As Galahad's cousin, he would be second-in-command. Thus will he have the chance to do you honor, Maelgon, instead of bringing you shame."

Maelgon frowned and grumbled, knowing he had been outwitted, but pleased nevertheless at the result. At last he grinned and slapped the High King heartily on the back.

"Arthur of Britain! By God, I'm glad to have you as my commander! I'll take your bait if we can keep the truth a secret."

"We are all kin here. Let us swear an oath upon it."

The boys swore eagerly, the men solemnly, and afterward they drank another toast.

"Here, boy, take your dagger." Maelgon grunted. "I wasn't going to keep it. I know how precious you hold it. I wanted to see if you would give it up to me." He glanced at Arthur. "He's better behaved with you, my lord, than ever he was at home."

"That," Arthur said, smiling, "is the way of youth." He rose, and they all rose with him. "Galahad, see if Varric can find Percival some decent clothing before he steps outside in daylight. I am off to the wharf to greet the men who came ashore last night, and see to the horses. These creatures Riderch brought us are fit for harness only. Wait until he sees the animals Lancelot has bred!" And with a laugh of pleasure, he departed.

Maelgon laid a heavy hand on Percival's shoulder. "You'll be the death of me, boy, if you don't learn to obey orders. If you disobey Arthur, there will be no second chance." He turned and left, still grumbling.

Galahad and Percival found themselves alone in the High King's tent.

"There. What did I tell you? Arthur listened to you, and outmaneuvered your father. You'll get to stay and serve Arthur as Prince of Gwynedd."

Percival grinned. "I knew if I stuck to you everything would be all right."

30 ⊕ THE MEETING

Kerrec was a walled town set on a low hill at the edge of the thick Breton forest. The old Roman road led straight from the harbor to the great gates, but centuries of neglect had taken their toll and the once-level highway was cut by gullies, overgrown by scree, reduced in places to little more than a rutted track through the overgrowth. Nearer the town the forest fell back before cleared fields and pastures. Here among the cattle stood ranks of standing stones, black and silent sentinels of a time gone by.

In a hundred years the town had grown beyond its original stone walls. Now a second embankment had been thrown up, topped by a palisade, around the fields, houses, gardens, workplaces, and streets that comprised Kerrec New Town.

Galahad and Percival rode side by side in the train of Arthur's troops as the army passed in a long file through New Town and up the ramp to the ancient gates of Old Kerrec. Percival's mount, a bony carthorse scrounged up from somewhere at the last minute, had such an awkward gait it took all of his concentration and a good grip on the mane to stay on his back.

When the procession halted before the gates, Percival looked up from his horse's withers and looked around. "Is Benoic as big as this?"

Galahad shook his head. "Benoic's not even half this size."

Percival laughed as a posy of wildflowers landed in Galahad's lap. "You never told me you had admirers in Brittany! What pretty girls!"

Three young maidens had stepped forward from the gathered onlookers and now stood gazing up at him, wide-eyed and giggling. Reddening, Galahad brushed the flowers to the ground.

Percival winked at the girls, but to Galahad he said soberly, "Where is Lancelot? In the king's house with King Hoel?"

"I suppose so."

"That's wise of Arthur. To arrange it so that Lancelot and Gawaine meet for the first time while he's there watching."

"Arthur's nothing if not wise."

"What will you do if Gawaine challenges him?"

Galahad shrugged. "I'll watch, like you. Lancelot can take care of himself." Another posy landed in his lap and Galahad's face flamed. He flung the flowers to the ground without taking his gaze from between his horse's ears.

Percival felt a tug on his sleeve. A slender, fair-haired girl looked up shyly at him. "Please, good sir, to tell us the name of yonder handsome knight, your friend, who turns his back on us?"

Percival grinned. "You can't really think he's handsome, can you? With his face so red? Galahad, do you hear? They admire you for your beauty, of all things—they don't even know who your father is! His name is Galahad, maiden, and he's Prince of Lanascol."

The wide-eyed girl curtsied to the ground. "Sir Lancelot's son! God be thanked, and keep him safe from harm." The crowd grew quiet at the mention of Lancelot's name, and many among them bared their heads.

"You do me no favors, Percival," Galahad snapped. "I should have let you starve in the forest."

A rider trotted down the lines, reining in his horse as he came alongside them.

"Galahad. Percival." He inclined his dark head politely as he addressed them. Galahad sat unmoving, looking him steadily in the face. Something flashed in the rider's black eyes, as if this was not behavior he expected, but he spoke courteously to them both. "The King has given the order to set up camp near the east gate, next to the Franks. Percival, you are bidden to find your father and stay with the men of Gwynedd until the King sends for you."

"Very good, my lord. I will."

"Galahad, you are bidden to attend the King. We go in to greet Hoel." The black eyes narrowed as a small smile touched the rider's lips. "And Lancelot. See you don't keep him waiting." With that, he put spurs to his horse and cantered back up the lines.

"Who was that, wearing the dragon cipher?" Percival whispered anxiously. "And why didn't you bow your head? I saw his face—he was affronted."

"That," Galahad replied stiffly, "was Mordred."

"Oh! So that's Sir Mordred!" Percival lowered his voice. "I heard one of the soldiers say he's the High King's son but not the Queen's. Is he a bastard, then? And heir because there is no trueborn son?"

"It's worse than that," Galahad said through clenched teeth. "Mordred is abomination."

Percival glanced quickly about them but none of the bystanders had heard. He leaned closer to Galahad. "Why is that? Is his mother so ignoble?"

Galahad glared at him. "Don't you get any news in Gwynedd? Or did your parents keep you in the dark on purpose? His mother is Queen Morgause of Lothian and Orkney. Gareth's mother. Gawaine's mother."

Percival brightened. "Brother to Sir Gawaine and son to the High King. He is nobly born, indeed."

"Brother and cousin," Galahad said bitterly. "Queen Morgause is Arthur's sister."

Percival paled. "You mean—"

"Yes. Bishop Landrum says Mordred is damned on account of his birth. He's a fiend in prince's trappings. He's abomination."

"Keep your voice down, for pity's sake," Percival urged in a whisper. "You're speaking treason!"

"I am speaking nothing but the truth."

"You're calling the High King's son a fiend! It's as much as your life's worth if anyone should hear you."

Galahad shrugged contemptuously. "Mordred knows what he is. He can never be High King."

Percival's eyes bulged. "Of course he can, if he's the High King's heir."

"He will never wear Arthur's crown. I have sworn an oath before Bishop Landrum that if he attempts it, I shall slay him."

Percival's jaw dropped. "You'll *what?*"

The horn sounded and the procession began to move.

"Cousin!" Percival cried, but Galahad ignored him. Soon they were trotting and the effort of staying in his saddle took all of Percival's attention.

Double wooden gates set into thick walls of dressed stone guarded the entrance to Kerrec Old Town. As he passed within, Galahad saw rank upon rank of soldiers' barracks and workmen's shops of every kind: smiths, coopers, carpenters, engineers, and masons—one could tell their skills by the sounds inside, as well as by the signs upon their doors. The tanners, saddlers, and bootmakers he could smell. The narrow streets thronged with people who had come to greet King Arthur. They stared as the men rode by, now and then calling out a greeting to the King or to a man they knew, and blessing him in the name of whichever god was sacred to them.

In the forecourt of the king's house Arthur's company dismounted. Unlike the fortress of Camelot, the king's house was not a castle of stone but a large, rounded, timbered dwelling with a roof of tiles patched with thatch. Servants brought them basins of water to wash with and they cleansed themselves of the dust of travel. Galahad followed the men down an ill-lit hallway until they came to a set of double doors. Suddenly he heard the High King's voice. "Where is young Galahad? Bring him to me."

"Here I am, my lord!" The press of men pulled back to let him through. Galahad looked up at Arthur. The High King wore his crown, a simple crested band of beaten gold that shone bright against his dark hair, lighting the dimness. Although the day was warm he had donned his scarlet cloak, pinned at the shoulder with the dragon brooch. At his side hung wonderful Excalibur, the great emerald in the hilt glinting as he moved. *Long life!* it signaled, *Victory to Britain!* No one could mistake the message: This was the High King of all Britain, the One Unconquered, awesome, aloof, and powerful, who held all their futures in his hands.

"Galahad, I want you near me. Stand here, behind Mordred and Gawaine, as we go in." The dark eyes met his. "Remember your promise to me." A swift glance at Gawaine. "Both of you."

Arthur gave the signal and the doors opened. The hall was packed with soldiers, the Breton commanders and officers on one side, Franks on the other. A narrow passage opened between them; down this walked Arthur. Galahad could feel the tension in the men he passed. It was more than the distrust of ancient enemies newly allied. All their eyes were on Gawaine of Orkney. Galahad wondered suddenly if Gawaine's word could be trusted. The Orkneyman walked stiffly, head up and eyes forward. But his hands, held at his sides, were bunched into fists. His reputation as a fierce fighter had obviously preceded him across the Narrow Sea. Would his hot temper get the better of him, despite the vow he had made to Arthur? Mordred had thought it possible. Was this the spectacle all these men had come to see, a fight to the death between Gawaine and Lancelot? And what would Arthur do when Lancelot killed him, the last living of Lot's children, his own sister's son? Galahad's palms began to sweat and he schooled his face to show nothing.

At the far end of the hall upon a low dais King Hoel of Brittany sat in a great, carved chair. He was old and frail, with thin gray hair and sagging flesh that had onced housed a larger body. Even thick robes of rich velvet could not hide the thinness of his frame. But his eyes, light blue and quick, missed nothing. To his left stood Childebert, King of the Franks, a stocky man of middle years, sharp-featured and ill at ease, whose eyes flitted restlessly over the congregation and whose jeweled fingers played nervously around the hilt of his sword.

In sharp contrast, Lancelot stood as still as stone on the other side of Hoel's chair, tall, lean, and self-possessed, his eyes on Arthur. Galahad saw at once the change in him: five years had aged him ten. There were silver threads in his black hair and his temples had gone gray. The crown of Lanascol encircled his brow, a silver band set with garnets. His clothes were plain and self-effacing, and he wore no badge, but the hawk had been beautifully stitched in silver threads on the breast of his dark tunic. Who had done that? Galahad's mother never would have and his aunt Adele was not so skilled with a needle. Suddenly he remembered the fine stitching upon the sword hanger in the king's room in Lanascol, and the beautifully embroidered cushions in Arthur's library. A cold draft pricked his skin. How did Lancelot dare wear that tunic to greet the King? It was a badge of shame, and yet he wore it like a badge of honor.

Then his throat went dry as he saw that his father was not wearing a sword.

"Welcome, Arthur," Hoel grumbled as Arthur bowed, and the endless formal greetings and introductions began.

Galahad stood quietly and listened, but all his senses were attuned to Gawaine, beside him, and to his father on the dais. He could feel Gawaine's hatred like a wave of heat, sweeping past him, engulfing everything in its path. Mordred must have felt it, too, for he took a half step forward in front of Gawaine and hooked his thumb casually in his swordbelt.

Arthur and Childebert exchanged civilities. The High King took his time and spoke to Childebert in his own tongue. Childebert visibly relaxed and nodded, pleased, to much of what the High King said. Where had Arthur learned to speak the Frankish language? Galahad knew a few words himself, swear words and name-calling, mostly, but he, who had grown up a week's ride from Frankish lands, he could not speak as fluently as the High King. Hoel looked tickled and interjected once, slapping his knee and laughing outright. At the end of the exchange, Childebert stepped forward and took Arthur's hand, lifting the great Pendragon ruby to his lips. A shout went up from all the gathered men. No stronger sign of unity could be given from king to king.

While cheering filled the air, Arthur turned at last to Lancelot, who came forward and bent his knee. But before he could kneel Arthur raised him and embraced him, hugging him and speaking softly, while Lancelot's face lit with joy.

Mordred stepped forward and began to kneel, but Lancelot gripped his arm in the soldier's embrace.

"Arthur's son does not kneel to me," he said roughly in a voice heavy with emotion. "How are you, Mordred? It is good to see your face again. You grow more like him with every passing year."

"In spirit as well as flesh, I hope," replied Mordred with a smile. "You are looking well, my lord. We have missed you in Camelot. Arthur speaks truth when he says that without you we are a ship without a sail. All the men look forward to fighting beside you."

Lancelot smiled and glanced toward Arthur. "He does me too much honor." The smile faded. "I hope I shall see battle. But that is up to Gawaine."

The hall quieted instantly as Lancelot stepped in front of Gawaine. Slowly, while every man in the room held his breath, Lancelot sank to both knees and bowed his head.

"I beg your pardon, Gawaine of Lothian and Orkney. I have done you a grievous wrong. For the deaths of your brothers Agravaine and Gaheris I am responsible but guiltless. But for the murder of Gareth . . ." He stumbled over the word and his voice choked. He drew a long breath to steady himself. "For the murder of Gareth I am alone at fault. He was innocent of wrongdoing and I slew him. I carry this stain upon my soul until my death, and God will judge me for it. I beg your forgiveness. I will submit to any penance you see fit to give me."

There was a long silence while Gawaine struggled for the control to speak. No one moved. Arthur stood at Lancelot's side, a hand upon his shoulder, and stared hard at Gawaine. That redheaded warrior visibly shook with anger, looking down on Lancelot's bowed head, but he dared not touch his sword. Finally, he spoke.

"I do not forgive you, Lancelot. You're very clever to come to me unarmed and try to make your peace in public. I do not require penance. I require your life." Arthur stirred and Gawaine said quickly, "But I have promised my uncle the High King that while we both fight in his service I will not harm you. For this long, you are safe from me. Fight, then, Lanascol, fight for Britain and fight well. For at battle's end you shall meet me. You owe me a life."

Lancelot rose sorrowfully and bowed. "At battle's end, my lord," he said wearily. He turned away, but Arthur caught his arm.

"Stay, Lancelot. There is more ahead than grief. Turn around."

Lancelot turned and Arthur beckoned Galahad forward. He stepped out from behind Gawaine and saw Lancelot's eyes widen.

"*Galahad?* My son." Lancelot wrapped his long arms around Galahad and embraced him. Galahad stiffened. His head hammered. His breath stopped in his throat. And then he saw Arthur's eyes. He dropped his gaze obediently and allowed Lancelot to kiss his cheeks.

"I did not recognize you—you have grown three handspans in five years! What a comely lad you have become—you have your uncle's beauty and your mother's eyes."

"And *your* skill with a sword," Arthur interjected, smiling, with an arm about Lancelot's shoulders.

"That should be no surprise, my lord, after nine years in Camelot training with the best in Britain."

"Alas," said Arthur in a low voice, "these last five years the best has been in Lanascol, not in Britain. How we have missed you, Lancelot! But your son does you great credit. He learns everything as fast as we can teach him."

"Commendation from the High King is praise worth having. You make me proud, Galahad, to be your father."

Again, Galahad felt the pressure of Arthur's stare. He bent his knee. "Thank you, my lord. It is my wish to be worthy of the expectations you and the High King have of me. I pray God I may do Britain honor."

"Well spoken, son." Lancelot stepped closer. He raised Galahad and looked into his face. "Are you here to fight? Will you fight for Lanascol? You can do Britain honor now on the battlefield if you fight with me."

Galahad flinched under his gaze and shot a look at Arthur.

"He has sworn an oath to serve me," Arthur said lightly, "and I have put him in charge of the house guard, such as it is. As both you and Gala-hantyn want to be in the front lines, I thought it best for Lanascol to do this. I dislike to disappoint you, Lancelot, but it is better so."

The two men looked at each other and some message passed between them that Galahad could not read. Lancelot nodded slowly. When he looked at Galahad again, his gray eyes grew sad.

As the kings of Britain came forward to greet Hoel and Childebert, Galahad retreated into the crowd. It had all happened as he had thought it would. Arthur had protected him as promised, and Lancelot knew that but for his own presence there, Galahad would gladly have fought with Lanascol. It had all gone smoothly.

Then why did he feel so wretched? Why did he feel as if *he* had done something wrong? *A good man is like a white robe.* Everyone present knew of Lancelot's transgression. Gareth's murder was only a part of it. How could they still love him? And how could Arthur, who knew firsthand the wicked-ness of seduction, who himself had fallen prey to a woman's corrupt desire when he begot Mordred, how could Arthur welcome the very man who had betrayed him? Who wore, to greet Arthur, a tunic embroidered by the lov-ing hand of Arthur's wife! Was he, Galahad, the only one in this hall of men who recognized the enemy? Could he alone see the tawdry truth for what it was? A lump rose in his throat. *Sin is anathema, and those who commit it. Put them all away.*

With tears in his eyes he spun on his heel and pushed his way out of the hall.

31 ✝ LANCELOT'S CURSE

In the darkest hour of the night Galahad awoke in a sudden sweat. He gasped for breath, his chest tight, and pushed himself upright. His bedroll was soaked—dew on the outside, sweat on the inside. He glanced hurriedly around. The torch in its stand outside the High King's tent was nearly out; it must be close to dawn. Bryddon was frankly asleep on his feet, leaning on his sword and snoring softly. Gabral nudged him with a toe.

"Nightmare?"

Galahad gulped, and nodded. "I guess so."

"It be Frankish air. Bad for Britons."

"Nonsense, Gabral. We're in Brittany. We're a long way from Frank-ish air."

"Too much feasting, then." He grinned. "Too much wine."

Galahad shook his head. King Hoel's feast had been a good one, and the wine had been sweet and unwatered, but he had partaken lightly of Hoel's offerings and knew that the source of his distress lay not in what he ate or drank, but in his dreams themselves.

He passed a shaking hand across his brow. It was the third time in the week they'd been in Kerrec that he'd had this dream just as he awakened. No, not a dream, but a memory, for the horror was real. It had happened just before they had left Camelot for Brittany. While he was awake he could keep the memory dark, but in his sleep it was liable to return to him with all the power of the original event. He covered his face with his hands.

It was a soft, spring evening in Camelot. In the dim quiet of the chapel the burnished altar cross glowed in the gilded light of candles. Outside in the town and in the meadows, the fortress thronged with crowds. They spilled out beyond the walls onto the slopes of the hill itself, the armies of Britain gathered for war with Rome. The chapel was a refuge, a place of peace and rest, a place to pray and to think without interruption.

As Galahad arose from his prayers he was startled to find he was not alone. A slender woman in a dark cloak knelt in a corner, hands clasped, head bent in fervent prayer. There could be no doubt about who she was, for her bright hair escaped from her hood like sunlight from a storm cloud. Only one woman in all of Britain had hair like that.

Suddenly he was beside her, looking down at her bright, hooded head. He did not remember moving his feet. So great was her concentration, she did not hear him. He caught a whisper of her prayer: for Arthur's safety and speedy return, well and whole, to her arms. And for Lancelot's life.

His blood began to race. With a trembling hand he pulled his cloak tighter around his body. The movement disturbed her, and she finished her prayer, crossed herself, and rose. Drawing back her hood, she faced him.

There was nothing angelic about her. Her beauty was so startling because it was tangible, physical, so completely flesh and blood. The scent she used clung to his nostrils; her sapphire eyes, so deep, so clear, swamped his reason; the flawless silk of her complexion reduced his bones to water; the full curve of her lips robbed him of breath. He stared at her in wonder and in silence, for he had completely forgotten what he had come to her side to say.

"Galahad." Her voice, calmly sensible, steadied him. "If you wish to speak to me, speak, and I will hear you. . . . Well? . . . Time presses upon me. I beg you, my lord, speak or let me go."

Renounce my father and let him be! The words rang clearly in his head but his lips refused to let them pass. He looked into her calm, perfect face and cursed himself for a coward and a fool. There was no trifling with her and no getting around her. He wished now he had never risen from his knees.

Worse still, the effect of her beauty did not ebb as time passed in silence between them, but rather increased. He was a crab trapped on the melting beach and she was the full, inflowing tide. In another moment she would drown him.

The candlelight threw his shadow against the wall, where it towered over hers. For a brief moment it gave him a kind of courage. "For my father's sake—"

Anger sparked her dark blue eyes, but he knew she would not chastise him for his presumption—he was Lancelot's son. It had always been, with her, the most powerful weapon he possessed. But she, too, knew her weapon. She leaned toward him until his breath stopped and he waited, awash in dread, for her lips to touch his face. The edge of her cloak brushed his body with the gentleness of a caress.

"For your father's sake, I forgive you," she said softly against his cheek. "Judge me not, Galahad. Look into your own heart before you seek to know mine."

With that, she sidestepped him adroitly and walked away. And he stood there, engulfed in rampant longing, wondering desperately if this physical curse, this disobedient body that had leaped to life at her nearness, was his inheritance from Lancelot or God's punishment for his raging, covetous, wanton desire. *Your very daydreams may betray you. You may be damned for what you long for.* He threw up an arm before his face, but too late. Like it or not, he was flesh of Lancelot's flesh and cursed with Lancelot's curse.

It was the last time he had seen her until the day of departing. Then she had stood between the great dragon doors with tears in her beautiful eyes and a crown on her bright head, and had kissed Arthur good-bye while the armies raised a great shout of joy around them.

All his life Galahad had known that Lancelot lived under a curse; he had heard his father say so. Father Aidan had told him what it was. Long ago in Benoic, the Lady of the Lake had prophesied to Lancelot:

> *You will seek love;*
> *You will find honor.*
> *Glory shall be your reward*
> *And the sins of the flesh your undoing.*

He had never understood how a man as strong and disciplined as Lancelot could succumb to weakness for a woman. He had imagined that women must possess devilish powers and enchantments to so enslave a man. But since that night in the chapel of Camelot on the eve of war, he had known that he, too, suffered from Lancelot's curse. It was a weakness in the fiber of his being, in his body and in his thought, a thinning of the blood, perhaps, a taint of spirit. Were his dreams not proof of that?

It was not an inheritance he wanted, but what could he do to fight against it? He had already vowed, before Bishop Landrum and before God, that he would never marry, would never lie with a woman. Yet the oath had not banished this shrinking fear that melted his innards and dissolved his powers of speech. If anything, it had grown with passing time. He had been powerless before Queen Guinevere. He did not want to be powerless before any woman ever again.

Suddenly he remembered a courier who had arrived in the middle of King Hoel's feast, and the dire news he had brought. Perhaps this was his chance. If he could do something courageous, if he could put a woman in his debt, make her bow, make her scrape, make her recognize him and ac-knowledge his superiority, then perhaps he could break Lancelot's curse and be free of this fear forever.

With controlled deliberation he pulled on his boots, rose, and belted on his sword. By the dim light of dying torches he found the tent he sought. He poked his head inside the skins.

"Ssssst! Percival!" Fifteen boys lay sleeping, bedrolls crowded together, indistinguishable in the darkness. "Percival!"

Nearby a sleeper moved, waked. Percival sat up and rubbed his eyes. "Galahad?"

"Come with me. Can you?"

"Of course, cousin," Percival replied in alarm, coming fully awake and pulling on his boots.

Galahad drew back into the shadows as Percival crawled from the tent. "I've news, cousin. I need your help."

"What's going on? Did something happen at the feast last night? Did Gawaine challenge Lancelot? Did—"

"No, no. This has nothing to do with Lancelot and Gawaine. They were civil enough, at opposite ends of the table." Galahad led Percival into an open field where they could not be overheard. "While we were at dinner, a courier arrived for King Hoel and gave him a message that put him in a fury—"

"What's happened?"

"Hoel's niece has been kidnapped. She was on her way home to her fa-ther on the far side of the Perilous Forest after a long visit in Kerrec. Hoel sent her and her nurse with gifts and cattle, and a company of soldiers for protection. The courier was from her father—she never arrived."

"How long ago did she leave?"

"A week. It's but a two-day journey."

"Then she is dead. Else someone would have heard from her by now."

"So he fears. He was in a terrible rage. But he cannot ignore the chance she may yet live. And in any event, he wants to know what happened. He must tell her father something. King Arthur volunteered to find out."

"That's no surprise. Who goes with him?"

"Lancelot and Bedwyr, my uncle Galyn and our cousin Bors of Ganys, Prince Mordred and Sir Gereint."

"And not Gawaine, because Lancelot is going." Percival grinned. "That will rub some salt into the wound."

"I need your help, Percival. I want to go with them. Can you pack a week's rations into my bedroll unobserved while I get Rouk ready?"

"Of course I can. But you'll not go without the King's leave?"

"I'll meet them on the outskirts of the forest; by that time, it will be too late to send me back unescorted. Arthur will take me. I know he will."

"When do they leave?"

"An hour past dawn."

"Then we've plenty of time." Around them the night was black, but the gentle dimming of the eastern stars heralded change. "I'm glad you'll be riding with Lancelot. You've avoided him all week and he's noticed it."

Galahad sighed wearily. "Why can't you accept that I despise my father?"

"Because I don't understand it. He's the most honorable of men."

"He is not. You don't know him. My mother did, and hated him. Every minute of every waking day."

"Hate is a strong word."

"But a true one. He ought never to have married her."

Percival looked at him curiously. "But he had to."

"Nonsense. Who forced his hand?"

"You never heard the story, then? He got her with child. By mistake. He was drunk, and she had disguised herself as Guinevere for the purpose."

"That's a lie!" Galahad reeled. "That's a foul lie!"

Percival flushed. "It isn't, but I meant no insult. Where's the harm in it, anyway? He married her."

"Harm!" Galahad's voice shook. "You accuse my mother of whoring and deception, my father of drunkenness and fornication, and you ask me where is the harm? Are you a half-wit? If the tale is true, I'm bastard bred!"

"Oh!" Percival gulped. "I didn't think of it's being you. Perhaps she miscarried the ill-begotten child. But it doesn't matter now—"

"Ill-begotten!"

Percival hurried on. "What matters is that he married her, after all."

"Why would my mother deliberately seduce a man she never liked in order to betroth him?"

Percival reddened. Galahad grabbed his tunic. "What is it? For God's sake, tell me, if you know!"

"She seduced him . . . as revenge upon the Queen. To make her weep."

Galahad stared at him. "That's ridiculous! To throw away her future for a moment's spite?"

"She didn't throw away her future. She became Queen of Lanascol."

Galahad let go of his tunic. "She hated Lanascol. It can't be true. She wasn't a fool. She— Don't you dare breathe a word of this to anyone else, do you hear?"

"But, Galahad, if the tale has reached our corner of Wales you can be sure it's already known all over Britain. We're *always* the last to hear the news."

"I've lived nine years in Camelot and never heard it! Perhaps your mother made it up!"

"All right, cousin," Percival said quickly. "Perhaps she did. Anyway, it's a long time ago and it doesn't matter. And look, Lancelot continues to honor her by not taking another wife. There are women all over Britain who'd stop at nothing to catch his eye."

"That has nothing to do with honoring my mother and you know it perfectly well. He'll never remarry unless he can have Guinevere. That should be obvious to anyone with eyes."

"Listen, Galahad," Percival said softly. "I know this bruise is sore to the touch, but try to see it sensibly. All the world knows Lancelot loves the Queen. There is no dishonor in it. He's not waiting for her."

"Don't be a half-wit. There is nothing *but* dishonor in it."

Percival drew a long, uncertain breath. Around them night dissolved into steel-gray dawn. Grasses heavy with dew trembled in the cold half-light. "What are you saying?" he whispered. "Are you accusing your father of treason?"

"Yes," Galahad snapped.

"No. No. I don't believe you."

"Don't, then. It is all the same to me."

"The High King is not a fool. He's not blind."

"Indeed he is not. Both his eyes are open."

"Well, then. You are exaggerating."

There was a long silence. Percival shivered and folded his arms tight across his chest. Galahad stood as still as stone.

"The High King sees clearly into my father's heart. Yet he forgives him. For the Queen's sake. But I do not."

"Galahad, he cannot have betrayed Arthur's bed—Arthur would not keep him near and value him so if that were true!"

In the growing light Galahad's eyes looked black. "It is a mortal sin to covet your neighbor's wife. And in his heart he has lain with Guinevere a thousand times."

"In his heart?" Percival gasped in relief. "In his heart—but not in his flesh."

"Even if that were so, it would not excuse him."

"Of course it excuses him, if he did not do it!"

Galahad shook his head, the bitter memory of his own dreams lending acid to his tongue. " 'Whosoever looketh on a woman to lust after her hath committed adultery with her already in his heart.' There is no difference in God's eyes between the intent and the deed. A man who lusts after a woman the way my father does is as guilty as if he lay with her. How else should covetousness be a sin? Actions are nothing without thoughts. It hardly matters if he has lain with her, or caressed her, or kissed her, or only spoken softly to her under the summer moon. In his heart she is his wife, and no other woman ever has been."

"Hush," Percival whispered, "or someone will hear you!"

"She is the passion of his life. In his heart they are one, man and wife, and it is his own friend, the High King Arthur, who betrays him."

"Oh, hush! Stop! Guard your tongue! This is treason!"

"Yes," Galahad said miserably. "And my father knows it. Even Arthur knows it. But they bear it. For her."

Percival's mouth was dry. "This cannot be."

Galahad wiped the back of his hand across his eyes. "What's worse, this is not a sin he will repent of. He holds it close and cherishes it, though it is his damnation. 'No whoremonger nor covetous man hath any inheritance in the kingdom of Christ.' "

"Do you hear what you are saying?"

"If he'd been faithful to my mother it would all have been so different! But he does not even regret his transgressions. To repent of sin you must give up the benefit it gains you. And this he will not do."

"What benefit?" Percival demanded. "That awful night gained him nothing and cost him much!"

"I'm not talking just of the night he killed Gareth. But even so, you are wrong. It gained him a great deal. It gained him the undying devotion of the Queen and, because he saved her life, the complete forgiveness of the High King."

"Complete forgiveness? Arthur banished him. What more do you want Lancelot to endure?"

"Arthur banished him to send him where Gawaine could not easily come at him. It was done *for* my father's sake. As for saving the Queen, if he hadn't been in her chamber in the first place, they'd never have attacked him. And now he sits on the throne of Lanascol, revered by all the nobles in Less Britain. What punishment is that? He ought to publicly renounce the Queen forever; he ought to get down on his knees before Arthur and beg his pardon. But he never will."

Behind them the sun rose, sending long shafts of light across the dewy grasses, steaming away night's tears.

Percival plucked at Galahad's tunic. "Come. Come away. I'll go pack your bedroll. You'd best get something to eat."

They turned together toward the line of tents, visible now as dark humps in the summer meadow. Percival slid his arm through Galahad's and led his reluctant cousin back toward camp and the company of men.

32 ✝ THE SEARCH

They rode in single file along a narrow track, dark and overgrown, through the heart of the Wild Forest. Gereint led, being most skilled at tracking, with Bedwyr following and behind him Arthur, Lancelot, and Mordred. Galahad was made to ride behind Mordred, while Bors and Galyn brought up the rear. They went silently now, for they were nearing the end of their quest and the outlaws they tracked might be lying in ambush anywhere along the tangled verge.

Galahad was glad of the need for silence; at least he would not have to talk to Mordred. Earlier in the day the Prince of Britain had forced him into conversation as they road abreast, forced him to polite address and thereby to recognition of Mordred himself, of who he was, of what he would someday be. This was a torture that took all Galahad's concentration to endure. He suspected that Mordred did it to annoy him. Certainly the man took joy in his discomfort; more than once Galahad saw amusement light his black and secret eyes.

It had not been so bad the first day out. Although the men had not welcomed his company, they were polite to him once Arthur agreed that he could come. He had wanted to ride beside the High King, but Arthur rode with Lancelot and they talked all day about armies, battle dispositions, alliances, and plans for the future. So he rode instead with Bors and Galyn. He had to apologize to Bors, of course, for frightening Cordovic, but Bors forgave him readily enough, calling it a boyhood squabble and complimenting his swordsmanship.

They followed the tracks of the Princess Elen's convoy—wagons, mules, horses, and cattle—well into the forest. It was easy to find the place of ambush. The soldiers who had formed the guard lay lightly buried and rotting in the damp soil not ten feet from the track; by the buzzing of the flies they found their bodies. They had been stripped of clothes and weapons and robbed of jewelry. Death had at least been swift. All of them had been beheaded.

Arthur's men took time to give them a proper Christian burial and say prayers for the salvation of their souls. Galahad watched out of the corner of his eye while the High King spoke the benediction. Only Mordred and Bedwyr did not make the sign of the cross. Bedwyr, who worshiped Mithra, made a sign of blessing. But Mordred made no sign at all.

Close examination of the damp earth told them some of what had happened. Five men—only five!—had attacked the party, slain the guard, captured the princess and the cattle, and led them all away. One of the men was a giant with a footprint so large it looked barely human. Gravely, they remounted and pressed on as fast as they dared. Every man rode with a drawn sword. The deeper they went into the forest, the darker it became. At last, it seemed, they could smell the sea. They had to be near the end of their quest, Galahad thought, unless these men were pirates. But they had cattle with them. They could not be far away.

At dusk they rode up to the edge of a tidal pool, a large, open lake with an island in the middle. The shore was muddied with the tracks of men and beasts and in the dim light Gereint could not determine which way to go. It was Mordred who spotted the boat, pulled up well past the tide line.

"My lord," he cried, "here is their means of escape!"

Arthur stood on the shingle and gazed out at the little island, hands on hips. "Can you row us, Mordred?"

"Certainly, my lord, if I can find the oars. Here they are, in the underbrush. A poor attempt to hide them—they must have been in a hurry."

"It is my hope they know they are pursued," Arthur said quietly.

"If they are not on the island," Galahad wondered aloud, "then why do we go there? Shouldn't we try to follow their tracks?"

Lancelot turned swiftly with a rebuke on his lips, but Arthur put out a hand and stopped him.

"If they are not there now," he said patiently, "they have been there, and I wish to know what they have left behind. We will not lose much by stopping here tonight. They are slowed by the cattle and the wagons. And now that we are close, we must defend against attack ourselves. I'd prefer to camp on the island where we will have notice of their coming, especially if we have taken the boat."

Galahad flushed. "Yes, my lord. I see. I'm sorry."

"No need," the King said kindly. "You are here to learn. That's why I let you come. Gereint, Galyn, Bedwyr, will you swim the horses? I doubt this boat will take more than six."

Mordred, who had been raised on the Orkney seas, rowed the rest of them across. A heavy silence fell upon the company as the island drew nearer.

Bors shifted his weight uncomfortably. "A likely place for a rape, by the look of it."

Lancelot drew in his breath sharply, and Arthur, his face grim, turned away.

"By the grace of Almighty God," Lancelot whispered, "it is not unknown."

Stunned, Galahad stared at them. Camelot abounded with stories about the Queen's abduction by an ambitious king, years ago, early in her marriage. She had been taken, they said, across water to an island. Lancelot had rescued her but not, the rumors whispered, in time to save her from King Melwas. Galahad had never given these tales the smallest credence. Had it been so, surely Arthur would have put her away!

"In that case," he said aloud, "she were better dead."

Mordred looked up, aghast. Lancelot turned to him a stricken face. "Silence!"

Arthur stirred and said in a low voice, "Whatever her state, I pray we find the poor child alive."

Galahad opened his mouth to protest, but Mordred leaned forward over the oars and hissed, "Say another word and I'll toss you overboard. You can swim ashore or drown."

Galahad sat still and stared at all of them, dumbfounded. The grief on all their faces could mean only one thing. How could they honor her still? How could they? How could the High King ever have taken her back? How could Lancelot love her after such disgrace? Were they mad?

The island proved to be no more than rocks and sand and scrub. A hundred feet from shore they found the ashes of a campfire only recently put out, and a cave with bones of cattle and clear signs of recent habitation. In the rocks above the cave they found a spring.

"It's a good hiding place," Lancelot remarked. "Not a bad spot for head-quarters. These must be the bandits Hoel told us about, who have terrorized the forest these four years past. But now we have found them, we will free the land of this scourge." He paused, lifting his chin like a hound who scents his quarry. "They are not far. And they are afraid. Let them await us."

"This is where they slept," Gereint called, bending down to examine the cave floor. "There is blood here, Arthur."

"Cow's blood?"

"I doubt it. Look!" He lifted in his hand of strip of cloth, dirty and crumpled but finely woven stuff with pale embroidery worked upon it.

Arthur took it and frowned. "Bors, you and Galyn tend the horses and make camp. Get us a fire going. Everyone else, spread out and search. For anything. We have but half an hour before the light fails."

It was Galahad who found the nurse. He almost stumbled over her where she lay, huddled against the rock face. Her clothes had been ripped from her body, and her scrawny arms clutched a few tattered, bloody rags to her withered breasts. Her face was pressed into the dirt, and her gray hair, stringy and unbound, was streaked with blood. There was blood between her legs, too, and down her flaccid thighs, old blood, dried and dark. Galahad gagged and turned away. His shout brought the men running. Arthur knelt down and took the old woman gently in his arms, cradling her head against his chest.

"She breathes!" he cried. "Water, quickly!"

Galahad watched as the High King washed her face with gentle fingers, and spoke to her in a low voice full of tenderness. It was as if he never even saw her ugliness—her age, her bruises, her wanton nakedness. To him, she was a soul in need, although the mere touch of her dirtied his tunic and soiled his hands. When the water revived her she grew rigid with fear, staring wildly at them, then turned her face into Arthur's tunic and wept ragged, bitter tears.

"We are here to take you home," Arthur said softly, bending his head close to her ear. "Can you tell us what happened? Does the Princess Elen live?"

"Mother of God!" she croaked, clinging to Arthur. "She is gone to Heaven, my little one, my precious child. The Lord heard her prayers and took her before the brute was done. She is out of her pain. Oh, God!"

"Hush, mother. I will ask you no more. You need rest."

At that she looked up at him and ceased her weeping. Her faded eyes darkened with anger. "I am not going home, kind lord. I will die here with her. So you must take this tale back to her kin. Tell the king. Will you promise me?"

"I promise it. Rest assured, mother, that we will kill her murderers before the sun sets on the morrow. We have tracked them long and are almost upon them."

Her lips parted in an attempt to smile. All her teeth were broken. "You are the one they fear. I heard them talking. You are the One Unconquered."

"So God has blessed me."

"So it has been foretold." She closed her eyes. "The giant Grile. He is the leader. Thick as an oak, and as strong. He's a monster. The others are nothing without him. My poor little Elen. She did not believe, even when they brought us here, that he would . . . The brute stripped her in front of everyone, that they all might behold her beauty, then he . . . right there in the cave, the cowardly dog! I begged him—me, a grandmother—I begged him to take me in her place. He only laughed and set the others on me. Oh, sir, spare him not, though he beg for mercy! There is no mercy in his heart. I hear her screams, even now, waking and sleeping, I hear her screams. She was virgin and he killed her."

"Hush, mother," said the King, lifting her in his arms. "Tell us no more. I will not spare him, I promise you. Let me take you to the fire and warm you. Later you must tell us where her body lies, that we may give her Christian burial."

She had buried the girl's body in the sand as soon as the bandits were gone. She had no tools but her fingers and it was the only earth soft enough to move. She herself had dragged the child's body from the cave, the little girl she had reared and tended for fourteen years, and whose cruel death she had been forced to witness. It had taken the last of her strength and all but the last of her will. Before moonrise she died.

The men worked solemnly well into the night, digging graves in the sandy soil by the light of crude torches, saying little. Galahad was glad of the silence and the dark. Nearby lay the body of the princess, washed clean of sand and blood. They had no cloth to cover her, and in the flickering shadows of torchlight the marks of death were dimmed; her flesh looked young and firm and rosy, her body lying as if she idled, waiting for a lover.

Galahad wiped the sweat from his brow. He should never have come. This rescue had not gone as he'd planned. Instead of wielding his sword in an heroic act and proving himself superior to a sixteen-year-old girl, he wallowed, powerless, in a sea of rising distress. He fought against the physical excitement that gripped him, for it terrified him. What if Lancelot's curse was a crown of thorns he would wear forever? Surreptitiously he glanced at her body again. He would see her in his dreams, alive and beckoning, he knew it with certainty. He would see those budding breasts, those curving hips, those pliant thighs—with an effort, he forced his thoughts away. He should have stayed in camp with Percival. He should have stayed inside his bedroll. He should have stayed in Britain.

"Enough, Galahad!" He stopped abruptly. They had all finished digging and were looking at him. "Enough," Arthur repeated gently. "We can bury them now and give them rest."

The High King said prayers over the women's bodies, anointed them with oil from his saddlepack, and sent their souls to God. Everyone blessed them on their journey, making signs over the gravesite, everyone except Mordred. But as they turned away from the mound, Mordred clutched the amulet he wore around his neck and his eyes shone unnaturally bright in the torchlight. Arthur slung an arm about his son's shoulders.

"We'll lie here tonight," the High King ordered, "and be off at dawn. Tomorrow we will catch them. Tomorrow they will pay for what they've done here. I swear my oath upon it."

Galahad watched them walk away. He stood alone and looked down at the raw earth of the girl's grave, his face hot with shame. Every man there had seen his rampaging emotion and had recognized it for what it was. Like the burning thirst of a man stranded in a wasteland leagues from water, his horrific lust was something solid, physical, overmastering. Was there no way to redeem his honor? He could think of only one. He could find the men who raped her, and make them pay.

33 ✠ THE SOLDIER

At dawn they swam the horses back. No one spoke. Tracks showed clearly where the gang had split up, each man going his separate way. The giant had taken the cattle and the wagons.

"We will divide into pairs," Arthur commanded. "At sunset, meet back here and we'll count our spoils."

"Galahad," Lancelot said quickly, "will come with me."

Arthur nodded. "Bedwyr, go with Gereint. Bors with Galyn. Mordred, come with me."

Was it Galahad's imagination, or did Mordred smile at him as he rode by? With a grimace of distaste, Galahad turned his horse to follow Lancelot's into the heavy brush. They rode all morning, Lancelot stopping once or twice to examine the trail.

"He has joined up with a friend," he whispered once. "Now you may be sure you will see action."

About noon Lancelot stopped and signaled to him to dismount. They tied the horses to the trees and slung their waterskins about their shoulders. "We go on foot from here on," Lancelot said softly. "I don't believe they're far. In this undergrowth we're faster and quieter without the horses." He looked hard into Galahad's face. "Are you ready, son? They're desperate men. They've raped and murdered the King's niece. They know what punishment they face."

Galahad drew his sword and held it firmly. "I am ready." He hoped his voice did not betray him.

Lancelot looked at him sharply, then slung an arm around his shoulders in a brief hug. "Let's go."

They slipped silently through the dark forest. Galahad was amazed at his father's skill, at how swiftly he moved and how sure he was of his way. He himself was lost after fifty paces; he was not even certain he could find the horses. Suddenly Lancelot stopped and beckoned him forward. Between the sloping branches of a pine they could see two men in a clearing. They spoke in furious whispers, brandishing weapons, arguing about whether to split up or stay together. They were both dressed in patched and filthy rags. The older of the two had gray flecks in his beard and a belly over his sword-belt. But he carried himself like a soldier and held a Roman sword. The younger man, armed with sword and dagger, had thick, matted hair and a wild look about his eyes. He was quick of movement and looked nervously about, scanning the trees.

"The younger man's more dangerous," Lancelot muttered. "He's mine. The other's had training; you'll know what to expect. He's heavier, but slow. You can take him."

"Yes, my lord," Galahad replied, his heart pounding.

"For the glory of God, for the glory of Britain, for the glory of Arthur," Lancelot whispered, crossing himself quickly, and broke through the trees with a wild yell. "Yield in the King's name, or die!"

With a cry, the young man bolted into the woods and Lancelot tore after him. The old soldier turned adroitly, sword up, and faced Galahad. His eyes widened.

"Why, you're a beardless boy! Who is with you? Come, come, you can't expect to take me by yourself."

Galahad said nothing. He circled slowly, his heart in his mouth and his head pounding. He feinted right and left. His father was right: the man had been trained in some king's army. All his responses were familiar.

But the soldier disdained him. He smiled slowly. "Who are you, boy? Where is your mother? Who let you out without your nurse?"

It was an old trick, provoking one's enemy into a rash mistake by hurling insults. Galahad smiled. The soldier lunged. Galahad lightly dodged the blade and nicked the man's shoulder, drawing blood and a howl of pain. This shocked him. Good soldiers did not cry out so. Clearly, this man had not been worthy of the army. He was easy meat.

The soldier glared at him and spat. "Bitch's whelp! Mewling puppy! Whose bastard are you? Whose sword have you stolen? You're naught but the son of a Greek whoremonger; I can see it in your eyes! You filthy little fornicating sodomite—" A fire began to burn within Galahad, and the soldier began to smile. He circled, ignoring Galahad's feints, watching his eyes. "A strapping bugger, aren't you? A lady's man already, I've no doubt. Have you ever had a woman, boy? Or better yet, a maiden, straight from her nurse's lap?" He smacked his lips. "Can you imagine anything so tasty? Such a pretty face, such red lips, such firm, round breasts, just big enough to fit in your hand, little hard nipples under your thumb—"

"Shut up!" Galahad cried, reddening and gulping. "Shut up!"

The sword came in fast, too fast; Galahad rolled and dove and missed it by a hairbreadth, springing to his feet, finding himself backed closer to the trees with less room to maneuver. There was no time to collect his thoughts; he parried a blow, and another, and another. The man was stronger and heavier and kept advancing. He had to have more room!

"Firm thighs," the soldier gloated, licking his lips and coming closer, "pale and tender, little round belly, curls as soft as goose down against your cheek—"

"Stop! Oh, God! Please!" Galahad backed, sweating, the sword hilt suddenly slippery in his hand.

"Can you feel it, son? The burning in your loins? I can see you do. Think of it, son. She's yours. So young. So frightened. So wild and warm and sweet—"

"Aaaaargh!" Galahad's vision went dark. He did not care if he lived another heartbeat. He attacked without thought, without feeling, and let his limbs move where they would. The soldier blocked him, parried, spun, and feinted, but these were moves he knew. He dodged and whirled, nicking him here, slicing him there, making him howl, leaping and dancing, making him pay.

"I yield! My God! Are you mad? I yield!"

The man was on his knees, weeping, clutching his bleeding hand. On the ground at Galahad's feet lay the man's sword, two fingers still wrapped around the grip.

"I don't know who on earth you are," the soldier sobbed, "but you're demented. Spare me, boy, and I'll make it worth your while. I'll give you treasure!"

Galahad stood over him, fighting for breath. Slowly his vision cleared. "Get up." The soldier rose awkwardly, mumbling thanks. "Take down your leggings."

The soldier stared. "What?"

"You heard me."

"But . . . I can't . . . my hand—"

"Do it. Or die now."

Whimpering with terror, the soldier struggled to obey. His maimed hand sprayed his clothes with blood as he fumbled, shaking, with the knotted thong that held his leggings up. Coolly, Galahad stepped forward and ran his sword tip down the man's legs, barely scratching the flesh but slicing the leggings free. The soldier cried out in horror, more afraid of the skill it took than of the deed itself. "Who are you? What do you want of me?"

For the first time, Galahad met his eyes. "My name is Galahad. I want your manhood."

The soldier stared at him unbelieving, then backed away and began to blubber as Galahad stepped forward and raised his sword. "You can't! My God, you are mad! No, no! Have mercy, I beg you! Kill me, then! Aaaaah!" He tripped over a root and fell on his back, weeping as the sword came down.

With a swift stroke Galahad sliced off his genitals and held them in the air for the man to see. The soldier began to scream. Galahad held the bloody flesh aloft and raised his eyes skyward.

" 'See the rage of mine enemies! Let the wickedness of the wicked come to an end!' "

"Kill me!" the soldier howled. "As you love God, run me through!"

Galahad tossed the severed organs on the ground near the soldier's face. Within moments two kites dropped from the trees and began to fight over the flesh. "I beg you!" The soldier wept. "Kill me and have done! Oh, God, oh, God!"

"Don't worry. You will die," Galahad sat flatly, watching the man bleed and writhe in pain. Carefully, he wiped his sword on the grass until the blade was clean of blood, then slid it home to its scabbard and looked down at the dying man. "You'll die as you've lived. Without mercy."

"Fiend from Hell!" the soldier croaked, gasping in his agony.

"Galahad! What in God's name is going on?" Lancelot stepped into the clearing.

"Good knight!" the soldier shrieked. "Have you a sword? Kill me, sir, I beg you! Save me from this demon!"

"Dear Christ!" Lancelot gasped, frightening the kites away from their meal. "What have you done? Why have you done it? Are you mad? Why don't you kill him?"

Galahad looked up calmly at his father. "As he sows, so shall he reap."

"Kill me! I beg you!"

Lancelot, sickened, regarded his son. "You are not God." He drew his sword and looked down at the soldier. "For what you have done you deserve death. By the order of King Hoel I take your life. Say your last prayer and go to your god." With a swift downstroke he dispatched the man, cleaned his sword, and turned to face his son. There were tears in his eyes.

"Galahad, are you ill?"

"He has received as he has given; justice is served."

"You were ordered to kill him."

"He would have died in time."

"Mutilation is not punishment for rape. He was a man, after all, and deserving of quick death. You owed him that much. What you did is . . . shameful." Galahad paled. Lancelot's face was stone. "You've grown up in Camelot. You know better."

"Don't," the boy whispered. "Don't be such an ungodly hypocrite!"

"Watch your tongue!" Lancelot snapped. "Have you forgotten your manners as well as your principles?"

"*You* speak to *me* of principles?" Galahad shouted, backing away as Lancelot stepped forward. Tears streamed down the boy's face and he could not catch his breath. "Remember the whore of Babylon, the mother of harlots—she rules the hearts of all who look upon her! Even me—I was twice almost beguiled. But you . . . you have embraced her where you had no right. You, who've always known the sins of the flesh would be your undoing! A wanton woman corrupts the soul! A good man is like a white robe—but you step into the mud with both eyes opened—you chose your fate!"

"Galahad. Son. Stop and rest a bit—I have water and bread—you are not well."

"Don't touch me! You are tainted with her very scent—I can smell it on you! You carry it with you like a badge of shame. Why will you not renounce her? She is damned, because of you. Can you live with that?"

"Son—"

"Look into your heart!" Galahad cried, pounding his chest with his fist. "Can you deny you love her? Can you look me in the face and deny you deserted us for her? You kiss the ground she walks on—you are drunk on the wine of her fornication!"

"What in God's sweet name—"

"God's name is blasphemy on your lips! 'No covetous man hath any inheritance in the kingdom of God.' "

Lancelot stopped in his tracks and stood completely still, staring at Galahad with narrowed eyes. The boy's voice cracked as his tears coursed down his cheeks.

" 'Whoso committeth adultery with a woman destroyeth his own soul!' This you know. This you have always known! 'Can a man take fire in his bosom, and his clothes not be burned? So he that goeth in to his neighbor's wife—' Don't you see what you have done? It is clear to all the world— even to Arthur—can you be the only one who is blind? Yet you pretend to honor. How can you look him in the face and call him lord and friend? Has she corrupted you? Then she is a traitor and a whore! She is damned for love of you! How can you, how can you live with yourself?" The torrent stopped as suddenly as it had begun, and Galahad stood sobbing in front of Lancelot.

Breathing heavily, Lancelot said slowly in a quiet voice, "Do I understand you aright? Do you mean . . . do you speak of Guinevere?"

"Guinevere!" Galahad wailed. "The whore of Britain!"

In a movement too quick to defend, Lancelot turned his shoulder and smashed the back of his fist into Galahad's face. The boy fell spinning to the forest floor, blood bursting from his mouth and nose. He lay facedown, stunned, as the numbness slowly ebbed and the pain began.

Above him, Lancelot struggled for command of his voice. "If I ever hear her name pass your lips again, I will kill you. Son of my body or no, I will kill you. Do you hear me?"

Through a fog of pain Galahad saw the long fingers around his mother's throat, heard again the growled threat.

"Do you hear me? Answer!"

"Yes."

"Lie here until I return with the horses." He paused a long time. When he spoke at last his voice was low and quiet. "This is Aidan's doing. Aidan's and Elaine's. He filled your heart with hate. She taught you that carnal love was no more than a weapon. God forgive her, she believed it herself. But this you have forgotten in your pride: 'Judge not, lest ye be judged.' May God help me. I cannot tell Arthur."

By the time they met the others at the lakeside Galahad's face was so swollen he could barely see. Every step his horse took sent waves of nauseating pain through his head. His cracked and bloody lips made drinking torture and speech impossible. He had lost three teeth, his jaw throbbed, his ear had been deeply cut by Lancelot's ring, and his nose still seeped blood. But he sat as tall on his horse as he could manage, kept his chin up, and said nothing. Everyone assumed he had gotten the better of a dirty fight and honored him accordingly. Lancelot did not enlighten them. So Galahad sat still and endured their praises and their warm congratulations, while they told of their adventures and displayed the weapons and booty they had won.

Arthur and Mordred had killed the giant Grile. They returned with ten head of cattle, a store of weapons, and the giant's head in a bloody sack to give to Hoel. Mordred told the story of the great battle: the monster felled, nearly killing him, and Arthur saving him at the last minute with a brilliant and daring attack. Arthur smiled to hear it retold, and made light of his own prowess. Together they all started back along the forest track.

No one seemed to notice anything amiss. Their thoughts were on their victory and the celebrations that lay ahead. Only Mordred, whose black eyes missed nothing, watched Galahad with more than curiosity. As the light began to fail he rode up next to the silent boy and looked him over carefully.

"You'd best see a physician when we get to Kerrec. That's a nasty cut on your ear." Galahad did not reply. "Fought foul, did he?" Galahad stared hard at the space between his horse's ears. Mordred smiled slowly and lowered his

voice. " 'A fool despiseth his father's instruction: but he that regardeth re-
proof is prudent.' " With a mock salute he turned his horse away.

Galahad stared openmouthed at his retreating back. The pagan Mordred spouting Scripture! Though he wept with the pain it cost him, he
turned his head, pursed his lips, and spat.

34 ✟ THE TREASURE OF MAXIMUS

Percival lifted the hot cloth from Galahad's ear and gently patted the
bruised flesh. "There. That's better. Sit still a moment longer. The
nard's right here." With great care he applied the soothing balm and then
sat back, cleaning his fingers on the cloth. "I love the smell of spikenard.
The ear is healing well; Gaius says there won't be much of a scar. You're
lucky your nose is still straight and the gap in your teeth won't show in a
smile. Gaius said you'll look the same as you did before when the bruising
heals."

Galahad shrugged. "It doesn't matter what I look like."

"So you say. Yet someday you'll be glad of the face you've got." Galahad
did not respond and Percival's smile faded. "Why don't you just tell me
what's the matter, cousin? You've not been yourself these last ten days. What
happened on that journey? That must have been some fight! Did you know
you are honored all over camp? Even the Franks know your name." Galahad
shifted uncomfortably. "Is it true he was a trained soldier, twice your size?
And that after you disarmed him, he fought foul? King Hoel's thrilled
to have the giant's head. He's got it stuck on a pole outside his window and
is so delighted he almost forgets to grieve. Just think, Galahad, to have
killed your first man, in single combat, and at fourteen! Surely the High
King must let you in the army *now*! I can't imagine what you're so glum
about."

"I hope you don't go around telling these tales to everyone. Why can't
you learn to keep your mouth shut?"

"Oh, all right, *don't* tell me! It's probably not worth knowing, anyway.
Prince Mordred rubbed you the wrong way again, I'll bet. That's all."

"Never mind it, Percival. Talk of something else."

"Why is Lancelot so angry? He's not said a word to you, and only nods
to me, since you got back."

"I said, talk of something else."

Percival frowned. "I thought I was. Well, tell me what tonight's meeting is about, then. Why does King Arthur want to see you and Lancelot alone? And why does Prince Mordred look at you so queerly?"

Galahad scowled. "That abomination! Don't speak his name to me again."

"You really ought to try to get along with him, cousin. He's—"

"He's unclean. He's born of incest. His mother was Arthur's sister."

"His birth is not his fault."

"His birth damns him. He has no right to inherit Britain. I have promised Bishop Landrum I will kill him if he tries."

Percival gasped. "You said that before, but I didn't believe you. You can't, Galahad. Arthur has a right to choose his heir."

"Not Mordred. Arthur sinned when he begot Mordred. It's his own doing his son is unfit to be his heir."

"Is that so?" a deep voice behind them asked. They whirled and saw Mordred, cloaked in black, standing at the entrance to their tent. "What gives you the right to pronounce judgment upon *me*? You, whose father sinned when he begot you."

Galahad swallowed hard.

Percival fell to one knee, shaking. "My lord! Please forgive us! He didn't mean it!"

"I think he did." It was impossible to read Mordred's face. His black eyes gave nothing back. "Since when is my begetting any concern of yours, Galahad of Lanascol? Since our beloved bishop took you under his wing? The man who has fathered more bastards than the kings of Britain combined?" He straightened slowly and came toward the quaking boys.

"You shame your father, Galahad. And mine, who has been generous to you beyond the call of friendship. I know you call me 'abomination' behind my back. Tell me, princeling, what kind of God is it you worship who damns men for things beyond their power, like an accident of birth? This is not the God my father worships. Yet you call Him by the same name." He paused. Galahad, still standing, trembled visibly. "So you plot to kill me, do you? Laughable as it sounds, I believe you would try."

"I will kill you if you try to take Arthur's crown."

Nothing moved in Mordred's face, but both boys suddenly backed a pace.

"You can try," Mordred said softly, "if you live that long." He stepped closer. His lips were inches from Galahad's ear. "I don't know who you think you are, who were conceived out of wedlock and by guile, as one woman's vengeance on another. What gives you, or any man, the right to stand in judgment over me? Is it your precious destiny that makes you so superior?" His fingers snapped. "*That* for your destiny! A witch's drugged vision and a selfish woman's bid for power, that's all your precious destiny amounts to!"

The black eyes glittered. "I await the day you challenge me, boy. The pain your death would bring to Lancelot and Arthur would not stop me. That weapon may work against the Queen—may the gods bless her sweet, forgiving soul—but it will not work against me." He struck his chest, once, with his fist. "My soul is iron. Forged in a fierce fire. And your vengeful God does not frighten me. What are you, Galahad of Lanascol, but a blight upon the name of Britain? You do nothing to bring her glory and you shame the men who would. You are a stain upon her honor she would be better off without." He looked Galahad over and lifted an eyebrow. "When you are ready, princeling, try me. I will be waiting."

He turned away. Suddenly Galahad found his voice. "If you want to kill me, do it now! If you dare. Or are you a coward, too?"

Mordred turned back and slowly smiled. "Hardly. But until you attack me I have no cause. I am Arthur's son, not Elaine's." He paused. "But this I *will* do: I will deny you the honor you most desire. You will never serve in my father's army. Nor in mine. I will see to that." He walked up to Galahad and placed both his hands firmly on the boy's shoulders. "Here is a prophecy for you: You will go your own way. Alone. Unwanted. Neither leading nor following. Belonging nowhere. The honor of your house will die with your father, who deserves a better son than you."

The hands fell from Galahad's shoulders. Mordred paused. "I came to tell you that the lamps are lighting and it is time to go to the High King." With that, he turned on his heel and walked out.

"My God!" Percival said under his breath when he dared to break the silence. "My God in Heaven! He's just about the most powerful man in Britain, and you have made him your mortal enemy!"

A thousand eyes stared at him as Galahad walked slowly toward the High King's tent. He forced his shoulders back and his chin up. Gabral and Bryddon stood, not at their customary posts, but a full ten paces from the entrance. Galahad knew what that meant—a private conference, and one of consequence. Guards had been posted out of earshot to keep everyone away.

Varric brought him to the inner chamber, where Arthur stood, hands clasped behind his back, beside a triple-flamed lamp. There were no skins upon the beaten floor, no stools, no fire, no warmed wine.

"Galahad." The High King nodded curtly as Galahad bent his knee.

"My lord Arthur."

"You're looking better."

"Yes, my lord."

"I am glad of that."

But he did not sound glad. In the shadows behind the High King, Galahad recognized Mordred's dark face. His palms began to sweat. The skins parted; Lancelot came in and knelt before the King.

"My lord Arthur."

"Lancelot." The King's glance warmed as he looked at Lancelot, but still he did not smile. Lancelot, too, seemed strained and ill at ease. There were dark shadows under his eyes and he looked as if he hadn't slept in weeks.

"Now that we are all gathered," Arthur said grimly, "I will tell you why I have summoned you here." He looked first at Lancelot and then at Galahad, who trembled under that piercing gaze. "There is something of importance you are keeping from me. Both of you. One has only to look at you to know this." He paused. "If it were a small thing that need not concern me it would have blown over by now. But it has not. I cannot risk the health of my commanders, nor of any who serve me, with the Roman army approaching and the Burgundians at the Frankish border. Tonight you will tell me what it is."

Neither of them stirred. Arthur turned to Lancelot. "I have spoken to the physician. He confirms what I suspected when I saw you at the lakeside. The blow that Galahad took felled him and would have meant his death had it been struck by his opponent."

Lancelot drew a deep breath. "You are right, my lord. I struck him."

Something moved in Arthur's eyes, but he stood very still. "Why?"

Lancelot looked away. "Sir, I cannot tell you. I beg you not to ask me. It were better not spoken aloud. It were better not known."

"Nevertheless, I command you to tell me."

Lancelot threw him a desperate look and his voice grew pleading. "Arthur, I beg you! Let it die. Punish me as you will, but let it pass."

But the High King was not moved. His face looked carved in stone. "You will tell me," he said slowly and distinctly, "what is between you. Else neither of you has a future in my service."

Lancelot drew a long breath and stared hard at the floor. "Very well," he said flatly. "It is my fault, from the beginning. The boy has grown up without a father, and that is my doing."

"I will be the judge of that," Arthur said sharply. "Just tell me what happened."

"We met two men; I followed one and left Galahad to take the other. I judged the man was well within his range of skill. In this I was right; he disarmed the blackguard without a scratch to his person. But when I returned . . . I found . . . the boy was raving, shouting Scripture—I thought he had gone mad. He insulted me, he . . . my lord, he insulted . . . others, he said terrible things. He did not mean them; he spoke only to wound me—I think the finding of the young princess turned his wits, else he would never have cut the . . . done what he did."

"Ah." Arthur watched Lancelot unmoving. "Now we are coming to it. What did he do?"

Lancelot met his eyes, pleading, but could not bring himself to speak.

Arthur turned on Galahad. "You tell me."

Galahad backed a step. "I gelded the man who raped her. I cut off his fornicating manhood." The defiant words fell loudly into silence; all three men stared. Galahad's voice began to tremble. "Quick death was too good for him. I did no more to him than he had done to her."

Not one of them moved. The lamp flames threw their shadows giant against the tent cloth, where they quivered and danced behind the rooted men. At last Arthur spoke. "Who killed him?"

"I did," Lancelot said flatly.

Arthur nodded. "Thank you for it. But the blow you struck your son was not to bring him to his senses. It was more than that."

"Yes," Lancelot admitted unhappily. "I struck him in anger. I hit him as hard as I could."

"Tell me why."

"My lord, please—"

"It's no good, Lancelot. You cannot spare me. Your very reluctance tells me all but the details."

Lancelot shook his head.

"Lancelot."

"I cannot."

Galahad gulped as the King turned toward him. "Can you tell me, Galahad?"

"Y-yes, my lord."

Arthur's cool eyes met his. "Then do it."

"He struck me because I accused him of . . . wrongdoing. I told him he was damned. I told him why."

"Tell me exactly what you said."

"Arthur," Lancelot begged, "don't ask him for it. Please."

"You will be silent," the King snapped. "Speak, Galahad."

Galahad's voice shook as the words were forced from his lips by the King's commanding eyes. "He has always known that the sins of the flesh would be his undoing. He has let a woman corrupt his soul. 'Can a man take fire in his bosom, and his clothes not be burned?' For her, he betrayed my mother! And he betrayed you, my lord! It is no more than everyone already knows. In his weakness he has betrayed us all! My mother wept, wept and suffered, and I couldn't help her—I couldn't keep him away! My mother hated the whore of—"

"No!" Lancelot cried. "Don't, Galahad!"

"Silence!" Arthur roared. He nodded curtly to Galahad. "Go on."

Galahad swallowed in a dry throat. "My lord, he struck me because I called her whore."

"Be still!" Lancelot choked. "God in Heaven, have you no thought for the King? How can you do it?"

Arthur's eyes blazed. "Am I to understand you accused your father of whoring?" Galahad nodded, lowering his eyes to evade that awful stare. "Never in his life." Arthur paused. "With whom?" Galahad did not answer. "Who is it you call a whore, boy? Speak up. I command you."

But Galahad's bowels had turned to water and it was all he could do to stay on his feet. In all the years he had served Arthur he had never known how men could fear him. Suddenly he understood it. The King took a step toward him, but Lancelot reached out and touched his arm.

"Don't, Arthur. I will tell you." Lancelot spoke lifelessly. "He's never understood. Like so many others. He meant Gwen. He started with the whore of Babylon, but at the end, he said her name."

Arthur stopped. His voice, when it came, was unrecognizable. "Guinevere!"

"He said it to revenge himself upon me, for the years of neglect he has suffered at my hands. But that was why I hit him." Arthur's face was gray. Lancelot slid to his knees. "I blame myself for the grief I have brought upon you. My lord, forgive him. He's only a boy; his teachers have all been priests; his world is free of shadows. My dear lord, remember what it was like to be his age."

Arthur shook himself and abruptly turned away. He took three quick strides toward the dark tent wall, waited, and took three slow strides back.

"Lancelot, I hold you blameless. You have behaved throughout with honor. I thank you for your honesty and for your defense of her good name. Return to your command and leave the boy with me. Mordred, you, too, may go. I bind you both to silence. Not a word of this leaves this tent."

When they were alone, Arthur called for wine and a pair of stools. Varric hurried to obey. From his stool Galahad watched nervously as the High King clasped his hands behind his back and began to pace.

Since that first day in Camelot, long ago, Galahad had always thought of Guinevere as Lancelot's illicit passion. She was the wicked woman who had stolen his father's love and ruined his mother's life. And lately he had regarded her as the personification of carnal desire which corrupted men. He had never even considered that the King himself might be more than the woman's victim. But he considered it now. Why would Arthur keep a childless queen? It was his right, even his duty, to put her aside. And if she had been raped by his enemy . . . no one would keep her but a man who loved her beyond all reason. Now he knew for certain the truth of the King's affection. A moment ago Arthur's face had looked like death.

Arthur waited until Varric had served the wine and drawn the tent flap closed behind him. Then he seated himself across from Galahad. His eyes were dark pits in a face pinched white.

"Galahad, had you been a grown man, had you been anyone but Lancelot's son, you would be dead now. No one calls my wife a whore to my face and lives. Do you understand this?"

"Yes, my lord. I . . . I'm sorry."

"I hope you are. But I fear you are only sorry that you spoke it in my hearing. In your heart you believe it."

Galahad gulped.

Arthur gazed directly at him. "It isn't true, son." He made an effort to soften his voice. "Since first she came to Camelot twenty years ago, a girl of fifteen, knowing nothing of the world, forced to leave her family and marry a man she had never even seen, people have talked about Guinevere. That is only human, I suppose, but it is a trial to bear. She was a frightened child of astounding beauty thrust into a prominence she had never wanted, even in her dreams. Envy and jealousy dog her like shadows. But because her closest friend in all the world was my friend also, rumors started. You cannot kill a rumor. You can only let it die. This one has not died."

"Because he loves her!" Galahad cried in spite of himself.

Arthur sighed. "Yes, he loves her. What's more, she loves him. I have known this for twenty years. How not? I love them both."

"That's not what I mean!"

"Ah," Arthur said softly, "but it *is*. Perhaps you are too young to understand it. Galahad, we cannot choose whom we love. But we can choose how we act. All these years Lancelot has served me and worshiped Guinevere. All these years he has put Britain's welfare, and ours, before his own. This is love. Had he been less than he is, he could have torn apart my kingdom. I could not have kept him from it. You think, you and all the gossipmongers, you think he has betrayed me behind my back. Then you must think me either blind or besotted." The dark eyes flashed and Galahad's throat went dry. "You are wrong. He is the last man on the face of the earth who would betray me."

Galahad swallowed. "He never loved my mother."

Arthur shrugged. "It happens. She ensnared him, else he would not have married. If he has harmed you in this, he is at fault. But he has done his best by you, Galahad. He brought you to Britain to be with him. He trained you."

"He did not take me when he left."

Arthur nearly smiled. "When I banished him? You were nine years old and full of righteous anger at the death of your friend. Would you have gone? All you wanted was to mourn Gareth and cast stones at your father. I remember that night well. Lancelot asked me, as he made ready to leave, if I would keep you and watch over you. You were always foremost in his thoughts."

Tears filled Galahad's eyes and he wiped them angrily away. "He *never* thought about us. All he did was make my mother cry! My lord, he left us alone three seasons out of four! He wanted to be anywhere but with us. He loved the Queen more than my mother. He hurt her cruelly. He ruined her life."

Arthur listened sadly and watched his face. "So you were angry with Lancelot. I see that. But why did you mutilate the bandit?"

Galahad looked away and clasped his hands together. "I don't know. Something came over me, something dark and . . . and powerful. I couldn't stop. It was like being swept away in a flood."

"Ah, yes," said Arthur softly. "The same thing happened to your father the night he killed Gareth."

Galahad nodded weakly and slumped on the stool. "I guess so."

"In the right place, at the right time, such blind passion could make you a hero of war. But discipline is better."

"Yes, sir."

"Control that power that grips you, tame it and bend it to your will, and you will become a warrior of the first order. There will be nothing you can't do. But without control you are little use to anyone. You know now, I hope, that it was a grave mistake to mutilate the bandit. We were sent from Kerrec to kill those men. Mutilation is a coward's tool."

"I didn't mean to do it. But he taunted me about the princess. About . . . about . . . about what it had been like . . . to do what he did." His face flamed as the words stumbled out, and Arthur nodded slowly.

"I see." The King hesitated. "That was cruel. It made you angry?"

Galahad flushed still deeper. "It made me want to pay him back in kind."

"Well," Arthur said gently, "it was probably a tactic to provoke you and gain him some advantage. It is perhaps your very youth that made you prey to such a stratagem. Had you been older, had you lain once with a woman—"

"No." Galahad started up, unable to abide the stool. "I never will. I have taken an oath upon it."

Arthur raised an eyebrow. "Never is a long time."

"Nevertheless, I have sworn it. I am determined to be clean of my father's sin."

"To love honorably is no sin."

"I don't know if that is possible. Women are nothing but trouble."

"Sometimes they are. But it seems to me that nine times out of ten it is men who cause the trouble, because we value them so and guard them so jealously. And why do we value them? Women can be wise in ways beyond a man's wisdom. All of them, Galahad, as different as they are, young or old, lovely or unsightly, highborn or low, virtuous or wicked, all of them understand love. It is in their souls, I believe. It is a great gift, and not to be discarded lightly. Don't stand by your oath for the wrong reason."

Galahad realized he was standing while the King sat, and sank bank onto his stool. " 'Blessed is the man that endureth temptation, for when he is tried, he shall receive the crown of life.' That is the better road for me, I think."

Arthur smiled and emptied his cup. "We will see. There is no shame in breaking an oath made in ignorance. Come to me in five years' time and talk to me again about the virtues of abstinence."

Galahad colored. "I cannot change who I am, my lord."

"Nor are you set in plaster at the age of fourteen. You can grow and learn. You have in you the makings of a great man if you can keep mercy in your heart. You've all of Lancelot's strengths: his skill with a sword, his quickness, his courage, his devotion to right, his idealistic soul, even his beauty. Be as like him as you can. Be such a man as that, Galahad, and you can have any future you want." He flashed a quick smile. "Or any woman."

"My father didn't get the woman he wanted!" Galahad flared, and then paled at his own temerity.

Arthur looked at him gravely. "You're wrong about that, too. There was a time when he could have had her. All he had to do was ask." He rose suddenly. "The path to knowledge is a crooked one with many turnings. It is important to learn from mistakes. As you must do now. Are you ready to receive my judgment?"

Galahad slid to his knees and formally bowed his head before the King. "Yes, my lord."

"Very well. Galahad of Lanascol, for your treatment of the bandit, whom it was your duty to kill, not to maim, I remove you as my personal guard. You disobeyed my orders. I cannot yet trust your sword. You will sleep with Percival and the other pages in their tent. Prince Mordred will give you your daily orders. You will obey him." He paused. "Your other offenses are more serious. You have shamed your father, who is the most honorable man I know. You have insulted the High Queen, who has done nothing to harm you and whose honor I am sworn to defend. In insulting her you have insulted me. If you were older, I would fight you on a field of honor. But yours is a life I would not take willingly and I am glad you are too young. As it is, I should ban you from my service. It is what you deserve, but I am loath to take a weapon from my arsenal this close to war."

Galahad froze, pressing his palms together, a small sweat breaking on his brow. He looked up, eyes swimming, as the High King turned and walked beyond the lamp into the shadows, and stood, head bowed, hands clasped behind his back. He stayed so, statuelike in his stillness, for a long time. At last he sighed wearily, crossed himself, and turned. Quickly Galahad bowed his head again.

The King came back into the light and stood above him. "I will keep you in my service because you are Lancelot's son and I owe him my life many times over. And because there is nobility in you which I would rather honor than shame. You mean well. Where you err, I believe it is from ignorance, not intent. In time, your goodness will shine out with a clearer light."

Galahad fought back tears. His tunic was damp with sweat.

"But although you will serve me," Arthur continued gravely, "I cannot keep you near me. After the fighting is over, if we both live, I bind you to performance of a duty."

"Name it, lord; it shall be done!"

"Do you know the tale of the great Magnus Maximus? Ancestor of Ambrosius?"

"Yes, my lord. He was Emperor of Britain and your ancestor as well."

Arthur took a deep breath. "You will find, and bring to me, the rest of Maximus's treasure. The Grail and the Spear that, along with Excalibur, Maximus took with him when he attacked the King of Rome. When he died, his lieutenant brought these treasures back to his wife in Wales. The Sword she could not bear to look at, considering it the very cause of his ambition. So the lieutenant took it and hid it in a sacred stone, protected by gods, until I came to draw it forth. But she kept the Grail and Spear. Since her death they have disappeared, lost, known only in song. And since her death Britain has not been whole. With Excalibur and the help of Britain's kings, we have kept the barbarian wolf from our throat. But the future is uncertain." He spread his hands out in an inclusive gesture and then dropped them to his sides. "When we are dead, will those who follow be as strong? Legend holds that when all three lie together, Grail, Spear, and Sword, in the hands of her king, then will Britain be unconquerable for all eternity. This is all, Galahad, that is left for me to do. While Magnus Maximus held them, he was Emperor of Britain, and neither Gael nor Pict nor Saxon could conquer us." Arthur paused. "The Lady Niniane tells me these treasures can be seen in dreams, from time to time, by men of virtue. But only someone with a stainless soul can find them. Perhaps you—"

"My lord, I have seen them!" The words burst from the boy as he stared, glassy-eyed, at the King. "I saw them in a vision! In a red stone! Years ago! A shallow grail, and a long spear, haloed in light!"

Arthur looked startled. "Indeed? Niniane believes these things lie in Britain. But that is all I know about them."

Galahad prostrated himself at the King's feet. "My lord, I will do it! I will find them for you! You will be the greatest King the world has ever seen! You will hold Britain safe forever!"

Arthur hesitated. "That's in God's hands," he said gently, bending down to raise the boy. "We all do what we can for Britain. The rest is with God. Go now, Galahad, and get some sleep. You, too, have suffered much these past ten days. What we have said, we two together, will stay a confidence between us. I will share it with no one. You have my word."

"Thank you, my gracious lord."

"I will let you know when it is time to start this quest. Await my signal. Until then, obey Mordred."

"Yes, my lord. I will do it. Even that. I will do anything you command."

When Galahad had gone, Arthur stood looking at the space where he had been, his brow furrowed in a frown.

"May God forgive me such a host of lies," he whispered, "legends, myths, enchanters' chatter—but something must be done about you. You are a bright and deadly weapon, but you have no grip on the truth. Mordred was right. For all our sakes I must send you away. I pray that in your seeking you will find the sustenance your spirit craves. Poor unhappy boy. If only you had kept a little mercy in your heart."

35 ✝ THE LETTER

Galahad lifted the wineskin from its stand above the flames and began to fill the waiting cups. Varric, the High King's chamberlain, was abed with a fever and Arthur had asked Galahad to take Varric's place at council.

Gawaine, Bedwyr, Gereint, Galyn, Bors, and Mordred sat on skins around the low fire in the innermost chamber of the High King's tent. Only Lancelot was missing—Lancelot who was out on patrol because Gawaine was in camp.

"My lords," Arthur began, when suddenly the skins parted behind him and Bryddon's gruff voice interrupted.

"A courier, my lord King. With a letter."

Arthur rose. "Let him enter."

Bryddon saluted smartly and stood aside as a young man pushed past him, still dusty from the road. He fell to his knees and kissed Arthur's ring.

"My lord King, I come from Camelot with an urgent letter from the Queen." He drew from his tunic a scroll with the dragon seal.

Arthur took it and said quickly, "Is she well? What is amiss?"

"My lord, the Queen is well. I am charged with no message, but before I left the word went round that Constantine of Cornwall was on the move, and with troops."

The King's face darkened as the men broke into angry murmurs. He thanked the courier and dismissed him. Then he sat upon his stool, broke the seal, and read. Everyone watched Arthur's face. His grave expression seemed to freeze, then slowly harden into anger. He read it twice, and passed the scroll to Mordred.

"I am a fool!" he snapped, running a hand through his hair. "I misjudged him. I have played into his hands and left her to face him. Alone and practically defenseless."

"No, my lord, not alone," Mordred murmured. "She has troops. Handpicked and loyal to a man. And as you well know, her native wit is worth three of him any day. She is not defenseless."

Arthur shot him a swift look of appreciation, but shook his head. "No doubt he lied about the number he kept for Cornwall's defense. She will be outnumbered. If they can't take the fortress, they will sit down before it and cut it off from Britain. Either way, it is disaster. He will be king in all but name; he will do whatever he wills."

"I take it," Gawaine cut in, "you are talking about Constantine, Uncle? What's that black-hearted bastard done now?"

Arthur began to pace. "Guinevere has had word from the Lady Niniane that Constantine is coming up from Cornwall unannounced, and with troops. When this message was sent he had not yet reached the border of the Summer Country and committed himself to treason. But clearly the Queen fears it and Niniane expects it."

"He sees his chance to regain his birthright," Gawaine remarked bluntly. "With you and Mordred both away, he must think the kingdom is his for the taking."

Arthur scowled at his want of tact. Mordred rolled up the scroll and tucked it in his tunic.

"He knows well it is not his birthright," Arthur said flatly. "I made his father my heir only in default of an heir of my body. I was fourteen then, with no wife or family and the Saxon wars ahead. If he grew up expecting to be High King, he has fed upon false hopes. This he knows." He stopped and faced them. "I must send one of you home with troops to safeguard the Queen or rescue her, depending upon what happens."

The chamber erupted with voices as every man among them volunteered. Their eagerness astonished Galahad. Did every man there really want to leave King Arthur's side, and the prospect of the most glorious battlefield of their lives, to sit home in Britain and guard the Queen? He withdrew to the darkest corner and watched the King.

"I thank you, one and all, for your offers. I am sure any one of you could defeat Constantine, or hold Camelot against him. The Queen asks only for a loyal commander and a hundred men." Arthur paused. "I will send Mordred with five hundred."

Mordred's face lit and in his corner Galahad felt a weight lift from his shoulders.

"Here are my reasons. First, he is my heir, and his presence in Camelot removes any excuse Constantine might put forward about protecting the Queen in my absence. Second, it is fitting that if Constantine attempts to usurp my power, the rightful heir to it should face him and deny him. Only Mordred, ruling as regent, can put an end to his ambition. Third"—and here his voice softened—"next to me and Lancelot, Mordred is the one she would like best to see. Let us not forget that whoever goes, stays. Now that Constantine has revealed the treason in his heart, Camelot will never be safe from him." He looked around at the upturned faces. "Are you agreed? Has anyone a better plan?" But of course no one objected. Galahad wondered if any of them ever disagreed with Arthur, so accustomed had they all become to his good judgment and his wise rule. Twenty-six years he had been High King of Britain, and there was not a man who knew him who did not love him. Even Cerdic, the Saxon king, gave him such honor as it was in a Saxon to give.

Mordred knelt before his father and kissed his ring. "My lord honors me with this commission. I promise faithfully to fulfill it and hold Britain safe and whole until you return."

Arthur raised him and embraced him. "I have not a doubt of it. You'd best begin the preparations. Send to the harbor to make ready your ships. Take good horsemen—you will have more need of cavalry than I. Later tonight, come to me. I will have a message for you to give her."

When Mordred left, Arthur sighed and took his seat. "Now, we must reconsider the Roman commander Hiberius and his request that we send him an embassy to negotiate terms of peace. Bedwyr, you will lead the negotiations in Mordred's stead. Bors and Galyn go from Lanascol, Riderch and Oltair from Brittany, the three Franks Childebert has chosen, and from Britain, you, Gereint, and Gawaine." He paused, his face hardening into his warrior's expression. He looked at each of them in turn with eyes of metal. "Gawaine will lead the embassy." He said it defiantly, but no one objected. "He is my kin. Hiberius will be insulted if the leader is not from the royal house of Britain. Hoel and Childebert send their sons."

Gawaine leaped to his feet and accepted the High King's offer before it could be withdrawn. He proposed a toast to Arthur and swore his loyalty to all the King's commands. Everyone raised a cup and drank. The talk turned general and Galahad made the rounds again and again with the wineskin.

"You wait and see," Gawaine said to Bedwyr as the gathering at length broke up. "Your reservations are unfounded. You keep them busy at the conference table and I'll get a look at their numbers and their arms. Leave that to me. I can do anything but talk gibberish I don't believe in."

"I worry more about your saying too much than too little." Bedwyr grunted. "See you keep your tongue still until we are back in Kerrec." With a swift bow, Bedwyr departed.

Galahad bent over the Orkneyman's empty cup. Gawaine grinned. "Well, young Galahad, you've certainly set the army by its ears. It seems I missed something by not coming with you into the Wild Forest. What's all this I hear about your gelding a bandit and provoking poor Lancelot into a fury? Speak up. Cat got your tongue?" Galahad kept his eyes on the wine, but his face flamed. Gawaine leaned closer until Galahad could smell his dinner on his breath. "Is it true you two had words before the High King? I tell you now, boy, if you are ready to disavow your father, you'll find a friend in me. I'll stand by you. You know my reasons. You don't have to tell me yours. Say the word when you are ready, and we'll take an oath together to revenge ourselves upon him. What do you say? Eh? Think about it."

With a slap on the back, Gawaine drained his cup, turned away, and strode out into the night. Galahad looked swiftly about. The only men left inside the tent were deep in conversation with the King. No one had overheard. He raised a trembling hand to the tent flap and stepped outside into the cool evening air.

His heart hammered in his ears and he drew a deep breath to steady himself. Alliance with Gawaine! This was an offer worth considering. Lancelot might defeat one of them, but never both. This was his chance to revenge his mother for all her pain. *I will not rest easy, in Heaven or in Hell, until he is dead.* Not so long ago he would have jumped at the chance. Why now did his spirit recoil as if something unclean had just passed by?

Late that night, curled in his bedroll at the foot of Varric's pallet, he awoke to voices talking in the inner chamber. Mordred was bidding his father farewell.

"My lord, I still think it is a mistake to put Gawaine in charge."

"All the others are of your mind, as well."

"Well, then, will you not reconsider? Give him some title, some ceremonial post that will content his pride and do Hiberius honor. But do not let him command the embassy. I fear his short sight and hot temper will end in some disaster."

"You are afraid he will insult someone, or start a fight, from which retreat will necessarily mean war?"

"Exactly."

"Well, Mordred, I am content with such an outcome. I suspect it might be the best thing that could happen."

"My lord!"

"Listen. This is for your ears only. There will be war, Mordred, as surely as the sun rises. There is no hope of averting it. There never has been. Hiberius has come all the way from Rome to subdue the Franks and Bretons; he will not be content with less. I have allowed my commanders to believe in the chance for peace because I want Hiberius to think our embassy is sincere. I want him to believe we are unwilling, or unready, for the battle he is planning. The truth is, he is not quite ready yet himself. The Burgundian forces under his command are chancy fighters. They shout loudly and are eager to brandish weapons, but they have no staying power. Hoel's spies have news that when he learned of our own arrival on Breton soil, he sent to Rome for reinforcements, and these have not yet arrived."

"They fear you, sir, even in Rome. He fears to meet the Dragon of Britain unless he outnumbers you three to one."

"Whatever the reason, I would prefer to force his hand before those troops arrive. If Gawaine accomplishes this for me, however innocently, so much the better."

"My lord, I am glad you told me. I will leave with an easier heart. Does no one else know?"

"Hoel knows. And Lancelot, of course. In a week's time, Mordred, as you are riding through King's Gate and into Camelot, we might well be marching to Autun, and destiny."

"You will have victory that day. No one doubts it."

"I'd be well pleased if that were true. . . . Well . . . give her my love, son. Tell her I think of her often during the days, and every night she visits me in my dreams. It is true enough. She will be lonely, Mordred. Say what you can to comfort her."

"Yes, my lord. With pleasure."

"I shall be lonely, too. But I will be busy."

"Ah. That reminds me. There is one more thing."

"Yes? Well? Why do you hesitate?"

"Forgive me, my lord. But—from son to father—sir, Hoel sends me with a message."

"Yes?"

"In short, he worries that you allow yourself no pleasure. He has three maidens, he tells me, who would gladly come to your tent. I have seen one of them—a raven-haired beauty of seventeen—yes, I thought you might laugh."

"How old is Hoel?" Arthur chuckled. "Seventy, if he is a day, and still his appetites are undiminished! He has my admiration and my thanks. But even if the girl is willing—"

"More than willing, my lord. Eager. And she *is* a beauty."

"I've no doubt, Mordred, or you'd not have noticed her yourself. But no, thank you. A man who has been used for twenty years to the nectar of gods cannot after a mere month look forward to local brew."

"I hinted as much to Hoel, but he was adamant I make the offer. He thinks you have looked tired of late."

"Not tired. Worried about Lancelot."

"I thought that was settled."

"He cannot forgive himself for his son's words to me. He feels responsible."

"Galahad is old enough to speak his own mind. Lancelot is too quick to take blame upon himself."

"Yes, and always has been. He will work it out in time. But I worry that we do not have time. If he carries this guilt into battle, he is likely to take chances and endanger himself without need. He has done so before."

"I knew that boy would cause trouble if you brought him."

"I could not leave him home without dishonor both to him and Lancelot. He is learning, Mordred. It's a difficult age."

"Please, my lord. At his age you were crowned High King of Britain."

"Well, it is more difficult for some than for others."

"For him it is impossible. I think he's mad."

Arthur paused. "When I learned about the soldier's mutilation, I wondered myself. But I think perhaps he is a lonely boy, with a great soul and a great need, lost in the world of men. I wish I knew how to give him ease."

"You can't. He doesn't know what ease is. He knows only trouble."

"No. But he has a single eye."

"Send him back with me. I will keep him busy and get him out of Lancelot's hair."

The King's voice came softly through the tent cloth. "And take him away from Percival? No. They need each other now. This is a gift from God to both of them, this friendship. I would not disrupt it now for all the world."

"You have heard what the soldiers call them? Nemesis and Bumpkin! An ill-made match, it seems to me."

"Yes, I've heard. The men are cruel; they're only boys. The match is not so ill-made as it appears."

"Well, if you are so determined. You know best. You always have."

"Mordred. My son."

"Arthur."

"Go with God."

Footsteps retreated and silence followed. Galahad crept from his bedroll and parted the cloth, peeking into the inner chamber. Arthur stood like stone, staring at nothing. At last he sighed and crossed himself.

"If You love me," the King said softly to the empty air, "let me live to see him once again. It is all I ask."

For reasons he could not fathom, Galahad hid his face in his hands and wept.

36 ✝ AUTUN

Like a hungry serpent slithering toward a long-awaited meal, the huge army snaked through the wooded hills and down onto the rolling plain of Autun. Here and there in the clouds of dust they raised, the summer sun glinted off spear tips and helmet studs, caught a flash of color from the myriad banners lifting in the soft June breeze, shimmered on the glossy coats of horses, and set alight the great Red Dragon on a field of gold. They wound through meadows where wildflowers grew rampant, glorying in brief beauty, waving and bowing as the soldiers passed. Galahad saw all around him a rich land, green and growing, and wondered if within the week this soft and fertile earth would be bathed in blood.

If there were ever an army which could beat back Rome, this was the one. How Arthur had done it, Galahad did not know. In the month since he had arrived from Britain, the King had won the trust and the allegiance of all these foreign troops. Childebert loved him as a brother. To a man, the Franks would die for him. Was it his air of confidence and power? He let everyone know he never doubted the battle could be won. Was it his fairness? He had settled so many disputes to everyone's satisfaction, he was now the only arbiter the soldiers would accept. Was it his prowess as a warrior? Grown men half his age sat in awe to hear the stories of the Saxon wars. Perhaps he merely charmed them all; he let them see their cause was just, and he made them feel beloved. When men looked at him, they took heart and believed.

The embassy to the Romans had ended in disaster, as Arthur had foreseen, before it had really begun. No sooner had Bedwyr and his fellow diplomats retired inside the meeting tent than Gawaine ran afoul of a Roman youth who ridiculed his atrocious Latin and called him an ignorant savage. Gawaine had drawn his sword and run him through before anyone had time to blink twice. Utter chaos followed, and the Britons had barely escaped with their lives, for the murdered youth turned out to be Hiberius's own nephew.

Toward sunset the allied armies came to the banks of a river. The High King set his tent upon a small rise and the armies coiled protectively around him. At every campfire men sharpened their weapons, polished their buckles and armbands, mended leather straps and scabbards, and checked over their equipment one last time. They were ready now, poised for the enemy's approach. The scouts were out and Arthur and his commanders met in council to go over, one more time, the battle plans.

Two days later when the Romans came to Autun, the armies of Britain were well rested and deployed to be deceiving in their strength. From the hill where Arthur camped, all Galahad could see on the night of the Romans' arrival was a sea of tents and campfires from horizon to horizon. Before council broke up that night a great cheer was raised for the glory of King Arthur, but the commanders, when they left to join their troops, went silently.

Lancelot sought out Galahad and brought him to his own tent. He dismissed his servant and served Galahad wine himself. Then he stood, head bowed, before the seated boy. The lamplight threw shadows across his face, picking out the fine line of jaw and cheekbone and making deep pits around his eyes.

"Galahad. My son. This is the eve of your first battle, and perhaps of my last. At such times a man thinks of odd things." He paused and clasped his hands tight together. "He thinks of all the things he cannot change—of the harm he has done others without intent, of what he might have done that he did not do." He cleared his throat awkwardly. "I know there are things between us—a history of mistakes and misunderstandings—but I wish to do what I can to clear the air. I need to speak to you. Will you attend me?"

Galahad nodded and placed his winecup on the ground.

"Thank you. What I have to say has been on my mind for some time. If I am killed in battle, these are things I wish you to know." Lancelot drew a deep breath. "Life is short and often bitter. But God has given us choices. If you are wise, you will choose the honorable road, however hard that is. Do what you ought, not what you want. Then someday, when you are as old as I am, you may look back and at least know you have done the best you could. If you are lucky you can even be proud that you have served Britain. I have been luckier than most men—I have lived in Arthur's time; I have served him both as friend and as soldier; I have known the generous love of the two most loyal hearts in all the world."

He paused and took a turn around the tent. "I know that Arthur has dismissed you from your post, that he is sending you away. It grieves him deeply to do this. But you still serve him, Galahad. And in his service, as in no other, you will come to glory." He smiled briefly. "I, too, remember the prophecy. Do not fret that you are not in Arthur's army. Perhaps your way lies along a different road. From your earliest years, you have always been different from your fellows. It is not a curse to be so; it is a gift."

Lancelot stopped. He searched Galahad's face, but the boy sat still on the stool, gravely attentive, waiting. "Learn mercy, son. Not every man will measure up to your standards. Learn to forgive the ones who fail. When you are building Britain, do not worry that your workmen have dirty hands or soiled faces—in their hearts they are the same as you. Keep your eye upon what it is men have in common, as Arthur does. It is the path to greatness, and to honor. Accept men for the weak and sinful creatures they will always be, and look beyond."

Lancelot paused again. "You have had words with Mordred. Whatever the cause, set aside this enmity and put things right between you. He is not a bad man, and when Arthur is gone he will be your King. Britain needs you both."

"He will never be my King. He is abomination."

Lancelot regarded him sadly. "He is a reminder to us all that we are Adam's seed. Even the greatest among us stumbles and falls. 'There is not a just man upon earth, who doeth good and sinneth not.' " His voice grew soft. "Even Arthur."

The words hung heavy between them in the ensuing silence. Beyond the tent walls came the low call of voices, the distant jingle of tack and mail, the occasional whinny, the soft thud of boots hurrying past. The night seemed to hold its breath, stretching moments into hours, as the lamp flame burned steadily in the still air.

"Men are imperfect," Lancelot said quietly. "Even the best of them. I am, perhaps, less perfect than most. But whatever else I have done, I have always striven for the glory of Arthur and of Britain. If you are to have a future, Galahad, this is where it lies. Serve Arthur with your very life. Make him your example; be as like him as you can. Take your eyes off the sins of men, and see their goodness. When we are gone, Arthur and Bedwyr and I, Britain will be in your hands—yours and Percival's and other men your age. Be steadfast, Galahad, in your endeavors. Let nothing deter you. " Lancelot passed a hand across his eyes. "These sound like the words of an old man who is afraid to die and is trying to make his peace," he murmured bitterly. "Nevertheless, it's good advice."

He picked up a dagger from the table at his elbow and twirled it absently in his hand. Galahad watched with admiration the swift play of his clever fingers, the delicate touch, the balance and agility he could so unthinkingly command. With deliberation, Lancelot replaced the dagger on the table and, drawing a deep breath, faced his son.

"I have always loved you, Galahad. I give you my blessing and wish you well. If you . . . if you should change your mind and want to fight, I give you leave to join me. Arthur would not mind. There is not much honor in scavenger hunting."

"There is honor enough for me."

"The offer is good any time."

"Thank you."

"Ah. Well." Lancelot dropped his gaze. "Will you pardon me, son, for the wrongs I have done you?" he asked suddenly, stiffly, dragging his eyes back to the boy's face. "Can you forgive me for Gareth?"

A lump rose in Galahad's throat. "Yes, Father. I have . . . I have put that grief away."

"Lucky boy," Lancelot whispered.

Galahad looked up at his father's shadowed face. "I beg your pardon for shaming you in front of Arthur."

Lancelot exhaled slowly and his look lightened. "Thank you for that. It has lain heavy on my heart. For my part, I forgive you. That Arthur has not killed you means he has forgiven you as well."

Galahad rose. "The woman is all that remains between us, Father. Renounce your affection for her and I will fight with you. Proudly."

"This has nothing to do with the Queen." A spasm of pain crossed Lancelot's face. "I speak of the wrongs I have done you."

"It has everything to do with her! She is the root cause of all our suffering. Yours and mine."

"Don't be ridiculous!" Lancelot retorted hotly. With an effort, he calmed his voice. "She has never been mine to renounce," he said slowly. "And what is in my heart is not within my power to deny. It can only be forgiven."

"I can forgive it if you will give it up."

"It is not within my power to give up," Lancelot whispered.

"Then why did you marry my mother? Why did you beget me? Is it true, what they all say behind my back? That you lay with her because you thought she was Queen Guinevere?"

Lancelot looked at him a long time. At last he stepped forward and took his son in his embrace. "God keep you, Galahad. Defend Arthur with your life. I think you had better go."

At dawn, when the call to battle sounded, Galahad hurried down to his place behind the lines and organized his company of boys. Dimly, he heard the blare of horns and felt the earth shake beneath him as the armies moved. "As David was to Goliath," he prayed quickly under his breath, "so let us be this day to Rome."

His little corps, some of them hardly more than children, readied themselves to go onto the battlefield once the lines moved forward. Their chief duty was to protect their wounded men from scavengers until the orderlies could carry them from the field. Wounded men were easy pickings. After every battle ragged men crawled out from everywhere to scavenge among the dead and dying, robbing them of jewels and weapons, sometimes dispatching any who tried to resist. This Galahad was sworn to prevent. He and his troops had been trained by Gaius Paulus, the chief physician, on how to detect the signs of life, how to know when a man could not be saved, and how to give quick death. They would be first among the fallen and would call the orderlies to tend the living. Scavengers and Romans they would kill.

Percival looked pale as they stood nervously in formation. The ground shook; the din of clashing swords, screaming men, and pounding horses blasted their ears.

"Galahad!" Percival cried, leaning toward him. "Tell me truly—what is it like to kill a man? Is it hard to do?"

Color washed Galahad's face. "The men we kill will be half-dead already. Don't worry about your skill."

"It's not that," Percival said bravely, squaring his shoulders. "I will do what I must do. But I am afraid to look into their eyes."

For half a day battle waged fiercely over the green plain, retreating and advancing, going this way and that. Outnumbered though they were, the Briton armies gave no ground, and toward noon the Burgundian lines began to waver. Men fell, and bled, and died in unthinkable numbers. The hospital tents were full by midmorning, and still the wounded came. The orderlies could do no more than lay the moaning men on pallets in the shade and give them water.

As the sun rose and the sweet stench of blood simmered in the heat of the long June afternoon, Galahad's young army straggled, exhausted, back and forth across the field. Scavengers abounded. There were too many bodies and too few boys. Suddenly, in midafternoon, when numbed men could hardly move one foot before the other, the Britons attacked and broke through the Roman lines. Within the hour the battle turned. Everywhere the Briton lines pushed forward, commanders screaming orders to keep their troops together in the rout. Arthur of Britain had prevailed yet once again, but at a heavy cost. And hours of mopping up still lay ahead.

So tired he no longer felt his pain, Galahad moved slowly among the bodies, bloodied sword held ready, scanning the gray faces of the men who sprawled in the red mud. He had learned to recognize death. He knew now what a man's body held inside it; he had seen gray-white bones buried in dark flesh, he had seen green innards spilling out while their owner's dirty fingers tried frantically to push them back inside. He had seen hearts beat-

ing, heads opened, blood spurting rhythmically from glistening vessels, severed arms with fingers still groping, eyes hanging from their sockets, mouths
and noses filled with vomit, ears filled with blood.

He was beyond feeling anything at all. His sword had lost all vestige of
finesse. When he found a dying man or came upon a Roman, he struck
down at the throat with all his strength. He often stumbled and sometimes
fell, but the fear of lying there and being stabbed himself brought him to
his feet, shivering, moving onward. There were so many! It was impossible
to save them all before dark. His voice was hoarse from calling for the
orderlies.

It dawned on him slowly that all the bodies in his view were Roman.
The Britons had moved on—they must be winning. He lifted his head and
saw he was a long way from the trees that stood above the hospital tents.
There was no one about to ask. Some distance away he saw a scavenger
crawling furtively, a dagger between his teeth. Even as he watched, the
man stopped and tore the armband from a body, then grasped his dagger
and struck viciously downward. Swearing under his breath, Galahad moved
toward him. He staggered, his legs heavy as blocks of wood. He had killed
over twenty such vermin already.

"Sir! Mercy!" screeched the filthy thief, taken by surprise. With a
stroke, Galahad sliced his head half from his shoulders and stooped to take
the stolen armband from his hand. Then he saw the face of the man the
thief had stabbed.

"Cordovic, my cousin!" His stomach heaved. He looked around.
"These are all Bretons! This is Lanascol!"

A slow anger began to burn within him, bringing feeling back. He
knew all these faces with staring eyes. He knew them well. Nirovayne,
Hebes, Palomides. Movement caught his eye—another scavenger fumbled
at a soldier's tunic, prying loose the shoulder badge. Galahad staggered
toward him, but the man heard him and leaped to his feet.

"Go away, boy! My children are starving. Let me keep this badge and I
will trouble you no more!" In his hand he brandished a dagger. Without
thought, Galahad's left hand whipped his dagger from his belt and threw it.
The man fell, choking on his own blood, the dagger in his throat.

"That will teach you to steal from dead men!" But when he pried open
the twitching fingers to retrieve the badge, he froze. There was the Hawk,
silver on a field of black enamel, with a ruby eye.

"Father," he croaked, looking down at the long body in the mud.
"Father!"

Unbelievably, the body moved. The gray eyes opened and looked up at
him, glazed and unseeing. Stiffly, the lips formed a word.

". . . Arthur . . ."

"Father! Don't speak—I'll get you water. Orderly! Here! It's Lancelot! Quickly! Father, where are you wounded?"

Lancelot was covered with mud and gore, but Galahad saw no wound. Kneeling by his side, he felt his body gingerly for broken bones. When he touched his left leg, Lancelot cried out and fainted. Then Galahad saw the gash across his thigh, mud-filled and seeping blood. The ground beneath him was already a liquid pool. His hands, his face, his flesh were gray and lifeless. Already that day Galahad had killed men less desperately wounded, knowing they could not live. Two orderlies arrived with a crude stretcher, but when they saw Lancelot, they swore.

"Why have you called us here? He is a dead man."

"See his face, boy? He cannot live. We are three hours behind as it is. He'll not last twenty minutes. Use your sword."

"He *must* last! You must take him straight to Gaius! This is Lancelot, King of Lanascol! Bind the leg—go on! It's not pumping. If you do not, I shall see the High King learns who it was who killed his dearest friend!"

Wearily, the orderlies obeyed him, bound the leg, and carried Lancelot away. Galahad sat heavily in the pool of his father's blood, too numb for thought, too exhausted to go on. The late-afternoon sun sent his shadow long over the trampled ground and, in the distance, tipped the new-leafed trees with gold. He could not watch any longer. His head was spinning. Slowly, he lowered his head onto a dead man's chest, closed his eyes, and let go.

37 ✞ THE VICTOR'S SPOILS

He woke to darkness and the sound of pouring water. Someone thrust a soaking cloth into his mouth. He sucked it eagerly, his throat aflame. As memory flooded back he struggled to rise, and thin arms pulled him upright.

"Percival?"

"Here, cousin. A moment and I'll have a light." A candle swam before his eyes and Percival's mud-streaked face came into view.

"Is it over?"

"Aye. Drink this. Gaius made it for you. Go on, it's only water with healing herbs to give you strength."

"I'm strong enough." But he drank it thirstily. "Gaius mixed this for *me?*"

Percival nodded. "Because you saved Lancelot's life."

Galahad let his breath out slowly. "He lives?"

"For the moment. He awoke near sundown as they prepared to sew his leg. They had to stun him with smoke to do it. He's very weak. I should tell you that Gaius does not expect him to live much longer. But he wouldn't have lived this long if you hadn't found him."

Galahad sat very still. "Now I have paid him back for the gift of birth."

"So many scores are settling fast."

Galahad brought the candle closer to the younger boy's face. Beneath the dirt and gray fatigue he saw marks of grief. "Percival, what has happened?"

"My . . . my father's dead."

"Maelgon slain? I'm sorry." He slid an arm around Percival's shoulders and hugged him gently. "It is a most honorable death, fighting for Britain against an army of Romans who outnumbered us five to one."

"That's . . . that's not all. Arthur is missing and Gawaine with him. Lancelot is dying—and so many are dead! Urien of Rheged, Prince Riderch and his son—even poor Gabral and Bryddon. Bedwyr leads us now—oh, Galahad, how everything is changed! What will become of us?"

Galahad felt his throat tighten until he could scarcely speak. "What do you mean, Arthur is missing?"

"No one can find him. He has sent us no word. When Lancelot awoke, he was in a panic. He said he had seen the dragon banner fall. By the stream near our left flank, where the hard fighting was at the end. He was half out of his mind with pain, but he would not let Gaius stun him until they'd sent a search party out to the place the King had last been seen. They found the bodies of his companions, but not the King. They found"—he gulped—"they found his sash and his badge. Lancelot was wild with worry on account of the Saxons—"

"The Saxons!"

"Yes, because all their treaties are with Arthur, and if news got out that he was . . . missing . . . the treaties would be void and they might attack. And with the army out of the kingdom! Lancelot sent a courier to Mordred to tell him what had happened. And to tell him that, failing immediate news, he must be king."

"What! He has lost his wits!"

"Only the High King can renew the treaties, Galahad. Lancelot feared to leave Britain unprotected until we discover what has happened to Arthur."

"But he can't! It's treason!"

"I don't think so. According to Sir Bedwyr, Arthur had planned for this."

"Not Mordred!"

"Who else, then? Constantine?" He spoke bitterly and Galahad paused. This was not the same boy he had comforted that morning. In a single day, how much had changed!

"He had no right to send that message."

"He had every right. He had given his oath to Arthur that he would, if Arthur fell."

"He has not fallen!" A heavy silence hung between them.

"Then," Percival whispered, "where is he?"

Galahad wiped his eyes with the back of his hand. "I don't know. But he'll be back. I know he will."

"If he lived, he'd have sent a message. It's every commander's duty. But no one has come. . . . Can you stand, do you think? Sir Bedwyr wants to see you as soon as you are able."

"I'm fine. Where is he?"

"In Arthur's tent."

"He presumes too much!"

"For God's sake, Galahad, someone has to lead the troops and treat with the Romans! He is doing no more than he must. Go look at him, if you think he enjoys it."

Bedwyr had aged ten years since morning, his face drawn dark with grief and his movements labored. His right arm rested in a sling; near the shoulder a dark stripe of blood soaked through the bandage.

"Ah, Galahad, I am glad to see you. Come in."

"My lord Bedwyr." Galahad bent his knee. "I am at your service."

"Only temporarily, I pray, but I thank you. Do you know that your father lies gravely ill?"

"Yes, my lord."

"I have sent for a priest of Christ. Gaius gives him little chance of living through the night."

Galahad's gaze slid to the silver token Sir Bedwyr wore on a thong about his neck, a symbol of Mithra, the soldier's god. "Thank you, my lord. You are very kind."

"It's the least I can do. Lancelot is my friend." He paused. "Do you wish to attend him? If you do, I will make the arrangements." He saw the reluctance on the boy's face and added, "He's not alone. Your uncle Galyn sits with him now."

"In that case, my lord . . . I . . . I would rather do something useful. I'm sure I could be of no use to my father."

Something moved behind Bedwyr's dark eyes. "Very well. I can use you." He turned and led Galahad to the inner chamber of the tent, where great piles of weapons, armbands, necklaces, and badges were stacked. Three men were sorting these belongings under Gereint's supervision, and two scribes were labeling them with the names of their dead owners.

"Until we carry these effects home to the families of the men who died, they must be guarded," Bedwyr explained. "We have lost thousands. I judged this to be the safest place to keep them, the easiest place to guard. Arthur valued your skill with a sword, Galahad. Will you do us all this service and guard these treasured belongings home to Britain?"

"Yes, my lord. May I have Percival to help me?"

"You may appoint anyone you like to the duty. I leave the choice to you."

Percival shook his head when he heard the news. "It's because they all think you are mad, you know, that he chose you."

Galahad stared. "What do you mean? Who thinks I'm mad?"

"The whole army. They know your skill with a sword and they fear it. On account of what you did to the bandit before you killed him."

Galahad froze. "Who told you that?"

Percival shrugged. "You know how soldiers gossip. Sir Bedwyr has certainly heard it. Your new reputation will serve us well. No one will dare to come near the men's effects. You are the perfect choice."

Galahad found himself breathing hard. "And you, cousin? Don't you fear Nemesis, too?"

Percival laughed. "You're not *my* nemesis. And you're not mad; you're just single-minded. Bumpkin is perfectly happy to accept the protection of your sword."

"How brave of you." Galahad spoke bitterly, and Percival laid a hand on his arm.

"There's something else they say about you, cousin. They say you are chosen. That God has called you to some special service which will bring you either to an early death or to glory. Because you are not like other men."

Galahad began to breathe again and color flooded his face. "Don't be silly. Nobody says that about me. They're only repeating that wretched witch's prophecy. How could she possibly know what will happen?"

"They say she predicted this war," Percival said slowly, "and . . . and the death of Arthur."

The two boys stared blankly at each other.

Three days passed. A great gloom descended on the army as they went about the grim task of finding, stripping, and burying the dead. Every time a horseman rode by the men looked up in hope. When they paused from their labors they scanned the battlefield, the sparse woodland, the distant meadows. Everyone prayed to whatever god he worshiped that Arthur would not be found among the slain, but it would take a week to clear the field. And if he had been robbed or beheaded, what would be left to know him by?

To Bedwyr fell the task of dealing with the Romans. He kept Arthur's absence secret from the envoys and negotiated terms of surrender as he knew Arthur would have done. He demanded no gold, no hostages, no recompense for the trouble Rome had caused, but he returned Hiberius's body to his countrymen with the words, "This is all the tribute Britain pays to Rome." He left the Romans free to return home unhindered and demanded only Rome's oath to leave Britain in peace for a thousand years. He signed the document "AR"—*Arturus Rex*—and sealed it with Arthur's seal. The Roman commander praised his virtue and his mercy, and declared he had proved his reputation as a fair man. Beyond that, all Bedwyr could do was watch them as they gathered and buried their dead, and send scouts to see them off on the road to Rome.

For three days Lancelot lay in the world of shadows between the living and the dead, gray and frail, unmoving, unwaking, shrinking, it seemed, before their very eyes. Gaius shook his head helplessly. "If he cannot wake to take water, he will die."

Galyn sat by his brother's pallet and bowed his head in grief. So many were dead from Lanascol! Bors had been slain by a spear through his belly, Cordovic's throat was slit, and a hundred others as well loved were gone forever. If only Arthur were there, Lancelot might rally. But if Arthur lived, surely he would have sent a messenger to Bedwyr. Like as not, his body had been ravaged by scavengers and picked apart by kites. They might never find more than his bones. In despair, he covered his face and wept.

Inside the High King's tent, Galahad watched the stacks of belongings mount day by day, talismans of the heavy cost of victory. He and Percival stood guard in shifts, sleeping and taking their meals by the pile of treasure, stepping outside only for brief respites while Bedwyr himself was there in council. It was onerous duty, but no worse than grave digging or bearing the dead from the field.

Percival's grief for his father was barely within his command. He spoke little and sometimes wept when he thought no one could hear. Galahad mourned Gabral and Bryddon. He desperately missed their nightly banter, the half-wit's teasing and Bryddon's dour replies. Daily he visited the ditch which held their bodies, along with a thousand others, tossed wildflowers on their blanket of raw earth, and knelt in prayer until his knees ached so he could barely stand.

At twilight on the third day a whisper began among the troops, low and fitful at first, passing from man to man, and then, gathering strength, ran through the camp like wildfire on a swift wind.

"Arthur! The King returns! Arthur lives!"

Men raced out onto the plain, abandoning their campfires, their dinners, their work, to stare as a small group of men emerged from the distant woods, crossed the stream, and came slowly toward them. Two horsemen led fifteen foot soldiers. They carried no banner but, limp and ragged as they were, they marched in formation.

"By Mithra!" Bedwyr whispered, standing before the tent and shading his eyes from the setting sun. "Could it be Arthur and Gawaine? Galahad, look! Your eyes are better than mine. Can you see them?"

"I know the horse, my lord! It is the High King's!"

Even as they watched, men dashed across the open ground and knelt at the rider's side, kissing his boots, weeping as he passed. There could be no doubt; it must be Arthur. But the man himself, gaunt, bearded, and weary, Galahad hardly recognized. Gawaine, too, looked pale and exhausted. They approached the camp while the host of soldiers cheered and wept for joy. Arthur slid from his horse. Bedwyr embraced him, tears in his eyes, and kissed his cheeks.

"Arthur! By the light, I am glad to see you!"

"And I you, Bedwyr, my dear companion. Fate has proved a fickle friend. We sent a messenger to tell you we were off to catch the ruffians who ambushed us, but on the way back we came across his body. You have been three days without news?"

"It feels more like three years!" Bedwyr cried, managing a smile. "Come inside and rest, my lord, and let me tell you about the Romans—"

Arthur lifted a hand. "In a little while. First, take me to Lancelot."

When he sat at the side of his old friend, Arthur wept. He took Lancelot's frail body in his arms, held him close, and spoke into his ear. Lancelot stirred; his lips moved. Quickly, Gaius lifted a cup to his mouth, and he drank. Lancelot could not open his eyes, or speak, or move his hands, but as long as Arthur held him, he drank the healing broth and breathed more easily.

"When he can be moved," Arthur ordered, "bring him to me."

By morning a new tent was raised adjoining the High King's; Lancelot's pallet was set next to the tent cloth so that, should he awaken, he could hear the High King's voice. And Arthur, while he went about his business, could listen for sounds of progress or distress.

Arthur's first action was to send two couriers to Mordred with the news of his return, not trusting merely one to get the message through. His second action approved all the decisions Bedwyr had made in his name. He confirmed Galahad at his post and did not ask him if he preferred to be at his father's side. He took Percival aside and spoke to him privately. When the boy emerged, his eyes were red and he wore his father's swordbelt and his badge.

"Galahad! The High King has confirmed me as my father's heir. Provided I allow my uncle Peredur to act as regent until I am fifteen, I am now King of Gwynedd."

"Now you outrank me, my lord Percival." Galahad smiled, bowing low. The light left Percival's face. "If I did, I'd command you to attend your father. You haven't been once to see him. Your absence has been marked. He's senseless, you know. Why don't you just go in and kneel at his side?"

Galahad looked quickly away. "It doesn't matter what others think."

"Of course it does."

"Let it be, Percival. If God wants Lancelot to live, he will live. My presence at his bedside makes no difference."

"I will pray for him," Percival whispered. "I will pray for you both."

38 ⛨ THE DRAGON AND THE HAWK

In ten days the dead were identified and buried, their effects sorted, and wagons made ready to carry the treasure. The army was rested; the wounded were healing; it was time to start for home. But Arthur would not move. After gaining strength and awakening, Lancelot had fallen into a fever. His injured leg swelled and grew hot. His brow burned. He slipped into delirium, moaned, and tossed about. Gaius, having learned better, said nothing about his chances but lanced the leg, poulticed it to draw the heat, cooled his brow, gave him water, and waited. Arthur paced about his tent, listening to the dreadful moans, knowing by the sound of his agony that his friend still lived.

The days grew hot and the plain dusty. Men rode far afield to hunt, fished the streams, and set snares for ground fowl. Tempers began to wear ragged. But alone of Arthur's men Gawaine voiced his discontent. He hung about the High King day and night, badgering him to leave Lancelot with Gaius and start for home.

"You dare not leave it too long, my lord. You will tempt Mordred past his bearing. I grew up with him and I know his nature—he's an ambitious man."

"I know him, too, Gawaine. He will not steal my crown, if that is what worries you so."

"He won't be able to help himself. It is all he has ever wanted, to rule Britain in your stead!"

"Nonsense. He was a grown man before I made him my heir. That is treasonous talk—watch your tongue! He is my son."

"And my brother. I know his heart. He—"

"Enough. I will hear no more. I will not leave until Lancelot can travel.

Possess your soul in patience, if you can. If you cannot, take your prattle somewhere else."

Gawaine left, but he always returned, and always with the same song upon his lips. At the back of the tent, behind a curtain of skins where the men's effects were piled, Galahad and Percival heard these words and exchanged long looks.

They were there the day a letter came from Britain. The courier who brought it told a harrowing tale of a wild wind that blew from the north across the Narrow Sea. His ship was nearly wrecked upon the waves, so fast did she fly before the wind. But he would have to wait until the fury abated before he could return. No ship bound for Britain could even leave port.

Arthur paled. "How long has this been so?"

"My lord, the gale has blown nigh on a week, and shows no sign of weakening. It's a strange sight, for the sky is clear. The sailors' superstitions are aroused. Not a man of them will put hand to an oar."

"This means," Arthur said slowly to Gawaine when the courier had left them, "that the couriers I sent could not get across. They do not know in Britain that I live."

Galahad and Percival peeked around the edges of the curtain and held their breaths as the High King unrolled the scroll and read, his face lining with worry and his eyes growing cold. When he had finished, he looked up, his gaze far away, and then read it carefully once more. At his side Gawaine fairly danced with impatience.

"What does it say, Uncle? Is it good news or ill? Who is it from?"

Without a word, the King handed him the scroll and began to pace. Using his finger as a guide, Gawaine laboriously worked through the Latin script. "Why, it's from Constantine of Cornwall! And it's addressed to the leader of the Briton armies. 'To the most noble commander, King Arthur, if he liveth, or to whomever now standeth in his stead, greetings from Constantine, Duke of Cornwall.' "

"Notice," Arthur cut in thinly, "he does not style himself 'heir of Britain' as he was once wont to do. That is because Mordred has repulsed him, and because he is not sure that I am dead."

"He says . . . he says . . . your presence is urgently required in Britain, my lord. Because—let's see—how his scribe does beat around the bush. I can't see Constantine himself taking this long to say anything. Because—I knew it! Mordred has done more than make himself regent! He has made himself High King!"

Galahad and Percival exchanged frightened glances as Gawaine swore furiously and shook the scroll at Arthur.

"I told you, my lord! I told you he was ambitious! The traitorous dog has usurped your power and your name!"

"Call him that again at your peril, Gawaine. He is my son."

"But, my lord—"

"He is following my orders. Nothing more. The night he left Kerrec I told him that if I fell, he must assume the kingship without delay and treat with Cerdic. Surely you see the sense in that."

"But you have not fallen!"

"He does not know that. He has had only Lancelot's message, not mine."

"But Lancelot did not report your death! He knew only that you could not be found. Yet Mordred has crowned himself without even waiting for confirmation!"

"Nonsense. There has been no crowning. He has taken the title, as he must, until the courier gets through. Otherwise, Britain bares her neck to the Saxon fang."

But Gawaine could not be stilled for long. "My lord!" He gasped, staring hard at the scroll. "What is this? Constantine calls the Queen a vixen!"

"Read on," Arthur replied evenly, "and you will see."

Gawaine flushed as bright as his flaming hair. "Mordred is *courting* her?" He looked up, stunned. "Uncle, the duke says here . . . he says they are to be married! Oh, the vile dog! He thinks to solidify his power by taking your widow to wife. I'll have his head for this! I'll—"

"Gawaine." The King's voice froze Gawaine in midsentence. "If anyone will have his head, I will. But stop a moment, and think before you speak. Consider who writes the letter, and what he has to gain or lose by lies. Do not take every word as truth. Consider Constantine."

"Do you think he lies when he says Mordred is gathering his own army? I believe him. It is just what Mordred would do."

"Perhaps he is. But recall why Mordred went home to Britain. Constantine was on the march with troops. Mordred was sent to prevent the taking of Camelot. He has obviously succeeded, and Constantine is angry. If you were Mordred, with an angry war leader and his troops loose on the land, would you not shore up your own forces, for safety's sake? Thus far, what Mordred has done makes perfect sense."

"But these men are loyal to Mordred now, not to you."

"They are loyal to the High King. To Britain. Why must you see Mordred as my enemy, Gawaine? You know he is not."

"No?" Gawaine cried, tossing the letter to the ground. "How can you deny it, when he is betrothed to your own wife?"

Arthur ceased his pacing and stood very still. "It isn't true."

"How do you know? He has always loved her, Uncle. You know that."

"I know Guinevere. And I know Mordred. It isn't true."

"He solidifies his backing, and she holds on to power—"

"Consider the source, Gawaine. This barb was meant for me. Constantine wishes to divide us and is using Guinevere as the wedge. If he can bring me back to Britain as Mordred's enemy, he stands to gain much and lose nothing. It's a crafty tactic, but it will not work if I don't believe it."

"Are you so sure it is not true?"

"Yes."

Gawaine shrugged. "You have much to lose if he is right."

Arthur stood as still as stone. "If he is right it is already lost."

In the heavy silence that followed, Bedwyr stuck his head through the tent flap.

"My lord Arthur, have you a moment?"

Wearily, Arthur nodded. "Come in, Bedwyr. Gawaine is just leaving." Gawaine scowled, but obeyed, and sketched a salute to Bedwyr on the way out. With a deep sigh, Arthur sat on his stool and motioned Bedwyr to sit beside him.

"You look tired, my lord," said Bedwyr anxiously. "Have you eaten?"

"Later. Later. I have no stomach for food while Lancelot is ill."

"That is why I have come. Gaius expects the crisis to come tonight. By tomorrow his fate should be decided. He has a body of iron. If the fever breaks, he might live."

Arthur rested a hand on Bedwyr's shoulder. "And if not, not. Ah, Bedwyr, I cannot envision a world without Lancelot. He is a part of me. As are you, my old friend." Bedwyr nodded and bit his lip. "But he has a will of iron, too. I put my hope in that. Tell Gaius I will come at sundown. I will stay until it is over."

"Yes, my lord."

Arthur sighed. "You might as well know the latest news." He pointed to the crumpled scroll. Bedwyr retrieved it and slowly read. When at last he looked up, his face was grave.

"Constantine is your enemy, Arthur. These lies might be believed by credulous men."

The King's smile was bitter. "Indeed. They already are."

"Gawaine?"

"Of course. I am glad to know you have more sense."

Bedwyr tapped the letter. "Clearly, they do not yet know you live. For Britain's safety, Mordred might assume your command and raise an army. But this about the Queen is slander."

"Gawaine believes it."

Bedwyr shook his head. "If ever anyone made such an accusation about the Lady Ragnall, Gawaine would kill the man who told him for allowing the mere words to pass his lips. How could he say such a thing to you?"

Arthur folded his hands and stared hard at the floor. "Let us not forget he is my nephew, and stands to gain if my son can be discredited."

"Arthur! Do you mistrust him? He has been at your side these many years and always treated you with honor. Does he now plot against you?"

"No, no, do not misunderstand me. As much as is in him, Gawaine loves me. I do not doubt him. But he has an abiding jealousy of Mordred and would, I think, be pleased to find these lies of Constantine were true."

"Well, they are not," Bedwyr repeated firmly. "But one thing is certain: The sooner we get to Britain, the better. It is past midsummer now."

The King rose, and Bedwyr rose with him. "We will stay until Lancelot can travel. We will escort him to Lanascol with honor. Not until Gaius assures me he will live will I return to Britain." Bedwyr frowned, but Arthur's tone brooked no opposition. "Britain will come to no harm while Mordred is king."

Bedwyr bowed low and handed back the scroll. "As you will, my lord."

The King held the scroll to the lamp flame and watched it burn, then ground the ashes into the dirt with the heel of his boot. "So much for Constantine. Come, Bedwyr, I feel the need of sweet air. Let's go out to the troops."

When the sun set the High King went to Lancelot's tent. Galahad sat on a stool by the treasure he guarded and Percival huddled nearby in his bedroll, unable to sleep. They were near enough to the tent cloth to hear voices from the vicinity of Lancelot's pallet and to see the shadows cast by Gaius and his assistants moving back and forth in front of the light.

For a long time nothing happened. Lancelot continued to thrash about and moan while Arthur sat still at his bedside. Bedwyr came in once or twice to confer with the King. Gaius and his assistants kept applying heat to Lancelot's wound and cool cloths to his brow.

"God forgive me the thought," Percival whispered. "But what will you do if he dies? Have you considered it?"

"No."

"You will be King of Lanascol."

"You are King of Gwynedd. What are *you* going to do?"

"Go home, of course. And when I'm fifteen, serve Arthur."

"That sounds sensible."

"And you?"

Galahad shrugged. "Uncle Galyn can hold Lanascol easily enough. He's done it for Lancelot for years. I wouldn't be needed there. I'll stay with Arthur. Until—"

"Until?"

Galahad looked at his friend. Percival lay propped up on one elbow, his face solemn in the dimness, not quite a boy's face any longer. He had a gravity about him that was new. Galahad glanced at Maelgon's sword in its polished scabbard, wrapped carefully and placed just within Percival's reach. Not for the first time, he marveled at the power of weapons to transform the men they served. When he himself had belted on Gareth's sword, he had grown, by degrees, into someone different: a seeker of revenge. But when he had used the sword for that purpose he had wronged everyone. Even the blood of Autun had not cleaned the weapon. He knew, more viscerally than consciously, the sword was not for him any longer. But he had no other.

Percival, on the other hand, had found the sword of his kingship and he had grown, almost overnight, from a clumsy boy into a royal youth.

"Until what?" Percival prodded softly.

"Until," Galahad said slowly, "I must leave on the quest he has sworn me to perform."

Percival sat up. "You have been talking to the High King about your future, and you never told me?"

Haltingly, Galahad told Percival what Arthur had said to him during their meeting in Kerrec.

Percival's eyes grew round as shield bosses. "I knew you were different for a reason. This must be what you were born to do."

"Lancelot told me being different was a gift," Galahad said quietly. "Aidan said that someday I would learn about my destiny, and the High King himself gave me this quest. It's as if the prophecy was beginning to—"

Lancelot groaned. They saw the High King's shadow on the tent cloth, crossing himself quickly.

"Arthur's afraid that Lancelot will die," Percival said softly. "He hasn't been the same since he returned and found him ill."

"There are worse things than death if one dies unrepentant."

Percival glanced at him swiftly. "Don't start that again. He's shriven. Sir Bedwyr found a priest, remember?"

Galahad watched his father's shadow twist and thrash. "He would never tell a priest about her. Not the truth. Not about Guinevere."

Hours passed without a change in Lancelot's condition. Percival fell asleep and Galahad kept watch alone. Toward the middle of the night, when the earth fell quiet in the solid grip of darkness and stars burned still as breathless candle flames, Galahad gradually noticed that Lancelot was struggling. His moans grew wilder and more frequent, his breathing came hard in sharp, rattling gasps, and his delirious babble took shape into occasional words.

"Arthur!" he cried out. The King's voice came through the tent cloth, calm and soothing, but Galahad could not make out the words. He knelt down to Percival and shook him gently.

"My turn?" yawned the boy.

"Something's happening."

Percival instantly awakened and stood beside him, shivering in the dark, listening. The boys could see Gaius's shadow moving before the low lamp and they heard water poured into a basin amid the muffled, urgent whispers of his assistants.

"Guinevere," Lancelot moaned. "Beg Guinevere come near. I must see her face again. My sweet Gwen." The High King's shadow held steady at Lancelot's side, bent over the racked body, beseeching him, holding his hands.

Lancelot twisted on the pallet. "Galahad." He sobbed aloud. "Galahad. Son, forgive me!"

Galahad trembled and Percival gripped his arm. The King murmured something, but Lancelot turned away and moaned. Gradually, as his voice began to fail, he spoke in breathy shudders words wrenched from his desperate soul.

"Gareth!" he croaked, clutching at the King. "Murder! Gareth is dead! My God, my God, I'll kill the man who did it! I'll have his heart out! Arthur!" He gasped, "Who is it? Tell me!" But he did not pause to hear the King's response. "Gareth, Gareth, my beloved. Where is Gareth?"

The sweat stood out on Galahad's brow as he heard these words and watched the tossing shadow on the tent cloth. Lancelot's breath rattled in his chest. The King bent low and kissed him, and held him in his arms. After a long silence, while Percival and Galahad stood rooted, Lancelot's voice came clearly.

"Forgive me my sins, Arthur."

"My dear friend, you are forgiven."

"Tell Guinevere . . . I love her."

"She knows it well."

"Forgive me for it."

"There is no need. I forgave you long ago."

"Arthur . . ."

The King gripped him firmly by the shoulders. "Lancelot. I command you to live."

"I . . . I cannot," came the agonized reply. "Gareth. Galahad."

"Thou art clean of sin." Arthur spoke the Latin words slowly and clearly as he made the sign of the cross in the air above his head. "Now live."

But Lancelot's body slumped in his arms and the High King, choking back tears, began to pray. Gaius stood motionless behind him. It was suddenly very quiet. Galahad and Percival could no longer hear his breathing.

Slowly Galahad sank to his knees. "He is gone. My father is dead."

Percival knelt and put his arms around his cousin's shoulders. Sobs rose one after the other in Galahad's throat, broke in harsh waves upon his lips, and spilled out uncontrollably into the waiting night. He clenched his eyes and fists against the torrent but his will was a tiny thing, fluttering and useless against the never-ending springs of grief. After a long while Percival led him to his pallet and, dazed and exhausted, he slept.

He awoke to the touch of gentle hands, a touch so familiar that for a moment he was carried back in memory to another grief, another darkness. Strong arms lifted him and hugged him close.

"Galahad," said the King's voice in his ear. "Galahad, my brave lad. Rejoice with me. He lives!"

Galahad looked up into Arthur's face. All the King's weariness had vanished. He looked young again, radiant and strong, alight with joy.

Percival sat up and rubbed his eyes. "Sir Lancelot lives?"

Arthur's smile lit the chamber. "Yes, Percival, by the grace of God he lives! I heard your grief"—he turned back to Galahad—"and knew you thought him dead. After crisis comes collapse. If death comes, it comes then. But to the lucky comes peaceful rest after the hard struggle with fever. Lancelot struggled a long time—his rest now will be as long. But Gaius says he will recover."

"Thank God!" Percival cried. "It is a miracle!"

Arthur laughed for the sheer pleasure of it. "All of life is a miracle. Anyone who has been to war knows this."

Arthur embraced Galahad again and then looked into his face. "I knew that in your heart you loved him," he said very gently. "Now you know it, too." He smiled again. "God works in mysterious ways, does He not?"

PART II
The Return of the King

*In the twenty-sixth year of the reign
of Arthur Pendragon*

39 ✟ THE CROSSING

Galahad stood in the bow of the ship well forward of the great sail. He still could not believe they had finally put out to sea. Two whole weeks they had spent in Lanascol after the long trek from Autun, and three in Kerrec, penned in by the wayward wind. The storms that had assailed the seas all summer still played havoc with sailing vessels. Every second boat leaving harbor in a calm sea later foundered in a freakish wind. There seemed no end to it. Even Arthur's temper had begun to wear a little thin. King Hoel had advised them not to attempt a crossing, but Arthur was impatient to get back to Britain. They had readied their ships and camped at wharfside, waiting for the seas to slacken. And now, three weeks short of the autumn equinox and four months after they had left for Gaul, they were finally returning victorious to Britain.

He heard his name and turned. Percival made his way carefully between the neat coils of braided hemp. "Where've you been? I've been looking for you. Guess what I heard about Prince Mordred?" He lowered his voice. "I overheard Sir Gawaine telling one of his men what passed between Arthur and King Hoel back in Kerrec. *We* thought we were waiting for a wind, but it seems the High King was negotiating for Mordred's future."

Galahad glanced right and left but no one else was near. "Go on."

"Well, King Hoel was in a bad way, as you know—he couldn't get over his grief at Riderch's death, and his grandson Oltair's as well. All gone in a single stroke! He told Arthur he had no one to leave his kingdom to. His second son—did you know Prince Riderch had a brother?—is a man of forty named Grayvise who spends all day among his scrolls and studies music. He's a master on the lute and harp but, according to Hoel, has not a warrior's bone in his body. He's not wed, but neither has he an eye for women. Boys are more to his taste. And King Hoel wept because he had no one but Grayvise to leave his kingdom to. So guess what King Arthur suggested?"

"I don't think I want to know."

"Hoel has named Prince Mordred as his heir! Arthur and Hoel are cousins, so it's not as if Mordred had no right to it."

Galahad grimaced. "Better Grayvise. Better even a woman. Oh, I see what Arthur is about. He thinks to unite the Britains when both he and Hoel are gone."

"And in the meantime, the King promised Hoel, it means Brittany will be well defended."

"More to the point, it gives Mordred something to do when the High King takes back his crown."

Percival nodded. "It's not a bad idea, Galahad. If Prince Mordred has been High King all summer, and if he's as ambitious as Gawaine thinks, it won't be easy for him to give it up, even for Arthur. This is tempting bait. I think it's very clever."

Galahad shook his head. "It's madness. However clever it is, it will never happen. Gawaine probably invented half of it—he's been itching for trouble ever since we left Lancelot in Lanascol. If Arthur hadn't been there, I doubt his sense of honor would have kept him from attacking my father in his bed."

The breeze freshened suddenly against his cheek. On the horizon he could see the shore of Britain shimmering in the heat of late summer. They were nearly home. Behind them sailed the ship Bedwyr commanded, and somewhere in Bedwyr's wake were three more vessels—what was left of the army could return in one crossing, while it had taken three before.

Suddenly the ship lurched, throwing them off balance. They collided, stumbled, and clutched at the rail. In a few heartbeats the sea had heaved itself into gray, froth-decked mountains as a gale struck from the west with icy breath.

"Come on!" Percival shouted, grabbing Galahad's arm. "Let's get below!" Together they staggered aft as the spray-soaked sailors swore and sweated to reef the sail. There was not a cloud in the sky, yet the wind was whipping the seas, turning the day dark, and staining the water black. The ship rolled violently, flying eastward as the sea poured over the deck. The captain fought to keep the laden rig upright, but he was powerless to steer her course. Eastward and landward they flew, the sail in ribbons, faster and faster toward the looming cliffs and the rocky bays below. Men lashed themselves to the mast, to anything that might withstand the water's onslaught. At every wave crest they caught a glimpse of the rockbound coast fast approaching. They all shouted to their gods to save them, but the sound was borne away to nothingness before it was past their lips.

The breakers flung them past a rocky point and into a shallow bay. In the lee of the land the wind died, and silence deafened their ears. The ship rose on a crest, then fell, swung hard to starboard, and smashed against a sharp shoal of rock. Timbers groaned and snapped. Men shouted, wailed, and wept. Through it all, the High King's voice came calmly. "Brychan, open the hatches. Vorn, line up the men. We will go below before the ship breaks up and get the horses out."

Drenched and freezing, shaking so hard he could barely stand, Percival grabbed Galahad's arm.

"Galahad! I am lost! I cannot swim!"

Galahad held him up. "Don't worry, the horses can. Come on. Stay with me. I'll get you ashore."

Like many of Arthur's men, they were saved by the horses. Frozen and exhausted, they reached the stony beach clinging to a halter or a mane. By late afternoon two hundred men and thirty horses huddled shivering on the shingle.

"If this is an omen," Percival chattered, "I like it not!"

Arthur and Gawaine organized the ragged army; they salvaged whatever floated ashore, took stock of what men and supplies remained, and filed slowly up the narrow track to the top of the low cliff. From the promontory they looked down upon another beach, where two more ships lay foundered, men and horses huddled in dejected groups or roaming aimlessly. But someone was organizing them and putting things in order. A small figure looked up, waved, and raised a shout.

"Bedwyr!" cried Arthur in relief. "Thank God he was spared! Gawaine, move this group off the cliffs toward yonder woods. We're too exposed here. Make camp and get fires going. I'm going down to Bedwyr to get his news and help them up here."

"Yes, my lord." Gawaine spun on his heel. "Galahad, you're just the one I want; you're a wizard with horses. Take charge of the cavalry and set some horse lines. Find them fodder and water, if you can. You, Percival, take a troop and get us firewood. Let's go before we freeze to death in this cursed wind."

But the storm was spent, and passed away as quickly as it had arisen. By sunset they were camped, the horses dry and grazing, and had small fires going. Spirits everywhere were low. Such a homecoming was an inauspicious omen for men victorious in war. Arthur had not returned; they had found no fresh water; they had lost the ship and over fifty men to the cruel sea.

And then Percival spoke. "Who are those people? What funny clothes they wear!"

Galahad looked up. Gawaine shot to his feet. Away to the east a procession of small figures marched up another cliff from the shore below. They were not Britons. They wore skins and leggings crisscrossed with thongs and carried packs upon their backs. To Galahad they looked like peasant farmers trudging home from the fields. But the sea lay behind them. Suddenly the strangers saw their campfires. For a moment, everyone froze. Then the newcomers began to scurry about in panic until a tall man ran up the cliff and stilled them. Bronze-skinned and golden-haired, with a magnificent yellow mustache and a leather helmet adorned with gold, he strode among the farmers like a god among mortals, and soon had them organized into a small circle. Then he turned and faced the Britons, alone, hands on hips.

"By the Goddess Herself!" Gawaine spluttered. "Saxons!"

"Saxons!" Men leaped to their feet at the ancient battle cry and grabbed their swords.

"Are you sure, my lord?" Percival ventured.

"You ignorant puppy," Gawaine snapped. "I know a Saxon when I see one. They will regret the day they broke the treaty and ventured onto Briton soil! Galahad! It's time to put that bloodthirsty sword of yours to Britain's defense. To horse! We'll take them before they're all up from the beach!"

Percival grabbed Galahad's sleeve and held him. "Wait for Arthur, I pray you! What can we lose? We outnumber them; few of them look armed— stay his hand!"

Galahad looked back at the Saxons. They were aligning themselves in some formation; the leader shouted orders; more warriors ran up from the beach.

"Let go, Percival! We cannot wait for Arthur! In a moment they will be ready for us!" He jerked his arm from Percival's grasp. "There are few things left I'm certain of, cousin, but I'm sure of this: Arthur is good, Mordred is evil, and the Saxons are our enemies."

He ran to the horse lines where the grooms were throwing saddles on the backs of weary animals, and leaped bareback onto his stallion. Already the men were falling into formation as Gawaine exhorted them, igniting their fighting spirit and calling upon their pride as Britons to defend their homeland. Galahad cantered up and saluted. Gawaine flashed him a fierce look. "Bareback, eh? Even in battle? A real son of Lancelot, a show-off! Show me your skill, then, princeling, and guard my flank!"

In tight formation they wheeled toward the waiting Saxons. There were a hundred of them now, armed and ready, and everyone could see the weapons they carried. They swung their bright, two-headed axes over their heads in great, glittering arcs. But although they threatened, they did not advance. They waited.

The earth trembled to the thunder of galloping horses.

"Arthur!" the soldiers cried. "King Arthur is here!"

Arthur's great white stallion slid to a stop next to Gawaine, followed at a distance by Bedwyr and Gereint. The King's face was pinched with anger. "What's the meaning of this, Gawaine? Who gave the orders?"

"I did, my lord. Look yonder! Saxons!"

In the failing light they saw the bright ax heads twirling. Arthur looked startled. "By God, that looks like Cynewulf himself! What's he doing here?"

"Just what I intend to find out, my lord."

"Who's with him?"

"Two hundred warriors. Five hundred others. Farmers, by the look of them. They came from the beach."

"Longboats! But what are they doing *here*? No. I don't believe it. We have a treaty. They wouldn't dare."

"My lord!" Gawaine cried, losing patience, "they think you are dead! This is the invasion you feared!"

"Nonsense. And there are not so many of them. Cynewulf has been to the homeland to bring in more settlers, that's all. But the treaty forbids them to land in Britain."

"But, my lord—"

"No, Gawaine. That old fox Cerdic is cleverer than this. If he wants to test the treaty he will do it where Mordred can see him. No one could know we would be shipwrecked here." Arthur's eyes narrowed. "I wonder— perhaps we were blown too far east. These might be Saxon lands."

"My lord!" Gawaine shouted, trembling. "It is impossible! Do not de- lay! Look—they advance!"

Arthur squinted. "They have not moved—it's a trick of the light. We will attempt a parley. Wait here, Gawaine. I would speak with Bedwyr."

He wheeled his horse and cantered away. The troops Bedwyr led were running up from the beach. Someone had raised the Red Dragon, limp with seawater but still recognizable.

The Saxon leader pointed to it, and his men lowered their weapons. Gawaine pummeled his saddlebow in frustration. "He's getting old!" he wailed. "He's past his best! Time was, the mere sight of a Saxon savage would rouse him to a fury. Nowadays, it's talk, talk, talk!" He leaned over his horse's withers and spat. "That's the Queen's doing, Galahad. The bitch has made him soft. Before he married he was the deadliest warrior in the kingdoms. He'd never have let a chance like this go by!"

Galahad looked at him in amazement. It was the first time in his memory Gawaine had spoken sense. "Women are cowards, my lord."

Gawaine laughed. "If Ragnall could hear you she'd have your balls on a platter! *Some* women, Galahad. Not all." He stiffened, staring hard at the Saxons. "Look! The traitorous dogs are advancing! Where is Arthur? Still talking! By God, I'll not wait upon a lily-livered king!" He turned in the saddle. "I say we kill the heathen savages! Who is with me?" He raised his sword high overhead and the men behind him raised a shout. "Kill the bas- tards!" Gawaine bellowed, and set spurs to his horse. The soldiers broke into a victory paean. The whole line moved forward. Galahad followed without a moment's hesitation, riding hard on Gawaine's flank. There was no time for thought. They charged headlong into the Saxons, swords drawn, screaming.

He had never lived such a moment. Time slowed down and all his wits grew sharp. He saw every sweating brow and flying wisp of yellow hair, heard every shout, every snarl, every anguished cry, felt the press of bodies, the slither of sweat on his horse's sides, the jarring of his arm as the sword went home. It was slow and silent and easy. His legs felt warm and strong against the horse's body, his grip upon the sword hilt cold and hard. Axes whirled and swung about his head. He kept his eyes on them and let his body guide the horse and sword where it would. Tall blond giants fell before him like sheaves of grain at harvest time; blood splattered everywhere. A great, hot excitement swept him, a glorious rage, an ecstasy. This he was born for. None of them could touch him.

Too soon for him, it was over. The farmers knelt, crouching in submission, while the few warriors left living raced for the shelter of the wood.

"Enough!" roared a commanding voice. Galahad, breathing heavily but alive in every sinew, looked up to see the pale, glowing blade of the King's sword, Excalibur, raised high in the air. "Sound the retreat, Pelles. We are not here to murder unarmed peasants. Fall in, men. Has anyone seen my madman nephew?"

No one answered. Galahad stared in amazement at his own sword, glistening with bright blood right up to the hilt. He had killed today—his first battle! He had killed for Britain. He had denied Mordred's prophecy and fought in Arthur's army! He had slaughtered heathen savages and acquitted himself with honor before God. He crossed himself solemnly. "For the glory of God, for the glory of Britain, for the glory of Arthur."

"Galahad!" The King's voice came sharply at his elbow. He looked up as Arthur thrust his own sword, shining and unblooded, home to its scabbard. "Where is Gawaine?"

"I . . . I don't know, my lord. He was . . . off to my left somewhere. I was guarding his flank."

"And how do you guard his flank when you don't know where he is!" Arthur snapped, wheeling his horse. "An army of children! All of them blind!"

"King Arthur! King Arthur!" Behind them in the field of fallen bodies Percival knelt, waving frantically.

"By God!" Arthur muttered. "There's at least one man who's kept his head!"

Bedwyr ran to Percival, raised a hand, and signaled Arthur.

" 'Strewth!" the King cried. "Gawaine!"

Galahad watched him race away, unable to believe his ears. He looked again at his bloody sword. He had killed Saxons, forty of them at least! Whatever ailed the High King, that he did not rejoice? He dismounted and carefully cleaned the blade on the trampled grass. Nearby Gereint regrouped the foot soldiers and led them back to camp. He did not look in Galahad's direction. Alone, Galahad gathered his reins and walked to where Percival and Bedwyr stood in the deepening dark, looking down upon Arthur.

Arthur knelt at Gawaine's side, gray-faced. Gawaine lay still, looking up, his left arm severed at the shoulder by a Saxon ax, blood still pumping feebly from the wound.

"Gawaine," Arthur whispered, gently raising his head and putting his own waterskin to the dying lips, "my sister's son. I have enemies to face and you will not be with me."

Gawaine choked, swallowed, and gripped the King's hand. "My lord. Uncle. Listen to me. I've not much time."

"Speak, then."

"Tell Lancelot—"

"Yes?"

"I forgive him."

"Ahhh." Arthur bowed his head. "Thank you."

"Send for him, Arthur. You need him. Promise me—you will send for Lancelot. Make haste. The time is near." He stopped, gasping, and his head rolled back on the King's arm, his eyes empty below their lids. "Enemy. Mordred. Traitor." He sank back and Arthur, in silence, laid his hand upon his face and closed his eyes. Above the unmoving breast he made the sign of the cross. Then he rose and addressed them.

"You heard his last words. Before his death, my nephew Gawaine of Lothian and Orkney forgave Lancelot the killing of Gareth. You heard this from his own lips. Now go and make it known." He turned on his heel and strode off into the night. Bedwyr looked down at Gawaine's body and sighed.

"I'll organize the burial parties," he said under his breath. "May Mithra forgive him, if he doesn't do more good dead than he ever did alive." He shrugged and looked at the staring boys. "What a crossing, eh? And they say disasters come in threes. Come on, lads, one of you get the High King's horse and let's get started. It's going to be a long night."

All evening Galahad and Percival worked side by side with the soldiers digging graves, while Arthur sat before his tent, dry-eyed and fierce, hacking a cross from two pine boughs with a Saxon ax. When he had finished he bound the two arms of the cross together with thongs from his own tunic and locks of his own hair. Late into the night, as they worked to bury all the bodies and say prayers over all the dead, every man in the camp could hear, monotonous and unending, the heavy *thwonk! thwonk!* as Arthur pounded the rough cross into his pagan nephew's grave.

By dawn they had finished. Arthur stood for a long moment above the naked earth that clothed Gawaine. Bitterness and fatigue etched his face; his broad shoulders slumped forward; the sigh he sighed seemed to come from his very soul.

"Earth to earth," he muttered, "and dust to dust. Go to your gods, Gawaine. May you at last find peace." Wearily he turned away, saw Galahad, and paused. "I'm surprised you obeyed him. You are not in my army; you did not have to. What did he say that made you do such a foolish thing?"

Galahad gulped. "He said the Saxons were our enemies, my lord."

"Enemies with whom we have treaties for peace. You have made a mistake we will all live to regret."

Exhausted as the army was, they got no rest. The King ordered camp struck and led the march from the cliffs into the thick woods, north and west.

"We need water more than rest," he observed aloud to the men, and then, under his breath to his companions, "Give the Saxons time to collect their dead and send them to their gods. If we linger, we keep them from it. And if through us their gods are dishonored, we shall be sorry for it later."

"My lord," Gereint ventured, "do you really think we are in Saxon lands?"

Arthur shrugged. "We will know tomorrow."

Toward sunset they found a shallow valley with a slow stream running through it. Here they camped, watered the horses, set the watch, and finally slept.

Galahad took his former place outside the High King's tent, now that the treasure he had guarded lay on the bottom of the Narrow Sea. No one stopped him. The new night watch, a pair of Cornishmen, were strangers to him. They saluted him and bowed when he passed, but they did not speak. He missed Percival's company. But Percival slept now in his father's tent with the remaining men from Gwynedd. They had elected him, an eleven-year-old boy, to lead them in Maelgon's stead.

By dawn they were on the move again. The King quick-marched them up the valley, then cut through the forest, heading northwest. In late afternoon they came suddenly out of the deep woods into an open land, tilled and rich with harvest. Cattle grazed in meadows by the banks of a lazy stream, low huts with thatched roofs clustered behind a wooden palisade. Naked towheaded children played in the mud of the sties, and plump, round-faced women with bright, braided hair looked up from their labors in the fields, and gaped. Arthur brought the army to a halt. Screaming, the women ran for their little ones, snatched them up, and raced for the huts. Men began to appear, old and young, some with clubs, a few with axes.

"Well," Arthur said grimly, "now we know. We are on Saxon land." He raised his hand in greeting and spoke a few halting words. The Saxons stared at one another. The King took a silver armband from his own wrist and tossed it to them. There was a scramble for it, but it was handed with ceremony to the village headman, who examined it carefully, grinned, and bowed, stretching out his arm to encompass the whole fertile valley.

"Success," Arthur muttered. "Safe passage granted. Pass the word through the lines, Gereint. No bloodshed. No booty. No women. Not even a hostile word. We are guests here. This is not Britain."

They were not always so lucky. In their headlong race toward home they were set upon more than once by young, outraged Saxons tired of peace and eager for glory. When they were offered fight, they fought; and when they fought, they won. The weary troops expected nothing less: The magic of Excalibur defended Arthur still. In these skirmishes Galahad began to learn the art of war from its master. As he grew more disciplined, his skill drew praise from the commanders and he began to feel that the High King, who had been decidedly cool toward him since Gawaine's death, might warm toward him once more.

As Galahad waxed in pride and confidence, the High King's spirits waned. Daily he grew more bitter and more angry. If a day passed without Saxon opposition, he smiled at dinner. But after every deadly skirmish he grew somber and quick-tempered. "Dear God!" he was heard to exhort the heavens, "get me to Britain before Cerdic gets Cynewulf's news!" North and west they marched as fast as they could travel, a war-weary army, hungry, ill-shod, with no desire for battle and all their thoughts upon home and peace and rest.

Every night the High King called his commanders to council. They had shrunk to a mere handful: Galyn, Bedwyr, Gereint, Meliodas of Cornwall, Percival, and Galahad: three men near forty, three boys not yet twenty.

"We are not far from Britain now," Bedwyr offered as they settled in a circle and Varric lit the small fire in the center of the High King's tent. "A day's ride, no more, should bring us to the Great Plain."

"Then we are closer to Cerdic's stronghold than we have yet been." Arthur looked at his men. The flames shed dim light and sent their giant shadows shivering against the tent cloth. "We'll send scouts ahead and go prepared for battle."

Young Meliodas spoke hopefully. "Perhaps he hasn't learned about us yet. Perhaps he is afraid to break the treaty."

The King's lips thinned. "It is *we* who broke the treaty. We are here without his leave; we attacked without provocation; we have killed his people. What would you do, Meliodas, if you were Cerdic and your people cried out to you for vengeance?"

Meliodas dropped his eyes. "I'd come after you, my lord. I'd have to."

Arthur nodded. The men looked at their King. In the week since Gawaine's death he had grown old. The lines from nose to mouth, and from mouth to chin, spoke of deep grief and wretched weariness. The ready laugh had vanished from his voice and the spring of youth from his step.

"There has been plenty of time for a courier, my lord," Bedwyr observed. "But as yet, he has held his hand. Perhaps he understands what happened."

Arthur's face, half in shadow, looked carved in stone. "Even if he understands it, he cannot stay his hand. He dare not do it. He is beset by warriors who thirst for Briton blood and would be glad to replace him with his own son Cynewulf at the first sign of weakness." There was a long moment of silence as they each envisioned what a future without Cerdic might mean. Britain had been at peace for twenty years; they had long ceased to regard the Saxons as a serious threat.

The King rose and began to pace. "Here is how the matter stands. If he has time, Cerdic will gather an army and come against us. It hardly matters whether or not we are on Saxon soil. Before we get home we will have to face him. But what I wish to know is, what will Mordred do?"

At the mention of Mordred's name the men went still. Bedwyr looked quickly at Gereint. Percival stole a glance at Galahad. Arthur stopped his pacing and looked down upon them. "You are my council. Tell me what you think."

Bedwyr cleared his throat. "He must know by now, my lord, that you live. If he is ruling as High King, as Gawaine believed, he knows he must yield the title back to you once you confront him. He loves you dearly. I don't think Mordred is a threat to any Briton, least of all to you."

Gereint straightened. "There is not a man in Britain who would follow him if he tried to stand against you." Arthur's eyes slid to young Meliodas and back again. Gereint followed his thought. "That includes Constantine."

Meliodas gasped. "My lord, my father would *never* side with Mordred! Why, just his very presence on a field of battle would be enough to make him take the other side!"

The older men smiled to hear a naked truth so boldly stated. Arthur took another turn about the room. When he stopped before them, his face was grave.

"None of you has considered this from Mordred's point of view. He is in a difficult position." He paused, and they watched him, waiting. "Let us assume he has been acting as High King in my absence. The first thing he would do, after assuring Constantine of his ability to rule"—he arched an eyebrow at Meliodas—"would be to gather an army about him that stood a chance of defeating a Saxon attack."

"But every man of fighting age came with us!" protested Gereint. "Who is left to form an army?"

"Young men. Second sons with little hope of glory without battle. All those who have grown dissatisfied with peace." He gestured in Galahad's direction. "Let no one say a youth not yet fifteen cannot acquit himself with skill and honor on a battlefield." Galahad flushed and Percival squeezed his arm. "Next, he would renew our treaties with Cerdic, to safeguard Britain's borders. Mordred values our treaties with the Saxons as much as I do. He has done this. I am sure of it." He looked around the circle into every face. "He is Cerdic's ally."

The men glanced nervously at one another. "Perhaps he is," Bedwyr admitted. "That does not mean he would join forces with Cerdic against *you!*"

Arthur looked at him in silence a long time. "Cerdic will go carefully. I know the man. His hand is forced, but he is a cautious old fox. He will not believe the first reports brought to him. Once he has spoken to Cynewulf himself, he will protest formally to Mordred. Mordred will not know if it is truth or trap. But he is bound by the treaty. He is bound to keep Cerdic sweet while he finds out." He paused to let the implications sink in. "I have kept a steady course northwest to make our route predictable, in case either he or Cerdic wished to send us a message. But as you see, no one has come. Tell me, my lords, what this means."

They all looked at one another. No one spoke.

Meliodas broke the silence. "I suppose that Mordred's loyalty is without question, my lord?"

Everyone's gaze dropped but Arthur's.

"Yes."

No one breathed. Arthur's eyes flicked from face to face, hard with anger. He turned and paced back and forth, hands clasped behind him, mouth set in a grim line. Finally he stopped. "All right. You are my council. I will listen. Tell me about Mordred."

None of them met his eyes. He stood over them, waiting.

"Bedwyr? You know him best. Speak."

Bedwyr rose and faced his friend. "My lord, I do not doubt that Mordred loves you as much as he loves Britain. He is a good man, quick-witted and careful, a brilliant administrator, a fine commander. But—"

"But?"

Bedwyr drew a deep breath. "He is your son, my lord. Ambition runs in his veins. He must be first and best in everything he does. Any prize, once gained, will not be yielded lightly. Gawaine saw this in him and feared it— so did Lancelot. I would be less than honest if I told you I did not fear it also."

"For this reason, I have secured him Brittany. What do you think he will do?"

Bedwyr shook his head. "I don't know. But I don't think he could ever raise a sword against you. My guess is, he will fortify Camelot and wait to see what action Cerdic takes."

Arthur turned from him abruptly. "Galyn?"

"My lord knows well there was never any love lost between me and Mordred. I am not so certain that he would not stand against you." His voice began to quaver at the look in Arthur's eye. "He has followers, I know—mostly wild, pagan youths from outland kingdoms, those who found themselves leaderless when Lancelot killed Agravaine and Gaheris—and I do not think that if he has indeed had the effrontery to assume the king-ship, he will be able to give it up. To anyone." On his shoulder badge the hawk trembled, wings outspread, as if it would take flight. "Cerdic's anger may serve Mordred well. He can join Cerdic's cause, giving out that he is bound by treaty, and come against us. If he loses, he has lost his crown, which he must have relinquished in any case. But if he wins"—he gulped— "if he wins, his future is secure. My lord, I grieve to wound you, but it would not surprise me to see him riding side by side with Cerdic on the field of battle."

Arthur's nostrils flared, but he stood very still. "Thank you, Galyn," he said quietly. "That took courage. You think him a traitor, then?"

"Not yet, my lord. But I think it may be in him, whether he knows it or not. And if it is true that he has taken your Queen—"

"It is *not* true!" The King passed a hand over his face. "Even this? Must I consider even this?" He sighed and dropped his hand. "If Constantine's vi-cious slander is the truth, then my son is indeed a traitor. If he has married Guinevere he has no choice but to destroy me." His voice trailed off to nothingness. No one dared move. Slowly, the King turned toward Gereint. "Come, Gereint. Let me have truth. Galyn is witness I do not kill the mes-senger who tells me what I like least to hear."

"My lord King, it will not happen. Mordred is too good a soldier to risk what such a battle would mean. It would tear the very heart out of Britain, whoever won. He loves Britain. He would not do it."

Warmth returned slowly to Arthur's eyes. "Thank you, Gereint. Now, Meliodas of Cornwall. You do not know Mordred, but tell me what you think your father will do."

Meliodas colored. "My lord, my father thinks Mordred is born of the devil. He would never join him."

"Would he join me against him?"

The youth paused, then shook his head. "Probably not. If Prince Mordred were to come against you, my father would probably stay fast in Cornwall and wait it out. He would lose nothing, and might gain much."

Arthur's lips twisted in a bitter smile. "You are an intelligent young man, Meliodas, to see your father so clearly. That is exactly what he would do. Indeed, it is what he aims at. Well, and Percival, King of Gwynedd, young as you are, you have sense. What is your opinion?"

Percival blushed and struggled to still the tremor in his voice. "My lord, I don't know Prince Mordred, but from what I have seen, I think he is a loyal son. It will be all right, my lord," he added earnestly, "once you see him face-to-face."

At this Arthur's features softened, and he smiled. "The voice of youth, untouched by the seductiveness of power. It is refreshing!"

Finally he stood before Galahad, who rose. "Galahad, Prince of Lanascol. Son of my right hand. The finest swordsman in the King's service, after your father. You have lived nine years in Camelot. Tell me what you think of Mordred."

Percival jabbed Galahad hard in the legs with his elbow. Galahad passed a tongue over dry lips. "My lord." His voice came out in the barest whisper. He squared his shoulders. "My lord. It is not his fault, perhaps, but Mordred is—" Percival jabbed him again and Galahad staggered.

"Let him be, Percival," the King said icily. "Go on."

"Mordred is abomination."

Everyone froze.

Arthur drew a long breath. *"How do you dare?"*

"The bishop says he was damned from birth. He was conceived in sin."

"That is my fault, not his."

"Nevertheless, he is corrupt."

"Do you condemn him so swiftly? He has battled all his life to prove worthy of my trust, that I might forgive myself for the night that I begot him. It was I who wronged him. He is innocent."

"The bishop says we are none of us innocent."

"He will not betray me."

"If he yields back the throne of Britain, I will . . . I will bend my knee to him. But if he tries to keep your crown—"

"Galahad, please!" Percival gasped, tugging at his leggings.

"He loves the Queen, my lord. I have heard him say so. If he has gained her bed—"

Arthur raised a hand. "That's enough." His breath came fast and his color was high. No one dared breathe. For a long moment the King searched Galahad's face; then his mouth set in a thin line and he spun on his heel.

"Ungrateful whelp!" Bedwyr spat. "After all the King has done for you, to reward him so! Where is your charity? Where are your manners?"

"Silence!" Arthur strode out of the shadows and pointed to the dirt floor at his feet. "Get down on your knees, Galahad." Instantly, the boy obeyed. "Bedwyr, be still. I asked for his opinion. And I knew what it would be." He looked down at Galahad's dark head. "Do you hear me, Galahad?"

"Yes, my lord."

"I knew what you would say. I had hoped that bringing you to Brittany, letting you live among men and be treated like one—I had hoped it might open your eyes. Do you know why you are on your knees?"

"I have offended my sovereign lord."

"Oh, God!" Arthur cried, raising his arms skyward. "I am lord of *nothing* beyond this limping army! No, Galahad. You kneel because I want you to thank God with all your heart that your father did not hear your words to me." He ran a desperate hand through his hair. "For the first time since I have known him, I am glad he is not with me. And that is your doing."

"I'm sorry, my lord."

"You are not sorry. You believed what you said."

"Then forgive me, my lord."

"God grant me strength, I will try. Better you should appeal to your Creator—I have no time. He has eternity." He spoke bitterly and looked at his men. "We approach our destiny. And we come to it, not a victorious army crowned with the glory of defeating Rome, but a hungry, homesick herd of shipwrecked soldiers who have lost our way and attacked our allies—we are a shadow of what we were—and now we must face an angry Saxon force. How I miss those men who lie buried beneath the earth of Autun!"

Bedwyr slowly approached the King, laying a hand upon his shoulder.

"My lord, you know it was necessary. Had we not stopped the Romans they'd be in Britain now. And our best chance of stopping them lay in joining forces at Autun. You had to go. And stop them we did. Arthur, you have done what no Briton has ever done, not even Maximus! You have defeated Rome! And as for the Saxons, Cerdic knows he can never take you. All his men know it and so do ours. While you are King we do not fear the Saxons."

Arthur's hand slid unthinkingly to Excalibur's hilt. "But at what cost?" he whispered. He looked into their faces but no one answered. Turning away, he nearly stumbled over Galahad, who still knelt at his feet.

"Get up, Galahad. You will fight beside me when we go into battle, you and Percival—yes, you, Percival—I will need every sword at my command. But afterward"—he paused, and straightened—"afterward, our ways must part. I am out of patience; you cannot insult my wife and son and serve me."

With that, he strode out of the tent.

"Sir Bedwyr," Galahad whispered, "I have put the High King out of temper—I apologize, my lords. I did not mean to."

"Don't flatter yourself," Bedwyr snapped, "it isn't you." Then he shrugged. "He is angry with you, but that is a small thing compared to this black grief that hangs upon him after every battle."

"Grief for Gawaine, my lord?"

"Not exactly." Bedwyr sighed. "I suppose you are too young to understand it. It is the burden a king bears, this King more than any other. He grieves for all those who fell in battle, who gave their lives for Britain and for him. They are his responsibility. Give it a little time and it will pass. But just now he feels like their executioner." He shook his head at the boy's bewilderment. "Lucky indeed is the soldier who fights under such a commander. There is not another like Arthur."

In the morning the High King addressed his troops and told them what they faced. To a man, they cheered him and cried out for Saxon blood. The younger men had grown up on tales of the glorious Saxon wars and were eager to fight where victory was assured. They sang as they marched and boasted of the great deeds they would do. Bedwyr smiled to hear them, but nothing could lighten the High King's countenance.

Near noon the King's scouts returned with the news of an approaching Saxon army led by a graybeard.

Arthur nodded curtly. "Cerdic."

"Aye, my lord. That's my belief, though I've never seen him."

"How many?"

"Three thousand at a guess, from the dust they raise."

"Horses?"

"Sixty. Most are small, puny things better suited to plowing, but a group of them have handsome mounts."

The second scout saluted. His face was white. He licked his dry lips and glanced nervously at the first scout. Arthur saw the look.

"What else? Out with it, man! This is not the time to spare my feelings!"

"There are . . . two armies, my lord. Saxon and Briton. Riding together."

Silence fell upon the commanders, while Arthur's face grew slowly hard and cold.

"I don't believe it."

"M-m-my lord, I saw the standard. The Red Dragon, raised beside the Saxon white."

Behind his back, Bedwyr made the sign against evil. "Are you certain, man? How close were you?"

"Close enough to see them riding side by side. Cerdic the Saxon king and Mordred the Usurper!"

All eyes turned toward Arthur. Slowly, he gathered up his reins.

"Gereint, give the orders. Quick-march up the ridge. Once we are in position . . . then we shall see."

"At once, my lord."

"My God," Percival whispered, as the King moved off, "you and your uncle Galyn were right, and I was wrong. Oh, Galahad, what will come of it? Briton against Briton, with the Saxons watching?"

"Son against father," Galahad said slowly, "with the whole world watching."

They were in position in plenty of time to see the Saxon force come across the plain. Horsehair plumes danced on their helmets while ax heads and spear tips caught the sun. Hidden in the thin woods along the ridge, the waiting Britons watched them silently. The Saxon force exceeded their own in number, but as the scout had reported, they were not alone. Side by side with Cerdic's massed foot soldiers marched a small but orderly British force led by a cavalry as fine as Arthur's own. At its head, under the Red Dragon of Britain, and nearly knee-to-knee with Cerdic himself, rode Mordred. From his position on Arthur's right flank, Galahad could see the High King's face. Not a muscle in it moved; not an eyelash blinked. Closer they came, and closer, until the flank of Cerdic's force rode hard by the ridge where the Cornishmen under Meliodas lay in wait.

"Raise the standard," Arthur said in a deadly voice. "Then wait for my command."

The standard-bearer rode forward through the sparse trees. One among Mordred's cavalry called out, pointing. Mordred lifted his head and raised his hand to halt the march. His own troops obeyed him, but the Saxons kept coming. Mordred shouted. Cerdic turned and gestured, raising an angry fist. Mordred spurred his horse to the Saxon king and grabbed his arm, talking swiftly. But the Saxons had seen their enemy and begun their war chant. Cerdic shook off Mordred's arm, glanced up into the trees, and spat upon the shoulder of Mordred's horse. Mordred reined back.

A great bellow burst from Arthur. "What! Are you coward as well as traitor? Ye gods bear witness—he is no son of mine!" He raised his arm, tears flowing unchecked into his beard, and brought it down. With one voice they raised the victory paean and charged down the slope. Galahad saw Mordred whirl, gather his men, and quick-march them back across the plain as fast as they could go.

The Saxons fought viciously and well, but they were no match for such a seasoned army, better mounted, better led. After two hours of bloody battle, Cerdic was forced to withdraw to save his men from slaughter. Angrily, he turned in his saddle and shook his ax at Arthur. The High King lifted Excalibur into the air and with a long look at Cerdic, spat upon the ground. The old Saxon grinned suddenly, gestured a mock salute, and galloped away.

Again they spent a long autumn afternoon burying the dead. The High King sat on a tree stump at the edge of the woods, motionless, silent, staring at the ground. Percival worked side by side with Galahad, too excited to feel his own exhaustion.

"You saved my life again, cousin! God bless you for it! I never knew the man was behind me, only at the last minute did I see the ax descending— you must have eyes in the back of your head, I swear it!"

Galahad smiled. "No, but I see more clearly in a battle. Everything is sharper—hearing, seeing, the sense of danger—it's so clear and real, yet so slow and silent, like a dream."

"Slow! Are you jesting? It went at lightning speed!"

"Not for me. I can't explain how it feels. Slow, and . . . and somehow easy. My sword leaps forward of its own will, and men go down before it."

"Dear God!" Percival stopped his digging and stared in admiration. "To everyone else it's hot, hard work, and to you it's easy! And you looked like it, too, you and Arthur, never a wrong step or a missed stroke—isn't he wonderful to see? So cool, so calm, when everything is mayhem—"

"Not so cool today," Galahad murmured. "Look at him yonder. The heart's gone out of him."

Percival lowered his voice. "He thinks his son has betrayed him."

"And so he has."

"But Mordred didn't stand against him after all."

"No, he turned tail and ran like the coward he is!"

"But if Cerdic is his ally Mordred *had* to come along, at least to find out if it was really Arthur. But we attacked before he had the chance to parley."

"Parley!" Galahad snorted. "He could have come alone if he'd wanted words. But he brought an army."

At sunset Bedwyr brought Arthur the news that all their dead were buried. Only the Saxon dead and dying still lay upon the field. The King sat motionless, as if he had not heard. Bedwyr repeated his report. Arthur's cold eyes flicked upward to his face and stopped Bedwyr in midsentence.

"What is the name of this place?"

"I don't know, my lord."

"Find out."

Bedwyr bit his lip, watching the King with anxious eyes. Then he shrugged. "Yes, my lord."

When he returned soon after, Arthur had not moved. "My lord, the name of this place is Cerdices Leaga."

"Cerdices Leaga," Arthur repeated slowly. "Cerdic's field." He rose suddenly and drew a long breath. "Burn it."

41 ✝ ON THE PLAIN OF CAMLANN

Hands shook Galahad awake out of a deep sleep. He looked up into Varric's face.

"My lord Galahad, the King would see you."

Galahad blinked. Above him the black night blazed with stars. "Now?"

"Aye, my lord. Now."

The camp lay sleeping around him. He smelled the acrid scent of charred stubble, where the grass fires had swept Cerdic's Field in violent fury. In the distance he could still see the line of flames driving inexorably eastward toward Saxon lands.

Inside the tent Arthur was alone. A wineskin warmed above a low fire and two animal skins lay flat on the floor on either side of it. Arthur came forward from the shadows. "Sit down," he said quietly. Galahad bent his knee. With his own hands the King poured wine into a horn cup and offered it to Galahad. He took nothing himself but sat down and waited. Gone was his vibrant energy, the familiar pacing, the warm speech of welcome. This was a silent man, still to his very soul, with eyes that burned with a consuming anger.

"I need a courier, Galahad. A discreet one."

"My lord, I am at your service."

"This needs courage. And stealth."

"My lord, I will do it."

The King drew a scroll from his tunic, sealed with candle wax and imprinted with the royal ring itself. "I want you to take a message to the Queen."

Galahad met his eyes. A protest formed on his lips and died unspoken. He nodded.

"Secretly. Travel by night and ride in daylight only if you are hidden. You must get around Mordred's army and into Camelot without being seen. And you must get out again."

"But I thought Camelot was built to be impregnable."

"So it is, except to stealth. Merlin built me a bolt-hole, just in case. I will tell you the secret of it. But you must get into the Queen's garden your-self. I do not have the key."

A sudden vision flashed before Galahad of a thong Lancelot had once worn around his neck. On the end of it had hung a small bronze key. He had bragged to someone, laughing, that it was the key to Paradise.

Galahad's cheeks burned. "I will manage it, my lord."

"You must swear an oath before me that you will be as gracious to the Queen as if she were your own mother come to life. Put aside your judgment and be polite. I require this of you."

The angry eyes bored into his soul, forcing his will. Galahad drew a deep breath. "I swear it upon the Word of God."

Arthur handed him the scroll. Galahad saw that his fingers trembled.

"Do you require an answer, my lord?"

"No." He sat very still. "After you have seen the Queen, ride on to Avalon. Get an audience with Niniane. Tell her I must see her. I *must*, do you understand? This is a command." He reached up and unclipped the dragon cipher from his shoulder. "Give her this as a token. I am in dire need of her advice."

Galahad's hand shook as he took the badge. "Yes, my lord."

Arthur exhaled and sat back. "I am grateful for your service to me, Galahad. You fought well today. You have grown into a soldier of the first order."

"Thank you, my lord."

"But your service has come to an end. In the battle that lies ahead your sword will not matter. It is in God's hands." The King paused. "This is a mo-ment for plain speaking. When I told you, Galahad, a lifetime ago, before Autun, when I told you about the Grail and Spear—"

"Yes, my lord?"

"I confess I don't know the truth of the matter. I fear that any quest I might send you on would be a waste of your time." He stopped, staring into the distance. "The things themselves are real enough, if Merlin is to be be-lieved, but what I said about their power to preserve Britain is fabrication . . . myth . . . legend." He passed a weary hand across his face. "I would give my right arm if it were so. But Britain's fate is in the hands of men."

"And of God, my lord."

Arthur smiled wearily. "I must be getting old, Galahad. I used to have your faith. I used to love riding out to battle. Now I dread it."

"But," Galahad whispered, "the battle is over."

"Oh, yes. The Romans are defeated. The Saxons are conquered. All that remains are the Britons."

"But *you* are King of the Britons!"

The ghost of a smile touched Arthur's lips. "Am I? I *was*."

"And will be again, when we get to Camelot!"

"The once and future King," Arthur muttered, gazing into the distance. "So Merlin called me once, long ago. But that's not what he meant by it."

"You shall take back your crown from the traitor Mordred, and your name shall live forever as Britain's King!"

Arthur looked at him. "Is this a thing you must believe? Perhaps it is. We must all have dreams. But my dreams came to an end on Cerdic's Field." He rose. His voice was tired. "Well, Galahad, we come to our parting. When you have delivered your messages, seek what fortune you will. Promise me only to keep Britain's honor bright."

Galahad knelt before the King. "My lord, I will find the Grail and Spear for you. I believe the legends. I will find them for you and you will be King forever."

Arthur's voice softened. "Find them quickly, then, for I am running out of time."

Under the trees at the edge of the plain of Camlann it was pitch black. In the distance Galahad could see the campfires of Mordred's army, glowing in orderly formation around the central cluster of tents. Beneath him his stallion pulled at the bit, eager to be going. He could smell home. But Galahad held him back a moment more. He knew Mordred would have scouts out and he needed to know where they were.

Suddenly the stallion's ears pricked forward and his head lifted. Galahad drew his sword. Nothing moved. He waited with held breath, but nothing happened. The night waited with him, dark and still. Somewhere an owl called softly, and was answered. The horse relaxed and went back to playing with his bit. Galahad exhaled.

North and west beyond the River Camel he fancied he could just see the foothills of Caer Camel, where beyond the rising ground the fortress of Camelot grew straight from the living rock. There the High Queen waited, secure in her citadel, while both her champions led their armies toward one another. He shuddered. The horse shied. A fist gripped his wrist and wrenched his sword free. Hands grabbed him, pulled him to the ground, forcing his face into dirt. A knee dug into his back; his arms were wrenched behind him and bound tight—all before he could manage to draw a second breath.

They pulled him roughly to his feet. There were three of them, he saw, all wearing the shoulder badge of Camelot troops. Two stood before him and one rode up through the trees, leading horses.

"Give us your name and family," growled the nearest of his captors, a thickly built young man with a fringe of beard. "Where are you bound for, and who sent you?"

Galahad ignored him. His eyes were on the slender youth who brought the horses forward. "Rhys!" he whispered.

A thick hand slapped his face. "Shut up! Answer us or we'll run you through! If you're not with us, you're against us! Who are you?"

"Go to hell," Galahad snapped.

The second soldier laughed and drew Galahad's dagger from his belt. "Let's kill him, Orrin."

"Wait!" The rider slid off his horse and came forward, peering at Galahad. "Don't kill him. I know him. He's Galahad. Lancelot's son."

Both soldiers straightened. "Lancelot's son! I'll be damned."

"We'd better take him to the King."

Rhys came closer, searching Galahad's face. "Hello, Galahad. I've not seen you since you left the bishop's schoolroom to go to Brittany with Arthur. This is a strange meeting, eh?" He spread out his hands. "Look at me. I'm a soldier after all."

"What happened? I was sure by now you'd be in a monastery."

"My father went with Arthur. I was forced to take his place. It was the only honorable thing to do. When he returns I'll be able to go back to my books."

Galahad shook his head slowly. Sir Caradoc, commander of Caerleon, who had publicly denounced his only son for his desire to be a priest and not a warrior, had gotten his way in the end. "I'm sorry, Rhys. I'm afraid your father won't be coming home. He died at Autun."

Rhys drew a trembling breath and crossed himself. "May God bless his embattled soul. I feared it. Was it quick?"

"Oh, yes."

"Shut up, both of you," Orrin demanded. "This isn't a council meeting. We've work to do. What are you doing here, son of Lancelot, on the plain of Camlann an hour before midnight? Spying?"

"No."

"What then?"

Galahad was silent. The third soldier raised the dagger again.

"He went with Arthur," Rhys said quickly. "He could be a messenger."

Galahad shot him a furious glance and Orrin chuckled. "Search him, Rhys. I'll wager you've hit it on the nose."

Rhys put a hand inside Galahad's tunic and withdrew the High King's scroll. He glanced at it quickly. "Who's it from?"

"Your sovereign King," Galahad replied acidly. "Arthur of Britain."

"Who's it to?" Orrin asked.

Galahad just stared back at them unmoving. The man with the dagger grinned.

"Take his weapons," Orrin ordered. "Rhys, you take the scroll. We'll see what King Mordred has to say about this."

"*King* Mordred!" Galahad gasped. "Then it's true! I knew it! He's a traitor!"

Orrin raised a fist to strike him but Rhys held his arm. "Let be, Orrin. These are only words, and not without meaning. Take him to the commander before you break his jaw. He might have valuable information."

Galahad was thrust onto his horse and led into the camp. Men stared curiously as the three soldiers marched him toward the central tent. Orrin gave the password and a brief message to the guard outside, who bowed and disappeared within. Minutes passed. Galahad glanced at the curious faces around him. They were strangers, all of them. He had never seen any of them in Camelot. And they were all young, some of them as young as he, too young to grow beards. This was Mordred's army! An army of beardless boys! He smiled in contempt, and then suddenly remembered Arthur's words: *Let no one say a youth not yet fifteen cannot acquit himself with skill and honor on a battlefield.* He wiped the contempt from his face as the guard reappeared and gestured them inside. His captors pushed him ahead of them into the lighted warmth of Mordred's tent.

At first he thought the tent was empty. A wineskin hung over a small fire in the center, a handful of crimson cushions ringed the firestones in a neat circle, but no one was there. The three scouts shuffled uneasily behind him. One of them coughed. A shadow on the far wall moved. It was then Galahad noticed a partition at the other side of the tent. A lamp burned somewhere behind it and a tall man paced before the lamp.

The shadow became a presence, a dark silhouette lit from behind. Against his will Galahad began to tremble. The dark figure stepped forward until the firelight touched his face.

"Well, well, well," Mordred said softly. The scouts went down on one knee. Galahad remained standing. Firelight lit the planes of Mordred's face and threw his eyes in shadow. The grim expression, the steady stare, the power that fit like a second skin, the hint of explosive rage and grief—this was the same face he had confronted two nights ago under the stars on Cerdic's Field.

Mordred nodded to Orrin, who gave a brief report of Galahad's capture.

"Where are his weapons?"

"Here, my lord." Orrin handed him Galahad's sword and dagger. "He's a messenger of some sort. We found a letter."

Rhys held out the scroll. Mordred examined it carefully, staring at the seal, his mouth set in a grim line. Slowly he looked up.

"You've done well. Excellent work. All of you. Back to your posts now and keep a sharp lookout. My father's been known to send two couriers when the message is of dire importance."

They bowed and hurried out. Mordred stood looking at Galahad, who trembled under his gaze. He hefted Galahad's dagger in his hand.

"Turn around."

His lips moving in quick prayer, Galahad turned his back to Mordred. If they killed him no one would miss him. They could toss his body in a wayside ditch and he would never be found. Arthur would think he had gone on about his business, Percival would think he was off on his quest. No one in Britain would think to look for the bleached bones of a lost Breton boy. They all had more important things to think about. He jumped at the touch of hands.

"Calm down," Mordred said quietly, "I'm only cutting your bonds."

When his hands were free he rubbed them together to rid them of their numbness. His raw wrists were starting to swell.

"Cranach!" Mordred called.

A guard poked his face into the tent. "Yes, my lord?"

"Let no one in. No one. Until I give you leave."

"Yes, my lord."

Mordred hesitated. "Come with me." He led Galahad past the partition into a small bedchamber. A gilded double-flamed lamp stood above a stool and a low table. A weapon stand held Mordred's sword, his brass-studded fighting vest, his leather helmet with the King's gold circlet on the brow. Against the other wall was a simple soldier's cot with a single dark blanket of combed wool. The furnishings were plain enough, but by the standards of Arthur's ragged, shipwrecked army, they were luxurious indeed. The knowledge that until recently Mordred had been in Camelot only heightened Galahad's resentment.

"Sit down." Mordred pointed to the stool and Galahad sat. The fine hands, so like Arthur's, poured a cup of water from the carafe on the table and handed it to Galahad. Mordred placed the unopened scroll with Galahad's sword and dagger on his own cot, sat down, and leaned forward with his elbows on his knees. "So. My father really *is* in Britain."

Galahad stared at him. He wasn't sure what he had expected, but it wasn't this. "Of course he is! Do you pretend you didn't know it?"

Mordred looked at him steadily. "You called me a traitor to Orrin. Is that what they think of me, then? Is that what my father thinks?"

"Of course," Galahad cried hotly. "What else *could* he think?"

Mordred bowed his head and passed a weary hand across his face. Galahad felt a stab of acute anguish. He had seen that gesture a hundred times before.

"Your men called you King. You wear the crown on your helmet. You can't deny it."

"It's by my father's order I took the title!" The admission burst from Mordred with a force that shook the tent. He rose, unsettled by the violence of his emotion, and began to pace back and forth across the small space. Galahad heard nothing in the ringing silence but Mordred's soft footfalls—

no soldiers' voices, no laughter at the campfires, no jingle of bridles or tramp of boots. The whole camp waited while Mordred paced, his lined face as cold and pale as marble.

"Tell me," he snapped, "what happened at Autun. I've had reports from couriers, but they have proved unreliable. The last one we had told me Arthur was dead."

His voice quaking, Galahad reported what he had seen, the source of the confusion, Arthur's return and Lancelot's near death, Constantine's letter—here Mordred's face grew pinched, but he did not interrupt—the procession to Benoic, the crossing home, Gawaine's death, the battle and the burning of Cerdic's Field. As he finished, he glanced at Mordred, who stood half turned from the lamp, clutching the amulet at his throat, his eyes closed.

"I see," he said slowly. "I see how it happened." He sat down on the cot again, as still now as he had been restless before. When he spoke his voice was calm and clear. "Where are you bound for with this letter?"

Galahad did not reply.

"Never mind. That's an easy guess. Camelot. This is Arthur's message to Guinevere." Mordred smiled at Galahad's expression. "I know my father well, you see. Do you know what he says in the letter? Does he call me traitor to her?"

Galahad passed a tongue across dry lips. "I don't know."

Mordred nodded. "Well. I will have to take my chances with that." He picked up the scroll and tossed it back to Galahad. The boy stared openly.

"You . . . you aren't going to read it?"

"No. It's not meant for me."

Galahad looked down in amazement at the scroll in his hands. The seal was unbroken. He tucked it back inside his tunic with the slow, clumsy motion of a man in sleep.

"Do you know," Mordred continued, "what his plans are? Is he willing to parley or is his heart set against me? I'm certain he's heading toward Camelot, but I need to know his intentions."

Galahad swallowed. "He is coming to take back his crown."

"Well," Mordred whispered, "it is his for the asking."

Galahad stared at him blindly, unable to speak. Mordred rose, picked up Galahad's weapons, and handed them to him.

"You're not going to kill me?" Galahad croaked, sliding to his knees on the dirt floor.

Standing above him, Mordred smiled. "No. Once I wanted to, for pride's sake. But there's been water under the bridge since then. And even if I wanted to, I wouldn't. You're my father's courier to his wife. You're free to go."

"But . . ." Galahad's world began to spin. "But why not? I have sworn to kill *you*!"

"If you want to kill me, draw your sword and take your chances. But you should know"—he reached down and raised Galahad—"I have held Britain only in his absence and at his order. I will not oppose him. He is my father and my King. I will yield to him as soon as I can meet him face-to-face."

"But what about the Queen?" Galahad said under his breath. "Constantine's letter! Aren't you married to her?"

Pain stabbed Mordred's face and his lips twisted in familiar bitterness. "Don't you know slander when you hear it? The gods know I've loved her since first I saw her—so have Lancelot and a thousand others—but she is Arthur's wife, not mine." His voice dropped in weariness. "And if I were the last Briton living, she would not have me. There is not a truer heart on earth." He turned his back on Galahad. "Go on. Get out of here."

But Galahad's legs would not move. They were rooted to the floor. "I don't understand—you show me mercy, but . . . you are my enemy."

"Oh, yes," Mordred replied softly, facing the shadows, "and abomination, too. Your God, Bishop Landrum's God, is a cruel god. I wouldn't have Him as a gift."

"He is Arthur's, too. There is only one God."

"Arthur's God is merciful. He forgives. Yours doesn't." Mordred turned and spread his arms out in a gesture of inclusion. "Do you still think me evil, Galahad? Are these the actions of an evil man? You don't know how lucky you are to have an honorable destiny. Everyone who hears Niniane's prophecy will honor you for it, although you have done nothing to deserve it. My destiny"—his voice shook—"is a bitter gall to me."

"Your destiny?" Galahad repeated dumbly. "I never heard . . . I never knew . . . who foretold it?"

"It is the curse of the witch Morgause, Queen of Orkney. My mother's curse. Few know." In the heavy silence Galahad could hear the flutter of the lamp flame, the held breath of the waiting night. The words, when they came, hovered on the edge of sound. "I was born to be my father's doom."

Galahad gasped. Mordred's black eyes burned. "Ever since I met him I've spent my life trying to avoid this unwanted fate. I love Arthur. I honor him. I would not knowingly harm a hair on his head. And yet, and yet . . ." He closed his eyes and his features creased in anguish. "I feel it coming fast upon me. I feel it breathing on my neck. Like a boulder some unknown hand has already set in motion down the slope."

Galahad found that his eyes were wet. "My lord, can I take a message . . . can I let him know . . . surely what you fear can be averted."

Mordred's lips twisted. "I've already sent a message asking for a parley.

My fate—his fate—is in his hands. And you are *his* messenger, Galahad, not mine. But I thank you for the offer. You have changed, I think, since I saw you last."

"Everything in the whole wide world has changed, my lord."

Mordred nodded and shrugged, grim amusement pulling at the corners of his mouth. "The wheel of time has turned again. Niniane said it would happen at Autun. It must have been a slaughter. . . . Well, I will not hold you here. You must be off to Guinevere. When you see her"—his gaze softened and he looked quickly away—"do not tell her about my fears. Don't alarm her. Tell her Arthur is on his way and Lancelot is healing. That is all she'll want to know."

"My lord, I cannot tell her about Lancelot."

Mordred looked at him in surprise; then his gaze narrowed in a long, assessing look. "So that's it. I knew there was a barb in you that pricked your spirit. I never knew it was Guinevere." Galahad avoided his eyes. Mordred sighed. "You believe the rumors because your father loves her."

"And she loves him. The High King told me so."

"Yes," Mordred said evenly. "My father believes in facing facts. What he did not tell you, I imagine, is that she loves him more than Lancelot; she loves him more than life. She had a chance to choose between them once, years ago, after her abduction. Niniane herself put the choice before her. She chose Arthur." Galahad's eyes widened and Mordred smiled. "Do not imagine she and Lancelot are lovers bereft, pining for each other behind the King's back. They would laugh at the very idea. The center of their world is Arthur. And it always has been."

"But she has been the cause of so much misery—"

Mordred laughed quietly. "Every lovely woman is. Don't take it to heart so. No one can make you unhappy, Galahad, without your consent. Don't listen to gossip. Take men as you find them." He raised his arm in a gesture of dismissal. "I apologize for the sermon. The Queen awaits you. Take up your weapons and go on your way. And may your God go with you."

In a daze Galahad buckled on his swordbelt and stumbled from the tent. The army of boys watched him with open curiosity. A groom held his stallion ready. They had watered the horse, picked his feet, and groomed his coat. He rode unmolested out of camp, unable to speak, unable to pull his whirling thoughts together. Of his own accord the stallion headed toward the Camel ford and home. *Mordred loyal!* It was the only thought his mind could summon, and it stunned him. *I'm sure of this: Arthur is good, Mordred is evil, and the Saxons are our enemies!* How was the world turned upside down in so short a time! A lightning flash lit the sky. For the space of a heartbeat he saw the dark silhouette of Caer Camel rising in the distance, her summit pricked with light. Then the world went black. Thunder rumbled ominously in the distance.

"Come on, Farouk, old boy. It's a night of revelations—nothing is as it once was." He put his leg to the horse's side and the animal broke into an eager gallop. *Who knows,* he thought as another flash ripped open the brooding sky. *Who knows what awaits on such a night?*

42 ✟ THE QUEEN OF CAMELOT

Galahad stood in the Queen's garden in a drenching rain. A fitful wind tore at his cloak and stung his face. It was the middle of the night, but a dim light shone above him from the Queen's chamber. A shadow passed before the light, a slender shadow, pacing. Still, he paused at the bottom of the steps to her terrace. His ebullient mood seemed to have dissolved in the pelting rain. Now that he was here, he would rather fight a hundred Saxon savages than face this one woman. Every man he knew had fallen victim to her charm. Yet she was not an enchantress; she had no magic; her power over men was a fully human kind of charming. He was determined to make his visit short. He would climb the steps, deliver his message, give her news of Arthur, and depart. He was only a messenger. There was no reason to linger.

He shifted his shoulders and water streamed from his cloak. Still, he waited. The storm had broken well before he reached Caer Camel. He had cut through the woods at the base of the high hill, tied his horse at the spring, and approached the secret entrance by the route the King had described. No one had seen him. It had been easy. Not so easy to scale the wall into the garden, but not difficult for a strong youth on an urgent mission. He looked up and saw the dark shadow of a woman standing by the terrace door, gazing out. As she turned to draw the curtain he saw a glimmer of her face—it was not the Queen. Swiftly, he ran up the steps and scratched at the glazing as she pulled the curtain closed. How many times, he wondered suddenly, had Lancelot done the same?

The curtain parted. A slender, plain-featured young woman stared at him in surprise, a candle in her hand. Galahad opened his cloak to show he carried no sword, no knife, no weapon of any kind. He reached into his tunic and showed her the scroll, then beckoned her urgently to open the latch. She hesitated, watching his face. There was no hint of beauty about her, but she had wide, intelligent eyes, and she had poise. She lifted the candle to get a better look at him, and then slowly unlatched the door.

"Who are you?" she whispered fiercely as he stepped forward. "Quickly, man, or I'll call the guard!"

"I come from the King," he whispered back, shaking the water from his cloak. "I bear a message for the Queen. In secret."

"King *Arthur?*" she said softly, wide-eyed. "Does he live?"

"Of course he lives! Did you not know it?"

"Praise God!" she quavered, crossing herself with feeling. "We have heard only rumors. We don't know what to think. Mordred is High King now."

Galahad shook his head. "Not for long."

"Where is the King? Is he without?"

"No, but he is coming. Only Mordred still stands between him and home."

She covered her mouth with her hand.

"Anna!" a voice spoke from behind them. "Who is there?"

Anna whirled and Galahad dropped to one knee. "Queen Guinevere."

She stood in the doorway but her presence filled the room. Robed in dark cloth, she was invisible among the shadows but for her white-gold hair and her alabaster skin. She crossed the room with quick steps and stood before him. He bent his head.

"I know your voice. Who are you?"

To his amazement, his body trembled. He, who had killed a hundred men that very week, he had to draw upon his courage to face this woman! He raised his head and his hood slipped back.

She drew a quick breath. "Galahad! What does this mean? How did you come here?"

"By the garden gate, my lady, and up the stairs. In my father's footsteps." He instantly regretted his impudence, but her very presence made him fling up his defenses like a hedgehog.

"You presume too much!"

"Forgive me," he murmured. "It will not happen twice."

Her scent filled his head, sweet and enticing. The hem of her gown lay inches from his boot. The fabric trembled. He struggled against the familiar soft pit in his stomach, the growing lassitude in his limbs, the slowing of his thoughts as the small thrill of excitement deep in his gut blossomed into a beating ache.

"My lady!" Anna gasped. "Arthur is alive! This is his messenger!"

The Queen went still. For a long moment the only sound was the lashing of rain against the glazing of the door. Then she said, very softly, "How does my lord? Fares he well?"

Her tenderness swept over him like a wave of heat. Her nearness forced him into one mistake after another. If he knelt another minute at the hem of her scented robe, he feared he might press it to his lips. "May I rise?"

"Will you behave?"

He nodded. He did not have to stay long—he would endure it some-how. "I am tamed, lady. Your lord and husband has bound me round with oaths. I am harmless." He opened his cloak. "I come without weapons."

She reached out her small, slender hand and raised him. The skin of her palm was cool and firm. "It is not your weapons that I fear. Tell me about Arthur. You traveled with him? You were aboard his ship?"

"Yes," he replied, avoiding her beautiful eyes. "I have been at his side since we left Britain. I guard his flank, now that Gawaine is dead."

She went still. "Gawaine dead? When? Where did he die?"

"On a Saxon beach. He led the charge and I was right behind him. Cynewulf's ax got him. He died in Arthur's arms."

"So . . . you have fought for the King after all?"

He nodded. "I owe the King my life twice over. Would I could be so cool in battle!"

She looked calmly up at him and he shifted his weight uncomfortably. He could almost feel the silk of her skin beneath his fingertips. The urge to touch her grew irresistible. Something moved behind her eyes. With the smallest smile, she turned away and gave him peace. "Yes, my husband is a warrior to his soul. How does he fare? Does he sleep? Eat? Is he weary?"

"He is angry. His allies have attacked him and bar his way."

She shook her head impatiently. "You don't understand it, Galahad. We *had* to reestablish treaties with the Saxons." She stopped. "Well, no matter now. Tell me about Arthur. Has he his health?"

Her long, slender neck, pale in the dimness, reminded him of the wild lilies in the fields outside Autun. A stray wisp of white-gold hair crept from her net and nestled against her cheek. He opened his mouth to speak, but no words came out. She raised an eyebrow in a graceful arch. He cleared his throat and prayed silently for fortitude. "He is sick at heart and weary of war. There is a knife in his back. He thinks his son a traitor, and it kills him."

"Traitor!" she cried. "Mordred is no traitor!" Her pretty hands, clasped tightly together, were shaking. She crossed herself and gripped the bedpost for support.

"Even so, we saw him, plain as day, come take the field against us—against *us*—and beside Saxons."

"Dear God!" She sank to the bed. "The end has come." Anna ap-proached, but Guinevere waved her away. "Surely Mordred never raised a sword against him? He swore to me he would not."

"No. The King attacked and Mordred withdrew his men from the field. King Arthur took it for cowardice. It broke his heart."

She bowed her lovely head and covered her face with her hands. Anna hugged her shoulders. Galahad straightened. It was the first instance of frailty he had ever seen in her. But when the Queen looked up, her eyes were dry.

"One more thing," she said slowly. "Does your father live?"

Now that the moment was upon him, he could not tell her. He wanted to believe Mordred. And Arthur. But it was easier to believe that they, along with Lancelot and every man of his acquaintance, had fallen victim to the power of her features, her form, her voice. He knew he could not bear to see the look upon her face when she learned that Lancelot was alive.

"Bedwyr lives and fights with us. Of my father, I say nothing."

She could not control the anguish on her face. "Please," she begged. "Please, Galahad. Give me a word only. That's all I ask."

"What happened to Lancelot is no concern of yours."

"No concern!" While he watched, she seemed to harden and grow cold by slow degrees. She rose. There was nothing frail about her now. She walked up to him with all the majesty she could summon and stared him down.

"Give me your message."

He was aghast to find how his fingers shook as he drew forth the scroll. In taking it, her hand touched his. Her beautiful eyes seemed to collect him and drink him in, drowning his resistance, whirling his thoughts into confusion, drawing him down into a maelstrom of molten longing. He could scarcely breathe. He burned in every sinew. Without willing it, he took a half a step forward and saw her lips lift in a knowing smile. He could do nothing but stand rooted to the spinning floor and curse himself for a willing fool. She controlled the beating of his blood, the very breath that fed his body.

She backed away, smiling as he flushed scarlet and broke out in sweat.

"It will pass," she whispered. "Give it time."

He stood unmoving, unable to move, in a hot flush of shame.

"Are you going back to Arthur?" she asked him quietly. "Will you take him a word from me?"

"I . . . I . . . I"—he gulped—"I'm going on to Ynys Witrin. The Isle of Glass. To Avalon, to seek audience with a witch—"

"With Niniane, Lady of the Lake?"

He nodded. "The King has a message for her. After that . . . I . . . I . . ." His voice trailed off uncertainly.

"I see." She held the scroll to her breast. "Then this is good-bye."

He was unsure whether she referred to the King's letter or to himself. He bowed quickly, awkwardly, and fumbled with the latch to the glazed door.

"Galahad." He looked up and saw her standing straight and very pale. "Go with God."

He raised his hand and made the sign of the cross in the air above her head. Then he turned and ran.

43 ✝ THE HARBINGER OF DOOM

Wearily, Galahad reined in his horse and slid to the muddy earth. He was soaked to the skin and so cold he could no longer feel his fingers. Steam eddied upward from his stallion's dripping flanks; the horse lowered his head, stretched his neck, and shook, spraying water everywhere. Galahad smiled and laid a hand on the streaming coat.

"No matter, Rouk, old boy, I couldn't be any wetter. God in Heaven, what a night! The causeway was half underwater, there isn't a star in the sky—more than once I was afraid we'd have to swim for it." He looked up at the smooth white walls of the Lady's shrine. Rain pelted his face relentlessly and a sharp wind lifted his sodden cloak. "Still," he muttered, "I'd rather sleep out here on the ground than ring the bell. But an oath is an oath." He reached up and pulled the bell cord that hung by the gate. "Perhaps they're asleep. Do witches sleep, I wonder?"

The horse nuzzled his chest and blew warm, sweet breath against Galahad's cold cheek. The boy reached up and scratched his ears, blowing his own breath gently into the horse's nostrils. "From one enchantress to another the High King sends us. I hope he reckons it's worth it." The stallion lowered his nose to the ground and began to crop the grass. Galahad grunted. "I tell you, Rouk, I pray this one is plain. I am burning alive from that beautiful woman's fire."

He was suddenly aware that eyes watched him from the dimness beyond the gate. An old woman in a dark robe set her hand to the latch.

"It is late for travelers," she began in a high, cracking voice. "This is the Lady's shrine at Avalon, lord. Follow the road up yonder and you will come to King Melwas's stronghold. He is away at the wars, but his cousin will provide shelter for you and your horse."

Galahad took hold of the gate as she tried to close it on him. None of them yet knew Melwas was dead.

"Madam, I have no wish to disturb you, but I come from King Arthur with a message for the Lady Niniane. It is urgent. I am instructed to give the message in person."

"From King Arthur?" She began to tremble, but whether from age or cold or shock, Galahad could not tell. "Have you proof?"

Galahad dropped the dragon badge into her hand. "Give this to your priestess. I will wait out here for her answer."

The badge disappeared into the fastness of her robe as she swung the gate open and beckoned him inside. "No, no, we are not so inhospitable as that. Come in, young lord, and bring your horse. There is warmth and a dry place for both of you to wait while I take this token to the Lady. Come in, come in. Do not be shy. We welcome all comers, even Christians."

Half an hour in the porter's lodge before a wood fire was enough to warm him, if not to dry him. At least he felt presentable by the time two pages came to escort him into the Lady's presence. They were no more than young girls, robed in white, with slim bare feet in simple sandals. They neither spoke to him nor looked at him, but led him silently along ill-lit hallways until he stood at last before a small, curved door. One of them reached out and pulled the latch with a slender hand. As she stood back she peeked up at him. He saw wide, hazel eyes in a pretty face and heard her catch her breath as she dipped him a quick curtsy.

"My lord may go in now," she whispered, and then the two of them turned and disappeared, whispering and giggling, into the labyrinth of corridors.

Galahad paused. He would have given everything he possessed to be back in Arthur's camp, in the companionship of men, where he could think straight and where his body obeyed his will. When this last interview was over, he would ride up the Tor to the Christian monastery near the summit and beg for a sleeping space among the brothers. He would be safe there.

Squaring his shoulders, he pushed the door open and strode into the room. He wasn't sure what he had expected—a dais, perhaps, or a gilded chair, a priestess bedecked with ornaments and surrounded by acolytes—but what he saw surprised him. Two women worked at a trestle table, potting plants. The sleeves of their white robes were rolled up past their elbows, and their hands were filthy with dirt. At the end of the table sat a basket full of plump, green apples, and beside it, the dragon badge. Nearby, tall candles lit their work and shone upon their faces, absorbed and content. One woman was past thirty but still lovely, pale-skinned and dark-haired. The lines in her face respected her beauty, and spoke of purpose as well as of power. The younger woman was the first to look up and see him. She was thin to the point of frailty, with rich brown hair and large, warm brown eyes that dominated her other features. As he met her eyes Galahad felt a shock of recognition, although he knew well he had never seen her before. She sat perfectly still, staring at him, hardly breathing. He felt her fear clearly across the distance between them.

"Yes, Morgaine, I know," the older woman said softly, pushing the soil in place around the edges of a glazed clay pot. "The Harbinger is here. Give me a minute longer."

Without looking at him, she dipped her fingers into a water bowl and cleaned her hands upon a towel. Then she rose, and at last lifted her head to look at him.

This was Niniane, Lady of the Lake. He recognized her from her visits to Camelot during his boyhood. Always close to the bishop's side, he had learned only disdain for the pagan witch who was Arthur's chief advisor. But he knew her face. He had not intended to kneel—he was Christian, after all—but he suddenly found himself with one knee on the floor.

The faintest of smiles touched Niniane's lips. "Prince Galahad of Lanascol, if I am not mistaken."

"I am he, Lady. I come from King Arthur, bearing a message. For you alone."

He had the impression of violent movement, but they were both perfectly still, the standing woman, the seated girl.

"From Arthur." She whispered it, then turned to her companion and motioned her to stand. Together they came around the worktable and stood before him.

"Arise, Galahad. Be welcome. It's a nasty night to be out riding. We will give you comfort here."

"Madam, I do not come here for comfort. My lord King bade me bring you an urgent message."

"Yes." The word was clipped, and for a moment her face grew hard. Watching Niniane, Morgaine's brow wrinkled in worry and again Galahad was struck by a sense of recognition. Morgaine turned to him. At once he felt a soothing touch upon his spirit, a sweet caress of love, of patience, of care. She held his gaze with a will stronger than his own. He could not look away.

"He has been to see the Queen, and she has left her mark upon him." He heard Niniane's voice, amused. "Yes, Morgaine, go ahead. Give him peace."

The young woman approached him until she stood only inches away. Galahad's temples pounded, his breath came short, but he was held frozen in place and could not back away. Gently, she reached out and touched his temples, then his chest, his stomach, and, very lightly, his thighs. He could not prevent her; he was bound by invisible bonds. At her cool touch the fever in his body slowly died, excitement and longing dissolving into gentle calm.

"Thank you," he whispered. She looked back at him and smiled. He knew that smile! Who was she?

"This is Morgaine," Niniane said, reading his thought, "daughter of Urien of Rheged and of Morgan, his queen." Morgan—Arthur's sister! This amazing young woman was Arthur's niece. Galahad smiled in return. Those were Arthur's eyes he recognized, and Arthur's smile. He bowed to her.

"Lady Morgaine. I am in your debt."

"Morgaine does not speak," Niniane said. "But you will hear her voice with the ears of your spirit when she desires it. She is known as the Queen of Avalon for her healing hands." An eyebrow lifted. "We do not get many callers. Few of them are male. Fewer still are Christian. Here we honor the Great Mother, who made men."

"I was sent," he said quickly, "by King Arthur."

Sadness swept her features and again her face grew cold. "Your coming has been foretold. You are the Harbinger."

Neither woman looked at him but he could feel their fear across the space between them.

"Harbinger of what?"

"Of doom." The words rang loud in the small, still room. "Time is turning. The low are made high and the mighty fall. Morgaine, you must be ready."

Trembling, Morgaine nodded.

Niniane addressed Galahad. "When Arthur has no more need of me— when my time is past—she will be Lady of the Lake after me. She is a healer, as I am a giver of dreams. Her sight is far-seeing and always true." She paused, her lips pressed close together. "She will be the last."

"But the King *does* have need of you," Galahad broke in, "he sends for you. He would see you as soon as you can come to him. It is urgent. He commands you."

A single tear formed slowly in her eye, spilled over the lid, and crept down her ivory cheek. "I will come to him," she whispered. "On the plain of Camlann I will see him again."

Morgaine reached out and touched her arm. Niniane shook herself.

"Your message is delivered, prince. I thank you for the pains you took to bring it. We would be pleased to offer you rest tonight in our guest pavilion."

"Thank you. I . . . I know it is an honor, but I will go on to the monastery farther up the Tor. This is not the place for such as me."

Niniane smiled charmingly. "And take your poor horse from his dry stall out into this weather? He will founder if you do." Galahad paused, not sure whether this was warning or prophecy. "Besides," she continued pleasantly, "through Morgaine, the Goddess has done you a kindness. You owe Her a night in Her house." Although he intended to resist, Galahad found himself nodding in acquiescence. Niniane reached into the basket of apples and handed him one of the shining fruit. "Morgaine will guide you to your chamber. Sleep well, and dream a true dream."

The cell was small, but comfortably furnished and scrupulously clean. He fingered the soft wool blankets on the bed as Morgaine set the candle down. To sleep in a bed again, after months of soldiering! And a pillow stuffed with down! Through the narrow windows he smelled the rich scents of a land at peace: stacked salt hay from the marshes, new-cut grass, and the heavy sweetness of ripening fruit. Apples from the orchards of Avalon were prized throughout Britain. He looked down at the one he held his hand. What he longed for was a heel of bread with meat broth, but shied from mentioning it to Morgaine. It was well past midnight; the kitchens must be closed.

Morgaine stirred and he looked up. Slowly, she reached out and placed her palm against his chest. Her eyes closed, and she began to lightly hum. She was a tiny thing, frail and fragile. *A reed for the god's voice.* The words came to him from nowhere, out of the dark. Perhaps he had heard it said of Merlin long ago—he could not remember—the weight of his flesh grew heavy and he sank down upon the bed. His hunger died. He wished only to eat the apple and go to sleep.

Morgaine took a clean towel from the bedstand and moistened it with sweet water from a carafe. Pushing his hair from his brow, she gently washed his face, and then his hands, even his fingers, one by one, with care and attention. All the while he watched her face. She was pretty in a delicate, elfin way but not remarkably so. She certainly had nothing of the kind of beauty Guinevere possessed, that set men afire and turned their wits. Hers was a peaceful loveliness that soothed his restless longings and filled him with contentment. Yet her power was real enough. Her presence commanded his attention; while she was there, he could not look away.

When she finished her ministrations she retrieved the apple and handed it back to him.

"Thank you, Lady Morgaine." He smiled and she returned it, shyly. "Will the Lady Niniane send me a dream tonight?" *Yes, young lord.* He heard her voice, clear as a silver bell, in his thoughts. "Long ago, before I was even born, she made a prophecy about me. Can I . . . I mean, I would like to know more about it. Because I don't understand. Anything at all." She smiled again and turned to go. *You will.*

"Will I see you in the morning?"

She shook her head. He tried to school his face, but something must have shown upon it, for she came near to him again and with a gentle finger traced the sign of the cross upon his brow. Then she was gone.

When he rose at last from his prayers he ate the apple. Sweet and juicy, it satisfied both his hunger and his thirst. He lay on the soft bed, feeling oddly free and light, and let his thoughts drift. The dark walls dissolved into the darker night, and he slipped silently on magic wings into the beyond.

* * *

He rode out of a dark forest by the banks of a flowing river. In the middle of the river stood a castle on an island. . . .

44 ✝ DAY OF DESTINY

"O ur Father, which art in Heaven, preserve this youth and heal him. Bless this young prince— Hell's bells, I've spilled the gruel! Oh my, I'm sorry, Lord, take no offense! Bless the boy, if he isn't waking, and I've got this goo all over his fine clothes. Where is Brother Gervase when I need him? Oh, Lord, grant me patience!"

Galahad heard these words dimly in a deep sleep and struggled to awaken. He was lost in a leaden fog which weighed him down and clogged his throat.

"There now, this rag'll do. P'rhaps he'll be too sick to notice. Lord, I warned You I was not the man for nursing. You never listen to me. Ha ha! And a good thing, too, I can hear You saying. Well, he'll recover, I'll be bound, but it'll be no thanks to me. I'm better in the garden than the sick-room. Although— Confound it! Be gone, little vermin! Out, out! I told Gervase weeks ago to get us a cat that made itself useful, and what does he do? A litter of kittens good only for cuddling and more afraid of a mouse than I am of a woman! Ha ha! I'm sorry, Lord, take no offense, but I believe You've made a mistake with Gervase. He means well, there's no denying that, but he never gets things right."

Galahad opened his eyes. He lay on a bed of bracken over a hard dirt floor. The room was small and mean and bare of furniture. In the hard, gray light that spilled in from a single window he saw his companion, a short, heavy monk in a filthy robe who busily wiped and straightened Galahad's tunic, chattering steadily.

"Brother, who are you?" His lips moved but no sound came out, and he found to his dismay that he could not raise his head.

"Well, well, that will just have to do. P'rhaps by the time he wakens, he'll be dry. Gervase will have to fetch him another bowl of gruel. Oh!" The monk looked up and saw blue eyes watching him. "You're awake at last, my son. May the Lord be praised, we thought perhaps you'd sleep forever. Here, rest against me; I'll raise you up a bit so you can drink."

With surprising skill the monk maneuvered him to a sitting position and deftly spooned what was left of the thin gruel into his mouth. It tasted foul, more like medicine than food. Had he been ill?

"Can you take more?" the monk inquired earnestly when he was finished. "I'll call Brother Gervase to mix another batch. It won't take but a moment."

"No," Galahad whispered, pleased to find he could speak a little. "But some plain broth, perhaps? I . . . I feel so weak."

"And no wonder!" the monk exclaimed. "You've been here the best part of a week with only water for sustenance—all we could get down you in your waking moments."

"Waking?" Galahad stared. "A week? But the last I knew I was abed at the Lady's shrine!"

"You remember nothing of it? Well, it takes some that way. You're not the first young man who's come to us in sorry shape from the gates of Avalon. They must have sent you a dream."

"A dream?" Galahad frowned. He could remember nothing but the thick fog of sleep that had nearly drowned him, yet the words struck a sharp, familiar chord. Had the witch cursed him with a dream and stolen a week of his life? He recalled only a vague sense of joy, of overmastering awe and excitement, but he could not remember why.

"Oh, yes," the monk went on, "they're great dreamers down at the Lady's shrine. Sees visions day and night does the Lady Niniane. Don't worry, son; it will pass."

"I remember nothing. Where am I now?"

"Why, you're at the House of God on Ynys Witrin. My name is Ignacius. And yours is Galahad—oh, my, forgive me, my lord; I forgot to address you proper—it slipped my mind when you awakened."

"Never mind. But tell me, Ignacius, how did I get here?"

"On horseback, of course. A young lord like yourself need not walk. And a fine steed he is, too."

"Ignacius!" Galahad gripped his sleeve. "Are you telling me I *rode* here?"

"Settle down, there's a lad, it's all right now. Your recollection will return to you anon. It always does. Rest now and I'll send Gervase for some broth."

Galahad forced his voice stronger. "Did you say a week? I rode here and have been asleep *a week?*"

Ignacius's strong, capable hands held him still, and he had not the strength to struggle.

"Yes, my lord, that's what I said. Usually they don't sleep for so long. You must have brought the Lady Niniane bad news."

Memory crept slowly back. "I brought her news that the High King would speak with her." And he remembered how still she had gone when he told her.

"Well, my lord, she rode out this very morning to greet him. He and his army sit camped out yonder on the plain of Camlann."

On the plain of Camlann I will see him again. And as she spoke, a tear had fallen from her eye. Why should such a message be bad news?

"They say there'll be a battle soon. Perhaps today. No doubt she rode out to warn the King."

"Mordred!" Galahad cried, struggling to arise. "Is Mordred there?"

"Aye, my lord, but—"

"I must get up! I must avert the battle! I must go to the High King and tell him about Mordred!"

But his efforts cost him his strength and he fell back against the bracken as Ignacius clucked worriedly and the darkness overtook him once again.

He awoke late in the afternoon. Through his window the mid-September light shone golden and the air bore the first cool hint of coming evening. He rose and found his legs unsteady, but serviceable. A heel of bread and a jar of water lay by his bed. He ate the bread eagerly. His window looked out on a verdant meadow bordered by woodland. The trees threw long shadows eastward. Feeling better for the bread, he looked around for his sword and his dagger. It was time to be going to Arthur, if he could sit his horse. He found the weapons stacked neatly in the corner by his pallet, along with his cloak and badge. He checked the badge and was relieved to see the Hawk of Lanascol and not a cross of red. He stopped suddenly. Why on earth should he expect his badge to change? His hand began to shake. In his mind's eye he saw clearly the red cross on the white field, and knew it was his.

"Never mind," he muttered, donning his cloak and fastening the Hawk to his shoulder. "I want no more dreams or visions. I must find Arthur."

He opened the door onto an empty hallway. Not a soul was about. An unearthly silence made everything about him seem unreal. He jumped as a flight of ravens went overhead, cawing, and a frisson of horror slid up his spine.

"Galahad the Brave!" he sniggered, adjusting his swordbelt. "Afraid of ravens!" Nevertheless, he crossed himself for protection. It was well known ravens could scent a battlefield fifty leagues away.

He walked down the corridor and passed more cells, all as mean and dirty as his own. Vermin scurried from sight as he approached and he shuddered. He had lain a week on the floor of that horrible cell and he would wager his birthright he had not been attended every minute. At the end of the corridor a piece of half-rotted canvas hung across the doorway. Lifting it with care and holding it away from his cloak, Galahad stepped outside.

He stood near the edge of a steep slope with a view of the winding road down the Tor. To his right he saw a chapel with a wooden cross nailed above the lintel. It was a primitive structure built of roughly cut timber, patched with wattle, and roofed with thatch. Low outbuildings hunched behind the chapel, and near the meadow, under a branching oak, a cluster of small wooden crosses marked the burial ground. Nowhere did he see a living soul.

All around him the golden daylight deepened and cooled in utter silence. Even the birds were still. Beyond the bend in the road the Lake of Avalon glistened blue, distant and serene. Beyond that lay the marshes, and the causeway to the mainland. And beyond the low rise at the end of the causeway the river Camel ran through the plain of Camlann.

Galahad shivered in the unnatural quiet. The hairs on his neck and arms bristled like a dog's who senses the storm's approach. Suddenly he heard chanting. Low and dolorous, it oppressed the very air. He walked to the chapel and poked his head in. Two candles burned upon the altar— thriftless extravagance for such a threadbare monastery! But perhaps the good brothers had been suddenly called away. By the dim candlelight Galahad saw the swept dirt floor, the tattered hangings, the crude but lovingly polished crucifix, the carved altar, but the place was empty of people.

As he closed the door the chanting grew louder. He turned. A slow procession came into view up the roadway. Six monks carried a bier upon their shoulders, staggering slightly under its weight. Behind the bier limped a single soldier, weeping, followed by twelve monks chanting in two lines. Galahad frowned as they drew closer. The limping soldier looked familiar— tall, black-haired with graying temples, the sword, the badge . . . His mouth went dry. It couldn't be Lancelot! He was home in Lanascol! But it *was* Lancelot, and he wept shamelessly, openly, tears coursing down his cheeks in a steady stream.

Galahad's eyes flew to the bier. The body was that of a tall man, washed and scented with sweet herbs, shrouded in fine white cloth. The right arm hung lifelessly over the bier, swinging in slow, dreadful time to the monks' steps. On the hand was a golden ring with a great red stone. Galahad's chest tightened and his throat closed. He fumbled with the latch of the chapel door and flung it open. The procession passed slowly by him. He saw the High King's face, gray and shuttered, eyes closed, mouth grimly set, his spirit long departed. Above his ear the side of his head had been opened by a sword blow.

Galahad tasted the salt of his own tears. Lancelot's arm wrapped around his shoulders, drawing him forward into the chapel, leaning on him.

"Thank God in Heaven you are here. We two alone are left to bury Arthur."

In the long, dying twilight they gave the dead King what honor they could. The abbott spoke the sacred blessings in the rich, calm voice of one who is certain of Heaven's reward. Galahad and Lancelot mumbled their responses, half weeping, holding on to each other. And together, as night descended, they dug his grave with their own hands under the chapel altar, while the monks chanted solemnly around them.

"He must lie where the Saxons will never find him," Lancelot muttered. Galahad avoided looking at the High King's face. The head wound was ferocious. He felt his innards rise and worked furiously to keep those thoughts at bay. He said nothing, and Lancelot was most of the time beyond speech. The monks burned incense as the abbott intoned prayers of blessing and benediction. By candlelight they lowered Arthur's body into its grave. Lancelot took his friend's cold hand and kissed it.

"I have done what you asked," he whispered, pulling the ring of office from Arthur's finger. "Rest in peace, my dear lord." Grabbing Galahad's arm, he drew him outside into the cool, clean evening.

The first stars had risen in the east, while in the west a halo of deep blue ringed the horizon. Lancelot eased himself slowly onto a flat rock by the roadside, propping his injured leg out in front of him. Galahad stood beside him, too numb for thought.

"He is gone," Lancelot said gruffly. "The greatest man of our time, of any time. He is gone."

With an effort Galahad cleared his throat. "How did it happen? How did you come here, Father? When I left the High King a week ago all was well enough."

Lancelot shook his head. "He sent you away because his fate was upon him and he knew it. Oh, Arthur! Most merciful of men!" His voice cracked and he stopped.

"When did you get here? Tell me, tell me what happened!"

"I came as soon as I could walk. Something told me Arthur needed me. Urgently. Adele tried to stop me on account of Gawaine's threats, but I came as soon as I could walk."

"Gawaine is dead. He died the day we landed back in Britain. Killed by a Saxon. Before he died he forgave you for Gareth and asked Arthur to send for you."

"Did he? God have mercy upon his pagan soul. His dying sight was truer than he knew. I headed straight for Camelot and found them, father and son, facing each other at its very door. As Merlin foretold it."

"But how did it happen? I spoke with Mordred. He swore he would yield to Arthur."

"He tried," Lancelot whispered. "But it was not to be. Against his will, he carried out his fate."

"What do you mean, he tried?"

"They parleyed. Niniane arranged it. They met in a tent upon the battlefield and talked it out. When they emerged, they embraced. Everyone could see that all was well. The High King wore his crown upon his helmet and Mordred was bareheaded. I don't know what Arthur promised him—"

"I do. Brittany. Hoel's successor."

"Ah. Well. It was enough. They made amends."

"Then however did the fighting start?"

Lancelot sighed wearily. "I don't know how it began—an exchange of insults between foot soldiers, most likely, a sword raised without thought— but the battle began of its own will. Men started fighting without waiting for a signal from either commander. Arthur and Mordred's arms were still around each other's shoulders when they found they were at war."

Galahad remembered Cerdic. "They couldn't stop it?"

Lancelot shrugged. "How?" He moved his injured leg and winced. "Perhaps Arthur could have—Mordred tried—but I think . . . I think Arthur knew it was the end. He drew his sword, saluted Mordred, and joined the battle. He left Mordred no choice."

"Was it Mordred who . . . who—"

"Yes," Lancelot said slowly. "Mordred slew him at the last. A sword to the head. Arthur saw it coming. And he slew his own son in the same moment." Lancelot passed a hand across his face. "Only twice in his whole life was he unworthy of himself. When he begot Mordred, and when he killed him. Now he has paid for those sins."

"At least," Galahad said, "his death was quick."

But Lancelot shook his head. "Mordred's was. A spear thrust through the heart. The King was a veteran. But Arthur suffered. I lifted him from the ground and he still breathed." Galahad saw his father's eyes brim with tears. "I carried him toward Avalon. There was no one left standing. I thought perhaps the Lady of the Lake could heal him, as she healed me long ago of a grievous wound. So I carried him there."

"On horseback, surely."

"There were no horses."

"You carried the King on foot all the way to Avalon? But it's an hour's ride and you are wounded!"

Lancelot shrugged. "God gave me strength. I carried him, and he spoke to me." Lancelot's voice broke. Galahad looked up at the moon, rising white and shining in the east. His cheeks were wet. He stood in the still beauty of the night and listened to the tale of Arthur's death.

"He bade me take Excalibur from his hand and throw it into the Lake of Avalon. I refused at first. But he pleaded with me. He said it must be done, and there was little time. He said his head hurt him." Lancelot's voice quavered and he roughly cleared his throat. "I had gotten as far as the causeway across the marsh. I threw the sword as far as I could, so far that I lost it in the light and did not see it hit the water. But I heard it go in, as smoothly as a blade home to its scabbard. Soon after, a boat appeared, I suppose from the Lady's shrine. I don't know how they came there. They had no pole. There was no wind. I wasn't watching. I was with Arthur. He could no longer see, but he told me to wait, that they would come."

"That who would come?"

"Three queens to fetch him." Lancelot glanced up. "I thought he was wandering, but I was tired, so I pleased him and waited. In the boat were three women dressed in mourning, white-robed, white-veiled. One was Morgan, the King's sister, Queen of Rheged. The other was Niniane, the Lady herself, Queen of the River Isles. The third I did not know. Young, frail, rather pretty. Something familiar about her."

"Morgaine," Galahad supplied. "Queen of Avalon. The next Lady."

Lancelot grunted and shifted his leg again. "Three queens. They had prepared the craft to receive him, lining it with cushions and velvets and rich trimmings. I carried him into the boat and laid him down upon the cushions. He was covered with blood and grimed with dust. They said they would take him to Avalon and tend him. The youngest took his poor bleeding head and cradled it in her lap. What an angel of healing she must be, for when she stroked his head he opened his eyes and saw me again. He spoke to me one last time as the boat pulled away from shore. He . . . he called me a true friend." Lancelot covered his face with his hands. "Oh, my King, my King, let me follow where you have gone!"

Galahad swallowed hard. "But they could not heal him."

"No. They bade me send for the monks and await them at the gates of Avalon. They cleaned him and dressed him as you have seen, and they sent him here for the rites, but they could not give him life."

Galahad sat down beside his father.

"You said . . . you said there were none left standing? Was everyone killed but you? What about Percival?"

"I'm sorry, son. I do not know. Galyn, my poor brother, Bedwyr, Kay, Gereint—all are dead. No one answered when I called out. If any lived, I did not know it. And the ravens . . . " He shuddered. "Ravens came from all over Britain. The ground was black with them."

Galahad crossed himself. "Dear God," he whispered, "protect Percival if he lives, and preserve his soul if he does not."

Lancelot's hand came down gently on his shoulder. "I'm sorry I did not look harder. All I could think of was Arthur."

Galahad nodded. "What happens now?"

Lancelot drew a long breath. "I am going home. I will not serve Constantine. He did not lift a hand for either side, but waited in safety while they destroyed each other. He's a traitor to Britain."

"Is he King now?"

Lancelot shrugged. "Who else? There is no one left. Pendragon is no more." He paused and looked at Galahad. "And you, son? Have you had enough of war? Will you come home to Lanascol with me and learn what I can teach you of the craft of kingship? Or"—Lancelot's voice went suddenly gentle as he watched Galahad's eyes—"or will you kill me? You have wanted to, off and on, since you were five years old. Or don't you remember?"

Galahad drew breath sharply. "I remember."

"If you think my blood will assuage your poor mother's troubled spirit or avenge you for Gareth, then kill me now. I will not stop you. It's as good a time as any—I've little left to live for. Bury me here, beside Arthur. Then perhaps my soul can rest."

Neither of them moved. Galahad's throat was dry and his blood hammered in his head. Once, everything had been so clear, so clean, so well defined. But now . . . the world was a place of shadow and disguise. Nothing was as it seemed to be. Men were slippery creatures; they grew, turned, changed before one's very eyes, and were no longer the people they had been. Galahad looked into his father's eyes, as cool and gray as a sword blade, and remembered the night Lancelot had returned to Lanascol, remembered sitting on his father's hard bed, watching him as he prayed, hour upon endless hour, for the forgiveness of his sins.

Galahad exhaled and shut his eyes. "I cannot kill you. I never could have. And it has been a long while since I have wanted to."

Lancelot raised his head and looked up at the stars. "It's my fault you ever felt so. It's my fault Aidan thought he could use you as a weapon. I injured him when I was young, although I did not know it then, and he spent his whole life consumed with the desire for revenge. You and your mother were his tools."

"How do you know this?"

"He confessed it when I finally found him."

Galahad stared. "You found Aidan? When?"

"About a year after I brought you to Camelot. My men discovered him hiding in an old, dilapidated mill in a hamlet on the edge of the Wild Forest, starving and half-mad. He still had his golden cross and silver goblets. Stolen from a Breton church. The bishop of Kerrec was delighted to have them back."

"Did you kill him?"

Lancelot's hard gray eyes glittered. "Of course. But his death was swift. A kinder fate than he deserved after the agony he inflicted on Elaine and the unborn babe. He poisoned them. And he killed your dog. He confessed that, too."

"*He* killed Valiant?" Galahad repeated blankly. "Why?"

"To spur you on to kill me." He smiled ruefully at Galahad's expression and then sobered. "Had I stayed in Lanascol instead of Britain, so many, many things might have turned out differently. And I went to Britain not only to serve Arthur but to be near Guinevere. Can you forgive me for this, son?"

Galahad's chest tightened. "Tell me . . . first, tell me why . . . why did you marry my mother? Is it true you lay with her because you thought she was Guinevere?"

Lancelot shook his head. His voice was heavy with fatigue. "Galahad, the sad truth is, I was so drunk I could hardly see my hand before my face. Arthur and Guinevere held a feast on the night of the summer solstice to celebrate the fifth year of their marriage. She was twenty, and so beautiful— so beautiful she set every man alight. I wanted her more than I wanted life. But she had eyes only for Arthur. There was something between them that night, something wild and vivid and true . . . I got drunk because I could take no part in it. She never once looked at me, but I could not take my eyes off her. I don't know what I wanted of her; she owed me nothing, but I burned for her that night with a fire I couldn't control. So I went out walking to cool my ardor—and found Elaine." He bent his head. "It is true she looked like Guinevere. They were cousins, after all, and much alike. And part of me tried to pretend she was Gwen. I won't deny it. That is my sin. But in my heart I knew it was Elaine. How not? I had known her for seven years. And I was content that it should be so. I betrothed her that night, and I spoke to her father, Pellinore, in the morning. You were never bastard bred, son; you were trueborn. And that is the whole truth of it, although God knows the gossips would have it otherwise."

Galahad took a deep breath of cool air, the first breath of a new life. "I forgive you, Father. I've been so wrong about so many things . . . you, Gawaine, Mordred, even Guinevere . . . I don't know who I am, anymore."

Lancelot smiled briefly. "That is life's great adventure. Finding out. You stand at the edge of a mystery it will take your lifetime to solve. I almost envy you. But I have not the energy for it anymore." He sighed. "What will you do? Serve Constantine?"

"I don't know. I must find Percival. If he lives, I will travel home with him to Gwynedd. If not, I will bear his body there."

Lancelot nodded. "As good a plan as any. My time is past, Galahad. My days near their end. Do what you wish, but make ready to be king."

Galahad looked up at the rising moon sailing high and clear among the stars. *Time is turning,* Niniane had told him. Everything would change. Arthur no longer had need of the Grail and Spear. On the thought, the memory of his dream returned to him, complete in every detail, and he gasped aloud.

"What's the matter, son? What is it?"

He had *seen* the Grail and Spear! He had seen them with a force and clarity that belied the dream itself. His heart began to pound as he recalled the flashing pictures in the Cross of Visions—the gleaming spear, the dazzling krater—it was a true vision, after all!

"What is it, Galahad?"

"My lord—Father—I've seen a vision of . . . a vision of something I must find."

Lancelot frowned. "What sort of vision?"

"I don't know. I saw it in Aidan's stone when he thought he was showing me something else. A grail—so full of light! I saw it in the dream Niniane sent me. Even Arthur told me of it, although he had doubts about its power."

Lancelot shrugged. "Arthur was only a man. But he believed, as I believe, that men can work miracles themselves, if they only believe they can. If you want badly enough to find what you have dreamed of, then search for it. You will find it." The corners of his mouth lifted. "Perhaps in the last place you expect."

"But that means I must stay in Britain."

Lancelot struggled painfully to his feet. "In that case, I will knight you, that you may face Constantine, or any other lord, with the honor due you. You are young for it, but you are worthy and there is no time. Kneel at my feet and repeat these words."

Solemnly by starlight Lancelot spoke the ritual words that bound a warrior to his sovereign lord, and Galahad repeated them. When it was over, Lancelot gave his son his formal blessing.

"And this shall be your token, for we have no witness." He handed Galahad his own sword, with the cross of rubies in the hilt. Awed, Galahad took it.

"Your own sword that Arthur gave you?"

"It has served Britain faithfully these many years, and now will again. Arthur would want it so. I don't need it. I will face no more Saxons now. Let me have Gareth's weapon in exchange. It is only fitting. He lives, day and night, in my heart."

"Thank you, Father. It is a gift beyond price."

Lancelot smiled sadly. "With Arthur gone, little is precious to me any longer. Will you lend me your arm as far as the Lady's shrine? I would speak a word with Niniane, but I fear my leg will not carry me that far."

"I will do better than that. I will bring you my horse."

As night deepened Galahad led Lancelot down the long winding road, past the mean dwellings of the poor Christian brothers, past the mighty portals of Melwas's empty castle, past the orchards heavy with ripening fruit, to the door of the shrine itself. The same old portress opened the gates.

"Welcome, Sir Lancelot, Sir Galahad. You are both expected."

"We would see the Lady Niniane, good sister," Lancelot said.

"Ah, sir, alas, this very day she is gone from Avalon. She has left the Mother's service. But the new Lady expects you and will heal your leg besides, before you go on your way."

Lancelot winced as he slid from the horse. "If she can do that, she will have my thanks indeed. Where did Niniane go, do you know?"

The old woman nodded uncertainly. "Home to tend her husband, King Pelleas, who was wounded in the battle."

"Well, I am glad to know someone else survived it."

"We have several wounded men in our House of Healing." She turned to Galahad. "One of them has been calling out your name, my lord. Is he a friend of yours?"

"Percival?" Galahad cried. "Percival of Gwynedd? Does he live? He is here?"

The old woman smiled and rang a bell. "I think that is the name. Petra will know. She will take you to him."

Lancelot turned to his son and embraced him. "If this should be our parting, Galahad, I thank you for your service to Arthur, even unto the last. Such sorrow as I feel can hardly be borne, but seeing you today has made it bearable. There may still be a future for Britain while you raise a sword in her defense. Let us part as friends and forget those things which have been between us."

Galahad returned his embrace. "I owe you much, my lord, and I wish with all my being I had been a better son."

"And I a better father."

"After you have seen Morgaine, will you be off to Lanascol?"

"To tell poor, sweet Adele my brother is dead." Lancelot looked down and opened his hand. By the light of a torch Galahad saw the golden glitter of the High King's ring. "Before I go home," Lancelot said slowly, "I must take his ring to Guinevere."

Galahad stiffened. "Leave it here. The sisters will see it gets to Camelot."

"She is not in Camelot. She fled to the monastery at Amesbury."

"She was in Camelot a week ago. I saw her."

"Did you?" Lancelot looked up. To Galahad, the tenderness in his eyes was a blow to an old bruise. "But she is not there now. Arthur sent her a message, secretly, to fly from Mordred and seek shelter at Amesbury. He told me this himself as I bore him in my arms. He bade me see her."

So that was the message he had carried! Galahad found his voice suddenly unsteady. "It was unfair of him to ask you. Father, whatever was once between you and . . . the Queen, surely it is time to give it honorable burial."

"I will not refuse Arthur his dying wish."

"But if you go . . . now that she is no longer his wife, you will sully your name . . . and hers—" Galahad's voice shook and a bud of anger, hot as an ember, began to blossom and burn within his breast. Desperately he fought to regain the calm, the peace they had so newly built between them. "Besides, you're in no condition to ride to Amesbury. You'll inflame your leg."

Lancelot smiled sadly. "It doesn't matter."

"Father!" Galahad reached out to touch him. "Promise me you will leave her in the convent. You will not take her to Lanascol."

"I will ask her, certainly. But I don't know if she will consent to come."

"Oh, please!" Galahad whispered fiercely, gripping Lancelot's arms. "Please don't! Be strong, Father! Bypass Amesbury! Throw the ring in the lake, after the sword! Let the woman be!"

Lancelot looked down at his hand. Arthur's ring shone upon his finger, gold and bloodred in the torchlight. He drew a trembling breath. "He asked me to see her. He sent me with words to say."

"He is dead."

"She does not know it. I should be the one to tell her."

"She will learn of it in time. This is certain."

"She will not learn it from the lips of a stranger! You are cruel to wish such a thing upon her."

"Father! Listen. She lives in a house of God. She is not alone. Come away from her now and let her be."

Lancelot slowly shook his head. "I will see her. I promised it. And I owe it to them both."

Galahad dropped his hands. "If you wed her and take her to Lanascol, I will not come home. Ever. This is the end between us."

Lancelot's shoulders sagged. "Be merciful, Galahad. Forgive us if you can."

"I *have* forgiven you! But you will not let her be!"

Lancelot put a hand on his arm. "You have your destiny, son. And I have mine. Guinevere is part of it."

The page arrived and beckoned them inside. "The Lady will see you now, Sir Lancelot. And I will take you to the House of Healing, my lord prince. Follow me."

"No," Lancelot said suddenly. "I have changed my mind. I will not stay. If you can loan me a horse for a silver coin, I'll be on my way."

The girl's eyes widened. "Of course, my lord! We've been collecting them from all over the plain and the marsh. Take your pick of whatever's in the stable."

Galahad watched Lancelot search in his pouch for a coin. "Then go," he said roughly, wiping his sleeve across his eyes. "Go if you must. I am not your son any longer." He spun on his heel and followed the page inside.

Lancelot turned, the coin in his hand, as the gate closed behind his son. He gazed at the retreating figure with sorrow upon sorrows, sketched a salute, and whispered, "Go with God."

✠ BOOK THREE

PART I
Three Women

*In the seventh through tenth years of the reign
of Constantine*

45 ⛨ THE GIANTS' DANCE

A storm rolled over the Great Plain, where the armies of Constantine and his allies gathered before the Giants' Dance to plan their defense and wait nervously for dawn. Five leagues east a sprawling Saxon host hunched by their campfires in the blowing rain and practiced their victory paeans.

In an upper room of a roadside tavern just over the northern rise, Galahad knelt at a window and crossed himself. He could hear Talorc of Elmet pacing the room next door, and he wondered whether Talorc, alone of all the men of the north whom he had brought south to Constantine's defense, had foresworn the wineskin in order to go to bed early and sober. Most likely the rest of them would be drinking all night. He hoped the landlord had locked up his daughters.

Bowing his head, he thanked God the men of the north had honored their pledges and come. Without them Constantine had little hope. The Saxon force comprised five federations, while Constantine had been able to raise less than three thousand men. But this time the Welsh were there. The courier had been specific: all the Welsh had come in a single federation, all five kingdoms led by Gwynedd. But whether he had Peredur or Percival to thank for that, he did not know. The courier had not reported. In Camelot they'd had no news from Wales in years. And for the last six months he himself had been in the north twisting the arms of kings who needed persuasion, even at sword point, to keep their pledge.

He might, of course, have gone to Wales himself to seek out Percival, if Constantine could have spared him. But he had not even sought permission. He did not know exactly why. Did he wish to avoid a meeting that would be awkward, even tragic, if Percival had not succeeded in claiming his birthright? Did he prefer to remember the adventures they had shared as boys and not risk confrontation with a different Percival, a man of eighteen who might not be a friend? Did he wish to avoid being questioned about the Grail? He would have to admit that nothing—absolutely nothing—had happened in the last three years that could be taken as a sign. Or did he merely wish to keep his distance from Percival's meddling sister, Dane?

Galahad shook his head in vexation. He could not pray. His mind would not stay on anything, but roamed his memory, sifting through dross for gold. He recalled the day when, outside the gates of Avalon, he first learned that Percival had survived Camlann. When he had turned his back on Lancelot and followed the acolyte down the whitewashed corridors of the Lady's House of Healing. She had shown him to a small bedchamber, spotlessly clean and herb-scented, warmed and lit by an applewood fire. The body on the pallet, still as a corpse and bereft of color, had looked more like a beggar than a prince, something hard used and then discarded when its essence was exhausted. For a frantic moment he had thought they had made a mistake, or that death had sneaked into the room before him. Then he saw the fresh red stain in the shoulder bandage, and exhaled. He was on his knees at the bedside when dark eyes opened in that stretched, white face—and Percival smiled.

Galahad pushed open the shutter and gazed out at the lashing rain. Somewhere out there, perhaps camped in the shadows of the standing stones, his cousin might even now be meeting with his captains, sharing wine around a fire, or readying for bed. Tomorrow he might find him, *must* find him. If they both survived.

At dawn the Saxons swept across the Great Plain. The Britons waited in the shadow of the great stone ring they called the Giants' Dance. Each man on the field that day prayed fervently to whatever god he held holy for victory, life, or quick death, and Constantine, watching the road north, prayed he would see Galahad's red-crossed shield and the banners of the promised northern armies behind him. But time was running out.

Cynewulf, knowing Constantine awaited reinforcements, attacked him on both flanks as soon as he had light enough to see. Within an hour he pushed the Britons back until they were nearly surrounded. In desperation they withdrew to a defensive formation around the Dance, when at last the men of the north appeared on the horizon, galloped hard into the Saxon flank, and, after long hours of bloody fighting, drove the invaders from the field. The day was Britain's, but the cost was high. Cynewulf himself survived to lead his ragged army back to his own land, to regroup and plan the next attack. But Constantine's army was cut to half its size.

Constantine greeted the northern lords with words of praise and welcome, smiled into their faces, and toasted them at the victory feast, but his heart was filled with bitterness. So many of his own lay dead, while so many of theirs still lived, all because they had not answered his call until Galahad had forced them. Had they come last year, or the year before, a pitched battle might have been avoided.

"Couldn't you get them here any sooner?" he grumbled to Galahad as they parted after the victory celebration. "Those pagan dogs nearly had us. At least they all came—Elmet, Lothian, Gorre, Rheged, Strathclyde. Without them we'd not have had a chance. Thanks are due you, boy, for that service."

Galahad stiffened at the condescension, familiar though it was. "Our cavalry is inept and slow. Victory should not have taken so long. And you should have been able to keep them longer at bay. My lord."

"We've not the horses Arthur had," Constantine snapped. "And I hope you're not going to tell me, as everyone else does, to send across the Narrow Sea for Lancelot! Let him keep his precious steeds, much good they do him. I will ride a mountain pony into battle before I'll send for help to that Breton bitch's whelp!"

Galahad schooled his face. "My lord knows best."

"Don't sneer at me, princeling! I'm not in the mood for your high-and-mighty ways. You've only been back six hours and already I've had more of you than I can stomach. Who do you think you are, to stand there and recite to me my shortcomings? If you'd found the Treasure of Maximus for me, there needn't have been a battle at all!"

A whiplash of anger flickered in Galahad's eyes. "Who am I? I am the Knight of the Seat Perilous. You made me so yourself. As for the Treasure of Maximus, you're not worthy of it." He drew his sword from its scabbard and offered it to Constantine in the gesture of surrender, the flat of the blade lying across his palms. "I have done all you asked and more, for three long years. Britain is safer and stronger than it has been since Arthur died. But now we are finished with one another. I beg leave to go."

Constantine froze. Color drained from his face. He made no move to take the sword. "Now, now, Galahad, easy does it. I meant no offense. I'm just on edge. My son Markion was nearly killed today. Put that away. I've . . . I've got business to attend to just now. Sleep on it, why don't you, and come to my tent in the morning. We'll discuss these matters then."

Galahad sheathed the weapon. "As the king commands."

"That's my boy. Good night, then, Galahad."

Galahad turned and walked alone down the lanes of tents, past campfires redolent with the scents of roasting fowl and thick, bubbling stews, past the pleasant sound of voices talking eagerly together, sharing the warm companionship of soldiers who have faced death and come away. No one called out to him to join them. For three long years no one but Constantine had willingly sought his company. Whether they believed the miracle of the Seat Perilous or whether they had been part of its staging, did not matter. They all kept him at arm's length.

Out on the battlefield work parties were busy digging trenches for the dead. Their rhythmic dirges floated on the night air, dolorous and slow. He found himself walking to the beat of their music as he headed toward the Welsh encampment beyond the Dance. Night drew down and the black sky burst into stars, filling the heavens with a light more welcoming than campfires. Ahead of him, darker shadows in a dark night, marched the timeless megaliths of the Giants' Dance. He walked toward them.

No one knew who had built the Dance. For eons men had revered it as a sacred place, gathering around it at solstice and equinox with their chants, spells, and sacred fires. Christians left it alone, believing it haunted by the spirits of Uther and Ambrosius, who lay beneath the kingstone at its center. But it did not frighten Galahad. The great giants, marching in pairs and topped by capstones the size of Saxon ships, spoke to him of high endeavor, of courage and faith, of the dauntless pursuit of dreams. He had sat alone near the kingstone twice before, ringed by the awful giants of an unknown past, and felt their power round about him. Though built by men at the dawn of time and raised again by Merlin the Enchanter, the stones held the spirit of the living deity. Galahad had worshiped there in the open air and felt the free flowing of his soul, the release of confession, the joy of granted grace. He remembered well the blessed peace that followed, bathing his soul in light. This was what he needed after the filth of battle, after years of compromise and loyal service to a cruel and greedy king. Somehow, somewhere, he had lost his bearings. His old dreams of glory were as dead and difficult to remember as last year's May Day ribbons, discarded in some long-forgotten corner to gather dust. How slowly and inexorably it had come upon him, the stiff boredom of political life, the constant scheming for gold, men, and power. It had deadened his senses and sullied his soul. He had lost something precious at the center of his being and did not know how to get it back.

He quickened his pace toward the outer ring of stones, when suddenly, out of the dark, he heard his name.

"Galahad!"

He knew the voice, and turned. "Percival?"

Out of the shadows stepped a soldier with a bandaged head, taller and broader in the shoulders than Galahad remembered, but still the eager companion of his youth.

"Galahad! Cousin! It's really you! After all these years!" Percival embraced him and thumped him on the back. "My God, I wondered if I'd ever see you again! I heard you were here. Were you at the feast? I didn't see you. How well you look—and without a scratch! Where are you camped? Let me send a servant for your bedroll—you must stay with me. I've a million things to tell you—and a million to hear as well, I'll be bound. Why haven't you ever come to see us?"

"I should have, cousin." He glanced sidelong at Percival. "Why haven't you ever come to fight for Constantine before this?"

Percival smiled. "So that's it. It's easily explained—if you'd ever come to ask us, you'd have known. Come with me and I'll tell you all about it. Don't look so stern; I'm here now. And I got here before you did, this time!"

"And were wounded for your efforts. Is it bad?"

"Little more than a scratch, but you know physicians. The more bandages they apply, the bigger their glory. Come, you look famished. Follow me."

Percival's tent lay in a place of honor at the center of the Welsh encampment. His own standard hung on a pole outside the entrance, the Gray Wolf of Gwynedd on a field of blue. Percival himself seemed unchanged in all but stature and attire, with jewels at shoulder and waist, and wristbands of silver. But leadership changed men and brought boys to manhood. Would this new Percival be his friend?

"I suppose," Galahad ventured, "you are now King of Gwynedd in more than name."

To his surprise, Percival laughed. "Indeed, cousin, that is why I'm here. Come, come, sit down. Make yourself comfortable. Drachan, we'll have the wineskin." He winked at Galahad. "That stuff Constantine served at the feast was little more than flavored water, but I think you'll appreciate this."

The wine was neat, mellow, and better than Galahad had expected. He leaned back against a cushion and began to relax. "How is your family? Your gracious mother, Queen Anet, and Peredur, your uncle?"

Percival raised an eyebrow. "My mother's well enough. You have not heard about my uncle?"

"I have heard nothing. What happened when you went home?"

Percival smiled. "You were right, you know. I suppose it's really a common sort of tale until it happens to oneself. He'd held power since my father sailed to Gaul with Arthur, and no one could blame him if he didn't want to give it up. I'll say this for him: although he didn't give two pins about Constantine, he had Gwynedd's best interest at heart. Even I could see the strength of his arguments. A grown man of five-and-thirty with experience behind him could rule the kingdom much better than a lad of fifteen."

"Your experience—at Autun, at Camlann—outshines anything he has ever done."

"Yes and no. Don't forget, the only army I ever commanded vanished, died, down to the last man. That's not a record of great leadership."

"No one can blame you for Camlann. That was the devil's day. All of Arthur's army died as well, and no one can contest *his* leadership."

"Ah, but Arthur died with them. I did not." He paused. "When I went home at fifteen and demanded my crown, my mother and sister supported me and he yielded. But as soon as I was crowned King of Gwynedd, I began to see that I was king in name only. Peredur's commands were the ones that were obeyed, not mine. He led the men, not I. He seldom even asked for my opinion, but just went about his business the way he had been used to doing. He was always polite, always reasonable, always able to show that everything he did was for the welfare of Gwynedd, and therefore for me."

"Yes," said Galahad slowly, "he always had a fluid tongue. I remember him well."

Percival grinned. "And he remembers you."

"But tell me how you came into your own. Is he dead, then?"

"Oh, no." Percival smiled and refilled their winecups. "No, he rules as regent while I am away. I gave him leave." He smiled at Galahad's surprise. "There is more than one way to skin a cat. I'll tell you all about it, but first . . ." He hesitated, watching Galahad's face. "There is a member of my family you neglect to ask about. It was *her* doing I finally took power. It was all due to Dane."

Galahad grunted and downed his wine. "I beg your pardon. I meant no offense. How does your sister?"

Percival laughed. "Well, very well. I'll wager you a gold coin you'd not know her. I'm sure she'd love to see you, if only to ease her conscience. Poor Dane is convinced she is the reason you left Gwynedd. She has never forgiven herself."

Galahad shrugged. "Let that pass. Tell me how a mere girl brought you into kingship—that should be a good tale."

"I swear upon the Book of God it's true! And you know well Dane is no mere girl. She persuaded me that the only way was to win the men's respect and diminish Peredur's—against his will he would find himself without power. That meant a swordfight."

"You challenged him?" Galahad's interest awakened. "Good man. Tell me about it."

"I followed Dane's plan. Last year on my seventeenth birthday I stood up at council and read him a list of grievances and challenged him to settle the dispute with swords. He smiled at first, and gave me every sort of reason why I should not risk myself and the future of Gwynedd against him. But in the end he had to consent, or the men would think him the coward I had called him."

"Since you bested him, why did you not kill him and have done?"

"Kill him! What need was there to kill him? He is my kin, *our* kin, and besides, he is useful." Percival frowned at Galahad. "You have been too long at court, I think. In any event, that is not my way. But let me tell you how we did it. Dane had planned it since the summer. All the long winter she engaged Peredur in games whenever she could. He loves games almost as much as hunting, and when she let him win at chess he grew merry and boastful, and wanted more. So he hunted less, and drilled less, and put on weight. Ennyde smoked out that plan, and began to badger Peredur to keep fit. To silence Ennyde, Dane found the miller's daughter—a pretty lass, golden-haired and plump. She employed her in the castle. Peredur went for her like a pike for a minnow. He hardly stirred from his chamber for days at a time, and Ennyde was so furious she refused to speak to him. It took him only three months to get the girl with child and send her packing with a dowry, to her father's great delight—and by that time he was positively sagging around the middle. But I went four hours every day to the swordmaster—not Maldryn; he died of flux the year after we left. This was a new man—and practiced until my sword arm turned to iron and I beat the swordmaster himself nine times out of ten. The soldiers watched—the wagering was fast and heavy, I can tell you! And Dane even taught me a move she had seen you do, one you never showed me, a neat escape done with a twist of wrist and hip."

Galahad's face flamed. "I remember."

"And one or two she had thought up herself and said would take him by surprise in a pinch, they were so unorthodox."

"I can imagine."

"When the day came, I bested him fairly in front of all his men. I spared his life and he had to pledge me his allegiance. With their own ears the soldiers heard him swear loyalty to me. I have had no trouble since."

"He has never tried to take back any power?"

"No." Percival paused and then smiled. "Perhaps I should mention that I sliced his sword arm in the fight, and that although he has recovered the use of it, it's not as strong as it used to be. It's good for hunting, but not much else."

Galahad smiled and toasted him with his winecup. "I congratulate you, Percival, on a job well done."

"And well conceived and planned."

"Yes, I congratulate your sister, too."

"She would be happy to hear you say that. Where are you headed now? Why don't you come back to Gwynedd with me? We are hosting a convocation of northern kings this winter—actually, since they have come south to fight, I hope to persuade them to travel to Gwynedd on their way home."

"Why? To form a new alliance? To widen the reaches of your power?"

Percival grinned. "Only in a manner of speaking. They come as suitors. I intend to get Dane a husband."

Galahad choked back laughter. "I wish you luck."

"It's her own idea. Wales is strong enough, and now, under my leadership, fights for Constantine. As you well know, the north is a fairly solid coalition, and it takes all your own powers of, um, persuasion, to convince them to lift a hand for the rest of Britain."

"One thing I promised them was help against the Anglii. Elmet is beset by them again. Would you travel so far to fight that battle, Percival?"

"Of course I would. I did once, didn't I? And I am here, am I not? Dane thinks we need to help Constantine win over the northern lords. If she can be queen in one such realm, it is a start. I wager none of those boneheaded kings could withstand her logic or her energy for long."

Galahad did laugh. "I've no doubt of that. You know, Percival, it's not a bad plan. And you say it is Dane's idea? Is she so eager to leave Gwynedd?"

"No, but she is eighteen and ready for marriage. I'd trust her with the reins of power in Strathclyde, Gorre, or Lothian before I'd trust the kings who rule there now."

"Who are her suitors?"

"Owaine is foremost among them. His first two wives died in childbed and he is looking for another. Alliance with Gwynedd would please him greatly. He is past forty, but still has life left in him. Valvan of Lothian is interested, unfortunately. I loathe him. My cousin Kastor is still unwed. He's said he'll come and take a look. Rydor of Rheged is my best hope. That's a handsome match to my mind. Rheged's not so far; we could still see each other from time to time. Rydor's still a young man and looking for a bride who can bring him something."

"I know one you have left out. Talorc of Elmet. A good man and a fine soldier."

"But he has a wife."

"No longer. He put her away when he discovered his sons had been fathered by the captain of his guard. He tells me now he believes she bedded half his army behind his back. He's still bitter about it and in no hurry to remarry, but he is a good man and a friend. Ask him to come along."

"Indeed? Then I will. It's my hope I can persuade them to return to Gwynedd with me and we can get this settled before the snow flies. They can make their offers, she will choose which suits her best, and in the spring she will be married." He gulped. "It's going to be awfully hard parting from Dane, but we've always known it had to happen. I'd be grateful for your company, Galahad. Stay the winter with us, if you can, but at least come back with me."

Galahad hesitated. "I will not be as welcome there as you expect."

"Dane has not forgiven herself for what she said to you that day and would give anything in her power to make amends. Please at least give her the chance to apologize. Once she leaves Gwynedd, who knows where she'll be?"

"Well, cousin, it has lately been in my mind to break with Constantine. I shall come. But not for the winter. I have stayed in one place too long. I prefer to be on the move."

Percival leaned forward and lowered his voice. "I ought to have asked before, but I was so full of my own news—did you see the sign?"

"What sign?"

Percival stared at him. "Have you given up the quest, then?"

Galahad felt heat rush to his face. "No . . . I don't know. Nothing's happened in the three years I've served Constantine. I've seen no sign."

"No tests?"

"Nothing."

Percival clapped a hand on his shoulder. "Then it's time to leave. The Saxons should be quiet for a few years after this defeat. Come to Gwynedd. We'd both be glad to have you for however long you can stay."

Galahad put down his winecup and rose. "It is for you alone that I go to Gwynedd again. And if I were not persuaded your sister's attention will be elsewhere, I would not go, even for you."

"For heaven's sake, Galahad, whatever happened between you?"

Galahad shrugged his cloak into place and faced his friend. "Let it be. I would rather forget it. Now let me pass, cousin. I have a longing to be out in the night air."

Out in the dark he breathed deeply and looked across the black expanse of emptiness toward the Giants' Dance. Too late now to seek that refuge. Talorc would be waiting at the inn, anxious at his absence. The others would be wondering, perhaps with lifting hopes, if he had left them for good. He realized suddenly that he had come to a fork in the road. One path led to Gwynedd, to the renewal of Percival's friendship, to the warmth and friction of social intercourse, and to the roiling stew of political alliance, the grubbing for land and power. The other path, the nearer path, led to the Giants' Dance, to solitude, to prayer and peace, and perhaps a return to his quest. He gazed at the Dance with an ache in his throat, but he had made Percival a promise. Slowly he turned and started on the long road back to the inn.

46 ✝ THE FISHER KING

On the way to Gwynedd, Percival's party stopped at the fortress of Caerleon, standing on a hill above the River Usk well inland from the Severn estuary. It had been a military fortress since the Romans rebuilt it and had been fortified before that time out of mind. Arthur had enlarged it and built a fine house there on the ruins of a villa. Here Percival and all his train were welcomed by Sir Lukan, the commander, who was delighted to have such armed strength around him. It was harvesttime, and the country roundabout had been beset by bandits who stole from the hard-working villagers and then seemed to vanish into the woods and fens. But now, with six kings visiting and all their retinues, *and* with the fearsome Sir Galahad as well, they might be able to get through the harvest in better shape than they had for years.

"Pray stay, my lords. Rest and refurbish your provisions. The country hereabouts is rich with game and waterfowl."

"We can't stay long," Percival replied, looking around with satisfaction at the orderliness of the compound, at the old barracks all in good repair, at the roadways new-laid with stone and the new thatch on the stable buildings. "We can't stay long, but we'd be more than happy to bide a while. You've done well, Sir Lukan. The place looks as it did in Arthur's day." This was the highest compliment one soldier could give another, and Sir Lukan bowed low.

While the northern kings were getting settled in their quarters, and their troops in the barracks, Percival pulled Galahad aside. His eyes danced and his whole body trembled with suppressed excitement. "Galahad, you must come with me tomorrow—early—on a secret journey. I have something wonderful to show you!"

"A journey? We just rode in."

"You will count it worth your while, I wager." Percival grinned. "But I will not tell you more ahead of time. That would spoil the surprise. We'll start at dawn."

"How far away is this wonder?"

"Half a day's ride up the Usk. If you balk, I shall go without you. Mark me, nothing can keep me from it."

Galahad looked at him closely. "You act as if you were off after a woman."

Percival blushed faintly. "I cannot tell you another word. If you want to know my secret, you must come with me."

Dawn broke through a rose mist that hugged the trees and lightly kissed the calm, slow-moving river. Dewy grasses soaked the horses' fetlocks as the young men rode along the bank in silence, listening to the early birdsong and the occasional splash of an unseen fish. The sun lifted, tinting the leaves orange and yellow; the day lightened; the land grew steeper and the going slow. Near midmorning they came to a swift-flowing tributary and turned to follow it upstream, picking their way through the tangled overgrowth with care, swords held ready. Nowadays bandits were always a danger off the best-traveled roads. The path grew steep and rocky and the roar of the tumbling river filled their ears.

Just when Galahad felt numbed from the beating sound, without warning the dense forest fell back and they rode out onto a grassy verge. In the middle of the river stood a castle on an island. Galahad's mouth went dry. He recognized it. Percival rode forward, but Galahad could see no bridge, nor any fording place. The river swept by, deep, swift, and silent, and the castle beckoned.

At the edge of the river, Percival turned in the saddle and waved him forward.

"How are we to cross?" Galahad cried. "The ferryman's not here!"

Percival stared at him. "How did you know there used to be a ferryman? They haven't kept a ferryman for years—too many bandits in the forest."

Galahad shook his head to clear it. "I don't know . . . I saw him once, I think—"

"Saw him! Then you have been here?"

"Yes. No. I don't know. What place is this, and how do we get across?"

"This is the home of Pelleas, King of the River Isles. When he dispensed with the ferry he built a bridge. But it is invisible, and can carry only one at a time. You must follow me carefully."

"What do you mean, invisible?"

"Don't excite yourself; it's not magic. He built it underwater. There is a path to the island, but you must be given the secret to know the way. Follow me, but follow me exactly. Your horse is not afraid of water?"

"Farouk? He's not afraid of anything. Lead on."

In single file the horses entered the flowing river. The current frothed and swirled about their legs, but they walked through the water knee-high on a zigzag path, heading first this way and then that, eventually climbing out on a gravel beach. Grooms appeared, saluted the men, threw blankets on the horses, and led them away. Percival turned to Galahad, his eyes shining. "A neat trick, is it not? Keeps the king's enemies away and his knights sober. Come on, I will take you in. We are expected."

"How is that? Did you send a message?"

"No need." Percival grinned. "I see you do not remember. Good King Pelleas has the dubious honor to be wed to an enchantress."

Galahad paled. "Oh no! Not—"

"Yes. You *do* remember. The Lady Niniane."

"By God, Percival, I'll have your hide for this!"

"You can't get back without me, cousin, so make the best of it while we're here. You won't regret it. This is Corbenic. You must know the legend: In this castle you will find your heart's desire."

Percival strode up the stone steps and rapped loudly upon the door. After a long moment it swung slowly open.

"Sir Percival!" the porter rasped. "Be welcome, my lord! And Sir Galahad, good day to you. The king and queen await your coming. My lords, follow me."

The porter was an old man with a bent back who leaned upon a staff. His wrinkled face was familiar, too.

"Thank you, Hector. It's good to see you." Percival clapped a hand upon the old man's back. "Is my lady well? Tell me now—I cannot bear the waiting!"

Hector grinned, showing gums. "Aye, my lord. Nothing ails a maid her age but loneliness. She'll be well enough presently, I'll be bound."

Percival laughed and followed him into the darkness of the corridor beyond. Galahad hesitated, looking around the hallway, up into the rafters, back out the door. It was all just as he had dreamed it. He knew the walls, the stones, the corridor; he knew the turns and steps and bridges; he knew the labyrinthine path to the hall of the Fisher King. He did not need to follow Percival and the porter. His heart began to thud as excitement coursed through him. For the first time in years he began to hope.

"Come on, Galahad, hurry up. The way twists and turns. You'll get lost if you don't follow closely."

Galahad smiled to himself. "Not even blindfolded."

They came at last to a pair of gilded doors. Hector stopped, pushed them open, and bowed low. "Sir Percival and Sir Galahad."

Within, it was just as Galahad remembered: a cavernous hall with the rafters lost in darkness, a long table set upon a dais, a white cloth laid upon the table, and candles everywhere. King Pelleas and his lady rose to greet them. Galahad recognized the man at once, the silver hair and beard, the blue-green eyes, the left arm hanging lifeless in its sling.

"Sir Galahad, how good of you to visit us." Tall, dark, still lovely, the enchantress Niniane looked at him with eyes that read his soul.

Galahad struggled to mask his face in the hope of deflecting that powerful gaze. He bowed politely. "Lady Niniane."

The knowing eyes narrowed in amusement and Niniane smiled. "I remember well last time we met. I am afraid the memory is not pleasant to you."

Under the pressure of her gaze Galahad forced his lips to move. "Nor to you."

Her smile saddened. "No fault of yours, my lord; you were the Harbinger of Doom. You trailed behind you the first dark shadows of Camlann. Morgaine and I saw them hunched like vultures on your shoulders. . . . But let us not talk now about such great grief. Tell us instead about the battle at the Giants' Dance—who was killed and who survived, and how Britain stands."

Galahad stared at her blankly. This was the woman who had inherited Merlin's powers—how could she not know these things already?

"Do not chide me, sir," she said gently, laying a hand upon his arm, "for as my lord Merlin bequeathed to me, so did I bequeath my gifts to the Lady Morgaine. With Arthur died my power. I know no more of events than you choose to tell me."

With more relief than regret, Galahad joined Percival and Pelleas at the table. Servants brought them cool water in silver cups, bowls of fruit fresh from the vine, and loaves of new-baked bread. While they ate, Percival eagerly recounted everything that had passed upon the Great Plain, naming the princes who had fought, and with how many soldiers, using cups and bowls to draw Pelleas a map of the battlefield and demonstrate the armies' dispositions. The two kings talked about terrain and battle strategy while Niniane gazed covertly at Galahad.

For three long years she had held hard to her patience and waited for the next chance to draw Galahad to her. But Constantine, that arrogant Cornish maggot, had not only robbed her of success three years before, but had kept the Breton busy fighting Saxons in the east, south, and north, far from the borders of Wales. As time passed and the reaches of her power shrank until she was barely able to see or summon beyond the lands Pelleas controlled—a bitter gall, indeed, for a woman who had once had all Britain at her command—she had paced hour by hour in a frenzy of frustration. Lately even her crystal had gone blank and quiet. She knew the gods did not wait forever. She knew that time was running out. And now, today, with hope gone, with ashes for memory, and without so much as a breath of omen, here the man was on her very doorstep. She managed to keep the excitement from her face but could not still the frantic racing of her heart. Here he was, a gift of the Goddess, and she must be ready—today, now—for her last act of power, if she could summon it. The future of Britain lay again in her hands.

Suddenly Percival broke off in midsentence. His face flushed and then instantly paled. Galahad turned to follow his glance. A maiden stood in the doorway, breathless from exertion, a sheaf of bright chrysanthemums in her arms. Her skin shone white as alabaster, her hair as black as a raven's wing. Her rosy lips parted in a delighted smile.

"My lord Percival!"

Percival leaped to his feet, upending his water cup. "Blodwyn!"

She made him a pretty curtsy and Percival glanced sideways at Galahad, his face aglow. When he pressed her fingers to his lips, he lingered, bending toward her, and whispered something. He was rewarded with a shy smile. She wore a necklace of tiny, polished seashells and earrings of mother-of-pearl. Her gown was the color of the waters that passed outside her door: blue-green and gray, ever changing in the dappled light.

"Galahad," Percival said softly, "this is Princess Guinblodwyn. In Welsh that means 'white flower.' Is she not aptly named? She is the girl I have seen in my dreams ever since Avalon—I knew her at once. We have been betrothed since midsummer."

Galahad bowed low to hide his face. He had seen her in his dreams, too, carrying the Grail! "You have kept your secret well, cousin. And you have an eye for beauty. My congratulations."

The girl dimpled charmingly. "You did not tell me your cousin was so handsome, Percival," she murmured.

Percival eyed him warily. "I allow that he's grown. But he doesn't smile—he can't be handsome."

"Why, then, you are blind."

"Put it, rather, that I have eyes only for you."

She smiled and blushed and Galahad politely looked away. The girl was pretty enough, and certainly highborn; but he ached for the old days—how long ago they seemed!—when he and Percival had sworn brotherhood together and had no use for women. And yet, this was not just any woman, if dreams held true.

Niniane's finger brushed against his hand. "Come, my lord. Accompany us for a moment. These two would cherish a moment alone, and Pelleas and I have something to show you."

Obediently, Galahad followed her out the door and down a short hall, Pelleas behind him. Niniane led him to a kind of porch built on stilts over the river which encircled a deep pool of still water. She leaned against the railing and stared down into the glimmering depths, while silent Pelleas stood at Galahad's side.

"I see you are wounded in your shoulder," Galahad began, pressured by the awkward silence into saying the first thing that came into his head. "In what battle did you fight?"

"In all of Arthur's battles," Pelleas replied gravely. "But this wound I received at his last. Camlann."

"Camlann! Why, that was full seven years ago! Is it not yet healed?"

"No," Pelleas said lightly. "It may never be whole. Niniane tells me it is beyond her power to heal."

Galahad glanced in amazement at Niniane, who straightened defensively.

"I told you I relinquished my powers to Morgaine." Then her voice softened. "It is a wound of the spirit as much as of the flesh. He was cut that day by the sword that killed Arthur. And when the life went out of Britain, the life left his arm. He will not be whole until . . ." She paused, holding his eyes.

Galahad found that he could not breathe. "Until?"

Ninane's gaze slid back to the water and her pupils widened. Her voice wavered on the edge of sound. "Until Britain is whole. Until Arthur comes again."

Galahad trembled and held hard to the railing. "Arthur is dead."

Niniane's eyes fluttered closed. In the complete stillness the only sound was the wayward chuckle of the river passing. Niniane's whisper floated across the deep eddy between them. "Not dead. Sleeping."

"That's impossible," Galahad said. "I saw him. I buried him. You yourself just now admitted he was killed."

Without speaking she beckoned him forward and his feet moved. She pointed down into the pool and his head bowed. Deep in the green depths he saw a great golden stone, dim and wavering at the bottom of the pool. *Watch.* The command, unspoken, claimed him and he obeyed. Gradually the great stone grew brighter, as though lit from within, although Galahad could perceive no ray of sun, no source of light, through the dark, shifting depths. As it brightened the unevenness of its surface began to emerge, lines and curves with shadows thrown into deep relief. It began to take on the image of a human face. Galahad bit his lip to still the sob that rose from the center of his being. The face that seemed to rise through the light to greet him was a well-loved face, strong-featured and warm, with a smile of welcome on the lips and a laugh already forming in the wise, brown eyes. His heart went out to greet it. *Arthur! My lord King!*

Close in his ear he heard the unvoiced words: *Look for me, Galahad. I am coming. Britain's future lies in my hands. I will return.*

Speechless, Galahad gazed into the pool as the face receded and the light slowly died. When Niniane touched his arm he jumped. His joints were stiff from straining and his face was wet with tears. She said nothing, but her wide, dark eyes soothed him, balm on a burn.

"Is it true?" he croaked.

Niniane nodded imperceptibly.

He cleared his throat. "How? How can I know this vision is real and not just a trick of your magic?"

She smiled briefly. "The line between life and death is not so absolute as you Christians believe. And even Christians believe it can be bridged. Did not your suffering God rise from his burial place?" Her eyes slid past him to the river. "I know several who have returned from the Otherworld. Merlin himself did, if you remember, to safeguard the rest of Arthur's reign. Wherever Arthur is, he speaks to me and he speaks to others. Ask your father, when you see him, if he has not heard his voice."

She turned to link her arm through Pelleas's. "You are the only one, Galahad, who can bring about the High King's transformation. Without you he will never be seen again by living eyes."

"Me?" Galahad turned white. "How?"

"Only you can find what is lost. Only you can restore him and so preserve us all."

Restore. Preserve. His eyes closed. He did not need to ask her what she meant.

Her lovely, low voice washed over him in a gentle wave. "When all three are in his keeping—the Vanquisher, the Preserver, the Restorer— Arthur will return. It was foretold long, long ago. Now the time is upon us."

She exhaled slowly and Galahad opened his eyes. Niniane seemed to glow with an ethereal light, a shining skin. The slender arm that stretched forth to touch the coming future wavered in his vision, like a staff underwater. "Find them, Galahad. I will give you the key. Attend me."

His heart racing, unable to move or speak, Galahad listened.

"The Vanquisher lies dark and deep; the Restorer and the Preserver lie in brilliants. Find them, Galahad, these otherworldly treasures. Then will Pendragon return to us as Merlin foretold it. The once and future King."

Galahad trembled. "What brilliance? Where? You speak in riddles— how can I understand you?"

"Take heart, Galahad, and believe. This is your destiny."

Her voice sank to a whisper that nonetheless reverberated over the sound of the river's passing. "Go, and seek the Blessed Gifts for Arthur, for all of us. My power is waning fast. Had you come to me three years ago— But let be. Trust Morgaine for the Sword. Direct your single-eyed strength to finding the Grail and Spear. Time is running down and you have not much left."

She read the question in his white, pinched face and tried to smile. "Follow your heart. That is the key. You are being carefully forged in a withering fire and your aim will be true. Follow your heart and you cannot go astray."

Pelleas tugged at her arm. "Take care, my dear. Do not say more than is permitted."

Without another word she turned, soundlessly, and accompanied her husband inside.

Galahad stood by the pool for a long time after they had gone, staring into the shadowy depths. At dusk he turned away. His head ached and his joints had stiffened in the cool damp until he moved like an old man. Since Niniane's departure all he had seen in the pool was a deep, slow swirl of cold green water, with nothing at the bottom but hope.

47 ⊕ THE BRIDE OF GWYNEDD

G alahad stood by the narrow window and stared sullenly out at the darkening hills of Gwynedd. Behind him the murmur of voices engaged in casual talk washed back and forth, constant and repetitive, meaningless and dull. They had lit the torches but it was not really dark. The hills still burned gold in the failing light, aglow in their autumn glory; the evening mists had yet to creep up from the sea; the stars were not yet out. He wished he were out fishing in the hill ponds, not milling around in aimless waiting. At this time of day the trout were just rising for flies.

Somewhere a shepherd's pipe played off-key. Queen Anet's voice sounded suddenly behind him. "Where is Sir Galahad? Have you seen him, Percival?" He hunched closer to the window, wishing suddenly he were anywhere else in the known world but Gwynedd. It was all right for the host of kings who waited for the appearance of Percival's sister—they had come for a purpose and had a prospect to amuse them—but what was *he* doing here? He ought to be long away. Since he had seen in Niniane's pool the sign he had so long awaited, he was eager to be off on the last stretch of his quest. The end was near, Niniane had said, and there was not much time. However, he owed Percival obedience to his promise. Without Percival he would never have found Corbenic. Or a future.

He stood with his back to the room, watching the night draw down, and thought again about Niniane's words. In the years he had fought for Constantine, run his errands, led his troops, won skirmish after skirmish, and saved Britain herself in battle after battle, he had learned firsthand about the Saxon strength. He knew that Britons fought in a losing cause. Every year the Saxons grew stronger and more numerous. Every year the strength of Britons waned. Unless they united as they had under Arthur, defeat was inevitable. It was only a matter of time unless—and here his spirit stirred and lifted—unless Arthur himself should truly come again. He tried to still the eager beating of his heart. It was hard not to be impatient. He was oppressed by the need for hurry.

"Well, well, what a brown study, my lord Galahad!" a voice said at his shoulder. He turned to find Owaine, King of Gorre, standing beside him, his breath already sour with mead. "What do you see out there in the dark?"

"Nothing, my lord."

"This wench we come to inspect is your cousin, is she not?"

"If by that you mean the Princess of Gwynedd, she is."

"Come now, no offense. You will learn in time all women are wenches. Do you have a high opinion of her? What is she like?"

"My lord, I knew her only in childhood. I have no idea what she is like now."

"Is she greedy? Does she hunger for a man's power? Your grandmother Alyse was such a one. I'm not looking to marry a rival for my throne."

"Queen Alyse was a wise woman."

"And raised two bold, headstrong females—your mother and the High Queen Guinevere. I do not want another such."

"If my lord wants a sheep for a wife"—Galahad bristled—"you should look outside in the pens."

But Owaine only laughed and slapped him on the back. "You endorse her, I see. Good, that is all I wished to know. I assure you, if the wench is ripe for bedding I am content. I am past forty with three daughters. It is time to get myself an heir."

Galahad wrinkled his nose as Owaine moved off. Dane would get what she deserved if she chose him.

"Something smell bad?" Talorc asked, coming up. "Why do you hide here by the window when the girl is due down any minute? It won't save you from Owaine's attentions."

"Or yours," Galahad replied with a light smile.

Talorc grinned. "As you see. You've been so solemn ever since we came down from the mountains. Did Percival twist your arm to get you here?"

"I came of my will. His family are my kin."

Talorc grunted. "You don't act like it. You behave as if they all were poisonous vipers. Tell me the truth about this woman, your cousin. Has she a head on her shoulders? Can she think for herself? Has she courage?"

Galahad raised an eyebrow. "Yes on all counts, if she is as she was. You are truly interested, Talorc? Or just curious? I thought you had had enough of women."

"That was my pride speaking. I have not your joy in abstinence, Galahad. I need a wife, but I do not want a vain or silly one. I want a companion. And a queen."

"Well," Galahad said slowly, "you have come to the right place."

"I am glad to hear it."

"Remember that Percival has foolishly placed the choice in her own hands. It will not be as simple as you think."

Talorc smiled. "Oh, I don't mind courtship. I may not be as rich as Owaine, or be able to offer a kingdom as large as Rydor's or Kastor's or Valvan's, but I have something none of the rest of them have—respect for the sex. And if she is anything like her grandmother, I do not worry about my competition."

"I wish you well, then."

Talorc turned away as a group of women appeared on the landing, and the men crowded around the bottom of the stairs. Galahad returned to the window. Dusk had fallen and the sea mist had begun to weave its way through the woods and meadows. In the deepening sky the first stars blazed overhead.

He wondered if he had told Talorc the truth. He had not seen the girl in seven years, and girls at eleven bore little resemblance to what they would become at eighteen. Perhaps she had grown meek and silly; perhaps her bold nature had turned domineering. Most likely she had turned into a proper harpy, but it was also possible her tongue had lost its sting. He grimaced. He would never forget the words that had driven him out of Gwynedd: *What would you call a woman who conspired to have her cousin raped? What would you call a woman who tried to trick the High King to her bed? She was false!* He shuddered. Nor would he forget her parting curses: *May your arrogance consume you, may your road meander! May you follow in your father's footsteps and love a woman you cannot in honor have!* It had been a mistake to come. He never should have promised Percival. He should have turned the other way when he heard his cousin's voice, and spent the night under the Giants' Dance.

Laughter and the sound of voices raised in celebration interrupted his thoughts and he turned. Dane must have made her entrance at last. All the lords clustered about Percival and Peredur, bowing low as they were introduced. Galahad glanced toward the great hall, where candles blazed and servants busily piled food upon the tables. No doubt the feast would last all night, with more eating and drinking and noise than he could stomach. At least Percival had hired an excellent bard. He had heard Hawath before at Camelot; the man knew every tale ever told in Britain, and everyone's lineage back to Druid days. He would end, as he always did, with the Lay of Arthur, and bring tears to everyone's eyes. It would be worth whatever else was ahead to hear him.

The press of people swept forward and engulfed him. "Galahad! There you are!" Someone grabbed his arm and swung him around. Without warning he found himself face-to-face with the glowing girl on Percival's arm. Around him the light and bustle faded into haze; in utter silence time paused. And stopped.

She was a beauty. She had skin like new cream, warm chestnut curls that strayed from their pins like a living thing resisting capture, and large gray eyes flecked with devilish green. As she stared up at him her lips parted, she caught her breath, and a slow blush rose from her throat to grace her cheeks.

"Can it be . . . Galahad? Cousin, is it really you?" She made him a low reverence; another of her chestnut curls came loose, and fell in a graceful curve across the breast of her gown. "My lord, I am honored by your coming."

Awkwardly, he put out a hand and raised her, but the words of greeting dried upon his tongue. She rescued him. "I have so much to say to you, cousin, now that you are here. But you . . . I'd not have known you, but for your badge."

"Nor I you."

She smiled. "Girls change more with time. I don't know why. Sit near me at dinner, Galahad, if you will. I would be honored."

He could not take his eyes from her. "Well, I . . ." The heat rose to his face and he bowed to hide it. "As you will."

Percival led her away. Galahad drew breath and the noise and light suddenly returned. The lords swept by him in her wake, following her into the feasting hall. Galahad stood rooted to the floor. His legs would not obey him and his brow was damp with sweat. He looked around swiftly and found Talorc smiling at him.

"Come, Galahad. Hold hard. We must go into dinner."

"No, I . . . I think I'd better not—"

Talorc laughed softly and took his arm. "You must, you know. You can't insult these good people. They're your kin. Besides, the lady has reserved you a seat at her side. Be brave, lad. Pretend you are facing Saxons."

Percival raised a toast and all the kings in their turn raised others, each one praising the charms of the princess Dandrane, each one waxing more eloquent than his neighbor on her eyes, her hair, her figure, her lovely smile. Galahad, seated at her side, did not detect a single blush. He was relieved to see she recognized this praise as the opening gambit in the courtship competition and did not attach truth to the words, although to himself he admitted that their praise hardly did her justice.

Throughout the long feast that followed, the lords vied for her attention, each one working to outdo his neighbor in the size of his boast, the cleverness of his jest, the magnitude of his compliments. Only Galahad sat silent, his eyes on his plate, unable to eat a mouthful, unable to speak a word. Across the table, Talorc watched him and secretly smiled.

Dane shone as the center of attention. She could match any man wit for wit and wasted no time in letting her suitors see what manner of woman she was. And as far as Galahad could tell, they relished the challenge. Even Valvan, the weasel-faced king of Lothian, could not help smirking whenever he looked at Dane. And Percival, a victorious king on his first night home, who was, after all, the host of this celebration, was dimmed to nothingness beside her brilliance. He seemed content to listen as the kings praised her beauty and toasted her good fortune. Like his guests, he sat filled with admiration and basked in the glow of excitement she shed around her.

Once or twice she found a moment to speak to Galahad. "I have heard much of your doings, cousin. They call you the Savior of Britain, which is a title only Arthur himself used to bear."

Galahad flushed and looked away. "I was a cavalry commander under Constantine, no more. I've done what I promised him I would do. I have finished with him now. He is weak and corrupt. There is no honor in serving him. He can do nothing for Britain but postpone her death."

"Well, I am all for that postponement. But what is our future then?"

"Our future blows in the wind, as the bards say. There is a hope—a small hope—we may regain what we had under Arthur."

Dane's eyes shone. "That is what I wanted to hear you say! How will we achieve this, except through unity?"

Galahad met her eyes. "Yes. Unity is the only way."

Dane regarded him closely. "And now that you have left Constantine's service, how will you work toward unity? By going home to enlist Lancelot's support?"

Galahad looked away. "Certainly not."

Dane hesitated. "Are you still at odds with him?"

"We have little to say to each other."

She reached out and covered his hand with hers. "Cousin, I beg you will let me apologize for my behavior the last time we met. I am aghast at the things I said. I was a very young and very stupid girl. That is all I can say in my defense. It was unpardonable."

Galahad gazed at her. In the lamplight her eyes shone as green as the sea. "You were never stupid."

"I was forward and spoke of things that were none of my concern, and of which I'd heard only rumors. I don't blame you for being offended. I beg your forgiveness."

"I forgive you. What you said about my mother was . . . not without foundation."

She exhaled in relief and let go of his hand. "Thank you. You are very gracious to say so. Time has improved us both, I think. But if you do not serve Constantine or Lancelot, whom do you serve?"

Galahad paused. He longed to tell her about the Grail, about Niniane's promise that Arthur would return, about how the future of Britain lay in his own hands. But his lips would barely move. "I serve no one now."

Her eyes narrowed in laughter. "Still looking for Macsen's Treasure?" He frowned at her and she colored charmingly. "There are stories about you and your quest all over Britain. You will be a legend soon."

"Not if I don't find it."

"Galahad . . ." He looked up and found her clear eyes searching his. A wayward strand of hair curled softly against her cheek. To his own astonishment his hand had actually lifted to brush it away, when the hall erupted in cheering. Hawath had arrived.

Percival rose. "My ladies and my lords! We are here to celebrate the coming nuptials of my sister, the consolidation of all Wales with your northern federation, and the crowning of a new queen among the men of the north. Within the month, I promise you, my sister, Dandrane, shall choose a husband from the host here assembled." The kings rose and bowed, their companions cheered and stomped their boots upon the floor, crying, "Dandrane! Dandrane! Long live Gwynedd!" Percival bowed. "I thank you. I thank you all," he shouted above the din. "In honor of the event, let us hear again the songs we heard in our youth, when Britain was united under one, strong king. I give you Hawath."

Not until Hawath took his seat and bent his ear to tune his harp did the noise die down. The bard waited until all eyes were upon him, bent his head toward Dane, and, with a knowing smile, gave them the old tale about an ancient beauty men had died for: a queen who was abducted by a love-struck foreign prince and whose countrymen put to sea in a thousand ships to get her back, waging a war that lasted a decade and decimated both royal houses.

Fighting Saxons was a noble calling, but Galahad could not imagine waging war over a woman. Agamemnon could not have been a very good king. Arthur would never have done such a foolish thing, even for Guinevere. He looked sidelong at Dane and was surprised to find her smooth forehead puckered in a frown. But Percival sat dreamy-eyed, stirred to his soul, and the other lords listened with rapt attention.

Dane glanced his way suddenly, caught him watching her, and wrinkled her nose. When the bard's last note faded and the men called out their acclamations and stomped their feet, she leaned toward him and whispered, "Arthur was worth a thousand Agamemnons, don't you think? To destroy your royal house and all the noble youth! And for what? A woman who had lived ten years with a foreign prince? If she'd had any sense of honor, she'd have killed herself. I'd never have gone after her if I were king!"

"That is just what I was thinking. But Percival would. Look at his face."

The smile she flashed at him seemed to strike him in the center of his chest and stop his breathing. "Ah, but the young fool's in love. And I hear you have met her, Blodwyn the beautiful, Blodwyn the innocent, Blodwyn the flower of earthly delight. Quick, while the bard takes his refreshment, tell me, did you like her?"

"Not much."

Although nothing in her expression changed, he sensed that she was pleased. "Pray tell me why not. Come, I will keep every word a secret, but tell me."

Galahad shrugged. "She was young and foolish. You know. The way girls are."

This time he had pleased her greatly. "Thank you. I have thought it must be so, from things Val has told me. But he is so smitten he does not see it. Don't worry, I would never try to come between them. But it helps me to know this—she will be queen here within the year, and I must do what I can to organize things so she can run them, so Val can think her brilliant and the scales will never fall from his eyes."

"That is not what I thought you were going to say."

Her eyes mocked him gently. "You thought I would behave like a jealous fishwife and wish her to fail? Galahad, you have a low opinion of women."

"But she will replace you in your brother's eyes."

"Never. You don't understand. He is more than my brother; he is my other half. How could I treat him so and live with myself?"

The bard struck a new chord and Dane sat up straighter. "I hope he gives us one of Merlin's tales," she whispered. "My favorite is 'The Once and Future King.' "

Galahad caught his breath. There it was again, as clear as a clarion call: the beckoning of his destiny. He seemed to see the Grail already in his mind's eye, shining like a sacred relic, a treasure more precious than all the gold in Rome, for it would summon Arthur from his sleep and return the King to Britain in the hour of her need. As the liquid notes filled the hall and the bard's clear voice rolled past his ears in flowing phrases, Galahad's heart filled with longing. It was time to seek what only he could find. He could not break his promise to Percival to stay for Dane's betrothal, but at month's end he would leave Gwynedd and all his obligations. He would set out and find the Grail and Spear that, with the Sword, would bring Arthur back to Britain.

The month passed slowly. He tried as best he could to stay out of everyone's way. When they went hunting, he went fishing; when they competed in swordplay in the castle courtyard, he rode out. He came always last to dinner so he could take the farthest seat. He was always first up in the morning and gone while they were still at breakfast. Talorc of Elmet took note and laughed. Percival, however, was annoyed. He complained to Galahad that his behavior bore the marks of rudeness. Did he intend to make Dane weep at night, thinking she had offended him again? With an air of resignation, Galahad joined the others in their daily games, hunts, and feasting, but he began to detest the suitors' company. Even Dane seemed to enjoy their attention less and less as time passed. Gradually she grew pale and silent, her buoyant humor fading into melancholy smiles. The few times Galahad came upon her unawares she flushed to the roots of her hair, lowered her eyes, and could hardly speak a coherent sentence. He wondered at the change in her—she had never been at a loss for words before. He put this down to her suffering at the thought of leaving Gwynedd, but when he voiced this observation to Talorc, the King of Elmet hooted. "Think that if you like, my lord. She is suffering, certainly. But I wager it has nothing to do with Gwynedd."

"What, then?"

Talorc smiled sideways at him. "If you don't know, it is not my place to tell you. You will find out soon enough."

One night after dinner, when the lords and their companions were drinking and singing lewd songs in the hall, Galahad stood before a log fire in the small chamber where the family often gathered for privacy. Anet sat on a cushioned bench, bending over her needlework. Peredur reclined on a couch with a tankard of mead. He smacked his lips and grinned up at Galahad.

"Well, nephew, how do you think it's going? She has barely a week left to make her choice. Which one of 'em do you s'pose she fancies?"

Galahad shrugged unhappily. "I'm sure I've no idea, my lord."

Peredur laughed. "And I'll wager you a king's ransom, neither does she! She's sorry now she sent for them."

"Do be still, Peredur," Anet said crossly. "You speak in ignorance."

"Do I, madam? Then tell me what you think. Young, blind Percival thinks it's all going swimmingly. He dreams of alliance with Rheged or Gorre. His ambition has clouded his perception."

Anet put down her needlework and sighed. "I agree with you there."

"Surely, Galahad, *you* must have formed some opinion." Peredur smiled up at him. "You've dogged her heels these last weeks. Tell us, does she favor one of them above the others?"

"I'm sure I couldn't say," Galahad replied stiffly. "She seems to me to be equally attentive to all."

"Well, she's not a fool," Peredur asserted, draining his tankard and thumping it on the floor to attract the servant's attention. "She'll keep them hanging, to see what they will offer. Owaine's made the handsomest offer to date, I hear."

"Your ears, sir," Galahad said evenly, fighting a sudden urge to cuff his uncle, "have heard a great deal more than mine."

"Be still, both of you," Queen Anet urged, taking up her work and whipping her needle through the silken cloth. "There will be no wedding of any sort if we don't complete the bride gift. We've only five months, and there are mountains left to do." She looked up suddenly. "Besides, you are wrong, Peredur. She has made her choice. She has fallen in love with one of them, though she hides it well."

Sweat broke on Galahad's brow.

"Indeed?" Peredur cried. "Then tell us, who will it be? I'll place a wager on it tonight and be a rich man next week!"

Anet smiled secretly and shook her head. "Save your gold. It is Dane's secret and Dane shall be the one to tell it. Not I."

"Do you really know, then? Anet, you amaze me," Peredur began, when the door opened and Percival strode into the room.

"Good evening, Mother, Uncle—Galahad, you are pale. Have a pull at the wineskin and steady yourself. I've just come from hall—Lothian has upped his offer. So has Strathclyde. By God, my sister is a genius! In a week's time we shall double our cattle and our gold!"

Anet bent over her stitching. "Perhaps you are right, son. But bear in mind that you might be wrong."

"How so, Mother? I am with them every day."

"I fear you see what you want to see and nothing else."

"Nonsense," Percival muttered, "you are the one who always sees clouds on a sunny day. Anything Dane plans, goes well."

"Mmm," Anet agreed, "provided she does not change her mind."

Percival stared at her in bewilderment; slowly his features hardened. "She would not dare. Not now. Not after this. She would not betray her kingdom and make her brother look a fool."

Anet looked at him kindly, and put aside her work. "Percival, you are a generous man and you have done well to leave the choice to her. But remember, when the time comes, that it is her choice and not yours."

Percival shrugged. "I have not forgotten. Whichever of them she chooses, I am content. Even the lowest offer is a handsome one."

Anet said nothing, but glanced up at Galahad with compassion in her eyes.

"Excuse me," Galahad rasped, bowing quickly, "but I must have some air." He pushed past Percival. "Good night."

Percival stared after him. "What's gotten into him? Have you been talking about Lancelot?"

"Not likely." Peredur grunted, gulping his mead. "He's an odd duck, that's all."

But Anet, her eyes on the flames, smiled secretly.

Out in the cool, clean air, Galahad strode about the castle grounds, his hands clasped in an iron grip behind his back, his long strides eating up the ground. They were mad; they were *all* mad, the ignorant, mead-besotted uncle, the prying mother, the bully of a brother! Why couldn't they leave the girl alone? God in Heaven, wasn't it enough that she had offered to sacrifice her future for them? Must they count her value in pieces of gold behind her back? Had they no feeling, no appreciation for her suffering? Just the *thought* of her wedded to one of those aging, ox-faced, northern half-wits was enough to freeze the blood! Were they really going to let her throw herself away and lift no hand to stop it—nay, but encourage her to choose the highest bidder, by God, like a beast at the market fair?

He swung through a grove of trees and ducked under a trellis. The garden was dark, but the half moon hung above sleeping trees and he could see well enough to avoid the beds, pruned and banked for the winter. He strode back and forth across the dead lawn, his breath leaving a spidery trail on the cold night air. Only a week until he was free of this—he could endure it no longer. He did not care whom she chose. He wished it were over and done with, and long behind him. He wished he had never come. He would rather renew his service to Constantine than spend another hour in Gwynedd.

Suddenly he heard a noise from the far end of the garden: a shuffling, a gasp, and a loud slap.

"I'll not take that from any lass!" came a man's angry grumble, and then a woman's muffled cry, cut short. Galahad whirled. In a recessed bower he saw two dim forms, locked in a struggle. A soldier had a woman by the hair, her arms pinned and his mouth on hers. Even as he watched the man recoiled, blood streaming from his lips.

"You filthy bitch!" he bellowed. "You bit me!"

The woman wrested free and launched a well-aimed kick at her attacker's groin. But he saw it coming and half spun away, grunting as the blow landed across his thigh. He was on her then, felling her with a heavy swipe of his fist, pinning her with the weight of his body as he tried to force her kicking legs apart.

"You little whore! I'll make you pay for that!"

"Bastard!" the woman shrieked. "I'll see you dead first!"

Galahad's sword whipped from its scabbard, his legs pounded across the lawn, his blade lay trembling against the attacker's neck before his mind could register more than that it was Dane's voice.

"Get off her." The command, cold and inhuman, seemed to come from the chilling shadows, not from his throat.

The man backed away and rose, turning to face him. "Well, well. Young Galahad, the firebrand. Put your weapon down; I've not harmed her."

"Valvan!"

"In the flesh," returned the King of Lothian, straightening his tunic. "What are you doing here, virgin? Spying on me?"

Galahad could not speak. He fought to keep his gaze from the girl sprawled on the grass. His whole body trembled with the effort, but the

hand that held his sword to Valvan's throat was cold, steady, oddly disconnected from his roiling thoughts.

Valvan's small eyes narrowed and he laughed. "Put your blade down.
This is no concern of yours. It's hardly a thing a virgin could understand—
we had an assignation. But she had a change of heart."

"Lying snake!" The hiss came out of the darkness, a shadow flew past
him, and the girl flung herself at Valvan, oblivious of the sword, her nails
striking for his eyes. Valvan raised an arm to fend her off; the nails missed
and drew blood on his face and neck instead. "Kill him!" It was more a sob
than a scream. "Kill him! Why do you wait?"

Galahad reached for her, took her by the waist, and drew her up against
him. She shook violently and struggled to free herself, but her strength
had gone.

"Leave him to me."

"He sent a page to me saying Percival awaited me in the garden . . . I
didn't know . . . God, Galahad! I'd never have come down if I'd known it
was him!"

He pressed her shivering body closer to his warmth. "Leave him to me.
I will avenge you."

Valvan backed until he was pressed against the bower. "You dare not
kill me, Galahad—neither your cousin nor your sweetheart will live to see
the morning!"

"No," Galahad agreed evenly, "I will not kill you. But I will give you
something to remember me by."

Valvan's eyes widened. "I meant no harm. You must believe me. The
lady is beautiful, and I knew well she would never choose me."

"So you thought to force her choice? You contemptible dog."

The bright sword point moved slowly in the gloom, an inch from Valvan's body. Valvan watched breathlessly as it descended. He clapped his
hands to his groin. "Not my manhood!"

"No," retorted Galahad. "Your face."

Before the man could move, Galahad's sword tip flicked upward and
sliced a narrow bloody stripe across each cheek, from lip to eye, and slid
soundlessly home to its sheath.

"Now let's see what maiden will have you. If you wish to revenge yourself, Valvan, you have only to name the day. I will be waiting."

But Valvan had had enough. Pressing his sleeve to his face, he whirled
and fled.

Galahad looked down at Dane. "Will that do? He is marked for life."

In the moonlight she had lost her vibrant color. Her face looked
deathly pale against her halo of wild hair. "Why didn't you kill him?"

Gently, Galahad raised a finger to her glistening cheeks and wiped away her tears. "Because it would have meant war. Britain cannot afford it. That is why you and Percival invited these ruffians here, to unite for common strength. But you need fear him no longer. I wager he'll be gone before morning so he need not explain his scars to Percival."

"I'd have killed him before I let him force me to marriage!"

Galahad's arm tightened around her. "I'd never have let you marry such a brute. Not while there's breath in my body."

They gazed at each other. Then Dane lowered her eyes and looked away. Coming to himself, Galahad loosed his arm and backed away a step.

"Thank you, cousin," she whispered. "Once you were Percival's right arm and tonight you were mine. We both owe you more than we can repay." She made him a quick reverence and fled from the garden.

Galahad stood beneath the singing stars and watched her go.

48 ✠ THE CHOICE

The last day of November finally dawned. A great feast was in the making; the cooks had been busy for days at the stewpots and bread ovens, the chamberlains sweated with brooms and dusters, and servants lugged from the cellars great vats of mead. The lords put on their finery. The women shook out their best gowns. Hawath the bard rehearsed the recitation of the long list of heroes of Gwynedd, whose ancient lineages ran back into the depths of time. No one regretted Valvan's absence; his sudden departure gave hope to all the others. But when Percival approached Galahad he found his cousin in a surly mood.

"I'm leaving tomorrow. I've stayed too long."

"What! Tomorrow? Why, the celebration will last for another week!"

"I'm in no mood for celebration."

Early in the evening Galahad packed his bedroll and took it down to the stable. His stallion, rested and impatient, whinnied at his approach. Galahad stroked the silken coat and rested his face against the horse's warm neck. "Rouk, old boy, we set off again at first light. We've a quest before us now, and neither Constantine's soldiers nor wandering dwarves nor promises to cousins will keep us from it. We shall get out of this wretched country and back into the open air. Ah, Rouk, I've not slept a solid hour this week past. You must take me away, boy, as soon as she throws herself to the swine she chooses, for I shall not survive if you do not."

As dusk fell and the servants lit the oil lamps, Galahad stood at his window, formally dressed in his best dark blue tunic with his badge at his shoulder, ready for the feast. He had steeled himself, he thought, to endure anything. Then footsteps thundered up the stairs and Percival flung himself into the room.

"Galahad! Galahad! We are undone! Gwynedd is ruined!"

"Calm yourself, cousin. What has happened?"

"A disaster—a catastrophe! You must help us!"

"I will if I can. You don't need to ask. But what is the matter?"

"My sister has disappeared!"

Galahad stared blankly at him.

"She has vanished! Gone! Disappeared! Into thin air, it seems. No one saw her go. One minute she was trying on her gown and baubles for her hair, and the next she was gone! I tell you, I will wring her neck with my own hands if I catch her, unless some horrible misfortune has befallen, and she is dead already!" He pulled at his hair in distraction. "Oh, ye gods, I am beside myself! This is the long-awaited night—I cannot keep them waiting another day."

Galahad came forward and took Percival's arm. "Be calm. If she was here recently, she can't have gone far. Have you searched the castle? From top to bottom?"

Percival nodded miserably. "Oh, yes, we did that first. My mother has had all her women at it. When we found her horse gone from the stable, Mother said to come and ask you." Percival threw him a quizzical look, then took another pull at his hair and paced back and forth. "I don't know why she seems to think *you'd* know where Dane went. Do you? Will you tell me? Will you go get her? Oh, God, how could she do this to me? She'd never dishonor us all like this. It isn't like her. She's not a coward—I can't believe she'd run off at the last moment. Why would she do it? Something must have happened, but what? Galahad, will you help us?"

Galahad walked to the narrow window and stood looking out. He took a deep breath, and for the first time in weeks it came easily. "If she has ridden out, I think I know where she may be."

Percival was too relieved to wonder at this admission. "Would you go get her and bring her back? I'd go with you, but I can't leave—these kings are my guests; I must see to their entertainment. We can go ahead with the feast, and Hawath can draw out his tales until she shows. That's the best I can come up with. Can you do this for me, Galahad? Will you find my sister?"

Galahad was already fastening his cloak. "Cousin, step aside. I am gone."

It was not until he had galloped beyond the meadows and into the wooded foothills that Galahad realized he did not know the way. Rouk had found the place by accident all those years ago, by the scent of her mare, and he had left in such a hurry he had not taken notice of any landmarks. With a smile of chagrin he dropped the reins on the horse's withers. "All right, Rouk, it's up to you. Find her for me."

Without hesitation the stallion headed up into the low hills that lay at the mountains' feet. Galahad let the horse go where he would and shut his own mind to thought, content for the moment to enjoy the sheer beauty of the night, the frosted stars, the crisp, salt-scented air, the sleeping silence of the forest, and below it all, like the low thrumming of a harp string under the bard's song, the thrill of anticipation.

Steadily the horse climbed higher, walking faster, as if he, too, could scent the promise of the dark. As they ascended, the evening star burned bright over the treetops and the breeze stabbed suddenly cold. The stallion lifted his head, nostrils wide, and whinnied. From far ahead came the answering cry of the mare. Galahad dug his heels into the horse's side.

In the clearing they came to a sliding stop. Dane waited at the cave mouth, the light of the fire behind her making a bright halo of her hair. Darkness shimmered at the edge of the leaping flames; a fitful wind whispered a welcome on the edge of sound. The steady beating in his ears began to quicken. An owl called, the long notes drawn out in the sighing breeze, the bard's final thrumming. Without feeling his feet touch ground, Galahad slid off the horse and walked straight into her arms.

"Thank God you have come! I knew Percival would send you. You must help me, Galahad!"

As he looked down into her face the world beyond them spun silently away. He bent and kissed her. At the first, soft touch of his lips she yielded to him all the joyous warmth of her eager nature. Sweet and insistent, the night music eddied around them, flames, wind, owl, and wild longing.

She took his hand and led him into the cave. She had prepared a cushion for him by the fire and cup of watered wine. Through the wavering light, through the pounding in his head, through the sweet song of desire, her voice came soft and clear.

"Galahad, Galahad, you came to me. And you came here, where I attacked you so long ago."

"I forgive you," Galahad whispered, alive with the feel of her hand in his, entranced by the delicate line of her cheek against her glowing hair. "I told you that before."

"If you tell me Lancelot is a lecherous villain, I shall believe you. I will put my faith in your judgment. At the very least, I owe you that."

He lifted her hand and held it against his cheek. "Why did you run, Dane?"

Her dark green tunic fitted her as closely as her gown. She seemed to have grown curves everywhere. She lowered her eyes. "Galahad, I am in an impossible position, and the worst of it is, it is all my own doing."

The firelight lent her skin a rosy glow. The soft fur collar of her tunic lay open and at the base of her throat a tiny charm hung on a silken thread. He watched it move and wink in the shifting shadows.

She stared miserably down at her winecup. "Owaine regards me as a broodmare, not a woman. If I went to Gorre, I should spend all my time in his bed, either getting with child or delivering one. Kastor, my cousin, is a pox-ridden philanderer. He cannot keep his mind on anything longer than five minutes. He has already seduced three of the cook's girls. I could be powerful in Strathclyde, but I should be desperately unhappy. And Rydor, whom Percival favors, is an excitable man. When it serves his turn he is an easy liar. Half the time he believes his own fabrications. I could bear some faults, but I could not live with a man whose word I could not trust."

"Do you despise Talorc? I know him to be an honest man."

She smiled bitterly. "Aye, too honest, if you ask me. He has made Percival an offer for form's sake, but he has left off his wooing. He is a good man, but he no longer wants me. I should only embarrass us both if I accepted him."

"No longer wants you? How can you think so? He admires you greatly. He told me so himself."

Dane looked up. Her eyes glinted green in the firelight, sea green, like the rolling ocean in a high wind. "I put it to him," she said softly, "and he told me he would not take a treasure from a friend, even if the friend did not know he possessed it."

Galahad felt heat rise to his face.

"I have dishonored Percival, and he never will forgive me. I didn't mean to—I thought only to please him and bring honor and wealth to Gwynedd and stability to Britain. I never thought I should—" She stopped, clasping her hands together and looking away, "I never thought I would feel differently about it when the time came. And now it is too late. I cannot back out and I cannot go forward. In six months Percival will bring his bride here. I must be somewhere else by then—I could never stand in her shadow, and she must not stand in mine. Galahad, Galahad, what is the solution?"

He rose slowly, standing very still. He could find no words to say. She looked at him entreatingly, beseechingly, and he knew she wanted something from him. But all he could think about was the beauty of her firelit hair, the sweet curve of her lips. . . .

Tears glistened in her eyes. "How could I know I would loathe them all? I cannot do it! I will kill myself first, with my own sword!"

He jumped forward and caught her arm as she turned toward the ancient weapon against the wall. She was in his arms at once, warm against him, soft and eager. "Galahad," she whispered, "I choose you."

He kissed her lips and pressed her body close. Deep excitement, so long simmering unacknowledged in the center of his being, now exploded into consciousness, alive as liquid fire, overmastering his will. Just as in battle, time slowed down and he moved fluidly, effortlessly, freely in a world that was completely new to him. He had never known a woman's skin could be so soft. His hands seemed to move of their own will, finding the laces to her clothing, discovering the smooth, fine flesh she kept hidden, caressing the terrifying, secret curves, making her gasp. She drew him down, yielding with joy to his touch. He was amazed to find how easily his body commanded the knowledge he had so long feared to learn. The heat of excitement engulfed them both, and they clung together, one body, one movement, in the young, strong passion of new desire.

In the black night Galahad awoke. The spell of wonder held him still: the woman's breath blew soft and sweet upon his shoulder, and her arm lay lightly on his chest. He did not want to awaken, not yet. He closed his eyes and let his hand slide over her skin, glorying in the amazing softness of her, wanting to know every sweet secret of her body, letting his longing free in the delicious dark. She stirred. He stopped her mouth with his and then began to kiss her, letting his lips discover what his hands already knew. Slowly and deliberately he rekindled the flame of her excitement, rejoicing in his power and unsuspected skill, until she gasped his name and reached out for him. When at last he took her it was not with the heat of mindless passion, but with a warm, living love that had flowered within him, sprung up from nowhere, unsuspected and unacknowledged, but as solid and enduring as the rock that enclosed them both.

"Galahad, my sweet love," she whispered as her breathing slowed again toward sleep. "They have been telling lies about you."

He pulled her head against his shoulder, his hand buried in her wayward hair, and kissed her brow. "They know nothing about me." His hand slid to her throat, and he lifted the tiny charm on its silken thread. "What is this token you wear about your neck?"

Even in the dark, he felt her smile. "It is the Hawk of Lanascol and the Gray Wolf of Gwynedd, together. I had it made a month ago when I knew I loved you. I had it made small, so none would notice and discover my secret. But I think my mother guessed."

He held it between his fingers, such a fragile thing. "A month ago?"

"Do you remember the night of your arriving? I knew as soon as I saw you. I knew as soon as you saw me."

"Ah," he whispered, brushing his finger against her lips. "I remember. You took my breath away."

She laid her cheek upon his chest. His hand slid along her back in one long, possessive caress.

"What a powerful charm," he said.

When he awoke just after dawn he did not know where he was. He was cold, stiff, and his joints ached as if he had been sleeping on a rock. Rubbing his eyes, he sat up and looked about. He *had* been sleeping on a rock. Bedding and blankets had tumbled off the thin bed of bracken and lay twisted in a wanton huddle on the bare rock flooring of the cave.

The cave. He blinked. His hand touched the wolf pelt and he stared at it a moment. Not that cave. He shut his eyes tight and then, with a sense of foreboding, opened them again. Something dark and horrifying lurked on the edge of consciousness and he fought to postpone the moment he must face it. He had killed the wolf years ago, in a bigger cave, with room for a horse at the back of it. But he had not been naked when he killed the wolf, and he was naked now. He pulled on his leggings and his boots as quickly as he could, and cast about among the blankets for his tunic, as if speed could save him. But nothing could slow the tide of returning memory.

"Good morning, love."

At last he looked up. Dane knelt at the cave mouth, stirring a fire, her brilliant hair spilling over her shoulders and down her back. Her smile turned his innards to jelly and he exhaled carefully. She rose and came toward him, a clay cup of steaming tea between her hands.

"Here. To warm you up. There's frost on the ground." She smiled at him. "I nearly let the fire die. I must have been distracted in the night."

He shut his eyes. It had not been a dream, after all.

"Come sit down. I have made you a sweet porridge."

He followed her to the fire and sat down on the cushion she had arranged for him, but he could not eat a drop of the porridge.

"Dane." Even to his own ears his voice sounded like a stranger's. But she had returned to the pot on the fire and did not hear him. He watched the long curve of her back as she bent over the flames; it seemed to him he could still feel the smooth skin under his fingertips. His hand shook violently, spilling the tea.

She turned. "Galahad. What's the matter?"

"I must . . . take you back to Percival."

"Yes. We'll go down as soon as we've eaten. It'll be a shock to him, I'm afraid. I don't think he has an inkling, do you?"

"Of what?"

She laughed, and her joy was a power in itself that tugged at him physically and threatened to overmaster him. But if he did not keep a clear head now he would never get another chance.

She crouched down beside him and kissed him quickly. "Of *us*, of course." She touched the charm that lay in the hollow of her throat. "Of the new future we will make."

Galahad put down the bowl of porridge. "Dane. I meant, I must take you back to Percival . . . and leave you."

She stared at him and slowly rose to her feet. *"What?"*

He rose, too, and stilled the longing to take her in his arms. "I . . . I can't stay in Gwynedd. I'm promised elsewhere. I have to—"

"Promised?" Her chin lifted and her nostrils flared. "To someone else? Who?"

He shook his head. "To no one else. Surely you know . . . you were the first. And only."

She was in his arms then, her soft cheek pressed against his, full of apologies and protestations of affection. He could not help pressing her close. He needed the warmth of her eager, willing nature, for he was cold inside, and getting colder. He kissed her and held her until her trembling subsided. Then he drew a deep breath and said, "I am sworn to find the Grail, Dane. You know this. It isn't new. But time is short, and I've stayed too long already as it is."

Instantly she stiffened and drew away. "As it is? Meaning what? You are sorry you came to Gwynedd? Or to the cave?"

He reached out for her, shivering, but she backed away and he had to let his arm fall empty to his side. "No. Of course not. But—"

"But what? We are betrothed, after last night. You're not going to deny that, surely."

He looked away, then wrenched his gaze back. This was impossible. He would never be able to make her understand. He spoke very gravely and as clearly as he could. "The Grail—in the right hands—will bring Arthur back to Britain. It will keep Britain whole. United forever. But if that is going to happen, it must happen soon. If I don't go, all Britain is lost."

Dane's eyes widened and she tossed her head angrily, making her hair fly. "What rubbish! Arthur is dead. Who has been telling you such nonsense? Britain lost! If you *do* go, your honor is lost! I thought only a stainless knight could find the Grail. Isn't that what you told me when you brought my brother home? How stainless will you be now, if you debauch me and leave me here?"

Debauch! He winced at the word, at the vulgarity and brutality of it. It was not the word for what they had shared last night, and she knew it.

"I am the one who has been chosen," he said quietly, hating the fear in her face, wishing there were another way to tell her. "Arthur himself chose me. I can't fail him."

"But you can fail *me?*" Tears sprang to her eyes and she wiped them away so they would not fall. "Can't you hear how pompous and ridiculous you sound? A king dead these seven years has greater need of you than I do? Galahad, you have filled your head with the ravings of lunatics. Take a moment and think about it. We . . . we ought not quarrel. Take me down to Percival and he will square it with the other lords. They dare not challenge you. If you have some promised duty to perform, I'm sure Percival will let you go, provided you are back by spring. We must wed and be gone before he brings Guinblodwyn here. That is essential. I must be gone before the first of May."

Galahad turned away and covered his face with his hands. He could not abide her suffering, and her own, futile attempts to hold the future at bay. Perhaps it would be better just to go. He remembered the morning old Ban had drowned the rest of Valiant's litter. *The best way's the quickest*, he had said to the grieving boy. *Soonest over, soonest forgotten*.

He dropped his hands and faced her, but she read something of his thought in his expression and said quickly, "I love you, Galahad. I have given you proof of that; I have made it as clear as I could. Does that mean nothing to you? Or do you really mean to shame me in my own home?"

He forced his lips to move. "Dane, I cannot marry you."

She stopped as if slapped, and paled. "Coward! Blackguard! Fornicator! Your father is a nobler man; at least he married the woman he lay with and gave her child a name."

He took her insults without flinching but they rang inside his head like the hard echoes of a struck bell. As he backed toward the cave entrance her voice grew shriller, and her tears coursed down her cheeks unchecked.

"Monster! Ill-begotten bastard! Would you betray me? Then you betray your cousin, your uncle, your father! You make Percival your lifelong enemy! You are false to the bone, just like your mother. And what would your father say? Honorable Lancelot, whose name you do not deserve to bear! You shame the House of Lanascol."

Sweat poured from his body and dripped from his chin, yet he shivered with cold. He tore the badge off his shoulder and flung it at her.

"Take it. You may have the House of Lanascol and all that's in it, for all I care!"

Sobbing, she stooped to pick up the badge and held it to her breast. "I curse you, then, with all the power of a woman's rage." She raised her arms skyward and wailed, "May the sins of your flesh persecute you forever! May you not spend a night in peace, not a single night, until you have paid for this deed! May all your endeavors end in ruin, may what you seek escape your grasp, may your precious Grail be ever hidden from your eyes! Until you have given me back my honor!"

Stumbling, Galahad made for his horse, grabbed the reins, and flung himself onto the stallion's back. For the second time he was running for his life away from Dane.

49 ✠ THE TOWER

Horse and rider struggled to the top of the ridge in the pelting, late-spring rain. The thin trees gave little shelter and they both hunched against the onslaught as they made their way across rocks and broken scree. They stopped at the edge of broad gully where a landslide had scarred the hill. Trees and bushes gave way to a sea of soft dirt and pebbles which afforded a wide view of the surrounding country. Galahad lifted his head and gazed out across a vast expanse of stark hills dark with wet rocks, gorse, brambles, and the twisted skeletons of long-dead, stunted trees. The change in season had not touched these badlands. Heavy clouds lay like a shroud from horizon to horizon, casting a cold, sinister chill across the barren landscape.

He stared at the view a long time. Somewhere in his childhood he had seen a wasteland such as this, or dreamed it. He had known even then it was part of his future. The stallion pawed fretfully at the unsteady ground, and Galahad turned him away from the slide.

Rivulets of cold water coursed down his back. For the thousandth time he shut a mental door against memories clamoring for attention at the edge of thought. For eighteen months Dane's parting curses had rung in his ears and for eighteen months all his endeavors had come to ruin. What he sought still evaded his grasp. He knew, in that dark, interior place where he kept secrets from himself, that it was too late now to find the Grail and Spear. Time had run out. The trail was cold. He had missed his chance for glory. Yet he traveled on, and searched on, because he had nowhere else to go.

For eighteen months he had repented his night with Dane, stopping at every chapel, every holy house, every wayside shrine to bend his knee, firmly close his eyes, and pray for absolution. And for eighteen months God had turned a deaf ear to his pleas. He knew the reason. There was a penance to pay. There was a trial coming. He only hoped that it would come upon him soon. And that if he survived it, he would be free at last of this heaviness of heart, this terrible, formless burden which weighed him down so cruelly and made every day a torture. He had lost the clear-eyed vision of his youth. He no longer had dreams he could remember. The road he trav-

eled had once been straight and true, but now meandered. Once his name
had commanded the respect of other men, but lately no one had cared
much who he was. It did not matter; nothing mattered, for Arthur Pendragon would never be recalled from the mists that held him. That hope,
like the others, had died away. Failure lay behind him and suffering ahead.
He was as certain of that as of the air he breathed.

Thunder rumbled in the distance and he raised his head. Black clouds
piled on the horizon, and nearer, the sky took on a greenish hue. Lightning
forked once, twice as he watched, and a cold wind whipped through the
trees ahead. A storm was on the way, and a big one. He did not want to be
caught in the mountains and risk losing Farouk in a slide. He put heels to
the horse. With any luck at all they would get across the river before dark
and into such shelter as they could find in the valley below.

On the morning after the storm Megan threw open the shutters and leaned
out the tower window into the sun. "Ahhh, what heaven!" she said, feeling
the warmth on her face. "Lilia, come look! That wretched storm is over and
the moor is full of wildflowers!"

Her sister joined her, comb in hand. "It's about time. Let's ride out. I
can hardly bear another day in this awful prison!"

"Should we ask Father for permission?" Both girls glanced silently upward where, at the top of the tower, their father had spent the entire winter
in his chamber without once stepping beyond the threshold.

"He's ill," Megan said decisively. "We'll ask Germaine. She'll allow it.
She must be as eager to escape as we are."

Lilia nodded in agreement. "Hurry, Meg, and put up my hair. Let's not
tell Ariane or Bella. Let's go out ourselves."

Within the hour three young women cantered down the track across
the blooming moor. Ahead, across the narrow valley where the river slashed
its way south, they could see the barren badlands rising ridge upon ridge to
the hills beyond. The land began to slope toward the river and they stopped
in a sparse wood to admire the budding trees.

"Let's ride down to the water," Lilia urged. "Father never lets us go so
far, and once the grass grows tall we'll never find the ford. I want to make
sure it's still there, that it wasn't washed away by winter storms."

Megan tossed her red curls defiantly. "He doesn't want us to find the
way out. He wants to keep us prisoners until we're all spinsters and must
serve him till he dies!"

"Hush, Meg!" Germaine exclaimed. "How do you dare such words? Father is a noble man."

"*Was* a noble man," Megan corrected, pulling her mare's nose from the grass. "Now he's a recluse. Badlands on one side, the endless moor on the other—is it any wonder no one ever comes by our door? How shall we ever get husbands locked away in that godforsaken tower?"

A slow blush crept over Germaine's pinched face. She was the eldest of the sisters and already past her best years. She knew more about the wrenching longing for a husband than any of them, but thus far her longing had brought her nothing.

"Very well," she said at last, "we'll go down to the river. Just to look."

On the far side of the woods the land fell sharply away to the rocky riverbed. They heard the roar of wild water long before they came upon the river, but when they saw it they pulled up in astonishment. The storm had swelled the river to full spate and it thundered down from the distant mountains in a rage of froth and noise, bursting its banks here and there and flooding the lowlands with new lakes. At the edge of a swirling pool nearby they saw a fine black horse, fetlock-deep in water, standing over a lump of dark cloth half-in, half-out of the water.

"Someone's fallen!" Megan gasped. "He'll drown! Come on!"

"Slowly," Germaine warned, "or you'll frighten the horse."

They trotted up as swiftly as they dared. The black stallion's ears flicked forward and he screamed a challenge, but did not move away. At his feet lay the inert body of a tall man, facedown in the mud, his fingers dug into the earth as though he had tried in vain to pull himself from the water. The girls slid off their horses and together pulled the body clear of the rising pool. With an effort they turned him over on his back and Lilia wiped the mud from his face with her kerchief. Germaine lifted his wrist and felt for the beat of life.

"Ah, thank God, he lives," she said.

"Look at him!" Megan stared down like one entranced. "Just look at him!"

The man was young, broad-shouldered, narrow-waisted, long-legged, and beautiful. They stared in silence, not quite able to believe their eyes.

"Is he a gift from Heaven?" Germaine whispered.

"His clothes are the finest quality," Lilia added. "Just like his horse. He must be a prince. Or a king."

"Or a god," Megan said, crossing herself. "He's the handsomest man I've ever seen!"

"Which isn't many," Germaine pointed out. Few people ever crossed the badlands to their tower on the edge of the moor, and their father employed only two men in his service, a guard who had lost a leg in battle and could no longer serve in an army, and an elderly stablemaster too old to ride away. The three girls looked at one another, suddenly smiled, and then laughed aloud. "Let's take him home."

* * *

"What do you mean 'a man'?" Ariane demanded, setting down her winecup. "What man?"

Germaine sat at the head of the dinner table with Lilia and Megan, her two youngest sisters, on her left, and on her right Bella and Ariane, who were nineteen and twenty and even hungrier than she was for a husband. They had not yet despaired of finding one.

"Indeed, it is true. We rescued a man this morning from certain death. But only one man."

"Where is he, then?" Bella spoke with the casual authority of the ac- knowledged beauty. Alone of them all she had honey-colored hair and pale blue eyes. Her skin was as fair as Megan's, but without freckles, and her countenance was admired by all her sisters. *And* by Hugh, the one-legged guard, who was experienced enough to know a handsome woman from a plain one.

"He's in the storeroom," Germaine said quietly. "In the back. Hugh moved his own bed in there, bless his generous soul." She looked at her sis- ters meaningly. "We thought it best that Father not stumble across him, should he come downstairs."

The girls nodded. They all remembered the last time a stranger had landed on their doorstep seeking shelter. Two full years ago a wandering bard, thirty years old, penniless and bedraggled, had begged for a meal and place to sleep out of the wet. Gladly, they had obliged him with a hot meal, a hot bath and shave, a soft pallet, and plenty of wine. To thank them, he had taken up his lap harp and begun to sing of Arthur Pendragon and the glory days of Britain. Suddenly the door had opened to reveal Sir Fortas on the threshold, sword in hand. The bard was halfway to the riverbank in ten minutes' time. Fortas had restricted his daughters to bread and water for twenty days afterward and warned them against ever letting another stranger in. The girls had considered it a great disaster for Bella, for the bard had not been bad-looking and had admired her.

"Who is he?" asked Ariane. "What's his name?"

Germaine shook her head. "We'll have to wait until he awakens to find out. He was senseless when we found him. But he's not lowborn."

"You should see his sword!" cried Lilia.

Megan grinned. "You should see his face!"

"And his dagger." Lilia was not to be outdone. "It has a hawk carved in the handle."

"Then he is a knight." Bella toyed with a strand of her golden hair. "What device is on his badge? That would tell us whom he serves."

"Alas," Germaine replied, "he does not have one. We could find nothing of the sort in his belongings. Strange, isn't it? No badge or token, but wonderful weapons, a shield and an ancient drinking cup, and the finest horse I've ever seen. Long-legged and swift, like the ones in the legends."

"My goodness, Germaine," Bella drawled. "You've already gone through his belongings? Without a word to me or Ariane?"

"We didn't want to interrupt your beauty sleep," Megan retorted.

"Hush, Megan," chided Germaine. "This doesn't help us discover who he is."

"A knight in disgrace, perhaps," Ariane suggested. "He may be hiding from pursuit. If so, he may not tell us who he is."

"Perhaps." Germaine paused. "But his biggest problem at the moment is his fever. We think he tried to cross the ford and was swept away. We found him senseless in the flood. He could have been there half the night."

"You've been to the river?" Ariane stared. "Whatever possessed you, Germaine? You know Father will have your hide when he finds out."

"He will have *all* our hides," Germaine said smoothly, "if he discovers there is a man in the house." She looked around the table and gathered all their eyes. "But perhaps he need not know."

"Unless one of us tells him," Bella suggested slyly.

Megan and Lilia burst into vehement protest, but Germaine succeeded at last in hushing them. "Finish your dinners," she said to Bella and Ariane, "and we will take you to him. After you've seen him, if you still feel you must tell Father, we will not stand in your way."

"There's always the chance the servants will tell him even if we do not," Ariane offered.

Germaine shook her head. "Gillie would never. Nor Hugh, who helped us carry him in. Nor Old Cam, who took charge of the stallion. They have no reason to betray us." She looked at them each in turn. "It is as clear to them as it is to all of us that this man, whoever he is, may be a means of escape into the world for at least one of us. If any one of us is lucky enough to accompany this soldier out of the valley, she takes at least one servant with her. That is the bargain we have struck. Are you all agreed?"

Bella and Ariane glanced uneasily at each other, the fretful look of competitors nearing the starting pole. "Agreed."

The storeroom was a small, rounded room at the rear of the tower with one poorly shuttered window looking out on the desolate moor. None of the girls had been in it for years, as it was used only for storage of Sir Fortas's supplies of pens, inks, and parchments, and of broken furniture and the discarded belongings of their long-dead mother. Now, as they entered, they found the floor swept clean and strewn with rushes, a hastily beaten carpet hung against the wall to cover the crumbling stone, and a fresh set of hangings around Hugh's bed to keep the drafts out. A low table near the bed held a candle, a water jar, a bowl, and a cloth. As the girls entered, a stout, capable woman of middle years rose from a bedside chair and curtsied.

"Goodness, Gillie!" Bella exclaimed. "When did you do all this? The last time I saw this room, it was full of junk with a pile of snow against the wall."

"We've been busy, Mistress and I." She nodded to Germaine. "I've washed his tunic and his leggings and hung them out to dry. Old Cam is rubbing oil into his boots. And Hugh is searching the hayloft for that old brazier. It'll be chill again tonight."

Bella turned to Germaine. "You undressed him, then? Yourself?"

Germaine flushed. "Gillie helped. We had to bathe him. He was filthy from the muddy water."

"That was bold of you, for a spinster."

"I am not a spinster yet!" Germaine cried, feeling the heat in her face. "I am four-and-twenty, and as desirous of a man—of a husband—as you are!"

"But not as likely to get one."

"Come, come," Ariane chided. "Argue later. Let's have a look at him now." She stepped toward the bed and drew back the hangings. Her sisters crowded behind her.

"My God," Bella said under her breath.

The fevered man lay cocooned in blankets with only his head and one shoulder free. His eyes were closed; a lock of black hair shaded his forehead.

"Is he real?" Ariane whispered. She put out a finger and touched his hot cheek.

"You never told us he was beautiful, Germaine." Bella sounded stunned.

"There was no way to describe him," Germaine said simply.

They all stared in silence.

"Well?" Germaine asked softly. "Are you going to tell Father?"

"No," Bella said. "Not on my life. He is my pass to freedom."

Ariane nudged her aside. "Unless he chooses me instead."

"That's enough," Germaine said sharply. "Gillie and I have worked out a schedule for tending him. We will all take turns." She frowned at Bella and Ariane. "Short turns. Gillie and I will fix his meals. You are all still responsible for your daily chores, even when your turn at nursing comes at night. Is that agreed?"

All of them spoke with their eyes on the senseless man in the bed. "Agreed."

* * *

Upstairs in her chamber Germaine fell on her knees at her bedside and crossed herself. "Holy Mary, Mother of men," she whispered fervently. "I have ever been your servant. I have never asked for much. Please, Mother, let this man be the one I've been waiting for. He has the face of an angel, and I have already lost my heart."

After breakfast Bella met Megan on the stairs.

"Why, Meg, you little fox. If that isn't your best gown!"

"And that's yours," Megan retorted. "*And* your hair ribbons!"

Bella smiled indulgently. "Why would he look at *you* twice? You're barely sixteen."

"That's old enough to wed. Mother was sixteen when she married. Besides, I'm the one who found him. *I* suggested going out. *You* had nothing to do with it."

Bella patted her hair, which was perfectly in place. "Thank you for the gift."

Ariane's first turn at nursing came at midday. Gillie showed her how to sponge the patient's brow with cool water and taught her to hold the watercup to his lips and make him drink during the few moments he rose to semiconsciousness. Ariane sat expectantly for the first quarter of an hour but nothing happened. The man did not rouse; he did not even move. Ariane's fingers drummed on the table. She took a sip of water herself, then rose and stretched. It was a fine day out, she knew, but only ragged shafts of light filtered through the patched shutters, and no warmth at all. She unlatched the shutters and threw them open, filling the small space with brilliant light and a soft breeze redolent of blooming heather. Nearby, stuffed in the corner among the remnants of a broken couch, lay a long scabbard wrapped in a blanket. These must be his weapons, she thought, hastily bundled aside when the soldier himself had been brought in. She lifted the blanket and gazed at the plain swordbelt and ancient scabbard. Her heart sank. They were not so very fine. They were not even as good as her father's. The scabbard had been marred and nicked in a dozen places and looked on the verge of crumbling into dust. She picked up the dagger and drew it from its sheath. Now here was a lovely weapon! It lay in her hand, cold and bright, like a heavy jewel. Surely the man who owned this could not be base. But perhaps it was booty, plunder stolen from some worthy prince in the dead of night. As she put the dagger down, the swordbelt slipped and the hilt of the sword turned toward her. She gasped. The scabbard might be plain but here was a king's ransom in the hilt of his sword! Nine rubies burned in the sun; the flash of silver chasing hurt her eyes. No one could steal this sword and wear it openly. He would be instantly known.

She covered the weapons carefully and returned to the man in the bed. The flush had receded from his face and he looked, for a moment, as if he slept a natural sleep. Ariane leaned over him and brushed his hair from his eyes. Whoever he was, he was someone who mattered in the world, someone important, someone commanding. But just now he was helpless and in her power. She touched her lips to his in an exploratory kiss, the very first of her life. Was it her imagination or did he sigh? She took his head between her hands, her heart pounding, and kissed him again.

At dusk Bella entered the storeroom. Reluctantly, Germaine yielded her place at the bedside.

"No improvement," she said in a low voice. "In fact, he's worsened. His fever's raging again and at times his breathing is a little rough. Ariane opened the shutters this morning. I thought Gillie would strangle her!"

"Ariane's a fool," Bella said calmly. "She ought not to be allowed near him."

"It may be the death of him, yet. He was in a cold sweat all afternoon, but now he's on fire. If you need help, Bella, if he should start to toss or struggle, call me or Gillie."

Bella nodded absently, all her concentration on the flushed face against the pillow. When her sister had gone, she raised the candle high and observed her patient. He was nearly too tall for the bed. The one arm flung against the pillow was long, well muscled, and shapely, the shoulder curved and hard as rock. She put the candle on the table and bathed his brow with a cool cloth. He groaned, turned away, and mumbled unintelligibly. She pressed the compress against his neck, marveling at how quickly his hot flesh heated the cloth. Sitting on the bed and pulling the blanket down, she exposed his chest and, after a moment's admiration, picked up the bowl and with her fingers rubbed cool water into his skin. The beating of her heart filled her ears. The man, too, responded to her touch. He groaned again and moved, his limp hand falling against her thigh. Bella stared down at his long fingers, then covered his hand with hers and pressed it against her flesh. She caught her breath at the thrill of excitement that raced through her. What was happening to her? She had never felt like this, even when that poor bard had kissed her.

She pulled the blanket away from the burning body and stared at him. She had never seen the whole of a man before. She had seen Hugh swimming in a loincloth, but only at a distance. Her only experience of the sexual act had been watching the barn cats mating. Where, then, did the knowledge come from? She was not afraid to touch him—blazing excitement urged her on—and she was not surprised when his body responded to her caresses. His head tossed on the pillow and he called out a word, a senseless word, but his eyes remained closed and his breathing as rough as hers.

"Who are you?" she whispered into his ear. "I love you. I want you. Oh, sir, wake up, won't you, and show me how?"

But there was no response to her question, and eventually he began to shiver. She tucked the blanket around him again and, armed with her new knowledge, smiled down at him. "Tomorrow then. If you can't teach me, perhaps I can teach myself."

For six days Galahad lay in a fever, alternating bouts of icy chills with raging heat. In his dreams he wandered through burning landscapes, peopled with demons, followed by tracts of frozen wastelands where every step could plunge him deep into bottomless crevasses. Now and then a woman's face came near. The sweetness of her breath overwhelmed him and he seemed to wait, hanging on a thread above the abyss, for the warm pressure of her lips. Then would he float heavenward, light as a feather, flooding with joy at the touch of hands on skin, until the pounding in his temples made the very air throb with beating fire and he sought, vainly, to encompass the flames that devoured him, to master the powerful, overwhelming drive toward union.

On the morning of the seventh day he opened exhausted eyes. All he saw, above him and around him, was white. For an instant he wondered if this was Heaven.

"Water," he whispered.

The wall of Heaven rent and a fair female face surrounded by a halo of golden hair looked down on him. He could not quite bring the face into focus. He was more than half certain she must be an angel. "Water."

She reached out her arms and lifted up his head, pillowing his cheek against her breast. A cool clay cup was placed against his lips and delicious, sweet water poured down his throat. He looked up into wide, pale blue eyes. "Who are you? Where am I?"

The vision did not speak, but bent down and pressed her lips to his, a kiss of possession. A spark of fear ignited within his heart, but his fatigue overpowered him and he slipped back into the vale of sleep.

The next time he awoke the room was dark. The curtain at his side had been pulled back. By the light of the brazier and the candle on the table near his head he saw two young women sitting in wavering, golden shadows. One of them had auburn curls that strayed from their pins. The sight moved him deeply.

"Please," he began, but his voice was a shadow of itself. The other woman, plain-faced but kindly, spoke to him gently and gave him broth that smelled of healing herbs and spices. He drank it gratefully. "Where am I?"

"Sir Fortas's tower." She saw his confusion and smiled. It was a comforting, peaceful smile and held no torments for him. Relief washed through him like a shower of rain. Perhaps the rest had all been dreaming.

"Sir Fortas is lord of this land. He is our father."

"Do I know him? I don't remember. . . . How did I get here?"

"No, you have not met him yet, my lord. My sister Megan, who sits beside me, found you drowning in the river pool. Did you try to cross the river in the flood?"

Megan. That must be the redhead's name. His heart sank. Gradually his memory stirred and events slipped back into their places. Yes, he remembered coming to the ford well past dark, having failed to find any place to shelter from the wet. Farouk had refused to cross at first, but he had forced the animal out of sheer frustration and against his better judgment. "My horse—did you find him?"

"Yes, my lord," Megan replied eagerly. "He has been enjoying himself in our paddocks these seven days." She blushed suddenly. "We have only mares, and two of them in season."

Galahad smiled weakly and both girls watched him, entranced. "Good for Farouk. Let him have his reward. He has earned it."

"Who are you?" Megan asked, coming to his side. "Are you a prince?"

The elder sister shushed her. "Are you strong enough to eat some bread? You've been nearly a week without sustenance. We thought more than once we might lose you."

He shook his head. Sleep—calm, dreamless sleep—was pressing against his eyelids. "No one," he said softly, sinking rapidly. "I am no one of significance."

Ariane and Lilia had the evening shift. Now that their patient was reviving, Germaine judged it best that they should nurse him two by two.

"I think we should find out who he is, since he isn't going to tell us," Ariane announced as soon as they were seated. "No one of significance, indeed!"

"How can we? We know nothing about him."

"You wait here. I'll be right back."

Lilia sat by the bowl of steaming soup covered with a cloth and gazed at the sleeping solider. He was pale now, and his breathing was still ragged, but he slept a peaceful, healing sleep. She wished he would open his eyes.

Megan had told her he had eyes as blue as the sky in summer and a smile that could melt the heart.

Ariane returned with Hugh.

"Here," she said, placing the bundled weapons in his arms and drawing back the blanket. "What do you think of these?"

Hugh knelt on the floor, cast his crutch aside, and reverently laid the bundle down. Gingerly, he put his hand to the jeweled hilt and drew the sword. Both girls gasped as the long blade glinted in the candlelight, its edges honed to killing sharpness.

"This—" Hugh choked, then cleared his throat gruffly and began again. "This is a weapon I know. I could never mistake it. I fought with the Breton at Autun. This is Sir Lancelot's sword." He raised the dagger into the light. "See the carving? That's the Hawk of Lanascol. These are Lancelot's weapons."

All three of them looked toward the bed.

"Well, *that's* not Sir Lancelot," Ariane objected. "This man's not five-and-twenty."

Hugh grabbed his crutch and hobbled to the bedside. Not since he had helped carry in the senseless, mud-spattered soldier had he taken a good look at his face. He scanned it now. "For the love of God," he whispered. "If it isn't young Galahad!"

"Who?" Ariane and Lilia cried in unison.

"Galahad. Lancelot's son. Last I saw him was at Autun. He was but fourteen at the time. And that was, let's see, nigh on nine years ago. My God, I'd not have known him. Just look how the boy has grown!"

Ariane's face lit. "If he's Sir Lancelot's son and has his father's sword, that must mean his father is dead. And Galahad is king of Lancelot's kingdom."

Hugh shrugged. "Or perhaps retired. I'd heard he'd gone home to Lanascol after Camlann. But everyone knows that Sir Galahad stayed in Britain to carry on the fight."

Ariane frowned. "We didn't."

Hugh bowed politely. "Begging your pardon, I'm sure. It's tavern talk I heard in Battle Valley when I went in to buy supplies. Galahad is well known around Britain." He glanced at the girls' rapt faces. "Among other things, they call him the Virgin Knight."

Ariane gasped. "That must be a jest! A man like that?"

"Aye," Hugh said cautiously. "So you would think. But he's different. He's unattached."

Ariane burst into angry tears. "Oh, the cruel fates! Wouldn't you just know it!"

Hugh frowned, puzzled, but Lilia enlightened him. "That means he won't want to marry any of us."

* * *

When Galahad awoke in the middle of the night, he was alone. The candle had gone out and the brazier shed only a pallid light. Gingerly he pushed himself up, testing his strength. He could sit up; he could stand, although moving made him light-headed. Some thoughtful person had left him a wastepot. Feeling much better after he had relieved himself, he turned to take up the candle and froze. Across the table a pair of pale eyes glinted in the darkness, watching him. His hand went instinctively to his sword hilt, met his hipbone, and dropped loosely to his side.

"Who is there?"

Someone moved with a rustle of cloth. Out of the shadows came a slender young woman clad only in a thin linen shift. Golden hair fell about her shoulders and her pink lips parted in a smile.

He reached for the blanket to cover himself, but she walked up to him and pushed his hand away. "There's no need, for me," she said softly into his ear. "Not after what we have been to each other."

She pressed her lips against his and her body, so warm beneath the thin fabric, molded to his own. A groan escaped him. Shreds of memory surfaced. She had done this before. She took his free hand in her own and lifted it to her breast.

"Don't you remember?" she whispered. "My beloved Galahad? My sweet betrothed."

"Betrothed?" The word stung and he sank down on the bed. "How do you know my name?"

"Dearest." She placed a hand on each side of his head, a movement that seemed suddenly too familiar. "You told it to me. Don't you remember? Right here in this bed."

He paled as she kissed him, and pushed her gently away. "You must give me time," he said slowly. "I remember nothing. Not even your name."

"Bella!"

The girl whipped around and Galahad covered himself with the blanket. A middle-aged woman appeared at the edge of light, rubbing her eyes.

"Bella, you wicked child! Get away from him this instant! I beg your pardon, my lord; it seems I cannot so much as close my eyes before the little wanton is at her tricks again! Bella, you ought to be ashamed of yourself! In your nightdress, you little hussy? Where's your gown? When Germaine hears of this—"

But Bella only tossed her head, sat beside Galahad on the bed, and placed her hand on his thigh. "Never mind your hysterics, Gillie. There is no shame in nakedness between a man and his betrothed."

Gillie stopped dead. She stared at them unbelieving. Then she turned to Galahad. "My lord?"

Galahad's face flamed. He wished to deny it. He would have given a limb to be able to deny it. But the hand on his thigh stirred other memories, of blazing passion and seeking hands, of the glorious, soul-searing joy of union and release. Of dim light against the dark cave wall, of smooth skin beneath his fingers, of withering fever and things seen in the night. He lifted his shoulders and let them fall. "I'm sorry," he muttered. "I don't remember."

Germaine and Megan appeared at midnight when the watch changed. Bella released Galahad's hand reluctantly, waiting until she knew her sisters were watching before she kissed him a gentle farewell. Gillie stayed behind to murmur furiously to Germaine while Megan approached the bed.

"You shouldn't let her do that, my lord Galahad," Megan announced matter-of-factly, taking a seat in the nearest chair. "Never let Bella take advantage. She doesn't know when to stop."

"Does she ever tell falsehoods?" Galahad asked tentatively.

"All the time." Megan grinned at him. "You don't want to pay attention to anything she says."

Galahad attempted a smile. "I would like very much to believe you."

His eyes followed Germaine as she closed the door behind Gillie and came to his bedside. He remembered her calm voice and reassuring touch, but he had never really looked at her before. She was plain-featured and soberly gowned, with no special charms beyond her thick, dark hair and her cool voice, yet he found himself warming to her. Her manner was so open, so completely without artifice. He could detect neither fear nor desire in her, and none of that coy archness he so detested. "Germaine." Even her name sounded mellow on his tongue.

"My lord Galahad?"

"How did you learn my name?"

"Hugh knew you by your sword, or rather, by your father's sword. He fought with the Breton armies at Autun."

"Did he, indeed? Will you send him to me? I should like to speak with him."

Germaine smiled. "Of course. He is eager to be of service to you, and I know you must be tired of female company."

"Not of yours," Galahad replied, and then stopped as a crimson blush mottled her face. "Take no offense, Germaine. I only meant you are an easy companion. But one of your sisters"—he shuddered—"I would be happy to do without."

Germaine's color deepened. "I beg your pardon for Bella. I believe Hugh suffers from her attentions as well, as he is the only man around even near our age." She hesitated. "Hugh says you are called the Virgin Knight."

Heat rose to Galahad's face, then drained away, leaving him paler than before. "I cannot help what people call me. But I pray you will not—it gives me no pleasure to hear it."

Germaine came closer. "Is it true, as Bella claims, that you and she have . . . that you are betrothed to her?"

Galahad flushed. "The truth is, I know no more of it than you do. I remember nothing. I only know what Bella tells me happened between us."

Relief washed Germaine's features and she drew a trembling breath. "Gillie thought as much. It is Bella's own invention, my lord. Pay her no mind. It's just that, being five sisters alone in this prison, five sisters of marriageable age . . ."

"Are there are no men around at all, then?"

Germaine swallowed painfully. "You have hit upon the essential problem, my lord. I am afraid that you have come to a house of women—women so desperate for a husband, we alight upon any passing stranger like a spider upon a fly. It is not cruelly meant, but there is a degree of seriousness in it."

"I see." Galahad paused. "But where is your father? Surely he should be your protection and your support. Has he no interest in finding you husbands?"

"Alas, my lord, he does not. I am afraid his interest runs quite the other way. All he asks is to be left alone in peace to read his books. He would be perfectly content to be tended by his daughters all his life."

"He thinks only of himself." No sooner were the words out of his mouth than bright color washed his face. He recalled his flight from the cave and the abandoned princess, the auburn-haired beauty of his dreams, screaming curses at his fleeing back.

"Oh, but he is a good man," Germaine cried, misunderstanding the reason for Galahad's sudden discomfort. "It's just that he has never forgiven our mother for her death. But he is kind at heart. Or he used to be before grief settled on him."

"I should like to meet him."

Megan and Germaine exchanged uncertain glances. "I'm sure you will," Germaine said. "Sooner or later."

Galahad was two more weeks recovering his strength. The dousing he had undergone had settled in his chest and was a long time clearing. Hugh waited upon him now instead of the sisters. Galahad vaguely remembered him as a decent enough soldier serving in Sir Sagramor's company. Hugh was so elated at the honor of this recollection that he could scarcely contain his gratitude and begged Galahad to allow him service.

Having less opportunity to be near Galahad, Bella found her influence waning. None of her sisters believed her tale of betrothal. Germaine had even told him he was free to go as soon as he was strong enough to travel. Something had to be done. But Galahad was always in the company of Hugh, who worshiped him, or in the stables with Old Cam, or with Germaine. It was impossible to get near him, and he never so much as looked her way.

When he was strong enough to be on his feet all day, Galahad took walks along the moor with Germaine. Sometimes they talked; sometimes they walked in silence. He found that he could tell her things he had never told anyone. She listened, nodded, and kept her counsel. One day she asked him, "Why did you say you were someone of no significance when you are Lancelot's son?"

The question struck like a blow and he struggled with himself to dredge up the truth. "Because although Lancelot is my father, I am unworthy to be his son. I can never go home. I deny the relationship as much as I can. To spare myself."

Germaine eyed him thoughtfully. "That's an honest answer."

"It's a coward's answer."

"Hugh tells us, my lord, that you have a reputation which outshines that of any other knight in the land, including the High King. You cannot be unworthy. Surely your father must be proud of your exploits."

But he shook his head. He could not go further. He could still see Lancelot's face on the evening before the Battle of Autun as he asked Galahad to forgive him his transgressions. He could still see him standing before the gates of Avalon asking one last time for Galahad's forbearance. He could not yet acknowledge the wound he had given Lancelot, the depth of the pain between them. And he could not bare his soul to Germaine when he had not yet bared it to himself.

During the sixth week of his visit Bella began to pale. She was often absent at meals and when she did come to table, ate very little. One morning, when she did not appear at breakfast, Germaine asked if anyone knew why she was behaving so strangely.

Lilia shrugged. "Oh, she's always sick in the mornings. I told her to ask Gillie for some chamomile."

Germaine froze.

"Oh, no!" Megan looked like she was going to cry.

Ariane slammed down her cup. "She's faking!"

Galahad looked from one of them to another in frank bewilderment. Germaine saw his expression and smiled faintly.

"Don't worry, my lord. She'll be better shortly, I'll be bound. I'll speak with her."

Two days later, on his return from a gallop across the moor, Galahad found Germaine waiting for him in the stableyard. He slipped off the stallion's warm back and after a firm pat on the black neck, handed the reins to Old Cam.

"Good afternoon, Germaine. Isn't this a brilliant day? Why, what's the matter? You look as if you'd been weeping."

She hooked her arm through his without a word and led him to the far side of the tower where only one window, high up under the roof, overlooked them.

"I have bad news, my lord. I've been watching Bella closely. So has Ariane. Her sickness is real. I thought perhaps she was sticking her fingers down her throat, but she is not. The spasms are real, and she suffers from them."

"I am sorry for her suffering. Cannot something be done to relieve her of it?"

Germaine stared up at him, fumbling for words. "My lord . . . that is not . . . I don't know what you mean."

"I noticed an herb garden behind the kitchen. Surely she can take some concoction for her pain."

"A soothing brew? Ah." Germaine exhaled with relief. "That has been tried, my lord. But she cannot keep it down."

"Would you like me to ride to Battle Valley for a physician? I am strong enough now, and so is Rouk."

Germaine frowned up at him. Was it possible for eyes that guileless to deceive? "She will not need that kind of help until her time comes. What she needs, my lord, is a priest."

"A priest! My God, is she dying?"

Tears filled Germaine's eyes even as her lips split into a smile. She held his hands hard. "No, my lord. She is with child."

Galahad stood as if struck. No expression at all crossed his features. His wide eyes seemed to look into the next world, and beyond. Germaine let go of his hands and they fell lifelessly to his sides.

"I know you have no memory of it," she said gently. "But something must have happened between you in your illness. It is all Bella's fault, I do not doubt. But nevertheless, it has happened. And the child is your responsibility."

He nodded dumbly.

"The nearest priest is at the Christian monastery in Battle Valley. But the brothers do not come here anymore, since Father"—she gulped—"since Father took up reading his books on pagan magic and prophecy. So you must take Bella to them." She gazed into his eyes, liquid azure wells of infinite sadness. "She will be leaving her father's house still unwed. We must trust you, my lord, to do right by her. We must bind you with a ceremony of betrothal, and then let you go. You do see, don't you, that it must be done?"

Galahad drew a long breath, his first breath in this new world of eternal lamentation. "Yes."

Germaine nodded. "Then we will arrange it as soon as we can."

A noise overhead made them both look up. A shutter flew back and a gray head peered out the window above them.

"Who's that? Who are you, sir? By what right have you encroached upon my land? I'll set the dogs on you if you won't answer!"

"Father!" Germaine gasped, and then quickly, under her breath, "We have no dogs, my lord."

Galahad stepped forward and bowed low. "Sir Fortas!" His voice sounded strangled and he pitched it louder. "Sir Fortas! I beg your pardon for coming unannounced. My name is Sir Galahad. I have fought with Arthur and Constantine against the Saxons, and with the kings of Wales and the kings of the north against the Anglii and the Picts. I have come . . . I have come to ask for the hand of your daughter in marriage."

The old man glared down at him and finally scratched his head.

"Which one of them do you want? Not Germaine—I'll not let Germaine go! She's too much like her mother."

Galahad glanced swiftly at Germaine. The longing and regret in that fierce gaze robbed Germaine of breath and made her heart sing. "No, my lord! I ask for Bella."

The old man snorted. "Bella! Ha! Bella's a different matter. Are you rich, sir? Have you anything to negotiate with?"

"With your permission, Sir Fortas, I shall come to you and make my request formally. But . . . give me a little time."

The shutter banged shut in answer and Galahad exhaled. He found that he was sweating. His face a mask, he bowed to Germaine. "If you will excuse me."

A tear slid down her cheek. "Of course, my lord. Go. And farewell."

Galahad slid to his knees by the edge of his bed and clasped his hands before him. Outside, Hugh guarded the door. For a little while, an hour at most, he would be alone. After that, he must take the step which would change his life forever. How had he come to this pass? He pressed his forehead against the bed and shut his eyes. There was only one woman he wanted as a wife, and he had had the chance to wed her—he had *owed* her that wedding—and he had thrown the chance away. More, he had insulted her and her brother, his best—nay, his only friend in all the world. He had made enemies of the two people he loved best. And why? Because he had believed from childhood that he was better than other men. Niniane and her wretched prophecy. Elaine, his mother, and Aidan, her tool. They had filled his head with nonsense for their own ends. But he, Galahad, was paying for it. No, he would not blame them. He was a child no longer. If he was proud, arrogant, certain of his birthright, it was his own fault, not theirs. He had believed them for far too long. And he had ignored others who had tried, again and again, to steer him toward the light. Arthur. Lancelot. Percival. Dane. Ah, God, Dane! His body ached for her; his spirit wept.

Had he not known this trial was coming? Had he not stood upon the ridge looking down across the wasteland and wished for it? Here it was then, and with it, a chance to do things over, to get it right, even though nothing he could do now would ever help Dane. If he had abandoned the woman he loved, then it was only just retribution that he should wed himself to a woman he detested. As his father had done before him!

He cried out, and smothered his cry against the bedsheets. Dear God, Dane's curse upon him had prevailed! *May you follow in your poor father's footsteps and love a woman you cannot in honor have!* Had Lancelot loved Guinevere with the kind of burning passion he bore for Dane? He knew the truth of that. Lancelot's adoration had never wavered; nor had his allegiance. Arthur had told him the truth: Lancelot had married Elaine because he got her with child, not because he loved her. And he lay with her not because he cared for her, but because she seduced him by trickery. And now it was his turn. He could not turn away twice from the duty before him. Not if he ever hoped to be worthy of the appellation "Lancelot's son."

Stiffly, with aching joints, he pushed himself to his feet, splashed water on his face, and called Hugh to attend him.

With the butt of his dagger Galahad pounded on the door to Sir Fortas's chamber. His clothes were newly washed, his boots polished, his cheeks shaved. Hugh had belted on his sword. Germaine had combed his hair. Climbing the stairs to the top floor of the tower he had passed each of the sisters, standing flattened against the wall, faces grave, eyes averted, except for Bella. Her pale eyes, so large now in her overly thin face, had followed him with a hope so intense that he was moved to pity for her.

"Sir Fortas!" he cried.

"Go away!" a faint voice responded. He pounded again, harder and longer than before. At last the door swung open to reveal a slumped, disheveled man in his bedgown, peering at him with large, unfocused eyes.

"What's the meaning of this interruption? Go away, can't you, and leave me in peace?"

Galahad pushed past him into the large, round room. Clothes, scrolls, dried pots of ink, nibless pens, and dirty dinnerware littered the floor. Rats rustled under the unmade bed. A pair of pigeons shuffled on the sill of the single window, its shutter had again swung open. The room stank of smoke, ink, dust, rotten food, sour mead, vermin, dry rot, and urine.

"Sir Fortas," Galahad began with determination, "my name is Galahad. I have come to negotiate for Bella's hand in marriage."

The old man gazed up at him with watery eyes. "You're a fool, Galahad."

"Yes, sir. I believe I am."

Fortas laughed suddenly and closed the door behind him. "Have you any money?"

Galahad drew a linen bag from his tunic and dropped it on the table amid a mass of half-written scrolls. The clink of coins sounded loud in the silence.

Fortas hurried over to the table. "Is it gold?"

"See for yourself."

The old man opened the neck of the bag and fingered a handful of golden coins. "Well, son, if you want Bella, you may have her. Take three of the mares and any furniture you fancy. This is enough to keep me in pens and parchment for a decade!"

"You used to be a soldier, sir, a man with a noble calling." Galahad looked about the room and wrinkled his nose. "What happened to you, for God's sake? What do you do here?"

"I've retired. I am writing a history." Fortas shuffled closer. "My wife died."

"Sixteen years ago."

"No, no, you are misinformed. Last month, it was." He looked up suddenly. "I know who you are. You're the Grail Prince. But if you're here, you've lost your way. Have you come to me for help?"

Galahad's jaw dropped.

"I can tell you things, you know. It's all here in my books." He picked up an old and dirty scroll. "They call you the Servant of God. Or they will soon. What do you want with women?"

Galahad hung his head. "What does any man want?"

Fortas cackled. "And they call you the Virgin Knight as well. But that's a lie."

"Yes."

Fortas nodded. "Don't blame Lancelot and Guinevere," he said suddenly, bringing Galahad's head up with a jerk. "They've given their lives to God and spend each day on their knees. Look to your own soul before you worry about theirs."

"Sir, I—"

"Bella will not be able to give you that kind of love."

Galahad gulped. "I know."

"If you take my advice, you'll give her to the monks in Battle Valley. They might be able to train her to obedience. I never could." He thrust the bag of coins into his robe and waved a hand at Galahad. "Take Ariane as well. Although she's named for her mother, my good wife will not mind. We are better here together without such interruptions. All we need is coin for ink and parchment. Send Hugh to me. I will place an order with the merchant this very day."

Galahad bowed stiffly. "Sir, we have fixed the betrothal ceremony for tomorrow evening. We would be honored if you would attend."

Fortas returned his formal bow. "We'll both be there."

Shaking his head, Galahad returned slowly downstairs. A thought occurred to him, and bypassing the curious gazes of the sisters, he went to find Hugh.

On the following evening the household gathered in the main room on the ground floor for the betrothal ceremony. The women wore their finest gowns and dressed one another's hair with ribbons and wildflowers. Bella, whose illness had emaciated her and left a waxen pallor on her skin, glowed with a fragile, ethereal beauty in the golden candlelight.

Galahad stood across the hearth from them, formally attired with his sword at his hip and his dagger thrust into his waistband. More than once he glanced at Bella but she would not meet his eye. Gillie stirred a pot of spiced wine over the fire, and Germaine threw open the shutters to the warm summer evening. The scents of the summer moor mingled with the wine's exotic spices made Galahad's head pound. But he did not mind it. He felt curiously at peace now that he had decided on his course of action.

Footsteps sounded on the stairs and Sir Fortas appeared on the threshold with Old Cam behind him. The girls stared at their father. He looked ten times taller in his battle dress: leather leggings, Roman corselet, and leather tunic studded with sharp bronze points. His short cloak was fastened over one shoulder with a lion device they had never seen before. A thick silver torque encircled his neck, and a jeweled wristband adorned his wrist. Most astonishing of all, he wore an old swordbelt around his waist and the scabbard that hung from it, hastily oiled and not very clean, held a bright and deadly sword.

Germaine came hesitantly forward. "Father?"

Sir Fortas nodded at her but gazed fiercely at the others. "Where's Ariane?"

"She's making ready, Father; she'll be here soon."

"Where's Bella?"

They stood aside so he could see Bella. It seemed to take him a moment to recognize her.

"Look me in the face, girl."

Trembling, Bella raised her eyes to his.

"If you dishonor this man, daughter, I will kill you for it."

Bella shrieked and dissolved in tears against Megan's shoulder. Megan stared up her father defiantly. "Leave her alone."

Sir Fortas laughed. "Just like your mother, Megan. As feisty as the day is long." He turned his head to look around the room. "Where is Hugh? Why did Cam come for me and not Hugh? What's happened to him?"

"I sent him on an errand," Galahad said quietly, drawing the stares of all the women. "He promised to be back for the ceremony."

"Well, he's not."

Germaine stepped forward. "With your permission, Father, we'll start without him." She glanced quickly at Galahad. The black stallion was not in the stables and Hugh had been gone for over twenty-four hours. Something was afoot, but clearly Galahad did not intend that it should interfere with the ceremony. She took one of Bella's thin hands in hers, and reached for Galahad's with the other.

"We are gathered to witness the pledges of this man, Sir Galahad of Lanascol, and this woman, Bella, daughter of Fortas of Darkmoor, to marry each other as soon as opportunity permits." She joined their hands and dropped her own.

"Bella, make your pledge."

For an instant, Bella threw Galahad a look of triumph; then she cast her gaze to the floor. "I, Bella, promise to wed Galahad of Lanascol—"

"What's the matter?" bellowed Fortas. "Are you ashamed to be my daughter?"

Bella whimpered. "I, Bella, daughter of Fortas of Darkmoor, promise to wed Galahad of Lanascol as soon as opportunity permits."

Germaine nodded. She turned to Galahad.

Galahad drew a deep breath. "I, Galahad—"

"No!" screamed a voice from the doorway. Everyone whirled. There stood Ariane, hair disheveled, dirt on her green gown, clutching a small cloth bag in her hand. "Foreswear your pledge, Bella! I've found you out!" She raised high the discolored bag. "She's been false to you, my lord Galahad! If you wed her, you wed a lie!"

Bella collapsed at Galahad's feet, clinging to his hand. "Pledge to me!" she cried in a piteous voice. "Please! Do it now!"

But Ariane marched up to her sisters, waving the little bag beneath their noses. "Do you know what this is? Can you smell it? No, not stinkweed, nor rotten eggs. Goatsbane! She's been poisoning herself with *goatsbane* to make all of us think she was with child!"

"*What?*" Fortas roared.

Ariane laughed as Bella huddled on the floor, sobbing. "It would serve you right if you died from it! Monster!"

"Wait, Ariane." Germaine's cool voice cut across the clamor. "Be calm a moment. How did you find this bag? How do you know she used it?"

Ariane explained that she had disbelieved Bella all along, and when Bella's sickness started she had begun to watch her secretly. But Bella took nothing in the mornings to make her ill, so she started to sit up at night and watch her. Every night, long after everyone else was asleep, Bella crept out of the tower and spent an hour in the shed by the kitchen gardens. Then she returned. And was violently sick upon rising in the morning. Thrice Ariane had searched the shed but had found nothing except the cold ashes of a fire and a small clay cup washed clean of dregs. Not until tonight, as she dressed for the ceremony, had it occurred to her that Bella might have buried her secret brew, so she had spent the last hour digging up the dirt floor of the shed. And she had found it. Goatsbane. Enough of the weed left to identify with ease, and dregs in the cup this time, too. Bella had been poisoning herself with an herbal tisane.

Everyone stared at Bella, who writhed and sobbed, her thin body curled in pain.

"What is goatsbane?" Galahad wondered.

Germaine shrugged, her face gray. "It's our name for rankweed. We call it that because it's the only thing goats eat which makes them vomit. I suppose she reasoned that it would work for her, too." She knelt down to Bella. "Can any man be worth death, my dear?"

"That man is," Bella wailed.

The slither of metal made them all look up. Sir Fortas had drawn his sword and leveled it at Bella's breast. "Do I understand aright? Did you take this brew to deceive Galahad into thinking you bore his child?"

Galahad stepped in front of the sword, reached down, and lifted Bella into his arms. "Sir, do not punish the girl for my sake. It would be more than I could bear."

"Do you hear that, Bella?" Megan cried. "You have shamed him and yet he defends you!"

Sir Fortas pointed the sword at Galahad. The weapon shook viciously in his hand. "Did you ask me for her hand because you loved her or to give a name to the child?"

Galahad looked down at Bella. Her sobs had subsided and she gazed up at him with ruined eyes. Her lips moved against the shoulder of his tunic. "Tell him the truth."

Galahad faced Sir Fortas. "There is only one woman in all the world I would marry, if I could. But she is a thousand leagues from me."

The sword sank slowly to the floor and Sir Fortas staggered back and fell into a chair. "The wanton hussy. Just like her mother! I disown her. I will not have her in the house."

"Gillie!" Germaine cried. "Some wine! His color's not good!"

In the midst of the commotion a shadow darkened the door and Hugh stumped in. He took in the situation at a glance, met Galahad's eyes, and nodded. Galahad settled Bella on a bench near the hearth, asked Megan to tend her, and then went down on one knee before Sir Fortas.

"I have made arrangements, sir, for the care of your daughters by the brothers at the monastery of St. Ninian in Battle Valley. The abbott has agreed to shelter them—I made provisions for four, but he will not balk at five—and teach them writing, reading, and Scripture. You are welcome to go yourself, but if you prefer to remain here, they will send a brother to tend you. Old Cam has volunteered to stay. So has Hugh. You will not be alone. You will have money for pens, inks, and parchment; you will have access to the brothers' library; you will have someone to clean and look after you. But you cannot keep your daughters penned in this tower any longer. That way lies madness. You must see that."

Sir Fortas gazed at him a long time without speaking. The girls held their breaths. Even Bella, who stared at him in open wonder, did not break the silence.

At last Sir Fortas nodded. "Their mother will approve. Take back the bridegift you gave me and give it to the brothers for their dowries. Do not weep, Germaine." His eldest daughter, who had wrapped her arms about his neck, shed tears onto his tunic. "I will live to see your wedding." He smiled suddenly at Galahad. "She will wed on the day you meet young Tristan by the well. I know all about it. I have a book of prophecy."

Galahad frowned at this gibberish, but thanked the old man.

"You must promise me one thing, Galahad," Fortas said quickly. "When you get to the end of your journey, take care of the good sister. She is life to you."

Which sister did he mean? Galahad shrugged. "Sir, the journey I am on has no end."

On the day of departure Old Cam harnessed two of the mares to a rude wagon. The other three were already with foal. Farouk danced eagerly, neck arched and tail raised in front of his mares while the women loaded their meager belongings into the wagon.

But before they climbed in for the ride that would take them across the wasteland to their hearts' desires, they gathered around Galahad.

Germaine curtsied. "Here, my lord. We have a gift for you, the five of us. It was Bella's idea. Since you came to us without a badge, and we would not have others mistake you for a man of no significance."

In her hand she held a round badge carefully crafted of elmwood and bearing the emblem of his shield: a red enamel cross on a field of painted white. He thanked them solemnly and stood still while Germaine fastened it to his cloak.

"I shall wear it with honor," he told them gravely. "As a reminder that even in my darkest hour, I found people who believed in me."

Bella came up to him as her sisters headed for the wagon. "Wear it in good health, my lord," she said softly. "I shall never forget what you did for me. But if you wanted to make me really happy"—she glanced at him quickly and saw his face darken—"you would travel the thousand leagues back and marry that woman who has your heart." She laid her cheek next to his and skipped away before he could respond.

To hide the flush that sprang to his cheeks, Galahad swung onto his stallion's back and saluted Hugh, who stood at the door with tears in his eyes. Then he raised his arm and gave the order for departure. In a window high up under the roof, old Fortas leaned out to watch him go.

"Don't miss the ford!" he shouted, waving a scroll. "It's a test! It's all in my book!"

Galahad shook his head. *Do your best? At the fort?* What fort? What could the old man mean? Fortas might have moments of lucidity, but clearly the man was mad.

50 ⛊ THE FORD

G alahad stopped halfway down the hill and wiped his brow. The day was hot for September, the road dusty and seamed with pebbles. Farouk had thrown a shoe and for two hours Galahad had led the limping horse along the old road in search of a smith. Now, as they rested in the shade of a giant oak, he thought he could just see, beyond the stand of pines at the bend in the road, the sinewy, telltale line of willows that marked a river and, with luck, a ford.

He was sure to find a smith if he followed the road downhill. Mastering the art of shaping iron with fire was nearly as old as civilization, and for as long as men had lived together they had needed tools, and revered the men who made them. In Arthur's Britain nearly every crossroads, ford, or waters-meet boasted a smithy. Wherever two paths met the old, simple magic of the Ancients still hovered, hallowing the meeting of men, joining the ways of going. There smiths built their forges. They did not forget their roots, nor change with the changing times. They remained as they had always been, as solid and reliable as the earth herself, needing no protection beyond the awe they inspired. They served low folk as they served kings; they bowed to no man.

A thin stream of smoke rising against the far hill roused Galahad from his thoughts. "Come, Rouk. I was right—that's bound to be a forge. Bear that cracked hoof a little longer and we'll soon have it put right. If it's a comely place, we'll stay the night to give you rest."

Obediently the stallion followed him back into the road. They had just reached the stand of pines when they heard a woman's scream. The horse's ears shot forward. A man bellowed; a ruckus followed with shouting, thudding, the clash of swords. Galahad leaped upon the horse's back and the stallion sprang forward. Together they thundered down to the riverbank, splashed across the ford, and bounded up the other side. Horses scattered as they charged into a clearing. Two men were battling the smith outside his forge, one with a broadsword, one with a club. Galahad thrust his sword into one man as the smith dropped with a groan in a pool of blood. He pulled the weapon free, spun, and took off the other's head before he could raise his club to block the blow.

"Ai-eee! Ai-eee! Flee!" The cry came from behind him. Horse and rider whirled as one. Behind the hut at the clearing's edge four men ran headlong for their ponies. Galahad cut them down, one by one, and left them to bleed. He jumped off the horse and approached the hut cautiously. Somewhere he heard moaning. He pushed open the door and edged inside, but the hut was empty.

"Father!" The piteous cry came from the back of the hut. He ran toward the voice and found that what he had at first taken for a pile of soiled washing was in fact a woman, thrown on a waste heap, her clothes torn to rags.

He took off his cloak and knelt at her side to cover her. Large brown eyes looked up at him in a face twisted by pain. "Father!" she whispered. "Get Father! I will live—but see to him!"

The smith lay senseless and covered in so much blood it was difficult to see where he was injured. He was a huge man with the chest and shoulders of a giant. His right arm had three times the breadth of his left. Small cuts bled all over his body—his attackers had been cowards, indeed!—and a gash in his side, a dangerous wound, seeped steadily. Galahad searched the hut for a piece of sheeting he could tear into strips, and bound the wound as best he could. The man was too heavy to carry to the hut or lift onto a pallet. In the end he took logs from the stack against the forge wall and rolled the smith into the forge itself. There was a half-made pallet in the corner.

Apparently he had slept in here before. With the rest of the sheeting and the barrel of water near the door he washed the smith of blood, then covered him with his own blanket to keep off the flies.

When he returned to the woman at the back of the hut he found her standing, leaning against the wall, shaking uncontrollably. She had covered herself as best she could, but he could see teeth marks, scratches, and bruises over her breasts and hips. She cowered when she saw him.

"I will not harm you. Will you come inside where I can tend you?"

She shrank back, her eyes glazed and unknowing. In one swift movement he stepped forward and gathered her in his arms, ignoring her protestations, and carried her inside the hut. She was calmer once she lay on her own pallet, and while he cleaned her wounds she closed her eyes and made no sound.

Not so long ago, a mere three years before, when he been a battle commander in Constantine's service, he had feared even to look on a woman's body, had feared to touch it, had feared the very thought of intimacy. Now his fear had left him, and without the hindrance of fear he could do what needed to be done. He marveled at the change, but he knew well he had achieved it at a cost. He was like everyone else now. He had joined that fellowship of men who knew that a woman's body could be a source of pleasure, a well of joy. He wondered if this was how Adam had felt at the first bite of the apple.

"Father!" the girl said suddenly.

"Your father is alive. For the moment."

She closed her eyes and let him finish his ministrations. When he had covered her with his cloak she looked up at him. "Whoever you are, I bless your coming. They tried to kill him."

"Why would they attack a smith?"

Her face tightened. "Why, indeed, but to get at his daughter." She was not a pretty girl but her skin was unblemished, her eyes clear, and her rich brown hair long and thick. Galahad said nothing and in a moment she went on. "We've nothing worth stealing. As you can see." A tear slid down her cheek. "They raped me."

"Yes."

"It hurts . . . it hurts."

"Can I get you water? Or wine, if you have it?"

She shook her head. Tears squeezed past her lids.

With a gentle hand Galahad pushed her tangled hair back from her face. "Rest here for a while. Sleep if you can. You'll feel better later."

She controlled her tears and nodded. "You'll tend Father?"

"I will do my best, but I'm not a healer. Is there anyone about who can help?"

The ghost of a smile crossed her lips. "I can. Did they cut him?"

"Only once badly, but I'm not sure how bad it is. It may be mortal, or it may heal."

"Where is the wound?"

"Here. Across his side."

She blanched. "Bind it and keep it covered. Keep him warm. Keep the forge fire going. I will go to him when I can stand."

Galahad rose. "Is there no one I can send for?"

"You're not leaving?" She reached out a hand toward him. "Oh, don't leave us! We are at your mercy."

Galahad took her hand and held it. "I won't leave. I promise. I'll do what I can. I just hope it's enough." He smiled briefly. "I can't leave. My horse threw a shoe."

The smith was still senseless when Galahad returned to the forge. Finding him pale and cool, Galahad picked up the bellows and stoked the fire. It was hard work and his arms ached before he was satisfied with the blaze. He set some water to heat and then went outside, sweating. Rouk was grazing contentedly along the riverbank. Galahad slipped off the bridle, drew off his tunic, soaked it in the river, and cooled the stallion's sweated neck and back. He washed the tunic out, splashed his face, chest, and arms with the cold water, and hung the garment to dry on a willow branch.

Then he set about dragging the dead men into the clearing. All six of them were the type of rugged outlaws who lived hand-to-mouth among the hills, killing as they chose, stealing what they needed to stay alive. Like the men who had killed Sir Ulfin. When Arthur was alive he had cleaned the land of vermin such as these. In those days men had been glad to live under the High King's laws because they were fair laws, and the lowborn got the same justice as lords and princes. But nowadays the whims of petty kings ruled the country and no one without gold could expect a hearing, much less a redress of his wrongs.

Galahad inspected the bodies. Their rags were worthless, little more than ill-dressed skins. Two had leather boots worth having, probably stolen from someone else. All of them, even the youngest, had jewelry. Between them he collected four copper armbands, a silver wristband, three tin badges, an amulet made of shell, two copper earrings, and a woman's necklace strung with glass beads. A little distance into the surrounding forest he found a patch of pliable earth free of rocks and oak roots, and in the forge he found a digging spade. Burying the ruffians took most of the afternoon.

When he had filled in the pit, fashioned a crude cross to mark the place, said a prayer over the grave, and washed his hands in the river, the sun lay low in the west, painting the water gold. He collected his tunic and the bridle from the tree, slung an arm around the stallion's neck, and led the animal into the horse shed hard by the forge. The only other animal in the

shed was an old, gray gelding with a broad, sunken back. Galahad guessed
he belonged to the smith. He divided a bale of meadow hay between them,
brought them water from the river, and slid the bar across the opening.

Then he went into the forge to see the smith. To his surprise the girl
was already there, bending over the wounded man with a jar of thick salve
in her hand. He watched her quietly. Her hands moved with the quick, effi-
cient skill of a practiced healer; only the tears on her cheeks gave her away.

"Can I help? Is there anything else you need?"

"Hot water. Hot enough to burn."

He watched as she flushed and cleaned the gash in her father's side. It
was deep and still seeping. She filled the gap between the edges of the skin
with the thick, brown salve she had brought with her, then rebound the
wound with Galahad's help.

"Do you want me to try to lift him onto the pallet?" he offered.

She wiped away a tear and shook her head. "No. Not yet. He can't be
moved until that heals enough to stiffen. It will be days yet . . . if he lives."

"Do you think the wound is mortal?" Galahad asked softly.

She shrugged. "In a man half his size it would be. If something vital had
been cut he would be dead already. All we can do now is wait and hope the
fever does not kill him."

"Fever? He's cold. That's why I've been stoking the fire."

She smiled sadly. "Oh, it will come. It always comes after a deep cut. A
hard, sweating fever can draw the poison out, but it can also kill."

Galahad nodded, remembering Lancelot's leg wound at Autun, and the
following fever which had nearly taken his life. He knelt down beside her
and saw her shrink away. He backed up a little. "I've fed your father's horse
and my own. I wondered . . . I wondered if you had anything put by for dinner. Bread or meat or gruel."

Eyes averted, she shook her head. "No, I'm sorry . . . I was . . . it's bak-
ing day and I was fetching the flour jar when the . . . when they came at me
out of the woods."

"That's all right," Galahad said quickly. "I'll take care of it. Where do
you usually build your cooking fire?"

"Out there, in summer. Do you have anything to cook?"

"I can set a rabbit snare. This time of day it should not take long.
But"—he paused uncomfortably—"I can't bake bread."

He was rewarded by a small smile. "The kiln's in here. Father built it
into the forge, so one blaze feeds them both. If I could walk, I could—"

"Are you still bleeding? What . . . what can be done?"

She looked away. "I ought to sit in a tub of hot water."

"I saw such a tub out back by the horse shed. You tend your father.
Leave the rest to me."

He set his snares at the edges of the clearing, then stoked the forge to raging heat, filled buckets and jars with water from the river, and set them to boil. He brought the tub into the forge, rinsed it out, and, bucket by bucket, filled it with steaming water. Then he reached a hand down to the girl.

"Let me help you." But she recoiled from his touch and began to tremble. "I won't hurt you. I promise."

"I can't help it!" she cried, hiding her face in her hands. "Go away, please, go away! I'll be all right, but you must leave me alone!"

Galahad turned and walked out into the night. It was rapidly growing cool as darkness filtered through the forest, blinding as a sea fog after the brilliance of the forge. He gathered firewood and built a cooking fire outside the forge in an old pit surrounded by firestones. His snares yielded a pair of rabbits. By the light of the fire he skinned them, whittled sticks, and roasted them over the open flame. When he peered into the forge to see if the girl was ready, he found her bathed, dressed, and curled at her father's side, asleep. He retrieved a blanket from the hut, half-cured animal skins crudely stitched together, and covered them both. He stoked the forge fire again before he tossed his bedroll on the ground outside the doorway, and, after a quick meal, fell asleep.

The next few days followed the same pattern. He rose at dawn and fished for breakfast in the river, cooking what he caught and sharing the meal with the girl. She seldom spoke to him and seemed to fear his presence as much as his touch. All her concentration was on her father, who roused now and then to his senses, drank the water she pressed against his lips, and then lapsed into senselessness once more.

Galahad took the smith's ax and cut wood for the forge, for the girl seemed panicked at the thought the fire should go out. If she had lived here all her life no doubt she had never known a day without the forge furnace. She appeared to heal quickly, for she was soon able to walk about, to bake bread, to wash her father's bloodied clothes and arrange a more comfortable sickbed for him. Galahad contented himself with hauling water, chopping wood, hunting for game, and tending the horses, all at a distance from her.

On the fifth day the fever began. It also began to rain. Galahad sat just inside the forge doorway and watched the girl mop her father's brow, croon to him the old hill-songs of his youth, stroke his stiff and graying hair with her tender hand. She was afraid and used songs, balms, and healing herbs to keep her fear at bay.

In his mind's eye he saw another woman, ill-used and full of grief, alone with her pain and her fear. Did she shy at the touch of every man who came near her? Did she weep at night for the irretrievable past? Did she curse his name when she knelt at prayer? Did she cry out to her brother for vengeance on her betrayer? Or did she call upon some inner strength to put his memory behind her, and go on? In three years' time had the knife edge of hatred dulled? Or did she carry scars from her ordeal that would harden her heart in bitterness all the days of her life?

He passed a hand across his brow and bowed his head. There was sweat on his face. For so long he had struggled to ignore the shadows that trailed him, the unutterable sadness that fit him like a glove. But, like the repeated, resounding strike of a hammer on an anvil, the truth beat down the walls of his defense and forced itself upon him. He closed his eyes to shut out these thoughts—he was practiced at it—but they haunted him day and night, always springing forward in an unguarded moment, always demanding recognition. More than once he tried to pray—just for the blacksmith and his daughter—but although his lips spoke the words he meant to say, his heart stayed dumb. There was no release now in confession, no liberating sense of cleanliness in prayer. The weight he carried was too heavy to be lifted. He could only go on from day to day pushing it to the back of his awareness, hoping without hope that with time it would dissipate, dissolve, and fade away.

By day the smith slept, but at night he worsened. Then would he rant in his fever, call out to his long-dead wife, laugh with vanished drinking companions, sing snatches of old doggerel, instruct his daughter on the shaping of a plow as though she were his apprentice, call upon long-forgotten gods for ease of his pain. The girl wept to hear him. For days the fever raged, steady and fierce; his daughter began to pray aloud to the Great Goddess to let it break. Once, near panic, she urged Galahad to fan the forge fire to blasting heat, that she might heat her father's poker and reopen the wound, cleansing it by burning. But she collapsed in tears long before it could be accomplished.

On the night of the new moon the smith died in her arms. Galahad heard his death sigh, whispered a silent benediction, and rose from his place at the door.

"No-o-o!" the daughter shrieked, and threw herself across her father's body, clinging to his senseless form. "Get you gone! Get out with your filthy Christian magic, and let him live!"

Outside the night was cold and clear; the stars sailed overhead like fire-bright ships on a dark sea. He knelt in the shadow of a pine and bowed his head. His throat tightened. His mind closed and he strained to form the words. They would not come. Help for the woman's grief, strength for her suffering—that was all he wanted to ask. But the thoughts that hammered at his mind struck a darker note. *My shame is of my own making and cannot be forgotten or forgiven. Ah, God! Better I should never have drawn breath!* He buried his face in his hands. In all the years Lancelot had worshiped Guinevere, he had never publicly dishonored her. He had always put her good before his own. And he, Galahad, had considered this passion contemptible. What an utter fool he had always been! What he had done to Dane was so far beneath him, Lancelot himself would never believe it possible of his own son. Tears splashed down Galahad's cheeks and he fell to the forest floor, covering his face to hide from the gleaming stars.

At dawn the girl emerged from the forge, her eyes red, her hair in tangles, and her face puffed from weeping. She looked down at Galahad in his bedroll.

"I have strewn his body with herbs. Three days he must rest there. On the third day he must go into the ground. I have no right to ask it of you, but will you dig him a grave?"

Galahad sat up. "Yes. Where?"

She shrugged. "As hard by the ford as possible." Then she turned and walked toward the hut. At the door she looked back. "Don't let the fire go out. Please."

She must have slept, for when she appeared again that evening to take up her vigil at her father's side, she looked much better. She had combed her dark hair and bound it neatly behind her head. The gown she wore was her best one; it was not much stained and bore no patches or signs of repair. She walked past the cooking fire, where a pair of river trout roasted on their spits, and past the long, shallow ditch where Galahad stood with his spade, straight into the forge without so much as a glance to the side. For three days she sat beside the body, moaning and chanting, cutting off her hair with her father's dagger, neither sleeping nor resting nor taking food. Galahad came in from time to time to work the bellows and bring her water; she ignored him and he left without speaking to her.

On the evening of the third day she rose unsteadily and came out to where Galahad waited by the finished grave. Her beautiful hair was gone, reduced to wayward tufts that stuck out at awkward angles. Without looking down at the gaping hole, she made him a reverence and spoke stiffly. "My lord, I would be glad of something to eat."

He gave her a bowl of the stew he had made, rabbit, mushrooms, and wild onions, the staple meal that had supported him and Percival throughout their travels, and watched with the solemn pleasure of the cook as she ate it all. It couldn't be up to her own standards, for he did not know one herb from another, but she ate with relish and licked the bowl clean.

"Have some more, I beg you. There's plenty."

Soft brown eyes looked up at him. "No. Thank you. I shall be sick if I eat more." She paused and lowered her eyes. "I must observe the mourning period before I . . . before I leave. You are very kind, and I have no right to ask it of you, but would you wait for me?"

Galahad nodded slowly. "If you wish."

She rose, and briefly touched his hand. "Thank you. I owe you much and have given you little but grief. You are a good man."

Galahad flinched at her praise but she forestalled him by speaking again. "I would be grateful for your food, for I may not prepare it myself during mourning." She smiled briefly. "This is where it is difficult, not living in a community. The isolation we two always treasured is a burden now. And I'm afraid it must fall on your shoulders. For I may not leave the house, yet he must be buried and sent to his gods with prayers. I know by your badge you are a Christian and will pray to no god but your own, for that is the way of such men. It cannot be helped. A mention or two of Llud of the Otherworld would please my father's spirit. This is all I ask of you. Will you do it for me?"

Galahad bowed. "I will do it."

Tears glimmered in her eyes as she turned toward the hut. "One more thing." Her back was to him and he strained to catch her words. "You may let the fire die."

Every day for fifteen days Galahad prepared her meals and left them at the door of the hut. He buried the smith and said the required prayers. He fed and tended the horses, swam in the river, watched the wild geese flying south overhead, slept in the forge, and let the furnace slowly cool. It took twelve days before the last ember died. That night an autumn gale raged through the forest and he lay awake beside the hearthfire he had lit for warmth, listening to the wild roaring of the wind and the creaking protests of the trees. He let his thoughts slide idly by, paying little attention to them. This was a respite, he knew, between the agony behind him and whatever was to come. A time of waiting. A time of peace. He was content, so long as he could keep his mind empty of all but the sounds around him, the groaning forest, the flutter of the fire, the wind-whipped tumble of the river, the howling fury of the storm. He closed his eyes as the racket grew, and fell asleep.

At dawn on the sixteenth day the girl emerged from the hut dragging a sack that held all her belongings. She was dressed in an old pair of woolen leggings, a leather tunic, and an overlarge, thick robe that Galahad guessed must have been her father's. A kerchief knotted tight under her chin hid her butchered hair. She curtsied before him and smiled.

"Today we leave this place, my lord. I know a track through the forest that will take us to the town at the watersmeet in only a week's time. My uncle is the smith there and he will take me in."

"Where does the road go, then?"

"To the same place, but it takes ten days. It curves, you see, following the river, but the forest track is straight."

Galahad nodded. "I will get the horses." He bridled both animals and found a saddle and neck strap for the old gelding. When he led them from the shed he saw the girl standing over the frosted, raw earth of her father's grave. But she looked up dry-eyed when she saw him and came away. The forge she did not enter.

To his surprise she lifted his stallion's feet one by one and examined his hooves. "I will pull his old shoes," she announced. "He will go better that way. My uncle will make you a new set, for your care of me." He fetched her the tool and watched as she pried off the shoes with expert skill and filed the crack in the bare hoof.

"You must have been a great help to your father."

She nodded but avoided his eyes. "We were a support to each other. The only support either of us had." She paused. "He was so afraid of the day I should marry and desert him. He was so fierce to all the young men who came this way." A soft smile touched her lips. "Of course, I never would have left while he lived. Whoever wanted me would have to want him, too. I told him so often, but you know fathers. He never believed it."

Galahad lifted her onto the gelding, bound the sack to the saddle, and, taking both horses' reins in his hands, led them along the path she pointed out. She never looked back.

The journey through the forest proved uneventful. Galahad kept watch at the edges of the fire every night. Before dawn the girl rose, and he slept as she prepared his breakfast. It was a joy to eat her cooking; he blushed to think how proud he had been of his own preparations. His prayers, it seemed, had been granted, at least as far as concerned the girl, for her attitude was unwaveringly calm and cheerful and she often sang softly as she rode. On the fifth day out she sang a song that startled him.

> O hark and hear the sacred ravens sing
> For crownèd by the pricking blackthorn ring
> Alone and hidden under timeless stone
> Lies the hollow hill, Lord Myrddin's home.
>
> Waiting as the water weathers
> Ringed by pillared stones alight
> The emperor's most sacred treasures
> Awful in the burning white.

We wait for him at Llud's own secret gate
For him alone the dark door open waits,
The seeker comes! And lo, his blessing stays
Upon our Motherland a thousand days.

"My lord, you are pale." She smiled at him. "Did you not care for my song? It's an old one. I don't know many that they sing now in the towns, but I find singing passes the time and leaves the mind too busy for other thoughts."

"No," blurted Galahad, "it's not that . . . I mean, your voice is charming. By all means, sing. But I . . . I think I've heard that song before. No, not the melody, but the words only. Where did you learn it and what does it mean?"

She gazed at him curiously. "My father taught it to me. He learned it from the hillmen, the Ancient Ones. They often came down from their fastness in the hills to have my father sharpen their tools and pass on news of battles and kings in the Giants' world." She smiled. "That's what they call us, you know. The Strange Ones, or the Giants. They speak to few, for few men know their tongue. Smiths do, who live in lonely places like ours, who serve only the road. They had nothing of value to trade him for his service, so he demanded a song of them each time they came. That's how he learned it."

"And its meaning? Is it one of their legends, this seeker, this man who finds the treasure?"

Her eyes widened at his eagerness. "Why should you suppose the seeker is a man? I have always thought it referred to Lord Myrddin himself, the god of the hollow hills."

"Why should it be so wonderful that Myrddin find something in his own home? Who is the emperor? Could it be Maximus?"

She frowned in puzzlement. "Who is Maximus? I took the emperor to be Llud himself, King of the Otherworld. For Myrddin's homes are gates to the Otherworld. Everyone knows that"—she smiled slyly—"except Christians, who take no time to learn another's faith."

Galahad hardly heard her. He was back in Dane's cave, fourteen years old, listening to the poem she had learned from the local hillmen. Surely they had mentioned Maximus, or Macsen, as the owner of the treasure. His heart sounded loud in his ears as the pain of yearning struck him. What he would not give to believe again that he could find the Grail! To have no stain upon him which made him unfit to lift his eyes so high! He could have wept with the agony of his loss. But the girl was speaking to him.

"—thought you would have asked by now. Did you not wonder that I sing at all?"

With an effort he forced his attention to her. "Yes, I did wonder. I admire your fortitude."

She laughed lightly. "Oh, no, my lord, it is not fortitude. It is something very much deeper than that—wonder at the gods' ways, of the symmetry of things. My dear father died, but with your help I cared for him properly and sent his spirit on its way to join my mother in the Otherworld. I have done what I could for him. And even as he left this world, another life entered it, that I should not be alone but should have someone to care for me in my last years."

Galahad looked at her blankly. "Who?"

She laughed again, a laugh of honest joy. "The Great Mother has blessed me with child, my lord. On the same day my father was struck down, this child entered my body."

Galahad stopped dead in his tracks, bringing both horses to a sharp halt. "Do you mean to say it happened when those ruffians raped you?"

Pain washed her face. "Never mind them. That is a memory I prefer to keep dark. But that is the day the Mother blessed me."

"But . . . but . . . surely such a thing is impossible! One coupling only!"

She frowned at him. "What is the matter, my lord? You are pale as a nether spirit. Of course it is possible. Was not King Arthur himself conceived in a single bedding?"

"Yes, but . . . that was different. Arthur's coming was foretold! It had to be!"

"There is only one magic to begetting," she replied gently.

Galahad staggered as the prophecies of his childhood returned to him in a cold blast of clearheadedness. He, himself, had been foretold. In one single night of drunkenness Lancelot had lain with Elaine and begot upon her Galahad himself. The world spun around him. *Let it not happen to her! Let it not be!* A child! Dear God, the thought had never even crossed his mind! Sweat sprang on his forehead. It was too late for prayers. The thing was long past saving. If by some miracle she had conceived, he was already father to a two-year-old child!

"My lord, make haste! We must reach yonder bluff before the sun sets, or we shall not make it to my uncle's forge tomorrow."

The words forced him to action and he hurried on in silence, but it seemed to him that the shadows that had dogged his heels the last three years had suddenly taken on shape and substance. He seemed to hear behind him not only the steady plod of horses' hooves, but the lively patter of a child's step. His dishonor was complete.

Late the next afternoon as the shadows deepened, they came down out of the forest into a shallow valley where a growing town had sprung up at the meeting of two rivers. They passed plowed meadows lying fallow, rounded pens of cattle, sheep, and goats, walled with earthworks and closed with tangled briar. They passed sturdy houses set hard against the road, yards full of chickens, kitchen gardens cut and bound neatly against the coming winter winds. They passed an inn with the tavern door flung wide in welcome, the scents of roasting meat and the sounds of laughter wafting out to greet them. At the end of the town stood the smithy, where the ancient road crossed the river. An old black gelding waited tethered at the door, his head low, his dull eyes half-asleep. Smoke poured through the roof hole and from within the forge came the steady clanging of the hammer.

"Go on to the house," the girl urged. "He's busy. He'll pay us no mind until the job is done." Behind the forge, nestled in a stand of birch, sat a rambling wooden house. It was built in sections, each section added as the need arose, with little attempt at harmony with the existing structure. Yet it had a cozy look, with a fire going in the main house and candles lit against the fast-falling dark.

A stocky woman opened the door and stood on the threshold, cleaning her hands on her apron. "Who's there? Who's come at this time of day? The smith's busy and his dinner waiting. He can't help you for an hour or two."

Galahad reached up and lifted the girl down. She made a pretty curtsy to her aunt. "Aunt Mab, you'll not remember me, perhaps. I'm your niece Lynet, Savro's daughter."

"Lynet!" The woman clapped her hands to her mouth, and then outstretched them as she hurried forward. "Child, I'd not have known you! How you've grown! When were you here last? Five, six years ago? Skinny as a colt, you were, and look at you now! My, you've turned into a beauty!"

Galahad realized with a thrill of surprise that although he had lived a month with the smith's daughter, he had never known her name. The two women hugged and chatted, both talking at once, with more to say, apparently, than time to say it. He headed toward the horse shed he had seen behind the forge. There were four animals there already, but room for as many more. He got the horses settled and fed, but when he came out he found the women had already disappeared inside the house. He hesitated a moment. A huge silhouette appeared at the forge door and bent over the gelding's hind leg, a movement followed by the sizzle of burning hoof and the smell of hot iron. A dunk in the water bucket sent steam roiling upward. Eight smart taps and the nails went home. The gelding, lids drooping, was fast asleep.

"Hey, now, Blackie, wake up there! Back to the shed you go!" The silhouette moved forward and melted into the dark. Galahad heard the gelding stir, heard the smith moving around in the shed, heard his heavy steps hurry by him toward the house. The smith threw open the door and cried, "Mab! We have a visitor! There's a new horse in the shed."

Galahad followed him up the steps. The inner room was warm, filled with people and firesmoke. Mab, Lynet, and half a dozen children of various ages sat around the fire. Directly in front of him, the smith gesticulated eagerly. "A finer animal I never saw, delicate and strong—like the ones Pendragon used to breed! Who would own such a horse as that?"

Mab rose. "Come, Sandrin, don't excite yourself. No doubt it belongs to the lad who brought Lynet. Look who's here! Your own niece, Savro's daughter, come to us for safekeeping. But alas, husband, good Savro died a month ago."

That news steadied the smith. "Ah, no. May God rest his good-hearted soul. Of course we will take you in, Lynet, and glad to have you. Perhaps you can teach your cousin Merko some manners at last." A ruddy-faced youth in his teens, whose eyes had not left Lynet since she walked in, colored radiantly. Sandrin laughed. "Well, there's a silver lining to every cloud, they say. How did it happen, Lynet? Savro was a strong man and never sick."

"We were attacked by outlaws, both of us. A warrior rode down out of the hills to rescue us, only a moment late because his horse had thrown a shoe. He killed them all, Uncle, every single one. But he was too late to prevent the stroke that killed Father. He helped me with Father; he kept the forge going; he tended the horses and fed me, every day, through the fifteen Days of Passage." The children looked puzzled at her reference to pagan rites; from where he stood behind Sandrin, Galahad could see a copper cross hanging on the wall. "He buried Father and led me by the forest trail all the way here. He is goodness itself, Uncle. I took him to be a gift from the gods, and asked no questions. I do not even know his name."

"Where is he now, niece? We must thank this man—and I must ask him about the horse!" the smith boomed, just as Galahad stepped past him into the light.

The smith stared wildly at him, as if he had just materialized out of the smoke. He pointed a shaking finger at Galahad's badge. "Sir, I know who you are! Every traveler upon the road has tales to tell of your doings."

"I beg you," Galahad said quietly, "do not pass on those tales."

"But you are the Servant of God who travels across Britain in search of holiness! You are the savior of the helpless and the strong arm of the weak. Why, you are the talk of every village and watering place! All the people of Britain revere you for your kindnesses."

"Galahad," Mab whispered. "The Grail Prince."

In the stunned silence, Lynet slid to her knees and the children followed her example.

"Please," Galahad said, "please don't."

Mab curtsied to the floor. Galahad grabbed the smith's arm to keep him from bending his knee.

"Good sir, I have done nothing for your niece any passing stranger would not have done. She is the one you should be praising. She survived an attack by ruffians, tended her father when her own wounds were not yet healed, bathed him and treated him, fasted when he died, shut herself up for two weeks in her grief, put it behind her and set off with a cheerful countenance to beg your hospitality. There is no other woman in Britain, save one, so courageous."

At this Mab wept openly and Sandrin bowed low. "My lord, we are honored to have you in our house. We would be honored if you would eat with us and stay the night. It is not a hardship—we have plenty of room—but if it were, we would gladly bear it all the same to give you ease."

Seeing the expression on his face, Lynet rose and went to Galahad. "Uncle, have a care. To a good man, praise is as painful as a wound. Treat him as if he were your own brother come to life and he will be comfortable enough."

Galahad reddened, but managed a small smile. "Thank you, Lynet. I am not responsible for the tales about me; I am not the man those tales describe. I am an ordinary person, like any one of you."

They all smiled at him politely and in perfect disbelief. They begged him to sit with them and sup; they gave him pride of place around the fire and served him the choicest morsels from their meager fare. Mab showed him his sleeping place and brought water from the well for him to wash in. She packed the children and the smith off to bed, bade Galahad goodnight, and left him alone with Lynet by the fire.

They sat in silence, watching the dancing flames. When Lynet finally spoke her voice was oddly hesitant. "Why didn't you tell me who you were? Why didn't you want me to know?"

Galahad shrugged. "I liked it better when we had no names."

To his surprise, she nodded. "I won't tell a soul. But I can't answer for my cousins."

"No matter. I won't be here long."

"Where are you going?" He did not answer, but picked up the iron poker and stabbed at the fire. "I must thank you, Galahad. I owe you my life."

He shook his head. "I only did what anyone would have done. Give your thanks to God, not to me. He sent me across the ford."

"I have. And it is not true that anyone else would have done as much. You grieved. You did not even know him, and your grief was as deep as mine."

He said nothing, but stabbed again at the fire.

"I wondered, but I did not like to ask, who it was you lost . . . forgive me. It is none of my concern. Only . . . I would give anything I possessed to help you as you helped me."

There was no curiosity in her voice, only warm concern. He shrugged roughly. "I am beyond help."

"Surely not," she said, laying a hand on his arm. "Gods are not deaf; nor are they weak. If you need help, ask."

"I . . . I can't."

She nodded slowly. "Let me tell you what happened to my father when my mother died. He was out of his mind with grief. He could not eat. He could not sleep. He could get no peace from prayer, nor from his friends, his family, not even from his work. In his despair, he wished for death."

Galahad looked up. Her solemn eyes looked through him and spoke to his very soul.

"He railed at the gods in his anger, and dared them to make him whole. He was full of bitterness, rage, and sorrow. He went from shrine to shrine, packing me along in his saddlepack, poor man. And then one day a she-wolf came into our camp, lifted me from my blanket, and started to carry me away. Father killed the beast and saved me, and from that moment on, put his grief behind him. It was the beginning of our devotion to each other." She smiled tentatively and withdrew her hand from his arm. "It is a matter of focus, you see. Finding the true center of your heart."

Galahad bent his head. "The center of my heart is beyond my reach."

Lynet pointed to the copper cross on the wall. "Perhaps you need a longer arm."

In the dying light of the fire the cross glowed red and gold against the wattle wall. Red and gold. Arthur's colors. From a great distance Galahad heard her say, "It's a long ride, but Christians always claim that the monastery at Amesbury is the best place to go for peace of mind."

She rose and with a soft "Good night" left Galahad alone in the fire-shot dark.

PART II

The Once and Future King

*In the eleventh year of the reign
of Constantine*

51 ⊕ AMESBURY

Two children sat by the well in the midday sun. The elder, a girl of twelve or thirteen, splashed cool water from the bucket onto her face and hands. The boy, her cousin, a lad of six, bent over his sandal straps, attempting to repair what had already been repaired three times before.

"Never mind," the girl said kindly. "Have some water. It's so deliciously cool!"

The boy sprang to his feet and grabbed his wooden sword, lovingly carved from a pine bough, complete with hilt and sharpened point. "How dare you address me so, maiden! My name is Galahad! The greatest knight in all the world! Take that! And that!" He danced around her, thrusting and feinting, accompanying his attack with such grunts and exclamations, and raising such a dust cloud, that the girl fell to laughing and then coughing.

"Enough!" she cried, waving her hand before her face. "Enough. Good sir, I yield! Bless me, Tristan, I wish I knew where you get your energy. It's hot enough to fire clay in the open air."

"That's weak woman's talk," he retorted, sheathing his weapon in the rope sling that hung from his waist.

But the girl only smiled. "I'll box your ears; then we'll see how weak you think me! Are you going to help me with these buckets or not?"

"I'll have a drink first." He reached for the horn cup in its niche in the lip of the well and dipped it in the bucket, draining it all in one gulp. As he lowered the cup he happened to glance down the dusty road.

A lone knight on a black horse road slowly toward them. With each weary step of the horse's hooves small white puffs of dust sprang up, spread, and slowly dissolved in the shimmering air, until the whole figure, man and horse, floated like an apparition above the road.

The boy rubbed his eyes and stared. "Look, Ayn."

She turned. "Who is it?"

"I don't know. A stranger."

"A Saxon?" she cried, grabbing his hand.

But the boy shook his head. "Not a Saxon."

"A pilgrim, then?"

"He doesn't look much like a pilgrim."

The girl pulled at his hand. "Come on, let's not wait to find out. It's a hot day; he's probably stopping here."

Stubbornly, the boy stood his ground. "I want to see him."

"We'll run to the woods and watch from there. If he's a stranger, he won't know the woodland paths; we'll be safe."

But the boy shook his head obstinately. "You go. But I want to stay."

Ayn dropped his hand. "You know I daren't leave you. Mother would have my hide! Are all Cornishmen so stubborn? You know I'm not to let you out of my sight while you're visiting us. I swear to God, Tristan, if you get us in trouble I'll kill you with my own hands."

He looked up at her calmly. "Don't be afraid. I'll protect you."

"With what?" She snorted. "Your sword?"

But he had turned all his attention back to the approaching knight. The horse was not so old as he had thought, but it was tired, plodding with head down and neck outstretched, the reins slack across the withers. The knight himself sat straight, eyes half-closed against the glare of the long, white road. The boy's eyes widened. He rode bareback!

"Ayn," he whispered, "look who it is!"

Horse and man saw the children, and stopped. The stallion's head lifted and his nostrils flared as he scented water. The knight slipped lightly from his back and came forward. Ayn retreated to the edge of the well. He had black hair, sleek in the sun, and the bluest eyes she had ever seen.

"May a stranger and his horse drink from your well?" the knight asked gruffly.

"It's not our well," the girl quavered. "It belongs to all of Amesbury."

"We'd be honored," the boy spoke at the same time as the girl, and they glared at each other.

"Thank you." The knight lifted their bucket and set it before the horse. With an audible sigh, the stallion buried his muzzle in the cool liquid and great gulps slid up his throat in a steady rhythm. When at last he raised his head and blew gently, the knight lifted the second bucket and emptied it over the animal's steaming back. Within seconds they were all sprayed as the horse shook joyously. The children laughed, the knight smiled, and Ayn caught her breath at the dazzling beauty of his countenance.

"No," the knight commanded sharply as the horse began to bend his knees. "No rolling." Obediently, the animal straightened and, moving off toward the trees, lowered his head to graze. The stranger lowered the empty buckets into the well and brought them up refilled. "With your permission," he murmured, nodding toward Ayn, and stripped off his dusty tunic. He bathed quickly in the cold water, pouring it over his chest and his shoulders. He was brown from the sun, his skin smooth and unblemished. His arms were long and well shaped, his chest and back hard with muscle, his shoulders broad and his waist narrow. Something within the girl she hardly guessed existed awakened and stirred. He soaked his tunic and wrung it out. By chance, his eyes met hers.

"My lord." Flushed, breathless, she dipped him a curtsy.

The knight regarded her wearily and with a small sigh pulled on his wet tunic. He refilled the bucket once again, and bowed low. "Many thanks."

"Wait!" cried the boy, who all the while had been staring at the hilt of the slender sword in its ancient scabbard. "Here, my lord, you have forgotten to take a drink yourself!" He lifted up his own horn cup. For a moment the knight stood immobile; then he took the cup, filled it, and drained it.

"Thank you, son. May I know your name?"

"Tristan of Lyonesse," the boy said proudly. "I'm a king's son, and the grandson of a king. Like you, my lord."

The blue eyes flickered and the knight's lips twisted as he handed back the cup. "Don't put your faith in lineage or ambition. Nor in dreams." He turned and whistled for the horse, who came trotting. "Put your faith in the strength of your sword arm and in God. All else is mockery." He leaped upon the horse and gathered the reins in his hand. "God keep you, Tristan. Which way to the Christian monastery?"

"Straight ahead down the road, my lord."

He nodded to the boy, sketched a salute to the girl, and headed off. They watched him out of sight; then Ayn stamped her foot hard in the dust. "He did not ask to know *my* name!"

"You offended him."

"I did nothing to offend him! You saw me—what did I do? No, he is just ill brought up, however noble."

Tristan stared at her. "Don't you know who that was?"

"I know he was ill-mannered." Ayn sniffed, plucking at her skirt.

"That was Sir Galahad!" Tristan cried.

Ayn shrugged defensively. "I don't care who he was; he has no manners."

"Sir Galahad is the bravest knight in all of Britain."

"Just how do you know it was Sir Galahad? He wasn't wearing a white badge with a red cross. He wasn't wearing any badge at all."

"Didn't you see his sword? The rubies on the hilt? That's the red cross of his badge. It's the most fearsome sword in all of Britain. And I stood *this* close to it!"

"Well, if it was Sir Galahad," Ayn persisted, "why is he here? There's no grail here. Who's he come to see? He's hardly welcome anywhere anymore. Your grandfather Constantine calls him traitor, the men of the north laugh at him behind his back, and the King of Gwynedd wants his blood. Perhaps he means to hide out in the monastery and become a lay brother."

Young Tristan was scandalized. "Him? Hide out in a monastery? Not a knight like that. He's going to find the Grail."

Ayn squared her shoulders and lifted the water buckets. "He looked tired to me. Maybe he's given up. After all, he's been searching for years and he's never found anything."

Tristan turned his back on her. He stared down the road where a shimmering of dust still floated in the air. "Maybe," he said, "he's looking in the wrong places."

Abbott Martin took his evening stroll after vespers, leaning on the arm of his companion. The heat of the day had died with the lowering sun and he found it cool and pleasant to walk among the willows by the stream's edge. The Great Plain lay at his left hand, and the neat, tilled plots of the monastery at his right. Several of the brothers had gone back to work in the gardens, eager to make use of the long light of summer evenings.

"Tell me, Brother Marrovic," mused the abbott, "tell me what you think of our new lay brother, the man who wishes to be known as Joseph."

The young monk looked up quickly. He could read nothing in the abbott's face but his customary detachment. "He's a warrior, Father. Not a man of peace. He won't stay long."

"No? Does he make trouble? Come, give me your opinion."

"In one way, I wish we had more like him. He is the most industrious man I have ever seen. He has rebuilt the benches in the refectory and patched the stable roof. He helped Brother Dynas plow two new plots, and has repaired the footbridge that was partly washed away in the spring floods. With Brother Timon he has relaid the flooring in the chapel, and by himself has whitewashed all the eastern cells."

"All that," the abbott murmured gently, "all that in two weeks' time."

"He's strong as a horse and there's nothing he won't do. Why, Brother Howyll even caught him scouring the cooking pots, which was supposed to be Jacob's penance. Er—perhaps I shouldn't have mentioned that."

But the abbott only raised his brows. "Indeed?" He stopped, turning to watch the setting sun throw long fingers of color against the whitewashed walls. "Joseph's industry is plain. He drives himself but finds no relief in it. Why do you suppose that is?"

Marrovic shifted uncomfortably. "I don't know him well, Father. Nobody does. He holds himself apart. But he's a fighter and he's quick. The threat of violence is always there in his responses. He's not the kind of man you can jest with. As far as I can see he works and suffers and suffers and works. As if he has a debt to pay."

The abbott looked at him sharply. "That's perceptive of you, Marro."

"Why is he here, Father? And what makes you think 'Joseph' is not his name?"

The abbott paused. The rose-washed walls darkened slowly to lavender. The monks rose from their gardens, wiping their hands and chatting together. In a pear tree a nightingale took up its song. "He doesn't answer to it, you know, not at once. He's only had it a fortnight. It's still new to him."

"But why travel incognito? Is he a fugitive? An enemy of the King?"

The abbot shook his head. "I doubt it's anything so simple. He is in torment, not hiding."

They walked slowly back together in the thickening dusk. The abbot stopped to admire the evening star, clear and brilliant in the western sky, riding low over the courtyard where the women's quarters lay.

"Perhaps he has come to work it off," Marrovic suggested, "whatever it is. We've seen that often enough."

"It can't be worked off," replied the abbot sadly, "which he must surely know by now. He spends more time on his knees than any man in Amesbury, but his prayers avail him nothing. Dreams disturb his sleep. The demon in him has got his soul." He looked at the star again, and suddenly drew breath in surprise.

"Yes, Father? What is it?"

"God has whispered in my ear. I wonder . . . yes, I dare say it cannot hurt. Tomorrow, Marrovic, bring Joseph to me after prime. I think I will take him to visit the Good Sister."

"The Good Sister! But she sees no one."

Abbot Martin smiled. "She will see *him*, I think, if he is who I think he is."

Marrovic stared at him "You know who Joseph is?"

"I have a suspicion."

"Who?"

But the abbot shook his head. "Give it five minutes' steady thought and you will discover it yourself. But as it is not my secret, I may not share it."

"But the Good Sister is dying."

"Yes, that is so."

"Why send this stranger to her? What good can come of it?"

The abbot glanced up again at the evening star. "Two souls in such dire need may perhaps help each other." He smiled down at Marrovic. "I see you have your doubts. Well, Marro, so do I. Nothing may come of it. But this I know—God moves in ways mysterious to men."

Galahad demurred at the abbot's suggestion.

"A woman? But why? If she has lived here for years she can have no need of me. And I . . . I certainly have no need to speak with her. Please, Father, set me whatever task you will and I will do it. But I am not fit to see this holy woman." He spoke rapidly, nervously, as he walked at the abbot's side, slowing his steps to match the pace of the older man. "Surely there are other things I can do to serve you better."

"You have done much to serve us, Joseph," the abbott replied calmly. "It would be ungrateful of me not to do you a service in return."

"Then let me pray alone in the chapel, or seek solitude in one of your cells. It is all I ask."

"But nothing comes of your prayers, Joseph," said the quiet voice. Galahad looked at him sharply, but the old man's hood fell forward across his face and he could see nothing in its shadow. "God will not speak to you in the chapel, or in the solitude of a cell. But I think God may wish to speak to you through this woman." He spoke with authority, and Galahad did not answer, but stared miserably at the paving stones. "You would do me a service to see her, Joseph. This woman is dear to us, and is dying. Visit her for ten days, and after that you may do what you will."

"Yes, Father."

They advanced slowly toward the women's quarters. The cells they passed were small and bare, but scrupulously clean, with swept dirt floors and a few pieces of simple furniture. Wreaths of fresh herbs hung on the walls to sweeten the air, and through the uncurtained windows the warm breeze brought the scent of summer flowers.

"I will tell you something about the Good Sister. She is a widow without family who came to us many years ago for protection when her husband died. She never left. She has touched the life of everyone here and made it better. She taught most of our younger men to read and is more beloved among the women than the abbess herself. And I have found, over the years, that she has a great gift, though she knows it not. Very often God will speak through her mouth."

"Why is she not the abbess, then?"

"Oh, she has not taken orders. She is a lay visitor." The abbott smiled gently. "She is a worldly woman, Joseph, who has dealt with kings and princes. However much she may enjoy the peace of our small community, she knows she is not called to join us. She still mourns the death of her husband. It is a fetter which binds her to this world."

"She is highborn? Where does she come from? What is her name?"

"When she came to us, consumed by bitterness, pain, and grief, she put her old life behind her and began anew. She put away her name and her kin. We call her the Good Sister."

"Surely, Father Martin, you must know who she is."

The abbott stopped and turned toward him. "I do," he said gently. "But I think you can understand, Joseph, why some who stop among us might wish to remain anonymous." Galahad flushed and looked away. "We respect that wish," the abbott said calmly, resuming his slow progress. "Now God lays His hand upon her and calls her home. She has waited patiently for this, yet I worry that she is not yet ready to go. There is something unfinished, something left undone that she feels she must do, but is powerless to accomplish by herself. I do not know what it is. It is my hope, Joseph, that you may discover it, and do it for her, and let her die in peace."

"But why would she tell *me*, when she has not told you?"

Abbott Martin shook his head. "I don't know. But God has sent you here for a reason, of that I am very sure. And it is not to mend our roofs and plow our fields. Ah, this is the door."

He tapped lightly. The door was opened by a thin woman in a plain gown, well past her youth, who held herself very straight. Her narrow, sharp-featured face held widely spaced, intelligent eyes. She looked vaguely familiar—Galahad wondered if perhaps he had seen her somewhere before, but for the life of him he could not remember where.

"Good morning, Abbott Martin."

"Good morning, Anna. I have brought Joseph, a new lay brother, to see the Good Sister. How does she do today?"

"My lady is resting. She is weak today, but not in pain."

"Will she allow Joseph to come and sit with her awhile?"

Anna's glance rested on Galahad. Her eyes widened and she frowned. "Father, I don't think it would be wise."

"Would you ask her?"

Anna hesitated, glanced at Galahad again, then made the abbott a graceful reverence. "I'm sure, Father, she will see anyone you vouch for."

She stepped back from the door and reluctantly Galahad moved forward. As he passed her he felt her eyes on him and had the uncomfortable impression that she knew him, but he could not remember meeting her and had no chance to ask. The abbott drew Anna aside and left him alone in the cell.

At first he thought there must be some mistake. He had been brought to see a woman and no one was there. The room had only one bed, blanketed in muslin on a wooden frame, and a pine washstand bearing a clay pitcher and a horn cup. An old three-legged stool sat near the bed and a carved wooden cross adorned the wall. There was nothing about the room to signify that a highborn lady lived here. If anything, it was poorer than the other cells he had seen.

"Sit down, good sir." He jumped and drew a sharp, painful breath. The whispered words came from the bed but there was no one in it! Then the muslin blanket moved and he realized with a shock that it was a woman's robe, swaddled with care around a body so thin that nothing of her flesh was visible. As he watched, a small, frail hand appeared and beckoned him toward the stool. A white veil of mourning covered her head and face. He could see no more than a shadow behind it, but he had the impression of eyes watching.

"My lady," he managed politely, taking the stool. "Good morning to you. I come from Abbott Martin. My name is Joseph."

"I know your name and where you come from," the thin voice replied. Galahad waited, but nothing else came. It dawned on him she might have difficulty speaking. Unhappily, he tried again.

"Abbott Martin desires that I stay and talk with you, my lady, but in truth . . . in truth I do not know what about. Um, why do they call you the Good Sister?"

The muslin veil stirred. "I am sure Abbott Martin did not bring you here to talk about *me*." He heard amusement in the low whisper, and fidgeted uncomfortably. "How did you come to Amesbury, Joseph?"

"I, well, I was riding south, and it lay in my path."

"You had no destination?"

"I go from one place to another as I will."

"You are a man in the full flower of your strength, with a noble bearing and a wonderful sword. Yes, word has gone around about your sword. Surely, you are an accomplished warrior and have done battle for Britain."

"Yes, but . . . long ago I fought for the High King. But lately I have killed only outlaws and thieves who hide in the hills and torment villagers. In return, the people give me food, a place to sleep, and permission to pray in their place of worship. In the past year I have gone from holy house to holy house throughout Britain. It is . . . in many ways it is better than fighting battles."

"You fought for the High King? Do you mean Constantine?"

"Constantine, and before that, King Arthur."

"You must have been very young. Did you ever go to Camelot?"

"Yes, my lady. I was raised there."

She was quiet for so long a time that he began to wonder if she had drifted off to sleep. But at last, the soft whisper stirred the light cloth of her veil.

"Tell me about it."

"About Camelot? Have you never been there?"

"I was there once. But time dims one's memory. I should so like to see it again, through your young eyes. Tell me what life was like in Camelot, when Arthur lived."

It was easy, after all, to tell her. After a moment's hesitation, the words came tumbling out of him, as if they had been tightly locked in some old, dark trunk of his memory and she had found the key. Mainly he told her about Gareth, his dearest, his only boyhood friend. Gareth, who'd been fourteen when Galahad had come to Camelot at five, yet who had become his protector, his older brother, his teacher and his friend. Gareth had let him tag along everywhere, and had prevented the other youths from making him the butt of their jests. He told her stories of their gallops through the woodlands, of sword practice with wooden blades, of games with cudgels and bow and arrows—everything Gareth had shared with him. His heart lightened as he relived those times; he grew excited and eager, laughing at the picture he drew of Gareth standing in the River Camel with weeds dripping from his hair, smiling as he recalled Gareth stretched on the riverbank, fashioning a reed pipe and playing to amuse the birds. He was just starting on the tale of how Gareth stole two horses from the High King's stable and took him on a wild ride across the marsh, when the waiting woman returned and stood sternly at the end of the bed.

"Brother Joseph," she said distinctly, as if the name produced a bad taste in her mouth, "that is enough for today. You will tire my lady overmuch."

To his surprise, he found that he was disappointed. The tiny hand moved upon the muslin. "You will come again tomorrow?" the voice said softly. "It is wonderful to hear you speak."

"With pleasure, my lady." He glanced at Anna as he rose. "At the same hour?"

She grimaced. "If you must."

There could be no doubt about it any longer. She despised him. As he passed the door he thought he heard the whisper once more, but he could not be sure.

"Anna! You promised!"

52 ✝ THE GOOD SISTER

He went daily to visit the Good Sister. His sleep improved. Now his dreams were filled with Gareth, with Arthur, Bedwyr, and Gereint, and the other men he had worshiped in his childhood. He relived those times in their retelling and it brought him unexpected joy.

The Good Sister seemed to enjoy these tales every bit as much as he did. On his third visit he found her sitting up in bed, her slender hands folded in her lap while Anna scowled and frowned and fussed behind her. She seldom spoke, but sat and watched him, drinking in his voice from behind her mourning veil. Even moments painful to recall were possible to face when she was listening. She possessed a reservoir of inner peace, or strength, or serenity, that flowed out, surrounded him, and buoyed his spirit.

"What a fine swordsman Prince Gareth was," the Good Sister remarked, after one of his long encomiums on his friend's skill and daring. "He must have learned from a master."

"From the finest swordsman in all Britain," he replied with a touch of pride. "Surely you have heard of Lancelot."

Because she asked no questions and did not press him, he found himself wanting to tell her about his father. Even so, it was difficult at first. He grew clumsy in his speech and his face burned, but as she said nothing at all about Lancelot, either in praise or condemnation, gradually he was able to speak of his father with better ease. To his surprise, he found he viewed Lancelot more dispassionately in her presence. His deeds of bravery now seemed like efforts of heroic virtue, and his sins . . . suddenly his sins seemed no more than instances of the frailty all men suffered. Lancelot was a good man, a great man, worthy to be Arthur's second-in-command and deserving of the High King's trust and friendship. There was no one left in Britain of his stature.

As he sat stunned at his own eloquence, he noticed her veil trembling and wondered if she wept. He feared Anna might chastise him, but when he came next day she actually curtsied to him. He soon saw why. A heavy chair had been placed against the wall near the window and in it sat the Good Sister, waiting for him.

"Good morning, Joseph." Even her voice was stronger, having in it a thin reed of timbre, the whisper gone. He took the stool at her knees and kissed her frail hand.

"Good morning, my lady. How glad I am to see you feeling better!"

"Thank you, Joseph. You are very kind. It is your doing, I believe. I have been saying to Anna that I hope today you will talk to me about Arthur."

"I should be delighted. What is it you wish to know?"

She squeezed his hand. "Tell me, Joseph, about that last foray to Less Britain, when Arthur took the army to fight the Romans. Tell me what you know of it, what you saw. What was his plan? What went wrong? How did his son, whom he loved so dearly, come to be his enemy? How did he come to take twelve thousand to Less Britain, and return with fewer than five?"

Galahad frowned. "You sound bitter, my lady. I assure you, Arthur was a wise man and a great warrior. All the kings of Less Britain united behind him. He smashed the Roman army. All his strategies were successful. Never doubt his prowess."

She withdrew her hand and spoke with the first touch of coldness he had seen in her. "My husband was killed at Camlann. I suppose I have a grievance against Arthur."

Remembering the abbott's words to him, Galahad grew eager to comfort her. "Your grievance is against Mordred, my lady, not against Arthur. Arthur was a king returning to his kingdom and found it denied him."

"But we who remained in Britain knew it was not denied him. Mordred swore openly he would yield his crown to his father."

Galahad spoke very gently. "He did yield the crown, but too late. The two armies were already face-to-face. Battle could not be prevented."

She sank back in her chair and motioned him to continue. He told her the whole story of the army's adventures in Less Britain, leaving out only the small details which might have given him away. It was a long tale, but she attended closely and Anna did not stop him. Only twice did he pause. When he came to the night of Lancelot's near death from his leg wound, she stirred and crossed herself. And when he came to the battle of Cerdices Leaga, she interrupted him.

"So Mordred refused to fight against his father."

"That day, yes. He fled from the field and left the Saxons to fight us."

"Then he kept his word. Arthur mistook him."

"King Arthur did not know he had made any such pledge. None of us did. But we saw him take the field against us, riding beside Britain's sworn enemy, Cerdic the Saxon."

"With whom," she countered, "we had had a treaty of mutual defense for some five years."

Galahad grunted. Her husband must have been one of Arthur's men; she knew her facts. "He did not act like an ally."

"His lands had been invaded." She sighed wearily. "Arthur must have been very tired."

"Indeed, we were all well-nigh exhausted, what with the shipwreck and losing so many men and provisions, and the quick-march through Saxon lands trying to avoid encounters—and then to see those two armies coming against us. The King was very angry. But we won the battle. Mordred withdrew westward. And that night King Arthur sent me on a mission."

Beneath her veil he could see a shadow of her smile. "Perhaps to get you out of the way. You must have been young, and he knew what was coming."

He looked at her sharply. "Perhaps. He sent me with a secret message to . . ." Should he tell her of his first message, to the Queen? To that beautiful and seductive woman who had been his father's bane? No, he could not. ". . . to Niniane, Lady of the Lake."

She shuddered. "Do not speak to me of Niniane! She is a witch! With her foreknowledge she could have prevented the massacre at Camlann and saved them all! Yet she did not."

Anna laid a hand upon her sleeve. "My lady, do not distress yourself."

Galahad shook his head. "Niniane did try to stop the battle. I learned it later—she rode out to the plain of Camlann and counseled Arthur to arrange a meeting with Mordred. And they met. What happened afterward was not her fault."

"Did you also fight in that awful slaughter, Joseph?"

Galahad looked away. "No, my lady. I did not. The Lady Niniane placed a spell on me. I did not wake until the battle was over."

"Ah. Was that by the King's order, or was it Niniane's own idea?"

"What do you mean?"

"You said the High King gave you a message for her."

Galahad gasped. "You think *that* was the message—to put me to sleep until the battle's ending?"

"It might have been."

"But Arthur said he wanted her to come to him. He told Lancelot the same thing. That's all I ever learned of the message."

She moved sharply, straightening in her chair. "You saw Lancelot again? When? Tell me."

There was command in her voice. Anna laid a hand upon her sleeve, but found it shrugged off in an imperial gesture. Confused, Galahad continued hesitantly.

"After we buried Arthur—"

"You buried Arthur?" She was trembling all over now.

"Please, my lady!" Anna begged.

"Silence!" came the sharp hiss from beneath the veil. She extended a small, shaking hand and Galahad took it in his own. "Please," she whispered, "please, Joseph, tell me what you know. If I hear it, perhaps I may die in peace."

"Very well, if you are sure—"

"I am very sure."

"I awoke from my sleep at the monastery on the Tor just as the monks bore Arthur's body to the chapel. Lancelot attended him. They blessed him and said prayers over him. Lancelot and I buried him alone, that no one would know where he lay."

"I thought you told me Lancelot had been left behind in Lanascol, unable to walk."

"Yes, my lady, but as soon as he could sit a horse he returned to Britain, fearing what Mordred might do. He came to Camlann just in time for the battle and carried Arthur from the field when he . . . when it ended." He relayed to her all that Lancelot had told him on that still, eerie evening when they had sat and spoken calmly together, father and son, for the last time, with Arthur's spirit over them. She wept openly to hear it. Anna cradled her head and glared at him, but he found he could not stop. He told her everything: Lancelot's throwing Excalibur into the lake at Arthur's bidding,

Arthur's prevision of the three queens in the boat from Avalon, Lancelot's tears as the boat floated away, bearing Arthur with it, gone forever. At last, when he came to the burial itself, he stopped. He found he had run dry of words and could say no more. The Good Sister straightened and pushed Anna gently away.

"Only you and Lancelot know where he lies?"

"Yes. I am sworn to secrecy about the place, lest the Saxons should find him."

The white veil nodded. "Anna. Leave us."

"My lady?"

"Leave us. I am well, I assure you."

Anna acquiesced reluctantly. "Very well. I will be within call."

A great foreboding assailed Galahad as the door softly closed. If the Good Sister asked him for the secret of Arthur's resting place, would he be able to deny her? It was such a great relief to open his soul to her! Would he now be able to close it against her plea?

She took both his hands in hers and he braced himself. Her hands looked so small and pale and fragile in his own strong, brown ones; she was so thin and tiny, how could he deny her what she asked?

"Tell me, Joseph," she said quietly, "what you and Lancelot spoke about before you parted."

He looked up in relief. "You are not going to ask me where the High King lies?"

"Of course not," she replied in some surprise. "You have sworn an oath not to tell. But clearly you spoke to Lancelot when it was done. I would like to know what else he said. And when you parted company, and why. It seems you two were nearly all that was left of Arthur's army."

There was strength in her voice and a wholly feminine curiosity that he found surprising and amusing. "We spoke about Arthur, mainly. And what a king he was. And about . . . fathers and sons, and the things that divide them."

"Thank God," she said under her breath.

"But when we came to the future . . . he was going back to Lanascol. He gave up on Britain. I had to stay. My friend—"

"Percival, wasn't it? Anet's son?"

"Yes, my lady." Had he mentioned Anet? He could not remember. "Percival fought at Camlann and I didn't know whether he lived or died. I had to find him and take him home to Gwynedd, one way or the other."

"Ah. That was good of you."

"Lancelot and I went down together to the Lady's shrine. There we parted. Percival was in their House of Healing, recovering from a grievous wound. Lancelot went on his way."

"Where?"

He fidgeted. Why on earth would she wish to know?

"What is the matter, Joseph? Have I asked you a question you cannot answer?"

"No, I know where he went."

"Will it pain me to hear it?"

"Possibly. How can I know? He went to see Queen Guinevere."

"Ah." She held his hands tighter. "Did that distress you?"

"I thought it hasty. We had just come from Arthur's grave, and he could not stay the night in Avalon to tend his leg, which was bleeding, but must hie off after Arthur's wife."

"Surely, Joseph, it was not like that." Her voice was very gentle. He slid onto his knees and laid his head in her lap. She stroked his hair with a motherly caress. "They were true friends, by all accounts, Lancelot and Arthur. When a king dies, Joseph, it is news to all the world. Everyone talks about it. Perhaps Lancelot wanted to tell the poor Queen in person, that she might know it and have a chance to grieve before she heard it gossiped all about. And no doubt, as Arthur knew he was dying, he sent his friend with words to speak to the wife he could not bid adieu himself."

"That's what Lancelot said," Galahad muttered, "but there was more to it than that. He had always loved her, all his life. He wanted to take her home to Lanascol and wed her."

He heard her quick intake of breath and her hand stopped. "You can't know that."

"I do know it."

"Did he say so?"

"Not in so many words. I accused him of it, and in defense he said he doubted she would come with him."

"And did she?"

"I have heard that she did not. But he asked her. Of that I am certain."

There was a long silence while tears welled in Galahad's eyes, tears he could not keep back no matter how hard he tried. Her small hand stroked his brow and pushed the hair from his face.

"I am so sorry, Joseph, that it should cause you pain." Somehow, her very presence eased the hurt.

"It was his one great weakness, his love for the Queen. It colored everything he ever did. Even if it was a passion sent to him by God and was not a thing he could help, it might have been bearable, but—"

"But what?"

"He cherished it over the other things he should have loved."

"What things?" She touched his brow and he closed his eyes. What a wonderful thing it was to bare his soul to such a loving heart! The aftermath of glorious confession engulfed him, and he sank deliciously toward sleep. He made one last effort to dredge up what lay, aching, at the bottom of his soul.

"My mother," he whispered, succumbing. "He never loved my mother."

Anna met him outside her door in the morning.

"Anna, why are you frowning so? Pray tell me all is well with the Good Sister!"

But she merely curtsied and said coolly, "Follow me, my lord, and I will take you to her."

He followed her, not noticing the new address, down corridors and through a portal to the gate of the women's garden. There Anna left him. "I will come for her in an hour," she said. "No one will disturb you until then."

Galahad looked around the garden. Trees stood at the corners, shading the walks, while wild lilies, daisies, mallow, lavender, and larkspur grew in colorful confusion against the enclosing whitewashed walls. The Good Sister sat on a shaded bench, upright and still. As he approached her, she rose and faced him. She was taller than he had expected and stronger than he would have believed a week ago.

"My lady!" He knelt and kissed her hand. "How good to see you! You are certain you are well enough?"

"Perfectly certain. And you? You were so unhappy yesterday and I fear I might have been the cause."

He smiled. It felt like the first time in months. "On the contrary, I am very well indeed. Nothing you could do to me could harm me."

"Mmm. I hope you will still think so at the end of this hour. I must speak with you, Joseph." She patted the bench beside her and they sat down together. "Now, I am an old woman, past forty, and you must forgive me for what I am about to say. If I had not come to love you, I would not ask it." She paused. "You are running from something. It is why you are here. Tell me, is it a woman?" She held his hands as she spoke and the desire to confess it tugged at his soul.

"How could you know?" he blurted, reddening. "The world thinks I seek for holiness, or for a marvel. But what I seek is absolution . . . for an unpardonable sin." He was breathing hard. Like a moth too near the desired flame, he shied away. "And indeed, I have dreamed more than once of a marvelous vessel and spear that, if I could only find them and retrieve them, could restore Britain to her former glory and bring back her King."

"Bring back her King?"

"Yes. Restore King Arthur to us."

"What nonsense!"

"Niniane said so. To me. She said he is waiting to return."

She bowed her veiled head and said evenly, "Galahad, did Niniane send you on this quest?"

He leaped to his feet. "You know my name? Who told you?"

She looked up and the tenderness in her voice melted all his anger.

"My dear, you did, in a thousand little ways. Your voice, your eyes, your gestures—and your tales contained a hundred details only you could know. Do not fret, Galahad. I knew your name before I even saw you, as soon as I heard about your sword. It's Lancelot's sword. He would never have parted from it except to give it to his son."

"Does everyone know, then?"

"Only Abbott Martin. No one here cares who you are. And if you choose to stay among us you may remain as Joseph. I will not tell a soul."

"Thank you for that."

"I have heard of this quest, Galahad." She reached out for his hand and pulled him gently down upon the bench. "You must know . . . you must know that Arthur cannot return from the grave. Those dreams are phantoms. So what drives you? In the last four years the tales about you have grown into impossible legends. Galahad of the red-crossed shield is known to everyone in Britain. Up north in Battle Valley I believe you are worshiped as a saint. You said yourself you have spent the last year on your knees in holy houses. What are you atoning for?"

He looked away. He could never tell her without the armor of anonymity.

Her voice softened suddenly. "Shall I hazard a guess? There is no power on earth like love. You lost your heart to a woman."

He inhaled sharply, but still could not look at the shadowed face behind the veil.

She continued very gently, "Deep love, honest love, forces one to decisions that perhaps one would rather not make." He flashed her a wild look and instantly regretted it. He knew his face gave him away. "Marriage means burdens—a wife, a child, a return to Lanascol, reunion with your father—obligations that a young man on a glorious quest might consider to be entanglements. You chose another future, but every day of it you fight to keep the painful memory of your choice within bounds. The witch Niniane has given you the means."

He cried out in anguish. "By all that's holy, I never meant it to come to love! One moment we were talking by the fire, and the next—" He gulped. "I've tried to convince myself that it was *her* fault for seducing me, just as my mother seduced Lancelot. But I . . . I know the fault was mine." He fell to his knees, hands to his face.

She bent forward and cradled his head in her arms. "I know," she said softly. "It is an old, old choice. And you are right that women are seducers. At times we need to be. But what makes you think your mother was such a one?"

"Everyone tells me so." He choked on the words. "She seduced my father to take him from the Queen. Everyone says it was so."

"Lancelot never told you that."

"No, but Arthur did, once. And it explains so much about Lancelot, if it is true." He found he could breathe again, now that she had led him away from the flame. "I never believed it could have been beyond his will—until it happened to me." His whole body shuddered. "I was begotten as revenge upon the Queen."

"Nonsense." She bent and kissed him. He could feel her lips through the fabric of the veil. "You don't know how it was at all. Rise, Galahad, and walk with me awhile. I will tell you a little about your mother."

He rose and offered her his arm. Her weight against him was so light and unsteady, she relied on his strength even to stand. At first it pleased him to be her strong support, but as she spoke he realized he was trapped. He could not leave and let her fall; he could not speak while she was talking. For as long as she chose to walk about the garden, he must stay by her and listen.

"I knew the Lady Elaine, Princess of Gwynedd. I knew her well. She was a beautiful girl, full of life and energy. You have her eyes. Every one of Arthur's companions admired her, including Lancelot. They were standing in line to wed her. She was the most eligible maiden in the land, but she refused all her suitors. Do you know why? The truth should not surprise you. She loved Arthur." The grip upon his forearm tightened. "Now, they say that all the world loved Arthur, and that was true enough, but not as I mean it. She loved him as only a woman can love a man. She was drawn to him first by reputation and then, when she met him, by the sheer power of his presence. She was passionately devoted to him her entire life." They came to a fork in the path. The Good Sister raised her face to the sky, and sighed. "Surely no one can blame her for such devotion. Her only problem was Guinevere. You know the story."

They started down a new path. The way was uneven and she went slowly, leaning on his arm. "When Elaine was still a girl, her mother, Alyse, your grandmother, took in her sister's orphaned child and Elaine's cousin, Guinevere. And although Elaine was the more energetic of the two, always full of plans and mischief, she was also beset by an abiding jealousy. She was just thirteen the summer Arthur's companions began searching for his wife. Alyse and Pellinore were sure that at last Elaine's time had come. Even at thirteen she had blossomed into a beauty. I like to remember her the way she was that summer, awaiting her future like a spring bud awaits the rising of the sun. All her life she had been groomed to be a queen. All her life she had loved Arthur Pendragon. Now he was High King, nineteen, unwed, and looking for a bride."

The Good Sister stopped and slowly turned toward him. "Can you imagine how she must have felt the day Pellinore came home and told his daughter that it was her cousin Guinevere who had been chosen? No one had gone to Camelot to propose Guinevere. It all happened by accident and at the last minute. And to make matters worse, Guinevere had never wanted to be chosen. Like everyone else in Gwynedd, she had hoped and expected Elaine would be King Arthur's queen. She cared nothing for Arthur. In fact, she wept to learn she must leave her home to marry a man she had never even seen. The two of them wept together at the unfairness of it all. But what was there to do? Neither of them could protest the choice without shaming Gwynedd, Wales, even Arthur himself, who had taken no part in the choosing, but was willing to abide by the decision of his companions.

"When the time came for Arthur to come to Wales to take his bride away, Elaine had mastered her jealousy, even if Guinevere had not quite mastered her fear. But Arthur did not come. The Saxons landed in the north that spring and he was called away. In his place he sent three of his closest companions: Bedwyr, Kay, and Lancelot. You know already what happened. Imagine, then, how Elaine must have felt. First, her foolish cousin is given a gift she cares nothing for, but for which Elaine would gladly sacrifice a limb. Then her cousin falls in love with the best friend of the man she is promised to. Is there a sadder story in all the world? Elaine's heart broke. She felt unjustly treated, even betrayed, by the girl her mother had taken in as an orphan. Had Guinevere stayed in Northgallis, Elaine might very well have been High Queen. Instead, once they came to Camelot, Guinevere was first in everything and Elaine second. It was not a role she cherished. That first summer was a torture to her. Every day she saw the man she adored but he never looked at her, having eyes only for his bride. Yet the bride suffered secretly for love of Lancelot. Truly, it was laughable."

Galahad stopped. His mind was numb. He knew his arm was trembling, but he could not stop it. The voice he had not recognized continued. "Guinevere grew to love her husband, which was inevitable, I think, given the man he was. Elaine approved this. She felt it was no more than Arthur's due. But Elaine could see clearly what others were only beginning to guess: that Guinevere still loved Lancelot with the passion of first love, a love that was returned, though never openly displayed, never allowed to blaze, but kept at a painful, steady burn. Imagine how Elaine, faithful to her single, enduring passion, resented her cousin's plight! Imagine how desperate it made her! She lived in fear of this secret flame touching Arthur's honor. As time went on and the fire between them did not cool, she grew more anxious. It angered her that Arthur himself accepted it and trusted his friend and his wife not to betray him. But Elaine could not trust them. However honorable their intentions, she did not believe they had the strength to hold out forever. Sooner or later they must yield to each other and betray the King. So Elaine did the only thing within her power: She married Lancelot. You may call it a seduction if you like, but no man was ever yet seduced without willing it just a little in his innermost soul. Who is to say it was revenge? She might have done it for Arthur's sake. Perhaps she did it for Lancelot's sake as well. He was five-and-twenty, without children, without prospect of a wife. Other men his age had sons training to be warriors. For love of Guinevere he was letting the fullness of life pass him by. Elaine gave him new horizons and stopped the gossips' tongues. When she bore him sons, the focus of his life, which had been in Britain, then shifted to Lanascol. That was where his future lay. You, Galahad, are that future."

Galahad trembled from head to toe. He could not look at her. "If all that is true, then why did the High King banish her from Britain?"

"He did not. The Queen did. If you have ever faced a woman's wrath, you will know the truth of that." Galahad's face burned. "When one is in the midst of events, one does not see them clearly. Guinevere saw only personal betrayal. She accused Elaine of seducing Lancelot, whom she did not love, just to hurt her. She could see no further than that she did not want Lancelot to leave. And she, who was childless, did not want another woman to bear Lancelot's sons." She paused, and exhaled slowly. "It is all so long ago, so far away, like a tale told in a tapestry. Such violent emotions have lost their force and are now toned down to softer hues. Yet here you are, Galahad, living proof of the past, reliving those old wounds and bleeding anew. You must not blame your mother. If it is anyone's fault, it is Guinevere's."

He was shaking so hard he staggered and put out a hand to brace himself against a tree. The Good Sister stood perfectly straight, alone, unaided. It took all the courage he possessed to force himself to face her.

"There is only one person you can be," he whispered. He reached out and slowly lifted the veil from her face.

Her hair, so fair it was almost white, framed a face that time had hardly touched. But for the tiny lines at the corners of her eyes and mouth, she was the same astounding beauty the world had worshiped for over twenty years. And her magnificent eyes, dark sapphire blue, direct as any man's, beguiled him against his will, as they had done that first day in the High King's garden so long ago. Slowly, he bent both knees to the ground.

"It can't be. Queen Guinevere."

"Rise, Galahad." She plucked at his arm to raise him. "Don't kneel to me. There is no need. Not between us. I am not Queen any longer."

But Galahad knelt. "How can it be you? You . . . you have always been my enemy, my father's doom—"

"I have never been your enemy. You never knew what passed, or did not pass, between me and Lancelot. You only knew the pain it caused you."

"But I saw you—that first day in Camelot—I saw you together. He embraced you, he kissed you—"

"Ah, so that was it. I was always glad to see him when he had been gone from me."

"Arthur told me—he found me weeping—he told me to keep a little mercy in my heart."

Her voice fell to a whisper and tears filled her eyes. "He was ever the most merciful of men."

"But I have hated you, and feared you, for the power you held over my father. And over my mother, too."

"It was not a power I sought, Galahad. And I wielded it only once, when I banished Elaine. I ask you to forgive me for that."

"She deserved it if she is the one who betrayed you to Melwas. Did she? Was she as false as that?"

Pain flickered in the sapphire eyes and she took time to frame a reply. "It was never proved against her. I am sorry to know such tales are gossiped abroad. She does not deserve slander."

Galahad drew a deep breath and rose, taking her hands and pressing them to his lips. "I forgive you everything. You have given me back my father and my mother, if what you said is true."

"It is not the way I saw it then, but it is the way I see it now."

"When I was a boy she was all that I adored. I thought my father betrayed her. With you."

"He never did."

"And later, when I saw how he was revered, I thought that if he were blameless, then she must be guilty. I thought she must have been a demon, who seduced him and turned me against him for her own ends."

"Once, I thought her a demon, too. But she was only a woman who suffered greatly. Lead me to the bench, I pray you. What we have left to say, we can say sitting."

He lifted her in his arms and carried her to the bench. She weighed almost nothing and felt frail as a bird. What it must have cost her, that walk around the garden!

"Do all women suffer so for men they love?" he asked when they were seated.

Her reply was a smile of infinite sadness.

His voice sank to a whisper. "I have done something so far beneath me it is unforgivable. I wanted so much to be unlike my father—all my life I strove for it—that I did what he never would have done. I ran. You were right. I ran away."

"Galahad."

The tenderness in her voice brought an ache to his throat. He gritted his teeth against it. "I have dishonored the only woman I will ever . . . the woman who lives"—he struck his chest with his fist—"here. In my soul. Every day, every night, she haunts my dreams and waking hours. I cannot sleep; I cannot pray."

"Praise God," she whispered, taking his hand. "You have confessed it. God will forgive you if you repent."

A strangled cry escaped his lips. "How repent? I have tried every day these last three years and more! There is nothing to be done—it is all too late."

"You think little of our Lord if you think He has not forgiven worse sins than this. Only ask Him."

"I cannot!"

"Ah, I understand. First you must forgive yourself."

Galahad's broad shoulders shuddered. "How can I when I have shamed her, and all my kin? Her brother is Percival, a man whose friendship I betrayed. He is within his rights to have my head. Oh, God, I have made such an unholy mess of everything!"

"Anet's daughter?" Guinevere smiled. "How the wheel turns. Is she an honest girl?"

"I would trust her with my life."

"Then go back to her. If she loved you then, she loves you now."

"How could she?" he mumbled miserably. "She must hate the very sound of my name."

"You know very little of women's hearts. They are not so changeable. Has she married?"

"I don't know. I hear rumors from time to time. You know, the common gossip of the marketplace and tavern. But I have heard nothing at all about Dane. Percival has married Niniane's daughter. She is queen now in Gwynedd. That is all that I have heard. And that my cousin wants my blood."

"Anet's daughter will take you back if it is in her power. Trust me for that. I know more about women than you do." Guinevere raised a hand to lower the veil over her face.

He reached out and stopped her. "No one will see you here but me, and I . . . I would rather look at you. To remind myself that the woman I have always dreaded so can be—is—also the Good Sister. And it is, after all, a very lovely face." She paused, then acquiesced, but the dark blue eyes flickered in displeasure. "Is it true, what Abbott Martin said, that you wear the veil because you still mourn your husband?"

"Not entirely. I put it on when I first heard of Arthur's death, but I keep it on for anonymity, and for vanity."

"For *vanity?*"

"Look at my hands. When they were all you could see of me, you thought me the age I am. But my face looks as it did when I was twenty. Merlin the Enchanter laid a curse upon me in the guise of a blessing: He said I should be Arthur's child queen and never show my age. He has turned me into a freak, may he rest in his pagan peace. What a hideous old man he was!"

He heard amusement in her voice and was relieved to know her irritation was not deep. "Vanity is part of a woman's nature. And you are certainly a woman."

Her eyes surveyed him in as bold an appraisal as he had ever yet received. "And you a man." He colored under her gaze and wished he had let her lower the veil. "What is a man of your strength, beauty, and daring doing here in this backwater? Britain needs you, Galahad. Your father needs you. Anet's daughter needs you."

He looked swiftly away. "Britain has been at peace since the battle at the Giants' Dance. My father has never needed me. As for . . . Dandrane . . . I cannot go back. I am too ashamed. And I cannot continue my quest for the Grail and Spear. That is a quest for a man with an unsullied soul, a virtuous man, a virgin. "

Guinevere watched him thoughtfully. "You attach too much importance to abstinence, I think. Loving a woman does not detract from virtue. Neither does lying with a woman sully your soul. It was your denial of that love, your abandonment, that was a lie and a sin. And that, like all sins, may be repented, forgiven, and made right. All it takes is courage."

"Only the Stainless One may find the Grail."

"No man is stainless," she said gently. "But let me hear a little more of this grail you seek."

He told her haltingly about the dream Niniane had sent him, first at Avalon, and then again in Gwynedd and at Dinas Brenin. He told her about his visit to Corbenic, everything he could remember.

When at last she spoke, Guinevere's voice was cold. "Niniane told you that the finding of Maximus's treasure would bring Arthur back to life?"

"Back to Britain. She said they would restore him. I guess that means back to life. She called him the Once and Future King."

"Mother of God!" Guinevere snapped. "The wicked woman!" She shook in anger. "That's Merlin's appellation. All it means is that his legend will live on among our children's children. She can't possibly believe . . . No, I see what she is doing. Oh, Galahad, it is another long story. Niniane has spun you a tale with a purpose, and entangled you in her ambition. Listen, and I will free you of it."

She began, not with the tale of Maximus, which he expected, but with the story of Merlin the Enchanter. In his dotage this great man, Arthur's closest friend and advisor, who all his life had avoided commerce with women, became enamored of a young acolyte in the Lady's service on the Isle of Avalon. Niniane had been adept at magic from girlhood and when she saw Merlin's looks of longing, she saw her chance for power and took it. By slow degrees she wove a spell of powerful enchantment around the old man. To everyone else, including Arthur, it appeared that Merlin had fallen in love at last and had taken his lover into his house. But every day she spent with him she grew stronger and more powerful, and Merlin grew older and more frail. Merlin himself was fooled. He assured the young King that all was well; he was teaching his apprentice the magic arts that would enable her to serve him as the High King's enchanter when Merlin was gone to his final rest.

"She sucked him dry," Guinevere whispered, her gaze far away. "She robbed him not only of his power, but of all his secret thoughts and all his precious memories. She left him empty of all that made him human and he fell into a living death."

"Did this murder go unpunished?" Galahad cried. "All those years in Camelot she served Arthur and he honored her! How could he, if she killed Merlin?"

Slowly, Guinevere's eyes slid to his face, and a smile touched her lips. "Oh, nothing could be proved against her, of course. And Merlin did not die, exactly. What was left of him lived on for a decade. I do not deny she used her power well. She served Arthur honestly and faithfully, and was obedient to his command. She healed Lancelot of a grievous wound; she saved me from mortal sickness more than once. She single-handedly rescued Morgaine from a nightmare life and brought her into the Lady's service. And Morgaine is one of the sweetest people ever to walk the earth. Niniane is a woman of courage and high ambition. She got what she wanted. For fifteen years she was the High King's enchantress, complete with Merlin's powers, privy to every secret in the kingdom." Her lovely face hardened suddenly, and the dark blue eyes went cold. "The one thing Niniane could not abide was a challenge to her power. Arthur she obeyed. Me she tolerated for his sake. I can imagine that she abhorred the day Arthur died and she had to pass on her power to Morgaine."

Galahad remembered her frozen face the night he had appeared at Avalon. *The Harbinger of Doom,* she had called him.

"You will never convince me that she gave up to Morgaine all the powers she stole from Merlin. I am as certain that she kept back some for herself as I am that Arthur walks my dreams at night. No doubt she gave Morgaine what she herself no longer needed—healing, the Sacred Seeing, the power over the moon and stars, the wind and sea, the cold fire that summons spirits."

"You speak like a pagan!" Galahad gasped, unable to help himself. "How can a Christian believe these things?"

"I have seen them," she said simply. "God's is not the only power on this earth. Not yet. I will wager any amount you like, Niniane kept to herself the power to bend the wills of others to her ends. She was always adept at sending dreams, the kind of dreams that stirred men to action in the belief it was the will of God. I know of many who have gone to their deaths for Niniane's ambition and did not know it."

"You think she sent me such a dream?"

Guinevere sighed. "I believe it is more than likely. If, as you tell me, she is restricted to life at Corbenic—a tiny place, after what she has been accustomed to—with a husband who was crippled at Camlann, why, she must be near her wits' end! Constantine will not even have speech with her— I know that old blackguard well. How can she get back to the center of things?" She tilted her head and glanced at him in amusement. Suddenly she looked for all the world like a girl of twenty flirting with her courtier. He began to appreciate his father's predicament. "She is no warrior. If she is to regain her place of power she will have to use her magics. She will appear with wonderful symbols of power and a wonderful tale to go with them. It seems she has devised this tale already. Vanquisher and Restorer, indeed! She would dredge up Arthur's very sword!" She drew a deep breath and calmed herself. "Since she cannot herself be king, she needs a warrior she can control who, with these treasures, can be acclaimed the next High King. I wonder just whom she sees in that role: Pelleas, Percival, or you?"

"Me?" Galahad gaped. "I do not want to be High King!"

"It is probably either you or Percival. He has married her daughter, you see."

"Do you mean she planned that?"

The dark blue eyes grew suddenly sad. "It would seem likely, wouldn't it? What better way to bind a likely young warrior to her side?"

"But Percival loves Guinblodwyn!"

"I hope he does. I hope he came by it naturally and not through dreams." Galahad's breath caught in his throat. "She may also, through dreams or more directly, be fanning his ambition. When you go back to Gwynedd, you may judge for yourself."

"But . . . but Percival has sense. And he still serves Constantine."

"So do many others who want his crown. But perhaps it isn't Percival. Perhaps you are the one she has in mind."

Galahad colored under her steady gaze. What devil had possessed him not to allow her to lower her veil!

"She would know you are a young man with high ideals—everyone has known that from your youth. She would hold out to you the conquest of something truly glorious: an achievement that could be won only by a stainless soul, a perfect virtue, a pure heart. She would no doubt connect these things with the treasure of Maximus, since she knows where it lies and could guide you to it."

"She knows where it lies!" He could not breathe. "But . . . but Arthur connected them also. He . . . he once told me they were things of power, that if he held them, no one could ever take Britain from him."

She closed her eyes on that and a look of both pain and tenderness crossed her face. "When did he say this to you? When he was trying to send you out of harm's way, before Camlann? No matter, he might even have believed it. Niniane was with him night and day before he left for Less Britain. She might have told him anything. Because she carried Merlin's power within her, he respected her advice. Who knows? But I tell you, Galahad, it is a thin tissue of lies, fragile as a spider's web at dawning. Arthur cannot come back. It is his power she wants, not the man himself."

Galahad sat silent and slowly Guinevere lowered her veil.

"I pray night and day God will bless his immortal soul. There never was a man like him before his coming, and I doubt there will be again. To speak as Niniane does about him is blaspheming."

They sat still for a long time. Anna appeared at the garden gate, watching worriedly, but with a wave of her hand Guinevere bade her wait. Galahad did not know what to say. His thoughts were in a jumble. He did not know whom to believe. Who knew what those two women, both powerful, both beautiful, had been to each other? But he did not think the woman he knew as the Good Sister would lie to him deliberately.

"I will ask God to send me a true dream," he said at last. "Here in this holy Christian place Niniane's power cannot reach me."

The white veil nodded. "When you have your answer, Galahad, go back to Gwynedd. Don't let your pride keep you from it. Of course she will be angry, but you can change that. What can she do but call you names? Be proof against them. Percival's anger will abate when you have done his sister honor. Go back and make right the harm that you have done. You will regret it all your life if you do not." She gasped suddenly, and swayed, her hand to her head, and Anna came running down the walk.

"My lady!"

Swiftly, Galahad lifted her in his arms. "Lead the way, Anna, and I will follow."

"She is exhausted!" Anna wept openly, trotting before him. "Oh, I knew it! I knew it! I told her again and again to let you be!"

He looked down at the limp body he held. "For her own sake, she should have listened to you. But for my sake, how glad I am that she did not."

In his sleep that night he dreamed of Benoic, a bright green jewel embedded deep in the Wild Forest of Broceliande. He dreamed he knocked at the stone gate and was welcomed home as the new king. Where is the old king? he asked the people. In the chapel with his fathers, they replied. He went to the chapel to say a prayer before Lancelot's tomb, but when he got there he saw Lancelot himself kneeling at the altar. He was much changed. Old and bent with a face like a death's-head, he turned around and spoke with a ghostly voice: "Galahad, take me to Britain."

It was three days before the Good Sister was well enough to see him again. Abbott Martin was very worried. His eyes searched Galahad's face. "This is the last visit, Joseph. She asked specifically to see you one more time, or I would not allow it. You have five minutes."

A lump rose in his throat when he saw her at last. She was shrunk almost to nothingness, wrapped in thick blankets although it was midsummer. Her voice was gone. He had to kneel at her head to hear her whisper, and the sound of her labored breathing filled his ears. He took her hand. It was blue with cold.

"My lady, I bless you for all you have done for me."

"Have you had your dream?" she asked softly. He nodded. She struggled to draw breath. "Galahad, I am dying. I must ask you . . ."

"Ask!" he urged, squeezing her hand. "I will do anything—you have only to command me."

"Will you . . . go home and send Lancelot to me? I have asked God to let me see him once again, but . . . even if . . . there are things he must do . . . he promised Arthur . . . it is time."

Gently, Galahad lifted her hand to his lips. "I shall go. I will go as fast as I can."

Her fingers moved in his. It was all the strength she could command.

"You are worthy of him, Galahad. . . . Go with God."

He left Amesbury before noon, galloping south across the Great Plain toward the sea with tears on his face.

53 ✝ LANCELOT

He rode out of the Wild Forest on a cool day in late summer. Banks of clouds scudded across the sky, grumbling ominously, lending Black Lake a greenish cast and sending the swallows darting madly.

The sentries at the gate were young men who did not know him. They must, he realized with surprise, have come of age since Camlann. How sad to think King Arthur and his doings were the stuff of legend to them, no more real than ancient King Cunedda had been to him at their age.

"Halt, stranger! Declare yourself!" He pulled up, and looked them over. There were three of them, just growing in their beards. The tallest was a heavy youth with the look of a bully about him.

"My name is Galahad. I am Lancelot's son. This is my home."

The guards stared and exchanged glances. "Where is your pass, my lord? Where is your badge?"

Time was, he thought, when he would have answered such insolence with a show of swordsmanship. But the guard did no more than his duty. How was he to know Galahad had left the badge of Lanascol in a Welsh cave, and the badge of the Grail Seeker at the bottom of the Amesbury well?

"Send for my father. Or my brother. Sound the alarm. I will wait."

A page went scampering off. Thunder rolled in the distance. The big guard stepped forward. "You cannot be Prince Galahad. All the world knows he is in Britain. You must be an impostor. Get off your horse." He reached for his sword, but Galahad held up his hand.

"Don't." He glanced at the other guards, who shuffled nervously. "Do you treat all strangers with such disrespect? What has been happening here? Has there been trouble from the Franks?" The youngest and most frightened opened his mouth to answer but the bully cut him off.

"It's no business of yours." He drew the sword and leveled the point at Galahad's throat. "I'll find out who you are. Get down."

Galahad regarded him steadily. He felt no anger. The insult glanced off him like a spent arrow. Such armor the Good Sister had given him! Calmly, he slid off the horse. The sword point touched his throat.

"Am I prisoner, then?"

"You are. Until Prince Galahodyn comes."

He smiled slowly. "You are a brave man. If I were the Galahad you think me, you might be dead now. Had you thought of that?"

"But I am living. So you are not he." The sword point pressed, and he felt a trickle of blood at his throat. He drew an angry breath; the nervous guard trembled visibly.

"Merron! The horse is unsaddled! He might be the king's son, after all!"

"He's a lily-livered coward!" snarled the bully. "I've blooded him and he won't even draw his sword."

"Is that your measure of courage?" Galahad's voice fell steady and cool into the tense silence between them. "Tell me, Merron, how old are you?"

"Nineteen. What is it to you?"

"Nineteen. Then you were eight when Galahad last set foot in Benoic. How can you know I am not he?"

"That is easy. I have insulted you and you've done nothing to repay me. Everyone knows Galahad would never stand for that. He's the proudest man in both the Britains."

Galahad bowed his head to hide his blush of shame. "But pride goes before a fall, and men may change." He looked up slowly. "I suppose he is generally despised in Lanascol?"

"Oh, no, my lord!" the youngest soldier quavered. "He is revered by many, although . . . although some among the soldiers hold him in contempt."

"Indeed? Why is that?"

"Because he does not fight for Constantine any longer, or any worthy king, but, well, I know this is hard to credit, but they say he spends his days with poor folk, seeking for holiness, and sleeps on the forest floor with only branches for a roof!"

"He hardly kills anyone anymore!" exclaimed the third guard, pushing forward, "except for hill bandits and common ruffians. Once he upheld the honor of Lanascol to all the Britons."

"They say he betrayed the King of Gwynedd and will not lift a sword to fight for him or any other of Britain's kings."

"Perhaps they will not have him," Galahad said slowly.

"Then let him come home and defend Lanascol!"

He looked into their young faces and saw there the fear, the longing, and the hope of leaderless men. "I tell you now, that is what I have come home to do."

In the silence that followed, Merron's sword point wavered, and fell. The guards stood staring and uncertain until a voice behind them called out,

"Well, and it's about time! Welcome home, my brother!"

Galahodyn strode out through the gate and Galahad took him in his arms. Behind them, the guards saluted. "Hodyn! How good to see you!"

Hodyn grinned and pounded his brother's back. "I'm happier than I can say to see *you*. Why haven't you been home before, and what brings you here now? Never mind, there's plenty of time to talk. Come, let's get inside before the storm breaks. Aunt Adele will be so delighted! Ah, you've still got Farouk—he's keeping well, I see—and you yourself, brother, you're looking fit. Bring me up-to-date on all your doings."

By this time they were well within the fortress walls and the gate had closed solidly behind them. There was no one near and Galahad stopped. "What's the matter, Hodyn? You've not paused for breath while we were in the guards' hearing. What's happening here?"

The smile faded from Galahodyn's face. "It's not a grave situation yet, or I'd have sent for you. But the Franks are acting up. The Burgundians are led by a new king and they are pushing the Franks westward, eager to revenge themselves for the defeat at Autun. As the Burgundians push the Franks, the Franks push us."

"We have a treaty with them."

"Childebert died last year, you know."

Galahad had not known, but he kept the admission from his face. "Does that mean the treaty is annulled? Didn't Lancelot renew the treaty with the new king?"

Pain crossed Galahodyn's face and Galahad knew his answer before he spoke. "It was bad timing. Father wasn't able . . . I mean, he couldn't . . . he wasn't administering matters then."

"Who was?"

Galahodyn gulped. "I was. But they wouldn't treat with me. I didn't think they wanted peace, frankly, even at the price of help against the Burgundians. Aunt Adele agreed. But . . . the excuse they gave was that they would deal only with the king."

Galahad stood very still. His gaze traveled over the ordered houses, the garden plots and workshops, the fields and meadows of Benoic, his home, and up the winding roadway to the king's house upon the hill. "How long have you had to act as king in our father's place?"

"Eighteen months. More or less."

"Where is he?"

"In the chapel. It's where he lives."

"Is he ill?"

"His body is healthy enough. It's his spirit that torments him."

"Why?"

Hodyn shrugged. "He's a hermit, Galahad, a hermit in his own home. No one talks about it, but of course everyone knows."

"You should have taken the title, too."

"Me? King? I couldn't—it's not mine to take. It's yours. And until he dies, it's his."

"He has abdicated power. You should have taken it. Men need to be led."

"Well, then, lead them." Galahodyn's voice was near the point of breaking, and Galahad saw how deeply pained he was.

"Come," he said, more gently, "take me to Adele. Between us, we can bring him round. I must take him back to Britain before the storms close the seas."

Adele had grown old in his absence. He remembered her as a lovely, dark-haired girl with a brilliant smile and laughing eyes. Now, gray and faded, she seemed less than a shadow of her former self. She still grieved for Galyn, Hodyn warned him under his breath, still missed him after ten long years. Remembering Guinevere, Galahad believed it.

He found her dozing in the garden sunlight, swathed in shawls, while her attendant sang softly over her stitching. Galahad dismissed the girl, who stared at him, and sat down by Adele. She was overjoyed to see him and demanded to know what had kept him away so long. He told her something of his travels around Britain and about the state of things in general. "Cynewulf has yet to prove himself the man his father was, but as long as he holds power he'll keep trying. I see no end to it, Aunt Adele. The Saxon kingdoms grow bigger and stronger and Britain's defenses grow weaker and more scattered. There can be only one ending."

"Nonsense. That's just what everyone said in Uther's last years. And then came Arthur. All it needs is a leader of men."

"There will never be another like Arthur."

"Well, well, let be. It's good to see you again, Galahad. I hope you have come home to stay."

"I must return to Britain with Lancelot. After that, I will be back to stay."

Adele looked up at him sharply, and placed a bony hand on his arm. "Lancelot is going to Britain? You haven't seen him lately. He has changed, I am afraid."

"How?"

She closed her eyes and the life faded from her face. "Ah, Galahad, it is not an easy question to answer. Part of it is that being a man of honor and being a Christian, he has committed sins he would now expiate by prayer and by fasting, if he could. Part of it is that being a man of courage and high ideals, he feels he has fallen short, has failed . . . people. Part of it is that he can barely tolerate life without his dearest companions, Arthur and Guinevere. He is aging, his time is past, and he knows it; he is alone."

Galahad took Adele's frail hand and raised it to his lips. "I will do what I can, Adele. The times are certainly changing, but he may yet have a role to play. I have seen the High Queen. She is dying and has sent for him."

Adele gasped. "Dying? You are certain? Oh, Galahad, what fearful news!"

"He would return to give her comfort, would he not? He wouldn't refuse her call."

Adele exhaled slowly, and nodded. "If anyone can save him from his self-recriminations, it is Guinevere. Go to him, Galahad. Go and take him out of himself."

The chapel in Benoic was the only building made entirely of stone in all of Lanascol. It stood on a shoulder of the hill, a good way from the king's house, on what had been holy ground for generations. Lancelot's father, Galaban, had quarried the chapel stone in the Roman manner and built a Christian house of worship above the ruins of a pagan shrine older than his ancestors. The ancient sacred spring was well tended, although the marks of older deities had been replaced by carved crosses. The half circle of ancient standing stones in the surrounding birch grove was now mostly hidden by choking underbrush.

Galahad approached the chapel by the side path through the herb garden. He stood a moment in the shade of the marble porch, out of the hot sun, and listened. Nothing stirred but the late bees, busy among the berries. Turning, he went through the arched doorway into the cool dark of the chapel. It was deserted. He dipped his knee and crossed himself before the altar. The whisper of cloth, the scrape of boots on stone were the only sounds he heard, and they were his.

Light from the south door threw the altar half in shadow. Here, twenty years ago, Aidan and his mother had dedicated him to God's service. And how had he served God? First he had served Arthur, God's beloved. After Camlann he had done what he could to restore Britain to her former glory, but Britain would never be the same without those same brave men to defend her. Perhaps he should have stayed longer with Constantine, but for all his show of Christian faith, Constantine was not a good man. Three years in his service had brought Galahad the taste of dust in his mouth and blood on his sword, but little else.

He had thought he served both God and Britain in seeking the Grail, but what had he really been after? Personal glory? Fulfillment of a prophecy? Expiation of his sins? He had achieved nothing, and it was even possible he had been the willing tool of a misguided sorceress. Arthur would not return. He could not undo what he had done in Wales. And he had wasted years, vital years, while Arthur's Britain slowly vanished before his very eyes.

He had failed. So far from serving God, he had done disservice to everyone he loved. He, who had always thought himself destined for greatness, he had behaved meanly, selfishly, and had done things no honest man could countenance. His eyes had been too long raised to the pursuit of impossible dreams. The Good Sister knew, as he had never known, that his fellow men were more important.

With an aching throat he knelt on the cool stone. Was there still time to make amends? If Guinevere was right and there could be virtue and honor in loving a woman, surely it was through the faithful service of a life-time, not in a night's carnal pleasure, and never, never in the cruel aban-donment and shame he had brought upon the deepest love of his heart.

"O merciful Lord," he whispered, crossing himself slowly, "let me be forgiven."

From the altar came a sound, a movement. Galahad looked up to see a man standing in the shadows, a tall, gaunt man in a monk's sackcloth. He came forward, white-haired, gray-bearded, and gripped Galahad's shoulder with a gnarled hand. Galahad looked away as the old man knelt stiffly be-side him and took him firmly in his arms.

"God forgives you all your sins, my son, once you ask."

He recognized Lancelot by his voice. His black hair had gone com-pletely white, he had let his beard grow, and his bones had lost flesh, but, as the shaft of sunlight in which he knelt revealed, he was not yet old. There was still strength in his body and living determination in his face. But the gray eyes were sad with longing and regret.

"Father."

"Galahad. My dear son. What burden is this you bear? Lay it before the Lord and be relieved of it."

Galahad shook his head. "It is not that simple. If there is a remedy for the sin I have committed, only I can make it. But let that be. The answer to that trouble lies in Britain. I have come home for you, Father."

"For me?"

"To take you back to Britain."

Slowly, Lancelot rose and Galahad rose with him. "I am retired from life, son. Hodyn runs things now. I have tried so hard, prayed so long, to put all that behind me. . . . I cannot go back." A ghost of a smile softened his expression. "You yourself are the answer to a prayer. Galahad, I thought I had lost you."

"I *was* lost for a time. For a long time. But I've returned. I . . . I met someone who showed me the way."

Lancelot hesitated. Galahad noticed his hands trembling; he braced himself for what might be coming. "Galahad. Can you find it in your heart to forgive me?"

For answer, Galahad embraced him and kissed both his cheeks. "Father, I forgave you a long, long time ago. When I committed a sin more grievous than any which ever tempted you. You have done what honor demanded your entire life. I, who have dishonored what I love best, I cannot judge *you*."

Lancelot turned away, too moved for speech. Galahad followed him out through the herb garden and down the path to the spring. There, Lancelot lifted a silver cup from its niche in a small altar, filled it from the clear pool, poured a libation on the ground at the altar's feet, and drank deeply. He offered the cup to Galahad, who did the same. Then Lancelot sat heavily on a stone bench and regarded his son.

"You have given me what I have prayed for these ten years past."

Galahad colored lightly under his scrutiny. "It is no more than I owe you, sir. I have behaved badly toward you, and for that I beg your pardon. I was blinded by my own ambitions—blind to your virtues, blind to my faults. But the scales have fallen. We can, I hope, deal together now as men."

Lancelot nodded. "Have you come home to stay? To take up your rightful place?"

"In time."

"Why not now? It is time. I will abdicate."

"Father, I come from the Queen, bearing a message."

Lancelot froze. "From Guinevere?"

"I have been with her in Amesbury since midsummer."

Lancelot shot to his feet and began to pace around the spring. "You have been with the Queen? How so, when you despise her?"

"You misunderstand me, my lord. I do not despise her. I think she is the kindest woman, the sweetest soul I have ever known."

This brought Lancelot up short and he stared openly at his son. Amusement and relief swept his face. "And she can charm the spots off a dog. I see you've learned that."

Galahad smiled. "She charmed all of Amesbury long ago. They call her the Good Sister. There is something about true goodness, true, open-hearted, all-forgiving love that engenders a like response."

Lancelot stood very still. There were tears in his eyes. "You understand," he said softly. "At last, you understand."

"I understand. I had to come and tell you so."

Lancelot drew a long, tremulous breath. "Thank you."

"But that's not the only reason I have come. She is dying, Father, and wants to see you. I promised her I would bring you back with me. And we have not much time."

Lancelot sank down upon the bench. For a long time he was silent. "You have seen her? She is truly . . . ill?"

"Very ill. The abbott says she is dying. I believe him. She said something about a promise to Arthur you had made. That I must let you know 'the time has come.' If you have some duty to perform, I will do it with you."

Tears slid silently down Lancelot's lined cheeks and into his beard. "My sweet Gwen," he said, then bowed his head. "I thought it was behind me, dead and buried with Arthur," he said stiffly, as he gave his hand to Galahad and allowed himself to be helped to his feet. "I thought it all belonged to another life. And I thought she would feel the same. As if time and distance could ever touch what was between us. But I see now I have only fooled myself."

Galahad took his arm and they started back up the path. "I made the same mistake," he said softly. "I did not reckon with the power of love."

54 ✟ THE ISLE OF GLASS

All the way back to Britain, Lancelot talked. It reminded Galahad of their first trip to Camelot together, when his father's rising excitement at returning had made him garrulous. But now Lancelot rattled on feverishly, disjointedly, saying anything that came into his head, anything to keep his thoughts from what lay before him. Galahad recognized his terror for what it was, and let him talk. They had a smooth crossing and good horses, and came to Amesbury just two weeks after the autumn equinox.

"My God," Lancelot said as they trotted into the empty square beyond the well. "It hasn't changed a hairbreadth in eleven years."

"I have always wondered why the Saxons do not take it. It lies so close to their lands, and it's good, fertile farming."

Lancelot shrugged. "They can take it anytime they like and they know it. But they will not while Guinevere lives. They revere her. For her beauty and her bravery and her horsemanship. Cerdic once compared her to one of their goddesses, I forget the name, a warrior woman with a great and shining sword." Galahad, who had heard the tale a hundred times, let him tell it once more. He only half listened; he was wondering why there was no one about in the village, no children playing in the dust, no women at the well. As soon as they came in sight of the monastery walls, he knew the answer. The whole town was clustered at the gate, sitting in the bleached grass, waiting.

"My God, I am too late!" Lancelot reined in his horse and stared at the crowd, but Galahad beckoned him on.

"Hurry, Father. Abbott Martin will be waiting."

"It is a deathwatch," Lancelot croaked. "May the Lord give me strength to do what I must do." Galahad saw that he was sweating.

The villagers made way for them, bowing low and staring. The gatekeeper let them in without a word.

"Timon, what news?" Galahad whispered, but the hooded youth shrugged, turned away, and closed the gate behind them.

Galahad walked swiftly through the familiar halls, Lancelot close at his heels. As he passed the chapel he heard low chanting, but shut his ears to the sound. They could not be too late. God would not let that happen. At the entrance to the women's quarters he nearly collided with Abbott Martin. Behind the abbott, Anna was weeping pitifully, supported by a group of sisters.

"Father!" Galahad whispered breathlessly, grabbing his arm. "Tell me she still lives! I have brought Lancelot!"

Abbott Martin looked at them both with great compassion. "My lords, may God bless you both for making your long journey. Truly, it is an act of love. But an hour past, the Good Sister was called to her eternal rest."

"No!" Galahad cried. "No, it cannot be so!"

"Be easy, my son," the abbott said gently. "She resides in Heaven with the angels, and is at peace."

Lancelot's reassuring hand fell on his shoulder. "It's just as well," he said in a low voice. "She did not want to speak to me again. We said our farewells long ago, in this very place. But I promised Arthur I would bury her."

Fighting tears, Galahad wondered at his father's sudden calm. Through blurred eyes he watched Lancelot bend down and speak a word of comfort to Anna, then walk past her and into the Good Sister's room. He closed the door behind him.

"No, no, no," Galahad whispered frantically. "She must yet live! I promised her she would see his face again!"

Gently the abbott took his arm and guided him away. "Come with me into the chapel. We will pray for the salvation of her soul. But do not distress yourself, my son. Sir Lancelot is right. She wanted him here, but not to speak with. All her thoughts were with King Arthur at the end."

"How do you know? Were you with her?"

"Indeed I was. I seldom see a soul so ready to go home. She was free from pain at the end, and possessed of a serene calm that lit her lovely face. She told me that her beloved husband had come to get her."

Suddenly from beyond the walls rose the shrill, keening wail of the village women. Galahad shuddered and followed the abbott into the chapel.

Guinevere's body lay scented with spices and shrouded in fine silk on a bier before the altar for three long days. Galahad knelt beside her, refusing all refreshment, praying earnestly that he might be forgiven for the years of ill will he had borne her. Lancelot joined him only in the dark hours of the night. He spent his days making preparations for the long journey to her resting place, for he had promised Arthur, as the great King lay dying, that he would bury his beloved wife beside him when the time came. Now, dry-eyed and calm, he set about fulfilling his promise.

On a cool, fair day in October the small procession set forth from Amesbury. Galahad rode at the head, leading the two horses who pulled the wagon with the open bier. Two servants walked on either side, to tend the bed of ice she lay on, and Lancelot walked behind. His own horse carried saddlebags of spices, and they stopped at every town they came to for a replenishment of ice, for Lancelot was determined that she should suffer no change until she was in the ground with Arthur. The wagon carried a canopy of gilded cloth to shield her from the sun, with a layer of tenting underneath in case of rain. Sheaves of golden chrysanthemums lay in profusion all around her, so that she looked, Galahad thought, almost like a maiden asleep in an autumn bower.

As they passed slowly through the small villages of southern Britain, humble folk came out to greet them, to say prayers and pay homage to their well-remembered, well-loved Queen. Word spread throughout the land and as they passed, people joined in the procession, sometimes for a league or two, sometimes for days, sometimes in twos or threes, sometimes whole villages. And everyone, young or old, however poor, brought a gift. Some brought no more than fresh herbs or flowers or sweet straw for her bed; some brought trinkets of bronze or copper, or wooden carvings, or painted beads, or ribbons or rings or swan feathers tied with colored string—anything at all that they valued, they brought and laid reverently on her bier.

Unbelievably, the Queen lay unchanging in her serene repose. Whether it was due to Lancelot's precautions, or to the cool, dry weather, or to some old spell of Merlin's, Galahad did not know, but her face, which was all that was visible outside her shroud, remained as beautiful in death as it had been in life, the bloom of youth lingering on her cheeks. All who came to see her marveled, and crossed themselves if they were Christian, or made the sign against enchantment if they were not. She gathered the faithful of Arthur's Britain around her as she traveled, and as they walked beside her they told stories of the great days that were past, when Arthur and Guinevere were High King and Queen in Camelot. It astonished Galahad that this woman had touched so many lives. He was ashamed anew that he had lived beside her for nine years and had not known her.

Throughout the journey Lancelot said nothing, but walked behind her during the day, and slept beside her at night. He ate little, and grew thinner, paler, older every day. He walked as if in a daze; he seemed unaware of the crowds of common folk around him, and they, to do him honor, left him alone. Sometimes at night Galahad fancied he could hear his father's muffled weeping, but in the morning his gaunt face never showed any trace of tears.

In the third week the procession reached the Summer Country. If Constantine and his army were at Camelot, they gave no sign of it. By this time the procession numbered more than six hundred. They crossed the plain of Camlann within sight of the towers of Camelot, but no one from the High King's fortress rode out to meet them.

At last they came to the causeway across the marshes at the eastern end of the Lake of Avalon. Ahead in the distance rose the hill island, Ynys Witrin, the Isle of Glass, with the Lady's shrine at the foot and the Christian monastery atop the Tor. At the entrance to the causeway stood a group of women, robed in white, blocking their way. The smallest of them stepped forward and raised her hand. Galahad reined in. He recognized that small, dark face with the warm brown eyes: Morgaine, Lady of the Lake.

He slid off the horse and bent his knee as she approached him. Behind him the crowds fell silent. "My lady Morgaine, we bear the body of Queen Guinevere to her resting place. I pray you, give us passage to the Tor."

She placed her little hands on either side of his face, cool and soft against his skin. He remembered that she did not speak, but no one of her women stepped forward to speak for her. *There are too many. Remember, it is a sacred place.* The words flashed unbidden across his mind, and with them, a picture of the bier with only himself and Lancelot in attendance, the horses struggling uphill, a squat, brown-robed monk walking behind. *I will bless her. Then you must go on alone.*

The cool hands withdrew. Slowly Morgaine approached the bier. The people drew back, bowing their heads. Morgaine made the sign of blessing over the Queen's body, and anointed the pale, cold brow with oil. Facing the bier, she closed her eyes and stretched her arms skyward, lifting her face to the afternoon sun. *Go to your God, my sister. May the hopes and prayers of all those who have loved you bear you across the dark river and into the Otherworld where your beloved awaits.* She lowered her arms. Galahad found that he was sweating. He had heard the words as clearly as though they had been spoken aloud. He glanced swiftly back at Lancelot and saw tears on his face.

Turning away, Morgaine flashed a look at Galahad, and he suddenly found himself addressing the crowd of mourners.

"Good Britons, attend me. This is the end of your journey. I thank you on the Queen's behalf for your service and the marks of love you have brought her. As King Arthur will be long remembered, so too will Britons remember Queen Guinevere, for the love she bore him, for the love she bore us all. Let her go to her rest in secret, and lie once more with the King in his eternal fastness."

The crowd dispersed with very little grumbling. Some came forward to kiss the bier one last time; some whispered a few last prayers of blessing. The holy women returned to Avalon. Soon he and Lancelot were alone under the wide sky. But Lancelot was as a man in sleep; he followed blindly after Galahad and the bier, seeing nothing, hearing nothing, unresponsive. Galahad led the horses up the winding path, past the gates of Avalon, past the deserted fortress that once belonged to King Melwas of the Summer Country; up and up toward the ramshackle houses of the Christian brothers and the primitive sanctuary where Arthur lay waiting.

A fat monk sat upon a boulder by the path, dabbing at his moist face with his sleeve and mumbling to himself. Galahad halted the horses.

"Brother Ignacius, is that you?"

The monk looked up. "Eh? Eh? What's that? How do you do, my lord? Oh, dear, I see you have lost a loved one. Allow me to offer condolences, oh, yes, indeed. My, my, what a lovely face. Your sister, my lord? Er—I beg your pardon, but how do you come to know my name?"

Galahad smiled. "You did me a service years ago, when I needed help the most. Never mind, I expect you don't remember." He slid off the horse and helped the monk to his feet. "If you are headed up the hill, let me offer you my horse."

Ignacius grinned at him. "A kind offer, my lord, for which I thank you, to be sure, but my days of riding horseback are behind me. And even when I *could* get a leg up unassisted, I needed a saddle to stay there. No, thank you all the same, but I'll walk."

"Very well, I'll walk with you."

During the next half hour Ignacius, in an unbroken stream of commentary, gave a thorough account of all that had happened at the monastery in the last eleven years, "since the Blessing." He never used one word when three would serve, but his tales were full of warmth and a heartfelt delight in the simple joys of life, and Galahad listened with pleasure. It had been a long time since the rescue of a kitten, or the antics of a child, or the tale of a too-well-fermented cider drunk on Christmas Eve, had brought a smile to his face.

The monastery had grown and prospered, it seemed, since the event Ignacius referred to as "the Blessing." The mention of this event was accompanied by winks and nods, so that Galahad understood it was a secret thing, not to be asked into, but one which brought great honor and good luck to the Christian brothers. Before this great occasion, they had barely held their own against the pagans; since then, they had thrived.

"We are growing, we are growing," Ignacius said, puffing steadily uphill. "We may never have orchards to rival the good ladies of Avalon, but we will outnumber them in a year or two. Folk are giving up the old ways, the myriad spirits, the sorceries, the blood sacrifice, and the cold standing stones, and are turning to the True Christ. You wait and see, my lord, in thirty years Avalon will fade into the mists and a fine church will stand there in her place. Er, hem, I don't like to say anything, my lord, but is that fellow following us all right?"

Galahad glanced back at his father. "That's the chief mourner. Let him be."

"He don't look well, and that's a fact. How far's he come?"

"A long way, but we are almost there. Tell me, Brother Ignacius, what I must do to get this lady buried beneath the chapel altar."

Ignacius gaped at him. "Beneath the altar! But, my lord! That's impossible! That's where . . . you cannot . . . the abbott will never allow it!" His round eyes narrowed and he gasped. "Wait a bit! Wait a bit! Don't I know your face? Aren't you the boy? Aren't you the boy who helped Sir Lancelot that night? The night of our great Blessing?"

"I am."

"God bless my soul! It's been so long, I did not know you!"

"Neither did you know Sir Lancelot."

Following his glance, Ignacius turned around and stared. "May the angels in Heaven preserve his soul!" He groaned. "I'd not have known him. He's not in this world, my lord; he's already in the next." He looked anxiously at Galahad. "But you'll never get the permission that you seek. Who is this lady you ask it for?"

"Queen Guinevere. Arthur's wife."

Ignacius groaned again. "Oh, dear, I see. Died last night, did she? I didn't think she was living in these parts."

"She died three weeks ago at Amesbury."

Ignacius stopped, and began to shake. "Three weeks? My lord, that cannot be!"

"I promise you, it is. We have brought her to lie in peace with her husband. It was the High King's dying wish."

Ignacius turned and stared at the still body, the sweet face with its flesh still full and curved, hiding its bones. Trembling, he crossed himself and mumbled a quick prayer. "What power is this?" he whispered. "The Lord Himself is with her! His hand lies over her and guides her home. I see, I see. It must be so. But my lord, the new abbott is a cold man, if I may be forgiven for saying so. He will never allow a woman to lie beneath the altar."

Galahad frowned. Here was a stumbling block he had not foreseen. "Is there no way around him, then? May it not be done in secret?"

Poor Ignacius began to sweat. "I suppose it might. I suppose it will have to. But I don't see quite how. It's hard to put one past Father John. He sees everything. And he doesn't like me much. That's why he's made me a message boy, at my age! Why just this morning I've come all the way from Glaston, thanks to a boy with a donkey cart, with a message for him."

Galahad shrugged. "Well, I will have to think of something. Meanwhile, surely she can lie in the chapel and receive his blessing. We will have to tell him who she is. But do not tell him where she will lie. Perhaps he will think of it himself."

Abbott John was a tall, dry stick of a man with bright, suspicious eyes. He welcomed them formally to the small, Christian community of Ynys Witrin and arranged to have the Queen's body lie all night within the chapel. But in the morning she would be buried in the graveyard, albeit in a place of honor high on the Tor. Galahad said nothing. Lancelot seemed not to have heard. Ignacius chattered and fussed under his breath and Father John lifted a disdainful eyebrow at him.

But when Ignacius delivered the scroll he carried, the abbott's expression lightened and he almost smiled.

"I am sorry, my lords, that I will be unable to perform the services myself. I am called away to conference with the bishop at Caerleon. Brother Ralf, or even Brother Ignacius, will have to serve in my place."

In the dark of night, when all the monks had gone to bed, Galahad and Lancelot met Ignacius in the chapel. He had brought with him the digging tools, fresh earth still clinging to them from the grave already dug up on the hill.

"The abbott's a prompt man," he whispered nervously. "What a stroke of fortune, that message!"

Galahad grunted as he put his shoulder to the carved altar. "Fortune, indeed! Hadn't you just been talking about the Hand of God?"

Ignacius smiled. "All fortune is the Hand of God, my lord. But I still don't think we dare more than one light."

The single candle was barely enough to discern the shadows in the gloom, but by its low and secret light they moved the altar, and began to dig in the hard-packed earth below. Galahad would not let Ignacius help, but set him to reciting Scripture as he and Lancelot worked.

Since they had crossed the causeway to Ynys Witrin, Galahad had not heard his father speak. More than once that night, as they bent and straightened, he stole a glance at Lancelot's face. His features were set in a kind of stolid calm, alight with peace, as though he neared a long-sought goal. And he worked with a controlled frenzy, a wiry strength that Galahad had not suspected was left in him. He did not sweat; he did not gasp; he did not pause for rest. He was driven by an overriding purpose. Even Galahad felt its pull.

The iron shovel struck wood with a resounding, hollow *thunk!* Lancelot stopped. Ignacius stopped. Around them the sanctuary grew quiet, its secret dark drawing into a tight, encircling cloak, weighting their shoulders, sweating their brows. Galahad climbed out of the grave while Lancelot swept the dirt off the planking that covered Arthur. A superstitious fear caught at Galahad's heart, an ancient terror he did not understand. He clutched Ignacius and the old monk clung to his side. Together, they watched Lancelot struggle with the planking, lift it, and sadly sigh. Galahad leaned forward and peered into the crypt. All that was left of Britain's greatest King was a bare skeleton of yellowed bone and some shreds of colored cloth. The left side of the skull had been smashed; dark eyeholes glared up at them accusingly. Ignacius mumbled frantically under his breath, his eyes squeezed shut, "Hail Mary, full of grace, the Lord is with thee. Blessed art thou among women and the fruit of thy womb, Jesus. . . ."

"My dear friend." Lancelot's warm, kind voice rang out in the hallowed dark and pushed the shadows back. "My dear lord, I have brought you your heart's desire. I give her to you with my blessing, as a token of the love I bear you both. Take back your death gift, and be free forever." He reached into his pouch and withdrew a heavy gold ring set with a dark red stone. Galahad recognized Pendragon's ring of office—the great ruby with the Dragon of Britain carved small—he had kissed it on Arthur's hand a hundred times. Lancelot knelt and slid the ring over the bare bone of a long finger. Shivers ran up Galahad's spine. He opened his mouth to speak but no words came out. Lancelot hoisted himself up onto the chapel floor and went to the Queen's bier. He lifted her gently, bent over, and whispered to her as tenderly as if she were his lover asleep in his arms. He brought her to the edge of the opened grave, laid her carefully down, lowered himself in, lifted her, held her a long moment against his breast, and finally laid her down next to Arthur's bones. Galahad watched, unable to move or breathe. Before his eyes her flesh began to age, wrinkle, shrink from the bones of her face; her eyelids sank, the white line of her teeth began to show between her flattening lips.

"Quickly!" Lancelot cried, his calm composure beginning to crack. "Galahad, attend me!"

Together, they replaced the planking and shoveled dirt over the bodies. Ignacius, eyes shut tight, rocked back and forth, hugging his wide girth. "Hail Mary, full of grace, the Lord is— O God protect us! Blessed are thou among— O Lord, keep the devil at bay!"

In silence father and son filled in the grave, stamped upon the earth, moved the altar back into place. Lancelot took the herbs and flowers and trinkets from the bier and strewed them around the altar's feet to hide the signs of disturbance they had made. Then he knelt before the altar and prayed.

"Thank God it's done!" Ignacius whispered, sweating freely. "Poor lady, may she rest in peace. But whatever shall I tell the abbott when he returns? What shall we do with the grave upon the hill? Fill it in?"

Wearily, Lancelot turned. "We are in God's hands. He will provide an answer. Wait until morning."

Taking this as dismissal, Ignacius nodded and backed away. "Very well, my lord, I will get me to my bed. And I suggest you do the same. I have shown young—Galahad, is it?—where the guesthouse is. Get yourself rest, and I shall wake you at dawning."

Galahad clasped his hands and shook them. "Thank you, my good brother, for your aid. You have done Britain a fine service tonight. Trust God to keep us safe from discovery."

"You may count upon my prayers!" Ignacius returned fervently, and let himself out the chapel door.

Galahad turned back to his father. Lancelot knelt before the altar, the candlelight pooling in a dim halo around his head.

"Father," he called softly. "Father, it is done. Will you come away now? In the morning we can start back for Lanascol."

Lancelot looked up. His gray eyes were black pits in the shadows. "Not yet," he said slowly. "I will spend the night here. With her. With them both. You go on."

"I do not like to leave you. You don't look well. You need food, some hot broth, and a warm blanket."

A ghostly smile touched Lancelot's lips. "There is nothing you can do for me, son. You have already given me the greatest gift within your power. You came back to Lanascol. Don't you yet see? My life is past. I belong with Guinevere and Arthur. Without them I am nothing. We three—" His voice broke and he stopped to steady himself. Galahad stood above him, looking down. "A man who does not love a woman is but half a man," Lancelot said slowly. "She made us both what we were. We are bound forever, beyond death, by that love."

Galahad shook his head. "I don't understand you, Father."

"If you ever love a woman as I have loved Guinevere, you will come to understand it. My blessing goes with you, my dear son. Now leave me in peace."

Half-annoyed with himself for obeying, but too tired to protest, Galahad left Lancelot in the chapel and went off to bed.

He was awakened before dawn by Ignacius's urgent shaking. "My lord! My lord! Come at once! Oh, dear, oh, dear, what shall we do?"

"What has happened?" Galahad cried, struggling awake.

"I knew it, I knew it, I knew by the look on his face," moaned the monk, as Galahad threw on his tunic and reached for his boots. "It's Sir Lancelot. He's dead."

Galahad froze. "No."

"Aye, my lord, I fear so. How it happened I can't tell. There doesn't seem to be a mark on him. Oh, hurry, hurry, the brothers will be up and about in a moment, and whatever shall we tell them?"

Galahad ran to the chapel and threw open the door. Lancelot lay on his face, his arms stretched over the grave below. There were tear tracks on his cheeks and his limbs had not yet begun to stiffen. He had not been dead long.

"O my father!" Galahad cried, falling to his knees. "This was what you meant! I did not know it!" He gathered the old soldier in his arms and wept bitterly.

Behind him, Ignacius fluttered nervously. "My lord! My lord! Take care, it is nearly dawn! Whatever shall we do?"

Carrying Lancelot in his arms, Galahad rose. "Bring the shovels, Ignacius. We will bury him on the hill. He would prefer to be near his King and Queen than home in Lanascol. He told me as much last night. 'Without them I am nothing.' And see? It is morning, and God has provided us a body for the grave."

Ignacius followed as Galahad carried Lancelot up the hill to the graveyard. He lined the grave with Lancelot's cloak, and laid his own over him. He removed Lancelot's swordbelt—it was his uncle Galyn's sword—and his badge with the ruby-eyed Hawk of Lanascol, and his ring of kingship, which he slipped on his own finger. Ignacius spoke the prayers of blessing while Galahad kissed his father's hollow cheek and whispered his farewells. By the time the brothers appeared for morning prayers, it was finished.

Galahad swayed, leaning on his shovel. "Get me out of here, Ignacius," he begged. "I cannot stay another minute. The whole place stinks of death."

The little monk brought him his horse and Lancelot's, and placed the reins in his hand. "We think of death as the gate of Heaven," he murmured, patting Galahad on the back. "But you are too young to find that much of a comfort. Get you down to Avalon and get some rest. The Lady Morgaine is a great healer, if I do say it myself. No one suffers at her hands and you are better off there than here. Go with God, my lord king. Your secret will be safe with us."

My lord king. He was King of Lanascol now. The weight of it descended like an iron cloak. He did not feel ready to take up that obligation. *A man who does not love a woman is but half a man.* The ache in his heart was proof of that. As his head touched the pillow in Morgaine's guest pavilion, he saw before him a woman's face, with gray-green eyes and a glorious tumble of chestnut hair. *Go back and make right the harm you have done,* Guinevere's voice whispered in his ear. *You cannot go back to Lanascol without her.*

55 ✟ QUEEN OF GWYNEDD

Galahad rode north at speed. After weeks of sun, the weather now turned cold and damp. When it was not raining it was sleeting fitfully, or snowing thin, hard flakes. Morgaine had given him a thick cloak of soft wool as a parting gift, and he wrapped this tightly around him and pushed on, riding first Farouk and then Priam, his father's stallion, alternating horses to make better time. When Morgaine had said good-bye to him she had pressed her hands against his temples. *Hurry. Hurry. Hurry. There is little time. It may already be too late.* The words had sprung into his head and he heard them still, whenever the howling wind paused to give him a moment's peace. Too late for what?

All over Wales folk were readying for winter, storing their harvest, bringing in their sheep and cattle, patching their houses, stacking firewood, peat, and charcoal, nestling into the warmth of the earth while the north winds blew. Nobody else was on the roads. The few travelers he met were local men, hurrying home with clods of peat, bundles of brushwood, or strings of rabbits slung across their shoulders. Everyone stared at him, a single soldier with two priceless horses and two priceless swords. Wales was poorer than it had been in Arthur's day. Three times he had to defend himself against hill bandits who thought that outnumbering him was enough. Finally he crossed through the mountain pass and made his last camp in the heights above Gwynedd.

But sleep came hard. The horses huddled together for warmth under a rock ledge and Galahad lit a good fire against wolves. He sat staring at it most of the night, seeing in it a woman's face and wondering how on earth he could ever say what he must say. He awoke well past dawning and made his way slowly down the mountain track. Now that the moment was upon him, he was eager to delay. For the first time since Lancelot's death the sun shone long enough to warm the air, melt the frosts, and breathe a deceptive breath of spring against his cheek.

Around midday he came out of the low hills into the forests that bordered the meadows and tended fields of Gwynedd. When he came across a clearing hard by a stream, he dismounted to let the horses drink. Tethering them to a tree, he gave them fodder and seated himself on a flat stone in a pool of sun. A huge oak stood near the entrance to the clearing, and a laurel, sprung from nowhere, grew near the center. It was a peaceful place and he was glad to rest. He had been there some minutes, deep in thought, when he felt eyes upon him, and turned.

A child stood in the path at the other side of the clearing, a girl of about three or four, daintily wrapped in furs from her wolfskin cap to her fox-lined boots. Black braids hung over her shoulders and long, dark lashes shaded the bluest eyes he had ever seen. In the far distance he heard a woman's panicked calling, the nurse, no doubt, looking for her charge. The child stared at him with all the guilelessness of her age. She felt no need to speak, but walked closer to him to get a better look. He shifted his shoulders under the direct gaze of such innocent curiosity.

"Hello," he ventured timidly. "I am a stranger hereabouts. Can you tell me, am I in Gwynedd?"

She nodded.

He tried again. "Is it far to the castle?"

She did not move.

"Er—my name is Galahad. What's yours?"

For a long moment he feared she would not answer, but she was not shy, only consumed with curiosity about him. "Elen," she said at last.

"A pretty name. A Welsh name. A queen's name, too, if I remember aright."

The child nodded absently, absorbed by his badge, his cloak and tunic, his sword, his belt, his boots.

"Are you a princess of Gwynedd?" For of course he had placed her now. She must be Percival and Blodwyn's daughter. If they had married as planned, there was just time. She was handsomer than either of them, and blue-eyed—probably a throwback, he mused, to some ancestral Celtic beauty of wild Wales, perhaps to the original Elen herself, whose fabled loveliness had snared the Emperor Maximus.

As if she had come to some decision, the child looked up into his face and answered firmly, "Yes. Are you a king?"

"Yes, but only lately. I'm on my way back to my kingdom. But it's a long way off. Beyond the sea. And before I leave I would speak with your father."

Her eyes widened at that and she considered him, as if deciding whether or not he was telling the truth. The nurse's shrill cries came nearer. The poor woman sounded close to tears. The child paid her no attention.

"Tell me, my lady Elen, where is your father? At home or away at the wars?"

The wide blue eyes narrowed. "I don't know."

"Your mother, then, is she about? I must speak with your aunt." Galahad rose and held out his hand to her. "But first, I will take you home to your mother."

She gave him her hand tentatively. "Mama has a badge, too. Just like that."

He looked down at her fragile face from his great height and his heart began to pound. "Like *this*?"

At that moment the frantic nurse ran into the clearing. "Lady Elen! *There* you are! Why didn't you answer me? I've been scared half to death— Oh!" She saw him then, and gathered the child to her skirts. Galahad saluted her politely and gained enough control over his voice to introduce himself. The nurse flushed and curtsied. But the child watched him with her unwavering, assessing stare.

"I found him, Helda. All by myself."

"Yes, yes, and a great lord he is, too," the nurse agreed, patting her hand. "I imagine he's come a long way to—"

"He's my father."

The words fell like lightning bolts. The nurse gasped. Galahad's world began to spin.

"Nonsense, child. Do hush, now. You don't know what you're saying."

"He has a badge like Mama's." She pointed. "Like the one in the gilded box. It's my father's badge."

The nurse grabbed her and shoved a hand across her mouth, but nothing could disturb the child's tremendous dignity. She pushed aside the hand and stood calmly looking at Galahad.

"Never mind her, my lord," the nurse muttered hastily. "Bastards are always looking for their fathers. Pay her no mind." *Bastard!* "Thank you, my lord, for tending her when she ran off. I'll return her to the queen."

"Then . . . then she *is* Guinblodwyn's daughter?"

"Oh, no, my lord. Essylte is Lady Blodwyn's daughter. And the baby Melleas, her son. This is the daughter of Lady Dandrane."

Galahad's knees were jelly. "But . . ."

"My lord must be a foreigner. Here in Wales we call her Queen of Gwynedd because she is, in fact—I mean, she runs things for her brother, King Percival, being so able and not yet wed. Lady Blodwyn is the king's wife, but she does little else but bear him children. It's confusing, I suppose, to an outsider."

Galahad sat heavily on the rock, his head in his hands, staring at Dane's daughter. "Sweet Lord, I am justly served." He closed his eyes and hung his head. A light touch fell upon his sleeve. The child stood at his elbow and, for the first time, looked pleased to see him.

He lifted her onto his lap and kissed her. Her mittened hands encircled his neck. He held her gently, partly in terror that this precious, fragile creature might be crushed in his embrace, or worse, that she might suddenly change her mind. "Sweet Elen. Be my guardian and take me to your mother."

He brought the horses out and placed her on Rouk's back. She showed no fear, but grasped the mane and grinned at him. The nurse looked from one to the other in growing amazement.

All the way down the track to the castle the child chattered to Galahad, asking questions at every stride.

"Why do you have two swords?"

"One is my father's and one my uncle's. My father's sword was a gift from the High King Arthur—you've heard of Arthur, I suppose?"

She stared at him as though he were a half-wit. "Of course."

Galahad could not keep from smiling. "I'm glad to see your mother has not neglected your education. My father gave me this sword when he knighted me. My uncle died with King Arthur at Camlann, and my father took his sword for his own. I, in turn, took it when my father died. That was . . . barely two weeks ago. I am taking it back to Lanascol."

"Lan-scol? Mama said Sir Lanesslot is king of Lan-scol."

He reached up to cover her tiny hand with his own. "Lancelot was my father. Your grandfather."

A smile of joy lit her face and she looked down at him with great satisfaction. "I knew you would be a prince. I knew you would come back to get us."

"Your mother never told you anything? I wonder, after all this time, if she will see me."

"There are ways around her." The child spoke from a vast wisdom of adult behavior and Galahad felt his throat tighten. If only Lancelot could have lived to see her! If only he himself had found the courage to return before—how different things might have been.

In the castle courtyard he lifted Elen down and gave the horses to a groom. One of the sentries stared at him, reached for his sword, then thought better of it and sent a page running. Galahad let Elen take him by the hand and lead him into Percival's stronghold.

The early dusk was already drawing down. Servants were busy in the corridors lighting oil lamps and bringing up the evening's ale from the cellars. In all the bustle, no one paid them much attention.

"This way, Father." Elen tugged at his hand. But Galahad had seen a door fly open down the hall, had seen the commotion of servants, courtiers, and king's men, had seen Percival come out, turn, and stare.

Swiftly he bent down to little Elen. "Run along, my sweet girl. I must have a word with the king, alone. Run and send your mother to me—no, put it thus: beg her to attend me, for I have great need of her." The child, seeing nothing amiss, complied gladly, and skipped away. Galahad straightened and waited.

Percival strode angrily down the hall. Two guards, coming up behind Galahad, seized him and pinned his arms. He did not struggle against their cruel hold, but waited, watching Percival.

"Disarm him!" snapped the king, and the swordbelts were torn from his waist. "Bind him well!" A coarse rope was looped around his wrists behind his back and pulled tight, biting his flesh.

Keeping the pain from his face, he looked sadly at his cousin. "You have changed, Percival."

With a wrath that darkened his complexion, Percival drew back his arm and hit him. "How dare you! How dare you show your face here! Who in all of God's creation do you think you are?" He jerked his head toward a nearby door. "Take him in there."

Galahad was dragged into a chamber, bleeding from nose and mouth. He recognized it, he thought, as the meeting chamber, where so many years ago he had carried a sickly Percival in his arms, and taken Dane for a boy. The lamps were already lit and a coal fire was going in the grate. Percival and his courtiers followed him in.

Galahad fell to his knees. "Percival, I come to you as a suppliant. I beg your pardon. I have done you and your sister a grievous wrong and I will submit to any penance you see fit to give me. I bring no one with me. I came alone, and you have my only weapons."

Percival grunted. He was older and thinner, with sharp features growing sharper. "Two swords in your hands are as good as an army. You are right you have done me wrong! I cannot forget it. Bryll, Sebastan, clear the room and close the door. Luathe, stand behind him and look sharp. He's quicker than you ever would believe."

With only a handful of men in the room, Percival drew his sword. "I sent you to find her, that she might choose a husband." He brought the blade to the side of Galahad's face. Galahad closed his eyes, remembering the justice he had so smugly meted out to Valvan for a much smaller crime. "Had you brought her back yourself and wed her, I'd have forgiven you the liberty you took." The blade caressed his ear, slid to his throat. "She is my *sister*! My own flesh and blood. And you . . . you self-righteous coward! You must know that I have sworn to kill you."

Galahad felt the blade at his throat. Beads of sweat stood out across his brow, but he kept his breathing steady and looked up into Percival's face. "My lord king, I knew all that when I came here. I yield myself to you. Kill me and avenge your sister's honor, if you wish. I *was* the coward you call me—I was worse. I betrayed every principle I held dear. I betrayed our friendship, your sister's love and honor, which I cherish more than life; I betrayed the good name of Gwynedd before all the northern lords; and . . . and I made a bastard of my daughter." His voice broke, and he struggled to control his emotion. "I have no desire to live without your forgiveness, my good cousin, and without that of your sister, whom I have loved steadfastly every moment of these four long years. If you can find it in you to forgive such a wretch as me, I will make good the promise of my actions, and take her to wife, if she will have me. If not . . . if not, then do with me what you will."

"That's rich!" Percival snarled. "After all the evil you have done, you offer to become one of my family! I suppose you think we'd want you."

Galahad bowed his head. "My father is dead. I am King of Lanascol now. Let me wed her and give the child a name. Then kill me. I will not try to stop you. Let Dane keep the swords herself. Your sister and her child will have a kingdom—they need not have me."

Percival lowered his sword. "You strike true, at least." His features relented and he said sadly, "I am sorry to hear about Lancelot. He was a great
man and lived in a great time. All Britain will mourn his passing." He
looked over Galahad's head to the back of the room. "Well, Dane, you have
heard him. What do you think?"

Galahad stiffened, but with his hands bound and Luathe's sword point
at his back, he could not turn around.

There was a long silence. At last he heard her voice, cool and steady. "I
cannot tell, Val, until I have spoken with him. Will you leave us alone for a
while?"

"Are you sure you will be safe?"

"You have his weapons. I am proof against anything of his except his
sword."

Percival nodded. There was pride in the look he gave his sister, and
Galahad marked it. "Luathe, untie his hands. Bryll, take the swords." He
looked back darkly at Galahad. "The windows are shuttered, the doors
guarded. Do not be twice a fool."

They were alone. Galahad rose, rubbing his wrists, and turned around.
She was now two-and-twenty and a full-blown beauty. Her rich hair was
swept behind her, but crept loose from its pins here and there, just as he remembered, to frame her face. The slender neck, the curved cheek and clear,
creamy skin— His throat went dry and his breathing stopped. She held herself still and kept expression from her features, but the gray-green eyes
flashed with the fire that he recalled. She stirred him to his soul.

"It was a good speech."

"I meant every word of it."

"Indeed? But perhaps you have grown clever with your tongue." He
waited. He could feel her rage clear across the room, like a wave of heat. He
braced himself to bear whatever she threw at him. *Of course she will be angry, but you can change that.* He alone was responsible for all this pain. "Why
did you come back, Galahad? To claim your daughter? You cannot have
her." He said nothing, only watched her patiently. "Did you really think you
could walk in here, fling yourself before my brother, mouth an apology, and
be forgiven? Think again. I will not be bargained for like a cow in the marketplace." Her hands were tightly clasped before her, and they trembled.
"You owe me more than it will ever be in your power to repay."

"I know."

"You have destroyed Percival's marriage. Being heavy with child, I
could not leave Gwynedd when he brought her here. She was a sweet girl,
and left to themselves, there might have been something for them. But I
was between them. While I am here, he loves me more, you see. It is the
way with twins; he cannot help it. Now she is a bitter woman and they have

little to say to each other, except in bed. I tell you"—her voice began to shake—"I tell you I carry this guilt upon my soul, and it is your fault!"

"If they share a true love, they will recover it."

"How dare you speak to me of love!" she cried, her eyes flashing green and filling with tears. "How dare you!"

He strode across the room and took her hands, holding them firmly to his chest as she struggled to break free. "I was selfish, stupid, blind, a boor, an arrogant fool, and I deserve your wrath. But I love you, Dane, with a love that will not die. I have tried everything to kill it, to spare myself the shame. I have gone half-crazy with regret. But every day and every night you are there, in my very soul. You are more a part of me than the air I breathe. You can deny me—I wouldn't blame you. I deserve it. But let me give you Lanascol, let me make what reparation is within my power. Let me give Lancelot's granddaughter his name."

Her eyes widened and the tears spilled from them.

"You have forgiven Lancelot?" she whispered.

Slowly he lifted her fingers to his lips. "All he did was love a woman unto death." Unable to contain himself a moment longer, he took her shoulders in his hands and kissed her. All her young passion, held in for so long and at such cost, burst its bonds in an instant and she wept wildly upon his shoulder, hugging him tightly while he rocked her gently and caressed her hair.

So Percival found them at the end of the hour, in each other's arms, deep in whispers, oblivious to the outside world.

56 ✝ THE SAXONS

Horns sounded from the ramparts and the door burst open. Percival leaned in and tossed Galahad his swords. "Saxons! No time for words—take charge of the south wall; I'll take the west."

"Longboats?"

"Worse—they're at the very gates! Word had spread of your coming, and the sentries gathered at the guardhouse to hear the gossip. They'll pay for their inattention now!"

He was gone in an instant. Galahad strapped on his swordbelt and turned to Dane. In the face of fear she was cool and still.

"What do you want me to do?"

He handed her Galahantyn's sword. "Take this, and the child, and whatever else you might need for an escape. Take both horses—mine and Lancelot's—to the cave and there await me. But be quick, Dane, or you won't make it. Go on foot if you must. My darling." He kissed her fiercely. "Be prepared to use the sword. Don't let them take you. Death is better."

"I will wait for you until tomorrow dark."

"If I'm not there I am dead or taken. Go south to Caerleon as soon as you are able."

"My love, I will. But—live!"

She turned and was gone. Galahad drew a deep breath and raced to the south wall.

Percival's soldiers were well disciplined and trained, but the attack had been a complete surprise and they were shaken. Irish raiders were expected from time to time, but they had never thought to see Saxons on their coasts. Galahad organized a defense of archers and swordsmen, and had the pages running for buckets of water, in case of fire. As far as he could see, the Saxons swarmed over the grounds in a disorganized scramble, running madly from the woods, scaling the palisade, setting fire to the outbuildings, wreaking general havoc, and making only intermittent dashes at the doors. He could see no one in charge. In spite of their fearsome aspect—they were blond giants wrapped in skins, whirling axes and screaming uncouth paeans—he was sure that Percival's men could hold them.

"Sir Mabrig!" he called to the ranking Welshman. "Take charge here. See the archers keep them off the walls. They can't be this few, so far from home, and this poorly led. I expect a major attack within the hour, but I hope to be back by then. Lend me a man who's quiet and surefooted for a mission behind their lines."

A youth of seventeen named Erec volunteered. Together they made their way through the castle, alive with voices all calling at once and ablaze with torches. It was but the work of a moment to lift a torch from a hall sconce and escape unnoticed into the stableyard. With a sigh of relief Galahad saw the stables stood intact.

"Erec, find me two horses which are not afraid of smoke." A quick survey of the stalls showed him his own two beasts were missing. Bless coolheaded Dane, she had not panicked, but had obeyed him and escaped.

"Where are we going, my lord?"

"To the shore. You know the road—find me the quickest route."

"But won't the Saxons be on the road?"

"I doubt it. They haven't horses and they need cover. Courage, Erec. Saxons disdain roads. If they can't travel by water, they'd as soon make a straight line through field or forest. They're a direct race."

The boy, who was in awe of him, mounted his horse obediently and, carrying the torch, circled around the castle gardens, cut through the woods, and slipped quietly out onto the shore road. Galahad rode with his sword drawn. In spite of his assurances he half expected a good skirmish before they made the sea, but they met no one. When they came in sight of the ocean, Galahad pulled up and signaled Erec to dismount.

"Stay here and hold the horses. Cover their nostrils with your cloak. You must be perfectly silent. Give me the torch. If all goes well I'll whistle for you; if I'm taken, get out quickly; don't look back. Do you understand?"

Erec nodded, eyes wide. Silent as a cat and as stealthy, Galahad crept toward the thin line of trees that marked the edge of the woods. Five minutes behind a gorse bush showed him where the lookouts were posted. The first he beheaded; the second, who heard him at the last second, he gutted. The third he had to fight, but it was quickly over—he sliced off the man's wrist and killed him with his own two-headed ax. Sweating lightly despite the sea breeze, he turned to survey the beachhead and was staggered by the sight before him. Thirty longboats lay drawn up on the shore! Thirty! This was an invasion! What they had taken for attack could only be diversion. He looked up the wooded slope toward the castle and caught his breath. A full attack was under way—the early darkening sky glowed dully red and he could see the flicker of flames against the treetops. Gwynedd was burning, and he was not there!

Angrily, he whistled for the boy and fanned the torch into a greedy blaze. They secured the horses, fashioned a handful of crude torches from driftwood and beach grasses, and set about firing the Saxon ships. The craft were well made with closely fitted timbers sealed with pitch, an enemy to water but a friend to flame. They lit like tinder. The stiff shore breeze did the rest. The sails, once unfurled, burned easily enough, and they used them as giant torches, dragging them from one boat to the next.

"Keep your eyes open!" Galahad gasped as they paused for rest. "Sooner or later they'll see the smoke and know what we're about. If we're caught on the beach, we're dead men."

More than half the boats lay burning before they heard the cries of Saxons coming down the hill. Galahad signaled Erec and they ran to the horses.

"Thank God they have no subtlety about them!" he muttered. "Now, trot around the beach, tear up the sand, let them think the whole cavalry is behind them. Then take cover in the wood and we'll pick them off."

No sooner had they galloped into the trees than forty Saxons ran onto the beach. They stared stunned at their burning boats, shouted to one another, pointed frantically to the sand, and tried without success to douse the flames. At last, one of them took charge of the others, posted a guard apiece at the remaining boats, sent a runner up the hill for reinforcements, and began, with a dozen men, to track the horses.

Galahad grunted in satisfaction. "Take the runner, Erec. Then cut through the trees and get behind them. They're afoot. Between us, we can take them all." Eyes wide with excitement, doubt, and hope, Erec rode off, and Galahad hunted for a good place to ambush.

The Saxons came up through the trees in no good order, but spread out, each man looking to fight his own battle. Galahad gave them what they sought. The first men passed within yards of his hiding place; his dagger flew at the foremost and caught him in the throat. The man fell choking on his own blood. Before his startled follower could react, Galahad's sword was in his side, twisting. Galahad slipped from the horse to retrieve his dagger and take the Saxon's ax from his dying hand. He heard a shout, and looked up to see a third running at him, swinging an ax. But they were in a thick wood; the ax caught a branch and stuck. Galahad's dagger flew free and found its mark. Hurrying, he collected his dagger and jumped upon the horse. By the time the rest of the company arrived in answer to the shout, he was gone. The Saxon warriors stared about them but kept their wits. They closed ranks and advanced uphill together. Relying on the nimbleness of his sturdy Welsh mount, Galahad wove through the trees, before them and behind them, striking with dagger, sword, and ax, retreating out of range after each attack, returning to take another man unawares. He had killed six more when he saw two others fall, struck from behind. Through the shadows he caught Erec's grinning salute.

The doubling in strength of their half-seen enemy was too much for the Saxons—they took to their heels, even the leader among them, and ran. They soon lay dying on the forest floor, for men in retreat were easy targets. Galahad congratulated Erec, whose awe had only increased now that they two had defeated so many Saxons without a scratch. They robbed the bodies of their weapons and divided them in haste.

"My lord, should we fire the rest of the boats, or go to defend the castle?"

"Defend the castle! I'm happy to leave them some means of escape, if we can drive them to it. The last thing we want are stranded Saxons in Gwynedd. But we are only two and don't know how big their force is. Thirty boats—they might be six hundred strong."

"Two against six hundred?" Awed though he was, the boy paled.

"Not only two. Trust Percival to fight to the bitter end. This is his homeland. We must provide him a diversion. We'll make the Saxons think they are surrounded. Confuse them. Take them singly or in twos, whatever you are able. But cover is essential. Stay in the woods and keep moving, astride or afoot. See if you can't drive them toward the western wall, where Percival's archers have a better shot at them. And Erec—" Galahad gripped the young man's arm in the soldier's embrace. "Good luck."

The boy bent his knee to the ground. "My lord Sir Galahad."

They fought half the night. At first Galahad despaired of victory—they were so many, and the larger force was well organized and bravely led. Their archers were doing the most damage, sending flaming pitch-soaked arrows high over the walls, scattering Percival's men, so many that the fire buckets could not keep up. Galahad began by picking off the archers' guards. Five had died before the captain knew anything was amiss. He led them a merry chase through the woods and killed them, one by one. The last one to die was the captain himself, a huge, dirty, blue-eyed man who spat in Galahad's face even with a sword at his throat. Galahad slid the blade partway into his neck and then withdrew it.

"Die fast?" he demanded, "or die slow?" He pointed toward the Saxon forces. "Cynewulf?" He laid the blade against the Saxon's ear. "Who's the thegn? Cynewulf?"

The warrior, dazed and dull-witted, consumed with the effort of hiding his pain, struggled to speak. "Cynric," he muttered thickly. "Aelfric. Cynric."

"You have earned your quick death, my friend. May God have mercy on your blighted pagan soul." And he slit his throat.

After that, it was a game of strike-and-run, the game he and Gareth had played in Camelot the long, sleek summers of his boyhood. He would throw three daggers and take three archers. A handful of men would pursue him into the forest, and he would dodge and hide and pick them off. Then he would strip the bodies of daggers and axes, and with their own weapons start again. It took them a long time to realize it was safer not to chase him, but to keep a sharp lookout and try to defend the blows. Soon Galahad was out of daggers and his horse was tiring. But by that time the loss of archers had been felt, and the Saxons were moving toward the main gate in the west wall to launch a full-scale attack. Galahad was content to see them attempt it, for it was against that sort of attack that old King Pellinore had built the castle, and outnumbered though Percival's forces were, this gave them their best chance.

Staying well out of the torchlight, Galahad skulked on foot among the shadows and the charred ruins of the outbuildings, gathering weapons from among the fallen Saxon, dispatching silently those who still lived. He selected a hiding place at the edge of the forest, between the main gate and the sea, and waited. When the attack came, Percival's men were ready for it. Archers rained down arrows dipped in poison, soldiers poured vats of boiling pitch onto the swarm of blond heads below. Those who managed to scale the walls met the clean, cold steel of Roman swords. An hour before daylight, with the burning fortress still untaken, the Saxons turned. But they were hindered in their retreat by what they took for evil spirits in the forest, who struck them down, unseen, unheard, and just as they gained the beach, split Prince Cynric's skull with a two-headed ax. The survivors could not get away fast enough, muttering under their breaths as they strained at the oars, about the ill-fated, god-cursed, dark-haunted land of Gwynedd.

Dawn broke red in the east when Galahad stumbled wearily through the west gate.

"My lord Galahad!" the sentries cried gleefully. "You live! You've been taken for dead these past six hours!"

"I am well enough, and whole. Have you seen young Erec, who went with me?"

"No, my lord, no one's come this way all night. King Percival is within, counting his losses. He'll be overjoyed to see you, my lord!"

He found Percival just emerging from the guardroom, drawn and bleary-eyed, his face smudged with soot.

"Galahad! Praise God!" He flung himself into his cousin's arms and pounded his back. "You are unharmed? Thank God! I took you for dead— Mabrig said you went behind the lines, and we heard nothing after!"

He was all weary muscle, bone, and sinew; Galahad could feel his exhaustion through his tunic as clearly as he heard it in his voice. "Erec and I went down to burn their boats. He's a brave lad; I've not seen him since we split up—have you found him?"

Percival made the effort to collect himself. "Erec? Laymon's son? Why, yes, I believe the physician's with him now. A sliced arm, I think, but not deep. He'll be all right."

"Then my prayers are answered. Now tell me, how do we stand?"

The lines deepened in Percival's drawn face. "It was close to disaster, Galahad," he said. "As close as I ever hope to come. I've just taken report. We've lost half the barracks, the hall of meeting, all the living quarters on the north wall. Only the women's rooms and the gardens at the back are untouched. Everywhere else, the fire has gutted. And I tell you, Galahad, if the Saxons hadn't left off their fire arrows and gathered for attack on the west wall when they did, I don't know where we'd be. That's the miracle that saved us."

Galahad laid a firm hand on his shoulder. "Bless the foresight of your grandfather, King Pellinore, who built the place of stone. The king's house in Benoic is made of wood."

Percival attempted a smile, but only the corners of his mouth twitched. "He was wealthier than I am, and had more men. Those were the great days of Britain, when Arthur was King. Ahhh, God, Galahad, we shall not see those days again."

"Courage, Percival. We two, at least, are keeping faith with Arthur. If it is God's will that Britain should go down into the pagan dark, Gwynedd and Lanascol will be the last to linger in the light."

A shout brought their heads up. A sentry hurried toward them, saluted Galahad, and fell on his knee before Percival.

"My lord! A soldier has this moment stumbled into the yard, bleeding from an ax wound. He says a band of Saxons were left stranded on the beach—they fought like madmen! A handful got through our lines and have headed up into the hills behind us. Shall we pursue them?"

Galahad, white-faced, gripped his arm. "How many? How long ago?"

"Six or seven, my lord. They have an hour's start."

"They are on foot, though. Be easy, Galahad. The dogs will track them."

Galahad was already leaving. He turned back a moment. "Dane is up there. With the child and two horses. And one sword."

Percival stared at him, thunderstruck. "Dane is in the hills? Are you mad? She's in the cellars with the rest of the women!"

"No, Percival, she's not." They both whirled at the sound of a woman's voice. Anet came toward them with Guinblodwyn behind her, holding the hand of a blond toddler. A nurse followed with Percival's infant son. "This is what I came forth to tell you. She never came down with us, nor little Elen neither. She kissed me at the door. It felt like farewell."

Percival turned angrily upon Galahad. "If this is your doing, cousin—"

The look on Galahad's face stopped his words. "She's in a cave in the low hills. It's an old hiding place of hers. I know it well. If she hasn't lit a fire they may not find her. Come on, follow me."

Galahad, Percival, and a dozen others who were still able to take to horse mounted and headed up the track into the eastern hills behind the fortress. Galahad led Percival straight up toward the cave. The others fanned out in twos and threes and searched the surrounding woods.

They came quietly into the clearing that gave onto the lip of the cave. Galahad slid off his horse and signaled Percival to dismount. Silently he drew his sword. He crept forward, careful of his footing, feeling rather than hearing Percival's quick breathing behind his back. There was no fire. The hearth lay cold and filled with earth. She had tried to hide it—why? Galahad saw his own blade trembling before him and found he could not hold it still. He had opened his mouth to call softly for her when he caught sight of the thing that lay in shadow beyond the entrance, and he froze, every muscle in his body straining against his will. He put out an arm to keep Percival back.

"Cousin!" Percival said softly. "What *is* it?"

He pushed past Galahad's arm and stopped abruptly. The body before them wore thick leather boots, filthy leggings, and a torn tunic of poorly cured skins. The man lay on his stomach, his long, straw-colored hair bound in thongs and flung across his livid face. Protruding skyward from his back rose the gleaming blood-encrusted blade of Galahantyn's sword.

"Dead!" Percival whispered. "My God, she must have killed him!"

Galahad barely trusted himself to speak. He was staring at the second set of footprints beyond the body. They had been made by boots.

"There were two of them." He pointed. His limbs sagged cold and heavy. He did not want to know what lay ahead inside the cave. He listened, and heard a soft rustling, only a breath of sound. He could not tell where it came from, but it could come from only one direction. As soon as he moved forward, it stopped. Slowly they crept into the center of the cave, past woven baskets knocked on their sides with their contents spilling out, past the chest of scrolls, still closed and locked, although the lock had been tried with a dagger, judging from the scratches and gouges in the wood; past the empty bed—thank God!—although someone had lain there; the blankets were tumbled and the bracken broken—and on into the dark. Galahad paused. The candleholder was missing. The old sword was gone. He had no light, nor means of getting one.

Suddenly the toe of his boot stubbed against something soft and heavy. The breath left his body. He knelt quickly and put out a shaking hand. His fingers found flesh, cold flesh and—a coarse beard and long mustache! He nearly wept. In the dark he bowed his head and said a quick prayer of thanksgiving.

"Galahad!" Percival's voice, above him, trembled at the edge of control. "Who is it?"

"The second Saxon, cousin. Your admirable sister has killed them both."

He rose slowly. "Dane!" he called softly, cupping his hands around his lips. "Make a noise if you can!"

They held their breaths in the damp dark, the brightening day behind them only deepening the shadow in the cave. Gradually, a dim light crept through a crevice up ahead, a feeble flicker, but by it they felt their way along the sweating walls to the narrow split in the rock that gave onto the smaller cave Dane used as a stable. Galahad slithered through, heart pounding. If it was a trap, death lay beyond. He pushed out into the light, the sweet smell of hay and horses heavy in his nostrils. There was no one there. The candle in its holder lay on a ledge of rock; Rouk and Priam munched lazily, barely interested in his presence, rustling the straw as they moved. Sword at the ready, he looked carefully about him. Beyond the second horse the extra straw was oddly piled; if his eyes did not deceive him, a sliver of silver blade stuck out from it, trembling lightly and catching the candlelight.

Galahad sheathed his sword and ducked around the horses. "Dane," he

said gently. "It's over. My brave woman, come on out." The straw parted and
she rose, her eyes wide with fear barely held in, barely controlled breathing
fast and shallow. Her white fist clutched a bloody sword.

"Galahad!"

He took the weapon from her and held her in his arms. She began to
shake violently and clung to him. He kissed her hard, willing his passion
to pierce her terror. "My wonderful warrior," he whispered, smiling down
into her ashen face, "how did you ever do it with this old sword?"

She tried to smile. Her strained look lightened. "There never was a better weapon than a Celtic blade."

"Nor a more difficult enemy than a woman. Is the ch—our daughter—
with you?"

The horror receded from her eyes at last. "Elen, come forth." The straw
rustled; the child looked up at them, calm and trusting, her fear already behind her. Dane bent and lifted her, kissing her round cheek. "You're a brave
girl, my lady Elen. Galahad, she never uttered so much as a squeak."

"Well, may the good Lord bless us all. You look like a family." Percival
stood smiling behind them, the joy on his face at odds with the sweat on
his brow.

"Come," Galahad said gently, slipping an arm around Dane, "let's go
out into the sweet air. We'll get those two out of the cave, and you can tell
us what happened."

The story was simple enough. They had hidden all night in the cave,
huddling together on the bed under the blankets. Dane had rigged an alarm
with a length of string strung across the mouth, fastened to a pewter cup full
of pebbles and metal spoons. Early in the morning the Saxons tripped it. In
the case of such an event, Elen had been instructed to slip into the inner
cave and hide in the horses' hay. Alone, hiding in the shadows, Dane had
run Galyn's sword through the first man and retreated to the back of the
cave. She knew the cave well and went silently, hiding behind a small ledge
of rock. She knew the second Saxon had not heard her. He was a superstitious man who shook badly, his breath wheezing in his chest and his fingers
tightly crossed against enchantment. Yet he had stopped when he saw the
chest and pulled out his dagger to break the lock.

"He probably thought it full of treasures," Dane said. "And so it is, but
none that he could spend. But I was terrified he might break the lock and
spill the scrolls, so I made a noise, just a tiny noise, and he whipped around
and came at me." She drew a long, trembling breath and looked up at Galahad. "He almost caught me. It was perfectly black, but his night sight was
good and he had the sixth sense of a cat. All I had was this old sword you'd
made such fun of—I knew the tip was broken, but the length of the blade
was sharp. In the end—he was right in front of me, but had turned—in the
end I cut his throat."

She gestured toward the dark stains on her clothing, and shuddered. Galahad reached for her and Percival politely looked away. "What a magnificent hideaway this is! Galahad tells me you've been coming here since childhood. This explains all your mysterious absences—she used to be scolded constantly for disappearing whenever she was wanted—but why didn't you ever tell me?"

Dane smiled, her head on Galahad's shoulder. "I don't know. We shared so much, Val, I just wanted to have something private. And if I *had* told you, why then, you'd have known where to find me that night I disappeared."

Percival frowned. "So *this* is where you were! Galahad knew it and I didn't."

"I didn't tell him. I never told anyone. He found it for himself. Don't look so hurt, Val. I never kept anything from you but this."

Percival forced a smile. "And Galahad. I own you surprised me there. I suppose, cousin, you will want to take her away to Lanascol. And little Elen too, who is such a friend to my Essylte."

Dane reached out and took her brother's hand. "We are past the time we should have parted, you and I. I will miss you awfully—you are a part of me, a second skin. But Galahad is"—she colored prettily—"he is the breath of life to me, as Blodwyn was, and will be again, to you. Let me get out of Wales; she will be again the girl you married. Give her some time; she will grow into a queen."

Percival looked unhappily away. "More like, I shall lose you both, you to Galahad, and her to her children."

"She has more thoughts in her head than children. You haven't heard them because you haven't asked. You've had me to ask instead. I promise you, in six months you will be glad I've gone."

"Huh!" Percival snorted.

"Galahad." She laid a hand on his arm. "How quickly can we get going? I have provisions; I had them here, and stuffed the saddlebags."

"You're never thinking of going *now*!" Percival cried.

"I saw the fires burning, Val. I know you were victorious, but I know my home is gone. I really . . . I really don't want to go back and say a hundred sad farewells. Let me remember it as it was."

"But . . . but what about the wedding? And all the preparations! You have no clothes, no fodder for the horses, no nurse for the child—you must stay until spring, at least, and not risk a sea journey in winter—Dane, what can you be thinking?"

"I have a change of clothing here in the cave, and warm cloaks aplenty. Now that Elen has us both, she needs no other."

"We'll go inland as far as Caerleon," Galahad spoke up, seeing the desperation on Dane's face. "I don't trust the coasts with longboats about. There is a priest at Ynys Witrin who will marry us. We'll leave coins there for the tending of Lancelot's grave. The Lady Morgaine will give us housing until the weather clears and we'll take ship from Avalon. We're sure to find a trading vessel headed for Less Britain."

"But—" Percival gulped, his face reddening. "How can you . . . you cannot go . . . to leave in such haste—again!"

"No, cousin, not haste. This is a moment four years overdue."

Percival wiped his eyes. "Then let me leave you to it." He extended his hand. "Galahad, my dear friend, my cousin, my sister's husband, all is forgiven. Never was life so hard to bear as when I thought you my enemy. Take her with my blessing. I would rather see her wed to you than to anyone else I know."

He embraced Dane and hid his face in her flowing hair. "God has granted you your heart's desire, my dearest sister. I know you will do him honor; I pray he will make you happy. The Narrow Sea shall not keep us apart. If the wars allow, I shall visit you next summer in Lanascol."

"You are more than welcome, brother. Remember this: I am Welsh and part of me will never leave Gwynedd. And Percival," she whispered in his ear, "attend to Blodwyn. She loves you dearly, and you are breaking her heart."

He managed a smile, kissed little Elen, saluted them both, and left.

Galahad took Dane in his arms and kissed the tears from her face. "Come," he whispered, "it's time to go home."

57 ✝ THE GRAIL

On a cold morning ten days later, when frost had furred the late leaves and silvered the bare branches, when ice lay in a thickening skin across the hill ponds and at the edges of streams, when the warm breath of the horses froze into twin clouds at every step, the solitary trio came slowly down out of the stony hills of South Wales and into the valley of the Tywy. Dane rode first, her hood drawn close, the soft fall of her hair matching the thick chestnut coat of Lancelot's stallion. Behind her Elen rode bareback on her father's horse, his strong arm about her waist, the cold stinging her round cheeks with red. They seemed, Galahad thought, caught in a timeless bubble, slipping through the winter world without a sound, across mountains, across rivers, through dales and fields and fens, along woodland tracks within a silent cocoon of contentment. Nothing disturbed them—no hill bandits, no Saxons, no beggars, no wandering holy men. When they spoke no one heard them. When they slept the stars sang.

Toward noon they came to the outskirts of the little harbor town of Maridunum, huddling on the west bank of the Tywy a league inland from the tidal flats at the river's mouth. Here the old Roman road crossed the river and ran east to the fortress of Caerleon and the mouth of the Severn.

"Galahad, may we stop here to buy some bread and wine, and to give the horses fodder and rest? A harbor town is sure to have a tavern."

But Galahad was frowning as he scanned the distant buildings. "There's no one about. No one anywhere."

"There's smoke rising from beyond that hill. Perhaps they are all within, to escape the cold."

But Galahad shook his head. "It's not that cold." Handing Elen into her mother's care, he pushed his horse into the lead and drew his sword. A bend in the track brought them around the shoulder of the hill. Maridunum lay spread out below them, smoke rising lazily in thin columns here and there, and nearby from the charred timbers of a farm dwelling. The fields around were burned to stubble, and a lone cow, heavy with milk, lowed in discontent at the gate where her shed once stood.

"A sack!" Galahad breathed, reining in. "The Saxons were here last night!"

"My God!" Dane gasped. "So near! Should we head back up into the hills?"

"No. They've gone. They'll not be back. There's nothing left here for them. By the look of it, everyone's fled into the hills. The King of Dyfed had a garrison here—those must have been the barracks, that column of smoke at the river's edge. Let's go down to see if there's anything we can do."

"Mama." Elen plucked at her sleeve. "Can I have some milk?"

Dane glanced quickly at Galahad. "Can you give us twenty minutes? I can take two skins of milk from the cow, and it would ease her pain."

Galahad nodded. From what he could see of the little town—houses without roofs, boats smashed and sunk along the river, the acrid smell of cinders hanging heavy in the frosted air—there was no need for haste. Indeed, when they rode down to the Roman road they found the place deserted. The tavern at the quayside had been leveled to the ground; every house along the street showed signs of violence. The few boats still at anchor in the river had charred masts or splintered hulls. Not a living soul stirred within the town.

"Where have they all gone?" Dane asked with a shudder, gathering Elen closer in her arms.

"Scattered into the hills, like deer. Before Arthur, it was a common enough occurrence. Give them a few days; they'll come back. And rebuild."

"To think— Galahad, to think this might have been Gwynedd!"

"Without Pellinore, without Maelgon, without Percival it might. Gwynedd has been luckier in her kings than Dyfed."

"What shall we do? Dare we try the road? The light is already failing, and we can do nothing here."

"The bridge across the Tywy is undamaged. Thank God for good Roman stone. Let's get across to the other side and put this town well behind us before we head into the hills."

As dusk drew down they crossed the river and followed the road straight east between the foothills and the shore. They came to an old mill that sat back from the road, the miller's house half-burned and deserted, the mill itself still standing, but the grindstone wrenched from its moorings and smashed into one wall.

"This might do for shelter," Galahad suggested, examining the remaining timbers.

"No," Dane objected, "it's too close to the road and the sea. I'd rather do as we've been doing and trust to the hills."

Galahad nodded at the shepherd's track that wound past the millhouse. "Let's try that."

Up through sheep meadows and hardwood copses they rode, the path twisting around the hill, rising upward snakelike, growing narrower but not quite disappearing. They came to a fork in the track. To the right the thin woods opened onto grassland studded with gorse; to the left the trees thickened beyond a tangle of blackthorn, where a pair of ravens rose screaming at their approach. Without hesitation Galahad went left into the shadows.

Before he had gone twenty paces, he pulled up.

"Dane, look yonder. Do my eyes deceive me or is that a shelter of some sort?"

They dismounted and crept forward. Behind a hawthorn brake someone had built a rough lean-to with branches and thatch for a roof, a wide manger and a trough for water, and, unbelievably, fresh hay stacked in a corner.

"Why, it's a stable!" Dane whispered in amazement. "And fodder, too! Whose can it be? Do you think it might be safe to leave the horses here?"

Galahad looked up at the new stars springing to life in the twilight sky. He could not explain the sudden peace he felt, but he was certain beyond a doubt that they were safe. They filled the manger with hay and the trough with water from their skins. With a sigh, the horses settled down to eat.

"But, Galahad, now we have no water for ourselves."

Unperturbed, Galahad shook his head. "There's bound to be a spring about somewhere."

A narrow track, much overgrown, led away from the lean-to, up a cleft of rock and onto a grassy verge before the high, rounded entrance to a cave. Dane gasped in astonishment, but Galahad seemed unsurprised to see it.

"Did you know this was here?" Dane began, then stopped short as a deep sigh issued from the hill itself, breathing out a dark, smokelike plume that raced by above their heads. Elen cried out and clutched her mother's tunic; the plume swerved, rose, and fluttered past, a whisper on the very edge of sound.

"Bats!" Dane exhaled in relief, stroking her daughter's hair. "What a delightful cave this is; it even has bats. See, Elen, they have left on their nightly hunt so that we may have the place to ourselves."

"And look. Here is water."

Galahad pointed to a small stone basin fashioned out of the living rock to one side of the cave. Water seeped out of a narrow cleft above it and formed a clear, still pool in the basin below.

"A spring?" In awe, Dane ventured closer. "Galahad, where *are* we?"

"Don't you recognize it?"

She shook her head. "How could I? I've never been out of my own valley."

"Mama, there's a cup. May I have a drink of water?" Elen pointed to a niche carved in the rock above the pool. Half-hidden by a hanging bough was a horn cup of ancient make with a rune carved deep into its side.

Dane's voice sank to a whisper. "Galahad, look. This place is a shrine. A shrine to Myrddin, the god of the hollow hills. This is his mark." She looked up at him, puzzled. "Have you been here before?"

"No. Nevertheless, I know what place this is. And so should you. You are the one who told me about it." He smiled. " 'Ravens sing, Blackthorn ring . . .' "

She stared at him, then narrowed her eyes. "You have been different, Galahad, ever since we came down out of the hills this morning. As if you went to sleep last night in the Welsh mountains and woke up in another world."

"Say, rather, that our journey south has been in a different time, a different world."

"Yes, I've felt that, too."

"And this is the end of it."

She swallowed visibly but lifted her chin. "We are not going to Caerleon?"

"We are. Tomorrow we'll ride out on the Roman road and reenter the world of men. But tonight we'll rest in this protected place." He reached for Elen's hand. "Pagan shrine or not, this is a holy place. We will be safe here."

They knelt and said a prayer, poured an offering of the icy liquid onto the ground it sprang from, and drank thirstily from the spring pool. Then they entered the cave.

Dark and cold, it smelled sour with age and disuse, but it was not empty. On a ledge inside the mouth they found flint and tinder, and by the light of a makeshift torch they discovered an old brazier, a pile of bracken so dry it flaked almost to nothingness at a touch, and an old empty chest bound with leather straps now cracked into pieces.

"Someone lived here," Dane whispered, drawing her cloak closer about her shoulders. "The caretaker of the shrine, perhaps?"

"Not recently. Yet dusty as it is, it's been tended. The floor's been swept; someone put hay in the lean-to."

Dane's eyes, huge in the torchlight, looked up into his. "Then someone is expected? Galahad, whoever could it be? Everyone from Maridunum is already hiding in the hills—why, then, is no one here? Either they don't know about it, which seems unlikely, or it's . . . it's too sacred to set foot in."

Galahad drew her into his arms and kissed her softly. "Set your mind at rest. Whoever tends the shrine keeps the shed in readiness. We commit no sin by staying. Can't you feel the peace of the place? We were meant to find it. We are the ones who are expected."

Dane shivered and looked up at the vaulted ceiling. " 'Ravens sing, Blackthorn ring, Under stone, Myrddin's home.' "

Galahad brought up their bedrolls and saddlebags while Dane and Elen gathered firewood from the woods below. They warmed wine over a small fire and ate a meager meal of honey cakes and raisins.

"Mama, may I look around?" Elen asked.

Dane considered. "If this cave is tended regularly, no animals live here. And the bats won't be back till daybreak. I suppose it is safe enough if you stay within reach of the light." She looked uncertainly at Galahad, who nodded.

Dane watched her disappear into the deep shadow of the cave and glanced quickly up at Galahad. He gazed unfocused into the inner darkness as though he watched a dream unfolding. This man who had scowled and glowered at everyone in his youth, whose ideals were set so high he found fault with everything, now sat, accepting and serene, in a pagan shrine. Hesitantly, Dane reached out and took his hand.

"Galahad," she said slowly, "we have had so little time to talk, needing to be silent. Tell me what has happened to you since . . . since you left Gwynedd four years ago."

He reached out and drew her onto his lap, encircling her in his long arms. "Four years. It seems a lifetime. There is too much to tell."

"We have the night before us."

His lips brushed her cheek and he breathed into her ear. "I've no wish to fill the night with words."

She snuggled contentedly against him and lay her head on his shoulder. "At least tell me about the quest. Percival told me all about the tokens you found together, of course. But when he left you, you were looking for a sign that three tests lay ahead. What were they?"

Galahad frowned. "You don't want to put too much faith in black-smiths' tales. Those men are hemmed about with legends and speak, some-times, as if every event in life were magically preordained. I'm sure the old man was handing down an ancient rhyme, but as to its truth . . ."

"Then you don't believe the tokens you found were part of a trial?"

His arms tightened about her. "They may have been. But after I . . . I abandoned you, I came to realize I had failed the quest. I wasn't worthy of my father's badge. I certainly wasn't worthy of the Grail. Not with such a stain on my soul."

"My dear love—"

"No," he said quickly. "Don't make light of that sin. I will tell you where I've been and what I've done, and when you've heard it, you may think what you will."

It was not difficult, after all, to tell her. In the still silence of the night he held her in his arms and let the words spill out, all the tales of his adventures, of the people he had met and of the prayers which had gone unanswered. Dane listened, watching the fire, as aware of the steady beat of his heart beneath the fabric of his tunic as she was of his words.

At one point she turned her head to look up at him. "Queen Guinevere! I did not know she was still alive. You speak of her with tenderness—I thought she was your enemy."

"I was young when I thought so, and believed she had injured me. I believe now that I did her a grave injustice."

Dane held her breath. "And . . . and your father?"

Galahad pressed his lips against her hair. "You were right about me, Dane, from the very first. I will never be the man my father was. I am not fit to wipe his boots."

"Not so!" she said, clasping his hand tightly between her own. "But did you tell him so? Before he died, did he witness your change of heart?"

"We spoke, God grant him peace, in Lanascol, and all the way back to Amesbury. We understood each other tolerably well at the end."

"What a blessing you must have been to him! I should like to see his grave and say a prayer over it."

"Barring bad weather and Saxons, we should be there in under a week. But we must stop the night in Caerleon and report to Sir Lukan on the sack of Maridunum and the attack upon Gwynedd. If he does not already know it. Dane, would you like to be married by the bishop there?"

She smiled, and he caught his breath at her beauty. "I would rather be wed at Ynys Witrin."

"There will be little ceremony at Ynys Witrin. The monastery is a poor, bedraggled place."

"I care nothing for ceremony. But I would like to be married before that altar, if, as you have so carefully avoided saying, it marks the heart of Britain."

He drew her close and kissed her, filled with the ache of longing. "Have I been that obvious? But you always could see through me. I will marry you there, or anywhere you will. Oh, Dane, how dreadful life has been without you! You have driven me half-mad."

She smiled. "You deserved every second of such torment. And I have been half-mad as well, with no escape from Gwynedd but through a husband I believed I could never have. I thought I should die there. I thought I would never see you again."

He kissed her deeply, and they lay propped against the wall with their arms around each other until all fear of separation melted away in the heat of their embrace. After a long while Dane was able to say without trembling, "Tell me, Galahad, the answer to the question all Britain is asking: What treasure did you count more precious than a woman's love? I have heard you called the Grail Prince, the Knight of the Shield, the Virgin Knight, the Soldier of God, the Friend of the Poor—but I never knew what you were after. It couldn't have been old Macsen's feasting krater."

"That is a question not so easily answered," he murmured. "But you have the right to ask it."

"I forgive you in advance," she said, her lips against his throat. "The way I feel tonight, I am beyond hurt."

He half smiled and pressed her closer. "But I don't know how to answer. I don't know what the Grail is. I suspect it is no more than a mirror of the heart. People see in it what they wish to see. To Arthur, it was the remainder of Maximus's treasure, and like the Sword, a gift from God to his ancestor and thus to him. But Arthur was clay down to his fingertips. He saw only what he had use for: a simple treasure to fill his coffers or to use as a symbol for kingship, or perhaps no more than a ploy to get me out of his way." He shrugged lightly, and stroked her hair. "I heard later it was Mordred who dreamed up the quest and bade Arthur send me on it. It could be true. He was a clever man, and far-seeing."

"Percival told me you used to dream about it. And that they were true dreams."

"Ah, yes, those dreams. Sent me by Niniane, the pagan enchantress. I pity Percival, with such a sorceress for kin. What Niniane saw in the Grail was a tool to power or perhaps a path to glory, reflecting only what she most desired."

Dane twisted her fingers around his. "And you, Galahad? What did you wish to see? Somehow I can't imagine you deserting me on that hillside for a piece of old metal, however powerful."

"Sweet," he croaked, holding her tightly, "don't."

She raised her head and met his eyes. "Now that you are back, I don't mind remembering. What we shared that night was something rare and glorious. You were full of love, so full you glowed with it; you shone. Your radiance engulfed me. And I have been alight ever since."

She leaned into him and kissed his lips. The warmth of her body made his head swim, and he thanked God for the thousandth time for the courage to return.

"It was more than a piece of metal to me. From the day Arthur told me of it, I conceived it to be a sacred thing, hidden away by God, protected from the sight of mortal men, to be achieved only by a man of virtue, a stainless soul. For that is what I took my destiny to be." He shut his eyes and winced. "My mother's misreading of Niniane's prophecy, Aidan's fanatic hatred of my father and desire for revenge—they shaped my vision of my destiny. I was to be a perfect knight. Not sinning, but sinned against. It pains me to recall it. What a pompous mule I was!"

Dane breathed gently against his skin. "I remember that, too."

"I undertook to be the best warrior the world had seen. Perhaps I wanted to outshine my father—my mother had raised me to it, God rest her tortured soul. But I think—" He stopped, breathing hard, and Dane squeezed his hand. "I wanted to be important to Lancelot, so important he would give up his life in Britain and stay home with me. I wanted him to be glad I was his son." He cleared his throat gruffly. "I suppose I thought he might admire me if I could do all the things he did and some that he could not. I undertook to live without women in perfect abstinence. I was certain God would reward such virtue, so certain I was ready to believe any tale, any snatch of rhyme that seemed to point to my destiny. I led poor Percival around Britain and back for three whole years seeking shields, cups, scabbards, and elusive signs. All it gained me was the bitter knowledge that Arthur's Britain was crumbling fast. The night before I parted from Percival, I considered giving up all hope of the quest. But that night we met a dwarf, and he sent each of us a dream."

"A dwarf?" Dane looked up. "Was his name Naceyn?"

Galahad started. "Do you *know* him?"

"He's Niniane's servant. When she comes to Gwynedd to visit Blodwyn she always brings him."

"So that was it. It was Niniane who sent the dream, after all. Then Guinevere was right. She was trying to send me south, to Pelleas's stronghold. No doubt Naceyn would have led me to her if Constantine's troops had not intervened. But at the time I was content to go to Constantine, thinking that perhaps the sign I waited for lay in Camelot. He tried hard to buy my loyalty. He must have heard something about my travels, for he told me straight out he wanted me to find Maximus's treasure for him, and he staged some ridiculous trickery to impress me into compliance." He sighed wearily. "I also thought that our only hope of preserving Arthur's Britain was to unify against the Saxons. But Constantine is no Arthur. Three years spent in service to that greedy man shriveled my spirit. He was less worthy of kingship than the grooms who served him. My soul went numb. My dreams ran dry. That was when I followed Percival to Gwynedd." He paused. "I met you and my life changed. Poor, thickheaded ass, I took it for a curse and not a blessing. I then did to you something my father would not have done to any soul he knew. I betrayed you."

"Galahad—"

"Let me finish. It was an act so low it robbed me of honor. An act so far beneath my father, it made me unworthy to be his son. And it was *I* who had always held him in contempt for his love for Guinevere. It was *I* who had always censured *him*. Your curse upon me held: I followed in Lancelot's footsteps. But when *he* awoke to find himself in a maiden's bed, he married her. I ran."

"My sweet—"

"Shhhh." He touched his finger to her lips. "It is truth, although it hurts to hear it. Knowing myself unworthy of the Grail, unworthy of my family, of honorable service to anyone, unworthy even of human friendship—"

"My dear!"

"—I sought solace for my soul. I wandered from shrine to shrine, all over Britain. I visited every threadbare chapel, every hermit's cell, every holy place in every kingdom, many of them not even Christian. I could not find God anywhere." He shivered. "Once my goals had been so high—now they were reduced to achieving a simple prayer. But I could not pray. Everywhere I went people took me for an honorable man, even for a holy man. I could hardly bear it—the admiration of those good, plain people was like turning a knife in my wound. More than once, Dane, I wished for death."

She lifted his fingers to her lips and kissed them.

"I could not find God because I looked in all the wrong places. In carved images, in buildings, groves, and mountaintops. I ought to have looked to the people of Britain. God was too near, too low, too ever-present for this poor, prophecy-bound blind man to see. And yet, I knew Arthur. I had Arthur's example before me and did not heed it. Keep mercy in your heart, he told me. Love the lowly; all men are the same inside. Some lessons, my sweet Dane, come very hard."

She pressed her face against his cloak to hide her tears.

"Finally, I came upon a woman who endured such distress and displayed such courage throughout her long ordeal, that when she told me to go to Amesbury, I asked no questions but obeyed. God spoke to me through Lynet. He sent me to Guinevere." He paused. "*There* was a woman who understood love. Even her enemies she honored and forgave. She gave me back all I had forsaken—my mother, my father, my faith, my life. The courage to come to you."

Dane raised her head. "I bless her from my heart."

"I see now what was dark to me before. What matters is how we honor one another. Arthur and Guinevere and Lancelot showed me that by the way they lived their lives. Father even tried to tell me once, but I would not listen. If I cannot love my fellow men, however dirty their hands, how can I love the God who made them?"

" 'Inasmuch as ye have done it unto one of the least of these my brethren, ye have done it unto me,' " Dane whispered.

Galahad nodded. "But something that is always before your eyes is sometimes difficult to see."

Dane pressed his hands between her own. "You have restored your honor. Now you are truly Lancelot's son."

They looked at each other a long moment. A sudden rush of tenderness lifted Galahad's heart, growing and expanding until it engulfed him, and her, and the cave, the child, the hillside, Wales, Britain, and all the world beyond. How unutterably precious it had all become, of a sudden! He opened his mouth to tell her, but could not begin to find the words.

"You may have given up your quest," Dane said quietly, "but it has not given *you* up. You may have wandered aimlessly, but the road you traveled was straight, after all."

"What are you saying?"

"That you dismiss the blacksmith's tale too soon. You passed the three tests, all unknowing. You set free what ignorance had imprisoned when you led Sir Fortas's daughters out of that tower. You polished what fire had tarnished when you rescued the smith's daughter from her attackers and from her despair at her father's death. What kind of life had she, so isolated from folk at that forest forge? You brought her into the company of her kinsmen and gave her a future. And as for kneeling of your own accord before the virtue of a woman, I imagine you must have knelt before the Good Sister more than once."

Galahad stared at her. "Of course, but . . . that was no test."

"Not to you, perhaps. But the blacksmith said you had to pass the tests without recognizing them for what they were."

"But if that old rhyme is true, I should have received a sign. A sign I could not miss—those were his very words. Yet I received no such sign, unless you count the vision in the pool, one of Niniane's tricks."

Her smile was full of mischief. "You fell in love with me, didn't you? If you hadn't, would you have cared much what happened to Fortas's daughters? Would you have offered to marry Bella? Would you have felt for

Lynet's suffering and admired her fortitude? You did not think much of poor Marrah, as I remember. Would you have gone to Amesbury at Lynet's direction? Would you have even *spoken* to Guinevere?" She grinned at the look on his face and pressed his hands tighter. "I was your sign, Galahad. You had to learn what it was to love another person more than yourself before you could save anyone from anything."

"Perhaps so," he said, dazed with the wonder of it. "But if the old smith's tale was a true tale—"

"I think it was."

"—then the Grail is real as well. Yet I have not found it." He gazed down at her. "I am not looking for it any longer. I have no need."

"Then you *have* found it," she said softly. "You have found what you seek. To you it is not the forsaken treasure of an ancient king, nor a symbol to use in a bid for power. Your Grail, my dear, is the crown of life. The secret of holiness. The key to joy."

"You mean love," he said simply, holding hard to her hands.

A small sound from the back of the cave turned their heads. Out of the dark shadows stepped little Elen, her wide blue eyes alight with excitement.

"Mother, Father, I have found a palace! And a king at his table! Come quickly!"

Dane gasped. A thrill ran up Galahad's spine.

"What king?" Dane went to the child and knelt down to face her. "What have you seen?" But the child only gazed at her with blazing, starstruck eyes. "Oh, Galahad, has something wicked been done to her?"

Galahad rose. "No," he said softly. "This is not a wicked place."

"Then why does she speak so strangely? What does it mean?"

He held her close, taking Elen by the hand. "Don't you remember the rest of the song? 'Water weathers, Stones alight, Macsen's treasures, Burning white.' " Her eyes widened. It was his turn to smile. "There is something in the cave."

Elen nodded. "Burning white."

"Dear God!" Dane clutched at his arm. "It is *here?*"

His smile broadened and he led her forward. "There's only one way to find out."

"Won't we need a light?" Dane glanced anxiously behind at the fire.

"No," Elen asserted. "There's light everywhere."

Trembling, Dane followed her daughter and Galahad into utter blackness.

At first they thought the back of the cave was solid rock. But Elen, pulling at Galahad's hand, found the fissure and slipped through. Galahad and Dane went more carefully, pressed hard against the rock face with barely room enough to breathe. They struggled out onto a flat ledge of rock and stared in wonder at the sight before them. Light flooded a gigantic cavern roofed and pillared in shimmering crystalline rock. On a great stone slab rising from the gently sloping floor, like a table set for a king, a triple candlestand gleamed and burned. Light spilled over the still pool that floored the cave, ran up delicate crystalline pillars of pink, gold, bronze, and white that stretched from the vaulted roof to the glistening floor. Light fled up the shining walls, reflecting back into the pool, shimmered up the gleaming columns until the whole cave seemed to beat and pulse with the trembling candle flames.

No one dared breathe. The only sound was the soft, distant drip of water. Galahad pointed to the stone table. Beside the candlestand lay a long shaft of polished wood fitted with a spear tip honed deadly bright. He walked toward it through the shallow, icy water without knowing he moved. The center of the slab was hollowed out into a concave well of colored crystals—white, gold, purple—sharp and brilliant, stinging the eyes with light. With shaking hands he reached down and lifted a silver krater from the well. Wide-lipped and chased with gold, studded with winking amethysts, the shallow bowl seemed to float between his hands. Around the edge of the lip ran the writing he remembered. *Whoso thirsts, drink ye and be restored. Whoso wanders, hold me and find rest.* The Restorer. He glanced down at the spear. *Whoso trembles, take this and fear not. Whoso is lost, by my strength shall be preserved.* The Preserver. He wondered how anyone, seeing these beautiful treasures, could think of them merely as tools to power.

Dane's whisper echoed off the walls. "Macsen's treasure!" She lifted Elen and carried her through the pool to Galahad's side.

"Where is the king?" Elen asked. "There was a king here. He smiled at me. He was standing here beside the table."

Galahad replaced the krater in its jeweled well. "Brilliants," he said. "That's what she meant. It lies in brilliants." He turned to Elen. "What was he wearing, this king?"

"He had a gold crown. And his armor was shiny. And an eagle stood behind him on a pole. It was gold, too."

Dane let her breath out slowly. "Maximus. A Roman commander. Magnus Maximus. She saw Macsen himself, Galahad."

Galahad nodded slowly. "I suppose she must have. And this . . . Guinevere told me Niniane knew where it was. And the Ancients knew, all along. At the gate of the Otherworld, protected by the god of the hollow hills." He gazed around the pillared hall and the shimmering blaze that leaped up the walls and turned the pool, now alive with the ripples of their passing, into a dance of flashing light. "I should like to die here," he said softly, "when my time comes."

Dane shivered. "It's not a graveyard, even if it is haunted by spirits."

"But just feel the peace of this place. There's nothing to fear. It's the gate of Heaven. And the spirit which guards the treasure is the King's."

Elen asked, "Can we take that spear with us? And the bowl, too?"

"Certainly not," Dane replied. "They do not belong to us."

"They belong here," Galahad agreed. "I think this has been honored as a sacred place since men first found it. Someone tends it and lights the candles. We'll leave these treasures here in God's keeping. But someday we'll come back again."

Dane drew Elen closer. "Galahad, see how cold she is! The gooseflesh all along her arms—let me take her back to the fire and warmth."

He nodded. "Give me a moment to offer a prayer here, and I'll be right with you."

As Elen and Dane crossed the cold water and slipped through the fissure, Galahad crossed himself gravely and knelt before the stone ledge. This time his spirit seemed to soar through the pulsing light; his words flew upward of their own accord to the ear of Heaven. He asked for nothing, but blessed by name every man and woman he knew. When he finished he crossed himself again and knelt, head bowed, to let the joy of this moment swell and fill his being.

Then a voice spoke. "Rise, Galahad, my brother."

He trembled even before he looked up. He knew that voice! He rose slowly, clutching the edge of the stone ledge to prove to himself that he was not dreaming. For there on the other side of the Grail stood Arthur Pendragon, King of the Britons. In the flesh. He wore, not a golden breastplate, but a brown robe trimmed with marten and a plain, braided belt. Around his dark head shone the red-gold crown of Briton's kings. The very crown Constantine now wore.

Galahad gulped. "My lord Arthur?" The words seemed to reverberate in the radiant air. He was not sure if he had spoken them aloud or merely thought them.

Arthur's smile seemed to light him from within. "Welcome, Galahad. You have succeeded. I knew you would."

"Sir?" Galahad fought for breath. "Is this . . . have you . . . returned? Is this what Niniane meant?"

Arthur laughed a deep, joyful, human laugh. "If not, it will have to do." He extended his hand across the stone table, across the hollow lined with crystals, across the Grail. "I have much to thank you for, Galahad. For Guinevere. For Lancelot. For Britain's future."

"Sir, I have done nothing. I've made a mess of everything I tried to do."

Arthur gripped his forearm in the soldier's embrace. The King's flesh was warm and firm, his grip strong. Galahad glanced furtively at the side of his head, but above his left ear his head was whole, the hair not bloodied and matted but hanging straight to his shoulders as if newly brushed. The warm brown eyes watched him in amusement. Galahad swallowed in a dry throat, and Arthur smiled.

"You have done more than you know. You have found what you were seeking, and you have learned what it was you sought. And look, you have found me the treasures of Maximus."

"N-not the Sword, my lord."

"Yes," Arthur said softly, raising his hand in the air. "The sword, too." The great sword Excalibur appeared in his grip, the very sword Galahad had seen on the High King's hip a thousand times.

"But where . . . how . . . ?" Galahad asked in a strangled voice, staring at the weapon as if his eyes would burst.

"The Lady of the Lake, into whose keeping your father gave it when he threw it in the Lake of Avalon. Now all three treasures have returned to the earth from which they were made, the source of their power and protection. But for you, I could not have found them. I could not achieve this on my own. That was not my task while I was in the world; it was yours. You brought them to me. Thanks to you, Galahad, it has been accomplished. Britain will be forever undefeated."

"You can keep Britain safe, even though you are . . ." Galahad's mind reeled. He could not grasp what was before him. But Arthur's kind eyes understood. And forgave.

"Yes. Even though I do not walk the earth you walk. Britain will never yield her sovereignty again. I came to thank you for that."

The King let go of his arm and Galahad staggered against the stone slab. His arm was numb, his knees jelly.

"Never? What about the Saxons? The Picts? The Anglii?"

"Forget them. You cannot defeat them and now there is no need. For in time, in a very short time, they shall become as much a part of Britain as we are ourselves. They shall not rule over us; we shall be one great people and rule ourselves. That is our destiny. But it would not have happened without you."

Galahad stared dumbly as Arthur's face grew less distinct, as the cave wall, gleaming with moisture, began to appear behind his fading form.

"Don't go, my lord!"

"Farewell, Galahad. Go home to Lanascol and leave Britain to her future. It is a glorious one. And know this: Your name shall be remembered for as long as Britain stands."

He was gone, and the cold cave rang with the echoes of his voice.

Like a man in sleep, Galahad turned away from the Grail and Spear, waded through the icy water, and found the fissure in the rock. He paused for a moment, trying in vain to command his racing thoughts. On the other side of that rock lay the warm darkness of the outer cave, the loving embrace of his wife and child, the kingdom that awaited him, and the responsibilities that went with it. While behind him—he swallowed hard—behind him lay the glory of Britain, which he might never see again. Maximus. Arthur. The Grail, the Spear, the Sword. He smiled slowly, joy rising in him like an unruly fountain, wild and unstoppable. He laughed suddenly and without looking behind him, slipped back into the warmth of the world.

✝ THE DESCENT OF PENDRAGON

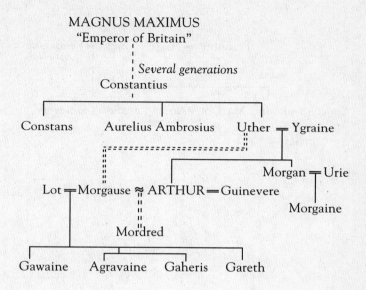

MAGNUS MAXIMUS
"Emperor of Britain"

Several generations

Constantius

Constans   Aurelius Ambrosius   Uther — Ygraine

Morgan — Urie

Lot — Morgause ≈ ARTHUR — Guinevere

Morgaine

Mordred

Gawaine   Agravaine   Gaheris   Gareth

⚜ THE HOUSE OF GWYNEDD

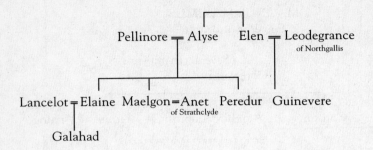

Pellinore ⲧ Alyse   Elen ⲧ Leodegrance
                                            of Northgallis

Lancelot ⲧ Elaine   Maelgon=Anet   Peredur   Guinevere
                           of Strathclyde

Galahad

✝ THE HOUSE OF LANASCOL

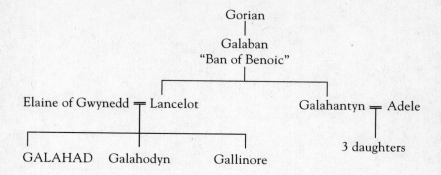

Gorian
|
Galaban
"Ban of Benoic"

Elaine of Gwynedd = Lancelot   Galahantyn = Adele

GALAHAD   Galahodyn   Gallinore   3 daughters